Kip Manley

CITY *of* ROSES

VOL. 4

–or BETTY MARTIN

SUPERSTICERY

PORTLAND • POINTS WEST

Supersticery Press
Manley, Kip
City of Roses Vol. 4: —or Betty Martin / Kip Manley
ISBN 978-1-7349452-6-3

Originally published as individual chapbook nos. 34 – 44 from 2020 – 2024.

Art is a Gift

www.thecityofroses.com

the TABLE *of* CONTENTS

a RECAPITULATION

SOMETIME LATER, IT IS SAID, Jo Maguire, Huntsman of the Court, Duchess of Southeast, did learn that one of her knights, the Harper, had been waylaid as he was delivering the season's allotment of dust to Wu Song, who kept watch along the city's southeast marches. A council hastily convened by King Lymond agreed to ask his sister, Queen Ysabel, to turn fresh dust to meet this obligation.

Afterwards, Ysabel and Jo held a dinner party for her majesty's inamorata, Christina Halliwell, who, with her sister Stephanie, made up a burlesque act known as Chrissie and Ettie, the Sœuers Limoges. Jo invited her old friend from the streets, Christian Beaumont, whom she had feared lost, only to discover he'd been doing odd jobs for Bruno, her grace's Shrieve. Ysabel hoped to announce her investment in the Sœuers' latest performance, but was outdone by Stephanie's date, Reg Davies, an aspiring developer.

Arnold Becker, Jo's former boss, lived happily with the Anvil, a knight of the court. Becker now worked at a day care center downtown, and was studying early childhood education at the community college. It seemed he'd found a cure, or at least a treatment, for his condition, of forgetting anything wonderful the next day, but that treatment drew the attention of David Kerr, occasional tregetour.

Philip Keightlinger, freelance occultist, was distressed by an apparent failure of the wards drawn to keep himself safe, and fled from his rented room to the first car he saw, a car driven, it turned out, by Ellen Oh, a friend he hadn't seen since their summer in Berlin. She took him home, to a blue room in the attic of a big old house, where he felt safe once more, but his handler, Frances Upchurch, found him nonetheless, and put him back to work.

Gloria Monday, née Suzette Wilson, encountered a difficulty in accessing her dead father's funds. An appointment at his lawyer's offices led her to Anna Nirdlinger, former amanuensis to the former Queen. They bonded over what they had in common: the answer each had given, to a question from Ysabel. Gloria took Anna to one of her father's properties, an abandoned warehouse, where she lived with Marfisa, the exiled Axe of the court, and Anna used her connections with the Glaive and the Guisarme to secure a line of credit from the Bank of Trebizond, so that Gloria might begin transforming the warehouse to an art studio.

Christian refused Jo's offer of a full-time job, and an apartment, but kept the money she offered, which he took downtown to bank with the xo, who kept order among the city's unhoused. The xo told Christian that Danny Moody, who'd been sent to prison a couple of years ago for one hundred and twenty-four months, was somehow back in town. Moody had gotten off a bus from Salem that morning and went looking for Winks, whom he found in the dirt caves under McLaughlin Boulevard. Winks had been holding onto Lucinda, a Fairbairn-Sykes poignard, that Moody then used to kill Winks.

Ysabel learned that Lymond's plans to revitalize downtown entailed the demolition of the Lovejoy Ramp, a bridge over the rail-yard. The Ramp's columns had been painted with figures and cartoons many years before by the yard's watchman. Ysabel went to the retreat of her mother, the former Queen and the loathly lady, to see what might be done, but her audience was interrupted by Mr. Keightlinger, about a mysterious errand for Mrs. Upchurch. Shaken, Ysabel sought solace in her weekly session with the Starling, but on a whim brought Chrissie with her. Ysabel asked Chrissie what she thought of the Starling, who, that night, was a perfect doppelgänger of the Queen. Ysabel hoped this might leave Chrissie unaffected, but it was Ysabel's question she answered, and so Chrissie succumbed.

At the spring Samani to honor the new knights of the court, the Devil, moved by the Queen's plea for the Lovejoy Ramp, made public her disagreement with her brother, and announced he stood with her majesty. The King charged his Huntsman, Jo, with securing an apology. She found the Devil in his morgue of clippings and photographs from defunct newspapers. He refused to apologize, and instead demanded a duel: a duel interrupted by Mr. Keightlinger, about his mysterious errand, who is in turn interrupted by David Kerr, on an errand of his own. The Devil dispatched, Jo wounded, Mr. Keightlinger disarmed, David Kerr is appalled to discover a wisp of quicksmoke clinging just above Jo's heart, the stuff released by the wizard Lier the winter before.

Jo spent a day or two recovering in her rooms on Hawthorne. Mr. Keightlinger spent a day or two recovering in the blue room at the top of Ellen Oh's house, and then told Mrs. Upchurch that he quit. Ysabel spent a weekend with the Starling, and offered her a portion of dust, free from the usual bonds of the court, but the Starling refused her gift. Ettie found herself at a group therapy session organized by Gloria, for women who'd answered Ysabel's question, and asked for their help in saving her pining sister.

The Harper, mocked by other knights for his treatment at the hands of the horse-headed brigand who waylaid him, attended a morning spar with her grace's band in an attempt at reconciliation, an attempt that too-rapidly spiraled into insults, drawn weapons, struck blows. Jo attempted to intervene, but the Cater was cut down. The Harper fled, and Jo, disconsolate, ordered her band to gather up what was left of the Devil's morgue, broken and scattered by their duel.

Mr. Keightlinger took himself to the Viscount Agravante, in the house of his invalid grandfather, the Count, to demand the boon that Lier had given the Viscount the year before. Mr. Keightlinger broke the boon open, but found it empty. Shaken by the encounter, the Viscount went on to take offense at certain remarks made by the Baron Medardus, concerning Queen Ysabel, and Annisa Beydoun, the Bride bought from the Court of Engines. The Viscount tasked the xo with sending a message to the Baron. The xo turned to Moody, now working the xo's crew along with Christian Beaumont, but his enthusiasm led to a struggle, and the Baron was struck down.

Court was held the next day, in the throne room of the house at King's Heights. Jo declined to attend, and sent the Mason in her place. The Viscount attempted to deflect any possible suspicion by airing the grievance of Gwenders, the latest victim of the horse-headed brigand, but the Mason, who'd fought the brigand, insisted that brigand was none other than the Viscount's sister, Marfisa, the exiled Axe.

Mr. Keightlinger compared notes with his erstwhile antagonist, David Kerr, who'd been terribly concerned by the wisp of quicksmoke he'd discovered. Mr. Keightlinger was more concerned by the empty boon, and Lier, somehow, released. David Kerr had a brutally simple plan to neutralize the quicksmoke, but Mr. Keightlinger was adamant that Lier must first be found. They parted without agreement. Mr. Keightlinger took himself to the warehouse, to ask Marfisa's advice in stealing into the house of her grandfather, the Count. David Kerr set his plan in motion, by suggesting to the Anvil that he take Arnold Becker to Goodfellow's that night, on a date.

After the disastrous assault on the Baron Medardus, Christian fled to George's, the home of the Porter, who put him to work sorting shoes. Jo found him there, and once more asked him to come with her, but the Porter discovered to her that Christian was no longer entirely what he had been. Dismayed, Jo seized the mask that was her badge of office as the Huntsman and went to confront Vincent Erne, the previous Huntsman of the court, and Erne's son, the King. Heartsick at what she's done on his majesty's behalf, Jo smashed the mask and resigned her office, swearing never to kill for the court again. The King accepted her resignation, as Huntsman, but asked her, as Duchess, to attend some business with him at Goodfellow's. Jo, reluctantly, agreed.

At Goodfellow's, David Kerr shucked Becker from the crowd at the basement concert into an upstairs room, and slipped a mickey into his drink. He then found Jo, and led her to that same room, hoping that, if Becker were to fall asleep before receiving his treatment, his condition, pent up for so many months, would return with power enough to neutralize the quicksmoke. But when the Anvil and the King burst into the room, Jo and David Kerr vanished, and the King collapsed.

At that moment, in the house of the Count, Mr. Keightlinger and Marfisa discovered what had become of the boon, and her grandfather, as some other shapelessness awoke, starving, and tore out Mr. Keightlinger's throat. Marfisa fled, leaving the Viscount to placate that other with domestics until, sated, the other settled into the form of Grandfather Count.

Becker awoke, remembering nothing of his love for the Anvil, or anything else of the past few wonder-filled months. All about the city, every last store of dust had lost its spark and become nothing more than pinches and piles of ash, and the King was no more the King, but a confused young man named Ray. The Queen brought Ray to speak before the court, but the Count and Viscount were there. Recognizing the smell of the other from her time as Lier's captive, the Queen denounced the Count as an impostor.

The other and the Viscount retreated to confer with the Lake Barons, still upset by the loss of Medardus. The Queen retreated with Chrissie in an attempt to turn a puddle of dew, to see if the dust might be restored. That attempt failed, but across the river, at the warehouse, Petra B, one of the women who'd answered Ysabel's question, revealed her secret to Marfisa: the night that Ysabel had become Queen, she'd been with Petra, who had ever since kept that first small store of dust, and that dust had somehow kept its spark. Marfisa left to fetch the Queen.

The Hounds of Southwest and the Lake Barons, believing the Queen to have gone mad, pressed their way into the house at King's Heights to secure her person, overwhelming her majesty's defenders, but then Marfisa struck. She threw the throne itself through a great picture window that looked out over the city, and leaped with the Queen down the slope.

Marfisa brought the Queen to the warehouse, where Gloria Monday and the rest who'd answered Ysabel's question discovered that, with the loss of the dust throughout the city, her power over them had also been broken. Petra B brought her the last of the dust, but rather than save it, the Queen spent it all in a celebration that united hobs and knights, artists and domestics, lovers and peers in a mighty burst of joy that echoed through the city. In the house at King's Heights, the other, still dressed as the Count, slit Ray's throat before what was left of his court, revealing their King to have been a mortal all along.

Two weeks passed. Becker, in a fugue of disbelief, left his life with the Anvil and took up a job in the phone room he'd once managed. Gloria Monday used her line of credit to support the community gathered around her warehouse, even as the Glaive and the Guisarme moved to divest her of the property. Marfisa kept watch, as Ysabel began a liaison with Chrissie, and Ettie, and the Starling, who'd lost her power to change her face. Then Jo Gallowglas fell from the sky, back into the world.

Jo found her band at Bruno's, and they fed her a breakfast of cold pizza. She showed them she had returned with Lucinda, Moody's poignard, and they caught her up with what had happened: the dust, the King, the Count, the Queen. Jo went to the warehouse in time to see the Queen's open court, hobs and clods, domestics and mechanicals, and her knights, convened to meet with the Glaive and the Guisarme. The Queen demanded as her majesty that the warehouse be given free and clear to Gloria Monday, and that the planned demolition of the Lovejoy Ramp be stopped. The Glaive and the Guisarme, in turn, offered up a case filled with shining dust, dust that still had its spark, dust that had been kept safe in their storehouse outside the city, to be portioned out with prudence by the peers. The Queen refused their gift, at first, but the outcry of the court was such she seemed then to relent, if the Guisarme and the Glaive would agree to join her. This tension would remain unresolved, however, for in the tumult, the presence of Jo Gallowglas was noted by the court, and her majesty, overjoyed, leaped into her grace's arms. In the flush of their reunion, they discovered that the mingling of their tears left behind tiny kernels of golden dust. The Queen called for a wooden tub, and some little dew from the court, and proceeded to turn with Jo's assistance more dust than had ever before in memory been seen.

The Queen ordered the tub to be set out in the open, in the middle of the warehouse, and her court to help themselves to it, and as they did so, in reasonably orderly fashion, Jo took herself

out to the sidewalk for a cigarette, where she met the new
Mooncalfe, not Orlando, but Zeina, who served the Marquess
of Northeast. An suv pulled up, filled with knights and peers,
Houndsmen in blue, but also the Chariot and the Mason and
others, who'd come not to partake, but at the behest of the
Count, to secure the Queen, and the dust. A fight broke out, and
Jo, horrified, found her sword once more in her hand, and
watched as the Mooncalfe cut the Serpent down. Jo laid down
her sword in the sudden lull, and walked away, as cries erupted
behind her, and light bloomed. The Queen, shining above like
a sun on the nighttime street, made her way past prostrating
knights of every color to catch up to Jo, and stepped down to the
pavement to ask a question.

Our story resumes as the Queen returns with her answer.

Portland, Oregon
2020 – 2024

ALL MY EYE (AND) BETTY MARTIN. All nonsense. Joe Miller says that a Jack Tar went into a foreign church, where he heard someone uttering these words—*Ah! mihi, bea'te Martine* (Ah! [grant] me, Blessed Martin). On giving an account of his adventure, Jack said he could not make much out of it, but it seemed to him very like "All my eye and Betty Martin" ; but there is no prayer known that fits this description, and the story is, on other grounds as well, absurd as an explanation. The shortened phrase, "All my eye," is very common.

—*E. Cobham Bewer*

Appearances do not deceive if there are enough of them.

—*Laura (Riding) Jackson*

NO. 34

" – up and Stand."

BRIGHTLY SHINING SUN – UNCERTAIN LAUGHTER
THE COLORS OF THE HOUND – EXACTLY AS YOU ARE
WHAT HAPPENED NEXT – A STIFLED SHRIEK – THAT FIRST SOB
ROLLING OVER UNDER UNTUCKED SHEETS – HANDS
BOURBON & BLUEBERRY – "HUNT WHAT?" – COMPROMISE
SOUTHERLY, FOR KOREA – TWO SWORDS, SIDE-BY-SIDE – DISAPPOINTMENT
ANOTHER WORLD – KEPT SAFE – WHAT MAKES IT TICK
A HOUSE THAT LOOKS MUCH LIKE THE OTHERS
EVERYTHING TO LOSE

SUNLIGHT SHINING SO BRIGHT from the corner that they lift their hands to shade their eyes in the otherwise darkness, turn away as they sink to their knees, and the Chariot lowers her gleaming head, and the Axle ducks behind his grimy collar, and Luys, the Mason, stares at the swords in his hands as their blades grow much too bright, and Sweetloaf up on the stoop isn't looking away, he's blinking rapidly as all that sunlight swells and leaps a sudden soundless shout so bright it burns away the shadows in the foyer behind him, and the Mooncalfe knocks her forehead against tiny gleaming tiles, and the Trident empty-handed sags against the muralled wall, so bright it washes out the neon colors through the arch behind him, revealing the glass tubes held in place along the floor by uneven strips of grubby tape, and the Shield kneels over his useless fauchon beside them, and the Stirrup blinks gormlessly in the doorway to the cavernous room beyond, so bright it banishes any dimness that might've lingered in the stalls to either side, and swallows cold fluorescents in a prismatic flare that sheens the lazuli lapels of knights stood over clenched and squinting coveralled domestics, and all those bright swords drooping, those lowering clubbed-up fists, and the brilliance zeniths as it lights on a wooden tub in the middle of them all, still overflown with mounds of golden dust that shine a dawnlight yearning up to blazing downcast

1

noon, and the Bullbeggar turns from it shoulders draped with fur, and Anna blinks behind her narrow black-rimmed glasses, and Gloria Monday in her black high-waisted gown lifts hands against this absent sun, and the Dagger in his pearly suit squared off against the Sapper in his navy, they straighten from their crouches, lift away their hands, and more domestics dun and olive, khaki and umber past them, and more knights in denim and slate, midnight and cerulean, all recoil, prostrate, gawp, the Anvil on one knee, Biscuit beside him, and Miriam black tie unclipped, the Guerdon behind her, under the big main overhead door rolled all the way up, the sword in his hand a-shine with the light that shines over all of them, through them, past them all, out onto the loading dock, discarded lengths of cyclone fencing woven wire starkly bright, and a blue struck from the glossy black of the suv parked at an angle there, and the Axehandle scrabbles around the fender of it, falling to his hands and knees in what should have been shade but the light, the light, the dusty asphalt bright below him all the tar-black leached away to gleaming mica, ancient motes of broken glass pressed by the weight of countless tires into pavement-dazzling sparks that fade, that stretching dim, and he looks up, sits up, shaking his white-locked head as shadows spill to pool in hollows left by that retreating brilliance, and the streetlight above once more begins to make a difference about him. He lifts his phone to his ear, "Mason!" he barks. And then, "Shield? Is the Mason there?" Pushing himself to his feet. "Was that," he says, "was that her majesty?" And then, hushed, "Do you have her?"

A footstep, snap of gravel, chime of chainlink.

He turns abruptly, lowering the phone. The figure stood there, halfway up the gentle rise of the block, shapeless grey coat, something saggy lolling from one hand.

"Sister?" says the Axehandle, Agravante.

She lifts what she holds up over her head to yank it down, a limply flopping oblong swallowing her cloud of white-gold hair in a rubbery goggle-eyed horse's head. He looks about, over the hood of the suv, but the loading dock's empty, and no one's under the overhead door anymore, "Cetera?" Uncertain laughter within, a brief scuffle, nothing serious. "Jamie!" calls Agravante, sharper now. He seizes the handle of the door of the truck. She's stepped out in the middle of the street, striding toward him, lifting an arm out to one side, an arm improbably lengthening, somehow slender, a bat slipping down to her palm. He clambers into the suv, "Luys!" he's shouting at the phone in his hand. "Fall back! Come to me, *now!*" Fumbling about, the steering column, the sun visor, the padded compartment between the seats.

Her first swing's a brusque overhead chop that dents the glossy hood, pops the corners, a bang that makes him jump and drop the phone. She steps back, horse-head a-wobble, shifting her grip on the bat.

"Marfisa," says Agravante. "Wait."

Her second blow crumples the front of the truck.

UNCERTAIN LAUGHTER – THE COLORS OF THE HOUND
EXACTLY AS YOU ARE – WHAT HAPPENED NEXT

UNCERTAIN LAUGHTER, and a scuffle. A knight in sleekly cobalt sleeves, a woman short and round, white apron over taupe, they're pulled apart without much trouble under buzzing fluorescent lights racked high above, the shine a harshly cool that somehow warming as it falls to buttery summery softness gathered in so many glimmering sparks clutched tight in hands held high, so many caught on fingertips, knuckles, lingering on lips and cheeks, so many drifting freely among the biding rustle of that wordless crowd. A tickle of strings, a rattle of sticks against the concrete floor, a crash of metal and glass somewhere without. Someone whoops. "The *hell,*" roars Gloria Monday, there before the raised stage, starting off toward the overhead door, but Anna Nirdlinger catches her arm, "It's okay," she's saying, as a ramshackle beat assembles itself from the clicks and strums. "Gloria, it's okay."

"Okay?"

No I would not, a ragged chorus dissolving in giggles as the incipient song redoubles, asserts itself, and then a great breath taken all at once, Carol in her slinky gown, the Blue Streak cross-legged on a crate, cradling his guitar, the Bullbeggar, Otto Dogstongue, knelt on the concrete, coaxing that popping lopsided beat from a couple of overturned plastic buckets, no I would not give you false hope, on this strange and mournful day, laughter still shaking their words, and the joy that dancing whirls about them.

Out in the middle of them all the great wooden tub set down on a couple of pallets and filled with gold, and over around behind it the Queen, sat upon the floor, her loose white blouse unbuttoned, white trousers rolled up past her shins, her bare feet caked with filthy gold. An empty aisle stretches away from her down the length of the cavernous warehouse, where no one dares to cross the line of golden footprints left wavering between the art-filled stalls to either side, up from the neon-brushed shadows of the arch at that far end, oh, little darling of mine, I can't for the life of me. Her clipped black curls matted with gold, and more gold splashed over lips that part in what might become a smile, and the course of a lifetime runs, but a beat skips, over and over it's falling a-clatter apart, over again as the song drops away to once more silence. She sits up. Pushes herself to her feet. Turns about.

Over under the overhead door a figure in a shapeless grey coat twirls and catches, twirls and catches a slender wooden bat. Atop the boxy shoulders a floppy horse's head, and the stiff fake mane of it sweeps this way, that, until a plastic sidelong eye catches sight of the Queen. One last twirl and catch. Limping, then, across the warehouse floor, past the silent band and watchful, into and through the crowd parting before, stepping back, up to the Queen there by the wooden tub. Clack of the bat planted on concrete before her.

"You're hurt," says the Queen.

"It is as nothing," words muffled by that mask. "The Viscount meant to seize and render your majesty." Unsteadily stooping to take a knee, that ridiculous head hung low. "Would that I could but have run him off."

The Queen lays a hand on a rumpled shoulder. "Have you come, then," cupping that crisply stiff mane with her other, "for your portion?"

"Lady?" that head tips up. The Queen caresses the snout of it, and says, "I would have given you salt." It's almost a whisper. "I would have given you bread, and oil." She tugs, lifting away the mask. Marfisa knelt before her shakes out sweat-clamped curls the color of clotted cream. The Queen lets the mask drop to the floor, and the sound it makes when it hits is shockingly loud. "I suppose," she says, a bit louder as she turns away, "gold will have to do."

"My lady," says Marfisa, though the words catch in her throat. "It has ever, and always," a squeak of wood on concrete, that bat a trembling pillar to support her slowly standing weight, "been you, that I serve," but "Tell us, though," the Queen's saying, "has there ever been such splendor?" Leaning lit up over the tub. "A hundred hundred knights," she says, "might satisfy their toradh," dipping her fingers in to stir the brilliance, "yet still!" Turning back. "We'd have enough to light the city!" Thrusting up her shining hand, the shape of it lost in a blare of gold, and her hair and her smile, her breast and the folds of her blouse a-gleam with the same sunny lustre.

"Your majesty is generous," says Marfisa, bare head bowed.

"Are we," says the Queen, closing up her hand, swallowing the light in a fist that, tipping, leaks a gleaming trickle, a shining thread that widens a spilling rush of falling gold to the floor between them. "Mark this!" cries the Queen, "and mark it well! Hawk or Hollow, Helm, Hare – *all* are welcome, here, to this, our court!" Stepping away from Marfisa, the tub, into the bated crowd. "Any one of them, any peer, or merest peon, *any* of them might bring themselves here, to this puncheon," a gold-dusted gesture swept back, at the tub on its pallets, "and each of them may freely take whatever they do need. But!" Her hand drawn back. Another step into the retreating press of them all. "If they do serve the Hound?" She's stopped before a young and slender knight, trembling in his suit of navy broadcloth. He looks away as she straightens his lapels, leaving them brushed with gold. "If they have found themselves," she's saying, "beneath the heel of that, that creature, that pretends it is our uncle," and looks back, over her shoulder, to Marfisa there by the tub. "Or that vaunting Viscount Lickspittle," and a shake of her head. Turning back to the trembling knight, who's tried to step back into the crowd that's stepping back from him. "Stay," says the Queen. "Doff your jack."

"Ma'am?" he squeaks, even as he sets about to shrug the coat from his shoulders.

"The colors of the Hound," she says, nodding at his salmon-striped tie. "Put them off." And then, as he hastily undoes the knot. "Your name, sir."

"The, the Sapper, ma'am," he says, letting the tie drop to join the coat.

"We asked your name," she says, "not your office, which is forfeit, for what you would have done this night."

The breaths taken, as the crowd around them at once presses close and falls away, as the warmth about them dims, as the light chills. Blinking, the knight says, "Jeffeory, ma'am."

"Present your blade, Jeffeory," says the Queen.

He lifts his empty hand, fingers working, readying themselves, a blink, and he closes them up about the hilt of a sword slipped shivering from the air. Lowering, kneeling, he offers it up, neveled across his forearms. She looks away, back once more to Marfisa. "Tell us," she says. "Would you, could you, withstand, the might of the oppressor?"

"Majesty?" he says, but does not dare to lift his head.

"Should you not restore what's right?" she says. "For all aggrieved by wrong? Stand firm, against guile, malice, and despite? And might you do this, in service to our court?"

"Majesty," again, he blinks, looks up, "of course, I have so sworn – "

"Then rise, good Sir Jeffeory! Sapper no more, but the latest Axe, of this, our Court of Roses! Tell them!" she cries then, to the crowd. "Tell them all! They have but to come to us, stripped of their blues, their blushing pinks – come to us naked! And we will make them new!" She leaves him there, knelt on the concrete floor, staring aghast at the blade across his arms. "Go on!" she calls, to the band there through the crowd. "Play on! We would have music!" Spangled with gold that flings off golden light as she turns and turns about, looking over the crowd, "Starling!" she cries. "Where is our Starling? Is she below? Someone, fetch her for us! We would have our Starling!" And then, stepping through them who scramble out of her way toward the band, *"Play!"* she cries, and Otto fumbles for his sticks, the Blue Streak picks his way into a chord, Carol blinking takes up the chorus, oh, oh-oh no, no I would not, I would not give you false hope, and the shuffle and slide of resumptive dances, the laughter and the whoops renewed.

Marfisa stoops to take up the fallen mask, brushing a glitterfall of owr from the mane. She pulls herself up, shakes out her limp, and smoothly, assuredly sets off, twisting and slipping through the dancing throng, shoulders, arm, the bat suggesting a path through the crush, away from the tub, past Jeffeory there, still kneeling, without sparing him a glance.

Applause breaks out, and cheers. There at the back of the unlit stage the Starling's stepping from the shadows, not so tall as she might've been before, more slender, draped in a chiton of smokey stuff, and glimmering through the clouds of it lines of silver along her arms, her legs, curled about her breasts now, sleeking her belly. Hands reach up to take her hands, her arms, helping her down, into the out of sight of the crowd. The band crashes into another song, Teakbois! they all shout, over the revving guitar, the whirling sticks, and Carol's scatting like a trumpet, but the dizzying swoop of the crowd's attention, the wave of deafening silence, the stumbled steps and turned heads, the murmurs and gasps have nothing to do with the band. Marfisa pushes on through a crowd no longer dancing out of her way, thumped and blundering into the cleared space before the raised stage.

Two figures stood there in the whickering, flannering, golden unfolding light, as the cheers break out, and the applause, the two same frames draped in satiny white and cloudy black, the same hips and thighs, the same olive faces with the same might-sometime smiles under the selfsame eyes of sharply green, and, now, the same hair thick and black and all of it long in artful tangles down past either set of similar shoulders, pressed together, and though the one of them's still limned in silvery paint, there's not a streak or smear of gold left gleaming the other.

"Lady?" says Marfisa, leaning both hands on the bat.

"Fret not, gentle knight," says one of them, the Queen. "We would make you new, as well. There's already a Mooncalfe running about, but it has been some little time, indeed, since we have had an Outlaw in our court."

"My lady," says Marfisa, clenching her hands to squeeze the folded horse's head beneath them, wrapped about the knurled end of the bat. "I've no need of an office, to tell me my duty, or my place."

The Queen lets go of the Starling's hands, steps away from her, right up to Marfisa. "Even this, you would refuse me," she whispers.

Marfisa does not look away, nor lower her head, she doesn't blink, nor does she say a word, but flinches, just, as the Queen takes a step too close, steps past her, headed for and along the crowd behind her, only to stop before a woman, there, sundress and motorcycle jacket, a hand knuckled to her downcast forehead. Muttering something, perhaps. Starting violently when the Queen takes hold of her other hand.

"It's good to see you here," says the Queen.

"Melissa," says the woman, shaking her head.

"We know your name. Of course we know your name. Did you think we could forget?"

"Please," says the woman. "Don't."

"We would never dream to hurt you," murmurs the Queen, soothing that trembling hand with both her hands. "You, Melissa, we would not make new," but "Oh, *hell* no!" a bellow from over by the overhead door, and Melissa looks up, over that way, but "look to us, sweet Melissa," says the Queen, unperturbed. "Look at me." Shivering, Melissa does, blue eyes blinking quickly behind thick lenses. "We would not change a thing," says the Queen. "We would have you exactly as you are: a gallowglas."

"You get away from," that bellow, cut off by a yelp and a scuffle. The Queen doesn't seem to have noticed. "I don't," says Melissa.

"We would have you," says the Queen, "as our Huntsman." Stepping back then, turning away, spreading wide her white-draped arms to fold them about the Starling's embrace, as the blinks and gasps, the steps aback begin to spread, and the mumbles, the looks, the questions, the shouts, the piercing shriek all loosed by what's been said, Ogilvye grabbing Cherrycoke's shoulders, Trucos demanding an answer of Getulos, Biscuit holding apart a struggling Trident and Dagger, Morcilla wailing, and Val there in her pink watch cap, as Gloria Monday shoves herself from Lustucru's restaining grip, and Anna starts after her, into the churning rough and tumble of the crowd. Under it all the guitar unseen chugs into a sawed-off riff, but the boom on the buckets won't fit, and Carol's singing something else entirely, dragging them in her wake, I'm not getting excited, 'cause the thrill isn't mine to invite in, and cheers break out over there, and applause, and an outraged shout as the twins severely blond strut onto the stage, kicking their long legs red and black, and hands reach up to grab them, help them down. Melissa's hands are in Gloria's now, their heads bent close, and rainbow-threaded Joli's there, murmuring something comforting, and Anna clutches Petra all in black. Marfisa still grips the end of her bat still planted on the floor, and bows her head a moment, in the light that falls about them, chill and pale, at once too thin and bright.

Then she takes up the bat, sets off through the hurly-burly toward the stage, toward the Queen who's kissing the Starling before turning then to Ettie, or is it Chrissie, pressed close for a kiss of her own. The clack of the bat planting itself is sharp enough to seize their attention, and they swivel and lift and crane to look to her, the Queen and the Starling, the Sœuers Limoges.

"Is there, as last, some little thing, that you would ask of us?" says the Queen.

"My lady," says Marfisa, as Chrissie's arm, or Ettie's, crimples the smokey gauze about the Starling's hip. "Why have you done this?"

"We have done a great many things, this night alone," says the Queen, her hand on the Starling's hand, tucked in the white satin crook of her elbow. "What, specifically, has you exercised?"

"You named that girl your Huntsman," says Marfisa.

"Because we would have it done," says the Queen.

"But you have," and Marfisa looks back through the crowd, to the tub there, shining. "All was," she says. And then, to the Queen, "Jo made it back. She has returned!"

The Queen steps close. "We would not," she says, quietly, "hear that name uttered in our presence evermore."

"But all was well," says Marfisa.

Chrissie murmurs something. The Starling leans against Ettie, who reaches to catch the Queen's hand, the Queen, turning her back to rest of them all as the band plays on.

High ahead the highway swoop and curl of offramp lit by sodium smolder against a dingy indigo sky. Down here the parking lot actinic behind her, striking cold sparks from the railroad tracks as she steps across them. An unlit building ahead, blank bulk dark against the rusted haze. She crosses the empty street, passing under the stoplights shining red above her, through a rank of sturdy bollards, white reflective stripes about their stubby tips. A broad swath of sidewalk ahead, an espresso bar closed at the corner, umbrellas furled, stacks of chairs and upended tables secured by padlocked cable. Slogging past, down the broad sidewalk that meanders the length of the unlit building to another file of bollards along a narrow drive, and then the mighty boles supporting the overpasses keening and moaning above. Crunch of gravel underfoot, her mismatched Chuck Taylors, her black jeans, and her T-shirt, her empty hands. Past shadowed columns the ground drops away into nothing, the complete abruption of the river before her. Across that lightless void the sudden leap of downtown, towers blazing bright enough almost to overwhelm the streetlamps sparse along the esplanade, the diffusing glow of the highway above, falling with the wash and thrum of traffic loud enough to drown any slap or chuckle of riverwater. As she steps out from under the overpass a bridge hoves into view, a line of lights shot straight just past the trees, held up by shallow arches across the river. At the far end vault two girdered towers, and high within each are caged the bridge's blocky counterweights, storeys of concrete painted red, held somehow aloft. She stands there, looking at them, one hand to her chest, fingers splayed along her collarbone, heel against her breast.

"You ain't got much time," somebody says, and she wheels about in the shadows much lower, closer, her jeans still black, her shoes mismatched, but she's stuffed in a puffy ski jacket of some filthy color impossible to name, "Like it's gonna," she snaps, but stops, blinking, frowning. "I don't," she says, "need, that much. Time. To pack." She's looking about, not at the skinny shadow in a long dark coat, but the apron of scruffily bare dirt that slopes from a blank retaining wall to a row of slender columns that uphold the bridge above, a file of proscenia framing not the river, but a quiet cross street, dimly lit, and narrow onramps rising either side. She heads toward the wall, away from the shadow. A couple of dome tents pitched right up against the concrete, where criss-crossed stripes of whitewash palimpsest graffiti.

"I didn't mean to scare you," says the shadow, as she crouches on a blue tarp laden with swollen garbage bags. "I said, I didn't mean to – "

"Fuck off, Christian," she says, perfunctorily. She's digging through the bags, yanking one open, tossing it aside. Yanking open another, digging in to fish out clothing, a pair of tights, some grubby underwear, a T-shirt, black. Stands abruptly, casting about for something, something else. Wraps her arms about herself. One of her sleeves leaks tufts of pale down fill from a freshly ragged slash.

"I just," says the shadow. "I never figured you'd, I mean, obviously I did, because here you are, but – "

"Where else am I gonna go?" she says. "Huh? Tell me that."

"Anywhere," says that silhouette of shoulders hunched. "Anywhere but here." A truck booms over the bridge above. When it has passed, "They weren't all out looking for you they'd be here. They'd be drawing you another circle in the dirt."

"But not you, huh, Christian?" She sniffs, she gulps. Her hair no longer sun-bleached, the tips of it stiff with filth pattering the shoulders of her jacket as she shudders. "You knew I'd come back." Her Chuck Taylors digging into the gravel, scuffed white toe half torn away on the one, the sock within spotted dark. "I've been taxed," she says. "What else is she gonna do?"

He snorts, and she looks up, alarmed. Skinny shadow in the shadows, there before one of those narrow arches between columns. "*She* ain't gonna do a goddamn thing," he says, "and you know it. She's making with all the sound and the fury, but *she* ain't the one you gotta worry about, is she."

She swallows. Takes a step off the tarp, toward him.

"That's it, isn't it?" he says. "The guilt. *You* got to get out. *You* got to live."

Arms still wrapped about herself, she doesn't say a word. A car turns onto the ramp to the left, headlights swiping over them, too suddenly bright and gone to reveal anything.

"Come on, Bambi. You know what happened next."

A deep breath, and she says, "I know you never said any of *that.*"

"So?" He takes a step toward her, but not yet out of the shadows. "I ain't the one got the order of things all wrong. You don't start rutting through the bags till about, oh, now," he says, and another step closer. Streetlight cuts across dusty black boots. "Looking for something to steal on your way out the door."

"What fucking door," she says. "Christian, I swear, I don't know what the," but "See," he's saying, "there's your problem, right there. You never give nobody their due. Christian." He snorts. "The hell kinda dead name is *that.*" Another step, and the streetlight slices up the dusty skirts of that dark coat, and grimy jeans. "You know what to say," he says. "You know the name," but he giggles, weirdly echoey loud in the breathless stillness. "Shizzt," he says, full of mirth, filled with malice. "Shizzt," he says, "the Drow."

"Who the fuck," she says, closing on him, four steps, five, and he smiles. Moody smiles.

A Stifled shriek – that First sob

Stifling a shriek she steps too hastily back, stumble-scuff the pavement of the esplanade, arms outflung, bare arms against a fall that doesn't, she's, her T-shirt's back to black, and cracked across the front of it a devil's leer. Moody's sitting on a stump with his back to the empty river, the shining city, smiling unctuously, black leather hat tipped up, his ragged jacket of army-surplus green.

"That's, that's mine," says Jo.

"Yeah?" he says, stuffing his hands in the pockets of it, pulling them out, setting his collar, his shoulders as he rolls his neck. "You got my shirt," with a jerk of his chin. "Took me way too long to put two and two together. You stole it. That night. Didn't you."

"How," she says, and a deep breath. It's all so quiet about them, even the overpasses behind and above. "How did that happen."

"What," he says, looking about, a performance of uncertainty, "all that?" undone by his smile. "Just now?" He points. "I live in your head, Bambi. Rent's awful cheap."

"You *live*," she says, "in *prison*," quiet and cold and definite. "You got *arrested*. You pled guilty, even if it was only a *tenth* of what you ever did. A hundred, and twenty-four, *months*," stepping across the esplanade toward him, sat there on that stump, "and I didn't have to think, about you," she says, "I haven't thought about you, not at all, not once since then, not till Christian went and said you, you were, back. Danny Moody's back."

He scowls, he shrugs. "I bet you don't believe in tigers, neither," he says.

"So, what," she's saying. "You wanna kick in my ribs? Slice me up? Fool around a little, maybe, before you set me on fire?" but he's laughing, roaring with laughter, he throws back his head, reaching up to catch his hat, settle it back in place. "Your favorite spot's a mile away," she says. "I ain't gonna go easy. That's a long way to haul somebody, by yourself."

"Look at you, Bambi." Still chuckling. "You got so *fierce!*" An exaggerated shiver. Planting his hands on his knees. "Truth is," he says, "I could do whatever I wanted, right here, right now, and there's no one around to say boo. Not a goddamn fig." Sitting back, a sigh. "I just come down to see what's what. That's all this is about. And I admit it, I was," he shakes his head, "trepidatious. Heard you was in it. Rolling deep. But now that I finally *see* you?" A thunderclap of laughter, shaking his shoulders. "I mean, *look* at you!" Throwing a gesture at her. She flinches. "Look at what you got left. Nothing. Nobody. You ain't *shit.*"

She says, "You were there."

Again, a shrug.

"You saw how it ends," she says, reaching behind herself, rucking up the bottom of that shirt. Pulling out a flat black leather sheath, undoing the flap of it to reveal a wire-wrapped hilt. "You," she says, taking hold with a wiggle, slipping the blade of it free. "Your belly slit open." The length of it shining even in this dull light, tapering to its ineluctable point. "Strung up by your guts," she says, looking up to meet his eyes. He's lowered the brim of that hat, and his smile's not nearly so broad as it was. "Bleeding out on the Fremont Bridge," she says.

"Yeah?" His voice emptied of all mirth. "You gonna do that, Bambi? All by your lonesome?"

"She came back with *me,*" she says. "Not you. Me. *I'm* the one."

"Well, if you say so. But," tipping back his hat, "if that's how it's gonna end?" One more shrug. "It ain't ending here." That smile is back. "You got yourself a nice T-shirt. You got a pretty little knife, I bet that's gonna come in handy. Good for you." Pushing back the army-surplus cuff of his jacket. "I got myself a new toy, too," he says, showing off the watch about his wrist, heavy and gold.

"You," she says, the poignard wavering, dipping. "You, if you, what." A deep breath, the blade back up between them. "What did you do to him."

Another shoulder-shaking, belly-clutching, hat-catching burst of laughter. "Aw, hell," he says, theatrically wiping his eyes, "when you finally figure it out? I wish, I wish to *God* I could be there, to see the look on your face." Hands on his knees he pushes himself to his feet, and she takes an involuntary step or two back. "But I got shit to do," he says. A gesture at his wrist. "It's got all these, dials and rings and, knobs, you know? I gotta figure out how it works. What makes it *tick.*"

"*Moody!*" his name ground to dust in her mouth, "get *back* here!" twisting, lash of the blade at his shadow, "you *god*damn sonofa*bitch!*" clawing climbing to a shredded shriek, she leans forward, arms wide, *"Moody!"* Wavering there with the force of that bellow over the roots of the stump alone. Blinking. Looking about. The empty, lightless river. The long, straight shot of the bridge. The overpasses far above, and the rush and thrum of the traffic back and forth, like wind. She takes a step but her duct-taped shoe crunches slipping down the crumbled edge of the esplanade's pavement, and she doesn't so much fall as sink to her knee, heel of one hand on the scrub of the river-bank, clink of poignard on asphalt. One shaking breath hauled in, coughed out. Holding herself a moment there.

Standing, limping away from the stump. The esplanade winds beneath the bridge where it gathers itself to cross the river, and she shuffles into its softened shadow. Working the dimmed blade back into its sheath, looking back, the stump, the lights of the city beyond. A stretch of cyclone fencing's thrown up here under the bridge, panels leaning drunkenly over the stretch of rumpled dirt it walls off, between esplanade and buttressing wall. A white tin placard's loosely wired to it, stamped with stern red capitals, NO CAMPING NO FIRES NO DUMPING, and then, in smaller letters beneath, Multnomah County Bridge Section. Across the esplanade the ground falls steeply away, calamitously littered with shadowed rocks, all brushed like the bare dirt with dim salmon light. Some time ago some of those rocks were pushed to one side or the other to clear a path down to the river, a boat ramp, though too long, not nearly wide enough for more than a canoe. Shuffle-stumble halfway down toward the water, but stepping aside there, off the path, picking her torturous way across the rocks. Hanging a moment with the effort of correcting for an overbalanced step, one shoe kicked out over the dusty earth.

A squared-off block of concrete, the mighty foot of the pier of the bridge above. She sits herself atop it tailor-fashion, hunched over her knees. The river still deeply black here under the bridge, but not so empty, not this close, the surface silkily limned by streetlight, bridgelight, a dully sullen glowering sheen of yellow and orange never to be found in any sunlight, but even here the lap and slop the sluggish current affords cannot be heard over the endless chords of rushing traffic so far, so high above.

Her first sob seems to take her by surprise, shuddering her, and she closes up her eyes, her mouth. The overflowing swell of it lifts her shoulders, tips her head, but she holds it until she can, slowly, and with some little effort, let it out. She's better prepared for the next.

ROLLING OVER UNDER UNTUCKED SHEETS – HANDS
BOURBON & BLUEBERRY – "HUNT WHAT?" – COMPROMISE
SOUTHERLY, FOR KOREA

ROLLING OVER UNDER THE UNTUCKED SHEETS, pastels tangled together, flush of teal, icy pink, a yellow startling in the sunlight, black hair abrupt against the one white pillow. Her arm tugged free still socked in black and white to brush some of that hair from off her face, to dig sand from the corners of her eyes. Not quite a groan, she takes in a breath, sits up, pastels falling away, pale waves crashing back to a rumpled ocean. "Hey," she says. Shoving the bulwark beside her. "Hey. Want some breakfast?" Reaching across herself to scratch her shoulder, dig under the cuff of the sock. Not a word or a breath from the bulwark. "I want some breakfast," she says, tugging the sock down, working it off.

He sits up sometime later, blinking thickly in the sunlight, pastels puddling his lap. Absently scratching the wiry black that mats his breast. She's over by a freshly assembled credenza, the only other piece of furniture in a room that still feels crowded. She's pulled on brief black shorts, a cropped white T-shirt pasted to the curves of her breasts and her belly, she's stirring something atop a little electric griddle. He sniffs, and again, deeply, closing his eyes. His mustache thick but neatly trimmed, the black of it hatched with white. "Oh," he says, "and is that speck you're frying?"

"If by speck, you mean bacon?" she says. "I'd offer you some." She shrugs.

"Just as well." He yawns. Another elaborate sniff. "Odor alone is almost enough, for a man in my condition." Slapping his jowls, shaking his head. He works his way out from under pastels to the edge of the great thick mattress. "Ghost of a pig," he says, scooping up a grimy grey union suit, "for a pig of a ghost." Working his way into it. She's tonging up slices of bacon, dropping them on a paper plate. Holds up the last one, charred and glistening, turns it about, lifts it for a bite. Hissing, "shit!" dropping the tongs to the credenza, the bacon to the floor, "The fuck," she says. "The fuck am I gonna do."

He pauses, stood by the mattress, trousers half-buttoned.

"This was supposed to be a place for people hurt, by her. And now she's," slapping the credenza, "I mean, it was one thing when she was just, sulking, in the basement, but last night? Last night was," looking back, over her shoulder. "What am I gonna do, Jim?"

"You could ask yourself a question," he says, doing up the last button. "Why is it, d'you think," wrestling his suspenders up onto his shoulders, "her majesty comes to find herself here, to be doing such things?" Tipping that head of his left, right. "Of all places." Rolling up the sleeves of his union suit. She folds her arms, leaned back against the credenza, "I don't know," she says. "Some fight or something, with," shrugging, "somebody's grandfather, hers, maybe, I don't know. I can't keep track. It's family and it goes back years, so I don't think anybody could really explain it, but there's probably a lot of money, which means lawyers," she sniffs. "Our lawyers."

"That's why she's not there," he says, casting about. "Why is it *here* her majesty finds herself?" He fishes a cracked brown boot from under drooping pastels. She snorts. "I haven't kicked her out yet."

"Sweetling," he says, sitting heavily on the mattress, "attend the line of inquiry with a modicum of the gravity I'd like to think it's due?"

"Here is where the action is," she says. "Simple. But now, she's got everything she needs, to fuck it all up. Again. And *that,*" she says, pushing off the credenza, "is the gravity of *my,* whatever the fuck it is." Scooping up the uncooked portion of bacon, still in its plastic bag, she opens one of the credenza's cabinets with a toe to reveal a mini-fridge. "My query," she says, squatting to stuff the bag away among takeout cartons, a jug of orange juice, a bottle of spumante.

"The point, my nonpareil," he says, working a boot onto his foot, "that must be taken into account, is this: even," tightening the laces with a grunt, "even the most capable skipper in all the world, with the sun itself that shines from his very arse," tugging on the other boot, "why, even such as he'd be utterly lost, at sea, you might say, useless, in point of fact," snugging the heel of it home with a sigh. "When stood by himself," he says, looking up, "at the wheel of a mighty clipper, without he has a couple a dozen of these," and he holds up his hands, the backs of them up to the first knuckles furred with wiry black, the heels of them and the palms edged with rough thick callus, and about the thumb of the left a simple ring of pale gold.

"She's here, her majesty's here, for you guys," she says.

"Who else, to wash her dishes, and fold her unmentionables?" He gets to his feet. "Light her candles when it's time, and snuff 'em when it's done? Beat the rugs and polish the glazing? Lay pipe, fit bolt to camlock, joist against beam, set brick atop brick? How else might her palace assemble itself?"

"And you guys," she says, and takes a bite of bacon. "You guys are here for me."

"Ah, my dimpled dumpling," he says, stepping close, "while I'd never be one myself to dispute your inestimable charms," a hand on her hip, the other her breast, a-stroke till she grips his wrist. "For what me and Marfisa put together, here," she says. "And Anna." Souring. "Even if there has been some mission creep."

Both his hands are on her hips now, and he presses a kiss to her cheek. "You're never out of sandwiches," he says, "and the coffee's always hot." Letting go, stepping back, "And I'm in need of a gallon or so."

"Go on," she says. "I'll be down in a minute. Soon as I find some pants."

Up on the unfolded table, then, boxes printed with sprinting cups that trail intricate curls of inked steam. Cackletub turns them about and squares them with the edge of the table so that over on the other side, Christian stooping can punch in the perforated holes toward the bottom of each, working out and securing the black plastic spigots, "Hang on," he says, pushing past someone pushing in to get at the boxes, the stacks of paper cups Cackletub's setting out, *"gimme* a minute," he struggles to reach the fifth of five and punch it open, but someone's got a cup already, and another hand on a spigot, and somehow in the jostling he's struck by a jet of coffee, "Jesus *Christ!"* he shouts, whipping his hand away, and everyone, the entire crowd, falls back, the aggressively jocular air let out of them all. Someone drops an empty cup.

"Oughtn't to say that, boy."

"Ain't for our likes."

"Sear your tongue, they will, words like that."

"Shattern," the word a boulder powdered by thunder.

"A fellow once I knew – stout Faber Iona, had a hand in the Oriental Fair, he did, and builded Balor's Dun – why, never could he keep the name of their Sweet Lord's Son – "

"Teeth," another boulder-word, uprooted by tidal spittle.

" – from out his mouth. Once he'd learned it, of course. Terrible shame, what happened."

"Really," says Christian, wiping the back of his hand on his sleeve.

"An nawt a'd say Horwendel'd steer yiz wrong."

"Jesus," says Christian, very deliberately. "Ever-loving. Christ." Working his jaw, his lips around, baring his teeth in a great big smile.

"Well," says the one of them. "Not right *away.*" And everyone starts to laugh, Christian loudest of all.

"Donuts?"

"What?" Christian looks up from the sugar dispensers and the pitchers of cream he's helping Cackletub lay out, the spoons and stirring straws that are snatched as soon as he lets go. "They're coming," he says. "The Flynn's on it. And Ned. You look all shook up."

"Oh?" says Iemanya, black hair askew, white apron crooked over her taupe blouse. She sets a paper cup on the table, lifts pugilistic fists, "Was *fun!*" she says through a broad grin.

"I bet." Christian hefts up a couple of bundles of paper napkins. Cheers from the big open overhead door, where somebody short's coming through dwarfed by the stack of boxes held before him, "Beignets!" somebody cries, skinnily sallow and tall.

"Blue Star," says the short man, setting his sagging tower of boxes on the table. "Bourbon and blueberry."

"Rosemary an raspberry," says the big man following after, a couple more boxes in one platter-sized hand that are seized before he can set them down. "Soup's on!" says Christian, stepping back. Cackletub hands him a paper cup filled with steaming coffee, black.

Out in the middle of that cavernous room, past the crowd a-jostle about the coffee and the donuts, there's the wooden tub, worn staves sawn off at just about knee-height, bound about by riveted iron hoops. A woman approaches it warily, looking about before gingerly planting a foot shod in beige orthopædic leather, thick-soled, velcro-strapped, on one of the pallets that holds the tub above the concrete floor. She leans over the light of it, reaching with painful care to suddenly seize a handful of sunlight, and the look on her face as she holds it up, to let it trickle into the plastic baggie held in her other hand. Looking about again, the empty stage the one end, shadowed arch the other, before dipping in to scoop another blazing dollop.

Sipping coffee, Christian looks past the tub and the woman to one of those art-filled stalls across the warehouse, this one lined with jewel-toned photos of houses and Dutch-angled store-fronts. Stood on the threshold of it a woman taller and more slim than the man before her, and she as cooly pale as he is brownly banked, her one arm sleeved in gleaming plate, pauldron and cop, cowter and vambraces, his thickset torso swelling a denim jacket. They say things to each other, much too quiet to make out, as others pass before them laughing, discussing things to be done, problems to solve, the wonders of donuts. Someone else sidles up for a pinch of gold. Christian sips his coffee, and watches the woman lean slowly down, hesitate just for a moment, as the man turns away, so that her kiss is pressed to his cheek, and not his mouth.

"A fine spread indeed," booms Big Jim Turk in his union suit, his dungarees, brushing his mustache aside before taking a glistening purple bite. "Who's to blame?"

"Brether Ned," says Christian, "and the Flynn," even as Ned's saying, "Aye." Jim fills a cup with coffee. The focus of the dispersing crowd shifts, from tables and pastries and boxes of coffee, to Big Jim Turk, downing that first cupful, reaching to fill it again, and nothing of his donut left but crumbs, fastidiously folded away in a napkin. "All right," he says. "I'm for the upstairs hallway west. Walls are stripped, and prepped for painting; it's but a day's job with a few to pitch in," a nod there, and there, "Hup" from another, he's taking note, but "Ah," says Brether Ned, those enormous hands of his tucked away in his back pockets, "was to taken cable, far ta sparken cellar, but day's en day are taken sod, fa hroof. Ull need anand."

Brows lift, eyes widen, "oy" and "ach" and someone says, "The roof?"

"Har majesty insisten," says Brether Ned.

"It'll go quick enough with enough of us, to take it in and haul it up," says Jim. "A break from the painting. What time's it coming?"

Ned shrugs. "Nuncheon, a thereanent."

"Herself's not with a meeting today," says Jim.

"And her majesty's below," says slender, sallow Melia. "Lunch'll be nothing more than it should."

"So there's the day," says Jim, throwing back the last of his third cup, and they're all milling about now, some headed off this way, or that. Christian busies himself with tidying up a couple of empty donut boxes, sweeping crumbs away. The thickset man, swelling his denim jacket, is making for him, across the warehouse, his hair a crisp circle of white about his brown bald head. "Let's go, boy."

"Stuff to do," says Christian, opening a fresh box of donuts.

"In case it had passed your notice, there's peers in the house," says Gordon. "They ain't need the likes of us." Watching, as Christian with a bit of waxed paper fetches out the last couple stragglers from yet another box, consolidating them, tidying, sweeping. "I said let's go, boy."

"I am not," says Christian, looking up, "your boy."

"We had our fun," says Gordon. "Now it's done. Cold light of day. Time to get back."

"Ain't nobody gonna be there," says Christian. "Look around! They're all here."

"All the more reason. Nobody to get in the way."

"'Cause they're all *here!* The coffee's *here!* The, the donuts are *here.*"

"That ain't what's to be done, boy."

"I am *not,*" snarls Christian, and his hands curl into fists that thump the table. "I'll be by," he says, then, "later. After." And moves to open another box of donuts, even though the one before him's still untouched.

Gordon steps back. "All right," he says. "After."

"At Berbati's, in the restroom, of all places."

"Yeah, we, we know, Melissa."

"Let her speak."

"It was, uh, last October? The Corner Laughers show, with Wheat. I was there with Julie, and her friend, from New York? Anyway. I went in to, to touch up, you know, and she came in. She came in, she was laughing like somebody just said something really fucking hilarious, but she was by herself? And, I mean, it was her eyes, you know? I looked up, just in time, to catch them in the mirror. Those eyes. And, okay, so maybe I was staring? But I'd already had, like, two of those baklava martinis, okay? And she just, without saying hi, or nice dress, or I really like that color, she just, she *asked*. And I. I'm not, I don't, I don't usually, but I, uh, I, I – "

"You said yes, Melissa. We know."

"Gloria."

"What?" Gloria Monday sits up on the grimy carpet, there before the escritoire. "No, seriously. What." She's pulled on a pair of slick blue shorts and a violet T-shirt that says Death & the Maiden & Horace. "What good is this doing. What good did any of it ever do."

"A lot," says Anna Nirdlinger in her white dress shirt, one hand on the back of the nubbled green armchair where Melissa's slumped, still in her sundress and her motorcycle jacket, but "Miriam's gone," Gloria's saying, "Jessie's gone, Star's gone, Joli left, Thorpe's buggered off God knows where, and Petra's out there *playing* with them, Addison won't return our calls, *Val's* gone, everybody's up and gone, and her fucking goddamn majesty," jabbing a finger at the closed office door, "is gonna make what's supposed to be *our space* over into her brand new goddamn *palace*."

Marfisa, leaned back against the wall there by the door, says nothing at all to any of that. Her tights are black, her tank is grey, her curls are sloppily knotted at the nape of her neck.

"I thought it was all over?" Melissa sniffs. Behind thick lenses mascara's dribbled and smeared about puffily red-rimmed eyes. "The dreams, and all. They stopped. Why did she, why did she go and *do* that to me?"

"She felt she had to," says Anna, but Marfisa looks up at this, "Jo Gallowglas refused her majesty," she says. "Her majesty has elected a new Huntsman."

"But why *me,*" says Melissa, buckles clinking as she leans forward. "What am I supposed to do? Hunt? Hunt *what?*"

"The Huntsman," says Anna, "is usually from without the court."

"He is a falcon, on the wrist of the King," says Marfisa, "that flies and stoops at a word."

"But there isn't a King, anymore," says Gloria.

"Stoops?" says Melissa.

"He will come back," says Marfisa. "He always does. But while he is away, the Queen might come to the Huntsman, and ask a favor of him."

"But she didn't," says Melissa. "Ask. Last night."

"That's not a favor," says Gloria, as Anna says, "She wouldn't."

"Once," says Marfisa, "when the Queen, perhaps, felt the passage of time more keenly than she liked," hands clasped before her, fingers interlaced, "she found herself become quite jealous of the youth, and beauty, of her Princess." Looking up and away from them all, in that windowless little office. Melissa sniffs. "And so she came to her Huntsman, and asked this of him: that he would go to her highness and, with such clever ruse as he might devise, urge her with him into the wood, where he was to cut out her heart, to bring back, to her majesty."

"Jesus, Mar," says Gloria, kneeling up on the carpet as Anna frowns.

"Wait a minute," says Melissa, sitting up, clink.

"What you are supposed to do, Melissa Gallowglas," says Marfisa, and she takes hold of the knob of the door. "Determine, for yourself," and she opens it, "when the time comes round for you: will you do as her majesty wishes?" Looking back, at them all. "Or will you refuse?"

Out onto the walkway, and the door gently shut behind. Below the cavernous warehouse diffused with cooly shadows against bright day without, submerging the sullen warmth of the tub on its pallets, and someone shouts, frustrated, and briefly she closes her eyes. The tables down there have been folded away to make room for three more pallets loaded in under the open overhead door, laden with rich brown rolls of turf stacked high, coiled within with startling green, and a half-dozen or more stood about in coveralls and dungarees, pointing, disputing, we can't exactly, crane's not even, swanning about! and but her majesty. Marfisa takes hold of the ladder bolted to the wall and climbs away, up and up to the makeshift floor tucked under the rafters, laid with dusty rugs and ceiled with tiny stars, green and blue and white, red, orange, mostly gold, though, thousands of them. She bulls her way past and through the awkward frame of a truss over dust-furred boards to a lone crate waiting under some sort of hatch. Steps up, reaching, the clack of a latch undone. Hauls herself into the blaring light of noon.

A field of pea stone stretches out to ankle-high parapets of brick on three sides. Behind her, the brick backsides of the buildings at the high end of the block, a couple more storeys each, sparsely windowed. Down the other end a frail gazebo's been erected, canopy of palest blue upheld by gauzily curtained poles. She cocks her head, frowns. Sets off toward it, pop and crunch of gravel underfoot.

In the shade of that gazebo Petra B's squatting over a matte black case, hefting a weighty matte black lens. "I don't usually shoot people," she says, fitting the lens to a slender camera body with a click. "And never like this."

"It's easy," says Ettie, knelt on a carpet spread over the pea stone, rocking forward as Costurere kneads gleaming oil into her shoulders and her back.

"Artless dolts do it every day," says Chrissie already glossy, as Aigulha brushes her severely yellow hair.

"It's just gonna take, ah," says Petra, thumbing on the camera's viewfinder, "some adjustment, okay?"

"Hold that thought," says Ettie, pointing with her chin. "Here comes Auntie Mar."

"What are you doing?" calls Marfisa, one hand shading her squinting eyes as she approaches this little island of coolth, the carpets haphazardly laid, the discarded white robes blued by gauzy light, and the whites of Aigulha's and Costurere's shifts. "Isn't it obvious, ma chère?" says Ettie, getting to her feet, taking Chrissie's hand. "We're making *art.*"

"The lobs and hobs must be about their work," says Marfisa. "They were to prepare the roof for turfing. Her majesty would have a lawn – you had them set this out, instead?"

"The lawn can wait," says Ettie.

"The sod is here!"

"We're here," says Chrissie. "The light is here."

"And they would make *so* much noise, ma pouliche," says Ettie. "Quite distracting."

"It will dry and die if it's delayed."

"Buy more," says Ettie.

"Her majesty would have our pictures," says Chrissie.

"Her majesty," snaps Marfisa, catching herself with a grimace. "You are to have this," waving, at the gazebo, the carpets, them, "cleared away, within the hour." Crunch and scrape as she turns to go.

"You really should try to be *happier,* chère!" calls Ettie to her retreating back. "After all – you won!" And then, without looking away as Marfisa yanks open the hatch at the far end of the roof, "It's really terribly simple, mon oisillon," she says. "Most stuff, as you say, like this," turning then to Chrissie, and she tucks a yellow lock more securely behind an ear, "it's merely a journalistic exercise," as Chrissie smooths a streak of oil over her clavicle. "Once, one golden afternoon, Dear Reader, I got to be in the same room as a beautiful girl."

"I told her what to wear," says Chrissie.

"I told her what to do," says Ettie, "and so on."

"Here's the proof," says Chrissie.

"Do something, anything, other than that," says Ettie, looking over Chrissie's shoulder to Petra B still crouched by the matte black case, "and we'll be fine. Today," turning away, without letting go of Chrissie's hand, "is all about contrast. Smooth and gleaming," she lifts a foot from the carpet, "rough and dusty," setting it with a twist in the pea stone, "brilliant shadows, darkest light. Or, I mean," frowning, "other way, anyway." Chrissie smiles. "Anyway," says Ettie. "Glorious black and white."

"Color," says Petra, getting to her feet. "I always shoot in color. Do the monochrome in post, if you want."

Ettie sighs, "Very well," she says. "One compromise at a time, I suppose," and steps from shade into brazen noontide light, and Chrissie follows after.

Red flesh and pink and clean white fat she tips the ribbed slab over, wrestles it about, clack and scrape against wood to fit a slender blade against the ridgeline of bone-stumps down one side. Slicing along it she pushes with her other hand the filade of bones away, slice again deeper and push a bit further, quick smooth strokes and sudden wrenching force, she's pulled loose a glistening fence of bone-posts bound by gristle and fat and redly striated muscle that she folds once and pushes click aside.

"I do hope you won't be throwing that away," says the woman on the other side of the counter. Not too tall, shoulders padded in a peach suit, hair all tiny corkscrew curls swept back, pinned up. "Neck bones chopped in a slow cooker, garlic and thyme and just enough vinegar, collards and macaroni," miming a chef's kiss, lips carefully painted the color of brick, eyes limned with threads of startling green.

"Feather bones." She scrapes red water and translucent scraps from the block before her. "Better if it's pork." Turning that slab over and about, chuck-end angled before her, taking up the slender knife again.

"Won't argue with that," says the woman on the other side of the counter. "Still. That's a pot of good stock just waiting to simmer itself down."

"Someone will be with you shortly," she says, counting off truncated ribs that can just be made out under the snowy cap. Fitting the blade between numbers three and four.

"Oh, that's all right, Ellen Oh," says the woman on the other side of the counter. "I'm vegetarian. Mostly. We can talk while you work."

The blade only hesitates a moment before smoothly splitting the third from the fourth.

"We met, once before," says the woman on the other side of the counter. "I must apologize, for the brusque tone I took at the time. It had been a difficult day." Stepping close, dark hand pressed to the front of the counter's glass case. "But I see you remember. I see that you remember me, you knew me before I stepped up to interrupt you, yet you have not asked a single question of me."

"People like you," says Ellen, taking up a smaller, stubbier knife. "You can't help but explain everything, sooner or later." She sets to shaving an ivory membrane from the backside of her cut. "Usually, sooner."

"And what do you know of people like me?" says the woman on the other side of the counter. "Oh, Philip, to be sure, and he knew you. But if I were ever to have asked him where it was you learned how to do *that*," pointing to the board, the meat, the knives, "he'd say something about the six weeks you worked one frigid summer in a restaurant in Patagonia. But *I* know." Leaning forward, her hoarsely rich voice lowering to a more intimate pitch. "It was a much hotter summer, and much earlier. The first time you ran away from home. You worked in Sutter Randolph's pit. He called you Ginsu the entire time, and you never punched him once."

Ellen sets the smaller blade aside, looks up, eyes dark, black hair spiky short. Sharp black curls of ink roil up from the open collar of her smock to shape branches that stretch up her throat to the point of her jaw, and intricately calligraphed leaves. "He was a mean old man," she says, "and his hands were hard. I did work in Patagonia."

"Of course," says the woman on the other side of the counter. "The best lies are always true." And then, "Philip is dead."

"I know," says Ellen.

"The author of his demise sits comfortably in a house in the hills, eats well every day, sleeps soundly at night. How does that make you feel?"

"If you do not like it," says Ellen, taking up the smaller blade again, "do something about it."

The woman on the other side of the counter smiles. "Perhaps I am," she says. Cocking her head, those corkscrews a-tremble. "Your ink is lovely," she says. "So precise. I almost," pointing, "recognize that bird," the beak, the beady eyes, the subtle crest just poking from her foliage. "A fairy-flycatcher, isn't it. Bit southerly, for Korea?"

"There are a few," says Ellen.

"Well," says the woman on the other side of the counter. She lays a card on top of the glass case, fnap. "Should you change your mind." Turning away, she heads off, past more chilled display cases filled with rounds and stacks of meat, knotted ropes of sausage links and cutlets already breaded with crumbs and cheese, ready to fry, rubied pucks of steak, misshapen lozenges and irregular tubes of aged salumi, whitely dusted with mold, still wrapped in twine. Ellen lifts the card, small but stiff, an ostentatiously plain linen stock, and blank. Turns it over. Frances Upchurch, say slender, sans-serif letters. Beneath them, in the same font, a simple, ten-digit number.

Two Swords, side-by-side – Disappointment
another World – kept Safe – what Makes it Tick

Two swords laid side by side on the glass-topped table. To his right the blade is long, widening from sharp tip shining clean and straight to the palm's-width ricasso, where a crude sigil once was stamped some time ago, a simple block shape worn and faded with time, a horn perhaps to one side, the suggestion of a foot, there where the shallow fuller begins its slope down the clear bright length of the blade. The plain cruciform hilt of it stolid and thick gleams even in this light with all the randomed nicks and dings and here and there a notch whacked into the quillions stretching simple and straight to either side, and then the grip, bound about with straps of tawny leather smoothed and darkened by much handling, and the pommel, a wide flat plain-faced coin, thicker through itself than the largest thumb, the beveled edges of it scratched and chipped, even here.

To his left the blade is shorter and more slender, a needle next to the other, shining but darkly, chased the length of it with coiling waves that swirl in the depths of the steel. The hilt is simple and straight, wrapped in dulled wire, and the quillions almost as long together as the hilt, but over and about them a glittering basket woven of wiry strands that meet in thick worked knots of steel all gathering together in a sternly singled cord that swoops to the great silvery clout of its pommel. Stamped above the quillions on what thickness the blade can manage a crude sigil, the lines of it still sharp, a horn clearly emerging from one side of the block shape, and the foot.

"Mason," someone says, and he looks up. Sweetloaf's in the doorway, shoulders sagging in his bomber jacket, pompadour a-wobble as he shakes his head, lips glumly pouched. He steps into that trapezoidal room, careful of the thicket of furniture stacked up the one wall, tables perched upon a sideboard, upside-down chairs interlocked, what might be a pew precarious in the shadows up there, and makes his way down the long oval table past emptied pizza boxes to the Mason, and those swords. He lays on the glass an empty scabbard of plain black leather, the throat and chape of it beaten metal the color of thunderclouds, and a loose black belt, undone. Sweetloaf steps back, but the Mason with a lurch seizes his hand, holds it, holds him still, that pale hand long and narrow caged by great rough fingers. Presses it to his cheek. Sweetloaf, blinking, frowns. A bit of leather's tied about the Mason's wrist. He lets go, and Sweetloaf steps back, his other coming up almost of its own accord to take, and hold, and stroke, the palm of it, with his thumb.

"Well?" says someone else. They both look up. The Shrieve in a tartan vest at the foot of the table, looking with stern expectation to Sweetloaf, who shrugs. "Her grace wasn't there," he says. "*Nobody* was fucking there."

"Sweetloaf," says the Mason.

"Place was even emptier than *here,* and *this* place is a fucking *graveyard.*"

"There's no need," says the Shrieve, and the Harper in the doorway behind him, yellow beard and sleeveless sweats, but the kid won't stop, "They're, all of them," he says, "all over at that fucking *ware*house with every-fucking-body else!"

"Enough," grits the Mason.

"Except for fucking us," says Sweetloaf. "And herself, I mean. Geeze."

"*Sweetloaf!*" the Mason. Both hands flat on the table before him. "She will come, back," he says, in a different voice, but the Shrieve takes a breath, hands tucked in the pockets of his trousers. "You will be disappointed," he says.

Slap, the Mason's hand on the glass. "She *will* come back."

"Perhaps," the Shrieve. "But if her grace does return – "

"*When.*"

A sigh, then, from the Shrieve. "When she comes, Luys," he says, "she won't bring with her the way things used to be. She can't return to us what we once had."

"She already has!" cries the Mason, and Sweetloaf abrupts, almost knocking the teetering thicket of furniture. The Harper's sidled up behind the Shrieve, who blinks. "She already has," says the Mason, again. "Come back. To the Queen, last night. Together, they turned the owr. After *weeks* of," looking down, for a word. "That much, Bruno," he says, "*so* much, *is* come back."

"They did," says the Shrieve. "That they did. But that's her sword, there, on the table, before you. And she's gone, again, and again no one knows where. And last night, after the owr was turned, the Queen – "

"Her majesty named a new Huntsman," says the Harper, folding his arms.

"Fuck," says Sweetloaf, in a breath.

"There's been a rupture," says the Shrieve, even as the Harper's saying, "Some mousey little nobody nobody's even heard of." The Shrieve favors him with a sidelong look, and he shuts up his mouth. "The world is," says the Shrieve, turning back to the Mason, "different. If we aren't prepared for that. If we don't take that into account," leaning forward, both hands flat on the glass of the length of the table between them, "you will be disappointed. Luys. Luys, listen," straightening, stepping around the foot of the table, past the more awkward corner of the room, "even if her grace were to come through that door in the next moment, and take up her blade, we'd still be where we are, right now: torn, between," he pauses, gripping the back of the chair before him, looking to the Harper, then back to the Mason. "On the horns of a thorny dilemma," he says.

"And nobody to take out the fucking trash," mutters Sweetloaf, glaring at the pizza boxes.

The Mason pushes back his chair, gets to his feet. "You'd have us choose, for her grace," he says, taking up the sword to his left, and the empty scabbard, "between her majesty," fitting the tip of the one to the throat of the other, "and the Count," slipping the blade home.

"I would have us be prepared," says the Shrieve.

The windowless room is not much bigger than the round table they're sat at. A white board covers one wall, most of it taken up by looping orange letters spelling out WinBank May 4.0 or Bust!!! "There's no sales, right?" she says.

"Ah," he says. "Well." Not much more than a kid, really, with his paper-laden clipboard and his unlit tablet computer on the table before him, his rumpled shirt patterned with tiny propeller planes in a brown and gold at odds with the pale blue and purple paisleys of his tie. "We don't sell anything here, that's true. Your performance isn't judged on, how many, ah, units, you move. There's no commissions, or anything like that. But." Sitting back, head canted. The knot in that tie's too wide for his skinny neck. "You will be trying to, talk people? Into doing something they might not necessarily want, to do? You know? And, I mean, isn't, in every interaction, isn't there something like, an aspect, of sales?"

"I, ah," she says, blinking. Blond hair pulled tightly shining back in a high ponytail, and the top two buttons of her plain white blouse undone.

"You," he says, "you're trying to sell yourself, to me, right now," he says, "and I'm, well, I'm trying to, sell you," he shrugs, "on the idea that, this is the kind of place where, if you work hard, if you, commit, you know, to what we ask of you, you'll be, you know? This'll be a good fit. Tell you what." He tugs a couple pages from the clipboard, pushes them across the table toward her. "Look this over. I'll go, I'll find someone to run them with you. If you can stick around," getting up, "who knows, we might even try you on the phones tonight." He holds up a hand. "I'm sorry, what was your name again?"

"Jessica," she says. "Vitaly. Jessica Vitaly."

When the door's closed she slips a pair of narrow square-lensed glasses from the purse on the chair beside her. Pulls the pages across the table, turns them over, brow cocking, eyes widening, lip curling. Something buzzes. She lets the script drop and hikes up in her chair to wriggle a clamshell phone from her pocket. Anna, says the little screen on the back of it, buzzing again in her hand. She unfolds it. "Hey.

"Yeah, well. What I said.

"What I said.

"Anna, listen," she leans back, "I," tips her head back, looking up at the serried tiles of the dropped ceiling. "Oh my God," she says.

"Oh my God.

"Is she, did you, did she, you, okay, okay. Okay. But," and she closes her eyes.

"This doesn't change anything.

"It doesn't! I mean," sitting forward, elbows on the table, "what the hell good do you think I could possibly," forehead pressed to her palm.

"Well that's a lovely thing to say. But you and I both know she could, and she has, so. She would. She will. So I'm not going to risk, I, I won't. I can't." Turning in the chair, hand on the edge of the table, "Anna," she says. "Anna, I know. I know. And I," a sigh, "I do, too.

"Yes. Yes, but. No. No," she says, "no." Listening. "Not yet," she says, finally, "not yet. Still – yes. Where else am I gonna –

"It's, I'm, I'm fine, Anna. I'm fine. I mean," and here, she takes up the script, "I already found a job. I think."

Becker drops the headset on the keyboard, untangles the cord of it from his wrist with a flick. Taps the enter key, pushes the mouse about, click, closing windows on the monitor, click click. All about others push back chairs, get to their feet, pull on sweaters and hoodies, light jackets, each before their own carrel of kelly green just barely wide enough for a monitor, a keyboard, a corded telephone. Up by the only desk in the office the kid in his tie laughs with a blond woman in jeans and a loose white blouse. Becker folds himself in his oversized flannel of zipatone plaid. "Thanks, Crecy," he says, to the older woman next to him, as she hands him a dark grey meshback cap she's scooped from the floor. He fits it over what's left of his hair.

Tinny from an unseen speaker jangling cheerful piano, somebody sings, always said no, then I turned around, saw someone smiling, Becker's eyes are closed, he's leaned against himself over and over in the tarnished mirrors reflecting mirrors reflecting pitted amber thrumming with the elevator's descent, and there's so many Denices in T-shirts and sweaters and all of those necklaces, and a crowd of reedy TJs green and grey, stepping into, the thinly croon, I stepped into, into another, and the elevator sighs to a stop. The doors grind open. The three of them step out.

Thinned salmon haze of streetlight softens an empty black sky, glare of the sign on the corner across the street, Danmoore Hotel, too bright to be in focus. Without a wave or a look back Becker crosses against the light, past a sandwich board that says Three Lions Bakery. The block after that's a little open plaza where tracks of light rail curl in a turn-around, power lines and guy wires supported in a complex criss-cross by concrete columns topped with deco glass. The next block lined with restaurants, Indian, Persian, Lebanese, Tibetan, a rowdy throng erupting from the taco bar on the corner, mostly women, shorts and skirts, T-shirts and halters, and so many brightly blazing loops of neon colors, green and blue, yellow and pink, orange and purple glowingly circling wrists, necks, twisted into shining crowns, kicking anklets. They wheel and swarming cross against the traffic, horns and laughter, pealing whoops. He waits with an angular sports car until the last of them tumbles off and it can turn, purring, before him. Shrugs out of his flannel overshirt, knots it about his waist.

Darker ahead, and quieter. He passes under a pedestrian bridge, short trees and greenly slender planted against the curb on his right hand, the windowed galleries of a reconfigured department store to his left. His head is down, crossing the next street past a brightly lit construction site, spinal column of an elevator shaft climbing by a mighty yellow crane, Now Leasing, says the sign on the corner, Fall Occupancy. Sogge Enterprises.

Through a little park, serely planted with more young slender trees about a giant chess board and an empty fountain, past quiet apartments now, red brick set with white-framed windows. Another park ahead, the trees much older and much taller here, more stately, stretched with great confidence over the street toward the silent, bricked-over arrière of a grand old theater, Portland's Centers for the Arts, says the unlit marquee over a side door. Raucous scraps of night sky suddenly fling themselves about, a subcommittee of crows registering displeasure and excitement as he scurries through, away and down a steeply genteel slope by another, much more recent theater, glassed-over ramps and stairwells at the corners and a sign for an Artbar in the lobby.

It's brighter here, out from under those trees, a haze of streetlight once more softening the sky. A couple of elaborately caged lamps ahead preside over a stern low gate, blocking this side street from the traffic ahead, Broadway, say the street signs, and Main.

Crossing with the light, past a courthouse, high steps softly lit, a parking garage, a bright fast-food restaurant set in one corner of it, crew bustling behind the counter. An astylar kiosk across the next intersection, four arches set in a square about a staircase leading down, under the sidewalk, warmed by the glow of Edison bulbs, and just past it a small shelter of brushed steel and glass in its own fluorescent pool, a sign before it listing routes, the 14, the 10. Becker's pulled his wallet from his pocket, he's slipping a bus pass free, when he stops, there, in the middle of the street, and frowns.

There's a man sat upon the shelter's bench, back against the glass, shoulders straining the jacket of a pale blue suit, the hair of him clipped close and iron-grey, and his mustaches long and grey, drooping to either side of his shaven chin, where the tips of them are caught and weighted by rough-shaped pewter beads.

Becker turns abruptly away, lurching off down the street between courthouse and office tower. Somewhere behind a bus is rumbling this way. Stepping onto the brick-paved walk, around the next corner between office towers, head down, wallet clenched in his hand. The Standard, say the signs about him. Live 95.5. No Parking This Space, Subject To Tow. Killian for Portland's Future. MARLO. Through the row of trees ahead, all the same scrawny undersize, can just be made out the figure of an enormous woman, clutching a trident, stooped over the front doors of another office tower. Across the street to the right the sandstone blocks of City Hall, and tucked up against it another bus stop, a single brushed steel pillar supporting a roof of cantilevered glass, SW Madison & 4th, says the sign, 4, 10, 14, 30. Becker opens up his wallet again, and waits for an SUV to pass before darting across.

That man steps out from where he'd been leaning against the pillar, his mustaches, those strong, broad shoulders, "Wait," he says. "Arnold Becker. I ask only that you hear me out."

"No," says Becker. "Go. Away. Leave. I don't," and he balls up his hands.

"Tell me," says that big strong man, "that you remember nothing." Quietly hoarse. "Not a moment. Tell me that you do not even know my name, and I will go. I will go, and trouble you no more."

"What if I *do* know your name," says Becker, viciously quiet. "What if maybe I *don't* know what happened, but I know, I know that if," looking away, then, looking for the words to come, "I take your hand," and he swallows. "If I take your hand, I would be so, happy, but, but any moment, any morning, I could wake up, again, I would have forgotten it *all,* *again.* I'd end up right back here. Again. And I can't. *I can't.*"

"Becker," the other man, barely more than a whisper. "My love. This, I swear: I will keep you safe."

"Yeah," says Becker, closing his eyes. "You will."

When he opens them, the man is gone. A deep breath, shoulders unhunching. Tipping back his cap. Turning, at the sound of an engine, the bus, turning the corner. 14, say the orange lights over the windshield. Hawthorne.

The glass before him full of yellow beer, the burger steaming on its bun, he dredges a jojo through ketchup but the ketchup's gone, the plate is gone, the beer, he's no longer sat in a blocky booth of smooth dark wood, lit by a single low-hung bulb, he's in a plastic-backed chair, chrome frame of it winking in utter darkness. He's no longer dressed in brown painter's pants or his anorak of chocolate-chip camouflage, but a white T-shirt laundered almost to translucence, and royal blue jockey shorts. A plop. Startled, he looks down at the splotch of darkness fallen on the junk mail littering the table-top. Another, it might be red, it might be ketchup dripping from the potato wedge in his fingers. He frowns, but lifts it to his mouth. Someone screams.

Slap of bare feet seizing a doorknob into a garage all shadows looming, a single lamp a-dangle brightly on the other side of a pickup truck, a meaty smack, a muffled gurgle. "Dad?" he says, or tries to say. His voice is gone. Another smack, a yelp, he heads around the front of that truck, squeezing between the bumper and the wall as words climb out of a snarling growl, barely discernible, "What you get," a sucking, bubbling breath, "is what I let! You! Have! What you," another wheeze, another, "what you, give me," the words scaling all the way up to a shriek, "is *everything!* Is!" and a smack, "my!" and a smack, "due!"

Another of those plastic-backed chairs has been set under the swaying trouble light, a man's sat in it, arms bound up behind his back with loops of bristled rope. Parked beside it a wheelchair empty but for a rumple of blankets, dingy grey thermal and a threadbare quilt. Crouched on the lap of the man in the chair is a much smaller man all elbows and knees and ears and Adam's apple and thin wild hair, hunching to clutch lapels and swing a flattened hand, smack! "Now *tell* me," snarls the crouching little man.

"Dad!" he yelps, one hand on the fender of the truck.

The man in the lap of the man on the chair looks sharply up.

"I really don't think this is necessary." He steps away from the truck, toward the chair. "You made your point." Dropping the jojo, flicking a splot of ketchup from his fingers. "Stay put, Jasper." There's somebody else in the garage, stood just past the reach of that weak harsh light, a shadow wrapped in bulky shadows. He reaches past his scowling father for the greasy rag stuffed in the mouth of the man in the chair.

"That ain't what you said," says the shadow behind him, "and that sure as shit ain't what you did."

He stops tugging the rag, but doesn't let go. He's looking at his father, crouched on the man's lap, skinny knees cruelly dug into the man's belly, that untucked shirt, the sharkskin jacket rucked by his father's clutching fists, fighting to haul in every breath before he shoves it out.

"No," says the shadow behind him, rustle and step, "you just came in. You watched, you didn't say a goddamn thing, and when you went and got blood all over yourself," and at that, the man in the chair with a whine starts to struggle again, yanking the rag away with a toss of his head, bucking enough to rattle and scrape the chair, and his father with a yelp rears up and savagely cracks his head against the bound man's nose and splatter, blood shining his father's forehead as he sits back up, and there are the spots of it, staining his thin white T-shirt.

"Well," says the shadow. "You excused yourself. You went back into the kitchen. You wanted to wash your hands. And then," another step closer, the light lapping the edge of a filthy blanket dragging the floor. "You told me not to worry."

"It's not mine," he says, half to himself.

The glass, full of beer. The glistening burger, pink tomato, the palmful of iceberg. The jumble of fried potatoes. The light hung low over darkly blocky wood, and sat in the booth across from him, "Moody," he says.

"Hey, Chad. How's it hanging?"

"The fuck, man? What the *fuck* was that?"

Moody's looking up and out, "Hey!" waving, "yeah, I'll have what he's having? This thing," he says, lowering his voice, hunching forward, "is *amazing,*" flipping back the cuff of his army-green jacket, holding up the watch on his wrist, "and she just *gave* it to me!" The xo looks from the watch all heavy and gold to Moody's darkly glittering eyes under the brim of that black leather hat. "I'm still fiddling with it, figuring out what it can do, and what happens when it does it," fingertips passing back and forth over the crystal of it, the ticking hands, the bezel, a conjurer's fillip, "but think about it, man." He's looking up at the xo, sharp eyes, sharp nose, sharp chin. "There is no way in *hell* that any of *that* was *any*where in her head!"

The xo lifts his glass of beer, sitting back, to drink it down in one unbroken swallow. Holds the empty glass upturned above his mouth a moment.

"Don't you *get* it?" says Moody.

The xo sets the glass with exaggerated care back on the table by the untouched burger. "No," he says, flatly.

"This thing has *power,* man. There is no possible way she could have known," a wave, at nothing in particular about them, *"any* of that."

The xo's fists thump the heavy wooden table, chiming flat-ware, jumping the plate. *"Who."*

"Jo fucking Maguire," says Moody, taken aback. "Who else?"

"And I'm supposed to believe," says the xo, nodding at the watch, "she just *gave* that to you."

"Well," says Moody. Shrugs. "Yeah."

A House that looks Much Like the Others
Everything to Lose

A house much like the others all along the one side of the street, low, demure, set close to the curb, only a shallow curl of driveway, a freshet of paving stones crossing the scrap of a yard to the front door. He pauses, one Chelsea boot on the front steps, glossy tobacco polish marred by dust, an ugly scuff across the toe. Looks back, over his shoulder. A high stone wall lines the opposite curb, lofting from dim pools of streetlight into thickets of shadow above, themselves swallowed by the looming slope of night. He's stood in the light of the lamp hung over the warm yellow door, his suit of a blue as dark as those shadows, his salmon shirt buttoned up to the throat, and no tie knotted there. His weird white hair swept back in matted locks long enough to brush his shoulders, just.

He opens the door, he steps within.

The unlit hall, a stairwell spiraling up to the right, a kitchen to the left, cold and dark. A great dark empty space ahead at the end of it that he heads toward, boots quiet on the dust-dulled floor.

No one stands watch at the hole smashed through the great curving wall of window. Jagged blades of glass still hang dangerously above, to either side, framing tree-shapes without silhouetted against the city's glow away off below down there, a vague brightness drawn in and caught by cracks that leap through the window in every odd direction, faint lightning frozen in the moment of impact creaking and scraping even at the gentlest breath of a breeze. He's headed for the glass balustrade mounted about the stairwell in the middle of that room, and the long straight flight of steps headed down. "More!" someone growls below. "C'mon! All of it!" There's light at the foot of the steps, hotly yellow-white but wildly uncertain, guttering, redoubling with a shocking flare.

A hand on the transparent railing, he begins his descent.

"My lord," an exhortation choked off, he hastens his steps, suddenly thunderous, down to the porch below, long table laden with blazing candles thick and thin, pristine and melted stumps, whites and yellows and oranges and sullen reds stuck atop varied candlesticks and candelabra, the light of them leaping and flaring, swooping with the wind of his passage down the line of them, past the two in blue, the one in pink stood back against the wall, not daring to look up as Agravante sweeps up to the other, sat at the head of it all, pouring the last of a bottle into an overflowing goblet, and runnels of whiskey spilling to spread across the cloth. Lifting a pink hand to pull from that mouth with a plop a bit of bone that's set, glistening, in a puddle of liquor. "Where in the hell," says the other, but suddenly scrambling pushes back from the table as Agravante doesn't come to a stop, as Agravante without faltering leans to clamp a hand about the other's throat, carried by momentum in a mighty half-stumbled shove that topples the chair slams the other back against the credenza, loomed out over the drop to dark trees below. Pushing further, squeezing. The other grunts, and a weird flicker and flash, that white shirt for an instant too bright, the hand lifted not a hand. "Go on," snarls Agravante, leaning into the other's bent frame. "The few who've stayed," quiet, gutturally close, "cling to but a single shred of doubt. Go on!" shove and squeeze, "take even that from them."

The other, wheezing, spittle bubbling, trembling, lowers what's once more a hand all pink, heel of it splat against the credenza. Turning a bit, "Leave us," spits Agravante over his shoulder, without looking away from the other. The hurried rustle, then. Footsteps away and up and out.

One last squeeze. Agravante steps back, throws wide his arms. The other a hand to that darkening throat, red blotches chased under sickly skin. "Where," a hacking spit, "have you been," the rush of words burred, unfinished.

"Out," says Agravante. Leaned back against the table, shadow leaping and faltering over the other, those elbows propped among a litter of unwashed crockery, shaking that wildly ivory-crowned head, *"Simple,"* and a cough, *"instruction. Bring her. To me."* Pushing suddenly swaying up, "That was *last night."*

Agravante shrugs. "I had to walk back. The car was, totaled, I believe, is the word," but *"Where,"* a growl over all that, *"is she!"*

"Safe," says Agravante.

The other launches off the credenza, roaring *"I! Will!"* and *"Eat! You!"*

"You'll lose!" shouts Agravante, hand up, palm forward. The other yanked to a halt, wavering. "Everything," says Agravante.

"You can't," spitting, *"you can't hurt me."*

"I can," says Agravante. "I have. I will." He plucks up from the puddled whiskey that bit of bone, glittering purple in the candle-light. "Move a finger against me," he says, "and I will have the Queen destroyed, and I will have the Princess destroyed, and you will lose everything you came here for."

"You couldn't," snarls the other. "You wouldn't dare."

Agravante shrugs, closing up his fingers about the bit of bone. Takes hold of the stem of the goblet. "Where the, hell, was I, you ask?" Tipping the goblet enough to spill some brimming liquor, then lifting it to his lips. "Making certain," he says, and sips. "I needed someone at the Queen's new court, now that her majesty's fecundity's returned. Someone I could trust with such a terrible charge." Sets the goblet down. "As for her highness?" He looks up a moment, then back to the other, and there is something almost sympathetic to his mien. "I've always had someone I could trust, outside her door. You really must come to appreciate the limits of rule by fear alone."

"Do it!" bellows the other, and Agravante flinches. "Go on!" Those pink hands flailing. "Destroy them both! Gut yourselves! See if I care! I'll just light out for another goddamn city! Another goddamn court!"

"But," says Agravante. "You might do that now, and without this fuss and furore. No," a deep breath. "You need us," he says, pressing his hand flat on the table. "We don't need you, but we can't seem to get rid of you." He lifts the goblet again. "But now? Now, we have a choice. We have options. So: I propose, a détente." He gulps down a mouthful of whiskey. The other, red-faced, trembles before him. "We will set about the business of determining," says Agravante, a magnanimous gesture with the goblet, "whether we might resume our dependence on the Perry line, or start anew, with our new Bride." That bit of bone still in his other hand, pinched between thumb and forefinger. "You, if you behave yourself," flinching again, the patter of slopped whiskey, as the other takes a step, just a single slow and heavy step, struggling against the gravity of some awful other place. "You might well avail yourself of the choice we do not take. Something," a deep breath, shoring up his tone, "or nothing. What will it be?"

"You," the word spat up as if cast off by the rocks that churn in the other's belly. *"You. Will. Regret. This."*

"Oh, to be sure," says Agravante. "Every day of all the days to come. But tonight," and he sighs. "Tonight, the evening's pleasant. And I find you spoil the view."

The other screams, once, as if in answer. Stomps away, floorboards creaking with every pounding step, toppling a thicket of candles with the sweep of an arm, flight of sparks and splash of wax and light, clang and crump of sticks. As those footsteps climb the groaning stairs, Agravante drinks off the rest of the whiskey in one long hissing swallow. Blots his lips with the pink cuff of his shirt. Looks at the goblet in his hand, cloudy glass with here and there an errant bubble trapped in the thickness of it. At the bone in his fingers, an oblong, pitted cuboid of a thing with a couple of smoothly concave facets, sheened purple in the firelight. He hurls the goblet away to smash against a baluster.

It stands. What? Yes. Say it stands. Had to up
in the end and stand. Say bones. No bones
but say bones. Say ground. No ground but
say ground. So as to say pain. No mind and
pain? Say yes that the bones may pain till no
choice but stand. Somehow up and stand. Or
better worse remains. Say remains of mind
where none to permit of pain. Pain of bones
till no choice but up and stand. Somehow
up. Somehow stand.

—*Samuel Beckett*

NO. 35

" – many Christian eyes – "

THE LIGHTS ARE OUT; THE CURTAINS DRAWN – ORDER 722
WHAT BECKER HASN'T DONE – THOSE SCRAWNY ARMS
THE SEMBLANCE OF A HOUND – UP UNDER; HIGH BENEATH – 157,185 SF
A DELICATE CLINK – "WELCOME BACK" – JACK'S DOG – THE FLY, THE FLY
LESS THAN A TWO-POINT-FIVE – EAST MULTNOMAH SOIL & WATER
DUTY – WARD, OR SIGIL? – SELECT PASSENGER – BEAUTIFUL MOUNTAIN
THE LAST OF THE INTERNATIONAL HARVESTERS
"SORRY ABOUT THE BURRITO" – THE VERN – EAST OF EVERYTHING
THE LIGHTS ARE OUT, THE CURTAINS DRAWN

THE LIGHTS ARE OUT, THE CURTAINS DRAWN. She sits in one of the two chairs there by the small round table in the corner, wrapped in a thin white towel, hair limply, darkly damp. Hand on a knee, elbow on the table by a slim black phone, screen of it cracked. She blinks. Neatly draped over the dull yellow coverlet of the one queen-sized bed a pair of black jeans, a sort-of folded black T-shirt. On the shag carpet at the foot of it a pair of Chuck Taylor hightops, one white, one black, both grubby, fraying duct tape wound about the toe of one of them. She draws a slow, deep breath. Lets it out.

There's a knock at the door. "Jo? Hey. Jo."

"It's open." She doesn't get up out of the chair.

A lowly ruddy flare of morning light as the door swings open, and somehow the room becomes smaller, wallpaper shot though with fraying metalled threads, dusty flat screen of a dead television, peeling veneer of the dresser, expressionist print of a football tackle askew above the bed. The man in the doorway heavyset and tall, leaning a shoulder on the one jamb, hand braced against the other, in the fingers of it a featureless yellow keycard. "I need the room," he says.

It's unclear whether she nods, or shrugs, at that.

"So I gotta kick you out," he says. Looking about the room. His hair is greasily brown and cut to no specific length, his

45

short-sleeved shirt a drably olive, his tie of mustard yellow. "Do you," he says, frowning. Shifting his weight in the doorway, still braced. Trying again. "Did you even get any sleep?"

"You don't get to pretend you give a fuck," she says, quietly, but clear.

"Jo," he says, and drops his head, shaking it vaguely. Hauls it back up with a deep breath in through his nose. "Room has to be cleaned and prepped by eleven," he says. "You, what, you just used the shower? Jo?" Looking away, shaking his head more definitely. "I can let you have it till ten. Do what you need. Get yourself some sleep, whatever. There will be a wake-up call."

"I need a charging cord," she says.

"You," he says. "You need a."

"I need to charge my phone," she says.

"You want me to get you a," he says.

"Just for an hour or two."

"This place?" he says, "you better not set on fire."

"I didn't," she starts to say, but closes her eyes. "Just for an hour. Or two," she says, opening them.

He drops his hand, takes a step into the room, onto the carpet dazed by all that light, reaching for the doorknob. "You don't get to make a habit out of this," he says, and pulls it toward him.

"Zach," she says, before the door shuts. "Thanks," she says.

"Lemme see about that cord," he says, and the click of the latch.

She closes her eyes again. Sat there, in one of those two chairs, by the small round table in the corner. Wrapped in a thin white towel, hands folded in her lap, bare feet nestled in the thick shag. Damp hair slowly drying.

"Good morning, welcome to Jack in the Box, how may I take your order?"

The guy in line ahead of her, tall enough to stoop and preternaturally thin, steps up to the counter and says, "Southwest Scrambler. With sausage. And a salted caramel shake."

"I'm sorry, sir. That's on the lunch menu, sir, the shake."

She's fishing from her pocket a medium-sized binder clip pinched about a five, a couple of ones. At her feet a black nylon duffel, limply empty, brightly new.

"We serve breakfast all day, sir. Lunch starts at eleven."

"Caramel whatsit, then," he says. "Coffee. Large."

"Southwest Scrambler, Caramel Iced Coffee, that'll be nine dollars eleven cents. Number seven twenty-one. Next?"

She kicks the duffel across flatly red tiles up to the counter, the red-jacketed clerk patient at the register, sizzle and pop and scrape behind, "Good morning, welcome to Jack in the Box, how may I take your order."

"The, ah, combos." She's peering at the brightly lit menu above, all close-up images of carefully assembled sandwiches, glistening fried potatoes, sweating and steaming cups of this or that. "Coffee's included?"

"And hash browns, yes."

"Okay," she says. "Let's have the ultimate breakfast, then. Combo." She's unclipping the bills.

"Ultimate Breakfast Sandwich Combo, four dollars eighty-nine cents. Number seven twenty-two."

She lays the five on the counter, takes the receipt and the change.

"Next?"

A low and narrow booth in the back corner. She's sat herself on one short vinyl-coated bench, stuck the duffel on the other, she's undoing with a rip the velcro of her fingerless cycling gloves, tugging one free, then the other. On the table by a paper cup of black coffee and three torn sugar packets is her phone, the screen of it lit up, 09:42, say the numerals of the phone's clock, Tuesday, May 15. 35%, the much tinier numerals by the partially filled icon of a battery, all of it floating over a photograph taken somewhere outside, at night, herself and Ysabel, cheek to cheek, Ysabel's hand at the upturned collar of her white coat under her lopping black curls, a coolly sidelong smile for Jo beside her, laughing, short hair tufted every which way, blur of her arm reached into the bottom of the shot where the corner of the glass is webbed with cracks, one of them jagging through the two of them up to the top. "Seven nineteen, order seven nineteen," blurts a voice from speakers up by the ceiling, and then, distantly, "Welcome to Jack in the," unamplified, "can I take your."

She presses the button at the bottom of the phone, gingerly taps in a code to unlock it. Touches the nested gears from among the icons that appear, sprinkled over their faces. Scrolls through a list of options till she reaches one that says Wallpaper.

"Seven twenty-one," the voice from the speakers. "Seven twenty-one."

Choose a New Wallpaper. Dynamic, Stills, Live, All Photos 152, Recent Photos 152, Favorites 0. Her fingertip dithers over Live, over Stills.

"Seven twenty-two. Order seven twenty-two."

Live. A selection of swirling cloudscapes appears, teal, indigo, stormy grey. She selects stormy grey, and the clouds fill the screen, squirming under her fingertip. Set, or Cancel.

"Seven twenty, and seven twenty-two. Orders seven twenty and seven twenty-two."

She looks up. Thumbs off the phone, stuffs it in her pocket. Heads for the counter, where a tray is waiting.

In the parlor, with the bicycles and the folded sandwich board that says Piano Lessons, Weekday Appointments, all glazed by morning light that drifts through high side windows, Becker's in a white T-shirt and grey lounge pants, one hand on the newel post at the foot of the stairs, he's taking a deep breath in through his nose, "Wow," he says.

"Yeah," says a woman away toward the back of the house, past the dining room opening off of the parlor, stood in the kitchen there through the archway, holding a great cast iron skillet.

"Is that," says Becker, and he sniffs again, "can I scam a cup?"

"I didn't make it," she says, staring at the skillet, heavy and wide and the yellow enamel of it pitted and stained, worn away with use. She tilts it, looking over the inside of it in the light, smoothly faintly glossy unmarred black. Becker bustling behind her, opening a cupboard, selecting a mug, looking over the electric drip coffeemaker on the gleamingly clean counter, carafe of it full and steaming. "Maybe it's Hollis's?" he says. "Hollis wouldn't mind. Would he?"

"Somebody *cleaned,*" she says.

"Somebody," says Becker, looking about, empty mug in his hand. The kitchen does sparkle, in this light, diffused though it is though the leaves of the trees without, glass jars of grains and beans lining the spotless countertops, faucet gleaming over an empty white sink, even the floor with a freshly mopped sheen. She's stood there, her oddly layered housedress, rainbow socks, her flamingo-headed slippers, that skillet in her hands, "Somebody *cleaned* my *pan,*" she says, aghast.

"Is it okay?" he says. She looks at him, then. Sets the skillet on an eye of the stove, and even the drip pan beneath the element's been scrubbed clean. "Oz," he says. "Is it okay?"

"It's perfectly seasoned," she says.

"Oh," he says.

"Nobody touches my pan," she says.

"I know, Oz. I know."

"Nobody *uses* my pan."

"I know." He turns back to the coffeemaker. Pours himself some coffee. The mug is blazoned with a dancing rag-and-bone man leading an elaborately laden horse. "Maybe it was Hollis?"

"Hollis didn't do this," she says.

"Well, *I* didn't," he says, sipping. "Dang, this is good."

"Pour me a cup," she says, and abruptly opens the fridge.

"So we're assuming it's communal," he says, getting down another mug, this one embossed with stylized chickens. "Oz?" He fills it with coffee. She's still before the refrigerator, one hand on the open door. "We out of oat milk?" he says.

Oz reaches both hands into the fridge to awkwardly, gingerly lift out a plastic takeaway dish to set it, quickly, on the counter, hands leaping away as if burnt. What's within can be made out, just, through the clear plastic lid, wide noodles set in a chilled red ragù, tumbled with glistening chunks of meat under a still-fluffy cloud of grated cheese and finely chopped herbs yet green. Giorgio's, says the label pasted on that lid. 5/14. "Oh," says Becker, peering over her shoulder. "I've been there." He frowns. "I think." Stepping back. It's a, fancy Italian place."

"Becker," says Oz.

"In the Pearl," he says.

"This is a vegan refrigerator, Becker."

"I know that," he says. And then, eyes widening, "Jesus, Oz, that's not *mine.*"

"*I* didn't put it there."

"I know, but – "

"Hollis doesn't eat pasta."

"Yes, but – "

"Jayfer's still out in Boardman."

"Maybe she came back early?"

"She would *never* violate the refrigerator like this."

"Maybe somebody's pranking you! I don't know!" Pushing back what's left of his hair. "I didn't, go, to a fancy restaurant, last night, and I'm pretty sure I didn't sleep-clean the, the kitchen, in the middle of the night, I never touched your pan, and that's *not* mine!"

"Can I have some?" says the man in the archway, pointing to the coffeemaker. "I am gonna need a cup or two before I can deal with this nonsense." Pushing between them both, reaching for a mug. "Hollis," says Oz. "Hollis! Somebody *cleaned* the *kitchen.*"

"Yeah?" says Hollis, filling a mug. "Did you notice the bathroom?"

THOSE SCRAWNY ARMS of his folded about himself as if for warmth, Christian Beaumont in a stained grey hoodie stands with one foot on the pallet, looking over the great wooden tub, staves of it worn yellow oak sawn off about knee-high, closely fit together and bound about by riveted iron hoops, wide enough across that he might lie down his full length within it, were he so inclined. The blues and indigos that usually plane his hunched cheekbones have ablated to oranges and reds in the candescent light of all the golden dust that fills it. "Go on," says Cackletub beside him. "Take some."

"And do what with it," says Christian.

"Have it," says Cackletub, taken aback. "Hold it. Let it warm the bones. Light the way. Shew again the colors we did lose. Crowd the mouth with flavors, the air with odors, that we forgot we ever knew. And the songs that can be heard, the deeds it makes it possible to do?" a gnarled finger lifts, thick-nailed tip of it pressed quick to Christian's forehead, and he rocks back from the touch of it. "Once you've known *that,* the old and deep and true of it, why – the world without seems cold and small, and empty, as it is."

"That's, um," says Christian, "yeah."

Someone steps up to the other side of the tub, the Stirrup in his brick-red vest, to dip a pyrex measuring cup in the golden dust. He holds it up, eyeing the level, pours back a slithering handfall, holds it up again. Shakes the cup to settle the owr.

"He's his obligations, as a knight," says Cackletub, leaning close. Christian starts. "You, you're the Porter's. He'd bring you your portion, but he's famously pledged: not one drop, nor yet a pinch."

"I'm the whose, now?"

"Gordon. The Porter. Who carries the mace, and opens the door."

"I'm not," says Christian, "his, I'm not nobody's," but *"Wisht!"* from Cackletub. "Not so loud. Not even in this room, so loud." Leaning close, "Gordon won't bring your portion, but you might take it for yourself." Christian's edging away, but Cackletub presses close, "You've been here a week, yet you haven't begun to wonder at why," a bony elbow in Christian's ribs, "go on. Her majesty's said."

Christian looks up and away at that, to the raised stage at the one end of the cavernous warehouse. Empty now but for the nubbled pea-green couch, where the Queen and her favorite hold court, the one sat up at one end, arm stretched along the back of it, the other laid the length of the couch, bare feet coquettishly crossed over the arm of it, black curls spread over the pillowing lap, and only the black lace and silver ribbon, the white silk and gold satin, to tell the two of them apart. Laid on cushions at their feet the twins in stockings red and black, Chrissie on her belly and her elbows, pinching and poking the screen of a tablet computer, Ettie perched over her shoulder, pointing and commenting. Synthesizer chords chime brightly cheerful from an unseen speaker, take me to the desert, some-one's singing, take me to the sand, show me the color of your right hand. On the floor before them, some few knights and others mingle, chatting quietly. Far off to the side of the stage, where the makeshift tabouret's been dragged, a woman in a black leather jacket is sat upon a stool, reading a tattered paperback. A greatsword sheathed and leaned against the wall behind her.

A bustle ruffles the disparate crowd, someone steps in from the daylight, stooping under the half-raised overhead door, straightening, the Guisarme in a light linen suit, his lemon shirt, his tie of lime. With him, towering over him, the Sovnya, shoulders of her white blouse crimped by a shining silver bevor. The Guisarme bows, deeply, to the stage, the couch, the Queen, then turns toward the tub on its pallets.

"A moment, Guisarme," says the Queen, voice pitched to carry. The milling comes to a sudden, jerking halt. The Guisarme, with a breath, swings back, the Sovnya close by his side. "My lady," he says, and bows again. "As always, it's ever a pleasure."

"Your third such, in but a sennight," she says, stroking the Starling's hair. "One should, perhaps, beware," and she looks from him to the tub behind him, "the risks, that attend to overindulgence," and now she looks to the Sovnya by his side.

"Needs must, my lady," he says. "And your majesty's gracious generosity does see to our every need."

"Our charitable concern, my lord," she says, "is it's your brother's needs that drive you, not your own."

He spreads his hands, he bows his head. "My brother's needs *are* my own, majesty."

"Your brother's coat's still blue, Welund," says the Queen.

"He does yet serve the Hound," says the Guisarme. "Would your majesty not agree that loyalty, that commitment, must, however difficult the course, stand firm against the lashings of such – "

"What he does serve," says the Queen, and her words ring in that cavernous room, "oh, it cringes when it's whipped, yes. It does bite the hand that feeds, though its yipping bark's more piercing than its teeth, and there can be no doubt, no doubt at all, it does return to its own vomit, for it is sick, quite sick – but not with gratitude, my lord. No. It has obtained the semblance and the seeming of a Hound, down to a trick, and it would have its day – but look into its eyes. Look deep within. You'll find no warmth, no adoration, and nothing of the Pinabel. Our cousin, Frederic? Is no more."

The Guisarme opens his mouth, but does not speak. All those gazes of the crowd, patiently impassive, yet focused all on him, those knights and others there before the stage, and the smattering behind him, there about the tub, the Buckler, the Stevedore, the Sequin and the Jackstaff, the Axe, the Flynn and Jenny Rye, Goggie, Luchryman, even the Sovnya at his side, chin ducked behind the shining bulwark of her bevor, and also Chrissie, and Ettie, chins in hands, and the Queen, her arm still stretched across the back of the couch, and only the Starling as she sits up from the Queen's lap's looking down, with a secret smile. The woman at the far end of the stage has not yet looked up from her book. He closes up his mouth, the Guisarme, and he swallows, and tries again. "Your majesty," he says, "cannot possibly be wrong, but is it not – "

"Are you not sworn to the Hive, Guisarme?"

He blinks. "Without question, ma'am."

"And your brother, the Glaive – is it possible he stands now at your side?" She makes a show of craning her head about, "But we do not see him. We haven't seen hide nor hair of him, in fact, for ten days and nine nights. Is it possible, that in that time, he's come to serve our Helm? Or salve our wounded Hawk? Can it be he's seen the light, and does now seek to soothe the Hare?" Leaned forward, elbows on her white-draped knees. "Or does his wind yet blow Southwesterly?"

The Guisarme, head bowed, says, "It is even as her majesty would have it."

"Until your brother changes his coat for a color we like more. Until he does come before us, and makes amends for his loyalty, his – commitment – to our bitterest enemy. Until such time. He will take no part of our bounty, with his hand, or any other's. This," she says, sitting back, "is how we," crossing one leg over another, "would have it." Shifting her arm from the back of the couch to the Starling's shoulders. "You may go." At their feet, Ettie ruffles Chrissie's hair, and Chrissie, annoyed, strokes it back in place. The Guisarme nods. They're all turning away from him, knights and hobs, domestics, peers, and only Sovnya with a nod for him in return, falling in smartly as he heads for the overhead door.

"Well, wasn't *that* a thing not to have missed," says Cackletub, turning away from the stage, but Christian isn't there.

Blue sky a seamless ceiling high above. Holding up a hand a moment to shade his eyes he peers across a half-empty parking lot. A simple arch at the far corner, a green sign that says Spring-water Corridor, hung over a narrow path between the railroad tracks to the left, the fenced-in yard of a gravel plant to the right, towering tanks and pipes, the lines and slants of conveyor belts silent, still. He sets off, thin robe loosely flapping, stripes of it in various colors that might once have been brighter, some few launderings ago, brown hair long and damply lank, redder beard quite full. Under the arch without a pause and past another sign that says Stop! Please Use Caution – Heavy Truck Traffic.

Beyond the plant the fence to the right swaddled in a heavy coat of vines, crowded leaves broad and darkly green affording only glimpses of the river, a muddy grey too gently smoothed to sparkle in the sun. To the left, past the rails, a slope rises steeply, shaggily, wildly green. Shadows ahead under a high bridge, and traffic booming and growling over it, the concrete pillars of it tattooed with graffiti, signatures, sigils, cartoons. "You could've," he's muttering to his trudging sneakers, "you could've been with me. Up above the river." He looks up, in the shadow of the bridge. "Under the earth," he says.

Calved from the bridge an offramp on spindly pillars curls through the air above to merge with a freeway along the top of that steep slope. "Echo," he says, "echo," eyeing it, and the bare fence between himself and the rails, "three, not ten," he says, and then, as he passes the last pillar upholding that ramp, "one," he says, "two, three, not ten, ten, six, eleven," he's counting fenceposts, "seven eleven, twelve," skipping ahead, "fourteen!" A hole's been cut in the next panel of cyclone fencing, close to the lush grass, where a green plastic bowl's been placed, and a clear reservoir with a bit of kibble still within wired to the pole. He stops, a faint breeze stirring the loose skirts of his bathrobe. Faintly happy cheers and a whoop from someone unseen on the river. Away ahead a cluster of bobbing dots, joggers growing as they approach. Grabbing the fencepost wire ringing under the kicking slipping soles of his sneakers he clumsily throws a leg over the fence, rolls himself over, drops to the tracks. Unsnagging his trailing robe with an irritated jerk. "You could've been with me," he says, and sweeps back his hair, combs his fingers through his beard, tugging loose a snarl. "Up under," he says, looking along the railroad. "High beneath." Darting across, into the brush, and up and up the grassy slope.

He finds a path, halfway up, half-hidden along a brow of earth. Shaggy trees lean heavily green out over the railway, the little herd of joggers passing by so far below. He braces himself against a crooked trunk, a balustrade to clamber the last steep hillock of path, onto the narrow top of the slope, between the trees and the shadowy galleries under the freeway so close above, regular bays between concrete walls that uphold the deck of it, floored with gravel-studded hardpack. A great eye's been painted on a wall of the first gallery, the iris of it elaborately paned, red paint squiggled over the pupil. He passes it quickly, stumbling over a low flat rock at the edge of the overgrown path, "One," he says, passing the next gallery, empty but for dust and what's left of a couple of dirt-raddled empty black garbage bags, "one, one, two!" and a dismissive wave for three kids clustered in the next, back denim and brown-tinged leather and red, hair shaved and sculpted in grimy hanks, ragged braids, in drooping petalled spikes, an unevenly gravid joint making its way from one hand to the next, "two!" he shouts again, scurrying past, "three!" as he jerks to a stop, there, this gallery empty but for a beige and brown dome tent pitched a-kilter in the sharp dark shadow of the freeway just above.

"Three!" he barks, under the rush of unseen traffic. "Not ten, fourteen, but three!"

Stood there, waiting, bathrobe snapped out behind by a sudden gust. Some baroquely intricate siege engine's printed across the front of his T-shirt.

"She could've been with me!"

Up past the tent, where the earth rises to meet the deck, the dirt's been tumbled, piled, a yawning mouth scratched up against the concrete piling. Hauling his robe back about himself he steps off the path up toward it, stomp, stomp, when the rolling wash of sound from above is cut by the drawn-out rip of a zipper. He stops, looks back to the tent, flaps of it parting just enough for a peering eye, "Hey!" he yells. "What are you, hey!" The tent shivers, flaps close up. "What are you *doing* here? Can't you *smell* it? Hey!" One last thrashing shiver, and the tent is still.

"Well," he says. "*I* can smell it."

Up to the empty darkness of the tunnel, laying a hand on the lip of it, thrumming freeway a ceiling too close. A deep breath. He ducks into the darkness.

Low, cramped, the floor unevenly rolling up into a wall he brushes with a shoulder, patterfall of loose dirt, he shakes that shaggy silhouette of a head. Shoves a hand in a pocket of his bathrobe, yanks it out, snap! A spark enough to show where he's stepping down and down and deeper within, stopping once, stooping, his unlit hand against the cleanly scraped wall for balance, face screwed up with disgust in the harsh glare. He snatches a fold of his robe up over his mouth and nose.

Shadows pool and spill ahead of his lit hand. The tenor of the dulled thrum hollows, opens, a space cleared off to the right where the wall falls away. He pauses. Coughs behind his robe.

The room unfolds itself from shadows in his light, back wall of pitted concrete, floor of it a sea of bags and sacks and plastic crates, a demolished cardboard box stuffed with blankets and trousers, coats and more, unidentifiable parcels and bundles and wads of fabric about, and so many empty cans and bottles, and bundles of newspaper trimly tied, and a body splayed atop it all, arms and legs at uncommon angles, torso bloated and collapsed all wrong beneath the pasted, blackened clothing, steeped in something long since dried and flaking crackled.

"I thought you got," he says, that one bright hand held high. "*You* thought," he says. "You thought he got the chair."

His hand drops, and darkness falls, complete, obliterate. Rustle and shuff, another pattering scrabble of falling dirt, crinkle of plastic, he's sitting, perhaps. A sigh. "You kept her safe," he says, to himself. "But."

And then, quietly, "This'll do."

A blue sky, utterly bereft of clouds, but nonetheless a haze has risen from some unfixable middle distance to diffuse itself between clearly here and soft, indefinite there, somewhere past the distant line of trees that edge the vast field to the right, still crisp, still sharp against the paling blue beyond, but somewhere yet before the mountain there, a single cuspid smaller, somehow, than it should be, to seem so much closer than it is, blued edges of its fading snowcap blurred by the bluing haze, its summit more inferred than certain, slipping away off behind those trees. More trees more closely planted not too long ago separate this narrow sidewalk from the field, this haphazardly patched seam-sprung walk that's more of an afterthought, really, too close to the wide straight cleanly painted road, where panel trucks and a tall van speed past, only a couple of feet away. Behind these trees, a low and temporary fence of two-by-fours and startling orange plastic sheeting's been pitched, one more straight line along with trees, sidewalk, road, relentlessly converging on a point off in that unseen, uncertain middle distance. A sign's erected awkwardly ahead, the framing lumber of the same fresh yellow provenance as the fenceposts. For Lease, it says. 157,185 SF. Call Now. It's close enough to the sidewalk she can slap it as she passes.

Her duffel's black, her jeans are black, her shirt is black, and across the front of it a devil's leering face, marred by silkscreen craquelure. Pause as a car whips past, dully grey, wind in the wake of it tugging at her, ruffling her hair, browner now, perhaps, indifferently cut. Starts out again, stops again, lifting her white shoe to kick it against the sidewalk. A pebble's dislodged from the cracked and duct-taped toe.

A semi blows past, one lane over, followed by another car, too close, too fast, top-heavy with a matte black cargo shell. She skips off the sidewalk at that, through the line of trees, past tummocky grass and raw bare earth, kicks a leg up over that startling orange fence and steps out, away from the traffic, out into the sun-bright field.

Flat and open and wide, but so much longer, stretched out alongside the road, grass of it thick and green and yellow, up about her shins, lined the four sides with greenly dark trees, exuberantly thicker at the ends and down the far side to the right, to the left that regimented rank all of the same tensed upthrust shape, branches too nervous yet to settle and relax, spaced with room enough between to grow, yet close enough to muffle passing traffic. She picks her way over roughly lumpy ground, one arm out for balance, the other tucked close, holding fast that shoulder-slung emaciated duffel. One last half-leaping step from deep grass to a rutted track, freshly churned by tires, or treads.

That track crests a barely perceptible rise to angle down the vaguest of declines, but this slight change in perspective's enough to reveal a broadly section of the field scraped clear of grass and rumples, excess earth piled indiscreetly here and there along the edges of it, and corners and points of perhaps some future interest marked with stakes, strips of that startling orange plastic tied to flutter and dangle about the ends of them. Traces of the track cross a corner of the lot, past overturned earth dried dustily dull, to where grass springs up again. The track, less freshly used here, angles further across the field toward that other bordering line of trees, thicker, more wildly lush, past a second lot much smaller, less officious, defined by trampled grass in a roughly ring about the charred remains of a bonfire, and a scattered detritus of food wrappers, discarded clothing, a lone heel-sprung running shoe, an untidy spill of unopened mail, stained and swollen by old rain, and above it all swirling silent eddies of flies and midges. The track resumes its parallel course, thick dark wall of trees to the right, the murmuring, whining road a ways off to the left.

Midges scatter, a dragonfly slicing their midst, stitching zip from point to point before her and she freezes to see it hung there, shivering, depended from the rainbowed whir of lacy wings. She tenses as it swoops quite close, then leaps away, a fleeting scrap too fast, lost in the soft blue sky.

There's someone away up ahead.

A quarter-mile or so up the track, not yet to the trees that cap that far end of the field, a cluster of half a dozen cars or so, and trucks, parked on the grass, and somebody there before them, arms swung in soundless claps, leaned forward, echoing after, a distant shout, "Oy!" And again, "Hey, oy!" Or maybe "Roy!"

Something bounds from flailing grass onto the track, making for her with alacrity, low shape galloping, a dog, much too slender for a dog, and brightly streaming. One or two others have stepped out from among the vehicles to watch. The shouting somebody's set off running up the track as well, after the spindly, long-legged whatever-it-is. She steps off track, kneels in grass, unshouldering fumbling open her duffel, "Roy!" the closer cry now, definitely "Roy! Wait!" as sharply patterfall too sharp for paws that cutting soil crisply little thunder wire-wrapped hilt in her hand but rocking back her heels she's blinking hand held up against a brightness not the sun but, but iridescent shimmering galumph a tiny horse not even a pony scampering past to wheel a tight curl whirling snorting halt, her one arm up and braced the sheathed poignard tucked behind her forearm, "Hanh!" she blurts.

"Roy!"

The horse, that tiny horse, leaps into the grass behind her and springs back out again, bucking on the track before her snort and whinny, four hands, maybe five at the most, dark-tufted fetlocks over dainty cloven hooves, pale glossy rose-grey coat, a skinny nearly hairless tail but for a sudden puffball shock at the end of it, as brightly shining as the mane, and iridescent, red in it, and yellow, shocks of green and sudden flares of blue as it tosses its head again, and its horn.

"He don't bite," calls the somebody, a boy, young man in jeans, denim jacket a-clatter with buttons. "Roy. Leave her alone. C'mon, Roy."

The unicorn, that tiny unicorn, takes a hesitant step closer to Jo. Trembling, flanks a-bellows from the effort of his galloping approach. The wire-wrapped hilt still in her hand, sheath still tucked behind her arm. She's lowering her other hand, reaching for the drily grassy earth before her, without taking her eyes off the unicorn taking another closer step, stretching out his neck, those black eyes liquid blinking, white-spotted lips, fine silky hairs about the black-rimmed nostrils, close enough his blown breath stirs her hair. She swallows. "Hey," she says.

"He's okay," says the young man in denim. "C'mon, Roy."

The horn of him's helically ridged, translucent as the inside of a shell, chased with as many colors as the mane but paler and subdued. It rises from just above his eyes, as long again as his neck, the tip of it trembling fixed to a point she has to look up from his eyes to meet. "Wow," she says. "That's, uh – "

The unicorn snorts, and lowers his head.

"Wait," she says.

The unicorn lowers his head, tip of his horn stretching just a bit further, just, to touch, to dimple her T-shirt there, above the devil's leering eye, to press. There's the faintest and most terribly delicate clink, and then a sudden extravagant flash of light.

"WELCOME BACK" – JACK'S DOG – THE FLY, THE FLY
LESS THAN A TWO-POINT-FIVE

"WELCOME BACK."

Jo lifts a hand, a shadow among shadows. Rubs her eyes, fingertip and thumb, pinches the bridge of her nose.

"Had us worried, girl. Come on. Sit yourself up. Water? Jack, fetch us a water."

Footstep, creak of springs, a slithering thump. "Careful, Jack," that voice, pitched high, creaky with smoke, or age.

"Ma'am," another voice, the young man. She opens her eyes. She's laid across a small and rumpled bed, legs bent over the side of it, feet somewhere on the floor. The space is long and narrow, dim despite the windows in every wall, for every curtain's drawn with differing colors and prints, reds and yellows for the cowboy hats and boots, purples and greens and blues and pinks for floral sprays, browns and oranges for squatly happy mushrooms, all backlit by daylight without. Someone's sat on the bed beside her, a dumpy woman, cardigan, what light there is catching rims and frame of heavy spectacles over her eyes. Jo sits up with a grimacing hiss, leaning over on one elbow, reaching to press a hand to her breast, rubbing, a soothing stroke.

"Here we go," says the woman beside her. That young man in denim's stood before them, holding out a short plastic bottle of water, cap of it already off. Jo takes it with a nod, sips, then drinks it down.

"Better?" says the woman. Jo holds up the empty bottle, but no one seems inclined to take it. "Where you headed?" says the woman.

"Away," says Jo, leaning forward, looking to set the empty bottle on the floor, maybe, but the floor is covered, piled with magazines, dozens, hundreds of them, neatly stacked here, collapsing in drifts there, Jack with his feet planted in some of the only cleared space available, a marginal meander from the bed in its nook up past a booth to one side under wide windows curtained with palm trees in pinks and yellows, a terribly compact kitchenette the other, and every available surface laden with more magazines, a helmeted warrior, an iceberg, a close-up of an eagle's head, a hedgehog curled in someone's hand, an astronaut, someone holding a pair of binoculars, someone scowling, hand tucked in the jacket of his uniform, The Battle of Waterloo, The New Europeans, Wild Pets, Is Anybody Out There?, The Tallest Trees, Planet or Plastic, Becoming Jane, Why Birds Matter, and all of them each of them every single one of those cover photos set in the framed by the same thick border of brightly jonquil yellow. Jo sits up, reaches past the young man, Jack, who twists aside, she seizes something from a scrap of countertop behind him, knocking off slippery flap a handful of magazines, "Careful, girl," a warning tone from the woman next to her.

"This is mine," says Jo, hitching up so she can tuck away the binder clipped about two dollar bills in a pocket, patting the others, "my phone," she says, looking about. "My phone?"

"You were flat on your back, dead to the world," says the woman next to her. The lenses of those heavy spectacles wrap around her eyes, lightlessly opaque. "Had no idea if we'd be calling 911, or what." A jerk of her head for Jack, who nods, leans over to fetch something from the magazines stacked on the table of the booth, hands it to Jo, her phone. She thumbs it on. 15:34, the numerals floating over her face, and Ysabel's. Quickly off again. "My bag?" she says. "The knife?" Holding out her hand. "The knife."

"You sure you're okay?" says the woman. "Collapsing out there like that."

"I'm fine, I'll be fine," says Jo, hand still out. "The water helped. Thank you. My stuff."

"Because I know it can't have nothing to do with Jack's cute little dog."

Jo's hand lowers. "Dog," she says, looking up to Jack, stood there in the meander. Behind him, up at the front of the space a single window, a windshield, curtained as well with plain dark burlap, a couple of captain's chairs, a steering wheel. Shadows render whatever expression his face might hold unreadable.

"Oh, Jack's got him done up all funny, sure. But he wouldn't hurt a flea, that dog."

"I promise," says Jo, "I won't tell anybody about Jack's," a sidelong look for the woman beside her, "dog. Okay?" Sitting forward, feeling for a clear patch of floor with her feet. "Just, give me my stuff, I'll get out of your hair, you've got nothing to worry about. Okay? Nothing."

"You sure?" says the woman. Jack's already leaning over the booth again, hauling up the nearly empty duffel, something heavy in it dragging one end. "You don't need anything else?"

"Water," says Jo, taking her bag. "Another water, if I could." Zips it open, roots about inside. The woman nods to Jack again, but he's bent over, peering through a gap in the curtains. Voices, indistinct, back and forth somewhere out there.

"Who is it?" The woman's gone from sitting to perching. Jack shrugs. She gets to her feet and somehow a step here, a step there, nimbly she's past him and headed up front without disturbing a page. A scrabble up there, one of the captain's chairs swinging about as she nears it, a flicker of colors, the unicorn's laid on the seat of it, legs awkwardly dangled. She leans over to scritch that brilliant mane. "Get her that water," she says, "but stay inside. Won't be a minute."

Opening the door, a sudden flare of sunlight. The unicorn snorts. The door closes up the light again.

"Dog?" says Jo.

Jack shrugs, looks back over his shoulder. The unicorn's perked up, looking up and over, the voices outside rising, a shout ringing over that creaky rasp.

"The hell?" says Jo, getting to her careful feet, "Wait," says Jack, but crumple slippy rippering step she's leaning against the tiny closet to reach "Jesus" for the counter past him lurching to brace himself against the ceiling, "You're gonna," but "Shut up," she snatches a curtain-corner, drags it ringing aside.

Another back-and-forth of voices without, lower, but as heated.

"Shit," says Jo Maguire, letting the curtain fall. Pulling the straps of the duffel up about her shoulder. Setting off tipping to lean from countertop to booth-table, making her way up the meander, eyeing all the while the captain's chair, and the unicorn sat upon it.

"May said stay inside," says Jack.

"Don't sweat it," says Jo, reaching for the door-latch. "I got this." A shrug. "I know these guys."

Yanking it open, into the light.

The first rolls of stuff high, ungainly wide, slick black plastic stiffly thick, creaking as they're wrestled into place under the aloof blue sky. A gentle hupf! not so much from any one of them but all at once they're tipped over, thump-thud, crunch on the grey pea stone. A breath of a pause, another, sharper ho! and they're off, slowly at first with the weight of them, pressing forward, unrolling to score wide black lanes side-by-side down the grey gravel length of the roof.

Even as they're still unrolling the second wave is setting up, more stiff ungainly rolls gallumphed to the gaps between lanes. Christian's wrenching his around, eyeing the placement when hupf! shoved over crackle and thump, he's wrestling the one end of his, checking the angle, hauling it back, ho! they set off, unrolling more plastic to overlap the first, Christian a little behind the others, filthy blue running shoes slipping and one long sliding step that leaves him on one knee on the stuff, scrabbling. Some of the others already returning, back over squeak and crack plastic to heave and let fall long green sacks of gravel from off their shoulders, weighting those unrolled strips. Christian steps off the plastic, up to a dwindling levee of gravel-sacks, and squats to get his knees under one, lifting with a scowl the weight of it, staggering back onto footsteps carefulling plastic past sacks already dropped, there, there, he lets his fall as soon as he can and bends over it, hands on his knees. Straightens. All about him they've set to ripping open sacks with shears, multi-tools, daggers, claws, spilling gravel out. He looks around, at his own bare hands, the long green sack on the plastic before him, weightily stuffed, of thick cord tightly woven. Here comes Charlichhold, hook-tipped knife out and ready, and Christian steps back, again, managing not to stumble over the drift of gravel already loosed behind.

Stripped to the waist, he kneels upon the grass.

Shaking his head he brushes gravel dust from the shoulder of his hoodie, making his way toward the other end of the unrolled plastic where tools have been piled, shovels, rakes. "The fly, the fly, the fly," someone's chanting, Trucos there by the small crane leaned out over the edge of the roof, and Getulos, "the fly, the fly, the fly," the two of them working the winch of it, muscles bunching and releasing across bared shoulders glossy with sweat, "the fly is on the turmut!" Christian takes up a push broom and joins the others, raking and shoveling, spreading the gravel, flattening out those piles over the plastic. "Was on a jolly summer's morn," someone's singing, "the fifteenth day of May," more joining in, "Jim Turk!" someone shouts, and a guffaw from Big Jim in the midst of them all, he took his turmut hoe, and trudged off on his way! For some delight in haymaking, and some they fancies mowing, but of all the trades we do like best, give us the turmut-hoeing!

Stripped to the waist he's knelt there, on rich green grass, lifting up his head.

Push broom turned over, bristles up, wooden head of it press and scrape, back and push. The gravel's more varied in color, generally brown, larger than the pea stone still visible, a pale strand of it lapping the base of the back brick wall, the reach of it left to stretch away the far end of the roof. For the fly, the fly, the fly be on the turmut! they're chanting, bent over with rakes and shovels, brooms, spreading the gravel from parapet to parapet until the last of the plastic's buried away, and it's all my eye for we to try to keep fly off the turmut!

And now come some, arms laden with stuff, rolls of speckled grey felt they drop and kick over, unrolling across the gravel, but also blankets and coverlets, ratty old quilts shook out, even sheets of cardboard, spatchcocked boxes tossed onto the rocks, now the next place as we went to work, it were with, and someone shouts above the others, "Brether Nedrick!" and general laughter, and a rough deep voice booms out, "An I vows an swares, an dizz declare, yar wiz an farst-rate hoer!" and the laughter then redoubles as they toss and stamp, flatten and spread. Christian steps back, nearly bumps into the Flynn, turns about, cardboard crumpling underfoot. Stripped to the waist he topples forward, hands and knees, clutching the trembling grass, "Shit," he hisses, trying to get himself out of the way, for it's all my eye as we do try to keep fly off the turmut!

He stuffs a hand in the pocket of his hoodie as they're stepping past, sprinkling water over cardboard and cloth from pots and jugs with ladles and cups and thumbs over spouts, dripping, dampening, dolloping, when we was ower at yonder farm, they sent for us a-mowin'! But we sent word back we'd take the sack, nor lose our turmut-hoein'! Over by the crane they've hauled up one pallet laden with plastic sacks that say FoxFarm and Sun Gro and Black Gold, and they're busily hauling up another with great wrenching twists of the winch, the fly, the fly, the fly! He's pulled his hand from his pocket, thumb-tip absently stroking grains of brightly gold against the blue-brown crease of index finger, shaking away a trailing thread from the frayed cuff. Suddenly elbows and wriggling Christian shrugs his way under and out of that hoodie, dropping it onto a patch of gravel, steps back with a nod as water's flung onto it, grabbing a handful of gravel to weight it down with the rest.

Stripped to the waist, a half dozen or so of them crouch and kneel, bared backs shining brown and glistening pale, ruddily bronze, jeans and dungarees, corduroys, work boots and knobbed bare feet, filthy blue running shoes, they spread and evenly scrape, tireless, chanting become a rolling thrumming nearly wordless hum-de-dum, the fly, the fly, the turmut as they press and tamp, rumpled and hillocked soil tumbled and spilt on the dampened cloth and cardboard mulched into the gravel spread over the plastic below, it's all left smoothly glossy in their wake, a rich black even field. There at the crane Getulos and Trucos, and Jim Turk with them, it's all my eye, it's all my eye as they winch up a pallet of turf-rolls, richly brown, coiled with startling green. Spread and scrape, press and tamp, shake off the sweat and breathe and blow, smooth and tamp and spread until, until, until shirtless he rolls onto his back in all the gingerly unfolded grass, under the high blue sky.

He sits up, utterly alone in the midst of that high new lawn. Not even a broomstick left behind, but his shoulders bare, and his jeans heavy with wet dirt.

"Hello, good evening. My name is Arnold Becker. I'm calling on behalf of Barshefsky Associates, an independent market research firm. This is, I assure you. This is not a sales," he closes his eyes, and rocks the handset back into its cradle. Sighs. Taps the tab key, toggling radio buttons next to listed items on the screen until he gets to Refusal (Hang Up). Presses tab again, to Refusal (Definite), then on to Disconnected, then back to No Answer at the top. Strokes his scratchily stubbled cheek. Reaches to press the enter key, but takes hold of the mouse instead. Moves the pointer on the screen to press the radio button next to Refusal (Hang Up). Sighs again. Hits enter.

A new number appears on the screen, ten digits, numerals bold and large. He reaches for the handset, rocks it forward off the cradle, and a dial tone leaks from the earpieces of his headset. Adjusts the mike of it with one hand while he taps the number on the phone with the other. Tips back his waiting head.

A click, followed not by the burr of a ringing phone, but the howling piercing gurgle of a modem, testing its connection. He slaps the headset from his ears to bounce against the keyboard, knocks the handset back into its cradle, cutting off the noise. The woman beside him spares him a scowl of sympathy, but she's speaking to someone on her headset, "no sir, not a sales call at all. Yessir. Jessie Vee. Well, that's great! Okay. And I know this sounds a little weird, but I have to ask, would you say you're the person who makes most of the financial decisions for your household?"

He lifts the headset off the keyboard, flicks it toward the back of his carrel. Pounds the tab key, down, down, until the radio button by Disconnected is lit up.

"And would that be all of the financial decisions, at least half, less than half, or none of the financial decisions for your household? I know, I know, it's a little weird. Trust me. It gets better."

Becker pushes back his chair, bends down to scoop up his messenger bag. Settles a dark grey meshback cap on his head as he gets to his feet. Rolls the chair carefully back into place before the narrow carrel, just enough room for the phone, the keyboard, the monitor waiting patiently for someone to confirm the status of this phone number.

"Becker," says the kid at the desk, "hey, Becker? What's up?" Voice pitched to carry just enough under the clatterous murmur of numbers dialed, questions asked, data entered. Becker's steps stutter, he shifts the strap of the bag on his shoulder, tightens his grip. Looks the kid over, his blue on blue check shirt, thick-knotted tie of brown and purple paisley. "You've only got six in the bag," says the kid. "That's less than a two-point-five. Becker? Becker!"

Becker pushes open the door, steps out into the cramped lobby, empty but for a couple of leather armchairs, the large copper letters of the logo on the wall, and, when the door swings shut behind him, so very quiet.

EAST MULTNOMAH SOIL & WATER – DUTY – WARD, OR SIGIL
SELECT PASSENGER – BEAUTIFUL MOUNTAIN

"THE EAST MULTNOMAH SOIL AND WATER CONSERVATION DISTRICT?" a plaintive bellow loud enough to be heard through the front door, even as he's unlocking it. "How, I ask, can we possibly *ever* be expected to bear the inestimably weighty responsibility of choosing the *directors* of such an august enterprise? With only *this,"* a rattling flutter, "to guide us?"

Through the twilight-steeped parlor, past the bicycles, the sandwich board draped with somebody's coat, the dining room's very bright, three people sat about the table piled with books and unopened mail. In the kitchen through the archway Oz is kneading something, shaking her head. A band of angels came to me, weeping, in the night, sings a woman from some unseen speaker, someone's phone, maybe. "Arnie!" cries a thickset man at the table, lowering the newsprint booklet he's been waving about for emphasis. "What a pleasant surprise."

"I've told you, Jimmy," he lets the messenger bag slip from his shoulder, "feel free to call me Becker, just like everybody else."

"Whatever it is you're to be called – on which point, you'll note, this jury is still out," Jimmy holds up a forestalling finger, "we'd been led to believe you'd be at work tonight. Thus, the surprise."

"Yeah, well," says Becker, letting the messenger bag slump to the floor. "I think I, ah, well. Quit."

Oz stops kneading. Hollis looks up from the paper on the table before him. Blood, color of the flower, emblazoned on your breast, sings the unseen phone. Jimmy blinks. "Forgive me," he says, "but one is usually a *touch* more definite about such milestones."

"I guess. I mean," says Becker, "I'm not going back. I'm not doing that again. So."

On the road to Jericho, sings the phone.

"A toast!" cries Jimmy. "An occasion so momentous must be marked. But with something more festive than kombucha," and a meaningful scowl for the brown glass bottle by Hollis's elbow. "It's *apple juice,"* says Hollis.

"Even so," says Jimmy, cocking a brow imploringly at Oz who's leaned in the arch now, wiping her flour-dusted hands on her apron. "No," says Becker, "that's okay, I don't, we don't need to. It's fine. So what is this? Some kind of, voting party?"

"Our civic duty!" booms Jimmy, sweeping a sweater-draggled arm over the ballots and booklets, the phones and the tablet spread over the table before them. "Third Tuesday in May, and evidence of the exercise of our franchise must be lodged with the appropriate authorities by eight o'clock this very night."

"We were gonna walk 'em down to the library," says the woman across from Jimmy. "Swing by the Bite after," says Hollis. "But doubtless, Arnie," says Jimmy, *"you* have long since posted your ballot by mail, and already confirmed its arrival with the county. Still. We might well benefit from your input, sir, in our deliberations."

"Actually?" says Becker, attempting a winsome shrug. Jimmy slaps the table. "My good lord, Becker," he says, "you do disappoint. You were fully intending to work your shift – which, if memory serves, typically extends to *nine* o'clock, on those evenings when you *don't* quit in the middle – without having performed your secularly sacral duty."

"Jimmy," says Becker. "I've had a day. I've had a *week.*"

"Leave him alone," says Hollis.

"I shall most certainly not," says Jimmy, holding up an admonishing finger, holding back a gust of laughter. "This must not, this *will* not stand. Arnie. If you are half the man I suspect you still to be, that ballot sits," and he pauses, pursing his lips. "Jimmy," says the woman across the table from him, but Jimmy shakes his head. "Not in your bag, no. It's in your room, unopened, isn't it. Not blatantly, out in the open, no: that'd be too on-the-nose. But innocuously stacked with other items you haven't gotten around to yet, but mean to, soon enough. So that you might relish the thrills of guilt – sharpened, perhaps, with an edge of self-loathing – that sweep over you whenever you inadvertently catch sight of the envelope's patriotically red embellishments. Reminding you of this obligation, to your neighbors, your city, that you failed to fulfill. Until you tire of the sport when its returns inevitably diminish over the coming weeks, and you finally toss it out with the recycling. So! Go on. Run away upstairs and fetch it down. Do this thing – not for the ideal of it, or the greater good: do it for yourself, Arnie. Redeem the day you've had. I feel certain that, in order to encourage such a rapprochement, between yourself, and your better self, Oz would be willing to break out the good stuff."

Hollis snorts. The woman across from Jimmy shakes her head with all her dangling, tiny braids. Oz cocks her brow, but she's smiling. Becker isn't. "James Frederic Madison Dupris," he says, "if that really is your name," and Jimmy's lips purse again at that. "I've moved," says Becker, "three times, since the last election. Most recently?" Looking about the dining room, the archway to the kitchen, them at the table, and Oz, "Less than four weeks ago. I don't *have,* a ballot. It's probably," throwing off a gesture, "sitting in a mailbox, back at my old place by the Lloyd Center."

"You failed," cries Jimmy, theatrically clutching his chest, "to update your *registration?"*

"I've been busy!" snaps Becker. "And who gives a damn about an election in May, anyway?"

"We gotta vote for Chloe," says Hollis, a hand on his ballot.

"It's totally gonna be whatsisname," says Becker. "Killian."

"But that's the point," says Oz. "Even if he wins, if he doesn't have a majority, there's a run-off in November," lifting a hand to make air-quotes, "the *important* election, right? So we'll have time, to – "

"To do what? Work for Chloe?" Becker hauls his messenger bag back up onto his shoulder. "She doesn't make the run-off. It'll be between Beagle, and Killian, which is basically just two different clubs of developers tussling over whose pot of money gets bigger next year. And Killian's still gonna win." The song picking its way through the air has changed, another woman's singing, he gave her a dime store watch, and a ring made from a spoon. Becker turns away, back through the parlor.

"Such cynicism, in one so young," says Jimmy. "You are not the man I thought I knew, Arnold Becker!"

"What can I tell you, Jimmy?" Becker calls back, over his shoulder. "I got layers."

Tock and clack of heels on tarmacadam, passing under a sign that says Springwater Corridor, between railroad tracks to the left, a gravel plant to the right, she makes her way toward the high bridge ahead, lit against oncoming night, glown white and sullen red with headlights and taillights to-and-fro-ing above the wheeling flares of red and blue that disrupt the shadows ahead. Those lights suggest colors hidden in the sleekly grey of her pantsuit, but do nothing to illuminate her face, or bring out the color of her corkscrew curls. She spares not a glance to either side, the dark slope to the left, rising to the freeway, the river away off to the right, disaffectedly rippled with light, nor does her stride falter as she rounds a slight bend in the path to see the source of those flashes, the police suv, the ambulance, parked one before the other to block the narrow path not far beyond the bridge. The suv's lights atop its roof, before and behind, all flash and sweep and stutter. The ambulance is dark.

A small crowd stood about, mostly beyond the suv, joggers and a couple of cyclists in athletic togs, somebody with a high, elaborate backpack, a woman in tights and a filthy T-shirt speaking with a couple, man and woman, both in dark suit coats. An officer uniformed in black by the rear of the suv, looking up the slope, they're all looking up the slope, where a couple of figures in white coveralls struggle their way down with some bulky burden. Still looking up, he steps away from the suv, "Hold up," he says. "Trail's closed."

"It's okay," she says, smiling. "I'm from headquarters." Reaching into her jacket she pulls out not a wallet or a badge but a small white card. "You're Officer Latif?" Holding the card not so much for him to see, but the tiny lens on the palm-sized camera clipped to his tactical vest. He doesn't look down at it, printed though it is with black squares scattered about a grid in a staticky random blot. He doesn't look away from her eyes, large and dark and neatly lined, friendly and welcoming. "Who've you got?" she says, tucking the card away.

"Guy who reported it," says the officer. "Didn't do it, but he's the closest we've got to anybody of interest. Most everybody else up there scattered." A sidelong look for the woman still speaking with the two in suits. The SUV rocks behind him, staccato thumps within, a muffled bellow. "Hey!" barks the officer. "We ain't got a full statement yet," he says, turning back to her. "He's, ah. Belligerent."

"He'll do," she says, opening the rear door of the SUV on a wordless howl, the dome light revealing a man, bearded, wrapped in a striped bathrobe, hands behind his back, kicking and hurling his weight about on the plastic back seat. "Stop that," she says, and the howl breaks, he holds himself, trembling, still, wedged back against the closed door behind him, head at an awkward angle, bare feet braced against the partition. "Can we talk?" she says.

Shivering, tense, still wedged, panting heavily enough to ruffle his overgrown mustache, trouble his rankly matted beard. He swallows. "Sure," he says, relaxing enough feet slipping on the plastic floor to settle back on the seat.

"Good," she says, climbing into the SUV, sitting herself on the bench beside him, pulling the door shut. "Hey, wait," he says, as the dome light clicks off. "You're, I, what? Who are you?"

"A moment, please." She's holding that card up so the printed squares face a smokey plastic globe high up on one corner of that partition between front seats and back. "Your pardon," she says, leaning across him to hold the card up before a similar globe in the opposite corner.

"What are you doing?"

"Just a moment." She's pressed the printed face of the card to the glass that windows the partition, criss-crossed with a wire grill, holding it still there a moment. "That should do it. Keep your voice down, just in case."

"You're not police," he says.

"Oh, I am, of a sort," she says. "What I'm not is a cop. I can't abide cops." Shifting on that plastic bench. "They'll primly tell you that the seats must be like this, to allow them to be cleaned, quickly, and easily, but they do not have to be so narrow, slick, unyielding. The discomfort is the point. Baked into the very design of the thing." Tucking that card back into her jacket. "It's, quite simply, cruel. And I can't abide cruelty."

"What was that, a sigil of some kind? A ward?"

"A QR code," she says, cocking a brow. "We don't have much time. Lean forward."

He does, but "Wait!" he blurts, as she reaches behind him, "what are you doing?"

"That zip-tie can't be comfortable."

"Leave it!" he says, sitting back, pressing back against the door, away from her. "Leave it."

"You found the body," she says. "You reported it." He nods. "But you didn't kill him," she says. "Her. Whomever."

"Of course not!"

"And yet," she says, "you're the one in the back of a police car." He shrugs.

She sits back against her door, perched on the edge of the plastic seat. "Is it in remission, then?" she says.

He blinks, and takes much too long to say, "What?"

"By your fundament betrayed," she murmurs, leaning toward him, eyes closed, for a long, savoring sniff. "You need a bath," she says, sitting back, "but not so much that it might mask what I can't smell." Opening those artfully painted eyes. "Do you know what it smells like? Metastasis? Take that thread of pleasant warmth you can find in the smell of shit, let it swell to the very point it twists into foulness – that's what I don't smell. The cancer that was eating its way, out of your colon, into your liver."

"I," he says. "I don't, what? What?"

"You've made a deal, Michael Sinjin Lake. The question is, with whom."

"Luke," he says, collapsing, slumped on the seat. "Luke. *She* was supposed to call me Lake. So I'd know it was her." He looks up, tentatively, something almost like yearning in his eye, but she's looking at his clean bare feet. "I have to be across town," she says. "I'd thought this to be a mission of mercy. I'd thought to find a dying, deluded fool. But you, Sinjin? Turns out you're a smooth operator," and she knocks on the window, sharply. "Operating correctly."

"Don't tell them?" he says, sat there on plastic, his striped bathrobe, his long and ragged beard, his hair, his hands behind his back. "I can do, so much," he says, low, quiet, urgent. "Please. Don't fuck this up."

The officer outside opens the door behind her. "Stay out of our way," she says, and climbs out of the suv. He resumes his howling, his thrashing, as the door's slammed shut.

He cuts through a parking lot under the blue-white light of a sign that says Motel 6, darting through a gap in the shin-high hedge, between a couple of startled trees out onto the street, looking up and down its carless length, a lane of it taken up by a set of tracks. A block up in a pool of streetlight waits a MAX train, and seeing it Christian breaks into a heedless, headlong run, leaping the scruffy median, up onto the sidewalk and down it, across the intersection against the light, the blatting honk of a yellow truck, and as the warning bell dings he manages to hurl himself through the closing doors of the first car, catching himself with one hand the railing by a couple of hanging bicycles. "Next stop," says a recorded voice, "is Convention Center. Puertas a mi derecha."

Bent over, settling his breath. His draggled jeans glossy and running shoes stiff with ground-in earth, his clean plaid overshirt too softly large for his skinny frame. No one in the thin crowd scattered throughout the carriage seems to have taken much notice at all of his last-second entrance. He allows himself a brief small smile, under those hunched cheekbones.

Next stop, he steps back from the doors to make room, just in case, but no one seems to want to get off, or on, not here, not through this open door. He looks away, through the opposite windows, small dim park across the street, two improbably slender glass spires lit up behind it, mere ghosts of skyscrapers. "This is a Green Line train to Portland City Center. Next stop is Rose Quarter Transit Center. Este un tren de la Línea Verde a Portland City Center. The doors are closing."

The MAX sets off, and now various passengers stir themselves, collecting briefcases, shopping bags, a suitcase, themselves,

"Puertas a me izquierda," as an overpass appears, approaches, swallows them, the train sighing to a stop in the attenuated salmon light beneath. Christian is first off the train.

A wide plaza, brightly lit, tangled with intersections, streets, rail lines, crosswalks, and all the stoplights. Up a low rise there past a scruff of trees just coming into their own the immensely spot-lit bulk of a coliseum, and under its pointed curl of roof by a stylized rose, a gigantic billboard of a basketball player preparing to take a shot, back-lit letters that say Rose Garden. A spur off all those intersections lined with idling busses, each with the same Warner Pacific University ad on the side. Away across the other side of the plaza, off toward the unseen river, more lights flare from the tops of a wall of concrete silos, and enormous letters painted along the rumpled length of them some faded time ago say amazon.com wouldn't fit here. Christian slips in among the flowing crowds, deftly navigating currents that turn away here up the sidewalks toward the coliseum, wash away there toward the busses, eddy at this corner or that, waiting until enough pressure's built up to spill them across a street, until only a few are left about him, headed toward another MAX stop behind a modest thicket of sculptures, slender white poles topped by skeletal cones suggesting lace, or coral, disconcertingly bright. He ducks around a ticket machine blinking to itself, Select Passenger, Select Passenger, slips past this person, that cluster settling themselves to wait, all the way up by himself to the end of the long slender glass-topped awning. Leans back against a brassy donut ringed about the awning's pole, just below hip-height, folds his arms in that oversized shirt, creases still clenching the front of it, and the sleeves, he's half-singing to himself, "all my eye for the fly, the fly," but he catches himself and he stops with a shake of his head.

There's someone else down at this far end of the stop.

Out past the edge of the awning she's stood before a tall red plinth, peering at the schedule framed on one of its faces, long full skirt and a trim little sweater, hair in a neatly tucked updo, and in her arms a broad round footed platter, a cakestand, all of milky green glass, intricately figured. Catching sight of him having caught sight of her, she offers a flash of a smile and the smallest nod before redoubling her attention to the schedule, clutching more closely her awkward bundle.

With a shrug, a sigh, he pushes off the pole, hands in his pockets, makes his way toward her. "It'll be along soon enough," he says. "You don't really need the schedule. They come every fifteen minutes, pretty much."

"What I don't really need," she says, and pauses, collecting herself. "Thank you, sir, but the operation of a streetcar schedule is within my capabilities."

"I didn't," he says, "I wasn't, I just," shrugging, hands still in his pockets, "looked like you were looking for something."

"I was," she says, reluctantly, "I seem to have gotten myself turned around. Where might I catch a bus on the Vanport line?"

"Vanport?" he says, shaking his head. "What number's that?"

"I don't know the number of any specific bus," she says.

"No, I mean," he looks up, turns away. "Where you going, north?"

"Vanport."

"I mean," he says, "maybe the six, but that's over on – "

"The six?"

"Runs up MLK."

"Em," she says, brow cocked, "ell, kay? Milk?"

"No," he says, drawn out. Tipping his head to one side, looking down. She wears a pair of saddle shoes, well-polished, and frilled white bobby socks.

"I had thought," she says, resettling her grip on the cake-stand, "to ride a trolley for a bit, until I recognized a stop, but," looking about, "this doesn't appear to be a stop for the Interstate line."

"Hey," he says, pointing to the stylized rail map on the plinth, straight lines of yellow, red, blue and green, orange, neatly twined about the simple cyan angle of the river. The stop almost at the top of the yellow line, there, labeled Delta Park and Vanport. "There you go," he says. "You're in the right, ah, place," but she's shaking her head. "I think I would've noticed," she says, "if they'd built a trolley out to my neighborhood."

"Yeah, well," he says, "pretty sure there ain't much of a neighborhood out that far. Just, like, a park, and a golf course. And then Jantzen Beach." The sound, rising about them, rush and whining grind, the train's approaching, long and white, sloping nose of it swinging about as it uncurls a curve under streetlights, the lights within shining out its windows. Expo Center, say the pinprick letter-lights along the top of the slanted windscreen, by a square of colored lights more orange than yellow. "Here we go," he says, turning to her, still stood by the plinth, clutching the cakestand, blinking.

"I think," she says, as the train sighs to a stop, clang of bell, "I'll wait, for a trolley I recognize." Doors slough open, down the length of it. "And must you keep staring at my shoes? Look me in the eye to say farewell, as anyone with manners should. Mister, ah," brow lifted, waiting.

"Beaumont," he says. "Christian Beaumont."

"The beautiful mountain." She shifts her grip on the cakestand. "And you might know me as Cora Bunch."

"All right," he says, stepping up onto the train. "All right."

Sometime later, a bell jingles over the door as Christian steps through into the dilapidated front room of the shop, counter there, worktable behind it mounded high with shoes of every shape and color and then some. Standing there in the middle of the bare scuffed floor, looking down at himself, mud-freighted jeans, filthy running shoes.

Clatter and clack from the back. He looks up. There's Gordon, strands of bead curtain draping and framing the bulk of him, his ragged sweater, shoulder-seam coming unpicked, his dark bald head with its circle of crisp white curls. "New shirt," he says.

Christian shrugs.

"You back?"

Christian heads up to the counter then, slips behind it. Pulls a plain brown moc-toed pump from the mound, holds it up a moment. Casts about for another.

"You're back," says Gordon. "Tea?"

THE LAST OF THE INTERNATIONAL HARVESTERS
"SORRY ABOUT THE BURRITO" – THE VERN
EAST OF EVERYTHING

THE LAST OF THE INTERNATIONAL HARVESTERS, say letters greenly sprayed across a sheet that's pinned to the beige and olive side of it, channeled like siding, studded with grids and hatches for outlets, hookups, compartments, and wide windows of flimsy sliding glass. Tires of it lost in the grass gown up about them. The scrub that blurs the line between field and copse has crept out over the bumper of it, seized hold of the radiator grille, stretched up to the dully staring head-lights, reflectors pitted by rust. Yellow-spined magazines can be seen through dust-streaked windshields, sloppily stacked in the gap between dashboard and curtains. There by it a small enough fire burns, haphazardly contained, licking an untidy pile of sticks in a scorched splotch of grass. She's bent over it, poking the flames with a crooked stick, light of them slipping red and gold a-sliding cross the blankly opaque lenses of her heavy spectacles.

"Girl's in it, you know," says the man sat in one of the lawn chairs by the fire. "You saw how she was with them boys. She ain't just in it, she's all the *way* up in it," waving a paper-wrapped bottle for emphasis, *"nothing* but respect."

"Up in what?" says the other man, leaned against the fender of a hulking pickup parked close by the stranded motorcoach. "What you got going on, Ma?" The dome light in the cab up behind him's dimly shining, and a song is playing within, faintly chugging bass and tinny soaring horns, than the first time you placed those stale smooth cigarette lips to my mouth.

"Shut that noise off," she rasps, but not unkindly, poking the fire again. He steps up on the running board of the pickup, reaches in through the open window. The song snaps off mid-swell. "Ma?" he says, stepping down. A cat yowls somewhere back that way, she stiffens, straightens, "That was Hot Soup," she says, holding up a hand. "Somebody's coming." Limps back to the other lawn chair, thick woven straps of blue and white, rickety aluminum frame. The man in the other lawn chair tucks his bottle away in the grass.

"I don't hear anybody," says the man by the pickup, after a moment.

"Ain't nobody coming," says the man in the other lawn chair, leaning down to pluck up paper crinkling his bottle for a healthy swallow. His T-shirt tight, hiked up to leave a hairy swell of belly above his sweatpants.

"Oh," she says, "and now you're the one who says what is, and what isn't." Leaning down for a stubby plastic bottle of water from the cardboard flat at her feet. "Cats don't make a noise like that, unless they have a reason. Better than dogs."

"Lo que, lo que," mutters the man in the other lawn chair.

"They *will* be coming back," she says.

"Ma," says the man by the pickup, plaid shirt neatly tucked into his jeans. "You got somebody messing with you? Do I need to stick around?"

"Oh, Mikey, hon, no," she says, hoisting her bottle to him, a waggling salute. "You've done enough. Get on home," but the whole time, those opaque lenses are fixed past him, the pickup, the sedan tilted beyond it, missing at least one wheel, the little runabout, hatchback sprung, the panel van, a tarp draped out from the side in a makeshift awning, the abandoned trailer rocked back on its wheels, hitch of it uselessly upthrust, past the handful of tents pitched among the cars, a couple of domes, the A-frame there, all vaguely lit by the ambiguous light of the boulevard across the vasty field, the office park beyond the boulevard, and a light flicks on in the A-frame tent, swinging about, blue-tinged, flicking off. Past all that, on the far side of this irregular little parking lot, there's a low, wide tummock of garbage, cinderblocks and upended pallets, what might be a toppled shopping cart, and light flickers within, another fire, perhaps, but also a brightness sharper, colder, quicksilverly tenuous.

"We'll be fine," she says. "Just fine."

"Sorry about that burrito," says Jack, gruffly. "They're pretty good if you can heat 'em up. Instead of," and he shakes his head, sort of laughs, "room temperature," he says. He selects a stick from the pile beside his knee and feeds it to the little fire before him, crackling up a prettily assembled cone of sticks and twigs. The slogans on some of the buttons a-clatter on his jacket can just be made out, Psychick TV, Born This Way, Keep Portland Weird, Sex Fossil, I Can't *Help* Myself, Stumptown Comics Fest. He looks up, over the low wall of garbage that's ringed about them, past the ragged darkness of the trees beyond, to the full moon riding clear and high in the brighter black above. "It'll be clear and dry tonight. Bit chilly. You can have the tent. I'll be fine out here." He feeds another stick to the fire, more of a twig really, and looks over his shoulder, to Jo.

She's laid back against a garbage bag stuffed with something that seems soft enough, sat up just enough to watch the unicorn. The rainbowed effusions of his mane hang brightly in the darkness, spikes and arcs of color that might almost be touched as he snuffles and grazes. He looks up at some distant sound, a yowl well out beyond their little paddock, and those colors whirl and dazzle, settling in gleaming new configurations. "That's just one of May's cats, Roy," says Jack. "You know that."

"How long have you had him?" says Jo, hand splayed over her belly, palm of it and wrist blocking the leering eyes of the devil on her T-shirt, thumb of it atop a small hole charred through, there, by her breast.

"A while," says Jack. His face isn't so youthful in the firelight.

"You've had a pet unicorn for a while," she says.

Another stick, a flare of flame. He places it, just so.

"Is that," she says, "a while, like, years? Months?"

"Weeks," he says, finally. "Couple of weeks."

The unicorn's returned to grazing, twitching that skinny, tufted tail, there by the toppled shopping cart half draped by a tarp, moldering pallet leaned against it, cinderblocks there, and garbage bags, the three or four milk crates, all piled just a bit higher than the unicorn's upraised head. "Is that," says Jo, "a couple of weeks, like, fourteen days, exactly?" Sitting up. "Or more like, maybe, closer to ten days." That garbage bag behind her, and her nearly empty duffle, by one bent pole of a low dome tent, orange and beige, set up atop some wooden pallets, the back of their little corral.

"Who were those guys?" says Jack.

Jo draws up her legs, folding her arms about them, chin on her knee.

"Because they sure seemed to know," says Jack, but "They were here for Roy," says Jo.

He looks at her directly for a moment, before turning back to the fire. "Were they," he says, then.

"He's a goddamn *unicorn*," she says. Roy, absently chewing, steps gleaming about the verge of the fire, black eyes blinking turned toward her. "What happened, ten days ago?" says Jack.

"That's not," she says, wrapping more tightly about herself as Roy minces ever closer. "It's got nothing to do with what happened today, when he," a sharp breath as the unicorn skitters a hop closer to her, lowering with a shake his shining horn, pushing those slender forelegs, those daintily cloven hooves, shivering stretching his full length out before her, for all the world like a dog. "When he did what he did," she says, swallowing.

"And what was that."

"Aw, no." Jo looks over at him not looking back at her. "Not even I knew you a fuck of a lot better."

The unicorn curls and folds his awkward legs, settling himself before Jo, laying out the length of his neck with a blowsy snort. Jack hikes up on his knees, shrugs out of his denim jacket, holds it out to her. "I told you," he says, when she doesn't take it. "It's getting chilly." His black T-shirt says Cadavers Left Around. Eyes on the unicorn, she leans over, gingerly, and takes the jacket from him, wraps it clattering about her shoulders. What Urge Will Save Us, says a button under her fingers, and another, Cruelty Is Always Possible.

"So how do you know those guys," says Jack.

"Who, Gradasso and," she pronounces it with exaggerated care, "Pwyll?" She shrugs. "They used to work for me."

A pop from the fire, a descending crackle. "You were their boss?"

"I was their Duke. Just for a bit."

Jack sits back. Looks down at the sticks left by his knee. "Duke," he says.

"Duchess of Southeast," she says. "The Hawk's Widow." She manages not to look away when he looks up at her. "Southeast," he says.

"Below Burnside," she says, "and, ah, sunward of the river. But really, practically speaking, only out to about Eighty-second or so. There's other guys, out past that, Wu Song, Končak, Hopper John, though, I mean, he's really out in Gresham, I guess," but she slumps, then, blows out a chuckling sigh. "Look," she leans away from the sleeping unicorn, reaching over, Jack draws back but she's snagging one of those sticks left by his knee. "I'll show you how it works. Portland," she says, "is divided into, well, I guess it's five fifths, now." Sketches a quick circle in the grassy dirt between them.

VERN, say red neon letters over the door. The sign that holds them's battered, dented, as if struck a mighty blow some time ago, and a T and an A hang lightless from the crumpled front of it. A taxi white and green pulls up beneath it, and the two of them get out, the one on the sidewalk in a red frock coat, puckered with intricate embroidery, and the other, street-side, in a short grey jacket with lots of little pockets and straps, and the sleeves pushed up past his elbows, shutting his door and slapping the roof of the cab, bang! It pulls away.

The bar within lit up in jukebox colors that do nothing to cast much light on anything at all, but the two of them push through without hesitation, past the bar to the right, tables to the left, the small crowd listening to a man on a stool in the corner, savagely striking a whirl-a-gig tune from his elaborately beautiful guitar, flinging chords over an insistently strummed bassline even as thumb and fingertips knock together a percussive floor of thumps and tocks from the soundbox. Past him, and a service window opening on a brilliantly lit white kitchen, through a low wide door into a side room, quieter and darker, even, a line of video poker machines blinking silently to themselves, an unattended pool table, green felt of it under its low-hung lights the brightest thing in the room. "Kern Gradasso!" booms Chilli-coathe, the Harper. "Cinquedea!" He waves them over to one of the red-upholstered booths tucked in the far end. "Pull up some chairs. Have a tot. What's the news?"

"Peg's with us, now?" says the Cinquedea, Pwyll, in his red frock coat. Gradasso in his grey jacket folds his arms. The enormous woman sat across from Chilli plucks a red-dusted tater tot from the platter in the middle of the table, her gnarl-knuckled fingers gleaming with glitter-painted scales, purple and grey. Chilli smiles somewhere in his big yellow beard. "Daisy here can clearly see which way the wind is blowing," he says.

"Keep playing with my name like that," she growls. "The wind will change."

"Oh, not this wind," says the third of them at the table, the red-headed man wedged against the wall, looking up to the woman beside him. "Can't you feel it?" His windowpane tie loosely knotted, tucked into his tightly buttoned vest. "A gentle breeze, perhaps, for now. Almost pleasant. But it's constant. It will not stop. And every day it blows, it blows away a little more of her majesty's great pile of golden dust. And every day it blows away a little more than the day before. It won't change. It will," he taps the table, "not" and again, "stop. And when that pile is done and gone," slam, the flat of his hand, "you think another will just, magically appear?"

Chilli lays his hand over that hand on the table. "Brother Stirrup will wax eloquent. But the plain and simple fact remains, Pegling Meg: the Queen is done."

"Done," she says, sitting back, booth creaking under her bulk.

"Has she a Bride?" says Pwyll, dragging a chair close to sit himself on it.

"What about toradh?" she says.

"What about it?" says Gradasso, leaning over for a couple of tots. "When any knob or churl might nip in off the street to fill their pockets, at any hour of the day, and no one to portion it properly."

"Any knob not of the Hound," mutters the Stirrup.

"She's exiled our own Duchess, Gretel," says Chilli.

"Actually," says Gradasso, licking his fingers, but Chilli's carried on, "She's taken Southeast for her own, and named another gallowglas to be her Huntsman!"

"No, but, Harper," says Gradasso, but Chilli's leaning over that platter of tots, finger pointed up at the woman across from him, "So who's to do for us, but us, Sweet Marguerite?" She cocks a skeptical brow. "Chiseauvert?" he says, and she sighs. But his smile's back.

"So, Harper, funny thing," says Gradasso, but that pointing finger's beckoning to the Stirrup, now. "Make with the map," says Chilli.

Gaveston, the Stirrup, presses himself with a grimace against the wall to make the room he needs to reach within his vest. He tugs out a colorful map that he unfolds across the table, heedless of the leaf that lops over the platter of tots. "Where'd you guys end up?" says Chilli, spreading his hands to smooth it out.

Pwyll hikes up in his chair to lean over the platter, the map, those hands, to plant a finger in the far upper right, by the thick blue river running along the top of it. "Airport Way," he says.

"Well Number Two," says Gradasso, and then, "well, the field behind it. Hard by the slough," as Chilli moves to make a careful x on the indicated oblong with a thick black marker. "Huh," he says. There are other xes on the map, a handful or so, but all of them down and in, close by the other river, that runs from bottom to top. "What was it?" he says. "Another by-blow?"

"What was what," rumbles Greentooth.

"The bang this morning," says Pwyll, sitting back down. She shrugs.

"What *was* it?" says Chilli, snapping the cap back on the marker.

"Don't know," says Gradasso, chewing.

"There was this, complication," says Pwyll.

"I was trying to say," says Gradasso.

"Then say it, blast your eyes!" snarls Chilli, but Pwyll leans forward to say, "More of a who," and picks out a tot.

"What?" says the Stirrup.

"Do tell," says Greentooth.

"*Who*," grates Chilli, glaring at Pwyll.

"Herself," says Gradasso, looking at his nails.

"Who?" says the Stirrup.

"Herself," says Greentooth, half a question.

"But this," says Chilli, perplexed, "this is east of *everything*." His fingers stray leftward a moment from the fresh x to tap a knot of access roads and ramps there, just before the yellow swoop of highway crosses the blue river along the top. "She was always more like to set up somewhere around Smith and Bybee," those fingers lifted, swept off to the left, a patch of green on the very tip of land where the two rivers meet. "When she wasn't up the island," he says.

"Her grace?" says Gradasso, frowning.

"Her awfulness," says Chilli.

"Herself," says Greentooth.

"No," says Pwyll, as Gradasso says, "Her grace never," and the Stirrup says, "Wait," and "Harper," says Pwyll. "You're twisted. Old Nineteen Names is still shacked up with the Gammer."

"She *is* the Gammer," mutters the Stirrup.

"We saw her *grace*," says Pwyll.

"Jo Gallowglas," says Gradasso.

"The Duchess Exiled," says Pwyll.

Chilli blinks.

THE LIGHTS ARE OUT, THE CURTAINS DRAWN

THE LIGHTS ARE OUT, THE CURTAINS DRAWN in the unlit parlor, but he moves with an easy confidence past bicycles, sandwich board, into the dining room, past the shadowy bulk of the table still piled with books and papers, under the archway, into the kitchen lit only by what's cast off from other lights without, just enough to gleam the jars that line the counters, to sketch the pots left on the stovetop, to limn the dishes in the sink, and slip over the rough-shaped pewter beads that weight the tips of his mustaches. He sets a paper bag and a larger canvas sack side-by-side on the counter by the stove, then stands there a moment, head tipped back, listening.

From the canvas sack he pulls a handful of cloth rags, a scrub brush, a small clay jug, a large, anonymous squirt bottle, a smaller spray bottle that says Mrs. Meyer's Clean Day, Orange Clove, and a pair of yellow gloves. From the paper bag he slips a plastic takeaway dish still vaguely steaming. Giorgio's, says the label pasted on the clear plastic lid of it. 5/15. Opening the refrigerator, he sets it carefully within, the fridge light washing over him, his blue jeans, blue denim jacket, his close-cropped iron hair, winking away as he soundlessly closes the door.

Then, tugging on the yellow gloves, taking up the scrub brush and the squirt bottle, the Anvil Pyrocles sets to work.

I muſt confeſſe many wilde thoughts may rise,
Opinions, Common Murmurs, and fixt Eyes
At my ſo ſtrange arrivall in a Land
Where true Religion and her Temple ſtand :

—*Thos. Middleton*

NO. 36

" – so powerfully strong – "

NORTH LEONARD STREET – BACK UP THE HALL
THE LIGHTS ABOUT THE MIRROR – A TIED GAME – THE AVANT-GARDE
A JOYOUS YAWP – "SO YOU'RE, LIKE, DEAD" – THE SOUND OF HIS NAME
EDDIE FRETS – TWICE ITALIAN – NOT ONE, BUT SIX – EVERYBODY
WHY THEY ARE THERE – THE FUTURE, AND THE PAST
THUS, THE NEWS – THE LIGHT IS CHANGING – FROM LIP TO LIP
THE CACHET OF CARDBOARD – ÖT PUTTONYOS
"WHAT TIME IS IT?" – A SHINING DETRITUS

N LEONARD 8000 ST, says the one green sign, and N St Louis 9100 Av the other, and she clings to the pole that holds them both, "Leonard, Moony!" she hoots. "Le-he-he-henny!"

"Minty," he says, laughing himself as he hauls her off the pole, "come on, *come on!*" Staggering away from pool to pool of streetlight slipped over arms clutched about each other's shoulders, pushing shadows out behind them, shadows that bobbing shrink to be swallowed by stumbling feet as they pass beneath the lamp above to seep out then before them, wavering, reaching, yearning for the return of darkness, "Lenny!" she yelps, and they laugh.

A house barely bigger than its garage, clad all about in pale blue siding, an enormous tree in the front yard of it that dapples streetlight into moon-bright coins spread over grass and sidewalk, pinking the finish of the pickup in the driveway, the late-model sedan on the grass. "Home sweet home?" she says, dragged behind, "on Lenny Street?"

"Avenue," he says, with a tug, but she won't step off the sidewalk. Hoisting a bottle in his free hand he waggles it, "Fuck you," she says, companionably, reaching for it. Taking the step. *"Fuck* you, Moody."

Open the door on shouts and gunshots from a big screen television there before the picture window, bursting with digital explosions, a bulky cargo plane heels over crumpling wing, in

89

the foreground ducking a couple of agents in tactical gear, guns up, "Whoa!" a guy on the couch, leaned away from the guy in the middle, controller in both hands swung wide, thumbs wildly twiddling knobs, "Shit!" and the guy on the other end of the couch clapping, "God *damn!* That was *epic!*"

"Danny Moody!" says the man in the leather recliner, "back so soon." Jaw salted with stubble, slick white scar tensing his expression into something ambiguous. "Who's this?" pointing with his chin, as gunfire chatters from surrounding speakers.

"Ada," says Moody, an uncertain gesture with his unburdened hand, "this is," waiting out another eruption of explosions, "God *damn!*" and "Hoo woo!" from the guys on the couch. "Runs pretty much every goddamn thing you'd ever give a shit about," says Moody, his gesture having woozily ended up toward the man on the recliner. "Chad?" he says, that hand swooping back to her there by his side, "Ada here took me in, when I was," both hands coming together, "out of sorts." Holding out the bottle, clear and colorless but for a pale green label. Chad takes it as more blasts shake the screen, rattle the window behind it. "Pisco?" he says, his expression resolving as a scowl, but Moody's tugged Ada out of that front room, through a short stub of hall onto an awkward landing, a short flight of stairs dropping into a kitchen. The treads of the steps have been chewed up, pale splinters left about holes gouged here and there, a couple of bent nails left where they'd been yanked. Moody's left his broad-brimmed hat on a linoleum table piled with pizza boxes and take-out cartons, he's headed for the fridge, there by a big sheet of plywood leaned up against the cabinets. Ada stands in the middle of the checkerboard floor, grey-callused slabs of her feet pinched by lime green flip-flops, shoulders slumped in her purple rain shell, laughter draining away as she looks about, garbage overflowing the can, food wrappers and wads of paper towels, empty bottles, crumpled cans, dishes clinking in the sink as more explosions rumble the house about them.

"Hey," says Chad, on the landing. "Bottle's half-empty."

"Half a bottle," says Moody, rifling the refrigerator, "better'n none." Ada looks back and forth, from the one, to the other.

"You know the rules," says Chad.

"She'll stay in the basement, with me," says Moody. "Least I could do. Where's the beer?"

"Everybody pulls their own weight," says Chad.

"Ada Minthorn," says Moody, tossing a carton over his shoulder, splat on the floor, "used to be an event planner for, uh, whatshername. Governor's ex-girlfriend." A plastic bag filled with something liquidly dark tossed aside, a foil-wrapped oblong scattering sandy crumbs. "Yeah?" says Chad, looking down at Ada. She shrugs.

"The things she could tell you," says Moody, straightening, slamming the fridge door shut. "She'll whip this place into shape in no time. Where's the damn beer, Chad?"

Chad looks up from Ada, then, over to Moody, that scar glossy in the light. "In the tub," he says.

Moody blinks. "The beer," he says, "is in the tub."

"On ice," says Chad.

Ada takes a breath. A treble fusillade occasions a basso profundo detonation, whoops and cheers, Holy *shit!* She opens her mouth.

"Ada," says Moody, still looking at Chad. "Get us a couple of beers. Anything in particular, Chad?"

Chad shrugs, without looking away from Moody. "It's all good shit."

"Back up the hall, down the left, other end of the house," says Moody. "Get yourself one, too. Should be nice and cold."

Turning, shuffle-snap of flip-flops, Ada trudges up the steps, past Chad pressing against the heavy bannister to make room. The scar makes it hard to tell if his scowl's become a smirk. Did for those camel-jockeys, somebody says in the front room, and fucko, that was Colombia, did you not see the fucking palm trees? The hall to the left is dark, couple of doors on the one wall, door at the end half-open on an unlit room. Stumbling over something, a pair of maybe pants left lolling on the carpet, "shit." Leaning back to kick open the door at the end of the hall, coughing, she lifts up an arm, back of her hand over her nose, "fucking *shit*hole fucks."

The bathroom's narrow, cramped, windowless dark. Might be a toilet there in the corner, a sink, the one shifting wall's a shower curtain, drawn. Sweeping her free hand up and down by the jamb, feeling for something, click of a switch and the sudden roar of a ventilation fan, she yelps, flicks another. The bathroom leaps into light, bismuth-pink tiling, brown mat, white towel, shower curtain printed with some old map of the world, and the seat of the toilet's up. "Fucking Moody." A four-footed orthopædic cane bent almost in half in the corner there, under the switches. She leaves the fan running, grabs the shower curtain to drag it open, and screams.

Pale pink tub full of melting ice, bergs and chunks of it stained purple and brown with trailing swirls of red and even pink in the water about bobbing cans and bottles lodged and a body, a small man curled up on his side packed in white and grey striated ice soaked in a gelid sludge of red and purple and brown about his skinny blue thighs, his crotch, his swollen belly plastered with a T-shirt that might've once been white, slashed and punctured, ripped about the ripped-out throat where the packed ice is darkest, the melt most red, head tipped up at an angle on a pillow of more ice, thin lank hair wetly dark, pasted to skull and ear and crumpled, wrinkled cheek, wrinkles that radiate from a sunken nose to snarl shut one dead eye, the other purpled, vacantly shocked.

"The beer's fine, Ada," calls Moody from the hall behind her. "Just wipe the blood off."

"You fucking *fuck!*" she shrieks. He's laughing, Chad behind him's laughing, she seizes a can from the tub and hurls it at them, thump and bouncing heavy down the carpet, "Shit!" yelps Moody, still laughing, Chad doubled over, trying to pull him back, "Your fucking *beer!*" she yells, throwing another bloody can.

THE LIGHTS ABOUT THE MIRROR – A TIED GAME
THE AVANT-GARDE – A JOYOUS YAWP

BULBS A-BLAZE ABOUT THE MIRROR, set in the frame to mercilessly light that face, the planes of it, those cheeks, the nose. Thin lips uncolored, unlined eyes with only a hazeled hint of green. Black hair brushed simply back, shorn at the temples to a stubble that seamlessly prickles the line of that jaw, and all in brightly sharp relief against an empty darkness that helps the light to chisel shoulders and collarbone, bare and hairless chest, long sinewy arms bent to lay those hands upon the table, backs of them starkly rumpled with veins.

"Now why, mon lapin," a voice slinks from the darkness, "would you want to go and look like *that?*"

The Starling smiles at herself. "Shouldn't you be asleep?"

"You never sleep, do you," that voice, purringly close.

"Sometimes I do." The Starling looks over her shoulder, away across the basement where the darkness is relieved by a dozen candles flickering before a bed, about a nest of cushions and bolsters laid on the floor, wraps and spreads and Turkey rugs and nestled among them two sleeping heads, the hair of them spread over pillows, black curls, bright floss. To one side a high-backed wing chair where Costurere sits drowsing, a snuffer in one relaxed hand, and Aigulha curled at her feet. The Starling turns back to the mirror. Over her other shoulder the shadows unfold a striking nose, a chin, a wicked, painted smile. "Do you find beauty, tiresome?" that voice, from those lips. "Pleasure, to be passé? Is that why you sink back to this, like a warm bath?"

"I am only ever what I want to be," says the Starling.

"You want to be what pays the bills, ma sucrette. And la femme's what's been engineered, over the centuries, to best provoke, and evoke, le plaisir. *If* you want to do it wholesale." In the mirror, fingers lift a shining strand of yellow hair, tuck it behind an ear. "It's not *our* fault. Just the way the world's been wired. Otherwise, you might well suddenly decide it's a great big mustache you want, to look like," a chuckle, "Big Jim Turk," as the Starling's stroking a knuckle along a lush mustache, gazing dourly from a face now smaller, in a head a touch more wide, sun-ruddied in the blaze. "Lord love her," those wicked lips twist wryly, "I do not see what she sees in that man."

"You don't?" says the Starling, shaking out long and jet-black locks, though the bangs clipped short are brightly pink. She's smiling again, apple-cheeked and dimpled.

"Oh, oh, no, that face, on that body – !"

"This?" The Starling shrugs, slumping in the chair, blue-veined breasts pink-nippled, broadly full, settling softly atop a soft swell of belly.

"Good lord," a hand comes up, those blue eyes in the mirror look down, "oh, put that away. That's cruel."

The Starling's fingertip strokes a delicate chin. "There's no cruelty in this, but what you bring."

"Oh?" Shuff and swoop in the shadows, shifting from stoop to kneel, head dipping to slip yellow hair behind a shoulder. "Do me."

"Do you."

"You never do me. Either of us. Do me."

A sigh, a stretch of a lengthened torso, hairless chest now once more flat, apples slipped from cheeks. "You already have a double."

"Do me. But slow. Slow enough that I can see you do it."

"Slow," says the Starling, licking wickedly painted lips. Turning away from the mirror and something, a trick of the light as it's passed over gleams the passing locks from loosely rumpled darkness to yellow pressed severely straight, slipping trimmed a strict straight hem, a gleaming lowered curtain. Those eyes, now blue, blink once. "Slow enough?"

"It's like," smiling up, "looking, at my sister."

"Not," says the Starling, smiling down, "a mirror?"

"You can't tell us apart, can you."

The Starling looks back to the mirror, as up beside her hikes that same face just below, same nose, same eyes, same severely yellow hair. "In pictures, no," she says. "I can't. But if I see you in motion, with each other. Or speak with you."

Ettie's smile in the mirror turns smirkward. "I can always tell when it's you, and when it's her royal majesty. It's some-thing," tucking a yellow strand of the Starling's hair behind an ear, "you do," she says, "or don't. Something missing. A lack," as the Starling looks to Ettie there beside her, "or the presence of," and tips her head to press a kiss to those murmuring lips.

The Starling sits up, lifts her mouth away, unsmudged, "a, a lack," Ettie continues, fingers lifted to her mouth. "I suppose," she says, "you think, it looks like the game is tied." The nails of them clipped close, shelled in the same glossy red.

"Are we playing a game?"

That hand to the Starling's knee, now. "Evoking, and provoking," says Ettie, seemingly to herself. "It's a matter of sensation," looking up. "I can guess, surmise, *presume,*" those fingertips further along the Starling's thigh, "but I can never *know,* not for certain, what this," back down the length of it, to the knee, "feels like, to you. All I can ever truly know," and that hand drops now to Ettie's lap, "is what it is *I* feel."

The Starling shifts in that folding chair, knees a bit further apart than before. "This is something you say to johns," she says.

"There are but two responses to this bitter truth," says Ettie, hiking herself back up, both hands on the Starling's thighs. The Starling sits forward, hands coming to rest on Ettie's shoulder, her upper arm, "This is just a thing," she says, lips coming close, "that you've cooked up, to have something to say to the ones who want to talk."

"Are you a john?" says Ettie.

Another kiss, that they both lean into, yellow heads together, turn and twist and dip and lift away with a hiss, the Starling's eyes closed, pursed lips now redly smeared. "One might," says Ettie, drawing her fingers up a shivering stretch of belly, "retreat," thumbing a nipple bluely pinked, "into the sensations one might feel oneself, the experience, of what one *does* know, for certain, to be real, or," lifting the Starling's hand from her shoulder, lick of a kiss for the knuckles, lip-print pressed inside the wrist. "Or, one might relentlessly pursue," turning the hand over in her hands, the nails of those fingers painted the same hard glossy red, but shaped to meticulous points, "whatever, hints, might be found," a kiss for the inside of the elbow, and then there, just below a breast, "that what one's doing to evoke," another kiss, wickedness askew about her mouth, "provokes," the Starling gasps as those lips close about a nipple, gently, and those sharp-nailed hands leap into the air to float a moment, aimlessly. Ettie's hands unseen, tucked away somewhere between them, "the effect, that one intends," she says, hiked up a bit higher, nose-tip brushing the Starling's nose.

"What is it you want," says the Starling.

"Haven't you been listening?" Ettie's hands still somewhere between them, smile broadening as the Starling shivers. "What I want. What her majesty wants. That's what I see, when I look at her. What I don't when I look at you."

"You're saying," the Starling swallows, eyelids sagging half to shut, "I retreat."

"I'm saying," Ettie leans close, looks up, "you don't pursue."

"Your sister doesn't, either."

Ettie looks away, looks down. "You tell me."

"You don't see that lack," says the Starling. "That need."

"That question," says Ettie.

The Starling, smiling, slowly shakes her head, lids lowered, shut away, "No," she says. "I do not love you, Stephanie Halliwell."

"Oh," says Ettie, still looking down, between them, "I think you want me. Well enough. I mean, it's not a *perfect* barometer, but." Between her hands in the Starling's lap a slender cock's been lifted pale and bobbing to a quickening pulse. "I didn't mean for that," says the Starling, hand slipping down Ettie's arm, "let me just," but Ettie shrugs the hand away, "All the more reason," she says, bent over.

"Didn't you have enough of that already?" grumbles the Starling.

"No," says Ettie, "no," stroking, kiss-smudged lips so close. "Not on this body," she says, and takes it in her mouth.

The Starling's hands come to the back of Ettie's head, but fall away with a grunt of something like frustration when Ettie sits back again on her heels. "Costurere?" she calls.

"What are you," says the Starling, but again, "Costurere," and over on that wing chair, Costurere starts awake. "Put on some music," says Ettie, "something soft, and bring yourself here. With Aigulha."

Stirs and murmurs, shaking awake, a click. A chorus hushly croons, caramel lips like hers, and a syncopation shuffles through the basement, so I could kiss them, but all she ever do is hurt, as the two of them in crisp white underthings approach the blazing mirror and the two of them, sat upon the folding chair, knelt before it. "I'd change my hair," says Ettie. "Color it black. And not so straight – not curls, no, something loosely full. However long you'd like. And, Aigulha? Something minimal, avant-garde – black leather. Straps. Buckles. I trust your eye. Don't lose heart, dear Starling," as with an "Of course, miss" Costurere steps up behind her, and a "Right away, my lady" Aigulha steps out of the light of the mirror, where racks of clothes-stuff crowd the shadows. "This won't take long," says Ettie, and she sighs, as Costurere runs gold-flecked fingers through already darkening hair, and lifts a silvery comb.

The Starling looks down at the erection in her lap. The sun keeps rolling in, that singing voice in the shadows, and the sea fog is great, and I smile, for a while.

Costurere steps back, and Ettie gets to her feet, shaking out a newly heavy helmet of black hair. Aigulha reaches under Ettie's arms to buckle a wide black leather belt about her torso, just beneath her breasts, cinching it tight, draping a yoke of braided data cables up over her sternum, about her neck, down the line of her back, plastic plugs of them twisted together a-dangle above the cleft of her buttocks. Costurere presses a finger to Ettie's lips, restoring the cleanly wicked line of red, but Ettie catches her wrist to lick a crumb of gold from a fingertip, turns it about to kiss the rough callus beneath a nail. Her other hand takes hold of Aigulha's, lifts for a kiss to the palm, and then, their hands still held in hers, Ettie turns her smile on the Starling, sat back in that folding chair, arm propped on the back of it, hair still yellow and severe, eyes yet blue and nose that nose, long lean legs crossed at the ankles, her softening cock a-droop. "Oh, ma crevette," says Ettie. "We'll have to do better than that."

"You want me, doing you, to fuck you, doing her," says the Starling, matter-of-factly.

"We've been over this," says Ettie, "you're doing my sister. You don't have it in you to do me. Do try to keep up." Turning to Costurere, "Go on, wake them," and then, to Aigulha, "Gently." Holding out a hand to the Starling as the two of them set out across the basement, toward the candlelit nest. "Well?" says Ettie. The music about has changed, someone's chanting over kiltered thumps, sad eyes, bad guys, mouth full of white lies, and the Starling takes her hand.

Wraps and drapes, shawls, scarves, chiffons drawn aside, the two women asleep on the rugs and cushions, the Queen a-sprawl on her belly, one arm flung over a purple bolster, profuse black curls a fan over her shoulders, a pillow for Chrissie's gleaming yellow head, curled on her side, an arm about the small of her majesty's back. "Miss?" whispers Costurere, knelt over Chrissie. "Ma'am?" Aigulha, bent over the Queen.

"Not *that* gently," says Ettie, plopping herself on the rugs beside Chrissie, gripping a shoulder, rolling her over, slithering yellow into her lap. "Hey," she says, conversationally loud. "Doodle. Wake up." Colorful cables a line down the curl of her back, she tugs Chrissie's silvery camisole back into place. Chrissie pulls her arms about herself, draws up her knees, gold-spangled lips a-twist in a grimace, "mmf," and "what?" and blinking thickly, opening her eyes, to see Ettie smiling down. She closes them again.

"Snug as a bug in a rug?" says Ettie.

"In a rug," says Chrissie, faintly. "The nicest insect." Frowning. Opening her eyes. "Your hair's different."

"I got you a present," says Ettie, sitting up, out of the way, to reveal the Starling stood among the candles, one arm up, hand of it laid against shoulder, fingers coiled in locks of yellow severe, and something uncertain in guarded blue eyes.

"I," says Chrissie, "what?" Looking over and up at Ettie, sleep-muzzled, confused, looking back to the Starling, who's starting to smile, whose other hand there by her thigh, "oh," says Chrissie, sitting up.

"Look at you, there," Ettie, sat up close behind Chrissie, chin over her shoulder, "such a big, beautiful sister." Those wicked lips so murmuring close. "Think of what you could *do* to your-self, ma moitié."

"Do you want this?" says the Starling, hoarsely.

"Do you?" whispers Ettie, and only a glancuing frown at the interruption. Chrissie's already shifting her hips on the rug, laying her weight back against Ettie who spreads her legs to make room, awkwardly propped on an elbow till Costurere kneeling a cushion slips beneath, tugging and tucking, stroking, soothing an arm, a shoulder, hair yellow, black, Ettie scowls, snaps "Go on," shrugging from under that solicitous hand. The music's changed again, a thumping, more insistent beat, my face is drawn, someone's sing-songing, my face is drawn with this num-ber two pen-cil. Off to the side a murmur, a rustle as the Queen sits up by Aigulha, the lickerish wick of a kiss, a sigh as Costurere scoots back, but Ettie's settled against the cushion, Chrissie's kissing her hand, Ettie bends lightly to press a kiss to Chrissie's forehead. The two of them look bluely up as one, as the Starling steps onto the rugs, sinks to her knees before them, cock wobbling, erect, those knees between Chrissie's ankles, falling forward, hands to either side of Ettie's hips. Swaying forward over their bellies, breasts brushing breasts, lifting to tilt a kiss for Ettie's mouth. Smiling. Pushing back as Chrissie lifts herself, and kiss and kissing again.

Ettie slumps back, and the look on her up-tipped face, a grunt like a laugh as they start to move atop her, and in her hand clutched tight is Chrissie's hand, so very like her own, the nails cut close and glossy red, even as Chrissie's legs twine about the Starling's legs so very like her own, long and palely lean, like Ettie's enwrapping them both. Ettie lifts her head back up by Chrissie's bobbing eyes closed Starling intent the two of them on the thing they're building, and all that slippery glassy gleaming yellow hair. Looking over, then, to the Queen close by, laid on her side on the rugs, an arm about Aigulha before her, a hand in Aigulha's lap, and Costurere knelt behind, the three of them watching intent on what happens before them, "Like, what you, see?" says Ettie, between gasps, but softly, too quiet for anyone else to hear, or even notice.

He laughs, a joyous yawp that startles her awake in the pastel sheets, "The fuck?" she rasps, blinking owlishly.

"Oh, sweetling," he says, "don't take it amiss," laid his full length atop the counterpane. "Merely the wonder of it overwhelms, at times. The living, as I've done, from the one end of the world, to the other." A hand still on the wiry black that mats his sun-ruddied breast. Shoulders red as well, quite red, and peeling here and there in lacy flakes among the shortly coiled hairs that riddle them. "As I'm doing," he says, absently scratching. Hips and legs untouched by sun, cleanly pale beneath more matting black, lank down the shins of him to his ankles, thinned about wide knees, thickening up his thighs in wiry whorls that converge on the tangled copse at his groin, an extravagant nest for the quiescent nubbin of his cock. "It will let itself out, from time to time." Smiling at her, and she leans down quickly to plant a kiss, there below his thick mustache. "Well, I'm glad you made it," she says, shoveling locks of black hair out of the way, over a shoulder, looking up, frowning, at the thin light seeped through dust-shrouded glass. "The hell time is it," she mutters, leaning out over the edge of the mattress to fish through discarded clothing. He rolls on his side after her, playfully slaps a jiggling buttock, "Hey," she growls, thumbing a rosy plaque of a phone to life. "Shit," she says. "I bet the sun ain't even up yet." Dropping the phone to the tangle of T-shirt and hoodie and tights, she rolls onto her back there beside him. "But here I am. Awake."

"If it's time you'd look to pass," he says, fingers trailed between her breasts. She pointedly lifts his hand away. "There's shit to do," she says, looking down the length of him, then back to his ribald smile. "Besides, you're not up for anything."

"But the work of a minute, and I'd be up for anything at all, with you," he says.

"It is entirely too early for anything that corny," she says, but he kisses her, and kisses her again, with a gentle fondness, and she shakes her head, trying not to smile, "Tickles," she says, lifting a hand to his face, but not to push him away. She strokes that thick mustache, black of it hatched with white.

"It's Sunday, less I've scrambled the weekly round," he says. "A day of rest, for all of us under the sun." A relishing smile, there below his mustache, her fingertips. "If you would not lie with me, then perhaps just lie, with me?"

She snorts up a giggle. "You're awfully proud of that one, aren't you."

"It's this blasted ebullience!" throwing up a gesture, hand dropping to her thigh with a slap. "I'm giddy with the wonder of it. And the joy."

"Is that what it is," she says, warmly skeptical.

"The wonder," he says, "and the joy."

"That's nice."

"You like it?"

"Yes, I, not that, wait, wait, too much. Just there. Like that. Like that." Lifting her chin as he dips for a kiss. There's a knock at the door.

He looks up, back over his shoulder, at the second knock. "Gloria?" calls someone through the door.

"Day of rest," she mutters, and then, "Who is it?" she calls.

"Ah, Melissa?"

He cocks a brow. She's shaking her head. "What's up," she calls.

The doorknob turns, the latch clacks, "Shit!" yelps Gloria, kicking her way under the sheets as he sits back against the pillows, arms folded, ankles crossed, watching amused as the door's swung open, a woman peering around the edge of it thick lenses freezing in the act of taking a step into the room, "Oh, I'm sorry," she's saying, as "Close the goddamn door!" shouts Gloria. "Jesus!" The door jerks shut.

A moment then, Gloria clutching the sheets about herself, Big Jim stretched the length of him nude atop all those pastels, and silence out in the hall. Then Jim starts to laugh, a gust stopped up behind the fist he lifts to his tight-shut lips, leaking in wheezing gasps. Gloria shoves him and the laughter bursts out, a blowsy guffaw.

"Sorry?" says Melissa, out in the hall. "Really. Sorry."

"It's not even *six,*" calls Gloria.

"I know, I, I couldn't sleep. I heard voices?"

Jim's eyes squeezed shut, shoulders shaking, he's only partially successful in not making much noise at all. "And?" snaps Gloria.

"Uh, Anna told me? Once, she said. You sometimes had. Bacon?"

"SO, YOU'RE, LIKE, DEAD. Right?"

Sizzle and pop six rashers of bacon on the little electric griddle, pushed about by tongs. "Melissa," says Gloria, there by the credenza. She's pulled on an oversized blue and grey hoodie, St. Mary's Football, it says, across the front. Undefeated Since 1859.

"What," says Melissa. Sat on the floor beneath the dust-glazed window in her motorcycle jacket, and leaned beside her a greatsword in a bulky scabbard of iron and dark wood and grey felted wool, the faceted pommel at the end of its long hilt laid up against a murky pane. "It's not like he's a hundred and seventy, a hundred and sixty, and lying there, looking like that."

Big Jim snorts, laid back against the pillows piled at one end of the high thick mattress, wrapped in a corduroy kilt, bare ankles crossed. "I'm as quick as you'd seem to see me," he says.

"I mean, you're the guy. You're the reason we have the Shanghai tunnels."

"Hardly," he says, and the merest shake of that big head.

"No, I mean, that's so cool!"

"They were never as extensive as the tales would have it."

"I took the tour. I've been down there, you know?" Leaning forward, hands on her knees, "Jim Turk's a *legend,*" she says. "Shanghaied a fucking wooden Indian. Found a basement full of guys dead from drinking ether, or formaldehyde, or whatever, and hired 'em all off to a captain before they were cold!

You're saying *you* did *that?*" but the shake of his head's more vehement, "No," he's saying, "that were the doing of Bunko Kelly, and I'll not have that bounder's sins totted up in my ledger."

"You've been alive a hundred and seventy years."

"Melissa," says Gloria a touch more sharply, flicking bacon onto a paper plate.

"I've read the obituary, printed on the occasion," says Big Jim. "Died in Tacoma, in ninety-five. Of a broken heart, no doubt." Looking down, away from them both. "Kate gone on the five years before, and it already being but certain my boys would never hold together what I'd built." Gloria stumps away from the credenza, thrusting the plate at Melissa, who looks up, takes it with a nod. "I don't recall a moment of Tacoma," Big Jim looks up, to Melissa, then Gloria. "What I do remember, like the last shred of a dream, is a little bell, jingling, above my head." Gloria's stood there, tongs in her hand. Melissa lifting a slice of bacon to her lips. "I was in the front room of a dilapidated cobbler's shop, and in my hand a tattered Persian slipper, half its spangles gone, embroidery threadbare, well worn by someone else's foot, much smaller than my own," and he waggles his hairy toes. "I've no notion where it came from, to be found there in my hand, but I held it up to the cobbler, who nodded and went to fetch something from the back of his shop. Porter, his name was. William Porter. I haven't thought of that in, in quite some time." Melissa, chewing slowly, listening intently. Gloria headed past the corner of the mattress to the credenza, her back to him. Wrapping the uncooked bacon in a plastic bag. "He returned," says Jim, "and set on the counter between us a boot, and a slipper, for all the world as if they was a pair. The boot being one of those heeled and tooled absurdities they wear in Pendleton, to get up fancy, and do so pinch the toes. But the slipper? The Persian slipper, yellow and orange threadbare, and more of its spangles remaining, perhaps, but otherwise a match for the one I held. They'd been worn, of a morning, by the same two delicate feet, fetching tea, perhaps, or every night to a sweet soft bed, that might've been my own dear Kate's." A wistful shrug of a smile beneath that mustache. "But I did know, even as I reached to pick it up, I knew, sure as the shilling at the bottom of a glass. I was crimped, to a captain unknown, for a duration as yet unspecified."

"Do you still have them?" says Melissa. "The slippers?" There's a knock at the door. "Who the fuck *is* it?" snarls Gloria.

"In a manner of speaking," says Jim to Melissa, as he's getting to his feet. "Gloria?" says someone through the door.

"It's Anna," says Gloria, to Jim, who's padding across the floor. "It's *Anna!*" she says, again. He opens the door with an unctuous fillip, "Welcome, m'lady," his jaunty intonation. Anna smartly dressed in herringbone steps into the room, mouth open with what she's about to say shut tight as she takes in what's about, shirtless and barefooted Jim, bare legged Gloria stooping to stuff the bacon away in a little refrigerator, Melissa sat by her sword. "I'm," she says, "sorry. I can come back," narrow lenses of her spectacles blanked by strengthening morning light.

"You're here," says Gloria, getting to her feet, "you're here. What is it."

Anna sighs, crisply. Holds up a sheet of official-looking letterhead, creased in thirds. "Apparently, this came yesterday. Did you see it?"

"I don't know, maybe, probably not," says Gloria, as if ticking off a list. Big Jim's settling himself on the mattress. "It's from Development Services," Anna's saying. "They've had a complaint regarding, as they put it, illegal occupancy. They're going to send a Fire Inspector to, ah," turning it about so she might read from it, "ensure the building is regulated according to its approved use, and the structure maintained in conformance with the Building Code in effect at the time of approval."

"Okay," says Gloria, blinking, after a moment. "They can talk to the lawyers. We own the building now. We own the whole damn block. They can," an irritated wave, "whatever!"

"The same lawyers who do serve the sworn enemy of our lady?" says Anna.

"Well, that's a," says Gloria, "a conflict of interest."

"And in what court would you plead that?" snaps Anna, but then almost immediately withdraws the edge, "you're tense," she says, folding away the letter. "You've had no coffee yet. I'll have some brought."

"I don't need," Gloria starts to say, but there's a wrenching scrape of iron on glass, *"Jesus,"* blurts Gloria, wheeling, "do you *have* to bring that fucking thing everywhere you go?"

Melissa, still sat upon the floor, resettles the enormous scabbarded sword she's just kept from toppling over. "Sorry," she says. "It's not like I can just, you know. Make the fucking thing *disappear*. Like you guys."

"Melissa," says Gloria, and there's the edge now, in her voice, but a shuffle in the doorway interrupts. She turns, glaring, to see Anna stepped out of the way of a stoop-shouldered man in a red apron, and in his hands a gilt tray laden with tall and steaming paper cups. Anna takes one with a smile. Limping over toward the mattress, he extends the tray toward reclining Jim, who takes the proffered cup.

"Right," says Gloria, with a sigh. "Coffee."

"Coffee?" says Melissa, scrambling to her feet, and scrambling to catch the scabbard again, scraping it back into balance against the glass. "Can I have some?"

He's already sweeping the tray toward her, turning it so that one of the two cups left is ready to her reach. Another bustle in the doorway as she takes it, "Majesty?" Anna's saying, and Big Jim's getting to his feet, and Gloria closes her eyes.

"Good morning," says the Queen, stepping into the room, a loose white satiny robe unbelted over white pyjama pants, black curls artlessly loose, bare feet smeared with gold. "How nicely convenient to find you all together."

"What's up," says Gloria, but the Queen's stepped up to the red-aproned man, "Is that," she says, suddenly delighted, "Cragflower! Could it be you?"

"My lady," he says, looking down and down, tray trembling just in his hands.

"You served my mother," she says, "you've served us, always, graciously, and well. It is a tremendous comfort to find you with us in this new circumstance."

"My own name," he says, wonderingly, as she takes the last cup from the tray, "never sounded so lovely, in my ears."

"Anna," says the Queen, turning away, "we would hold less of a court today, than a cabinet. Make some room ready for the purpose."

"Majesty," says Anna, with a nod.

"Don't we need Marfisa? For a quorum?" says Gloria. "Before we start changing things up?"

"The upper gallery could be," Jim starts to say, his words falling apart at looks from Gloria and Anna. "Dearest Suzette," the Queen's saying, as she turns to Gloria, who's stuffed her hands in the pockets of her hoodie, mouth snarled in a pout, but she doesn't look away from those green eyes limpid in this light, from the Queen's unreadably pleasant mien, and she doesn't flinch when the Queen lifts up that paper cup of coffee. After a moment, she takes it. Anna looks away.

"The upper gallery will do," says the Queen, turning to Jim, who, startled, bows. "Make it ready for a light luncheon. Good morning to you all."

Melissa says, "Ysabel?" But the Queen's already stepped out of the room, into the hall, away.

Over the brightening trees, away across the river, before hills already lifted into oncoming day, shadows wash away in strengthening gusts of light, and the windows of the houses that line and climb them gleaming white and silver, though the towers of downtown still steeped in dregs of dawn catch smoldering sullen brilliant red magenta glaring yellow and that wild mad light between them all too much itself to ever fit the rounding name of orange, sheets and flares that shrink to sparks but do not dim, shining more fiercely as they're compressed into the corners of so much window-glass and framing steel and aluminum resolving as the shadows about them drain away to differentiate shapes and styles, red brick crowned by a ziggurat, high coolly white the narrow windows dark, untouched, or all of dim glass all aflame, and the roof a tilted solar panel, there a spindled crane by a naked elevator shaft, skeletal articulation of a new building scaffolded about it, red-topped sandstone already shouldered into warm daylight, and there, off to the side, pink granite and amber glass clutch the last colors of dawn as full day breaks.

"That," says Abby Tinker, "was a good one." A long crackling drag from what's left of a hand-rolled cigarette. Curls of smoke leak from a corner of her mouth, a nostril, till she blows it out, a greyly olive cloud. "Not many of those left."

She leans over to set the cigarette on a glass saucer there, on the low table between them, of worn wood weathered and grey like their Adirondack chairs. Marfisa doesn't unfold her hands from her lap to reach for it. Creased and empty, tucked beneath them, a rubbery, floppy mask in the shape of a horse's head.

"It'll start raining, soon," says Abby Tinker. "Maybe today. Tomorrow for sure. You ever notice that?" Knob-knuckled fingers loosen the blue knit scarf about her neck. "We get a blast of summer, right at the beginning of May, enough to get a taste for it, and then," shrugging her shoulders swaddled in a puffy blue coat, under that scarf, over a fleecy sweatshirt. "Rain settles back for another month or so. Rose Festival's coming up," she laughs, "I swear. The dozen years I've lived here, ain't never been a Rose Festival wasn't absolutely *soaked* in rain."

Marfisa nods, or shrugs. Legs stretched out before her on the chair's extended footstool, long grey socks with white stripes over her knees, black running shoes propped out over dew-spangled grass. The chairs and the low table between them have been set out in the middle of the lawn atop the roof, the sun rising behind them, all of downtown spread before them, away across the river. Abby Tinker leans over to pluck up the cigarette for one more savoring suck over the saucer, holding the smoke with a beatific bob, eyes closed behind Coke-bottle lenses. She crushes the spark of it against the glass and sits back, seeping smoke like steam until she opens her mouth to let the last of it escape. "Very," she says. "Nice."

Marfisa smooths the mask in her lap, rubber puckered about the molded shapes of its snout, its teeth, its goggled eyes. The stiff black mane of it pricking her knees. "But Eddie will be here soon."

"That he will," says Abby Tinker. "Eddie will be here soon."

Leaving chairs and table, saucer and roach, they head back across the lawn, Abby Tinker, house slippers a-flap over thick wool socks, clinging to Marfisa's proffered elbow with leathered hands. One of the few windows in the back brick wall ahead has been left open, drawn curtains a gauzy scrim over the darker hall within. Abby Tinker crouches before it, leaning against Marfisa in a complexly hesitant maneuver that results in her head ducked under the sash, a slippered foot over the sill, shifting her inconsiderable weight with a slip and a scuff from without to within.

"It's a wonderful thing, having this outside my window," says Abby Tinker, drawing the curtains back with her inside. "He worries too much, Eddie does."

"He's very good to you," says Marfisa.

"Yes, he is. Eddie is," says Abby Tinker. "But so is this. Thank you." The light on her glasses makes it hard to say if there's a mischievous twinkle there, to point her vaguely pleasant smile. "Maybe next time."

Marfisa shrugs, and nods, gets to her feet. Helps Abby Tinker close the window between them.

Sitting tailor-fashion in a snug pair of boxer briefs, ink rippling her shoulders and her back, intricate etchings of leaves and branches, flowers and vines, and peeping from them here and there beady eyes, beaks and snouts, she's leaned forward, intent on one more shuffle of the cards, tap tap into an even deck. The floor and the walls to either side angled up in an atticked ceiling all painted the same clean eggshell blue, seamless, depthless, gleaming. She turns over the first card, fnap, a single unmarked, unmarred color, a dull flat sheenless grey. A second card set beneath it, a featureless field of brownly olive green. A third to the right of them both, magenta lurid against the eggshell floor. She regards them a moment, finger pensive against her lip.

A fourth card to the left, a rich dark hunter's green. The fifth, laid in the middle of them all, pearly silver, faintly iridescent. She closes her eyes. Sweeps up the cards and returns them to the deck.

Dressed now in a tank top and loosely flowing pants, Ellen Oh descends a grand dark staircase into a low-ceilinged room columned and beamed in dark wood, and none of the distant windows filled with leafy daylight as bright as the television in the corner, surrounded by beanbags, a low armchair, a ratty recliner, a couple of guys watching the wheeling blue that fills the screen, a camera chasing something over a lushly windswept field of grass. Past them into a long and narrow kitchen, where she takes a chocolate brown bowl from the dish rack by the sink, and a spoon, then opens one of the towering upper cabinets on a colorful clutter of clipped or twisted plastic bags, stuffed with all manner of chips, nuts, dried fruit. She pulls out a baggie of toasted peanuts, then opens a squatly yellow refrigerator on a profusion of bottles and cans, half-closed take-out boxes and plastic tubs of leftovers, to fish a single scallion from a drawer. Lays her armload on the counter before a blinking pressure cooker. Unlocking the lid of it, she scoops steaming white congee into the bowl. A rattling staccato with a great big knife renders the scallion to rounds and shreds of green and white that she sprinkles on top, followed by a scant handful of peanuts.

Bowl in hand, back to the low and dark-beamed room, the wash of wind from the speakers scattered about, and pleasantly hesitant notes plucked from an unseen guitar. "I don't get the point," says the one guy perched on the recliner, scratching gingery stubble on his chin.

"There's your problem," says the guy on the beanbag, tilting the controller in his hands left, then right, proxily steering something. The screen filled with flower petals, red and white and yellow and pink, tumbling in a gust along a line of immobile windmills.

"Tell me something," says Ellen. "The first thing that pops in your head. Whatever it is. Go."

The guy on the recliner frowns. The guy on the beanbag tips his head, intent on the screen, the petals, "Well," he says, "Abby Tinker – "

"A hatchet's a tool in most of Oregon, but it's a weapon in Portland, and you'll get cited if you open carry," says the other guy. He points at the screen, where the petals flutter to the ground in a burst of sunset light, and the turbines slowly start to spin in the background. "Either you just won," he says, "or you lost."

"Yeah," says the guy on the beanbag. "That is definitely your problem."

"What were you going to say, Dan?" says Ellen, taking a bite of congee.

"I, ah," he's setting the controller aside, "I don't know."

"Tell me," says Ellen, swallowing. "It was your first thing."

"Abby," he says, "Tinker, a minor writer, a Black writer, of the, ah, feminist, New Wave, ess eff," he shrugs, "she, she lives here. In Portland." His bulky grey hoodie says RCTID.

"Where," says Ellen.

"It was," says Dan, holding up a hand, "this introduction, she wrote, to – "

"Where, here," she says, spooning up more congee. "Not where you saw it."

"I know, I just," says Dan, shaking his head, "it's an apartment, over an old-skool Italian restaurant. She writes about how all the Reed kids go there, looking for Goodfellas, when meanwhile the real Mafia drinks at Hung Far Low's."

"Where," says Ellen.

"I'm," says Dan, closing his upheld hand in a fist. "Inner Eastside," he says. "She talks about seeing the fireworks, over downtown. And there's another Italian place next door, Costa, Spiaggia, something like that. She says how there's two Italian restaurants, on this one block, and only one Ethiopian restaurant in the entire city." Lowering his hand to his knee. "At the time. Anyway. That's it. That's all I've got."

"That's enough," she says. "I've got somewhere to go, and something to keep in mind." Dropping the spoon in the bowl, turning back toward the kitchen.

"Huh," says Dan.

"Gimme," says the guy on the recliner, reaching for the controller. "I want to try it."

NOT ONE, BUT SIX – EVERYBODY – WHY THEY ARE THERE THE FUTURE, AND THE PAST – THUS, THE NEWS

IT'S NOT ONE TABLE, BUT SIX, each of a length and a width, pushed together in two close lines of three tables each, and the tops of them of differing colors of formica, gleaming sunny yellow and dark red a-glitter with silver and black, lavender spun with threads of violet, a sturdy brown, pale institutional green flecked with more and darker greens, or blues, or greys, a buffed matte white, and Iemanya moves methodically about it, polishing the table-tops with a damp rag. The room about is dusty yet, littered with scraps of lath, ivory dollops of dried plaster and brighter scraggles of spackle along the drop cloth where Jim Turk's knelt, filling and smoothing cracks beneath the line of mullioned windows. There across the room Fildhine with a pair of needle-nosed pliers and Cherrycoke with a screwdriver confer about an exposed junction box. A line of them through half-opened double doors then, Teacup Tall and Charlichhold, Herwydh, Lustucru and Powys, deftly unfolding tray tables, setting down broad trays crowded with bite-sized snacks, and Powys hovering over them, prodding tartelettes back into place, resettling a mound of chips. "Wsht!" a hiss from Herwydh, as Big Jim gets to his feet, as Iemanya drops her rag into the bucket at her feet. The Helm Linesse has stepped through the doors, slender in a sleeveless tunic of gleaming grey, striding toward the trays, where Powys is still fussing. She plucks up a bit of golden crust twisted about a roasted fig, but doesn't take a bite.

"Chairs," hisses Teacup, and gesturing leads a number of them bustling from the room. Cherrycoke screws a cover onto the junction box. Jim sets to cleaning his trowel.

Next through the doors, Wu Song, soft white shirt buttoned up to his throat, tattoos at his temples blurred by stubble. A rumble rises behind him and he steps to one side, out of the way of Lustucru and Teacup and Herwydh and Fildhine, guiding a dozen or more wheeled chairs into the room, spinning and turning and pushing the thunderous ballet into place about the table. He steps over to the trays, and after a moment's contemplation selects a wedge of red pepper, dredging it through a ramekin of spice-speckled salt.

The Huntsman Melissa in her motorcycle jacket followed that herd of chairs into the room, and now, greatsword awkward in her arms, she's turning about to take it all in, "Wow," she says, just loud enough to echo, "this looks great, you guys have done a fan*tas*tic job with this," heading toward the trays, "this space, wow, these look *so* good. Thank you," she says, to Powys, who lurches up and back, blinking, "thank you all," Melissa's saying, as they step away from chairs, the table, heads down, looking away, "for *all* the work you," Powys already out through the doors, and Iemanya, Teacup Tall and Charlichhold, "do," she says, as the rest of them hustle and bustle away, and only Big Jim Turk, toolbox in hand, offers up a shrug. Linesse steps around the table, lays a hand on the back of one of the chairs. Wu Song's thick brows lift, bemusedly consternated.

"Excuse me," the Earl Alans, stepping in through the exodus. "Such a," he says. "Hey." His lightweight sweater asymmetrically patterned in earth tones, sleeves pushed up to his elbows. "You're the Xingzhe."

"Wu Song," says Wu Song. "You are the Earl among Barons."

"Well, we do for ourselves, over across the hills. Don't we," says Alans. "So, I'm an Earl. Not a Baron."

"And she's not a Duchess," says Wu Song, with a nod.

"No," says Melissa, exasperated, "I'm the *Hunter*." Snatching a tart criss-crossed with charred shreds of yellow carrot, she heads around to Linesse's side of the table, heaving up the scabbarded sword to drop it a-clatter on top, taking up most of the length of bright yellow.

"Yes," says Wu Song.

"Okay?" says Alans, looking over the trays, pursing his lips. "Could we get some water, maybe? Iced tea?" but trundle and chime, there's Powys returning, pushing a cart overloaded with bottles, flasks, pitchers, glasses, cups, Anna in herring-bone trousers at his heels with an armload of pads of yellow foolscap that she proceeds to lay out one by one on the table, and a pen with each. Melissa pushes her sword away with a scrape to make room. Gloria's slipped through the doors after Anna, hands stuffed in the pockets of her hoodie, headed head down for the chair at the one end of the table.

"Hey, um," says the Bullbeggar Otto, rubbing his ruddy head, "is this everybody?" His ripped black T-shirt says Stone and Salt across the front. Leaning over the trays, he dithers a moment, then selects himself a chip.

"Hello," says the Shrieve Bruno, stepping through the doors, his trousers, his vest, his jacket all of soberly differing plaids. He pours a glass of water from the cart.

"This, this must be everybody?" says Otto, gesturing a chip to take them all in.

"Not, ah, not quite?" says Alans, frowning.

"Good day to you all," says the Queen, there between the doors. Her white gown plain and simple, her loose black curls brushed back, her gold-stroked smile noncommittally pleasant. Linesse ducks her head. Wu Song nods. Anna bows, and Bruno bows, and Alans bows deeply. Otto lifts his chip, and ducks his head. Melissa, who'd just sat down, stands up abruptly, knocking her chair back squeaking on its wheels. Gloria looks over her shoulder.

"We are pleased you all could be with us today," says the Queen. "Take your seats, and we shall begin."

Walls paneled in rich wood, the ceiling of pressed tin panels between box beams, thick drapes drawn, and the only light from lamps with blue glass shades that line of middle of the polished table that nearly fills that close rich room. Ten high-backed chairs pulled close about it, and sat in them the Soames Twice Thomas, in a jacket of green tweed, the Wulver Hoseason, thick greyed hair pushed up from off his forehead, the Baron Alphons in an indigo velvet coat, underlit face warmly red, the Glaive Rhythidd in navy pinstripe, his tie of burgundy, the Baroness Clothilde at the one end in her black leather jacket, and at her right hand Sigrid in a black silk blouse, then the Mason Luys in red broadcloth, collar open, the Chariot Iona beside him in a track suit of dusty pink, her close-cropped hair chartreuse, the Guisarme Welund in a rich brown three-piece suit, and no tie about his neck, and there, at the head of the table, his royal blue shirt with collar and cuffs of spotless white, the Viscount Agravante, lifting a slender fluted glass. "Gentlemen," he says. "Ladies. Welcome."

"We would hear of the Marches," says the Queen. "How fares Northeast?"

"Beset, my lady," says Linesse.

"The rabbits tax you?"

"On all sides, ma'am. North, and south." Linesse shifts her gaze, sere and even, from the Queen, to Bruno.

"Shrieve?" says the Queen, and Bruno, puzzled, slowly shakes his head. "I know of nothing done to encroach upon Northeast."

"And yet," says Linesse. "Majesty, I must beg your indulgence. If we are to discuss this matter, properly, and in full, we would violate a stricture you have laid upon this court."

"Our indulgence is yours," says the Queen.

"On Friday, then," says Linesse, "the Gallowglas did come to my hall."

The Queen sits back in her chair. Gloria looks up. Melissa sits up, "You're not supposed to," she says. Anna looks down at her hands. "As an incursion?" says Bruno. "Or a conversation?"

"A complaint," says Linesse. "It would seem certain knights and bravos of Southeast," Bruno draws back his chin at that, "have been," she says, "threatening? Intimidating, a company of mortals camped in my demesne. She'd have it stopped." Looking from frowning Bruno to the Queen. "As would I, your majesty."

"Where is this camp?" says Bruno. "If the Marquess would be so kind."

"East of Williams," says Linesse, "north of Burnside. Which is enough. Had you not rather ask the names and offices of the offenders? Or perhaps they are known, already, to you."

"Ah, fuck," says Gloria, under her breath. Otto frowns, but not at Linesse. "This dispute," says Wu Song, gruffly, "should be settled in open court. Not private council." One hand laid flat on the green tabletop.

"This is a privy council?" says Alans, blinking.

"There's no dispute before us, my lord," says the Queen. "The Marquess will name these impertinent knights. The Shrieve will see appropriate action taken. We are all in agreement. There is no dispute."

"Helm," says Bruno, after a moment, with only a hint of a questioning tone.

"The Kern, Gradasso," says Linesse. "And your Cinquedea." Bruno looks away with a pinch of grimace.

"Shrieve?" says the Queen.

"Steps shall be taken, ma'am," says Bruno.

"There!" says the Queen. "As we have said. How else fares Southeast?"

Wu Song leans forward. "This one speaks for Southeast, now?"

"This one does," says Bruno, quickly, "in this room, today? Yes." Turning to the Queen. "Your majesty's presence, and generosity, are – "

"There have been many changes, of late," says Wu Song.

"And we," says Bruno, looking back to him, "keep up with them."

Otto says, "He, ah, he can speak for Southeast as well as I can, for North, or him," pointing to Alans, "for Southwest."

"But I *don't,*" says Alans, drawing back from the red tabletop. "Do I?" Looking about. "Is that why I'm here?"

"You are here, good Earl," says the Queen, "to speak of, not for. We'd have the news of each of our city's fifths and marches, North and East, West, South, all from those best suited to provide it." A hand on the yellow table to her left, a hand on the white table to the right. "Our friend Wu Song's correct," she says. "Change looms large in our affairs, of late. These last two peaceful, pleasant weeks of languid plenty were preceded by a fortnight of abject dejection, when all was lost, that we once more lightly hold." She sighs. "And even the wealth we have restored can't salve the loss of our cousin, Frederic Pinabel, nor the cruel joke played on us all, by the monster that's thought to take his place. Such blows must buffet the sturdiest of courts."

"Hell, I mean," says Gloria, at the other end, "you even went and swapped your Huntsman for another." Sat back, arms folded, brown table to her left, and lavender to her right. Anna glares, and lays a hand on Melissa's beside her. The Queen does smile. "It's precisely when all seems quietest, that we must listen the more closely for tell-tale signs of subsidence, settling – of cracks – and it is when all seems to still that we have room enough, and time, to make repairs. Thus," she lifts a hand, a gesture to them all before her, "we will listen, as you each make known what news you have, and when we've heard, we shall impart a newis of our own. So!" Turning to Bruno. "Good Shrieve. How fares the Southeast fifth of this, our court?"

A desultory piano echoes through the darkness, someone humming over it, the space of a breath, if you know me so well, sung over the gathering chords, tell me which hand I use, another breath, and then the piano falls into something self-consciously portentous. Three women sit in folding chairs before the blazing mirror, and each with the same blue eyes, and each with that same nose, and each with the same yellow hair severely straight, brushed back to lop behind those similar bare shoulders, before those same pale breasts. The one to the left in the mirror closes her eyes as Aigulha leans close to brush and shape the lids of them with a charcoal sheen. The one to the right lifts up her chin, lips pursed, that Costurere might limn and paint them balefully with red. Button up, that voice somewhere in the darkness, buttons that have, forgotten they're buttons. Well, we can't have that forgetting that. The woman in the middle leans over, then, to the left, in the mirror, to her right, eyes as yet unshaded, lips a dull uncolored pink, lifting a hand to tip the chin of the woman beside her up and over for a kiss too quick, and yet too softly gentle to be brusque.

"You're welcome," she murmurs.

The woman in the middle with a scrape pushes back her chair, gets to her feet, as Costurere takes up a shadowy applicator, as Aigulha finds a tiny brush. Pads away, naked, toward the racks of clothes-stuff crowding the shadows, with the piano, and the sudden swell of strings.

"She's clearly mad," says Twice Thomas.

"It's that Gallowglas," says Clothilde, there at the end.

"She is in pain," says Luys.

"She's deranged," says Hoseason.

"She's *depraved,*" says Sigrid.

"It's not just her majesty," says Agravante, at the head of the table.

"Not this again," mutters Alphons.

"Yes, this," says Agravante, setting down his empty glass. "And yes, again, if that's what it will take. It's clear to me, and should be, to you all, the Perry line's been broken."

"A canard," says Alphons, with a dismissive fillip.

"You would *use* this, as an excuse, to keep the Princess to yourself," says Sigrid with a sneer.

"Myself?" says Agravante. He lifts his slender glass, filled with something clear. "I assure you, cousin, I've no ambitions to be King, much less High King. I've ambitions to be no more than concerned, for the future of this city, and its court." He sips.

"Her majesty has turned owr," says Thomas. "In quantities not seen in years."

"Generations," says Iona, looking down at her hands in her pink lap.

"The future of our city seems secure, for now," says Welund, there to Agravante's left.

"Does it?" says Agravante. "Think back, but a year. What was the order then?" Holding up a hand, lifting a finger, one, "Her majesty, Duenna Queen," he says. A second finger. "The Princess Ysabel, Bride-to-Be of the King Come Back. And the Gammer Gerton, Arabella," a third finger, "all cozily ensconced Northwest, above the Pearl." A look for Welund, and for Rhythidd to his left, at the other end of the table, and then that hand's laid flat. "But today?" Agravante sits back. "Two gammers sit and knit on a couch in a house in the midst of the Northeast Marches, and our Queen, a-squat on a pot of gold in a run-down Southeast warehouse."

"That blasted Gallowglas," mutters Clothilde, slumping forward. Lifting a hand, a flutter of fingers. "Everything went to blazes when *she* found the favor of her highness."

"It all stems from a dalliance with a mortal, yes," says Agravante, knock of his knuckles on tabletop. "But not, I fear, the one you're thinking of."

Hoseason sweeps both hands through his already swept-back hair. "Well?" he says. "Which?"

"Our Viscount's showing off," says Clothilde, lifting the heavy cut glass tumbler by her elbow, filled with something honey-colored, and one great cube of ice. She sniffs it, nods appreciatively to Agravante over the line of lamps between them, and sips.

"Her majesty Duenna," says Agravante, with an accidental shrug. "Her love for her husband's Huntsman, that led to the birth of our Prince; the duel, that led to the loss of our King; the uncanny shadow that fell, of the loathly lady, that led to the desuetude of her majesty's gift; the murther of Gammer Gerton, that led to a new Huntsman, our first in many years; the return of the Prince Foregone, our King Come Back."

"And gone away again," mutters Hoseason. "Gallowglas did for him, all right," says Clothilde, and another big sip. "That's not," Luys starts to say, but "You all should note that some-one's fallen from this tale," says Agravante.

"The Bride," snarls Alphons, shrugging his velveted shoulders.

"We understood, Excellency," says Rhythidd, "that the Princess Annisa would stand as Bride. For all she's not been publicly acclaimed."

"Herself, a scion of the Perry line?" says Agravante, a touch too loudly for the room. "Flung so far afield she sprouted in the Court of Engines, and only now has found her way back home?"

Sigrid glares at Rhythidd across from her. "Her highness is promised to *our house*. She's to be *quickened* for *our* new court." Luys turns widening eyes to her there to his left.

"We have two hopes," says Agravante, quickly, "for our future, which some might say is more than most." Twisting his fluted glass back and forth. "But they are such slender reeds, bent already almost to the ground, by the winds of the storm that gathers itself about." Lifting the glass. "Either her majesty comes to her senses, and finds her dear Bride Arabella, who may well have been lost to us, to dust, to strife and murther," he tosses back what's left, "or. We somehow find it possible, in spite of all, to quicken up a new line for this Court of Roses."

"Having offered her highness up, a glittering prize for our affections," says Clothilde, "you now would snatch her back, to keep for yourself."

"We must not think of ourselves, ladies, gentlemen," says Agravante, "but of us all."

"Where is her highness?" says Rhythidd, then.

"Safe," says Agravante, setting down the glass.

"But where?" says Welund, to his left. "We meet, after all, in your grandfather's house," a gesture encompasses wood panels, pressed tin, drawn drapes, the blue-glassed lamps, "but without Grandfather Count."

"He remains at the house in King's Heights," says Agravante. "It likes him more, I think."

"With her highness," says Rhythidd.

"Yes," says Agravante, after a moment a moment too long. "Her, experiments. Have proven, difficult. To move."

"I see," says Rhythidd.

"One would imagine," says Welund.

Iona looks to Luys, beside her. Luys looks to none of the rest of them at all.

Puddles and splots of cold wax mar this table, and scattered broken candles, toppled sticks, stacks of mismatched plates still crusted with the remains of this meal, or that, a litter of roses scattered there, petals browning, withering, canes yellowing, snapped, some forgotten on the floor below, by an enfilade of empty liquor bottles, a discarded sock of thick grey wool, a crack-spined paperback splayed open, lolled pages curling in the desultory air, a slender phalanx bone sparked with silver, a long radius glittering magenta, what might well be a shard of ethmoid spangled blue, all in a clutter of shards of glass, swept with dust and dirt to a corner of the porch, before those wide-hipped balustrades. The Baron Euric stood halfway along the crowded length of it, disappointment somehow evident in the impassive thwarts of his features as he gazes upon the only other face in sight, pink-cheeked, crowned by a ring of wind-blown ivory, lost in the dazzle of sunlight behind, sat at the foot of that mess. Pink hands push away a stickily empty cup. "Where the fuck *is* everybody," mutters the other.

"Thus, the news of our marches, margins, fiefs, and borders, of our court, and all our people," says the Queen, "brought by you who know it best, to us that need it most. We hope to find our footing more secure, as we proceed together into this, our

bright new day. So much, then, for the business of our council."
Pushing back her chair, smiling a benediction upon Anna and
Melissa, Alans, Linesse to her left, and Bruno, Wu Song, and
Otto to her right. "Now to our pleasure," she says. "The news
we promised of our own is of a celebration. For many weeks
now, this generous house has been made a home for our people,
and our court. And for," a hitch then, in her breath, her voice,
"myself. Gloria," she says. "Dearest Gloria."

And Gloria, at the other end of the particolor table, lifts up
her head.

"Gratitude," says the Queen, "is not a sentiment we espouse."
Bruno frowns at that. Alans sits up, surprised. "The burdens it
imposes," says the Queen, "on both giver, and receiver, too often
and too rapidly redound unbearably." Wu Song looks from the
one end of the table to the other. Linesse is watching Gloria.
"But it cannot be allowed to go without saying, that were it not
for your open arms, your generous heart, this Court of Roses
would no more be a court. And so," leaning on the table before
her, pushing herself to her feet, "we honor not your gift, but
you, Gloria Monday," the others pushing back their chairs,
getting to their feet, even Melissa, at a nudge from Anna, "and
create you," says the Queen, "Chatelaine of this, our castle, a
fully vested office," squeak, as Gloria pushes back her chair, "of
the court," as Gloria gets to her feet, tugs her hood up over her
head, "with all the rights and privileges pertaining," says the
Queen, but Gloria yanks herself away from the table, and
stomps out through the doors.

"Thereunto," says the Queen. Lowering her head. "There's
food below, and wonders to be seen," she says, to the rest of
them, "the Bullbeggar's promised us music. Go drink, and eat,
and dance. Enjoy yourselves."

THE LIGHT IS CHANGING. She peers up beneath a shading hand as she steps off a number fifteen bus at the corner, there. The sun, having past its zenith, begins its inexorable descent toward a monstrous wall of rain-heavy cloud already stretched across one whole side of the sky, bulwarks that swell from stoney blues and greys up and up through warming browns to hazy, shredded palisades and parapets of ivory, and already the towers of downtown have been overwhelmed. The bus unkneels with sigh behind her, pulls away with a snort, on up the hill.

Across the street and down, a couple of similar brick buildings shoulder up three or four storeys together, the one at this corner higher than the one at the next as the street slopes before them. Above her, the skeletal frame of what had once been a grand awning to cover the sidewalk, though the wide windows of the storefront are newly, clearly clean. Inside, wide sheets of graffiti'd plywood neatly stacked to one side of the space, lengths of cyclone fencing laid upright against the other wall, and plastic signs lapped one atop another that say Wilson Properties, Sutherlin Bank, Anaphenics. Tools neatly racked against a bar back there, shovels, bolt-cutters, pry bars, and a fading mural on the back wall, of a leaning, red-roofed tower over sketches of olive trees. Lido, the letters cursive above. The next and lower storefront, windows similarly sparkling, and the letters on them freshly painted, red that's lined and edged with black, Monte Carlo, they say. Pizza. Steaks.

"Two Italian restaurants," says Ellen Oh.

A truck climbing the hill catches its breath with a gear-change, and in its wake the strikingly sharp pop of an actual drum being actually hit, the wash and murmur of a crowd. The side street by the Monte Carlo has been blocked with sawhorses painted orange and white, and a sign that says NO THRU TRAFFIC in officious sans-serif. Past them, the brick at the head of that block gives way to looming warehouse. The long windows of it, high above, stretched between concrete pillars, have been painted over with a mural of enormously exaggerated wildflowers, fiddlenecks and pimpernels, yarrow and verbena, angelica, camas, columbine and dogbane, sea thrift and manzanita, windflowers, all manner of thistles and lupines, hawksbeard, willowherb, brassbuttons and bog orchids, creamcups, gooseberry, stonecrop, redclaws and milkvetch, asters, nodding onions, each and all subject to the ministrations of busily stylized bees that seem to thrum in the light on the painted glass to gather and dust and throng in regulated streams to and from an abstract hive painted there, a honeycombed boteh above the overhead door. The street itself's been set about with picnic tables and wheeled carts here and there loaded with bottles of water and soda, kombucha, tea, beer and cider, with burritos and samosas, calzones, sandwiches and onigiri, and a thinly scattered crowd is sat or stood about, or mills along the loading dock down the length of the warehouse, where smaller overhead doors have been cranked open on stalls hung about with photographs, with drawings or paintings, shelves of sculpture, trinkets, knick-knacked figurines.

"This is a new one," says a woman into a microphone. She's stood under the overhead door, in a slinkily tight dress that can't decide in the light if it's purple or green or blue. "Well, an old one, but it's new to us." A simple drum kit's been set up behind her, but the drummer ruddily bald has taken up the keyboard of a melodica, fitting the mouthpiece to his lips. The kid beside her's started a licking strum from his big-bellied guitar, his head hung low, face obscured by a lone long lock dyed blue. "But we had to add it," says the woman into the microphone, "for our backup girls today, what did you go with," looking to her side, "the Triplettes?" Three women beside her, the same straight yellow hair, the same brief black dresses, the same knowing smiles from the same red-painted lips, "Stevie, Star, and Tina!" Politely smattered applause. The drummer's blowing a simple repeating phrase through the melodica, three notes, four, and like that the song's begun, she's my evil twin, she knows what trouble I'm in.

Ellen sidles in among empty tables on the verges of that crowd, toward a man stood there, quite short, a paper boat of nachos in one hand, licking cheese from his thumb. His jacket, his vest, his trousers all of soberly different plaids. We're a miracle, the backup singers leaning close to their one mike, genetic miracle. Ellen steps closer, putting on an ingratiating smile, "Abby Tinker?" she says.

He cocks his brow, looks about at no one else close enough, shrugs, shakes his head. "I'm afraid you have me mistaken," he says, but she's already turning away. She's my best friend, she's my girl, she's my girl's best friend. A stoop-shouldered man in a red apron clears empty wrappers from a table, pushing a little pot of cornflowers back to the middle of it. Applause breaks out, the backup singers bow, the drummer's already kicking a lumbering beat to life, as the kid swings his guitar aside, clapping along with the singers as they start up a shuffling, side-to-side dance, Imetun ímewoi ohuhan dem, they're chanting, imetun ímewoi ohuhan dem. A woman in a red-dappled sundress and a clinking motorcycle jacket dances unselfconsciously with a great long two-handed sword, the tip of the scabbard of it planted on the pavement. Ellen slips past, around another table, headed toward a barefoot woman perfectly still, necklaces of wildly colored beads layered over her brown breast. "Abby Tinker," says Ellen.

"Zeina," says the woman. "The Mooncalfe, of Northeast." Turning her head just enough to look Ellen up and down, grey racerback tank and the dark ink stitched across her shoulders, up her throat, loose blue yoga pants, bright orange running shoes. "You're not of the court, are you."

Ellen shakes her head. Rudan híókan eye, eye, belts the singer, as the shimmying triplets and the rest of the band clap and chant ímehú úlúhúge eyegerava, ímehú úlúhúge eyegerava. The clapping scatters, syncopating, as the kid swings his guitar back into place. Rudan híókan eye! The changing light has finally begun to dim as it has threatened, yellowing as the clouds green over the sky. A few fat drops of rain plop, darkening the street, glossing the painted tables, but the crowd such as it is seems unconcerned, still milling about, clapping as the kid launches a churning riff, and the drummer lifts his sticks, waiting, waiting, the singers all suddenly pressing close as out from under the overhead door behind them lines of men and women hasten, awkward in their arms great furled umbrellas that they hustle into place over carts and tables, this knot of audience or that, shoving them open, ribs and shafts of them strung with tiny lights of white and amber, already lit. The backup singers cluster close about their mike, oohing into it, as the singer lifts hers, give me your mascara and your phosphorous, holding out her free hand, not quite pointing to a woman there in the audience, sat beneath one of the freshly opened bumbershoots, the focus of one of the larger swirls of crowd, black curls brushed back, white gown plain and simple, beautiful queen, sings the band, with your beautiful gene, and here come the drums.

The sun struggles to return, gusts of light sweeping the street, flaring the dull brown hair of a woman across the crowd to russet and gold, and her white blouse too bright for a moment, fading as the sun relents. Beside her, a second woman unchanged by the changing light, her cloud of loose white hair still brightly, whitely gold, even as the drizzle resumes. Ellen makes her way toward them, past a portly man in peppermint seersucker, an older woman in various khakis, a pompadour'd boy in a brown bomber jacket. A woman all in black approaches the other two, heavy camera about her neck, and the brown-haired woman takes her proffered hand. They head together, the two of them, toward the warehouse, and when the thunder calls, it trembles in your belly, but Ellen doesn't swerve to follow, she keeps on, between a couple of carts, out to the edge of the crowd, "Abby Tinker!" she calls, as she approaches.

Marfisa turns with a jerk, a scowl, a step too close, too quick, "What do you want with her," she says, too tensely quiet.

"Nothing," says Ellen Oh, undaunted. "Not a thing. I'm fairly certain it's you I'm supposed to meet."

The only light seeps rain-soaked through mullioned windows over those six tables of a length and width pushed together, their tops of differing colors of formica. Gloria's slumped at the one end of it, elbows on lavender and earthy brown. She sighs, heavily, at the sound of a footfall behind her. "Is it over?"

"One oughtn't walk out on a queen like that," says Anna. She flips a naked light switch. Nothing happens.

"We interrupted them," says Gloria. "They never had a chance to finish. Was an illegal street fair *really* the smartest idea?"

"Her majesty," says Anna, stepping tock-clock toward the table, "did you a great honor today."

"Her *majesty,*" says Gloria, sitting up, "tried to *give* me my own goddamn *house.* That's gonna make anybody a little testy. And if she's gonna," turning about as tick-clack Anna crosses behind her, "if she's gonna *honor* anybody, with a title, or an office, or whatever, why isn't it, why didn't she," rattle of wheels as Anna drags over a chair, "it should've been," says Gloria, "you."

"I've slept in a filing cabinet," says Anna Nirdlinger, sitting down.

"I, ah," says Gloria, "what?"

"When I first started out, I slept in a roll-top desk with a dozen other girls. We each had a pigeonhole of our own. I've slept in a banker's box: spacious, and comfortable, but there's no cachet to it. Cardboard, you know. At Welund Rhythidd?" she takes off her glasses, "most of the paralegals sleep in the big bottom drawer of their desks." Wiping a bit of dust from a narrow lens. "I preferred the kneehole. It was considered," she sighs, "odd." Puts the glasses back on.

"But," says Gloria. "You, aren't a domestic."

"I was an amanuensis, for a time," says Anna. "That first night, after I first saw to her majesty, Duenna, that night when I slept in a bed, for the very first time?" looking away, in that underwater light. Gloria shifts a hand, reaching toward her, across the lavender. "Her majesty," says Anna, "would never deign to honor such as me."

"But that's not okay," says Gloria.

"Yet here," says Anna, and she smiles, "I sleep in a bed."

"We could," says Gloria, sitting back, "maybe," she shrugs, "see about getting you, a better one," hands up, a shrug.

Quick fingers, a needle, thin black thread, a delicate scrap of lingerie pinned to a padded board on tailor-folded knees, Aigulha bent over deftly seals a rip, seamlessly matching net-wise warp and weft of lace. "I liked the music," she's saying. "I liked the dancing." Gently tugging, fitting, pulling. Away over there through the darkness a shift, a sigh, a muttering, muffled moan.

"I," Costurere's saying, "liked the food," crinkily smoothing a paper pattern over a stretch of black pleather that shines in the glare of the trouble light hung above them. "Empanadas," she says, pushing a pin, "potatoes and cheese," and another, "ancho peppers," wincing at the sound of a slap. Someone laughs.

"You liked the beer," says Aigulha, smoothing fretwork with a fingertip.

"I did like the beer," says Costurere, reaching for a pair of pinking shears.

Away across the otherwise darkness between and among the blocky columns, fresh candles have been set before the empty bed, about the layered rugs and cushions, and two figures tightly curled about each other in that pillowy nest, one atop the other, curl of gold-streaked back, knees jackknifed about gold-smeared arms wrapped about hips, ankles crossed toe-flexing feet locked above and bracing below heads tucked between gold-spattered thighs, soaked yellow severe splayed over buttocks, shoulders, rugs and cushions, sip and slurp-smack shivering undulations, an effortful grunt.

"I wanted," says Aigulha, precisely trimming a leftover bit of thread with tiny silver scissors. "Would you want to go dancing? Again? Sometime?"

"Put up your work, girls," says the Queen, warmly magnanimous behind them. "You might have music and dancing, beer and pies, sweet cakes and kisses whenever you wish." Swish and sway of her gown stepped from the shadows, a hand against the glare of the trouble light. "They got started without us, I see."

"Ma'am," says Aigulha, and "Majesty," Costurere, as they scramble to their feet, laying shears and scissors aside. The

Queen spreads wide her arms, tips back her head, as fingers cleverly undo this knot, that hook, and her plain white simple gown collapses to the floor. She catches their hands in hers, and tugs them after, "Come," she says.

"But, my lady," says Costurere, looking back.

"The mending, ma'am," says Aigulha.

"We've said," the Queen pulls them both close. "Now's not the time for work." Lifting Costurere's hand in hers, her knuckle clotted with a curd of gold she presses to Costurere's lips. Smiling as Aigulha leans in for a taste. "Let's go," says the Queen, "and see what play they do inspire."

Behind them, as they head away toward the candles, someone steps just close enough to the trouble light to reveal black spike-heeled pumps, bare knees, a brief black skirt. Tick-click, tack-click away from the light, not toward the candles, but the darkness. Scrape of a chair. Snap of switch, lights blaze about the mirror over the dressing table. She sets down a stack of red plastic cups, a bottle half-filled with amber wine. Oremus Tokaji Aszú, says the label. Öt Puttonyos.

Sitting herself in the chair, she tucks a long and yellow lock behind her ear, but it twists as her fingers slip through it, coiling in darkening curls. When she reaches for the bottle her eyes are green, not blue. She pours a slug in a plastic cup, and another, then sits back, lifting the cup in something of a toast. In the mirror, up behind her, a bright wild knot of candlelight, the rugs and cushions, the Queen reclining, and Aigulha and Costurere laid with her, mob-capped heads in her lap, on her hip, watching intent that ouroboric knot of pleasure, something like it there before them, striving for, straining for, gasping, and a groan.

"WHAT TIME IS IT?" she says, sat up abruptly in pastel sheets. "Is that?" Rubbing her eyes. "Are you, is that, bacon?"

"Good afternoon," says Big Jim Turk, there by the credenza, stirring something about on the little electric griddle. "You'll note I didn't say good morning. It's late enough I thought I'd try an olfactory cue, as kisses and sweet nothings hadn't seemed to do the trick."

"Me and Anna were," she says, rubbing her forehead, "talking, you were already asleep when I, isn't that, like, a violation? Or something?" Complex calligraphy across the front of her T-shirt says The Mandarin Miranda. "The meat."

"If there's any sin," he says, pushing and turning, "these spatters of hot grease should prove penance, ow! enough." Thumbing the lop of his belly. His buttocks pale and hairless, flat, almost concave beneath the heft of his thickset torso. "Smell alone's enough to remind the likes of, tst! me, what I'm missing, but also," scooping slices onto a chipped blue plate, "enough to tell me, were I to take a bite," tap tap, and he shuts the griddle off, "what knots would twist my gut." Turning to hold out the plate, but she's already off the bed before him, taking it from his hand, setting it back on the credenza, wrapping him in a sudden hug. His hands up, startled, settle gently, awkwardly on her shoulders. He kisses the jet-black top of her head. "It's only what a Chatelaine deserves."

She shoves out of his arms, away, hard enough to rock him back a step. "Don't you start." Wheeling off toward the window.

"Gloria," says Jim.

Her back to him, both hands on the sill of it. The glass has been cleaned but painted over with blossoms, a nodding columbine in red and yellow, a suncup, an orange blanket-flower. Out beyond those colors, a rainy day.

"Stay in the game," he says, "or walk away from the table, but if you stay?" Eyes sternly direct over that mustache of his. "Then play."

"Thing is, Jim," she says. "I like the table. I built, the fucking ta-ble. I just don't like this game somebody else decided to play on it."

"And now," says Jim, "you're a step closer to being able to change it." She glares at him over her shoulder, and he chuckles, "I forget, sometimes," he says, "how very young you are."

"I'm a Sagittarius," she sneers. "You got nothing to worry about on that score."

"It's your impatience," he says, taking hold of her hand. "You can afford to be patient, Gloria. You have more time than you think."

Softening, taking his hand in hers, "And you made me naked bacon."

"I did fry you up some speck," he says.

"It's," she sags into him, and his arms come about her, "maybe it's the rain," she says. "It's back. It's gonna rain for weeks, now. At least until after the Rose, ah, Festival," she frowns.

"It's feast or famine, here in the Great Northwest," he says, looking down, dipping the better to see her turned-away face. "Gloria?"

"Something," she says, a distracted gesture, "I don't know. Probably nothing. Probably."

Leaned against the staves that make up that great wooden tub, Marfisa reaches out over the expanse of gold within. Brushes it with her fingertips. Draws them back toward her, furrowing the brightness. Shaking, flicking them free of dust. Pressing her hand to the inside of the wall of the tub, stroking the glossy oaken staves. Not much less than a palmspan above the level of the dust, the wood's not stained but brightened by a detritus of gold, all the way around the inside of that tub. She looks up to see Joan-the-Wad dredge a red plastic cup through the owr, drawing up a generous scoop as she laughs back over her shoulder at something somebody's said.

Marfisa turns away, taking a step to nearly collide with someone, a woman in a black dress a bit too brief for her height, black hair brushed back, unpainted lips, eyes with only a hazeled hint of green, nodding an apology as she turns away, tugging her skirt back down. "Starling?" says Marfisa.

Pausing, caught, turning then with a shrug and a smile, looking her up and down, loose T-shirt and tight shorts, low grey running shoes, white hair tied back. "Outlaw," she says.

Marfisa tips back her head, lips pursed, parting about something she doesn't say. What she does say is, "I wish to speak with her majesty. Here you are, without her. Is she, otherwise, engaged?"

The Starling looks away, shaking her head with something like a laugh. "The twins," she says, "complained of hangover, and are off away somewhere, sulking. Her majesty's below."

"Alone?" says Marfisa.

"When last I saw," says the Starling, and then, calling after Marfisa's retreating back, "but who can truly say?"

Away down the length of that cavernous warehouse, past stalls where here and there someone's tinkering, sketching, polishing, some sort of intricate contraption set in tensely whirling motion, splinters and sawdust being swept, clatter of dice and a token slapped triumphantly down on board, and laughter, teasing banter about an enormous steaming pot. Marfisa passes under and through a long low arch lit by strings of clear glass bulbs along the ceiling, out into a foyer floored with yellowing tiles. A scaffold's erected up one wall of the stairwell, a couple of painters wiping out the mural of a tree with great swathes of fresh white primer. She ducks under, past the corner of it, heading down instead of up.

But it's not dark, down there. She pauses a moment, hand against the wall, feet on different steps. It's quiet. She continues, softly, down.

Boxy work lights on orange tripods set among the columns obliterate shadows to starkly reveal the candles congealed about the skewed rugs, tumbled pillows, the wadded, crumpled throws and wraps before that big wide bed, pristinely made. Across the basement, past the dressing table where the Queen is sat, a dressing screen's unfolded, the frame of it of whitewashed wood, and panels of plain linen. The basement otherwise is empty.

"Where's the rest?" says Marfisa, so quiet in all that space.

The Queen turns about in the folding chair, white suit coat buttoned once, loose white trousers, black curls artfully tangled. Smiling. "Outlaw!" she cries, brightly. "How wonderful to see you!"

"I wanted to," says Marfisa, "talk," still looking past her.

"Of course! We must talk, and drink, dine, dance and sing, and laugh," says the Queen. "We should laugh. We've missed you. I, have. Missed you."

"You've been busy," says Marfisa.

"That's not an excuse. For either of us."

"And the clothing, and the costumes you'd been gathering? They're all," nodding toward the screen, white hair shining in this light, "there?"

"I've been debating whether to even keep this," says the Queen, with a gesture for the dressing table, the mirror over it, lamps about unlit. "I suppose it's important, to be able to check. Even if we know the looks will be perfect."

"And the seamstress," says Marfisa, turning away. "And the maquilleuse."

"They're well enough, I suppose," says the Queen. "Certainly more comfortable." Turning about, at the soft footfall as Marfisa walks away. "But, Marfisa," she says. "You wanted to talk?" Marfisa continues on, back down the starkly bright length of basement. "Marfisa? Outlaw? Outlaw!" Marfisa climbs the steps, away and up, without once looking back.

The Queen turns back. On the table, before the mirror, three or four red plastic cups stacked together, and a lone cup, crumpled, on its side, by a clearly empty bottle of wine. "Oh, I am regal," says her majesty, very much to herself. "I do rule."

The night is black and thick
I wander past your window
And I catch a cigarette thrown from a
    jewel-encrusted hand.

It comes on pretty quick
Exactly like a crocodile
In search of a mirage across the
    undulating sand.

—Robyn Hitchcock

NO. 37

" – and 'thirsty wilds' – "

"It all depends" – the import of Breakfast
Trinkets & Fallalery – the Work resumed – Looping the Pin
where It's going – Jumble & Clink – a Lug's business
a Bootlegger's reverse – the Gall they have – "Oh, it's you"
there'd be a Lawn – the Coordination of Intimacy – Bright Lines
the Shoe in Her hand – Kaffeeklatsch – Far be it
delicate Matters – "Force & Victory!"
You will be Warned

"And it all depends," says the radio, "on the nature of the day. Was it good?" A man's voice, unpolished, but not unpleasant. "Then it's all good, for one more day. Kick back. Relax. You've earned it. But if it was a bad day?" Groans from an unseen audience. Up behind the radio the wall's been tiled with old album jackets, color photos of men with horns, or keyboards, muted duotones of women crooning into elaborately caged microphones. "One bad day," the radio says. "Enough to take everything you've taken years to gather, and to build, to take it all and pull it down around you."

Out in the middle of the room a big round table covered in green felt, surrounded by a motley herd of armchairs and recliners, one of them laid flat. Curled apparently asleep atop it an old man in a brown suit much too big. "Our prosperity," the radio's saying. "Our security. The walls around us, the roofs over our heads, the floors beneath the very shoes on our feet, how secure are they? When all it takes is one bad day to lock it all away from us. How *real* are they, if one bad day's enough to make them disappear?"

One wall's mostly free of albums, taken up instead by an overhead garage door, a smaller door beside it creaking open on sullen afternoon. Christian squeezes through, sagging brown jeans, soft green hoodie, tugging the door shut as an afterthought. "In this," says the radio, "the richest country in the history of the world that ever was." He stoops, snagging empty cans from the floor, dropping them a-rattle into a blue tub. "Like many of you," says the radio, "I had my bad day," and murmurs swell, a general air of affirmation, "oh, indeed I did. I used to be an up-and-coming architect, what they call a starchitect, if you can believe it," and a pause for almost laughter. "But I can't show you any buildings I built, because I never built a one. Not while I was an architect. I told other people how to build them. And they're all garbage."

More empty cans, plastic cups, a bottle still a-slosh with dregs. Christian sets the blue tub down to pick his way through all those chairs toward the back wall, the shelf, the radio, "Everything," it says, "that, before my one bad day? I would've considered my life's work? Crap. All of it, I'm telling you, every building, not even crap. You see things differently, when it all comes crashing down."

It's old, the radio, sleekly rounded, a dignified brown overwhelmed by an ivory dial in the middle of its mattely translucent grille. Christian twists it, dissolving that voice in static, advertising yammer bent into woozy synths and a slapping pop, Nissan babes with the body burgundy, love my car same way I used to love key, "You turn that back!" snarls the old man from the recliner, and Christian jumps, knocking something over with a clatter on the shelf.

Pressure pressure pressure pressure pressure, from the radio.

"Now, goddammit," from the old man on the recliner.

"Best do as he says," from the man stepping through that smaller door, brown sack coat, grizzled cheeks, cream Kangol cap. "Yes sir, yes sir, what Duckie says," from the man following after, ducking his head, chewed-up brim of his old straw hat. Christian, scowling, turns the dial back squawking through babble, spoke fenders and two-way sneeze-through, a pirouette of sitar, elect had this to say, a whine and then "a bad day of their own," that voice.

"What on earth," says the man in the Kangol cap. "What's he going on about?" says the man in the straw hat. "What is this?"

"Found a dead bum," says the man sat up on the recliner. "Them tunnels, under the Ross Island Bridge. You know." An eyelid, his cheeks, a smatter of spots across his high forehead palely pink against the seamed and wrinkled brown. "The only thing," the radio's saying, "ever does any damn good."

Christian tips back enough to take in the rest of the clutter up there on the shelf, jars filled with nails and bolts and picture hooks, a loose tumble of wood screws and a gnawed nub of pencil, a long and slender copperly shining bullet that he sets back up on end.

"So he's giving a speech?" says the man in the Kangol cap, sitting himself in a soft plaid armchair. "On the radio?" says the man taking off his straw hat, turning it over in his hands.

"Community radio," says the man on the recliner, leaning down with a grunt to lever up the back of it.

Christian reaches past the bullet to a couple of fallen picture frames, lifting up the one, a scrap of paper behind the glass of it, a handwritten numeral four, we believe that if the white land-lords will not give decent houseing, Christian sets it upright by the larger frame filled with patches pinned to a white ground, an upraised fist blocked out in black, the letters BPPSD, a stylized leaping panther, a flag of red and black and green and gold, "to take away from this," the radio's saying, "what I want you to keep in mind."

"Who's dealing," says the man in the Kangol cap. "Who's got the cards?" says the man who lets his straw hat fall to the felt.

"Never leave the table," says the man on the recliner, leaning over the table to the middle of it, where there's a tub that says Aunt Ruby's Peanuts in faded letters, filled with flat washers and lock washers and nuts hexagonal and square, and beside it a greasy pack of cards he takes up in his suddenly nimble hands, clatter and ruffle. "Then who will do for us?" the radio says. Christian lifts the other toppled frame, a photograph within, blurred black and white on newsprint, dots of ink gone green on time-browned paper, kids at a table laughing over plates of food, two men, three, leaned over, stood behind them, a woman smiling with them, Breakfast, says the caption, at Highland United Church of, and the rest torn away. "That was Michael Lake," a suddenly different voice is saying, "speaking yesterday at Chapman Square."

"Where the hell is he?" says the man in the Kangol cap, leaning over to dig a handful of nuts and washers from Aunt Ruby's tub, and "Why's he always late?" says the man sitting himself in a wooden swivel chair before his battered straw hat, but even then the overhead door with a clanking grind has started rising. They look up, around, to see him, the boots, the denim overalls, the sharkskin coat, the broad smile and the laugh, "Ha *ha!*" he claps those big brown hands, and a generically jaunty funk vamp's kicked off from the radio. "I *can't* be late!" says Gordon, stepping into the garage. "It's my game!"

"Has a point," says the man scattering a handful of washers by his straw hat. The radio's burbling something about a proud co-sponsor of the seventeenth annual Portland Zine Symposium. Cards spin over green felt with deft wrist-flicks, two face-down there, two there, two more, and again. Christian's studying the scrap of newsprint, the men behind those happy kids, the one of them small and skinny, spots across his forehead clearly pale despite years-softened ink, grinning up at the man beside him, tight white T-shirt, big hands leaned on the backs of the chairs of the kids at the table before him, not yet bald, his hair a mighty round of tight black curls.

"Go on, boy," growls Gordon, pulling a wing chair around to the table with a scrape. "Finish up and get on out of here." Digging into the tub for his own handful, he lets four or five drop to the felt in the middle before spilling the rest by his cards. "Ante up, gentlemen! I'm here to take your nuts."

Shoulders shake with muffled chortles, and the one man slaps the table by his straw hat with a yelp. Christian puts the frame back by the radio.

TRINKETS AND FALLALERY, bangles and geegaws, furbelows, the occasional bagatelle all racked and scattered, sorted, spread over shelves in the glass case before her, sunglasses in silver, or tortoiseshells of blue, amber, green, or plainly classic black, candy-colored charm bracelets, a bowl of mismatched cuff-links, copper mule mugs and glittering shot glasses set before a couple of silvery cocktail shakers. She looks up, about the store, windowed walls that narrow to a point where glass doors propped open on a not especially sunny day. Deco to Disco, says the sandwich board on the sidewalk, 1960, the numerals painted in reverse on the clear glass lintel. Over in an odd back corner behind another glass case a clerk sits on a stool, reading a paperback. Poor People, says the cover. She coughs demurely. He doesn't look up.

Past a couple-three mannequins draped and posed in polyester finery to a small high table clouded over with filmy scarves printed with maps, cartoons, faux-embroidery and trompe-l'œil batik, twisted in infinite loops. She selects one spangled with toy rockets and flying saucers, slips it over her head, lifting out of the way her wild hair the color of clotted cream. She winds it twice about her throat, smooths it over the nubbled collar of her sheepskin coat, issues another, louder cough. The clerk turns a page, shoulder shifting in his pinstripe vest. His beard thinly patched.

Back to the glass case filled with baubles. Cocking her head to one side, the other, shaking out her hands, she plants her feet. Holds her right arm out, fingers wiggling. Something slips from the sleeve of her coat, a length of wood, finely turned and polished, improbably lengthening until those fingers close about the tapered handle of it, a baseball bat she twirls once and lifts above her head. One last glance for the clerk, who turns another page.

Splash of glass she drives the bat through the case, shatter and crash she twists it about, knocking loose the jagged shards so she might reach in to pluck a pair of sunglasses, thin wire frames, aviator gold.

"Hey!" the clerk's shouting, "Whoa! Hey!" Flinching as she rounds on him, sunglasses on her face, scarf about her throat, bat choked high. "The Shrieve," she snarls.

"Take," he says, "whatever, money," lifting to drop a cash-box on the glass, "there's, we're mostly cards, you know, debit, and – "

"Shut *up,*" and a shake of her bat. "Howling saayungkas, you aren't even in it."

"Take the money," he says, half-lilted to a question.

"Call your boss," she says. "Have your boss call their boss. Sooner or later you'll find someone who knows the Shrieve. Say the name."

"Sharif?" he says, blinking.

"Tell them Marfisa waits upstairs. Say that name."

"Mar," he says, "Marfissa."

"Tell them," she says, headed off toward the back of the shop. "But," says the clerk.

Kicks open a door at the back, rattle and skew a sign that says Employees Only. Hallway narrowed by boxes along one wall, a wooden crate at the end, an ottoman tilted on a broken leg. The lobby beyond, handful of steps to the landing of a steep staircase she quickly climbs, up and up to the very top, a single brown door, the numerals three and two and one hung above the peephole of it. Tap-tap she knocks, and listens. Bat swung restlessly down a chop at the air, back up and ready. She tries the knob.

Within an airy kitchen, cabinets white and blue left open on bare shelves, a countertop scrubbed clean. Past that three low steps down to an open room, windowed walls that narrow to a windowed point. The daylight seeping through's uncertain enough it's difficult to say how high the sun might be. And boxes everywhere, banker's boxes white and brown that cover the floor, the sofa, that barricade the great maroon chair in the narrowed point, and man sat tailor-fashion on the one cleared bit of floor before the coffee table. In one long slender-fingered hand a delicate pair of tweezers pinch a yellowed scrap of paper. The other readies a brown glass bottle of mucilage.

"What are you," Marfisa starts to say, when he blurts, "This one but does the bidding of her grace!"

"Her grace."

"Even so! The morgue was to be moved upstairs, her grace did say. In the event of rain."

"Rain."

"It's as her grace has said. And now," looking to tweezers, brush, the photo overturned before him, "the work resumes." Daubing the bottom of it with the bottle's rubber stopper, fitting the tweezed scrap of paper to the corner, setting bottle aside to take up a brush, carefully smoothing the typewritten scrap into place.

"When was her grace last here?" she says.

"Oh," leaning down to blow, gently, on the caption, June 7 1967, it says. MAC L-242 R. Perry, A. Gerton. "Not for days and days." Thump and bustle without, below. Marfisa turns back to the door half-open, footsteps pounding their way on up. She takes off the sunglasses.

The Harper Chillicoathe bursts through the doorway, bulky sweater and narrowed eyes, big yellow beard a-snarl with an ugly grin, "Oh, Outlaw," he says. "How kind of you, to bring me back my coat." He pulls from a flare of light a short but service-able blade. She shrugs. The man in the room below gathers with alacrity and care his tools, the photos, packing them away.

The first few savage chops aimed at her head, her arms, easily knocked aside by twitches of her upraised bat. Howling he jerks back, shoulders slung, both hands about the hilt above the heavy golden pommel as sidelong, shuffle-stomp, she flicks her bat at him. His hasty parry cracks her askew. She laughs.

He thrusts, she sideswipes, shifts back and back toward the three steps, one foot unsteady on the very edge. Shouting she swings a slap at his face he one arm cycling sideways ducks, feet slipping back into the kitchen. She follows with relentless jabs. He manages to snag the jamb before the hall to right himself, tensing pushing a leap of a lunge blade over her extended bat to punch a fold of her coat and lodge itself deep in her chest. She gasps. He braces to yank but she twists away, ripping the hilt from his hands to quiver there before her. Two heavy limping steps away. She leans a hand on the counter.

"Marfisa," he says, sternly edged.

Clatter the bat to the floor. Grips with both hands the hilt below that hammered golden pommel. Grimacing she pulls the slowly steely length from out her body with another hissing gasp. Sits back against the counter planted feet to lower the sword an ooze of something thickly white the length of it to dangle a moment from the tip.

"You are a thief," he says, "an accoster, and a budge, and I have proved it – "

"You wrecked my coat, is what you've done," she snaps, pulling away the lapel of it, eyeing the matted wool about the hole that glistens wetly.

"Outlaw," he says, but "Harper," she says, flatly. Pointing the sword at him with a bitter smile. "The coat," she says, "is mine. This sword, is mine. These rooms?" Lifting the tip of it to point, the one way, the other, "Mine," she says. Unwinding the scarf from about her throat. "Go and tell the Shrieve," she says, and wipes down the blade. Peers the length of it in this light. A sudden lurch at Chilli both hands on the hilt she jerks it up over her head a chop on the trembling verge of coming down, *"Go!"* she roars, and he's two steps back out of the apartment on the landing, hastening, footsteps receding away down the stairs.

She drops the sword to clang with a wince by the sink. Works her way out of the sheepskin coat to let it fall to the floor. Looks over the counter to the room below, the man still crouched behind a stack of boxes. "You," she says. "You may stay. A while, at least. You seem quiet enough."

Hand to her side, then, out of the kitchen, into the dim hall, away toward the doors at the end of it.

"If I am being honest?" says the gleaming amber phone, there on the unfolded writing surface of the escritoire. "I would have to say I do not know." Clear, loud, only a hint of crackle. "What you're saying is, she's back."

"She's been back," says Petra B, a hand on the back of the nubbled green armchair. "Ah, this is Petra. Anyway, she's been back about a month now."

"No," says the phone. "Well, yes. She is here. There. She is there, she has been there, we can set aside for the moment how honest you should have been with me, with us all, on this point."

"We haven't been dishonest," says Anna, white blouse crisp, sat to one side of the escritoire.

"She didn't," says Melissa, perched on the cushion of the armchair, "sorry, this is Melissa, she didn't, you know, have anywhere else to go."

"We shall set it aside," says the phone. "Put a pin in it. We'll loop back to it, but. The point I wish to make. That I wish to have made. What I mean, when I say, she is back." Rustle of paper. "You called it a spell."

"Yeah," says Melissa.

"It might be called that," says Anna.

"A spell, you've said, she cast," says the phone.

"Yeah," says Melissa, motorcycle jacket a-clink over a lacy shift.

"The question," says Anna, pushing her narrow glasses back up her nose.

"It's why we started meeting, in the first place. This is Petra."

"Sorry, this is, I'm Melissa," says Melissa.

"This spell was broken," says the phone. "When she came back. When she, returned, to your group. She no longer had this, *power.*"

Petra looks across the small close office to Anna. "Yeah," says Melissa. "I guess. Yeah."

"I want to make certain I have your frame of reference."

"It will do," says Anna.

"But now," says the phone. "What I am given to understand. What I'm hearing you tell me, is that. And this is the point I wish to impress. What you have said is that you believe, as of, a few days ago. What you have said to me is this power has been restored. And thus, that *she,* is back."

"Yeah," says Petra, and "Yes," says Anna, and Melissa perks up, "Oh," she says. "I get it. Uh, this is Melissa, sorry."

"And yet," says the phone. "It doesn't concern you. None of you is, concerned. That, having returned, being back, she might now, once more, put. One of you. Any of you. All of you, under that," again, paper rustles, "spell."

Anna looks to Petra B, who shrugs, "Not at the moment?" she says.

"She *wouldn't,*" says Melissa.

"But what," says the phone, "is the basis, for this assertion?"

"Sorry, this is Melissa?"

"She's focused on," says Petra, "ah, other. People."

"There's been a shift in the dynamic," says Anna.

"What I'm hearing," says the phone. "What you're saying. You have put your, trust. In this woman, who has, who had been, the *author.* Of every, heartache, of every," a sigh palpably blown from the phone. "Trauma, is not too heavy a word. In this context. That you, as a group, have aired, to me. To each other, these past few weeks. Forgive me. Is, have we heard from. Is, Gloria, on the call?"

Chime and clink Melissa tips back her head, rolling her eyes. Petra lifts her hand from the chair to adjust her thickly black-rimmed glasses. "No," says Anna.

"You must," says the phone, "understand. If I am being honest, I would have to say. This, is not, an appropriate, therapeutic. Posture." A deep breath in through the speaker. "Over a phone. But. Setting this, reluctance. Aside. As regards a decision, we can't. You can't. *I,* can't. Ask, the others," Anna leans over the side of the escritoire, "to, bring themselves. Into a situation such as you have outlined. With her," rustle. "Back."

"We appreciate your time, Addison," says Anna, to the phone. "Send your invoice. It will be paid." Taps the screen of it, cutting it off in the middle of "As you – "

"The hell," says Melissa, elbows on her knees. "We didn't even get to talk about the whole Hunter bullshit."

"Huntsman," says Anna distractedly, tucking the phone away.

"Hunter," says Melissa. "Huntswoman. Whatever," getting to her feet, "I'm *not* a guy. That is literally the whole fucking point."

"She's not wrong," says Petra. "Speakerphone's a terrible way to do group."

"It was a mistake to go ahead without Gloria," says Anna.

"Where *is* she, anyway?" says Melissa, reaching for the greatsword leaned up behind the armchair. "I mean, this whole deal is, like, her thing, right? It's why we're here? Why we started coming here, anyway. Is she just, blowing us off, now? Now she's shacked up with Daddy Jim?" Looking back and forth, from Petra to Anna. "What, am I speaking too bluntly?"

"It wasn't an I-statement," says Petra.

Anna opens her mouth to say something, but "Yeah, well," says Melissa, sweeping past them both, *"I,* have nothing to do, since her highness is off on some errand, so *I* am gonna find where she's stashed the liquor, because *I* say it's never too early to start day-drinking around here." Turning as she opens the door, scabbard awkward in her arms, walkway behind her, dim daylight softly through high and narrow windows. "You're welcome to join me," she says, stepping out, "but I don't think that's an *I*-statement, now, is it," and shuts the door behind her.

"Okay," says Petra B.

"The stress of what she's been through, lately, has doubtless – "

"Oh, stop. You really don't have to try so hard, you know? To find something nice to say. Not with me."

"Her position's rather unique, within our group."

"The whole quote-unquote Hunter bullshit?"

"The stress imposed must be relieved. Profanity can – "

"I swear," say Petra, "I don't know if it's because you're a lawyer, or because you're," a gesture, "you're, you know, but," that hand brushed back through her black, black hair, "the whole diplomatic thing, it's totally unnecessary. You don't have to go to the effort when I'm just, bitching about something."

"Someone," says Anna.

"Oh for God's sake."

"And," says Anna, turning back to the escritoire, "I'm not a lawyer." Taking up a small stack of mail, each envelope already neatly slit. Petra tips back her head, a bit of black lace at her throat. "See?" she says. "Diplomatic. Even when you're telling me to go fuck myself."

"That was certainly never my intention," says Anna, unfolding something on official-looking letterhead.

"And yet."

Anna tucks the letter away in one of the escritoire's pigeon-holes. "What troubles you?" she says.

"Where is this going?" Unakimboing, Petra leans a hand on the back of the nubbled armchair. "I moved in here, what, a month? Six weeks ago? Whenever. And, I don't pay any rent, which is great. Electric, cable, water, sewage, none of that crap I have to worry about, and that's great. Some of the stuff they have me shoot is, okay, is not, you know, ideal, but it keeps her happy, so that's a wash. And it's all I have to do. No hustling for waitstaff or bartending or barista gigs, no running PA errands for whatever basic cable producer just hit town, and whatever gear I want? I can just, order it? That, I mean, that's spectacular. I have *time*, Anna. I can do what I want with it. And that," a sigh, "that is, great."

"It doesn't sound as if it's going anywhere," says Anna. "It sounds as if it's where it needs to be."

"But for how long?" says Petra, stepping toward her. "How long can this keep going? *How* can it possibly keep going? I swear, Anna, I wake up in the morning, I just, *know*, like an ache, in my chest, I'm gonna open the door and everybody will be, gone. I'll come downstairs and it'll all be empty, the art all gone, the bazaar cleared out, that, stew that's been simmering for weeks, no more coffee, or donuts, the gold, Gloria, you, and, and then, then, what will I do, Anna? What could I possibly do?"

Anna gets to her feet, takes one of Petra's hands in hers. "That will never," she says, "would never, could never happen. A court such as ours can't pack itself up and steal away in the night. What has been built, here? Already? For ourselves, and her majesty, one day it might must come to an end, yes. But it will have lasted.

It already has." Lifting Petra's hand. "And if it does? Come to that end?" Clasping it to her breast, blinking behind her narrow lenses. "It will only be because we'll already have gone on, to whatever it is that's next."

"Do I," says Petra, "get to go, to wherever that is?"

"If you come," says Anna, "you'll be there."

Petra closes up her eyes behind her glasses. Tugs her hand free of Anna's. "Fucking diplomat," she says.

JUMBLE & CLINK – A LUG'S BUSINESS
A BOOTLEGGER'S REVERSE – THE GALL THEY HAVE

JUMBLE AND CLINK the keys in his hand, falling to chime on the pile of them in that wide-mouthed jar, seventy-five cents the price on the tag about it. Past the bins of loose handles and knobs, dulled nickel and pitted brass, wood smoothly turned to satiny finishes, white enamel cleanly bright but chipped, cracked, he stoops, there at the end of the aisle, over a low bucket filled with tiny dice like chips of ruby, sapphire, diamond, emerald.

"Anvil?"

He straightens, shoulders shifting in a blue-sheened coat a trifle tight. "Mason," he says. In one hand a worn brown leather satchel.

Back through an angled corridor more doorways than walls, out one of them into a courtyard crowded with birdbaths leaned companionably one against another, cold fire pits set before a line of chimineas, great earthen pots and planters and mirror-bright gazing globes, a clustered flock of spindly orreries and armillary spheres flanked by blocky concrete sundials poured from the same mold, and in the middle of it all a dry and empty fountain, the heavy-lipped basin surmounted by reticent angels. A low doorway opens on a steep flight of stairs to a cramped hall, lumpily carpeted and no angle entirely square. Luys knocks once sharply at a door, then opens it wide.

The office within surprisingly spacious, tall dimly shaded windows, spotless dark-stained floorboards, a brusquely modern desk in a corner, and behind it Bruno in a moleskin vest. "You weren't kept long?" he says.

"I did pass the time," says Pyrocles. "You've a great many distracting articles below." In the other corner an armchair, a low table with a single cut glass decanter, a dark shelf tastefully appointed, a dourly analog clock. "Someone would've met you direct," says Bruno, with a look for Luys hung back there, by the door, "but her majesty did need a car today."

"You'd have this business done most privily," says Pyrocles.

"I'd have it done as smoothly as it might," says Bruno, "an her majesty says it shouldn't."

"Her majesty," says Pyrocles, stroking with a knuckle those long iron mustaches from his lip, "forbade it the brother of the Guisarme, which is neither here nor there for – "

"It's been forbidden to any who yet serve the Hound," says Bruno. "As well we all do know. To think, it's come to this," a shake of his head, "the mighty Pyrocles would cloak himself in sophistry."

"Bruno," says Luys, crossing the office to lay a hand there on the desk, and Bruno sitting back. "Give it to me," says Luys, "if your delicacy forbids."

"It's not delicate," says Bruno, opening a drawer, "to be specific." Pulls out a rounded golden brick tight-wrapped in clingfilm. Lets it fall, heavily, to the desk.

"You'd press a point, but wouldn't break the skin," says Luys, a hand on that brick. "In this, we serve no Hound nor Hawk. We serve the Rose." Bruno looks away. Luys takes up the brick, turns to Pyrocles, who lifts up his satchel, holds it open, empty. Luys drops the brick within. Pyrocles hefts it with a nod, and zips it shut.

"We only delay what's inevitable," says Bruno.

"We provide," says Luys, "what stability we might."

"Stability," says Bruno, "sediments. The crack, when it comes – and it will come – will be all so much the worse, by how much more firm, how *stable,* all has seemed."

"You'd have us do nothing?" says Luys.

"I'd have us consider the implications."

"The desperate, Shrieve – the *hungry* – are the more likely to lash out. It's merely as simple as that."

"The comfortable, Mason, might be just as rash, if they smell a change in the wind. And the well-fed wield a stronger bite."

"Gentlemen," says Pyrocles, but "This," says Luys, a gesture flung toward him and the satchel in his hands, "nonetheless grants us time. A measure of peace."

"Is it peace we'd buy?" says Bruno. "Or a festering resentment?" A gesture of his own for the satchel, weightily a-dangle. "If this is a gift you'd have us give, the obligation's well beyond whatever we might bear. But if it's our duty? To the court, as you might have it?" A shake of his head, rhetorically slow. "You'd have us doling out their portion. You'd forge a bright new link of toradh. You'd set the Hound beneath the Hawk."

"We're neither of us the Hawk!" snaps Luys.

"Yet you did decide," says Bruno.

"And you did concur!"

"Gentlemen!" says Pyrocles, a bit too loud, a touch too quick. "I'd take my leave, if I have leave to take?"

Bruno's studiedly impassive gaze shifts to him from Luys, and Luys turns about, his frown a disconcerted blend of skeptical amusement and temper interrupted. Pyrocles lowers his head, muttering, "Levity was never my forte."

"Just as well," says Bruno. "A light Anvil's pretty much useless."

Luys snorts, once, his frown tipping over till a shake of his head recovers his expressionlessness. Pyrocles blows out his mustaches, pewter beads at the ends of them a-sway. "We forget ourselves," says Bruno. "From one servant of the Rose, then, to another, good Sir Pyrocles? Go as you might; make of it," a breath, "whatsoever you will."

"I'll," offers Luys, taking a step, but Bruno holds up a hand, "The Anvil knows the way."

A hand on the knob of the door, Pyrocles looks back. "He means well, the Viscount," he says. "They all do. Like you, they only want what's best. What's right, for all."

"Of course," says Luys, stood in the middle of the room.

"That may not be enough," says Bruno, behind his desk.

Pyrocles hoists the satchel up onto his shoulder, rumpling his coat. Out into the hall and down those stairs, the door at the bottom opening on a wide room crowded with the jetsam of abandoned bathrooms, bowls of old sinks stained and cracked stacked one within another along the floor, parched toilets crowded cheek by jowl, seats of them haphazardly raised or lowered. Coming up along another aisle the Harper Chillicoathe, scowling over his big yellow beard. A hitch in Pyrocles' step and the scuff of his footfall reaches Chilli, who looks up, over the toilets between them, his scowl becoming something more considered. "Hound," he says.

"Harper," says Pyrocles. Chilli's scowl redoubles, those narrowed eyes noting the satchel. "You had business with the Shrieve?"

"An I did," says Pyrocles, "it's none of yours."

Chilli looks away. Abruptly continues up the aisle, past tubs, over sinks, ducking through a low doorway, around a corner and down a couple of steps into a cramped hall, lumpily carpeted and not an angle entirely square, and Luys, who's shutting one of the many doors.

"Well," says Chilli, reaching to push open what hadn't fully closed. "He's awfully busy today."

"What?" says Luys, but Chilli's closing the door between them.

"You're early," says Bruno, still behind his desk.

"Better than late," says Chilli.

"Sometimes."

"What did the big lug want?" Chilli crosses the office, but toward the armchair, not the desk.

"The Mason?"

"There was another big lug?" Chilli plucks the stopper from the decanter, waves it under his nose. Cocks an appreciative brow. "Oh, you know Luys," Bruno's saying. "Hold on, hold tight, don't rock the boat, and soon enough her grace will set it right."

"Her grace," says Chilli, selecting a squatly heavy glass from the shelf, "seems happy enough in her tent, of late, with her boy, and his by-blow."

"You're keeping an eye on them."

"We're keeping an eye, yes, though it spreads us terrible thin. Peg Greentooth's out there now, and Gradasso next to spell her, and there's two who could be otherwise – "

"You're no longer interfering."

"No," says Chilli, pouring a slug from the decanter, "we're no more interfering."

"We can't have her riling the Marquess again."

"Relax, dear Shrieve," says Chilli, stoppering the decanter with a fillip, "neither you, nor our old dear friend Linesse, has any cause for concern. My associates and I take great, meticulous, horribly terribly *boringly* detailed pains," waving the glass, "not even to be seen, at all." He sips.

"Chilli," says Bruno, "who pissed in your whisky?"

Shoulders slumping, Chilli lowers his head. "Her majesty's bitch," he says, "has claimed her majesty's old pied-à-terre." He throws back what's left of the liquor.

"What?" says Bruno, after a moment.

"The flat," says Chilli, waving his empty glass. "Hawthorne and Twentieth, above the resale shop."

"No, I mean, you're talking about the Outlaw. Marfisa."

"Yes," says Chilli, setting the glass quite deliberately there, by the decanter.

"Chilli," says Bruno.

"She has my sword," quick and quiet and cross.

"You," says Bruno, looking away. "You lost a duel. Another. To the Outlaw."

"I didn't lose."

"She has your sword!"

"She cheated!" crossing from armchair to desk, "that woman, Shrieve, I, I found her, took her in when she wandered witless through a parking lot, she didn't have her *words,*" thump his fist on the top of the desk, "and in return she steals my coat, she decides it's *my* delivery needs hijacking, if it weren't for her, Conary would still – "

"If not for her," says Bruno, "you'd not be here, with me. We've spoken, Harper, about your propensity," he opens a drawer of his desk, "for squandering opportunity," dropping a plastic baggie swollen with gold to the desktop, "responsibility, good will," shutting the one drawer, opening another. "You really ought to look to that." Pulling out a small white note card, plucking a pen from the rack to one side of the desk. "See to it the Outlaw's removed from the premises. Do not do the deed yourself." Consulting a small black notebook, he writes out a ten-digit number. "This man," he's saying, "did scutwork for the Duke. Chad, though he's known as the xo." Pushing the card and the baggie across the desk.

Chilli takes up the baggie. "I want my sword," he says.

"There will be time and opportunity enough," says Bruno. "After."

"I want," says Chilli, but Bruno slaps the desk, "This is *not* an *exchange*, Harper," he says. "This is a thing for you to do. Make the arrangements to have your mess cleaned up. Keep me apprised of her grace's doings. We must know the angles, if we're to play them."

Now Chilli takes the card. "If I'm to make arrangements," he says, "on our behalf, perhaps some petty cash?"

Bruno takes a deep breath in through his nose, and opens a third drawer.

"Imagine, then, your majesty," says the kid behind the wheel, "the fucking look on *my* face," brown pompadour a-bob over the brass and leather goggles pushed up his forehead, "when I find out there's a whole fucking *kingdom* of Brooklyn, in the fucking Court of Apples, and *that's* the one he's fucking going on about," hurtling through an intersection, horn-blare dopplering behind, *"any*-fucking-way, *that's* the sort of shit that maybe ought to be seen to," twitch of the wheel edging left around a paused bus, back to the right before the startled windscreen of an oncoming truck, "if you'll pardon me for saying so, ma'am," eyeing the rearview mirror for a glimpse of the Queen in the backseat, bracing her jostled self as the car humps up and bouncing over a speed bump, "but *as* I was fucking saying, there's *none* of that horseshit to worry about up here! Even though North's not fifteen fucking blocks away," one hand flicking a gesture at the driver's side window as the other twists the wheel, bending them around a slow hatchback, "shit!" at the stuttering honk from an approaching van, hands leaping about, the one to twist the wheel right as the other yanks to downshift, engine whining, a slower floating rise and fall over another speed bump, and "Nothing, to worry," the Queen mutters as the engine roars.

Another intersection, squealing into a right turn. Squared buildings two and three storeys high and brightly freshly painted whip past either side, a bicycle scoots out of the way, a couple of pedestrians have second thoughts about a crosswalk. "Hang on," says the kid, flicking the wheel to the right then wrenching left, working the gearshift, engine yowling, rear end slewing all the way around in the middle of the street juddering drifting back a smidge to the side as he rights the wheel and stomps the parking brake. Sudden thunderous silence. "Here we are!" he cries. "Last free house in the Northeast Marches. Oh!" at the sound of the Queen resuming herself, squeak of naugahyde, squonk of springs, he's throwing open his door to dash around the trunk and open the passenger door smoothly, levering the front seat forward, offering his hand. "So I should announce you?" says the kid.

"This is more by way of a personal appearance," she says, her new white jeans, old boots, her long and lemon-colored cardigan. "Were it a matter for the court, perhaps, but," looking past the welter of bicycles along the sidewalk, thick hedges at the corner, to the building across the side street, two storeys of green clapboard and a neon sign unlit, Alberta Rexall Rose. "We'd be there. Not here." The house before them painted pink with mud-red trim, cramped front porch strung with tiny lights and crowded by a single enormous figure, an evidently empty suit of wicker armor topped by a great woven barrel of a helm.

"I'll just, wait in the fucking car, then," says the kid, shutting the passenger door, darting around the front of it, "just, it's as

I've said, ma'am!" Opening his door. "The fucking trains! Brooklyn Intermodal! Not the fucking Brooklyn of the Apples!"

Up the steps, onto the porch, she lifts her hand to the doorbell but thunk and clack the door creaks open, purple curtains a-sway. She spares a look for the suit of wicker armor.

Past the foot of the stairs, the hall butler hung about with all manner and type of hat, a derby and a Stetson, a floppy bonnet, a boater and a meshback cap, a dusty black stovepipe and a shako, elaborately plumed, set on the bench of it. Through the wide doorway into a dim, high-ceilinged room, drapes tight-shut and only a couple lamps lit, and seven or eight men and women, black turtlenecks and T-shirts, black tights and trousers, each of them fitted with a black beret, stood in two lines, an aisle that leads to a brownish-pink sofa, pulled away from the hearth, and two women sat upon it, leaned back against either arm, outstretched legs entwined beneath a couple of blankets and a quilt, the one her white hair bound and braided tight, the other white hair loose, undone, and both the same small crafty smile. The Queen's expression vacillates, amused, perplexed, widening in alarm as a little round man steps from his place right up before her, "Sic omnes lusere pii," he intones, savoring the orotundity, "Dionysius, et qui increpuit magno mystica verba sono." Those men and women all in black utter in a union mirthlessly polished, "Ha! Ha! Ha!" and then file past, one after another, out of the room.

"Well," says the Queen.

"It's not often we receive a head of state," says the one of them.

"Such occasions," says the other, "must be marked, with pomp and pageantry."

"You knew, that I was coming?" says the Queen.

"Oh, none of *that* was for your *majesty.*"

"Not specifically."

"It's something they've been working on."

"By way of," an airy gesture, "a statement of purpose."

"An artistic philosophy, expressed within, and by, the art."

"They did think you might appreciate it."

"They were quite," a brow, wryly lifted, "excited."

"And enthusiasm can be contagious."

"But also exhausting."

"Well. It can be exhausting."

"Will this take long, do you think?"

The Queen turns away, a shake of her head, "This was a mistake," she says.

"Is her majesty really such a coward?"

Pausing, in the middle of a step. "Do we seem afraid?"

"We seem a bit rude."

Turning back. "We'd rather not waste anyone's time," says the Queen.

"Then don't."

"Tell us why you've come."

"It must be terribly important, to have dragged you all this way."

"I," she says, "came," stepping back toward the sofa.

"*Thou* cam'st?"

"For your help," says Ysabel.

"But whatever could we *possibly* offer your majesty."

"Whose reign is one of plenitude, and peace."

Ysabel looks away, looks up, "When all," she says, "was lost," the picture molding crowded with wigstands and the heads of mannequins, each garishly painted with its clunically peculiar churlish buffoonish face.

"The owr," says one of them.

"The King," says the other.

"Our son." One hand squeezes another, there on the quilt.

"*Your* son." The hand lets go, withdraws.

"When all was lost," says Ysabel, a bit more forcefully. "They chose to stay. The hobs and clods, domestics all, some knights, and also the Starling, and Christienne, her sister, Petra and sweet Jessie, your old amanuensis, even Gloria, even," a breath, "Marfisa, my Outlaw. Though all was lost. Until Jo Gallowglas *came back.* And we did turn the owr once more. But." Looking down, to them on the sofa. "Just yesterday, Marfisa walked away from me. Again. And Gloria, Gloria's turned her back.

Jessie was here, with us, the one day, gone the next. And Jo," but here she looks away from them again.

"It sounds as if some few are left to you."

"Enough, at least, to crowd a queen-sized bed."

"This is not that," says Ysabel, quickly.

A serrated cack of a laugh. "Isn't it?"

"Of course it is," a rough-hewn chuckle.

"Do not think to mock me, Mother."

"Whyever not?"

"You openly consort with whores."

"And strumpets."

"I am the very Queen of Heaven!" cries Ysabel, flinging up her hands. "The Zenith, and the Acme! The Rose Arisen from our bitter tears! I will do, what*ever* brings me pleasure, when, and how, it please me!"

"And still, they have the gall to break your heart."

"That is *not* why I am here!" Turning, stepping away, arms folded about herself. "Gloria," she says. "We never, there was never," and then, "her entanglement with us was nothing but a cruel jape of the Mooncalfe's – yet such a lovely grace has come of it. The house, that she has made, and opened, to us all." Letting go of herself there, in the middle of the room. "We thought to create her a Chatelaine," says the Queen. "She spat on the office in our hands."

One of them says, "Then – perhaps – it's not the company you keep."

"Perhaps," says the other, "it's how you keep that company."

"Ask again, my pet."

"Be done with it."

"I can't," says Ysabel.

"You can't."

"Of course you can."

"I *can't*," says Ysabel. "I only ever asked when I knew what the answer would be. When I asked Jo Gallowglas that first time, I knew she would refuse. That's why I asked."

"Poor girl."

"Poor fool."

"She *saved* me, Mother." Stepping back toward the sofa. "She saved us all. And when, unbidden, she told me that, she loved me? A gift I never," blinking quickly, looking away. "The night that she returned? When we restored the owr? I knew, the answer. She'd told me her answer. But I was, greedy. I needed to hear it, once more. And so I asked again."

"And she refused you."

"For a second time."

Nodding, Ysabel takes a trembling breath. "And now," she says, "I don't know. Not anymore, not anyone. I didn't know what Marfisa would say, or Gloria. I look at the Starling, I look at Christienne, even sweetly stupid Melissa, I look at them and I do not know how any of them would answer. How, how is it, how can I not know? Mother, tell me, how do I do this? How, when I don't know that I'll ever know again?"

One of them says, "How, thou art."

"Why, the rule," says the other.

"Thou art regal."

"That is all."

"So it must be enough."

"Oh," says Eddie. "It's you," glowering over the taut-stretched security chain.

"Is she within," says Marfisa.

"The question you should be asking," he says, "is whether she's awake. As it turns out – "

"Eddie," a sternly quaver somewhere behind him, and he sags against the door. "Well," he says. "She wasn't."

The chain scrapes loose, the door swings wide, he steps back out of her way. A grandly overstuffed loveseat in the middle of the room, piled with pillows and a box or two and more of pads of yellow paper, leaves of them rumpled crimped and pressed by wavering wandering lines of ink that pinch and hump and curl to make the letters that make up words, words, words. Abby Tinker, bundled in a quilted housecoat, pulls herself to her feet at the one end of it, waving away whatever Marfisa isn't saying, "Don't mind me," she rasps. Eddie hustles over to offer an arm she leans on to work her bare brown feet into terrycloth slippers. "I don't sleep much, but it sure does take an awful long time to do it." Lifting an admonishing finger. "I'll be right back. No tomfoolery." Teetering only a little, she makes her way from the loveseat to the doorway in the corner there, a plank laid above it from one bookshelf to another, bowed beneath the weight of yet more books. Eddie watchfully monitors her progress until she's passed beneath, then turns balefully to Marfisa, "Why are you here."

She turns away, wild hair whitely gold, rainshell light and grey. "It does concern you both," she says, looking over the books close by, the names on the spines of them, Virginia Hamilton, Zenna Henderson, Basma Ghalayini, Eve L. Ewing, Kaiama L. Glover, Sonia Nimr, Grace Lavery, Katherine Kurtz.

"So tell me. I'll tell her when she's done. You wouldn't have to wait."

"Why are you here?" says Marfisa, looking to him then, his dwindling hair clipped close, his epauletted safari shirt the color of algæ. "You're not her son. Abby Tinker has no children."

"Oh, she's got lots of kids," he says. "I'm her mule."

"Mule?"

"I help her with the Forty-Acre Wood," he says, gesturing at the books, and then, glower resumed, "You people have *got* to keep it down, over there."

Marfisa blinks. "That's none of my concern."

"I told you, I would call the cops. Whatever it is you're up to over there, with all those people, it can't be legal. There's no way it's legal."

"Have you? Called the police?"

"They're not," he says, "exactly, rolling up. Are they."

"That's not exactly an answer," she says. A clash of contrary waters from somewhere deeper in the apartment.

"It's not your concern," says Eddie. "Why aren't you concerned."

"As I said," says Marfisa. "It concerns you both."

Eddie steps close, arms up and widening, "That's *not,*" he starts to say, but "This smells," growls Abby Tinker, there beneath the book-freighted board, *"distinctly* of balderdash."

Eddie drops his arms, hangs down his head, "I'm sorry, ma'am," he says. "She can be quite irritating."

"He told me to go," says Marfisa.

Abby Tinker shuffles across the room, back toward the loveseat. "I never," she says, "get tired, of hearing white boys call me ma'am. Bit mannered, maybe, too stiff to fold like money. But it's sweet in the ear." Gripping the overstuffed arm, lowering herself with a grimace. Peering up through her Coke-bottle lenses, looking for Marfisa. "Now," she says. "White girls? Are a whole *other* matter."

"I have found new rooms," says Marfisa. "We must determine a time when it is convenient to pack your books and things, and move them."

"You," says Eddie, "what?"

"I have found new rooms for you. In a building on Hawthorne, not far away. The views are excellent."

"You're kicking us *out?*"

"I would not kick you anywhere, Edward."

"You *gave* this place to us! You said it was ours, to keep!"

"These new rooms are also yours."

"Bullshit."

"I can take you there, and show them to you. Now, if you'd like."

"I knew better than to trust you," he says.

"What changed," croaks Abby Tinker. "What happened, that we aren't safe here anymore. Why do we all of a sudden have to leave."

"I," says Marfisa, and suddenly drops to one knee. Eddie takes a single jerk of a step closer. "I must," says Marfisa.

"Yes?" says Abby Tinker.

"I had thought," says Marfisa, "all would be well. She would be able, I had thought. She is the Queen." Shutting her bright blue eyes. "But she will fall. And you did trust me." Looking up, then, to those light-glazed lenses looking down. "You trusted me, but I did trust, I, I am." Swallowing a great breath. "I must, apologize," she says. "My lady, I am so, so very sorry."

Abby Tinker sits up in her quilted housecoat, hands in her lap, leaning over Marfisa bent before her. "Nobody's moving," she says, gently.

"I would do the moving," says Marfisa. "I would carry it all, from here, to there. You wouldn't lift a finger, nor Edward neither."

"You're gonna move all this," says Eddie.

"Domestics have packed up a house entire in one brief afternoon," says Marfisa. "This cannot but be easier."

"All my books," says Abby Tinker.

"Are there more within?" says Marfisa, looking to the doorway beneath the plank, and then, as Abby not unkindly laughs, "I will build you shelves! Shelves on every wall, in every room, and set your books upon them in whatever order you wish. And when I'm done, we'll carry you there, Edward and I, this couch a palanquin, and a wide-brimmed hat to shade your eyes from the sun."

Abby Tinker takes Marfisa's hand in her own, there on her lap. "But," she says, quiet enough the rasp is almost gone from her voice, "there wouldn't be a lawn."

"There is!" says Marfisa. "Not so large, but not so starkly new, either. And planting-boxes, for flowers, herbs, or vegetables, as you'd like. Oh, my lady, and a porch, and you might step from it direct onto the cool grass."

"It sounds lovely," says Abby Tinker. "But I'm not going anywhere."

"My lady," says Marfisa, but Abby Tinker's let go of her hand, she's sitting back, resettling the folds of her housecoat. "I'll stay right here," she says, and the rasp's returned, cheerfully rough. "Everything's fine, and it'll keep on being fine, until it's not. Same as it always was." Marfisa slumps back on her heels. "I am too comfortable," says Abby Tinker, "and too set in my ways. Which for sure means I'm too old, but there it is."

"I'll hold the rooms for you," says Marfisa, sitting up, hands on her knees. "And prepare them. This," looking up to Eddie, "I do swear. Stay here, my lady Tinker, but know that should you ever need it, you'll have another home to come to."

"That's, great," says Eddie. Abby Tinker takes off her glasses, rubs at her eyes, working her fingertips into the corners of them, pressing her thumb to a point just above the bridge of her nose, blinking sightlessly as she returns her glasses to their place. "Girl," she says, her voice gone quiet again, and gentle. "What you're trying to give me. It's, it's so much. Too much, for me to take."

"I would only ever ease your burdens, ma'am," says Marfisa, a hand on the arm of the loveseat.

"What would I ever do with so, so much," says Abby Tinker. Eddie scowls.

Fluorescents flicker above an oblong table, to starkly light the printed woodgrain peeling at the corners, the shelves stuffed with plastic tubs of abstruse gear, all tangled cords and anonymous shells and casings, black, grey, matte silver plastic, tagged with ragged strips of masking tape, O-DARK 13 and SHADOW UNITS, they say in handwritten scrawls, GIMP and FIDDLE-DEE PARTS, WTF 2ND, DO NOT TOUCH. "This is where we usually do department meetings," says an unobtrusive man, clutching a tablet computer to his chest, "if it was just one of you, we'd use Geoffrey's office, but that's even more crowded," and a distracted laugh. "Um," he says, pressed back to allow them room to pass, "I'm sorry," he says, "I don't mean to offend, or, but, you're, which, I mean who, I mean your names, I'm – "

"Stevie," says Ettie, dropping into a plastic chair at the far corner.

"Star," says the Starling, slipping into the chair beside her.

"Tina," says Chrissie, with a small smile, a little wave.

"Okay," he says, "so," tilting the tablet to glance at the screen of it, "maybe," a shrug, "name-tags? No, wait, I'm sorry, but, I mean, to keep track, maybe we, uh – "

"There's only the three of us," says the Starling. Her tight black T-shirt says Corduroy Queen.

"I think they'll figure it out," says Ettie. Hers says Suspiciously Cheap Lasers. Chrissie's says Bubbles O'Day & the Night. Their hair, the three of them, strictly yellow, rounded in blown-out bobs, their lips the same meticulous shade of dark rich red. "I, ah," he's saying, tipping the tablet away again, unfolding the case of it into an angled stand he sets at the one end of the table. "Did you know," he says, "when they first started shooting here, the, uh," the tablet falls flat. He sets it up again, muttering, "this might need to be higher," looking about. "Leverage," he says, reaching for a couple of thick black binders bursting with type-script, "used these offices," stacking them on the table, and the tablet on the binders. "The teevee show?" The tablet falls flat again.

"We don't watch a lot of television," says Chrissie.

"Well," he says, re-uprighting the tablet, "I'll just," but there are voices in the hall, "a *shit* about shit at this level," getting louder, "so get *off* my dick and go do whatever it is you *do* about it. *Jesus.*" A short and thickset man backs into the room, wide head shaved clean, turning about with a click and a switched-on smile. "Ladies!" he booms, and smack of his clapping hands. His violet wide-collared shirt undone a couple-three buttons. *"So* jazzed you could take this meeting. I was, blown away! By what I saw, a couple days ago at the street fair," offering one of those hands to Chrissie for a shake, "and I just *had,"* then the Starling, "to bring your magic," and Ettie, "to our show. Torni?" The pale and narrow man who's slipped in after nods, once. "All *right!"* Slapping both hands on the table. The unassuming man jolts. "All right." Sits himself across from the Starling, leaving Torni to squeeze between chair-back and shelves so he might work himself into a chair across from Ettie. "We're doing a couple-three things at once," the thickset man's saying, as Torni pulls out a phone to poke and scroll the screen of it. "Because, we've got the room on Tuesday?"

"That's it," says an older man, grey suit coat, trimly silver beard. "Non-negotiable."

"So plan on twelve, fifteen hours, call at six. We don't *usually* work days that long," as the older man sits with a shake of his head across from Chrissie, "but, like I say, we're really excited to bring your magic to our show," lifting his hands, he takes a breath, and "Hi!" says Ettie in the breach. "My name's Stevie, my sister there's Tina, and this is our good friend Star. Hello!"

The thickset man blinks, then laughs, slapping his hands back to the table. "We *are* going a bit fast! Okay, hi, hello, this is Aamos Torni, who's directing the episode," the narrow man nods without looking up from his phone, "directing most of them, this is our first season, and Al Smith here – "

"Call me Phonse," says the older man. "I keep the train on the tracks."

"Everybody calls him Phonse," says the thickset man. "Yes. And she'll be here in Stumptown day of, next week, but today she has to come to us from sunny LA, if Bob can ever figure out how to get the tablet to work, that'd be Terry Prudhomme, our intimacy coordinator. And I," spreading his hands, straining his violet shirt, "am Geoffrey Elliot. I am the showrunner; I run the show."

"Sorry," says Ettie, "to interrupt, again, but what is it, you said, the person who's calling in, does?"

"Intimacy," Chrissie starts to say, but Ettie holds up a hand. "It's one of the little things," says Geoffrey, "we're getting out of the way, today, just to make sure we're all on the same page. Setting boundaries. But you ladies are professionals! This won't be a thing."

"Professionals?" says Ettie. "Jeff, you saw us *sing*."

"Geoffrey," says Geoffrey. Torni pokes and scrolls. Phonse adjusts the jut of his beard. "Didn't Reg talk to you?"

"I don't know, Tina," says Ettie. "Did Reg talk to us?"

Chrissie sighs. The Starling says, "Her, ah, Ysabel. Told us."

"Ysabel's another friend of Reg's," says Ettie. "So tell us, Jeff, what – "

"Geoffrey, please."

" – what exactly *is* this magic you're hoping we – "

"Got it!" blurts the unassuming man, stepping back from the tablet, screen of it filled with a woman's lined, foreshortened face. "Geoffrey?" she's saying. "You there?"

"Bob," growls Geoffrey.

"It was," says the unassuming man, "the wifi back here is – "

"Bob," says Geoffrey, "my *suggestion* to you is to find something far away that keeps you busy long enough I can forget how very much I want to fire you right now. Capisce?"

"You let that boy alone," says the tablet. Bob, head down, slips out between a burly tattooed man and a guy in an aloha shirt, stood there in the doorway. Geoffrey turns to the tablet, smiling again, "Terry!" he booms. *"So* glad you could join us."

"Are they there?" Muffled thumps, swelling in the screen, dropping back, "Fuck's sake, Geoffrey, can you fix this thing so I can see what's going on?"

Geoffrey sits there, hands on the table, smile at half-strength. "Hello?" says Terry. "Geoffrey?" The Starling leans over to peer up at the tablet, but Ettie gently pulls her back. The guy in the aloha shirt steps into the room to adjust the tablet, peeking sidelong at the three of them, "Whoops!" says Terry. "There we go. Ladies, good morning, pleased to meet you," rustle of paper, "I'm Terry Prudhomme, intimacy coordinator for Shadow Unit, and you must be," peering down, "the Triplets."

"Triplettes," says Ettie.

"Got the new pages, Terry?" says Phonse.

"Brady's flashback?" Another shuffle of paper. "With the tulpas? I don't see Gus there. Is Gus there?"

"He's in Toronto," says Geoffrey, and then, a bit louder, "Gus is in Toronto, Terry."

"Fuck's sake! Geoffrey, we cannot *possibly* work like this."

"This is not," he says, as she's saying "over a goddamn video conference," and "this is not, you'll be," he says, and "with one participant entirely," and "day of, you'll be," and "not even present!"

"Terry!" he shouts, and restores his smile. "Day of, you'll be hands on. Choreography, rehearsal, the works. Today's just, dotting tees, crossing eyes for the streamer, the insurance, you know, the stooges in suits."

"This isn't busywork, Geoffrey. It's a process, and must be taken seriously."

"We understand, and hear, your concern," says Phonse, looking at his hands.

"We're going a bit fast, yes," says Geoffrey, "which we can, because, end of the day? We're all professionals. Ladies," turning his smile on the three of them, "what we have in mind is you'd appear in a flashback, and a coda. Agent Brady, one of our ensemble, he's played by Gus Kenworthy, you're gonna love him, he's telling Agent Lau about his first encounter with the anomaly, which is the Big Bad of our show. It's a one-night stand, with a woman who, played by you, one of you, is anomalous. Her desire generates tulpas. Thoughtforms. Physical manifestations of her mental state. So, we'd have our paramour," both hands presented toward the Starling, and then the one hand toward Chrissie, "her desire," and the other toward Ettie, "and her guilt, or reticence, or whatever. Shoulder-angel, shoulder-devil. Like that."

"But sexy," says Ettie.

"Think premium cable," says Phonse. "Hard R. But tasteful."

"Tastefully intimate."

"Ettie," says Chrissie.

"Stevie," says Ettie with a warning lilt.

"*Stef,*" says Chrissie, flinching at the look Ettie turns on her, but "This," she says, "it's no different, than any other scene or bit or shoot we've ever done."

"It isn't?" says Ettie extravagantly. "Well, all right! Let's set those boundaries. So, nudity: frontal, backal, or dorsal or pectoral or whatever, we're good with that, obviously. It's what we're here for. Contact? Well, anything with, whatsisname, Gus, would have to be either me or Star. Not Tina. That's a bright line. And as for anything between us?" Looking, then, to the Starling, and Chrissie. "Breast-play, sure. Anything genital, oral or digital, that'll be simulated, but we'll happily simulate ass or pussy, so you're good there. Dildos, strap-ons, any kind of toy, that's also simulated, there's to be no penetration on the day of, Jeff, there's another bright line, and if these tulpas get themselves into some kind of bondage scenario – tasteful, of course – there's some fuzz we'll need to work out, but we'll have plenty of time what with all the rehearsal and the choreography, right? But!" Leaning over to address the small crowd in the doorway, "Anybody in the audience, there's absolutely *no* touching the girls." Turning back to Geoffrey. "And if you're gonna sit in the front row, you're gonna tip. That's just common courtesy. Sound about right, sis?"

"Don't be a bitch, Stephanie," says Chrissie. Ettie closes up her eyes. The Starling, very still between them.

"Fuck's sake," says Terry.

"Well!" says Geoffrey, but Ettie's chair scrapes back, "oh, now, hold on," he says, as she gets to her feet, "let's not do anything rash in the heat of the moment," but Ettie's raising her voice over his, "Sorry, Ms. Prudhomme, Phonse," a brittle little laugh, "Mr. Torni, thanks, Jeff, but no thanks. We're just not feeling it," hand on the back of the Starling's chair, squeezing behind it, "come on."

"Don't say no in the room," says Geoffrey. "Take it home with you. Sleep on it."

"Come on," says Ettie, with a quick shove for Chrissie's chair.

"Geoffrey," says Terry, "what am I always telling you." Torni's tucking his phone away. Phonse has folded his arms. "It may seem chaotic today," Geoffrey's saying, and then Chrissie with a jerk seizes Ettie's hand, "but I assure you," says Geoffrey, trailing away.

"You want this," says Ettie, quietly. "This, is what you want."

Chrissie looks up. The Starling's hand on Chrissie's other arm.

Ettie yanks herself free. "Well, Jeff," she says, "I guess you get to see how much magic you get out of two Triplettes." Squeezing toward the crowded doorway, she mutters, "Jesus, can't a girl even leave in a huff anymore?"

"Everybody out!" roars Geoffrey, but she's shoving her way through them all before anyone can react.

THE SHOE IN HER HAND – KAFFEEKLATSCH
FAR BE IT – DELICATE MATTERS

THE SHOE IN HER HAND a soft-cuffed slip-on printed with checks of white and primary colors. Gordon nods. A piano boogies softly to itself somewhere under a chugging bass. She watches him looking over the cubbies, drumming her fingertips on the countertop in time. A dented cash register hulks at one end, a label freshly pasted at an angle to the back of it, The Order of American Mechanicals United, it says, Local 235. Gordon sets a pair before her, one a double-buckled pump in scuffed blue pseudo-alligator, the other a checkerboarded slip-on. "So," she says. "These are mine?"

"Welcome to Portland," says Gordon.

"They won't fit," she says.

"You'll figure it out." He sets the pump atop the mound of mismatched shoes on the worktable. The bell jingles as she leaves.

Through the pattering beaded curtain, into a cramped kitchen all scarred linoleum and darkly looming cabinets. Filling a kettle at the red tub of a sink, he sets it on a burner, cranks the knob to high, absently scratching the back of his head, where white curls ring his dark bald pate. "Too blasted many," he mutters. Opening a cabinet, he rummages for a thick-walled mug, a red plastic jar that says Folgers ½ Caff. The bell jingles, out in the shop.

He shuts the drawer he's opened, sets a spoon by the mug, "Better not," he mutters, pushing out through the beaded curtain, "if that's you, boy – "

It's the Marquess of Northeast, the Helm Linesse, stood in the middle of the shop, gunmetal hair cropped close, her two arms pale and bare the length of them. "Porter," she says.

"If it's titles and affairs of state you're after," he growls.

"It's clarity I'd have," she says, looking past him to the cash register. "Do we speak now Northeast to North?"

Following her gaze, his scowl curdles. "Rabbits always about, yipping and flexing, that's all it is."

"You haven't taken it down."

"They'd only put up another. And this is, after all, a free house." The hissing of that unseen kettle climbs enough to be heard over the softly music. "Could make two cups," says Gordon.

"You were worried, before," says Linesse, sitting at the small kitchen table.

"I never worry," he says, and dollops steaming water into mugs. "No future in it."

"You came to me, concerned," she says. "That their yipping in your shop might discourage your domestic kaffeeklatsch."

"We never klatsched," he says, dumping spoonfuls of grounds. Chiming as he stirs. "But I did come to you."

"You're no more concerned?"

He sets a mug before her. "Nobody here to discourage, anymore." Sitting himself across from her. "All of them what's loosed and fancy-free are down Southeast, taking their due direct from her majesty's own hand."

"You're alone?"

"Boy's about, time to time." Gordon sips his coffee. "He'd like a fight, but not with bravos. He's got beef with the mortal hounds, up St. Johns."

Linesse smiles at her mug. "There's a grocery on the line, at Fremont. The Mooncalfe duels there in the parking lot, most nights. Boasts she's yet to lose a bout." Lifts it, breathing in. "And you still take the shoes," she says.

"No one else to do it." Another sip. "Although," he says. "Last week, a man in a suit and tie, but dirty, frayed, shoulder sprung, accustomed to good barbering, but hadn't shaved in days. Had a saddle Oxford, grey suede gone brown, cream of it grey, and I didn't, Linesse, I didn't know it. Spent an hour or more, tossing shoes about. Nothing."

"The match hadn't come?"

"For all I know," says Gordon, "it never was."

"Come back with me," says Linesse. He lifts up his head, on the verge of a frown. "Come back with me," she says, again. "They don't come here for this, this building. Those shelves. They come to where the Porter is. Come back with me."

"I give no drop," he says. "I take no pinch."

"It would be as free a house as this," she says. "More. Never another morning coffee spoiled by preening hares." His shoulders lift with a grumbled snort. "I know a dozen storefronts that would do, on Going, Albina, Killingsworth. Come back with me, to see."

"A dozen," he says, sitting back. "This offer's not a whim. You came here to make it."

Those pale shoulders shrug. "There's no more bond between us, Gordon. Our eyes are clear on that. Unstiff your neck. Come back with me. Do your work in peace."

"To go, from Hare, to Helm," he says. "Your eyes may be clear, Linesse, and mine, but they're no more the only eyes in the world."

She's the first to look away, to the mug she lifts for one quick sip. "Blast and rot your pride, old fool," she says, and scrapes back from the table.

"Soon enough," he says. "And grace and beauty dog your steps, woman."

She's pushing through the beaded curtain, but the bell's already jingling, out there in the store. Tipping back his head, he says, "Again?"

But it's Christian, stood in the middle of the shop, Linesse off to one side. "Boy," growls Gordon, heading for the counter.

"George Honeycutt," says Christian, and Gordon freezes. Linesse lifts the back of her hand to her mouth. "That's your name, isn't it," says Christian. "That's why it says George's on the window."

"That ain't why," says Gordon, but Christian says, "It was the kids started calling you Gordon," says Christian. "At those free breakfasts you were running. Because you looked like the guy on Sesame Street."

"Who have you been talking to," says Gordon.

"People," says Christian. "Around. About. You're a goddamn hypocrite."

"Boy!" snaps Gordon, but Christian plows on, "Don't go home, you're telling me, you can't go home, your mother will never know you again, *boy,* don't even try, and here *you* are, playing poker every other goddamn night with your buddies from back in the day!"

"Stop this!" cries Linesse.

"You don't know what you're messing with," says Gordon.

"You're right," says Christian. "One thing I can't figure, it was, forty? Fifty years ago, when George Honeycutt up and vanished. You couldn't've been more than, what, twenty-five? So why the hell you look like that?"

"Boy!" roars Gordon, pounding the countertop.

"No," says Christian. "Damn your boy, and you," turning, heading for the door, "and all this goddamn bullshit." The bell, frantic at the force with which the door's yanked open, slammed shut.

"Blasted Duckie," mutters Gordon, "filling his blasted head with nonsense. What." Stepping back from the counter. Linesse staring wordless at him. "What is it, woman? What?" His one hand, both of them coming up to his forehead, the top of his head, and the look on his face when his fingers find there not a balding pate, but a mighty round of tight black curls.

The sidewalk whiles away through greenly thick top-heavy trees, a line of concrete shirred with drying mud. The Harper Chillicoathe picks his way along it toward a flatly sheen of water glimpsed through trunks. A sudden awkward decline ends the walk in a clean-scraped roundel, a railing jerry-rigged from old pipes at the very edge of the riverbank. A rope-lined tar-papered gangway angles over the water to a short but crowded wharf, a couple cabin cruisers and a smattering of motorboats, a line of sailboats nestled close, empty masts a white-branched thicket against more grey-green trees across the river, and a cul de sac of floating homes and houseboats. It's all astonishingly quiet against the distant endless thrum of freeway traffic. Chilli looks up to the closely ceiled wet-cotton grey of the sky, scratching his chin beneath his yellow beard. Sleeves of his bulky oaten sweater pushed past his elbows. The windows of the one house there scummed over all with dust. A deck beneath, boards greyly desiccated, long since out of true, the hot tub in the center of it filthily dry.

He sets off down the gangway, aluminum ringing under his boots, but halfway along he stops, looks back. A little man's stood at the top of the ramp, gazing down at Chilli with a blandly lack. Chilli shakes his head, turns with a sigh to go on, but the little man's on the ramp before him, much too close, and smiling about too many teeth.

"Cearb," says Chilli.

That smile somehow grows wider.

"You serve herself," says Chilli.

"So much depends upon a word," the little man says, conversationally enough.

"The loathly lady," says Chilli. "I'd ask of her a boon."

"And yet, you're here," says the little man.

"A by-blow," Chilli's saying, "just one, of which she still has dozens, I don't doubt. I had one, once, myself. A lovely creature. Not much I wouldn't do, to have her like again."

"And yet," the little man says, "you're here."

"I've business with these mortal hounds," says Chilli.

"Far be it from me to get in your way." The little man opens his mouth and those teeth, those teeth do part as he lunges for Chilli toppling backwards clang his one hand flung wide curling a fist to grip about nothing, nothing at all.

Slumped beneath the little man, the bouncing gangway slowing, gentling, Chilli winces at the polyp of slabber that dribbles to hiss close by his beard. Lips purse over those teeth, shutting them away. "Far be it from you," says the little man, "to draw a blade on me."

"I'm yet a knight," spits Chilli.

The little man shifts his weight, pushes up and back, "You'd threaten me with spurs?"

"I've more than spurs," growls Chilli, kicking shoving to roll himself over and out from under as the little man laughs, "Good!" the cry, somehow at once quite loud, yet far away. "You'll need it!"

Chilli gets to his feet on the jouncing gangway. There's no one else there with him.

A step forward, another, as the gangway settles again. He looks back over his shoulder to see the little man returned to the top of the ramp, smiling down with teeth too bright for such a cloudy day. "Eleleu!" he crows. "Eleleu!"

Chilli heads on down the gangway to the rough grey boards of the wharf, the small white cabin at the corner. Hayden View Moorage, says the sign over the door of it. Beyond, façades of floating homes and bows of boats crowd close to either side, the wharf a shadowed alley between, clink of sailboat fittings nudged by a fainting breeze, and the lap and sluff of water drowns the distant traffic's thrum. Boots loud on the boards he counts off moorings to his left, stopping at the fifth, a crooked gangplank propped between wharf and yellowing deck, the blocky snout of a houseboat snugged between a cabin cruiser draped with blue tarpaulins and an attempt at a miniature Queen Anne, the siding and spindlework a folly of lavender and teal. Chilli casts about, looking over the cleat wound about with thick grey line, the railing about the porched-over bow, the screen door blank against shadows within. "Hello?" he calls.

"The request," a voice lazily loud from within, "is for permission to come aboard."

"I was told to meet the xo here."

"You have but to ask," with a sing-song lilt. Chilli sighs. "Do I have it?"

"What's that."

"Permission," says Chilli.

"To?"

Looking about, arms akimbo, shaking his big yellow head. "Permission to come aboard," he says.

Thump, the screen door's kicked open. "There," that voice within. "Was that so hard?"

The cabin's dim, brief curtains drawn, a table to one side and a figure slumped over it, wrapped in a thickly bulk. A flag pinned to the back wall, red of it bright even here, criss-crossed with spangled bars of midnight blue. A sharply narrow man leans out to pull the screen door shut with a click. "So," says Chilli. "You're Chad."

"Chad's dad," says the man, dropping onto the table's other bench.

"You're Chad's, father?"

A laugh. "Nah, man, Chad *is* dad."

"I was told he was the xo."

"Meet Danny Moody," hand pressed to the lapel of his army-surplus jacket, "the new Executive Officer of this outfit." Chilli's eyeing the other figure, still unmoving, the swaddling an unzipped nylon sleeping bag. "Don't mind Jasper," says Moody. "He's a rusty old weathervane. Takes a hell of a gust to shift him, but he always ends up pointed the right way. So!" A clap too loud for that close space. "*I* was told you want somebody out of somewhere."

"Something like that."

"So we're in the neighborhood."

"It's a delicate matter."

"That you want smashed in a million pieces," says Moody. "Hey." He shrugs. "We're honest about what it is we do."

"What we want," Chilli takes a breath, "what I *need,*" tipping back his head, sighs. "Take your time," says Moody. Chilli shoots him a look. "I've changed my mind," he says.

"You *don't* want somebody gone," says Moody.

"I'll do it myself," says Chilli.

"You'll do it yourself. Okay." Pushing back the cuff of his jacket to check the golden watch about his wrist. "That it? Because, if so, ipso, you wasted my time, you wasted yours, you're wasting Jasper's, which, frankly, takes effort – "

"There's something else you can do for me."

"Which," says Moody, "would," leaning forward, sharp elbows on the table, "be, what?"

Chilli's hands in his pockets, looking down, yellow beard spread over his chest. "Watch someone for me. No smashing. No interfering, no contact at all. Is that something I can hire your hounds to do?"

"My men," says Moody, pointedly, and then a shrug. "What do you think, Jasper?" The slumped figure doesn't budge. "We can evolve, no question, but should we? Ought we?" Peering up at Chilli. "Ah, what the hell, buddy. We'll do it. Who and what and where and when?"

"A camp," says Chilli. "East of the airport, hard by the slough. You'll find her there," looking away, the flag on the back wall. "Among a dozen others or so. But," he takes a step toward the windows across the cabin, elaborate gingerbreading visible through the gap in the curtains.

"Let me guess," says Moody. "It's another delicate matter."

"This can't come back to me. To us. You can't be seen, and if you are, no one can know who asked it of you."

"It's a homeless camp," says Moody. "Right? Who's gonna ask?" Leaned away from the table, a hand on his knee. "Look, buddy, discretion's a watchword, but we need to know at a minimum who it is we're keeping an eye on, here."

"Someone," says Chilli, "who once was, highly placed."

A chime sounds. Chilli turns back. Moody's grin's quite sharp, and there's the flash of gold about his wrist. "Oh," he almost croons, and, relishing each word, "could this *possibly* be, the dear, departed, Bambi Jo Maguire?"

"You know her," says Chilli, each word distinct, deflated.

"Aw, man, me and her, we go *way* back!" says Moody. "She was the best man at my *wedding!* Aw, hell, buddy, I'd do this one for *free!*"

Slither and squeak, Jasper sits up, sleeping bag falling away from tangled matted hair and glaring eyes. "But the men, you know," says Moody, holding out a hand. "They won't."

Chilli pulls out a thick roll of bills wrapped about with a rubber band. Sets it, upright, on Moody's palm.

"Force and Victory!" someone calls, and Christian starts awake. "End of the line, y'all," whoever it is, the driver, at the front of the bus. "Ollie ollie oxen free!"

He's on a bus. Sat on a slatted wooden bench toward the front of it, passengers filing past and off, ducking their way out the front door, men and here and there an occasional woman in coveralls, lunch pails in hand, jackets slung from shoulders, hard hats still on a couple of heads, a man in a brown suit and a bow tie, shifting from one foot to another as he waits for the press to pass, a gaggle of kids in dungarees and sneakers, swaying poodle skirts, subdued perhaps the lot of them but clearly amused by some entirely private joke. Christian, smiling, frowning, shifts on the bench to look out the sunstruck window spotted with old rain. "Puertas a mi izquierda," he mutters, watching them make their way along the sidewalk, waving, laughing, calling out, trudging stoop-shouldered away, tipping back a head to smile at the still-high sun so bright, and in her arms a broad round footed platter, a cakestand, all of milky green glass.

Christian leaps to his feet almost to collide with an older woman veiled in black and hatted, clutching the arm of an even older man, his loosely double-breasted suit and tie of black, "Sorry," says Christian, hung back with a grimace, following after as they shuffle together to the front of the bus. Nodding to the driver as the couple works their way down the steps, the driver's uniform and cap of navy stripes on periwinkle, and the badge at his breast says Portland Traction Co. His dark-jowled face unaccountably amused. "Interesting sweater you got there," he says.

"What?" says Christian, and then, "It's a hoodie."

"Hoodie. Sounds like hoodlum, but I bet that's why you kids like it." The doorway cleared, Christian leaps down the steps, "Get on home!" the driver calls. Levers the doors shut. The sigh of releasing brakes, snort of the engine, the drably olive bus pulls away. Slipped through the milling crowd he turns about, a big band's strutting somewhere, led by a scratchy chorus of horns from the big wooden speaker mounted on a corner of a couple of rambling storeys, Vanport City Shopping Center, chrome letters in a cursive sleekishly austere. Across the way a flat-roofed building, United States Post Office, the sternly sans-serif letters across the front, Vanport, Ore. A flagpole high before it, and canted on the grassy curb a small round sign, Jay-Walking is a Grave Mistake. Another flagpole there before another ramble of a building, Administration, say the sternly letters by the glass front doors, and a slip of red's been pasted to the one of them. The only cars are parked, extravagantly streamlined, small windows, narrow wheels. The crowd from the bus almost entirely dispersed among side streets, footpaths, an aproned woman, box on her hip, left chatting with a suited woman in a skirt, a few of those kids share a furtive cigarette, that song still chugs from the speaker, you'd turn your back on a star, your heart is fixed, and you're against, the state of things as they are. No one to be seen that carries a cakestand.

"Okay," mutters Christian. "Now what."

Past the city offices the street curves along a slender stretch of water neatly edged by trim low trees and shrubbery to the right, and two-storey houses lining the left, each of a length, each with three wrought-iron porticos spaced along the front to shelter two front doors set side by side, and clusters of windows above and around, and each with the same low-hipped roofs, and the siding and the trim of each the same warm yellowing browns and creams. Curtains here and there, lace-trimmed, tied back, or roman shades, venetian blinds, or stark bare light-struck glass are all that might differentiate this apartment from that, or the blue tin wagon left by the one front step there, a nosegay wound among wrought-iron curls, but each and every one of those front doors has something red, a sheet of paper, pinned to it, or beside it, hung limply in the still and quiet air.

A distant peal of laughter, someone far-off calling. The street about him empty. No one to be seen, moving through a door-way, past a window. No cars at all, no busses, trucks. The slender water glassily flat.

Off the dusty street, over the grassy curb, a foot on the step lifting up to the narrow portico. Red paper flyers, pasted to the sidelight of the one door, pinned to the lower panel of the other, simply printed in big block letters:

REMEMBER

DIKES ARE SAFE AT PRESENT

YOU WILL BE WARNED IF NECESSARY

YOU WILL HAVE TIME TO LEAVE

DON'T GET EXCITED

The paper flutters. Christian steps back and back again, out into the street. The air's changing, rising to a sound, the rush and wash of tossing leaves, though the greenery about's unruffled, becoming as it does a rumble. Around the curve of the street here comes a pickup truck all bulbous fenders and slanted, bifurcated windscreen, the wood-paneled rear of it slewing about so slowly toward him as it rides a bubbling slurry of Christian's running, running, "Jesus!" gasping as his foot hits water, a puddle spread before him rising a-tremble with the swelling sound, waves skirl and spilling slosh before him ankle-deep, now stumbling shins arms wide his pell-mell slowed to frantic, kicking strides, the water climbing legs now sucking at his knees as there that pickup backward floats on by, fenders swallowed in froth. The first time he falls he manages to work his drenched way back to his feet. The next swell topples him, and when his head finds air his feet churn groundlessly beneath him. An enormous groan off that way, a mighty crack, "Oh, God!" arms flapping uselessly about, pop of glass a screaming wrench a splintering fusillade of snaps, "Oh, shit," water spinning him along, tossed and turned about to just catch sight of the first of those houses, curtains trailed in humped and bubbling rolls of white-grey water sloshing over sills of ground-floor windows, blundering through doorways beneath those porticos slowly turning, the whole long face of it swinging away from him, a building entire, shoved from its footing, stately to float away. And there, another, and another, jagged spars and broken wood at the corners shocking bright against staid colors of trim and siding, and there's one foundered broadside on the spindly legs of a water tower too frail, it seems, to bear up under the brunt and yet, and yet

Christian's hand finds a branch, seizing, pulling, both hands braced against the rush of water choking on the filthy spume his leg now crooked about an unseen trunk, breathing when he can as he holds, he holds, until sometime later he doesn't have to hold on quite so tightly, until some time again his sodden clothing no more floats but drags at him plastered against him shivering, relaxing, half-falling from his perch to find the muddy ground not even a foot below. All about the gentle patter of dripping trees, the particular crackle and lick of water as it seeps into the earth.

An old road paved some time ago, trees grown up where none had been, and not a splinter or shard, not a crumble of brick or rusted curl of iron, no pickup truck, no water tower somehow lofted high. A slender stretch of water glimpsed through the trees, mikily brown, and there on the raggedly overgrown bank of it, he blinks, one last lone bit of flotsam, tipped heavily back against the mud a statue of stone, perhaps, or molded concrete, an eagle's head much too large for an eagle, blank-eyed, starkly beaked, the rounded shoulders of its folded mighty wings.

Squelching he heads down the road toward the bend, blocked by a stretch of cyclone fence. A sign's hung high, Heron Lakes Golf Course, it says, and an arrow points right, North Gate Entrance. Beyond, hillocks and hummocks cloaked in shaved green grass roll away with politely shaded copses. Christian dripping wipes wet mud from his forehead, plap, fingers curled through the links of the fence. Faint laughter, thirty-three, can you believe it? Two men in brightly shirts, lemon yellow, salmon-belly orange, crest a not too-distant ridge, chatting companionably until one of them stoops to press a tee into serenely evened grass, and carefully sets a small white ball atop it.

But Reuel remembered the loathsome desert that stood in grim determination guarding the entrance to this paradise against all intrusion, and with an American's practical common sense, bewailed this waste of material.

—*Pauline Hopkins*

NO. 38

" – Ekumen ain't everything – "

THE TOILET – νεῶν κατάλογος – MIREPOIX – GIRLS RULE
A CHEAP PLANK, IN A VARIETY OF STYLES – THE FATE OF CAMELLIAS
MERCY, MY LORD – "SOMEBODY'S COMING" – FIXING HIS TIE
THE SOURCES OF WATER – "WELCOME!" – THE GLEAMING POIGNARD
EVERY TIME – INDIGO, FUCHSIA, APRICOT – THE SLOGAN
A LONESOME BANJO – NO, SHE DIDN'T – PINKISH-ORANGE LIGHT
MR. LOUDERMILK

THE TOILET in the light of morning sparkles, peach enamel, polished chrome, half-filled with water clear as crystal. Leaned over it Becker shirtless one hand braced on porcelain tile, sweatpants sagged below his buttocks and his other hand, his arm works quickly, with a rhythm, breath gone ragged rough but quiet, quiet, held, expression gripped with effort, a swallow interrupted.

The first jet splots the rim, the underside of the upraised seat. The second's less of a jet than an ooze that heavily falls to mar the water, a whitely oily bolus that unskeins itself apart, a creamy cloud thinning to watery milk, and Becker shivers. Sighs as he catches sight of his sticky fingers. Tears away a couple of squares of toilet paper to fold and wipe. Eyes the splotch left slickly glistening on the toilet rim as he drops the wadded paper in the bowl. Flushes. Lowers the seat, the lid, to hide it away.

Dressed now, grey trousers, blue-striped shirt, hastening down the stairs into the parlor, shoes in one hand, leatherette portfolio in the other. A messenger bag slumped on the floor there, and with a green-socked foot he toes open the flap of it to tuck the portfolio within. "Hail, the conquering hero!" calls someone from the dining room beyond, Jimmy, baggily soft pants in a zig-zagged profusion of bricky, earthen reds and oranges and yellows, his sideless T-shirt printed with a smiling cartoon, a monocled

179

brown face under a limp-brimmed yellow hat, a signature that says Panama Jack.

"That's what you're wearing," says Becker, slipping on his shoes, hoisting one onto the overwhelmed sofa to tie it.

"You know," says Jimmy, "it's a pleasure? To see your grasp of the obvious remains as firm as ever." Stepping into the parlor, dubiously eyeing the pile of coats, the crumpled cardboard box of books that Becker's trying not to dislodge. "You really think Oz wants you stepping on the cushions?"

"You told *me* to wear a tie," says Becker, setting both feet on the floor, tobacco wingtips, cracked but shining.

"I did," says Jimmy. "You have a job interview, and ties are appropriate for interviews. I, on the other hand, already *have* gainful employment, and this?" a gesture, for his own ensemble, "is appropriate for attending a riverfront carnival, which we shall do together, upon the conclusion of today's job of work."

Becker stoops, buckle-jangle as he scoops up the messenger bag. "You really think I'm gonna get it."

"Arnie," says Jimmy, brushing off Becker's shoulders. "They hired *me*, didn't they?"

Last of the water crashing about her feet, she leans a moment against the stained shower wrap, one hand on the knob, dripping head hung low until a growling ratcheting cough drives her up to hawk and spit at the drain.

Sunlight slices through an otherwise unlit office to brightly strike abandoned cubicle walls, slash shadows across empty aisles. At the one end, glass doors look out on a dusty lobby, and one of the cubicle walls has been wrestled into the stark hot light, meanly nubbled panel of it knocked out, and damp dark clothing draped over the top rail to dry, black jeans, a T-shirt, briefs and a limp grey bralette, a pair of once-white socks. Jo sits tailor-fashion on the carpet before it, back to the sun, hair still wetly dark despite the light, mud-colored eyes hooded in shadow. Laid before her a black glass phone, screen cracked, and a limp black leather sheath under a long lean knife, hilt wrapped in dark wire, blade of it tapered to an ineluctable point, but streaked and blotted with darkening orange. A stained bit of cloth wadded in the one hand on her knee. She lifts her other arm to sniff the black-haired pit of it. Tips back her head. Gets to her feet, snags the damp briefs from the rail to yank them on.

Quickly across a small and empty parking lot toward the overgrown verge, through high stiff grass, dark clothing mostly dry, small grey T-shirt plastered to her, it says something like Bicholim Conflict Diamonds in cracked and fading letters. Hair dried a stiffly indifferent brown. Jo crouches in the scrub and waits, as whipping past the road ahead, from left to right cars trucks and vans until a pause, a gap, she darts across the pavement to the narrow median, clutching the slender trunk of one of the shortly neat young trees planted there at regular intervals, watching, waiting for another gap in the traffic that roars by now right to left.

Crossing a wide field under a cloud-scraped sky, she's headed for the caravanserai in the far corner, the tilted sedan, the hatchback, the trailer rocked back on its wheels, all paying court among the tents and mounds of junk to the motorcoach stranded before the far line of trees, wheels tangled in scrub, sheet pinned to the side of it, a sign, The Last of the International Harvesters, letters greenly sprayed. Someone's calling, "Chit-chit!" a dumpy woman, shaking an enormous tub of kibble in both her hands, "chit-chit!" Her sweatshirt says The Thing, What Is It? in letters red and green across the front. Heavy black spectacles seal her eyes away. She sets the tub in the rutted dirt track as Jo approaches, and turns for one of the lawn chairs there before the motorcoach, as rustlings thread the grass all about, junk rattles and clinks, a draped tarp lofts, and cats, a dozen or more, streaming leaping mewling flowing yowling spitting gyring about as she sets the lawn chair by the tub, marmalade and mackerel, lilac and chocolate, spotted, ticked, tuxedo and torbie, cinnamon, silver, and scrabbling over the roof of the motorcoach an extravagantly filthy cream, one eye screwed-up and lost in a flat-nosed face. The dumpy woman sits herself, un-locks the lid of the tub, and reaches for a makeshift scoop, a milk jug with the bottom of it hacked away. Scatters kibble to the ground, over the roil of fur at her feet.

"Jellyroll," says Jo, pointing. "Handsome Boy. Whitman, Elimiel?" Squatting at the edge of the frenzy. "Elimiel. Jetson, Sir Snugalot. Tony P and Tony Q."

"Other way round," says the dumpy woman, "chit-chit!" scattering another scoopful.

"Tony Q," says Jo, revising her point. "Tony P. Hot Soup. Moonsault, Heisenberg, but I don't see Springbok?"

"She's around. Chit-chit!"

"That's Suplex, and there's the Majestic Mister Freel, right? And Archibald, and Inquiline, Ersatz, and this," as that filthy white cat ripples up to her, butting her knee, "is Malocchio, the Great and Terrible."

"Chit-chit!" The dumpy woman tosses one more scoopful, currents shifting among the cats to follow its pattering fall, and drops the scoop in the tub, starts locking its lid back down. Kibble-crunch and crack, an outraged hiss or two, a scuffle there, "So," says Jo, "ah, May? You maybe have something that's good for cleaning knives?"

"What do you have to clean off a knife?" says the dumpy woman, her eyes unreadable behind lightlessly opaque lenses.

"Rust," says Jo. "I think."

"Well, rust. You just need some vinegar. Let it soak a bit, then rub it down. It'll come right off."

"Vinegar."

"Might have some, under the sink." A calico leaps into May's lap, turns about once and leaps off again as she lift her hand. Almost immediately a blue tabby leaps up to luxuriate in her stroke. "Help me get this inside," she says, nudging the tub of kibble as Jo gets to her feet. "We'll see what we can find."

MIREPOIX – GIRLS RULE
A CHEAP PLANK, IN A VARIETY OF STYLES
THE FATE OF CAMELLIAS – MERCY, MY LORD

ONION, CARROTS, CELERY, the quickly even whicking of the knife reducing each to the same small regular dice swept neatly into segregated piles, white, orange, green. The onions tipped into the smaller pot on the camp stove, crackle and pop in the hot oil coating the bottom, stir and sizzle. A single bubble breaks from the richly surface of the stew that brims the larger pot beside. "An but Lily," says the old man, closely watching them at work, and none of the rest that mill about the warehouse floor, or the art-filled stalls. "Herself most powerful sad." A bucket hat rumpled in his hands. "Missin your ways about'n house. The marvelous scent a yon pottage." His eyes close beatifically. The Buggane with a shrug stirs softening onions. Powys dices the last of the celery.

"Lea this place," says the old man. "Come home wi me." Goggie, scattering a pinch of salt over the onions, timidly shakes her head. "Can't," says Powys, wiping down his knife.

"Can't?" says the old man, with a flash of heat. "Yer nawt suchen fool, a course ye'n."

"Can't," says Powys, eyeing the onions. "I never served your house."

That hat's dashed to the floor, "Nen matter!" the old man snaps, and then, relenting almost immediately, "Y'ars mended be done. Broths a simmer. Herself missen'em so, an all." He makes no move to retrieve his hat. "Ye'n your portion, ever an always. Bonds'n bond."

"We have our portion." Powys lays a hand on Goggie's, Goggie who's trembling, eyes fixed on that hat. "The Queen herself has seen to that."

"As unnatural! All yon standen about. An work needs done!"

"True, m'lord," says Powys. The Buggane spills carrots into the pot with the onions, stirring, stirring. Goggie leaps to stoop for the hat, darts behind the old man to set it on his seething head, smooth the rumpled brim, "Thar," he says, "good girl. We's go."

Goggie quickly shakes her downturned head.

"Ranh!" The old man shoves the smaller pot to topple off the camp stove spilling clatter and yellow, white and orange, oily splat at the Buggane's shaggy feet. "Enow! Herself's awaiten! Is't a-comin home, and back wi'me, anow!" Seizing Goggie by an arm she tries to yank away with a shriek. Powys turns away. The Buggane drops the spoon. "Hey!" says someone, someone else.

Scrape and clank she steps from the crowd that's gathered about, black motorcycle jacket over a flowery sundress, planting a scabbard the dull iron chape of it ringing on concrete, wood frame rising to a polished throat cuffed with felted wool, the mighty quillions of the greatsword within high and and wide enough she folds her elbows crooked to lean her weight on them. "We got a problem?" says the Huntsman, Melissa.

"Nar, ne problem," mutters the old man, letting go of Goggie. "Y'en move along."

"And who the hell are you, telling me to move along?"

"Gwenders are the Addition, miss," he says, touching the brim of his hat.

"And what, Gwenders, is the not-problem that made this awful mess?" A gesture, for the carrots and onions spilled to the floor. The old man turns away with a dismissive wave. "That's right," says Melissa. "Move the fuck along."

She hefts the scabbard up against her shoulder and, unsteady with the weight of it, makes her way on up the aisle, busy stalls to either side and a confusion of conversations, two and not three, herself with the veil in her, plum's a best for sweet smoke and, totaled indeed, it fell true! it fell true! and somebody somewhere is taking another run at a jig on a tin whistle. Up ahead, the wooden tub out in the middle of it all shines softly golden in the daylight, and someone slips up for a pinch, smiling as they do, and behind and above it all the upraised stage, empty but for the greenly nubbled couch, unlit.

An eruption of shrieks and screams and whooping peals of laughter, there under the overhead door, Gloria Monday in the midst of an overlapping swarm of engulfing hugs from a swirl of girls in summery togs, pogoing in their excitement, "Oh my God!" she's crying, as they break apart enough to turn about, "Oh my God!" Seizing the shoulder of one of them, tall and blond in a T-shirt that says Catholic School, Girls Rule, St. Mary's Academy, she bellows, "Where's your hall pass, young lady?" and the laughter climbs wildly higher. "You should be in your third period class!"

"Well, you should be in senior year!" shouts a girl in a magenta hijab.

"Basutāsōdo!" shouts a girl in overall shorts, pointing to Melissa there at the edge of them all, both hands clamped about the wooden frame of the scabbard leaned back against her shoulder.

"Big damn sword," says the girl in the hijab, as if explaining something, and "Is this one of your cosplayers?" says the girl in the T-shirt.

"She's the Huntsman," says Gloria, with a wicked grin, and Melissa glares. "But what's going on?" says Gloria, turning away, "What is this? Why'd you guys come here?"

"Why are we here?" says the girl in the hijab, as if offended by the very question.

"It's the last Thursday in May!" says a girl in white boots and expertly shredded jeans.

"CityFair, bitches!" shouts the girl in the T-shirt.

May's primly crouched over low stacks of magazines, head and shoulders swallowed by the lower cabinets of that terribly compact kitchenette, rooting around. Jo's stood in some of the only cleared space available in the motorcoach, a marginal meander from the bed in its nook in the back past the booth here, across from the kitchenette, up to the front seats there, windshield curtained with plain dark burlap. "You must have," she says, "just about every single one of these by now, huh." Every otherwise available surface is covered stacked piled high with magazines, hundreds, thousands of them neatly bulwarked against the wall, collapsing in drifts across the table, a shepherd on a donkey, a hippo plashing open-mouthed in shallows, a handful of geese in flight before two identically great blocky skyscrapers, distantly indistinct in dawnlight, the lavishly painted face of a sarcophagus, and a black leather glove clamped over the mouth of it, Inside Animal Minds, Along Afghanistan's War-torn Frontier, Puerto Rico's Seven-League Bootstraps, and every cover, each image and slogan neatly contained within the same rigorous border of brightly jonquil yellow.

"Oh," May's saying, "not hardly. They've been around since, oh, eighteen eighty-something? *There* it is." Backing out slowly, rickety, slither and thump of a glossy toppling stack. "Snake, it would've bit me." Holding up a filthy plastic jug with a scored and peeling label that says Heinz All Natural Distilled White Vinegar.

"Thanks," says Jo, taking it from her hand. "Not just for this, the vinegar, I mean, but. Everything, you know. Letting me stay. It's been, ah, it helped. A lot."

"Letting you stay?" May's smile a vague little thing, eyes hidden away behind those dark black lenses. "Come and go as you like. Who am I, that I could tell you to leave."

"Anyway," says Jo.

"And you and Jack have hit it off so well."

"I guess," says Jo.

"Use what you need," says May, and lays a hand on the jug. "Bring back the rest."

"Okay," says Jo.

Becker's pen, still uncapped, wobbles, pinched between thumb and forefinger. He looks up. The kid across from him, blondly sallow, too small for that brick red tie wound into an involuted knot, scratches dutifully away with his pen, and the woman to his left, the man beside her, his bowtie crooked, and the man at the foot of the conference table, black leather vest and three or four golden necklaces. Becker frowns at the paper before him. Employment Eligibility Verification, say the letters across the top. Department of Homeland Security.

"How is everything?" says Jimmy, looking in through the doorway. He's pulled a long grey cardigan over that T-shirt, a freighted clipboard in his hand, he's noting the nods and mumbled affirmations, and then Becker's hapless shrug. Jimmy, with a half-grimaced smile, crooks the fingers of his free hand. "Walk with me, Mr. Becker."

The hall without's made narrow by redwelds laid up along the one wall, stuffed each of them with neatly reams of printed paper, and the office there across the way lit only by the blinking lights of servers stacked on wire shelves. "I just, I don't know," says Becker, low and quiet. "I was expecting more of an interview. What do you even *do*, here?"

"It's right there in the name of the company, Arnie. LST. Litigation Support Technologies."

"But what does that *mean*."

Jimmy looks away. "What do you know," he says, "about pressboard siding."

"What?"

"Hardboard siding? Composite siding? Take sawdust, scraps, whatever you sweep off the mill floor, and instead of throwing it away, mix it with glue, resin, pour it in a mold, stick it in a pressure-cooker, voila! A cheap plank in a variety of styles and colors you can hang on the side of a house. Siding."

"Wonderful," says Becker.

"We are in timber country, Arnie. Don't scoff. The downside is, if any moisture's trapped behind the siding when it's installed – and, one must keep in mind, the only environment sufficiently desiccate to install the stuff might be found in certain craters on the Moon, well. It rots. It falls off the house. And thus: an insurance claim."

"Those," says Becker, looking to the redwelds on the floor.

"One hundred and twenty-five thousand thereof, so far. And each must be examined, capturing the essential information, claimant's name, location of the house, date of the alleged product failure, under what conditions, manufacturer and brand, was it Choctaw, Miranda, et cetera, and of course, which insurer's on the hook." He tucks the clipboard under his arm, reaches out to adjust the knot and drape of Becker's tie. "You have a pulse. You can read. There are twenty-seven keyboards on the coding floor here that have to be kept clicking for at least a month to get through all of this. There'll be a more, shall we say, precise, training, in about ten minutes. You start at fourteen an hour."

"Litigation Support Technologies," says Becker.

"We build databases for lawsuits," says Jimmy.

"And all this, this really helps the, ah, claimants? With, what, a class-action lawsuit or something?"

"Oh, sweet summer child," says Jimmy, clapping Becker on the shoulder. *"Plaintiffs* can't afford an operation like this. We work for the insurance companies. Mostly."

"All this is yours?"

"One of the perks of running the joint," says Gloria, trying the switch by the door to no effect. "I get a room for me, and a room for my stuff." She pulls out a great rosy plaque of a phone and pokes the screen, switching on a white light she shines over boxes stacked on the floor, a duffel bag, a couple of suitcases, four or five enormous blank canvases, leaned against the wall. "Where are you staying, these days?"

Melissa shrugs. "Here, I guess." Stood in the doorway, knee up, boot planted back against the jamb, enormous sword in its scabbard against her shoulder. "I haven't been back to my place in," watching Gloria pick her way across the unlit room, "uh, since," that thin brightness swept about, "Cinco," says Gloria.

"Really?" says Melissa. Her propped boot slipping to the floor. "Shit, I never even got any of my," lurching to catch the unbalanced scabbard, "shit," she says. "What are you after, anyway?"

"An outfit for tonight." Gloria lowers the phone, swooping the room into darkness. "I just had it out. You'd think it would be hard to misplace a thing that big."

"Just have somebody dig it out for you. Or make you something else! One of the, uh, sewing-people? Seamstress? Made me, like, a half-dozen of these?" Fingering the skirt of her flowered sundress. "I guess this is, my look, now, or something." Clatter and scrape as Gloria shoves something aside. "So," says Melissa. "You're going out? With those girls?"

"My friends, yeah," says Gloria. "It's something we do every year. First night of the Rose Festival, when they open the carnival in Waterfront Park." Taking a broad unsteady step over something. "I mean, I haven't gone out in," shoving a box aside, "Jesus."

"I have to go with you," says Melissa, nudging a ring at the throat of the scabbard, clink.

"What?"

"Her majesty said. If you go out, I go with you. To keep you safe."

"From *what?*"

Melissa shrugs.

"I swear," says Gloria, throwing up her hands, the light a wildly flaring beacon, "she is such a fucking," dragging the light back, shining it on something in the corner by the door. "Well, shit."

"You're, like, important, to all of this," says Melissa, as Gloria struggles back across the room. "But also, she, you know," as Gloria reaches a hunched shape in the corner, and the buzz of a zipper, "cares. About you. Whoa," as light glimmers over the stuff within. "I am gonna be underdressed."

Propped on the mantel a portrait in oils, a beagle, white, spotted with black and tan, stood proudly in a field. He eyes it, hands clasped behind his back, stiff dark jeans and a two-tone shirt, pale blue and cream, embroidered across the back with calligraphy that says Spare No One. Slick black hair tied back with a red scarf. His posture shifts at the footfall behind him, but he doesn't look away from the painting. Trees lower in the distance, and clouds fill the sky of it with brush-strokes.

"Your pardon, sir," says the man in the doorway, shoulders straining his blue T-shirt, mustaches long and thick, ends of them weighted with pewter beads. "I hadn't known our host to've been previously engaged."

The man by the mantel offers a gracious nod. "Your Viscount's quite the busy man. Perhaps he seeks efficiency."

"Then I must ask your pardon a second time – I am Pyrocles, Anvil of the court, but yourself I do not know at all."

"Joaquin," says the man by the mantel. "Late of Sacramento."

"The Camellia Court?"

"That court is no more, sir."

"I," there, in the middle of the room, Pyrocles folds his hands together. "I see. Your, Queen, is she – "

"It was quick," says Joaquin, "though it had been coming for some time."

"You're here, then, at the Viscount's invitation?" Rattle of china in the doorway, a glumly narrow man slips in to set a tray on the table low between wingback chairs, cups and saucers and a steaming clay pot, sugar bowl and tongs, dishes of cream and lemon slices. "What is it?" says Joaquin.

"His excellency," says the narrow man, a rusty croak, "does crave your kind indulgence – "

"The tea," says Joaquin. "What is it."

"Da Hong Pao," says the narrow man, chin tucked behind a high white collar. "A Wuyi oolong, from a mother tree." Nodding, he takes his leave.

"We're to serve ourselves, it seems." Joaquin tongs a couple of cubes of sugar into a cup.

"Efficiency," says Pyrocles.

Joaquin's smile is faint as he pours the tea. "So," he says, lifting his cup, "was it," even as Pyrocles is saying, "The last few months," and they both stop, interrupted.

"Difficult, but," says Pyrocles.

"Of course," says Joaquin.

"Gentlemen!" Agravante in shirtsleeves sweeps into the room, "excellent, excellent," a hand for Pyrocles to shake, and Joaquin, "you've had some refreshment, and accomplished already what I'd hoped to achieve, acquainting yourselves each with the other." His tie of pink and blue in a loose wide knot, and about his neck a bulky set of headphones, nestled under bobbing dreads.

"Joaquin tells us the Queen of Camellias has fallen, and the court there is no more," says Pyrocles.

"Indeed," says Agravante. "Bitter news. And of course our sympathies must be extended to them all – but from such generosity, opportunity does likewise grow."

"My lord?" says Pyrocles. Joaquin sips his tea.

"Despite our late King's efforts," says Agravante, "we're yet a number short of a court's full complement."

Pyrocles looks to Joaquin. "What office, sir, did you fulfill, in Sacramento?"

"Shootist," says Joaquin.

"Every modern court must have one," says Agravante. "But!" A gesture with the phone in his hand, cords lopping from it to the headset. "Acquaintanceship's not friendship. There's work yet to be done, if we're to be friends," a smile for Joaquin, "pleasant work, to be sure, but work nonetheless." Turning to Pyrocles. "It would give us all great pleasure, good Sir Anvil, I am certain, were you but to entertain our guest this very night. Show him the city as you know it to be, and he in turn might show himself to you."

"My lord," says Pyrocles, "forgive me, but perhaps, another night?"

Agravante frowns. "He's away tomorrow – quickly to return, no doubt," another gesture with that phone, at once forestalling and magnanimous, to Joaquin, who says, "I'm next for the Saltwater Court."

"They, too, wish to be modern?" says Pyrocles.

"I'm certain," says Agravante, after a moment a touch too long, "our Anvil will show you the best the City of Roses has to offer. Indulge yourselves!" Reaching up to settle the headphones over his ears, opening the phone in his hand, he turns and leaves the room. Pyrocles sighs.

"Subtle," says Joaquin, setting down his cup, empty but for a sludge of undissolved sugar.

A flatbed trailer, backed onto the grass, perpendicular to the river, parallel to the span of the bridge above, and a compressor kicks itself to chugging life. Squeal of an electric guitar, percussive keyboard riff, some handclaps all tinny from speakers mounted there, and there, on lofted poles all strung with lights, the wind blows hard against this mountainside, a soaring voice, across the sea into my soul, and roustabouts and teamsters hop onto the sides and tail of the trailer, looking over its hulking load, knocking this loose with a clang, shunting that home. Sigh and groan of pneumatics as two great girders red and yellow and green hoist themselves, hinged at the front end, up until they tower above the traffic passing back and forth along the bridge. Kyrie eleison, down the road that I must travel, kyrie eleison through the darkness of the night. Compressor-chug redoubles, another groaning sigh, and two more girders hinged at the tail end lift themselves and also the bulk of the trailer's load, a great stack of rattling beams lashed to those girders, capped at their lifting ends with neat white circles faced out to either side, Funtastic, they say, in fading rounded letters, Traveling Amusements. They halt not straight upright but at an angle, and with an overwhelming hiss of air released the first two girders at the front relax, fall back from their upright stance until with a proper thunk the tips of them meet the capped tips of the others, and there's an equilateral truss, hoisted up from the flatbed by the bridge.

Roustabouts busy themselves at the base of it, loosening the lashes of that bundle of beams until it sways depended from the apex of the truss, okay! Okay! Two of them seize the pair of beams on one side of the bundle and haul them swinging out toward the tail of the trailer, until there's room enough for the struts at the bottom to drop, clang! into place, bracing those two beams at an angle out away from the bundle, and even as they do two others have done the same on the other side, swinging that first pair out, away, clang! toward the front. The compressor's whine rises in pitch, chug of it now a flutter, and the whole assemblage seems to sigh, hup! shouts someone, and trembling the next pair of beams toward the tail end swing themselves out, away, as roustabouts yank down the struts, clang! and the next pair toward the front swing out, away, and so it goes, pair by pair erecting itself, segment by segment, wedge by slice, until the circle's complete, those first two pairs meeting high above the apex of the truss at the top of what's become a Ferris wheel. Another truck pulls up beside the trailer, and now the roustabouts leap to open the back of it, and begin unloading gondolas.

"SOMEBODY'S COMING" – FIXING HIS TIE
THE SOURCES OF WATER – "WELCOME!"

"SOMEBODY'S COMING," a warning lilt from the man in one of the lawn chairs.

"No one's coming, Hector," says May, in the other. "Cats would've said."

"Ask him yourself, then," says the man, with a wave off that way, past the front end of the motorcoach. Distant crunch of gravel, footfall yet loud enough to carry all that way. Jo, sat on the grass before them, hikes up on a knee. A man's approaching down the dirt track that's not quite a driveway, tall in trim black trousers and a bright white shirt, skinny black tie, and a pair of classic black sunglasses. "May," says Jo, and then, sharper, louder, *"May."*

"Go on," says May, without turning to look. "We got this. Go."

Up on her feet, jug in her hand, Jo heads away around the back of the motorcoach, out of sight of the track, into the scrub, to crouch under heavy, breathless trees. "Excuse me," some-one's saying, that man, "if you could give me a hand," maybe, and May's response can't be made out. "Looking for," the man's saying. Jo heads further into the deepening shade. "Johanna Draper," the last that can be heard.

She hauls herself from gnarled and crooked trunk to trunk, mismatched Chucks uncertain in the rootily treacherous under-brush. Winking in and out to the left a stretch of water coolly green, littered with fallen leaves and occasional twigs, a twitching cloud of midges on the penumbral threshold of the opposite bank, flickering as they pass in and out of the sunlight. She turns away from the water, up through the trees to the scrub that untidily edges the vast field, where she crouches, looking back. Mounds of junk, a couple cars now between her and the motorcoach, there's the tall man, black suit coat over his shoulder, genially chatting with May and Hector. Keeping low she darts across the field from mound to pile, from fender-shade to high-kicked trailer, past a tent, the tarp-awned side of a van, and someone sat on the floorboard of it, leafing through a tiny notebook. Ahead now the largest mound, a low wide tummock of cinderblocks and upended pallets, stuffed garbage bags, the torn remains of unidentifiable clothing, a wheelless bicycle frame, a bent torchiere. She sets the jug up as high as she can reach and follows it, feet choosing steps more stable than they seem, hands grasping holds that do not falter, over the top to hang a moment on the other side, the mound a wall encircling a little paddock cleanly scraped, green grass cropped close, the little dome tent beige and orange pitched atop some wooden pallets, and looking up at her, black eyes unblinking, the tiny unicorn.

"Roy," she says, "I'm just gonna," freezing when he steps toward her, chewing thoughtfully, maybe five hands high at the most, his palely glossy coat of rosy grey, the mane of him iridescent in the hot flat light, the horn even now the color of the inside of a shell. "I'm just gonna climb down," she says, lowering a foot, freezing again as he takes another step with a daintily cloven hoof. "Jack?" she calls, but quietly. "Jack!" again, with more urgency than volume. "You back? Tell me you're back."

A boot's thrust through the tent-flap, followed by a blue-denimed leg, another boot, probing for the ground, blue-denimed buttocks under the flap of a blue denim jacket tugged clattering down as he settles himself on his knees, wavering, "Jo?" he says, blinking, looking about.

"Call off your horse," she says.

Turning about he nearly topples. "Whoa," he says, "what are you," shaking his head, holding out a hand to Roy.

"Somebody's out there," she says, dropping to the grass, fetching down the jug.

"More of your guys?"

"They wouldn't dare." She edges along the paddock wall to a lap of cloudy plastic. Lifting it, peering through the rust-feathered mesh of an upended shopping cart. There's the motorcoach, the tall man laughing at something maybe Hector's said. "I don't know him," she says, "but I've seen guys like him."

"Looks like a cop," says Jack, close over her shoulder.

"Yeah," says Jo. "Asking about somebody named Johanna."

Jack blinks. Roy's nuzzling his distracted hand. "Not you?" he says.

"My name's not Johanna." And then, looking back at him, "Jesus, Jack, are you high?"

He grins. "Shit, I hope so." An enormous sniff. "Want some?"

"No," she snaps, turning back to the impromptu loophole.

Becker's working the strap of his messenger bag up over his head with one hand, repeatedly stabbing the Lobby button with the other. Settling the strap on his shoulder, untwisting it about. Music jangles, a quietly sashay, the lights are on, and someone's home, but I'm not sure if they're alone. A bare arm slips between the closing doors, tripping the mechanism that slides them open again, Jimmy, beaming, "Arnie!" he cries, shoving his way in, "it's five hours past the meridian! We've worked hard," leaning over to press the Lobby button firmly, once, "so now, it's time to play hard!"

"I, ah, I don't know, Jimmy," says Becker, squeezed back into a corner. It's not a large elevator.

"I said play hard, Arnie. Not hard to get. We're going to the carnival." Hauling his backpack up on a shoulder, Jimmy reaches to take hold of Becker's yellow tie, gently tugging it out from behind the strap of the messenger bag that crosses his chest. "It's but a short walk away through lovely weather, there's an alcohol pavilion, and as I'm management, the first round will be on me." Smoothing the drape of it with his fingertips. "One of those droits du seignuer they don't so much advertise." He's ditched the cardigan, and the pale swell of his belly there, through the gaps in the sides of that Panama Jack T-shirt, dark hair a touch too long, waves of it cresting in tufts and spikes that don't quite know what to do. "I just," says Becker, "can't see you as a manager." His smile a touch to genial to be a smirk. "Hit your rate, get me fifteen on the coding floor, stat! Who knew."

"What is it they say? We contain multitudes?"

"You were carrying a *clipboard*."

"A sight you shall take to your grave," says Jimmy. The doors slide open. "So tell me, Arnie," stepping out into the lobby, "what do you think of this industry in which you've found a new home?"

"I think," says Becker, following after, "I like how I didn't have to talk," frowning, slowing, "to anyone," he says, "on the phone," and stops, there in the middle of that cramped little lobby, that once had been richly appointed, brass trim and fittings pitted now, cloudy gold-veined marble chipped, spare deco chandelier in need of dusting. "Arnie?" says Jimmy, turning back from the vestibule doors. Becker's looking through another door that leads to a tiny storefront off the lobby, Moonstruck Café, says the darkly blue sign in the glass of it. A man on the other side, his brawny back to them, shoulders straining his blue T-shirt, and past him another, a wide red scarf tying back his hair.

"Who is that?" says Jimmy.

That man turns about, mustaches a-sway, as Becker opens the door, and "what," he's saying, "what are you, how did you, how are you here? *I* didn't even know I was going to be here. How did you know. How did you know where I was?"

The hiss and gurgle of a milk steamer. "My love," says Pyrocles, "though I've sworn to see you safe, it's not – "

"Don't," says Becker, "say that. Don't call me that."

"This is coincidence," says Pyrocles, "and nothing more."

"Your cocoas, gentlemen," says the woman behind the counter, pushing forth two white paper cups, each topped with a paper-wrapped truffle. "Habanero and sea-salt caramel, and Wild Card absinthe."

"We're here at my request," says the man with the wide red scarf. "I wished to try your chocolate." Taking the cups, he leaves a stack of heavy silver coins.

"Oh, but you're our guest," says Pyrocles.

"I insist."

"So," says Jimmy, there behind Becker, as the woman behind the counter picks up the coins with a frown, and a shrug, "Of course," says Pyrocles. "May I present Joaquin, of Sacramento, and of course, this is Arnold Becker."

"Of Portland," says Becker.

"Your pardon, sir," looking past Becker, "I haven't had the pleasure?"

"Oh," says Becker, "this is," but Jimmy's reaching past him, "James Dupris," he says, offering a hand to Pyrocles, as "Jimmy," says Becker, with a sigh. Pyrocles shakes Jimmy's hand, "And I," he says, "am Pyrocles, the Anvil."

"Ah," says Jimmy.

"We should probably," says Becker, turning, but Jimmy's hand's on his shoulder. "Out on the town?" he says, sprightly.

"I've found myself with time on my hands," says Joaquin. "The Anvil has offered to fill it."

"There's a carnival but a few blocks away," says Jimmy. "Let's make it a double date!"

Becker closes his eyes.

A cramped low space, lit by neon laser lines across the ceiling, vermillions and violets and bright lime greens that chase their reaching arms, their knees, that pulse in time with a loping beat under stabs of brass, an airhorn, die Wasserbetten durchzuroken und die Nachbarn zu schocken, "I forget," says the one girl, tall and blond, who's traded her school T-shirt for a halter of silver lamé. "Is it high pH that's good? Or low?" Perched on the edge of the padded bench that runs down the one long side, lifting and tilting bottles from the bar that runs down the other, peering at the labels in what light's afforded.

"This one's from glaciers in Iceland," says the girl in the hijab, magenta of it weirdly teal in this light. "Apparently, it's the first bottled water to be declared carbon neutral."

"Ooh," says the blond girl.

"It's all just tap water," says the girl in the overall shorts. "I saw it on Penn and Teller."

"Not all of it, Olivia," says the girl in the oversized dress shirt.

"There's also some fruit juice," says the girl in the expertly shredded jeans. "Oh, hey, kombucha!"

"The heck is yuzu?" says the girl with a clatter of beads and bangles about her wrists.

"They get the water from the sink, Edith, okay?" says the girl in the overall shorts.

"It's like a lemon, Lizzi," says the girl in the hijab.

"It *is* a lemon," says the girl in the jeans.

"Basically? You're paying five bucks for a label."

"Not tonight, Olivia," says the blond girl. "Wet bar's comped with the wheels!" Sitting back, grinning amidst the whooping and the laughter, "Little Suzie Wilson ain't the only one who can throw daddy's plastic around."

"Gloria Monday," says Olivia, grabbing a bottle that says Le Bleu, Ultra Pure.

"Sic transit blah blah," says the blond girl.

"It's her *name*, Chloe," says the bangled girl, grimacing as she tries to push the marble into a Codd-necked bottle of soda.

"Whatever. She's taking forever to get ready."

"You have to admit," says the girl in the hijab, "what she's got going on here's on a whole other level than covering transpo for a girls' night out."

"Please, Sanaa," says Chloe, rolling her eyes, "it's like a jumped-up community center or something. I was led to expect the second coming of the Holocene."

"It's not even six!" says the girl in the hijab.

"You think the joint starts jumping after dinner?"

"There was some music," says Olivia.

"Totally Riverdance," says Lizzi.

"Those little galleries are cool," says the girl in the oversized dress shirt.

"And the murals!" says the girl in the jeans.

"How true, Penelope!" says Chloe. "It's a McMenamins. What was I thinking."

"It's a sad leftover corner of First Thursday crammed into a dorm for homeless freaks," says Lizzi.

"Actually," says Sanaa, "the *preferred* term, these days, is *unhoused.*"

Chloe's the first to laugh, and Lizzi, Edith and Penelope, Olivia, as Sanaa just sits there smirking, an unopened bottle of lime seltzer in her hand.

"If this is what you get for banging a vampire," says Edith, "I say bring it on, Vlad."

"He was *not* a vampire," says Chloe, and "There's no such *thing* as vampires," says Sanaa, "I don't know," says Penelope, "did he sparkle?"

"He totally murdered her dad, is what he did," says Lizzi, to gasps and whoas and a forceful "He did *not,*" from Sanaa. Chloe says, "I thought that was a home invasion or whatever."

"Her father's dead?"

"Jesus, Olivia, keep up."

"It was a domestic thing, is what I heard," says Edith.

"How," says Penelope. "Suzie's mom was long gone."

"Gloria's," says Olivia, and "Whatever," says Penelope, and "It's her *name,*" says Lizzi. "It wasn't her mom," says Edith.

"Well, there wasn't a stepmom," says Chloe. "Or a girlfriend."

"Maybe, it was a boyfriend?" says Penelope.

"Maybe it *was* the vampire," says Edith.

"There are! No! Vampires!" shouts Sanaa, through the shrieks and clamoring peals of laughter, swigs and swallows, clacks and clinks of bottles toasted, the thumping beat, "So anyway," says Edith, adjusting the undone collar of her shirt, "when I tell you, believe me when – "

"Here she comes!" shouts Lizzi, leaned forward, peering through the heavily tinted window above the bar, and "Stations!" shouts Chloe. "Cue it up," to Sanaa, who's already grabbing a charm-bedecked phone from the bar, "get those sun roofs open," to Lizzi and Olivia, who reach for buttons set in discreet wall panels. The music stops to start up again, a stomping piano-driven hook, volume climbing as the lasers flicker away. Panels lift and slide apart to reveal the barely evening light, and they leap to their feet, pushing up and out.

The limo long and pink is parked along the loading dock, the smaller stall doors cranked up as people gathered about take in the improbable bulk of it, the music swelling from it, ain't being fun, an aggrieved voice sings, I know another bee's been in that hon, the girls popped up through the sun roofs, waving in a sort of unison as sweeping out from under the largest overhead door, Gloria Monday in a black high-waisted gown, arms socked in black-striped white, her jet-black hair threaded with silver ribbons and gathered in two great hanks over either shoulder, her bangs a virulent pink, her face lighting up with laughter that doubles her over, clutching Melissa beside her for support, as the girls in the limo bellow along with the chorus, "We miss that pussy, that pussy, that pussy, that pussy, no, no!"

Melissa in her motorcycle jacket, her flowery sundress, helps Gloria push herself upright, smiling, shaking her head, and Sanaa eyes them, frowning even as she waves, as Gloria shimmies toward the steps down from the dock, and Melissa's stumping after. Sanaa leans toward swaying Chloe there beside her to mutter, "Looks like she's bringing the babysitter." Chloe shrugs.

The gate, a skeletal stretch of scaffolding hung between two scaffolded towers, each wrapped in roughly woven tarps of this one black and that one red, and great yellow letters across the length of it, CityFair, they say, under a stylized rose. Beyond it over a stretch of flattened grass a couple of booths under signs that say Tickets in patriotic colors, but stretched across beneath a taut red ribbon holding at bay a crowd queued restlessly between spindly barricades wound back and forth to the sidewalk. Pop and crackle the speakers hung about, "Ladies and gentlemen!" a booming voice, "and those otherwise defined, developed, and endowered! It is with the greatest pleasure and the utmost pride that we are privileged here today to welcome you to the verdant sward of the Tom McCall Waterfront Park for our opening night, and you all know what that means," the cheers, the whoops, the claps, *"fireworks!* As soon as night falls, folks, but till then, we're about to open the gates, and you, yes, you, in your multitudinous and your splendiferously spectacular glory, all y'all here assembled, get to play the games and scream your screams as you ride our rides, the Kamikaze!" and bang! a burst of confetti from the black tower, "The Inferno!" and another burst from the red, "The Paratrooper, and the Hard Rocker!" and fluttering explosions from them both. "Alien Abduction! The Extreme Scream!" Ribbons dance upright in roaring gusts, and even more confetti, "and all your tested, tried, and true-blue favorites, the Scrambler, the Tilt-a-Whirl, and of course the tallest Ferris wheel this side of the Willamette!" The shrieks, the yells, the rattling of barricades. "And we have shows!" A sprightly riff starts revving from those speakers, and a brightly blat of horns. "Tonight only, on the RoZone Stage, we have Whenever Buckingham warming you up as only they can for the one, the only, Nu Shooz Orchestra! Admittance free with a wristband or a badge. Are you ready?" The cheers, the whoops, the applause. *"Are* you *ready?"* The music ratchets, the crowd roars, the streamers dance, the driver of a passing truck leans on the horn. "Then without further ado! Friends and neighbors! It gives us more joy than we could possibly hope to express or contain to throw open the gates to you, one and all, on the opening night of this, the greatest show on the riverfront, the wondrous, the fantastical, the serendipitiously stupendous, the exquisitely ecstatic and soaringly supreme, the absolute acme, the one, the only, the Portland Rose Festival CityFair!"

Pop! and the taut red ribbon leaps apart in a clap of sparks, a fluff of smoke, singed ends of it twisting, rippling, falling, kicked aside and trampled to the grass as the crowd surges in, waving armbands, flashing badges, heading for the ticket booths.

"Brought to you by Xfinity!"

THE GLEAMING POIGNARD – EVERY TIME
INDIGO, FUCHSIA, APRICOT – THE SLOGAN

THE POIGNARD GLEAMS in its makeshift cauldron, an empty garbage bag tugged open, bulk of it rucked up and cuffed to make a lip about a limpid pool of vinegar. Jo sits to one side, legs folded tailor-fashion, wall of junk behind her, and the deepening sky above.

"You sure?" says Jack.

"Yes," says Jo. Taking delicate hold of the wire-wrapped hilt, turning the blade over in its bath. Wiping her fingers on meagre grass.

"There's no," says Jack, "strings. If that, it that's what you're. Thinking?" Flat on his back in his button-dappled jacket, head pillowed on a rumpled sleeping bag. Smoke tendrils from the hand cupped on his chest.

"What I'm thinking," says Jo, "is I don't want any."

"Who doesn't like pot?"

She leans over cauldron, pool, blade, the vinegar faintly hazed, wispiest threads of rusty milk seeping from those orange blotches, fading to nothingness almost immediately. Her lips purse, her shoulders shift, a suggestion of a shrug. "Who," Jack's saying, clink of buttons as he lifts a hand, "doesn't," back of it hung above his supine face. Crunch of grass as Roy steps out from around the tent, chewing absently, dipping to nuzzle up another scant mouthful. "I was," says Jack, hand floating down to settle on Roy's haunch, that shivers at his touch.

"Maybe you'd better," Jo sighs, "just give me however much of whatever it is that's left, so you don't smoke yourself into orbit." He giggles, sputtering into a coughing fit. Jo's holding out her hand. "Come on," she says.

He's peering at a singed twist of paper and ash. "Ossifer," he says, "I think," more giggles, "you're too late, officer."

A sigh, a shake of her head. She lifts the poignard dripping from the vinegar, wipes the blade down with a bit of cloth, holds it up, sleekly flawless in the light. "Would you look at that."

"But," says Jack. "I mean."

She sniffs the wire-wrapped hilt, pats it dry with the cloth. "Never had to do this with my sword."

"You had a," says Jack, his frown growing more elaborate, "a sword?" He tries to sit up. Tries again. "You got blood? On your sword?"

"Not blood," says Jo, slipping the poignard into its sheath. She jumps at the rip of grass too close, Roy nosing a last lush tuft there by her knee, "Jesus!" she blurts, and Roy prances away, setting Jack off on another round of giggles. "You have *got* to keep him away from me," she snaps.

"You," says Jack, giggles subsiding, "have to relax." Making his way toward her on hands and knees, buttons a-clack. "I told you," says Jo, "I don't want any, and anyway, it's, it's all, used up."

"There are other," says Jack, plopping himself beside her, propped on an elbow, "ways," he says, hand placed quite deliberately there, on her knee, "to relax." She looks at it, half-swallowed by his jacket-cuff, knuckles delicate against the rough folds of her jeans.

Crunch of a guitar chord squalling echoes loud enough to drown a moment the shrieks, the screams, the cheers, the hissing groans and knocking chugs, the claps, the barking shouts, the whistles and dings and bleeps. Becker leans an elbow on a little standing table, there in a crowded corner roped off by yellow ribbon slung from flat-footed stanchions, No Alcohol Beyond This Point, says the sign facing all of them thronged within. "They'd keep us penned, as livestock," says Joaquin, setting by that elbow a red cup brimming with beer.

"And charge us ten dollars for the privilege," says Jimmy, a small clear cup of something dark in his hand.

"What'd you get?" says Becker.

"They said it was a Manhattan. I'm dubious."

"Maybe one of the lesser boroughs?"

"I'm afraid," Jimmy takes a sniff, "we're somewhere in New Jersey."

"Quien no recorre," says Joaquin, crumpling his empty cup, "no se corre! Shall we go and see what carnival this county fair affords, or order up another round?"

Becker eyes his own, still full. "What about, ah – "

"Mr. Pyrocles?" says Jimmy. Joaquin cranes up to peer over the shoulders of the crowd, "There," he says, pointing. "Still waiting to be served. I'll chivvy him along, and then, perhaps, we'll see what's to be seen." He sets off, strings of colored light striking gleams from his embroidered shirt, his slick black hair. Jimmy seizes Becker's hand. "You have *got* to tell me *everything.*"

"Jimmy," says Becker.

"Arnie. Yon Mr. Pyrocles is your mysterious silverback, or I'll buy a hat to eat." Becker closes his eyes, and Jimmy's smirk becomes something more considered. "Now." Nudging the crumpled cup between them. "What's with short, dark, and thirsty?"

Becker shrugs. "He's Joaquin, from Sacramento."

"I bet. Okay, give it to me straight: on a scale of one to ten, how," Jimmy looks up, away, for just the right word, "exciting," he says, "is tonight likely to get?"

"That's not," says Becker, lifting his cup, "that's not on me." Swallowing deeply.

"Get your head in the game, Arnie. You're here for a reason. Figure it out."

"You *dragged* me here, Jimmy F.M. Dupris!"

"Some people have all the class," says Jimmy, but he's looking past Becker, past the crowd, the lights, the trees and the fence to the parkway, the stop-and-go traffic, the halting limo long and pink in the thick of it, and the girls stood up through the sun roofs, cheering, dancing, waving.

"Wait," says Jo, drawn back, "wait."

"For what?" says Jack, shifted closer, over.

"You're sure."

"About what?"

"I, ah," says Jo. Rustle of grass, clack of buttons.

"Sure," she says. "Okay," she says.

Jack smiles. Another kiss.

"Where we going? Where are we going?" Penelope dancing ahead through the midway crowd, Olivia hastening after, and Lizzi her bangles a-clatter, "Tilt-a-Whirl!" cries Chloe, pointing, strings of tickets fluttering in her hand, but "Kurve!" shouts Edith, pointing somewhere else.

"We just gotta make sure we're in time for the parade," says Olivia.

"That's *next* week," says Edith.

"Every time," says Lizzi, and "We have to tell you every time," says Edith.

"We see the *parade* every time," says Olivia.

"Not on the first night," says Penelope. *"God,* Olivia."

"The Starlight Parade is not on the first night," says Edith.

"I," says Sanaa, "am getting me one of *those,"* as a kid traipses by with a stuffed giraffe not quite as big as he is.

"Tilt-a-Whirl *first,"* says Chloe.

"In this dress?" says Gloria, spreading her arms, full skirts a-sway.

"What, you're not gonna ride any rides?" says Olivia.

"Princess Gloria's here to be seen," says Chloe. "Enjoying herself would defeat the purpose."

"Like I'm the only one," says Gloria, with a look for Edith, who's unbuttoned her shirt to reveal a black lace bra. "I'm fine with rides. Just," pointing off toward the end of the midway, the imperially wheeling magenta lights, yellow and orange, brightly shining green, of the Ferris wheel. "Something more genteel."

"We," says Chloe, lifting her hands full of tickets, "will ride all the rides, win all the games, eat so much fried dough and tacos and all the cotton candy, we will scam drinks from pretty young men, and throw up behind the Honey Buckets, and we will *know* we had a *hell* of a good time, and we are going to *start* with the goddamn *Tilt-a-Whirl!*"

"Why not split up?" says Melissa. "If everybody," faltering, as they all turn their various attentions to her, "wants to, ah," a shrug, "different?" she says.

"We can do more damage that way," says Olivia.

"The point is, we do it to*gether,*" says Sanaa.

"We always have," says Chloe.

"Why are you even here?" says Lizzi.

"I, ah," says Melissa, a sidelong look to Gloria, who's balled up her fists, scowling, "She's my *friend,* okay? So fuck you, that's why."

"Whatever!" shouts Chloe. "Who cares." She starts handing out tickets, a string each to Olivia, Lizzi, Penelope, "Split up, hang out," she says, handing tickets to Edith and Sanaa, "whatever." Turning to Gloria, peeling a couple more strings away from the hank in her hand, fluttering as she waves it about, "CityFair, bitches," she says. "What's it gonna be?"

Plastic crinkle, splot and squish, "Ah," he says, "I got my knee in the, I'm sorry. Vinegar."

"Oh, shit, I meant to," she says, and "It's okay, I wasn't," he says, and they're both laughing. Scratch and scuff as Roy steps close, light shifting, and all the colors, as he lowers his head to snuffle the rumpled garbage bag. "Take 'em off," she says.

"What?"

"Your jeans. Go on."

"I don't think," he says, and "The smell," she says, and "Oh, like you're so," and "*I* had a shower," she says, "*I* smell fine."

"You do," he says, nuzzling close, a kiss for her cheek, the line of her jaw, her throat, "Are you sure," she says, "you're up for, whoa! Not there," grabbing the wrist of the hand well up under her T-shirt. "Not there. Don't."

"What is it," he says, muzzily, hands planted now in the scruffed grass, either side of her hips. "Why'd you, you're, so *scared,* of Roy. Why? Why did you – "

"He's a fucking *unicorn,* Jack!"

Rocking back on his heels, blinking once. Propping up on her elbows, shaking her head, "I'm sorry," she says, but "You *really,* need," he says, tugging at the waistband of her jeans. Roy steps daintily away, over toward the tent, watching as he undoes her fly, as she lifts her hips.

Canvas roughly stolid under his hand stroked back and forth, "Through here?" says someone behind him, and "He said it was this one," says someone else. "I should not have had that second beer," he says.

"Third," says someone behind him. He turns, blinking at a guy rope abruptly angled before him. "I thought," he says, "we were leaving? The alcohol tent?" Frowning. "Pavilion," he says, with great care.

"We did," says someone, now before him. "Are you sure it was this one?"

"The roustabout said. Look for the flap."

"Roustabout," he says, the word rippled by a chuckle. "Rostabit." He's laid a hand on the rope, too bristly thick, too tautly strung to pluck. "Your pardon," says someone, moving past him, a hand on his shoulder he reaches for, but doesn't clasp. "You're certain."

"No other tent like it is pitched on the field," says someone else. "There should be a loose flap." The canvas behind him wobbles as it's pushed, pressed, he looks up at it, rising taupely sere to a rumpled eave reinforced with dark saltires of gummy stitching and about it, beyond it, a vast emptiness of such an unearthly indigo. Slowly, tenderly, he lets out the breath he's caught.

Looking away from it when he can. Someone's to his right, and he smiles to see him. Someone else to his left, slapping the canvas wall, a jump of dust. He looks back, over his shoulder, turns about, "Where's," he says, "there was," a frown, troubling his face, "Jimmy?"

"*Here* we go," says someone else, lifting a weighty panel of canvas, and he turns back, someone's hand on his shoulder once more, to see the color within.

"Oh," he says. "Oh, my."

Fuchsia twirling lofted wobbles dropping clang and skip a-clatter rattling to drop a ring upended between the close-packed bottles, next to a green ring similarly trapped. A pink one there on the edge of the low wide bin that holds the ranks and files of tinted empty glass, an apricot ring bright against the grass below, and only baby blue is neatly snugged about a slim glass neck. "Five up, one on," says the woman behind the counter, rotely gathering up the rings. Her T-shirt, elaborately ripped and tied into a halter, says Ten Minutes of Gunshots across the front. "First tier only," she says, setting the rings in a stack on the counter.

"Again," snarls Sanaa, slapping a handful of tickets by the rings.

Close-quartered in a gondola high above the bustling midway below, the busy bridge behind, that stretches out across the river to the left, and unskeins to the right through the brightening lights of downtown. Thrum and groan, the Ferris wheel starts up, lurching the gondola down a few degrees from its perch at the top toward the darkening river, toward oncoming night, then groan and clank it stops again, setting the gondola a-sway. Gloria grips the pole behind her for support. Melissa's braced a boot against the spoked wheel like a table in the center of the gondola, careful of the stuffed and bustling overspill of Gloria's gown. "You guys do this every year?" she says.

"Since, ah, sixth grade. That was me, Chloe, Olivia. So." Gloria shrugs. "This is the seventh time, I guess?"

"And you always wore a prom dress?"

"No," says Gloria, "no, this?" Smoothing the satiny skirts. "This is what I wore to the Bellamy Bach show." Sitting back, tightening her grip as the great wheel thrumming groaning slips them down another few degrees, clank and groan and sway. "Me and Chloe, Sanaa, Edith, and Rod," she exaggerates the name, "with his fucking top hat," a sigh, another shrug. "Dolled up all gothic punk because, you know, Bellamy Bach. And there was this guy? This, beautiful man, sitting, all by himself, in a booth. And I," a shake of her head. "Chloe dared me, to go talk to him. So I did."

The thrum knocks up, clanks into a groan, the wheel turns, jerks to one more halt. Gloria lets go of the pole, leans forward, elbows propped on her skirt-clouded lap. "That," she says, "was the last time any of them saw me, until today."

Buckles chime as Melissa sits back, looks away, out over the downtown lights.

"And I mean," says Gloria, "it's not like we *weren't* little shits to each other, before. And it's not like I haven't done shitty stuff since, you know?" A corner of Gloria's mouth reaches for something sheepish. "But I started a, a support group. An art studio. A gallery. I'm running a fucking *palace* for a regular Mother Goose queen and all her fucking butchers and bakers and candlestick makers, and I," sitting back, round face softly shadowed, pink bangs struck by a flash, "I'm stuck in a goddamn pissy mood because it's like they never noticed I was gone."

Melissa says, "It's almost time for fireworks."

"Were you even," says Gloria, but once more the thrum, the grinding groan, it all slips into smooth acceleration, and their gondola swoops toward the bottom of the wheel's rotation, aways through bright fluorescent light past waiting riders cheering, jeering as they swing through climbing up over the trees that line the parkway, the sudden lights of the city, up and up toward the top again, and the midway spread below.

Crudescent light from one enormous lantern hung high up on the king pole, so bright, yet so intensely, insistently red, obliterating any other colors, leaving only outmatched shadows to suggest what shapes might move beneath, shadows, and here and there a sharply fleeting light-struck gleam of sweat on skin a-shift and push and sway and shove, and the effortful susurrus built from scuff of boots in dust, and running shoes, moccasins, clogs, the hissing shuck of denim on khaki, duck snagging jersey, chamois rubbing twill, the lop of belts undone, slither of vinyl, jangle and clank of unheeded buckles, rasp of flys unzipped, flap of plackets unbuttoned, and the sighs, the grunts, the groans, fragments of sentences too urgent to finish, too unnecessary to pay any attention, and also the wordless imprecations, but above all the slap, the pop, the slip and shuff, the lick and lap of flesh against flesh, with flesh, on flesh, but up he pushes himself and away, feet bare on trampled grass, trousers sagged about his hips, shirt long gone but his tie, his tie still somewhat knotted a mantle about his shoulders, and what's left of his hair awry. He laughs, half-swallowed, as a glove clamps about his upper arm to spin him not unroughly about, his own hand up to catch, to brace himself against a meaty shoulder. The other glove up between them tangles his tie about clumsy fingers, yanking him close with a chuckling growl, but shaking his head he pushes back, uncertain steps away, tie trailing fleurs-de-lis from a slackening grip.

The man, stood there, apart.

Blinking, heel of his hand wiping sweat from his eyes, he steps through all that light toward the man, his back to him, not so far away as he seems, nor so tall, squat legs thickly thewed and buttocks bare beneath a jacket black enough to insist upon itself in all that red, the slogan across the back of it legible only by the prick and pucker of embroidery, a single word, IRRUMATOR.

Something, a crackle of underfoot grass, a shout, a laugh, a pop in the hum of the lantern hung up high, something catches that man's attention, something enough to look over a shoulder, and smile to see him there, to turn, that jacket swaying open, close enough now to reach within, to lay a hand, to stroke the broad and hairless chest. That smile turns sinister, as horn-knuckled hands lay themselves on his shoulders, pushing, but he's already sinking on his own, to one knee, both, as one of those hands shifts to brush aside the weighty tail of that jacket, presenting a cock he takes almost immediately into his mouth, hiking up a bit to manage it, hard hands gripping his head as those hips, that cock, begin to pump.

Rumpled jeans a yoke about her ankles knees spread wide one low against the grass one high and him, he's awkward crouched above, clutching either side of her lap, the buttons pinned about his jacket clacking as his shoulders dip, I'm Not GAY I'm ANGRY can just be made out on the one, and Let GO When You GIVE another, and the back of his head in the darkness cants and nods. She's leaned back on her elbows looking up, and up, it's dark, so dark, the only light from a far-off parking lot, yet powerful enough to hazily pollute an empty, starless sky.

The only light, but also Roy, stepped close, those delicately cloven hooves back-and-forthing as he doesn't quite bring himself to stamp. A brilliant shake of his mane, a blowsy whicker, and stilling he plants those hooves. She looks down to see him there, too much too close, too bright, she blinks, nods absently with the rocking effort, her breath quickening, and meets Roy's darkly unblinking gaze, a lightless constant in the soft but relentless shimmer and pulse of iridescence that is his coat, and that horn held motionless above. She lifts a hand from the head in her lap to her breast, though there is no hole in this T-shirt, no gleam can be made out through the cloth of it, and he does not lower his unflinching horn. Still. She lays her hand on her breast, a gasp, and closes up her eyes.

Uncertain steps that don't quite manage to stumble under the vaulting radiant effulgences that bloom above, his baggy pants, his Panama Jack shirt, limp backpack slung from his shoulder, and clamped beneath an arm a messenger bag, "Becker!" he calls, and then, louder, to carry over intermittent explosions, "Becker? Becker!" What crowd there is at the edge of the midway mostly gazes raptly up, but here and there this person or that looks down, about, to see him there, who'd been calling, who's turning away with a shake of his head from the screams, the sparking whooshes, the bang and rattling pops above. He works a hand into a pocket of those pants, letting the messenger bag slip to dangle from its strap in his other hand, and hauls out a phone in a fake leather case. "Needs must," he mutters, working it nimbly with his thumb, the code, the app, the green-lit icon of a handset. Holds it to his ear, wincing at all the sound and light.

A muffled chime answers from below.

His lips purse, a grimace of realization, and he stoops to lay the messenger bag on the grass, opens the flap of it on a dim light, a chime unmuffled. He fishes out a second phone, glossy and black, Jimmy F.M., says the screen of it. Accept or Decline. His own phone says Arnold Becker, Calling, Mute, Keypad, Speaker.

"Well, shit." He thumbs the red button on his phone, and the chiming dies away. A fusillade of light fills the sky above, and oh, the applause.

A Lonesome banjo – no, She didn't

A LONESOME BANJO plucked and bent over makeshift percussion, a warmly disinterested voice, Burlington Northern pulling out of the world, she twists a key, shuts off engine, radio, headlights all at once. The only streetlight, a ways ahead, shines mostly on the rough stone wall that steeply rises to the right, the sidewalk narrow at its base. Across the street a curve of houses, demurely lit, and each at first seems discretely different from the rest of them about, yet all of them, every one, of a size, a type, with their scraps of yard, their brief driveways, their artfully unkempt flowerbeds and shrubs, that each ends up looking much like the others.

The key tucked away in her hoodie, she opens the toolbox on the seat beside her. Lifts aside a massive cleaver and a thinly elegant honing steel to pull out a tiny knife, the blade of it maybe half the length of its handle, whittled to a wicked point. She tucks it away in her hoodie. Takes another knife, as pointed but much longer, in her left hand, blade of it laid back against her forearm, and one more item, a lumpy wad of something rubbery and brown. Snap and clack the lid of the toolbox.

Quick across the street and up the shallow curl of driveway past a garage door shut up tight to the corner where she crouches, back to the house, silently panting through her wide-open mouth. Shakes out the wad, blankly goggled, blackly crackle, and, careful of the handle of the knife, ducks to slip it on, a horse's head, loosely floppy, a lopping wobble as she tugs it into place.

From the corner into darkness, through stiff hedge-sheaves with a minimum of rustle, then wary, sidelong steps down a steepening slope, fingertips brushing the wall beside her as the the bulk of the house lofts from the ground into darkness, just the hint of a flicker, candlelight, perhaps, ahead. When she can she ducks beneath, a step, two, criss-cross to a shadow solid enough to hold, a piling, and another, there. That weakly candlelight suggests by where it will not, cannot shine the shape of things, a sparse network of spindly piers lifting the enormity of the house above away from the falling slope, a wall there, a slender cellar of a sort, depended from that bulk, opening on an airy porch licked by that candlelight, slung out over a night sky only vaguely relieved in the distance by downtown's glow, hidden behind a shadow-scrim of trees.

Under the house, across the slope, slither of dry dirt, till her back's to the wall of the slender cellar, she waits out the silence. Careful steps, that wobbling snout a faint oddity in the shadows, tipped up to scan the joists and girders of the subflooring above, down to take in the cellar wall, ending abruptly to become the porch that itself takes flight, lifting in turn from the slope on piers of its own. She takes hold of the edge of that wall, breathlessly still until slowly, so slowly her other hand reaches up, candlelight glinting the blade of the knife swung away from her forearm, laid ever so carefully on the floor between two balustrades.

Nothing happens for a terribly lengthy minute.

Up and silently up her feet a-sway an elbow hooking the rail hunch and twist of hip a hoisted knee to soundless over the railing drop to the floor of the porch in a motionless crouch, arms wide, lop-muzzled head quite still.

The porch mostly taken up by one long table, thicketed with dead candles, only a handful at the far end burning, the rest of them sagged, leaned, melted in heaps of particolored slag, toppled and broken over bulwarks of filthy plates, glassware slimed with sticky dregs. Someone's slumped by those last few burning candles, the fitful flicker of them lapping at a bald head face-down in a tipped-up bowl, pink hand limply splayed.

She takes hold of the hilt of the knife on the floor by her knee.

Quietly down the porch, around and over the chairs shoved back from the table, that knife held out, away, to float over platters piled with limply rancid bacon, with furry blackened bread, with shriveled slices of tomato and withered herbs, a haze of gnats and fruit flies twirling, disturbed by the passage of the blade. Down to the end of the table and around to loom above the figure slumped there, pink-cheeked face turned sideways, pillowed on sodden noodles, shiny with coagulated broth, more flies a-whirl about an upright goblet, still cupping a wine-dark puddle.

She turns the blade as she lifts it, switching her grip from forward to reverse, up above her wobbling head as her other hand comes up to cap her grip.

Her shoulders lift with one deep breath. The other doesn't stir.

Thunk of blade-tip in tabletop a clinking squelch, the bowl rolling upright. The knife's pinned a shirt-collar, detached, yellowed with old sweat, there by a pink dish glove. She lets go. Steps back. Lifts away that horse's head, shakes out her black hair, spiky short. "Huh," says Ellen Oh. Looks up.

Frances Upchurch stands at the other end of the table, her pearly suit, her corkscrew curls. She lifts a finger to flawlessly painted lips, shush.

Then she turns and climbs the stairs into the house.

Leaving knife, collar, glove, the candlelight, the rotting feast, Ellen races up the length of the table leaping a toppled chair to follow her up those stairs, up and out into a dark and empty room, far corners of it and the floor vaguely gleamed by city-glow through the one great wall of broken glass. She shakes out the horse's head without stopping and tugs it back over her own, quickening her pace down a long and narrow hall, front door glancingly lit, a footfall to the left, above, a doorway enclosing a spiral staircase up to another hall, a light here and another at the end of it, past photographs hung on the walls, a rain-filled light-struck window, a twilit street of anonymous warehouses and power lines.

A padlock's bolted to the door at the end of the hall, but the shank of it's undone, hung loosely from the hasp. She reaches to lift it away, but something's clung to the rubbery felted stuff of her sleeve, a feather, long, a puff of white about the quill, vanes of it grimly barred with brown.

The goggled eyes of the horse head scan the hall, the walls, the darkness of the stairwell at the end. The feather drifts to the floor. She undoes the hasp, turns the knob, opens the door.

The room within's almost entirely walled away behind a canopy of netting. A single lamp is lit, and shadows lop and flutter, small and flimsily clumsy about a tall still silhouette. "Marfisa is the Horse," a light clear voice pitched low, "but you are not Marfisa."

"She said," says Ellen, a hand coming up to the cuff of the mask, "if I wore this, no one would stop me. But no one's, here," she says, horse-head turning away, dim hall barely visible between the light at this end, and at that. "Except," she says.

The silhouette steps closer to the netting, light shifting, shadow-scraps a-whirl. "What have you done."

Ellen lifts the mask from her head. "I killed him," she says.

"No." The silhouette steps back, and back again. "No, you didn't," she says, a darkness looming over the lamp. "Close up the door," she says, "and run." She shuts it off.

"Where did," says Ellen, looking away from the dark room to see the dimness trembling a blur that tumbles her prone to the dull carpeting. Bracing she kicks back but uselessly through a scribbled chiaroscuro that writhing grips and yanks, flipping her onto her back hands up that mask a-dangle to kick out again her free foot through air that ripples, whips away, resurges. Another kick at the shivering knot of light and shadow that's gripped her other foot. A howl roars the trembling length of the hall, displacing air to swell by yanks and jerks a monstrous weight that crumpling drops on her strangled grunt the dust that jumps from the carpet, and a wrinkled crease of light surrounds her head, wrenching up to slam her gasping back. Those are eyes now above her, burning beneath brows of guttering smoke, and that hole punched in the space beneath them becomes a mouth that yawning growling clenches in a sneer to drop a single word like a bullet, *"You."* The weight of the other above her blurring pulls from air and shadow and dust a torso, unfurls the arms that end in fists that hold her down, spins up a crown of wild white light to whirl above those eyes. "Who *are* you," words chiseled from the sound of grinding stones.

"Phil," she manages to say.

That weight rears up, improbably stretching those arms. "Phil?" and then, "Dr. *Kilo?*" Collapsing, floorboards groaning with the sudden burden, those fists squeezing her shoulders, that fizzing, hissing, sparking face too close. "Berlin," says the other, and that scramble of light and shadow sloughs away from pale lips licked by a grey-pink tongue, peels from ruddy cheeks below gimlet eyes, boils away from a crown of wild white hair adrift about a bald pink pate, the whole set oddly atop that trembling bolus of tight-wound light and air, dust and shadow. Those lips part, revealing sharp white teeth. "You aren't candy floss," says the other, leaning almost tenderly to bite, there, where her black-inked shoulder turns into her throat.

Her hand leaps up for one sharp blow.

A thunderclap lashing light that head snaps back, chin dark with blood but also the hair now lank about the temple, the once-pink ear, the hand that's slapping uselessly at the hilt of the tiny knife she's jammed into the side of that skull. The air, the light, the shadows unsprung, whipped free, wild blows that shiver photos from their hooks and crumple sheetrock, rake the carpet, knock her kicking knees askew and drive the breath from her as she manages to scramble out from under just as all of it implodes, a great intaken breath, swallowed away. Her feet under herself, a hand coming across to cup the blood that wells from her throat as the mewling other scrabbles the carpet strewn with feathers, a pinkly naked body much too small.

"You're alive," says the woman in the darkness behind the netting.

Ellen upright leaned trembling against the wall looks down at the other sat up on the carpeting, belly a swelling eructation pinkly plumped that pushes, pop! those arms now long enough to cradle a wailing, bleeding head. "I'm not done," she says.

"You're not enough."

Her one hand still clamped about the shoulder of her hoodie already heavy with blood, wincing as her other hand shuts the door between them. Closes up the hasp, fits the padlock to it. Snaps it shut. Turns back to the other but one of those arms too long too thin for the great swollen paw of a hand at the end of it swiping at her, she takes a skipping step away to stumble catch herself back braced against the wall. "Jyidshe," a sound that struggles from those lips, and she lifts a foot to aim a kick at that head, but the one great hand's being dragged back scuttling across the carpet, and the other's lifted, fingers spread to catch, to hold, to twist, and with a groan she pushes herself away, unsteady steps away, still leaned against the crumbled wall, smearing a trail of blood and gypsum in her wake as she heads for the darkness of the stairwell.

Feathers crackle as those hands flop to the carpet, grab and pull that body after her, tiny feet kicked uselessly, too slow, too slow, that swollen head the hilt of the knife still jutting from it lifting itself, a horrible sludgy wail of rage and frustration that manages to shape a word, *"Midch!"*

PINKISH-ORANGE LIGHT – MR. LOUDERMILK

PINKISH-ORANGE SODIUM VAPOR LIGHT strips details from the mural, and color, leaving only suggestions of flowers, gestures toward bees, the dark curl of the boteh over the shut-tight overhead door, and it blows out the brightness of the limousine turning the corner, leaving only a faintest blush to tinge the ungainly length of it slowing to a stop along the loading dock. The rear door pops open on jewel-toned neon and a thumping beat, a blazing fire, that's getting brighter, don't need nobody here that don't believe in me. Gloria in shorts and a blank white T-shirt wrestles out her empty gown, hauling it over her arm as Melissa half-falling follows, and a chorus from within of byes and love yous and see you next weeks cut off by the closing door. Gloria slaps the roof. The limousine smoothly pulls away.

Up onto the loading dock, Gloria losing an armload of gown for every armload she gathers back up. "Need a hand?" says Melissa.

"I got it," says Gloria, chin propped by the precarious pile.

Melissa opens a smaller door there by the large overhead. The warehouse within is quiet, dim, lit only here and there by this lamp still shining from a stall, that trouble light hung low, but mostly by the warmly golden glow of the great tub out in the middle of it all. Gloria turns about, chasing a trailing drape of skirt, turning about again at the sound of footsteps hastening close, "Chatelaine!" cries someone, Charlichhold, approaching. "Let us help you with your burden."

"Don't call me that," mutters Gloria. "Wait a minute." Melissa's headed off toward the unlit stage, where the shadowy bulk of the Buggane's sat, "Hey," says Gloria, setting off after her. "Hey!" Melissa leans to take the weight of what the Buggane lightly offers, her tremendous greatsword in its bulky scabbard. "You didn't have that with you?" Gloria says, an ell or more of her slithery gown trailing the concrete after her. "Why did you leave that here?"

"I was supposed to put it in my pocket?" says Melissa. "Strap it to my back and just, waltz through the gate?"

"What if somebody," says Gloria, yanking her armful of gown away. Charlichhold's trying to gather up the draggled skirts. "What if somebody went and pulled something? What were you gonna do, exactly, to keep me safe, without," twisting to yank again, "without," says Gloria, and then, blinking, blankly flat, "you weren't there for that at all."

Melissa shrugs, and a clink of the fittings about the scabbard's throat.

Gloria shoves the pile of gown at Charlichhold, who scrambles to catch it. "Her majesty didn't tell you to do a goddamn *thing*, did she."

"If I came to you," says Melissa, "if I said, hey, can I come out with you, and your friends, just to get out of here, for a night – would you have said yes?"

Gloria leans into an exasperated shrug, eyes wide, "Maybe!"

"Cleaned and mended by morning, ma'am," says Charlichhold, peering about a satiny fold of the heap of gown in his arms, "as well as ever it was."

"Whatever," snaps Gloria, stomping away.

"Hey," calls Melissa, "hey!" But she's looking to the tub, where someone's stepped up, blue robe and a great steel bowl. "You take what you need, right?" Hefting the scabbard up on her shoulder. "You really need that much?"

Past those murmurous, half-lit stalls, under and through the pitch-black arch, out into the stark fluorescence of the stairwell, up and up to the landing at the top. A brief hall, double doors to the right, to the left a corridor at this end and another at the other, paralleled, the both of them sparsely lit by brand new sconces, set in patchworks of wallpaper samples. Head down, Gloria heads down the one at the far end, but not too far along, to open a door on a room indifferently revealed by streetlight glaring through flower-shapes painted on the window-glass, a credenza there, and a high thick mattress laid upon the floor, piled with sheets and pillows rendered monochromatically pale, and the shadow rolling over in them, to sit up on an unseen elbow, "Gloria?" says Big Jim. She sits herself on the foot of the mattress, kicks off a shoe. "Did you," he says, and a throat-clearing rumble, "have fun? with your friends?"

She leans down to pull off her other shoe. "Fun," she says, "is for the bourgeois. I," she sighs. Lies back on the pale sheets. "I think I'm having an idea."

"Oh?"

"Oh, no," she says, rolling over on her belly, shaking her black-haired head. "Not yet. Not yet," pulling herself handful by handful of rumpled sheets toward him, "because," she says, and an edge to her smile, "I am going to give you such a kiss," closer still, "that you are gonna rise up and fuck the daylights out of me, and then we'll go to sleep, and then we'll wake up, and we'll have ourselves some breakfast, and then, maybe, maybe I'll tell you. If it's ready."

Those sheets fall away from his furred belly, his bare hips. "I await my lady's pleasure," he says, and Gloria starts to giggle.

Starting awake, a hand to her temple, Jack on his back beside her, snoring into an upflung elbow.

Out of the tent a rustle of mesh and canvas-flap, grommet-clink on pole. Crouched, hands clenched in close-cropped grass, listening. Flubbery snort from Roy, a dozing pool of impossible moonlight. Jack's snore tucked behind her, slowly gentle.

Silent to the wall of junk and up, black jeans, bralette, bare foot on cinderblock, fingers gripping sideways plastic crate to haul herself up top, laid flat, listening again. The schuss and whuff of distant traffic.

Twisting over and down, clatter abbreviated tink and click a thunk as something shifts, crackle of tarp she presses back against the junk-wall, shadowed, holding herself quite still. Once more listening. Waiting.

Further along the mound of junk, across grass lit indistinctly by a far-off blaze of parking-lot lights, a pale slice turns in the shadow of an abandoned sedan, opening out a white shirt-front that snaps into focus the negative space of a black black suit, scored by a skinny black tie, and she sighs, stands, steps out, "Hey," she says, and he jumps, black sleeve yanked up, across, a hand to his heart, "Jesus," he says. "Don't *do* that." And then, "You aren't Johanna, are you."

"That's," says Jo, "not, what it's short for."

"I, ah," he says, "I'm Mr. Loudermilk, and I'm looking for Johanna Draper. She has something," lifting his voice over the rising rumble of an approaching plane, "she *has* something she, ah, shouldn't have? And I'm pretty sure," looking to the mound of junk as the plane roars blinking overhead, and another shadow, enormous, shapeless, dislodges to swallow Mr. Loudermilk, crashing tangibly against the fender of that sedan as the plane dopplers away, struggle and jerk, a blow, a yelp, a brutal thump, "Hey!" Jo steps out onto the somewhat lighted grass, hands empty, ready, as the shadows resolve themselves, Mr. Loudermilk in his black suit held back against someone much larger, a swaddled bulk that barely registers his pushes and his strains, "Let me go!" slumping in that implacable grip. "I'm not gonna," he says, looking to Jo, "hurt anybody, but he? Needs to let me go."

"Oh, but Jasper's not with Bambi," says someone else. "He's with me."

Suddenly starkly lit, Mr. Loudermilk's white shirt a-dazzle, Jasper's matted hair a tangle over his scowl, and the man somehow in the midst of them all, sharp-honed smile beneath the brim of a big black hat. The flare fades, leaving the wire-wrapped hilt in Jo's hand of a leanly tapered poignard, and Danny Moody bursts into laughter, "Lucinda!" he shouts, "you perfidious *bitch.*" A step toward Jo, her blade up, free hand by it, elbow a bit too high. "Neat trick," says Moody, "but you forgot something."

"Excuse me?" says Mr. Loudermilk, and a strangled yelp as Jasper shakes him, once.

"I would've sworn," says Moody, *"you* swore a mighty oath never to do this kind of," a gesture, for her crouch, the blade in her hand, "work, again. Not for them. Not for anybody."

"If I could just?" says Mr. Loudermilk, and Jasper shakes him again, "How the fuck," Jo's saying, hands still up, that knife, "how is it you think you have any idea what I said."

"But I was there?" says Moody. "With you, and King Long Gone, and dear old Daddy Hook?" Slipping a hand in the pocket of his surplus jacket. "Whatever. There's another thing you forgot, which is what it is they say about knives," and he pulls something out, "and gunfights. Bambi, I'm telling you," pointing it at her, "you can't leave something like this," a stubby squared barrel, sprouted from his fist, "lying around where just anybody could think of it."

"Honestly?" says Mr. Loudermilk. "If you would," and then, peevishly, *"stop* that," to Jasper. "Look. All this?" A futile wave from a pinioned hand. "This is Agile Saffron business. Whole different ops profile. Now. I don't know where Dr. Uniform is," looking about at them all, "but me? I'm on a milk run. So if you'll just," but Moody whips around, dragging the mouth of the pistol with him, and the flash, the flash is quick and bright enough to show them all again for an instant, the pop an echoless crack, an afterthought, and Mr. Loudermilk jerks once in the wake of it. "Oh," he says, struggling to lift himself, sunglasses askew, "that wasn't," but he's already shriveling away, black suit collapsing into itself with a mildly disquieting rustle and pop! Jasper, blinking, lowers his empty arms.

"Huh," says Moody. Pistol still pointed where it had shot. "There's something you don't see every day."

"Danny," says Jo, "you didn't have to – "

"Sorry," he says, lifting his free hand, without looking away from what's no longer there, "Jasper, but," shifting the gun, just, "for this to work, you know," he says, "we have to have a body."

Another flash, lighting up Jasper's scowl as it becomes astonishment. Another crack, too loud, too quick. Jasper sags against the fender, and the patter of the blood leaping from his chest to his swaddled lap, and the slowly oozing of a second overflowing pump, and then.

"You didn't," says Jo, and then, "why."

"Okay!" shouts Moody, a matador's whip away in the barely light, and Jasper slumped against the sedan. "Step three? Call the cops!" He lets the pistol drop to the grass between them, and lifts a hand to his ear. "Or maybe I already did?" Smiling, sharply, at the thready, distant siren that's wailing louder, closer. "Be seeing you, Bambi."

Jo sinks to her knees. The gun there flat and black before her, barrel of it not much longer than the trigger-guard, grip wound about with glossy tape, and just visible in the darkness letter-shapes that say Kel-Tec, stamped in the pebbled metal.

Ain't nobody flying just because they fly here
You could trip sets
Real playas trip lightyears.

Tightrope time, twinkle-toes, and what?
Is you ridin or not? Everybody hands up.

Who they want? (*Who they want?*)
Game over. (*Game over.*)

Ol leech callin anyone who ain't sober.

—Daveed Diggs

NO. 39
" – Beautiful, we are – "

A RING CHARRED neatly in the floor about the sword, thrust in the middle of it, upright, short and straight the blade, of the width of two fingers from those cinders up and up to the quillions heavy and plain, the hilt wrapped about in overlapping straps of white worn yellow with hard use, up and up to the plainly beaten round of the pommel, as heavy, and as solid. Otherwise, the room is empty. The hearth there, dark and cold, swept clean, the windows blankly dark against the dark without, and only dim lamps lit in elaborately fronded sconces. From somewhere deeper in the house, below, perhaps, a basement, a confidently off-tempo guitar, a piercing soprano, gonna put on the stereo, as loud as we can make it go, and then turn the record over, over and over again.

The first of them steps from the kitchen, a brighter room off that way, walls the color of toothpaste. His rich red hair flops from a high widow's peak, his baggy ivory shirt open at the throat, his red check vest tightly buttoned, and his hands are warily empty. He starts at a creak above, but it's the second of them, making her way down the stairs, tall enough she needs to stoop, white tank top and a heavy leather kilt, her fine long hair a watery green. She nods as the third of them steps from the hall beneath the stairs, shabby velvet frock coat over orange coveralls, he's shrugging at them both, and applause smatters up from somewhere below.

The front door cracks open. The fourth of them tips in a grey-epauletted shoulder, followed by a quizzical scowl on a beefy face. The first of them nods, the third shrugs again, and the second steps off the stairs to yank the front door from his grasp, swinging it open to allow the last of them into the room, Chillicoathe, the Harper, who strides to the middle of it, his bulky sweater, his cargo shorts, his big yellow beard and his wide-eyed gaze, fixed only on that upthrust sword.

"Hey," says the third of them, the Cinquedea Pwyll, but Chilli waves him off.

"Now or never," says the second of them, Meg Greentooth, but the Kern Gradasso, the fourth, snaps up a hand, wsht!

"They're finishing up down there," says the first of them, the Stirrup Gaveston, but Chilli's already shaking out his hands, clapping them together, pop! to reach out for that yellowed hilt.

"Do you really," says someone, not any one of them, "want," a small and slender man, all in black, "to do that," there by the cold and empty hearth, delicate tulip of a cocktail coupe in his hand.

Chilli steps back from the sword as if stung, "Where," Gradasso blusters, as Pwyll insists *"I didn't,"* and Meg squeezes her enormous scale-knuckled hands into fists, opens them up again, pah! "Your pardon, Goodfellow," says Gaveston, over the others, "we'd no intention of disrupting your revels."

"I fear I've no pardon to give," says Goodfellow, eyeing his glass, "for there's none to be asked. This is a free house, Stirrup;" he lifts it for a sip, and then a gesture, liquor glinting in the light, "do what you will."

Chilli's eyes twitch, to this side, to the sword, to that. "And your will's not to stop me?"

"I'd only suggest, Harper:" says Goodfellow, "take a moment to consider whether you'd want this role, in that tale. If so," but Chilli's taken hold of the hilt, and a shriek of wood, a thrum of steel, he draws the blade from the floor.

"Well," says Goodfellow. "It'll be nice to have the room again, for dancing."

It's a complicated intersection, and the truck idles there a moment, under a red stoplight. A Balanced Life Healthcare, says the sign on the wall of the building to the left. Vicente's Pizza, over a florid red V, the sign on the corner of the building to the right. The main thoroughfare crosses before, and heads on down the hill, but here, here it's opened out a bit, something of a plaza for the lanes of traffic limned in paint that needs some touching up. Ahead to the right the low blank wall of a convenience store, 7-Eleven, says the sign that's bolted there, the brightest light about, and off to the left the dark bulk of an apartment building rises three storeys, four, The 20 on Hawthorne, says the unlit sign that swaddles the corner of it, Now Leasing, Units Available. Between them two more streets open up, one a dogleg off ahead, along the side of that apartment building, the other, there, cornering the convenience store, angled a diagonal rightward and down, into trees, among houses well-appointed. In the sharp slice of corner between them, the narrowed prow of an older building, painted a brown and darker brown gone almost black in the shadows, and not a window lit.

That truck idles through a full cycle of lights, green shone that way, then this, red lights this way, and that, and yellow on, then off, clicks of the switches audible over the muffled chug of the truck's engine. A car passes, quick along the thoroughfare, ignoring options left and right, engine snarling as it races to beat a yellow. Red becomes green, and that's when the truck lurches forward, but a blaring horn, a van there to the right, hooking about the convenience store, and the truck wrenches to avoid it, brakes screeching and rear wheels humping the curb as the van accelerates away. The truck wobbles on across the angled street to mount the lozenge of sidewalk lopped before the older brown building, coming to a gentle stop by a small young freshly planted tree, engine still a-rumble.

The driver's door pops open, and a cantering beat spills out under whirling, twirling guitars, a low voice chanting a beach for the waves of the world to crash on, you are the spilt wine, you are the spilt wine at the table of the gods, and a clap of drums. She slips from the seat, clings to the armrest on the door, and finding solid ground with her feet essays a step, but what she's stood upon's the curb of the low ramp from street to sidewalk, and the step she takes too heavy, too far down, and overbalancing, swung about, she topples to sit against the truck. What light there is gleams the blood that soaks the shoulder of her hoodie, blood slathered up her neck to the corner of her jaw, her cheek. There is a shining something, the voice is chanting, there is a shining something. Her head bobs with the effort of her breath, quick, quite shallow. Ellen Oh closes her eyes.

It's quiet.

It's quiet, and still, the music's gone, and the engine's chug. She opens her eyes to see a figure, bulky coat and wild white hair, stooped to squat beside her. "You're a mess," says Marfisa.

Ellen's lips part, her brow creases, but Marfisa's craning up, looking inside the cab of the truck, seat of it marred by a dark slick of blood. "Someone else will get this off the street," she says. "You need to get yourself inside." Lifting Ellen's arm, ducking her white head beneath it, heedless of the bloodied hand she grips within her own. "Can you stand?"

"I," says Ellen, gathering herself with a grimace, "I almost *died.*"

"You may yet," says Marfisa, bracing herself. "Come."

A Forest of Tattoos – what She could reach
for all to See, and anyone to Take – Rapprocher

Her tattooed forest hidden now by blood, and the ruddy golden crumbs that cake her shoulder and her throat, gleaming under harsh fluorescence. She's sat on the steps below the landing, bloodied hoodie a tangled stain on the floor, her T-shirt cut away, a sodden ruin in her lap. "You *lied* to me," she says, through her teeth.

Marfisa on the steps beside her scoops more golden dust from a plastic baggie. "I did no such thing." She presses it over the last visible edge of that ragged wound.

"You didn't," Ellen winces, "tell me the truth."

"And if I had?" Marfisa smooths the dampening, darkening dust with a knuckle. "Would you have listened?" Sits back, eyeing the almost empty baggie. "This will have to do."

"I need a shower."

"In time. Let the owr do its work. How does it feel? Don't touch."

Ellen shifts her shoulder. The clumped dust, settling, fuses as she eyes it to a cleanly golden shell, gleaming without slough or crack or flake. "You aren't human," she says. "Are you."

"No," says Marfisa, getting to her feet. "Let's get you upstairs."

Ellen takes Marfisa's hand to pull herself upright, working her shoulder back and up, forth and down, "That's just weird," she says.

"Don't touch," says Marfisa.

Up the steep stairs lofted from the landing, up and up to a plain brown door ajar at the top and into a brightly airy kitchen, "Can I at least get clean?" Ellen's saying, as she tries to hold up the blood-soaked lop of her T-shirt with a bloodstained hand.

"Find her some clothing," Marfisa says, curtly. "Did the truck get put away?"

There's someone else, a small man in a collarless shirt of faded green, there on the three steps leading down to a dark room crowded with shadowy boxes. He sighs, with some little gravity. "The truck might be said to have been secured."

"Is it clean," says Marfisa. And then, "There's clothing in the lobby. Destroy it. Clean the floor, and the steps as well."

"It is possible, perhaps," he says, "the lady misapprehends the particulars of a relationship with such a one as this."

"You served the Devil," says Marfisa, stepping away from Ellen, toward him. "Now you serve the Outlaw," as the small man sets off with a sigh, past her, his muttered "This one did but clean photographs for the Devil," trailing after him, "and not the scenes of crimes," out through the door that he closes behind him.

Marfisa's pressed the heel of her hand to her forehead. She scoops her white hair back, gathered a moment in a single hank, then lets it go to spring back to its cumulonimbal crest.

She opens a sparsely laden cabinet, takes down a blue-lipped drinking glass. Shoves aside with the sweep of an arm the litter on the counter, dirty dishes, tangled utensils, empty takeout cartons, wadded newspaper, an unsheathed sword, a couple-three fat little paperbacks, all to make room for the stainless steel bowl she hauls up.

"Is there a shower?" says Ellen, shivering.

"Don't touch," says Marfisa, crossing to the sink, where she sets to filling the glass. "I'm *not,*" says Ellen, turning with her, but blinking, wide-eyed, "whoa," she says, and sits, heavily, before the fridge. "Too fast."

"Drink," says Marfisa, squatting to offer the glass. And then, as Ellen, nodding, sips, "You struck your blow."

"I went in through the basement deck, like you said." She drinks off the rest in a gulp. "He was there, asleep, alone. I stabbed him," lifting her bloodied hand to point, "here," to the inked knob at the nape of her neck, "and," a wincing shrug, "he was gone."

"It wasn't him."

"She was there."

"Your wizard," says Marfisa, standing to take the bowl to the sink.

"Upchurch. She wanted me to go upstairs," lifting her voice over the rush of the faucet. "There's a woman, locked in a room full of moths?"

"Butterflies."

"And *she* told me it wasn't done. And then," looking down, at the seamless red-sheened gold that plates her shoulder.

Marfisa returns, careful with the weight of the bowl, "How did you escape," she says.

"I stabbed him in the skull."

"The skull."

"It was what I could reach," says Ellen. Marfisa dunks a dish-towel in the bowl, wrings it out. Ellen reaches for her wrist. "I didn't finish it," she says. "He's still there."

A drip from the dishtowel into the bowl, plink. "There is truly nothing of Grandfather left," says Marfisa. She leans in to daub the sticky blood from Ellen's breast, gently but firmly lifting the stiffening panel of T-shirt out of her way. Ellen tips back her head, looks up, to the dull white popcorned ceiling, "He bit me," she says.

"Yes," says Marfisa, scrubbing, wiping, scrubbing again.

"So, will I," Ellen rocks a little, absently, with the force of Marfisa's ministrations, "do I turn into something like that?"

"No." Marfisa dunks the dishtowel, staining the water in the bowl. Wrings it out again.

"Why did you let me go there by myself?"

"You," says Marfisa, blotting blood from there, and there, "would not be stopped."

"I had no idea what I was in for."

"Now, you do." Marfisa dunks the towel again. "Now we can make a plan."

Ellen scoots back, out from Marfisa's clasp, hard up against the fridge, her bloodstained hand between them. "If I hadn't made it," she says, her affect flat, her tone unchanged. "If I'd bled out in the house. Passed out and crashed, driving back."

Marfisa shrugs in her sheepskin coat. "It would be a different plan. What do you want from this, Ellen?"

"Vengeance," she says, almost immediately.

"And what will you do to get it?"

Ellen blinks. Lowers her hand. Marfisa leans in, to daub and wipe once more. "I should meet your wizard, next," she says.

"I've got a phone number," says Ellen.

"Does she answer?" There's a knock at the door, three sharp raps. "It's open," calls Marfisa. "I don't know," Ellen's saying, "I haven't called it yet," but Marfisa's sitting back, looking up and over to the unopened door, "That hod," she mutters, "will not – "

Three knocks, again, but slow, deliberate booms that rattle the door in its frame. Marfisa gets to her feet, frowning.

"It's him," says Ellen Oh. "Isn't it."

The door bursts open, splintering the jamb. Chilli takes a big step into the room, his boots, his shorts, his big yellow beard, the short plain sword in his hand angled to catch a flare of light the vicious chop at his head by the bat in Marfisa's hand, "Ha!" Shifting her grip the bat twirls back around and up, a jab at his chest he thwarts with an awkward downward whack, the sound of bitten wood. He wrenches, levering the bat to spin it free of grip and blade to fly across the clattering fall to the floor, "Ho!" as he loops the point of his sword to hang in the air before her throat. "It's steel must meet with steel," he snarls. "Fetch my blasted sword."

Marfisa's focus flicks from blade-tip to countertop, the hilt there visible among the litter. "Go on!" he bellows. "Make a move. *Make* your *move.*"

"Harper!" calls someone else. The broken doorway's crowded, Gaveston squeezing through past Pwyll into the kitchen, and Meg a-loom behind them. "There's a gallowglas on the field," says Gaveston, pointing to Ellen, but Chilli's blade doesn't waver. "There's a gallowglas," says Gaveston, *"bleeding,* on the field."

"Changes nothing," spits Chilli.

"It changes *everything,*" says Gaveston. "Put up. Step back. We'll try again, some other day."

"Yeah," says Gradasso, even as Pwyll's making shushing motions, "we ought to," but "Shut *up!*" roars Chilli, fury shredded to the edge of a shriek, blade still aimed at Marfisa's throat. "Pick," he snaps. "Up. That. *Sword.*"

"No," says Marfisa.

"Ranh!" Blade-tip leaps, settles, both his hands on the hilt held high. "Fine," he says, and takes a step, sidelong, another, turning his way about the kitchen, his sword a spoke, Marfisa, motionless, the axle. "Fine," he says again, his eyes still locked with hers. Reaching back for the counter with his off hand, sightlessly clumsy, fumbling about to close over the hilt. Drawing the second sword scrape against the counter, a blade in either hand now, and both of them pointed at her. "You've ceded the field. Take off the coat."

"No," says Marfisa.

"Take it *off!*" The blades shake in his hands. A step toward her, another, those points lowering just to touch the fleece of the coat's wide collar, there, and there, at either end of her clavicle. "I will *have* my *coat,*" he says.

"You'll poke two more holes in it," says Marfisa. "Go on. Deny the Queen her Outlaw. Render me to bone."

Gaveston swallows. Gradasso in the doorway raises, lowers an empty hand. Ellen looks from Marfisa, still, unmoving, to Chilli, settling and resetting his grips about the hilts of those two swords. Floorboards creak, as out there Meg steps back.

"I have your sword," says Chilli.

"That?" says Marfisa, with a nod for the sword to her left, short and simply plain, his right hand clutching yellowed leather. "That I stuck in the floor of Goodfellow's house for all to see, and anyone to take, who'd need of it."

He presses forward, deepening the dimples in the fleece. She takes in a quick sharp breath through her nose. "You will," he says. "Quit, these rooms." Takes back a step. "Get yourself to that warehouse of clods and boobs, I don't care. Take your books, your boxes, all your trash," another step back, toward the door, blades in either hand still high, "but you will leave that blasted, rotten coat, you hear me?" Yellow beard stirred by his panting breath. "And if you *ever* show that horse's head again, anywhere south and east of the Burnside Bridge, I'll strike it from your shoulders to set before the Queen, gallowglas or no. Are we clear?"

Marfisa's lips suggest the slightest smile.

"Gah!" Chilli stamps, whips both swords up and back, over either shoulder, pushes out between Pwyll and Gradasso, who duck to avoid the steel. Gaveston slips after. Meg leans in to swing the door shut with a massive, green-knuckled hand.

"That was," says Ellen.

"Yes," says Marfisa, stooping to pick up her bat.

"I lost that mask," says Ellen.

"We'll get more," says Marfisa, thumbing the freshly rough-edged nick cut deeply in the barrel of the bat. "Don't touch," she says.

Ellen's hand leaps away from the gold encasing her shoulder. The edges of it have gone lacey, darkly soft, crumbling here and there to pepper her breast and upper arm with flecks. "Marfisa?" she says, looking up. "What's a gallowglas?"

That long and oval glass-topped table, covered over with the detritus of many hasty meals, crumpled paper napkins, plastic cups stacked and toppled, crushed, glass bottles that had once held soda, beer, kombucha, an unsteadily towering stack of emptied pizza boxes, and crumbs and dregs and half-dried spills. Bruno favors it all with a rueful smile. "It's gotten a bit out of hand," he says. "Cachaça?" Setting a burlapped bottle on a relatively uncluttered patch, and two squatly heavy glasses beside it.

"Sweetloaf could see to this, surely?" says Luys, pulling out a chair, as Bruno uncorks the bottle, sitting himself, as Bruno pours a glass, "Would this be the first call of an industrious morning for you," he says, offering it up, "or the last stop of a long and wearisome night?" Luys shakes his head. Bruno shrugs, sets down the glass, and pours more in the second, the liquor clear and thin, the burble of it highly pitched. "So," he says, and sits himself across from Luys, lifting the glass in a one-handed toast. "The meeting's yours."

Luys nods. His chamois shirt is rumpled, brown, unbuttoned at the throat, his black cap of hair discreetly tousled. "We ought," he says, "begin to, discuss, what each we see as possible," a breath, "roads," he says, "to rapprochement."

"But Mason," says Bruno, smiling and frowning at once, "surely, you and I are friends."

"Between her majesty," says Luys, with a skeptically sour tang, "and his excellency," and Bruno nods at that, mouthing a silent ah, "But why's it we, who ought to do this thing?" he says, and takes a sip.

"Who else is there who might?" says Luys. "The Marquess, and the Soames, being at each other's throat."

"The Guisarme and the Glaive are brothers yet."

"And doubtless seek roads of their own. Should our discussion bear fruit, we'll no doubt share with them."

"And vicey-versey, I suppose?" says Bruno. "The fruit of the roads we might glimpse," he mutters, and swallows off what's left.

"Your pardon?" says Luys.

Bruno leans out over the table to uncork the bottle. "What of our lady?" he says, and pours himself some more.

"Her grace?" says Luys. "She is where she is. We must steward her demesne, as best we can, till her return."

"We," says Bruno.

"Yes," says Luys.

"You and I," says Bruno.

Luys frowns. "If you would put it bluntly," he says, his hand closing up on the tabletop. "But we do both have our help."

"You've the men," says Bruno, pointing with his glass, "I, the matériel," drawing it back, "to put it bluntly." He throws back the liquor in one quick gulp. "Too blunt?" he says, to answer the quizzical turn of Luys's mien. Sets down the glass, clack. "North," he says, tapping to one side of it. "Northeast," the other, fingers and thumb pressed together. "Southwest," he says, tapping to the one side again, "Northwest," the other. "Mason," he says, but this time does not tap, that hand resting over the empty glass, "and Shrieve."

"You'd set us both at odds?"

"I was not the one to call this meeting," says Bruno.

"A meeting to *discuss!*" cries Luys, throwing up his hands.

"Discussion," says Bruno, "takes two. Two points of view. Two sides, as it were. Sat across a table. As for rapprochement, well: there must needs be a gap, between the two, to be rapproched."

"You'd have us set at odds," says Luys, shaking his head. "With all that's happened, with all we have to face, between the Viscount, and the Queen, you want – "

"You've sat in privy council with his excellency."

"And you the Queen!" Luys falls back in his chair. "That's what best fits us to this task – our vantage, jointly, is ideal, to scout what ground they hold in common, and, with our counsel, bend their ears to bend their steps to seek it."

"We'd bend?" says Bruno. "The Queen, the Viscount, you would have us bend?"

"Away from senseless dispute? Back toward stability? Peace? Prosperity?" Luys leans forward, both hands on the cluttered table. "Every day, Shrieve. Each and every day, you take two deals, two angles, hands, and play them, to the betterment of both. This is what you *do*. This is your duty."

"My duty's to the Queen," says Bruno, simply.

"By which you mean to say that mine is not."

A moment passes, during which Bruno neither nods, nor shakes his head. Then with a sudden savage swing of both his arms Luys sweeps boxes, napkins, bottles and cans tumble crashing spinning clatter from tabletop to floor. Scrape as he pushes back his chair. "It's much too early in the morning for such nonsense."

"No, Mason. It's far too late to play at comity."

Luys gets to his feet. "That's it, then?"

Bruno does not look up, or back, as Luys stalks around the foot of the table and out the trapezoidal room. He leans forward, then, to take hold of the other glass, still full, and drinks it down. "That might have been a wee bit premature," he says, to no one in particular. Eyes the glass in his hand, twisting it back and forth. Reaches for the bottle, but pushes it away. Something rings, somewhere out behind him. "Mason?" he says, and gets to his feet.

"Shopkeep!" bellows someone away out there, and Bruno closes up his eyes.

Out in the big front room, floor of it unpainted planks lined and aisled with overflowing bins of fittings and hardware sorted by type, past the file of unhung doors leaned one against another along the wall, there's the counter laden with Mason jars filled with keys, where the Harper Chillicoathe bangs a service bell with his fist, "Shopkeep!" he roars again, through laughter, "we'd have our wares inspected!" Pwyll and Gradasso to either side, arms folded, akimboed, Meg there in the vestibule, hands up to brace her weight against the lintel, Gaveston leaning in to nudge, to point out Bruno in the angled doorway. Chilli turns, thrusts up a hand gripped tight about the yellowed leather hilt of a short straight sword, "See what I have brought!"

"A sword," says Bruno, still in the doorway. "All of you it took, to bring a sword?"

"With this," Chilli shakes it, once, "I went and got *this* back!" Thrusting up his other hand, his own sword with its heavy golden pommel. "I *beat* her, Bruno. The Outlaw's been rebuked. She'll leave the rooms on Hawthorne and, I swear, won't *ever* try to raid our portion again."

Bruno looks down, adjusts his cuff, the link a small coin, brassy with a silver center, Good For One Fare, say letters stamped about the rim. "And it took all of you," he says, looking up again, "to bring this thing about."

Chilli lowers both his swords. "It's been done," he says. "What does it matter – "

"Where is her grace?" says Bruno, simply.

"I," says Chilli, "her grace, her grace is fine, I'm sure – "

"That's *not,*" says Bruno, "what I asked." Stepping into the room, past a bin of filigreed hinges, "Where," he says, past a bin of coppery lock plates, "at this precise moment," up the aisle toward Chilli, "might I go," as Gradasso steps to one side, out of the way, "to find her grace," as Pwyll ducks into the vestibule with Meg, "the Duchess of Southeast," as Gaveston steps back, "Widow of the Hawk, Queen's Favorite," as Chill, blades crisscrossed before him, glowers, "where is Jo Gallowglas," says Bruno, "and why, under all the stars above, are you not watching over her, right now?"

A FOLDER NOT TERRIBLY THICK – MOTORVATION
LUSH WHITE SHAG

IT'S NOT A TERRIBLY THICK FOLDER she drops on the table, just a handful of freshly printed pages in a crisp blue jacket. Beside it she sets a spiral-bound stenographer's pad and two ballpoint pens, clack, tack, and last, a short brown paper cup with the tags of a couple of teabags peeping from under its white plastic lid. Scrape as she pulls out a chrome-framed black-cushioned chair, creak as she settles her bulk in it. Her slacks a slickly brown, her half-zip pullover softly grey, her silver hair close-cropped. She opens the jacket, flips back the cover of the stenographer's pad, takes up a pen, click-lick, click-lick, and squints at the woman across the battered table from her, younger, smaller, downright scrawny, wrists manacled to a bracket welded to the tabletop, arms bared and shoulders, shivering, dressed only in filthy jeans and a grey bralette, her hair-colored hair a matted, tangled curtain dropped before her face.

"Chilly?" says the silver-haired woman. Not even a clink of the cuffs in response.

"Okay!" Another click-lick of the pen. "This is Detective Sally Bauer, Bee Ay You Ee Are, on the Homicide Detail. Date is Friday, twenty-fifth May; time, oh-seven eighteen hours; case number," and here she checks the first page of the file, "two seven two, four nine eight. We are currently in an interview room in the confines of the Portland Police Bureau, Eleven Eleven Southwest Second, on the thirteenth floor." Turning a page. "State your name for the record." Looking up. That curtain of hair not even stirred by a breath.

"This strong and silent schtick won't get you anywhere, okay? We took your prints. You're in the system? We'll know who you are in not too much longer. You're not? Though, I gotta tell you, to look at you, this is not your first rodeo. Folks who, it's their first time? Never been through this before? Tend to be a little more," a shrug, "agitated."

A shiver strong enough to chime the manacles.

"You want a blanket?" Turning another page. "Cup of coffee?" Lifting the lid of the paper cup to hoist and dunk the teabags. Replacing the lid. "Give me a name. That way, when your people call, they can be told where you are, what's going on. You do have people?"

Removing the lid, setting it upside down on the table, she lifts out the teabags, squeezes them with a wince, drops them on the lid. Licks her thumb clean. "Look, the facts so far, not many of them, but, as-is, they're not bad for you. Play straight with me, everything checks out, you don't blow off Recog, you could be out of here by two, three o'clock in the afternoon. Not every day someone comes in with a body can say that." Turning another page. "Before we get any further in this, were you Mirandized? Because the form is here, but quelle surprise, it's unsigned." A heavy sigh. "So, out of an abundance of caution. You. Have the right to remain silent. Anything you say can and will be used against you in a court of law; you have the right to an attorney. If you cannot afford an attorney, one will be provided for you. Do you understand these rights as I have read them to you?" Shuff as she flicks the page across the table to fetch up by the bracket. "Here," tugging another pen from a pocket of her pullover, chucking it wobble to land with a limply flop on the page. "Gotta use one of those to sign it."

Not a twitch from the hands on the other side of the bracket, streaked with dirt about the knuckles, the yet-green smear of a grass stain.

"I get it. Shit happens, in those camps. They aren't safe. Big guy like that jumps you, in the dark? And maybe, we find out who he is, we find out he was off his meds, or should've been on some in the first place. There's a gun. It goes off. You walk away; he doesn't. It's self defense, straight up. Cut and dried. So help me get it over the line. Give me something. Tell me. Is that, how it, went down?"

Sitting back, with a creak, in her chair. Folding her arms. Waiting. Watching, until, click-lack, she leans forward, drags the piece of paper back to her side of the table. Marks an x at the bottom, scrawls the date beside it. Stacks it with the other pages, taps them into a neat bundle, slips them into the jacket. "Oh seven twenty-two," she says. "My shift ends at eight, which means about nine, nine-thirty, I should be done enough to get out of here, get a Denver omelet in me, get home and sleep for not nearly enough." Scrape of the chair she pushes back. "So if this is all it's gonna be?" Getting to her feet, closing the cover of the unused stenographer's pad. "I'd just as soon be getting that whole process jump-started. So." Tucking away her pens. "Your only chance of getting back on the street anytime today is about to walk out the door."

"I did," says the woman then, and Bauer starts at that, but blinking keeps any surprise off her face, "whatever it was I did."

That head lifting, tilting, matted hair falling away from her face, those thin pale lips, that nose, the mud-colored eyes. "You're telling me what's gonna happen because of what I did, it depends on how I talk to you, right here, right now."

"It tells me what kind of person you are," she says, "which, yeah, goes a long way toward figuring out what needs to happen."

"Doesn't sound much like justice."

Sally snorts. "Sister, all anybody ever can do is work the problem in front of them. Justice has to sort itself out in the wash. You said, it's mine. What were you talking about?"

Those flat eyes look away.

"It's the only thing in Dunbar's report that you said, to anybody. First on the scene, that's what you said to him: it's mine. What did you mean? What's yours?" A moment, a blink. "The gun?"

That head lowers, hair falling strands and hanks a curtain once again. Sally looks away, a grimace of chagrin. "All right," she says. "Fine," she says, and heads for the door. "The interview is over." Knocks loudly, twice. "Someone will be along to take you back down to Holding, in a bit." Somewhere without a bolt's undone, a knob is turned. "I'll see you again in a couple of days, I'm sure."

Head down, hood lowered, a soft green mantle about his shoulders, hands stuffed in his pockets, his running shoes once blue that take relentlessly one step after another, he makes his way down the block, across the street, down the next, past trim little bungalows in unassuming colors, and parked on the street before them bantamweight SUVs and beefy hatchbacks, many with ski racks or bicycle racks or ærodynamic carryalls fixed to their roofs. The sidewalk ahead's blocked by thrown-together panels of chain-link to fence off a construction site, hung about with signs that say Apartments Coming September, Crutchfield Evans, Anaphenics, No Parking This Space. He steps into the narrow walkway protected from the street by Jersey barricades in orange and white, down to the corner, across the next inter-section, without looking up or back.

Past the construction, more estate cars and bungalows, but also minivans and older sedans, and here and there houses more recently built, flatter, the windows of them duller, yards meaner, and what trees they have are yet too small to settle down behind. Music wafts his way, echoing chime of piano chords over a crisply languid beat. Up ahead, across the street, a half-dozen or so young men, boys, talking and laughing, shoving, mac 'n' cheese an a snotty nose, Motel 6, lame trappin an some shoddy hoes, somebody blows a cloud of smoke, somebody twirls away, dropping in a complicated tuck and stretch to a clap and a slap and an *ah*-ha, oh yeah. His shoulders hunch even higher to carry him on past, deliberately refusing to wince as the laughter redoubles, rising, joining, becoming a ragged revving chorus on the beat, *unh*-huh, *unh*-huh, ha-ha! and very much without looking like he's looking up or around he eyes the street behind him. A delivery tricycle's trundling up, big yellow box over the back two wheels behind the saddle, This trike eats hunger for breakfast, says the slogan on the side of it, Ask our rider about B-shares. The cyclist pedaling furiously, bright green helmet and a blue rainshell, "Go on!" one of the young men shouts, and "Fuck yeah, motorvate!" another, and "I *think* I can I *think* I can" over a couple of chorused chugga-chuggas that all dissolves in general hilarity. The cyclist's left hand lifts, bent at an angle, and the trike wheels into a right turn.

Head down, he keeps on.

A block or so later he darts across the street to the corner, the cross street here narrow, a low rise closely lined with smaller houses, cars and trucks parked heel-by-nose to either side. He heads down the slender single lane that's left between them, past here and there a tell-tale yellow envelope of a parking ticket tucked under the wipers, and pasted on a windshield there a faded green label, Tow Warning, it says, PBOT. One door, two doors, three doors down, and he comes to a stop, there in the middle of the street, his narrow cheekbones hunched much like his shoulders.

The house is small, pale green, the front of it mostly a shallow gable swooping to shelter a front door the color of cinnamon, and pushing up from the little porch before it to waddle down those concrete steps a portly brindle pit bull.

He squeezes sidelong between bumpers, around the blue garbage bin on the curb to kneel there, on the sidewalk, at the edge of the yard. "Goose?" he says, putting out his hand, and the dog's tail wags hard enough to unbalance its mincing hastening. "How'd you get to be so old?" The dog leans into his proffered hand, tongue-lollingly beaming at the scritches.

"You know him?"

He takes a moment, and a breath, before looking up. "He's just a good dog."

She's small, the woman on the porch, small enough her up-swept bun of honey-silver hair seems too ponderous for the rest of her, draped in a shapeless purple sweater. "About the only person," she says, "Gustav ever tolerated that from," scratching her chin, "was my boy." Folding up her arms.

His scritching's shifted to stroking, a couple of pats. "That so."

"Christian," she says. And then, "Beaumont. My son, though you wouldn't think it to look at him. Such a beautiful boy. You know him?"

A careful shrug, without exactly nodding, or shaking his head. "Did, ah," he says, eyes on the dog gazing blissfully up at him, "did something happen?"

"He was always running off," she says. "But he always came back. A wild boy, but not that wild. A few days, a week, at most." He's stopped stroking, but Gustav's tail still wags. "Been gone all winter, though. Eight months, now, this time. He sure has taken a shine to you."

He looks up again, blinking once, twice, to meet those pale grey eyes like water, like ice, faintly stern, vaguely suspicious. "I'm sure," he says, and swallows, and starts again, "I'm sure, wherever he is, your son, he's, he's doing fine, just fine."

"That so," she says. "Well. I think, now, maybe, you best be about your business."

"Yes ma'am," he says, getting to his feet. The pit bull gathers himself for a single baritone bark. "Gustav!" she chides.

"It's okay, Goose," he says. "You stay. You be a good boy."

She comes down a step or two, eyeing him as he heads past the garbage bin, away on down the sidewalk, hands in his pockets. Gustav still there at the edge of the yard, tail flagging, musters up one more bark. "Gustav," she calls, still watching. "Get on back here."

He sits up of a sudden, in that big round bed in the middle of the room, legs tangled in linens crisply striped with indigo. Leans forward, head in his hands, hands the heels of them rub at his eyes, shift as he sits up, slide down his cheeks, the faint rasp of yesterday's stubble, lifting to push back what's left of his hair.

He swings down his feet from the edge of the bed, bare feet that nestle in white shag carpet. Elbows on knees, bare knees, his head hung low. Up and standing then, all at once, stepping away from the bed toward the sweeping wall of glass. The sun is somewhere behind this room, blazing with daylight the city below, houses and low buildings across the bright river, traffic busy lined and crossed in a grid half-swallowed by green unruly overgrowth, and along this bank the towers of downtown deceptively sharp, brittle façades that shuffle themselves until it's difficult to pick out the shape entire of this brick ziggurat, that slit-windowed tower, and so many panes of cool rain-colored glass, and only the one lone tower of pinkly amber granite behind them all defiantly itself, windows of it struck to copper by the light.

Turning away.

The bed, in the middle of the room, striped sheets rucked and crumpled there, and the pillows where his head had lain, more pillows stacked beside them neatly, and the crease and drape of the sheets there undisturbed. Two small nightstands, one to either side, the tops of them both bare, and an empty stretch of thick white carpet, and the wall behind, a palely neutral blue that's almost white, the door there, left ajar, the shadowed hall beyond.

That hall jogs round a corner past a couple of closed doors to open out into an empty kitchen, unlit, dim haven from the dazzle of more white shag beyond, another wall of glass too bright. He leans a hand against the bare kitchen island and watches the big man move through all that daylight, stepping into a long low lunge of a stretch, twisting his torso the one way, the other, as he lifts both his arms out and up to the height of those thickset shoulders, muscles rolling and sliding along his broad bare back as he quite slowly supinates the one hand, pronates the other, looking away off to that side, and then just as slowly turns them about as his head twists to look the other way. Lowering his hands, then, straightening to his considerable height, iron-colored hair close-cropped, mustaches lush and long, gathered to either side of his close-lipped mouth by rough-hewn beads of pewter, and only a pair of snug white briefs about his hips. They share a look for one long wordless moment, and then those mustaches spread in a simple, guileless smile. "You remember," says the big man.

"I remember last night," he says, "astonishing enough. I remember," trailing off. He doesn't pull his hand away when it's taken gently in that larger, rougher hand. "I don't know what happened to my clothes," he says.

"Ah," he says, still smiling. "They're being found, retrieved, and seen to."

"Found," he says, looking away. "Is there any coffee?"

"There can be," he says, "and we have the makings of simple omelets, if you'd like," but he doesn't let go, and he doesn't pull away. They stand there, hands clasped, on either side of the corner of the island.

"I remember last night, and the carnival," he says, "and I remember you swore. You swore you'd keep me safe."

"And here you are," he says, "and you are safe."

"I remember forgetting you," he says, looking up again, looking back to him again, until he looks down, away, those weighted mustaches swaying. "I remember," he says, "how *much* I forgot," blinking rapidly as he looks back up to him, but he doesn't pull his hand away, he squeezes instead, and closes his eyes, and tips down his head. Lets him turn that hand over, lets a thickly grey-furred thumb stroke the back of it gently, once, twice.

"Well," he says then, thickly. "I'll have to make certain that never happens again." And he lifts that hand, to press a kiss to the back of it. To squeeze it with his own, another kiss parting his lips about the knuckles, a step to the side as he steps to the side, the corner no longer between them, pressing close, arms folded hands clasped between them as their lips meet in a kiss.

"MINE IS THE HAND!" – SALT *&* IRON, AND THE HEAT
A BRUTALIST LANDMARK – THIS IS HOW

"MINE IS THE HAND!" a howl from somewhere above. He looks away from the wide room ahead, back to the closed front door, the kitchen lemon-bright to one side, stairwell to the other, winding its way up. "Mine, the hand that writes upon the wall the name of God!" He swallows. Adjusts the knot in his tie of burgundy blue.

"Six are the wings unfolded from my face, and six times do they beat, and from them do I draw my quill! My ink!" That voice pummels the close walls as he climbs. "My ink the very dregs from your cups, and with it do I tally your numbers, many and all. Seven! Seven the wings that beat about my breast, but numberless the eyes within, and from them will I bring the scales that I must use to weigh you all, and find what you are wanting!"

He stops there, a handful of steps from the top, head down.

"Mine the mouth, to sheathe the burning blade! I am the one to draw it forth, when comes the time, and times, and the dividing of time!"

He resumes his climb, around and up into a ravaged hall, the carpet raked and tattered, crumpled walls smeared and splotted with ruddy brown. Two long ungainly feathered arms too skinny for the swollen hands at the ends of them, fleshy anchors twitching uselessly amongst fallen feathers and gypsum dust, and sat atop, a white-crowned pink-cheeked head, "My teeth, of iron! My nails of brass! I will devour, and break into pieces, and stamp the residue with my feet!" Spittle flecks those lips with foam, and spittle and tears shine the cheeks beneath wetly blazing eyes. "I will kill you all with death!" And jutting from the temple, he blinks to see it, the short plain handle of a knife, pale wood and two dull rivets smeared with blood, or something like it. "Minister to me! A thousand thousands, ten thousand times ten thousand stand!"

"Did you bring it?" says the Viscount Agravante, knelt at the other's side, stripped to his shirtsleeves. "Rhythidd?"

"What?" he says, and "yes, of course," lifting a heavy sack of blue velvet from a pocket. "Eagles and vultures," the other's muttering, "ravens and kites, and dogs. And owls."

"Go on, then," says Agravante.

"Yes," he says, "of course, I should," fastidiously hitching his trousers at the knee to kneel there, by the other. He tugs the sack open, and a horrid squeal wrenches from that jerking throat, "No! No! You cannot, will not, must not, no!" Rhythidd rears back from a skinny outthrust elbow rattling with pinions. Agravante leans his weight on fragile shoulders heaving, struggling to lift those uselessly enormous hands, "The blade, the pain, it's cold but clear, that clarity is all, but gold? Dehab?" struggling, those wet eyes widen as Rhythidd tips out a palmful of brilliant dust, "That honey's too, too warm, voluptuously sweet, do not, do not, you must not!" struggling uselessly.

"Go on," says Agravante, stark.

"The flakes of my flesh are joined together, shut up as with a close seal," the other, trembling with the effort of trying to lift that round little body those long frail arms against Agravante's weight, "my very, nostrils, seething smoke," twisting with a grimace from Rhythidd's shining hand, "and my eyes," a grunt, as Agravante shifts to free up a hand to grip that chin, those cheeks, to yank that head, turning the hilt back down beneath the gold, "the eyelids of morning," a mutter squelched by pinch-squeezed lips. Rhythidd tips his hand to trickle a shining thread that spilling loops about the hilt, the black and sticky crust, hissing to fill the wound. "Sorrow!" a yelp, and one last straining push from those wrong-braced slender arms, "withers to joy at my feet!" as the last of the gold falls from Rhythidd's palm.

"The blade," says Agravante.

"My lord?" says Rhythidd.

With a snarl for Rhythidd's consternated frown, Agravante plants a knee in the other's belly, seizes the jutting hilt, though there's no struggle now, no strain, just a drawn-out sigh as he draws it forth. Agravante sits back in a crackling flump of feathers, dropping that little knife. "More," he says.

"My lord," says Rhythidd, hoisting the sack. "There is no more."

"It's gone? All of it, gone?"

"Unless you wish to claw back what's been portioned."

"Even your Champoeg vault?"

"My lord," says Rhythidd, "we *must* maintain reserves, in case of an, emergency," starting, as with a plosive gasp Agravante giggles, a shivering mirthless whining laugh he stops up with the back of his hand.

"Actually," the other says, "I'm already feeling much better." Those hands, drawn back, no longer quite so large, as feathers drop from pimpled, thickening arms. "More myself."

"There," says Rhythidd, slumped against the crumbling wall, loose feathers lofted about the hand he lifts to his forehead. "Now, we might have this," an airy gesture, at the wreckage all about, "dealt with."

"Feel free," says Agravante, tipping back his head, his long white dreads in sagging disarray.

"My lord," says Rhythidd, consternation curdling. "I've no one here to see to it."

"You came alone?"

"I even drove myself," says Rhythidd. "On this, you were quite clear, and firm."

"Then we are as you see us. Mix up the plaster and find us a trowel."

"There's no one here, but us? What of the Princess?"

Agravante looks away, down the hall, the door at the end there, padlock shut upon its hasp. "Safe, for the nonce. You'd have her take up a broom?"

"Excellency," says Rhythidd, taken aback.

"His grace," says Agravante, "got greedy."

"The *hell* I did," snarls the other, sitting up with a grimace. "Horse-headed *asshole* was the one did this, only it wasn't your bitch of a sister." Pointing an arm foreshortened to smears of blood dried dark, dragged down cracked and broken plaster. "That? Ain't mine. Though it would've been. Should have been." That arm joining the other wrapping both to cradle a belly pinkly wrinkled. "I had her in my *mouth*. Salt, and iron. And the *heat,*" that last word folded in a drawn-out groan.

"I should, perhaps," says Rhythidd, but, "A moment," says Agravante, a hand up in forbearance over the clenched and rocking figure of the other, who coughs, a laugh, "I'm more, myself, yes, but," those small eyes squeezing shut, "not entirely. Candy floss." Nostrils flare. Those eyes pop open. "Better'n nothing."

"I must see to her highness." Agravante stands, brushing feathers from his trousers.

Those eyes, that regard, woozily unfocused, turns to take in Rhythidd, who shifts his feet, but does not get to them, who lifts a hand, but does not sit up. He skews his necktie in a brusque attempt to straighten it. "I should," he says, but doesn't, his expression, clarifying, scums over with a greasy sheen of horror as the other, featherless, slumps forward, pushes up, on hands and knees. That white hair has resumed its wild corona, matted only a bit there by the ear, where what gold's left drifts dustily to gleam a burgeoning shoulder. "My lord," says Rhythidd, trying again. "This is not your grandfather."

"This is necessary," says Agravante, halfway down the hall.

"What of," says Rhythidd, flinching as the other's hand crumples the shoulder of his jacket, clinging, "my brother's portion? How can you," as the other seizes his tie, "what will you, what will you!" as a grey-pink tongue slips out to wet those pale pink lips. "Without me," says Rhythidd. "He won't give it to you without me!"

"We'll make do," says Agravante, reaching for the padlock. "At the moment, it's come down to you, or me. My position's," looking back, "understandable."

"Please," says Rhythidd, the word stretched to a whisper.

The other chuckles, once. Feet kick, a briefly tumult in the feathers, and then the dull tock of a bit of bone, dropped to the carpet.

Ding the microwave, she opens the door of it, reaches in with a hot pad for a steaming yellow mug that says Ray of Fucking Sunshine. In she dunks a bright red seahorse infuser, dandling its delicate chain a moment. Color seeps.

Out of the kitchen, across the living room, dark wood paneling, grey-green shag, shuff of her bare feet into a shadowy nook of a hall. Nudging open a door into a small room filled with watery cloudy light from a sliding glass door, framed to either side by heavy curtains drawn. Around the foot of the great wide bed, messily unmade, to stand there by the glass, satiny tap pants in an antique beige and a scarf about her shoulders like a shawl. Sips her tea. Her hair's been shorn to a yellow fuzzing the curve of her skull.

Lopped open on the bed a bright blue rolling duffel, and stuffed within it, spilling out of it over the rumpled duvet, scraps and shreds of satin, silks, clouds of tulle and filmy lace, diaphanous rayons, workaday nylon and lycra in competitive colors, here and there white cotton knit. Setting her tea aside she turns to it, shoving this bit in, tossing that out, whirl of dangling straps, clatter of fasteners striking the wall. Leaping up onto the bed to step across it, angry squonk of springs, she drops to the narrow space on the other side. Shelves there, opposite the glass, haphazardly piled with more clothing, and she seizes handfuls of leggings, T-shirts, stuffing them heedlessly into the duffel, snags a translucent tub filled with balled-up socks, dumps them in after.

Outside, a bug-eyed little hatchback, bright red with racing stripes, swings into the space before the glass. She opens the passenger door, climbs out, transparent raincoat over a neon bandeau, baggily shredded jeans. Under the glassy hood, her yellow hair's cut short in back to swoop in lengthening, asymmetric sheaves about her face. She watches, for a moment, the room through the glass, before stepping up to rap it, smartly, with a knuckle.

She looks up from the duffel to see her there, without. Sets off around the bed, not over it, stooping before the glass door to pry something up, a sawn-off broomstick from the bottom rail, then straightening yanks on the unmoving handle, and again, rolling her eyes as on the other side of the glass she's pointing to the latch that, clutching the scarf about her shoulders, she's already undoing. The door slides open with an effortful squeal.

"May I come in?" she says.

"You still live here," she says, turning away.

"I, ah," she says, stepping within. "You cut your hair."

"Got tired of not remembering how long it was, on any given day." She shoves another handful of stuff in the duffel.

"We hadn't seen you, at the warehouse. Not since – "

"I haven't been to the warehouse. I got *this* done," a hand, lifted to her yellow fuzz, "at Rudy's, on Division. Paid Bethany seventeen dollars, plus a five-dollar tip. And you don't even know their names."

She draws back. "What?"

"When you went behind the screen, for the, coat, your hair, the, the jeans, what is that, cybergrunge? Did you ask for that, like, specifically? Or was it more of a dealer's choice?"

She looks down, transparent coat a-crinkle. "Aigulha," she says. "And Costurere. Of course I know their names."

"Well," she says. "You did fuck them."

"Is, is that what this is about?" Shaking her head. "That can't be what this is about."

"We *swore*," she says, that word shored up with something like cold steel, "we were *never* going to do," a breath, "that," she says, "again."

And at that, some uncertainty slips from the set of her shoulders. "It takes two to tango," she says, without smiling, and yet.

"But only one to wallflower." And then, before she can respond, "I push too far, you pull back, that's the balance, that's how we," turning suddenly away, resettling the scarf about her shoulders.

250

"Did you come here to get something, or," wadding up a scrap of lace, stuffing it in the duffel.

"I told you," she says, gently. "It's been a couple of days. You haven't answered your phone."

"I need to charge it," she snaps.

"Where are you going?" she says then, small and quiet.

She shakes out what she's holding, spandex tights the color of lemon sherbet, rolls them tightly to lay them atop the pile in the duffel. "LA," she says. "Reg knows somebody who knows somebody in Westwood, up in the hills. It's a landmark, of Brutalist architecture, he says. Anyway. Cameron's shooting there, next week."

"Prescott?"

"Dameshek."

"Wow. Just you?"

A shrug. "Three or four other girls. You know how it goes." She plucks out something, ivory satin edged with lace, and lets the scarf slip from her shoulders. "Flight's at four. It's only sixty bucks." Lifts it over her head to slip it on, a camisole.

"That's a one-way price," she says, once more small, and quiet. And then, shaking her head, "We're shooting next week, too. We got the show."

"Ah," she says, looking through the glass to the car without. The driver's still behind the wheel, anonymously hooded, a silhouette through the rain-spangled windscreen. "Turned out twins were enough, huh?"

"I'm sure he could make it work, if – "

"What about *our* show, Chris?"

"It could," she says, "still be three."

"Strippers," she says. "At an Exhibition. Remember? All our plans? What it was we were gonna do to take the world by the balls?"

"Pictures," she says, "at an Ecdysis."

"*Who cares!* Huh? Is it ever gonna happen, now? Ever?"

Staring then, glaring, each at the other, the one of them heaving angry breaths, the other preternaturally still. "What about the Queen?" she says.

"Oh," she sneers, "I think you got that covered." But then, blinking rapidly, she turns away, a shake of her head, hands casting about to settle on the duffel, close up the flap, zip it shut. "And anyway," she says. "I can't blow off Cameron Dameshek."

"You told him about the hair?"

"He knows about the hair. He likes the hair. You should maybe try it, next time you're in for a glow-up." Hauling the duffel off the bed, setting it upright on the floor.

"Stef," she says, her hand on the handle of the glass door. Looking up, across the bed, to her. "I love you," she says.

"Sure," she says. "Like that's got fuck-all to do with anything."

His one shoe propped on the pallet, nylon that might've been blue, and silver stripes long since gone lustreless, hands stuffed in the pockets of his oversized hoodie, green and softly new, he looks out over the great wide knee-high tub, bound about by riveted iron, wide enough his skinny arms stretched wide could never reach across it. Over on the other side, sharp Jenny Rye steps up, her dutiful scowl underlit by gold to shift and soften into something no less stern, but gone's all trace of pettiness, or of ressentiment. She favors him with a nod of recognition that startled he returns, and then she leans out to scrape a teacup through all that golden dust, draws it up to wave beneath her nose, careful of her chin, savoring something about it before she tucks it teacup and all away in a pocket of her coveralls. Up steps Brether Ned, ponderously kneeling to dip a hand, pinch up a goodly amount between spatulate fingers and thumb that he drizzles into an opened handkerchief, and paint-spattered Getulos, dunking a stripped tin can, and Trucos behind him, holding out both hands for what Getulos lets spill.

He shifts his shoe from off the pallet to squat, lean over, reach within but not to touch, the back of his closed fist no more than an inch above that warmly golden light. Unfolding his fingers, haze-edged silhouettes almost lost in the brilliance. Cheekbones hunching, he squints at the inside of the wall of the tub. Splays his hand along the oaken staves bound tightly, uncaulked, one against another. Difficult to make out in the effulgence, but a glimmer grits the gloss of the wood, up from the tip of his little finger, there, just above the burning surface, up and up to about the end of his thumb, a bit yet below the lip of it. He drags a fingertip up against the wood, gets to his feet as he eyes it judiciously, the pale pad glittering, granules of gold trapped in the whorls of the print. Turning away from the tub he nearly crashes clank and chime into a short woman peering thickly at him, leather jacket and something, a great big sword leaned up against her shoulder, "Hey," she says, "buddy, you okay?" He waves her off with his other hand, ducking his shoulders to swerve away, the one hand still held up to his nose, his mouth, his lips, that glimmering finger brushing his

"oh," says Christian Beaumont, turning to look back at that wide and shining tub, out in the middle of it all.

"Okay, everybody!" calls the woman with the great big sword. "Gather round! It's here, folks, it's here! Go on, open those up," one hand balancing the weight of the scabbard, pointing with the other to the stalls along the wall, the overhead doors in each of them, some of them already open, some rattling up as she's calling, and hands hasten to open up the rest, "let's go, everybody, here she comes, it's here!"

Down from the walkway above the empty, unlit stage, Gloria Monday's making her way down the skeletal stairs, baggy sweatshirt and knee-length purple tights, her bangs dyed freshly pink. She stoops under the rising big overhead door there, and everybody follows, out through the stalls and doors to the loading dock outside.

A battleship of a pickup's parked on the street, snugged right up next to the dock, black paint gleaming, dealer's sticker still pasted in a window. Hiked up over the tailgate a gooseneck hitch hooked to a long and empty flatbed trailer, clad in corrugated steel. Gloria nimbly leaps from dock to trailer, clang of the impact, "Okay!" she shouts. "All right." Lifting her arms to address them all, a benediction, an adjuration, a conductor's imperation, or a conjurer's. "This?" she says, "all of you, here, now?" and those upraised hands close in fists of acclamation, "this is *not* what I had in mind!" Those hands clap together, pop! "But that's okay! That's okay. This is not what *I* made, not at all. It's what we *all* have made, together," quick shake of her head, spreading her hands, allegro, vivace, she bulls her way through, "the, art, the food, the, the home! That we have made. The community! That we have all, together. It's, a wonderful thing! A wondrous thing." Lowering her hands, clenched again in fists, ritenuto. "And it should be *celebrated*. It should be seen! And this?" stepping back, to one side, "this is how," a sweeping gesture, mostrare, for the shining flatbed stretched beneath her feet, *"this* is how we make that happen!"

Some of them already coming down off the loading dock, the stairs there, and there, the ramp at the end, or just dropping down to the street, running their hands over shining corrugations, inspecting the hitch, the grimly oversized grille of the truck, and Big Jim leaning an elbow out the window of it, grinning under his thick mustache. "One week from today, from tonight!" Gloria's saying, "Downtown! The Rose Festival's gonna crescendo with the Starlight Parade! And *this?"* Clangingly stomping the flatbed. "This is gonna be *our float!* We are gonna ride *this,"* another stomp, "into the parade! Into *legend!* So! Start thinking up what we might wanna do, here. What are we gonna build? What's it gonna be? It could be, anything. *Anything.* Sky's the limit. Whatever you need to make it happen, lumber, lights, giant buckets of papier-mâché, I don't know, truckloads of flowers, tell me! And I will make! It! Happen!" Fists waved over her head, but faltering, lowering herky-jerkily, frowning at the lack of applause, the dearth of enthusiasm, the wholesale shift of attention from her, and the truck, and the trailer, to something, someone stepping out from under the big overhead door, dressed in loosely flowing whites, black curls undone, the Queen, making her way implacably through the crowd as it bustles to part before her, with curtsies, and with bows, heads ducked, hands folded, with fingers lifted to murmuring lips, with eyes that shine. She holds a hand up warily, as if to indicate her intended path, the palm of it and the fingers slathered with gold, and her gold-dipped feet are bare. She passes without comment or acknowledgement, down to the ramp at the end of the dock, white robe lofting behind her as she strides off down the street, each step a golden print to mark the dull black tarmacadam, and all the crowd left awestruck as she goes.

"What the hell was that," says Gloria Monday.

"You know, you know" – Exfiltration
a Failure of simile

"You know," she says, "you know, where it comes from. You know. You know. I had the papers. I had them. The, the, the, injections, the vaccinations, they don't, they don't inoculate, they don't, no, no! They don't, they don't put anything in, they don't they don't, they, sugar water. That's all. Sugar. Water. I had the papers. No," pushing back her hair, shoving back, down, stiffly crackle of too much old product, "no, what they do, what they do, they're taking *out*. They're taking it out. They're taking out," leaning close, "the *blood*."

Jo clutches a rough green blanket close about her shoulders, shifts away on the bright steel bench. Leans back against the slick-tiled wall. Closes her eyes again.

"I had the papers. I *had* the papers. They took my papers, they took, they *took* them. The papers proved it. The papers proved it, in a court of law. A court of law. They take the blood, they use the needles, they use needles to take the blood because they're scary, because needles are scary, they scare you to get the fight or flight, *fight*, or *flight*, to juice the blood, juice the blood with *adrenaline*, excite the adrenergic receptors, the papers, they took my papers, they took my papers and my laces." Shuffle-flop of undone shoe about a restless foot. "Fight or flight. Fight or flight. It burns adrenaline, it burns the adrenaline, tightening muscles, dilating pupils, juicing the blood, isozymes and transferases, it was in the papers. They took my papers. To burn the adrenaline. Burn it right up. Ox-i-dize it. Carbon. Hydrogen. Nitrogen. Oxygen, whoosh to juice the blood, they take it, they take it, they inject the sugar water, carbon, hydrogen, oxygen tangled, aitch-two-oh, they inject it so they can *out*ject, eject, *take* the blood, burning blood, adrenochrome, adrenochrome."

Jo opens her eyes. The woman at the other end of the bench sags forward, elbows on knees, ragged hem of torn-off jeans, grease-stained yellow blouse, light brown hair like straw. "Adrenochrome," she says, once more, her hands a-dangle below her lowered face. Across the room, past the empty steel bench stretched down the middle of it, the third steel bench against the opposite wall, three women side-by-side, puffy vest, vinyl skirt, cartoonish orange hair, baggy trousers, hiss and snap of a bubble of gum, slow whining whisper of a welling snore.

"It's pink," says the woman beside her, and the gum-chewer rolls her eyes. "It's pink, when it's first extracted, it's pink, but if you burn it, if you burn it, I had pictures, in my papers, they took my papers, but it's pink until you burn it, when you burn it, it turns brown, and then it's black, a sheet of black, but not like ash, it shines, ash doesn't shine, you burn it black until it shines, sticky and black and spread out on trays to shine and when you hit it," smack! of her fist against her palm, and the snoring woman starts awake. "When you hit it," she swings her fist again, stopping short of her palm, wavering there, relaxing, opening, "it shatters," she says. "And you hit it, and you hit it," clap, clap, "and you grind it, to a powder, when you do, it turns to silver, silver powder, piles and piles of silver powder. That's why they do it, for the powder. Juice the blood for silver, that's how lizards live forever. I had papers. I had the papers, in my folders, but they took them. They took my papers, and my pictures, and my laces, took my *belt*, they took the *blood!* Fight or flight to juice the blood, burn the juice for silver powder, I had the papers, you know I had the papers, it's all in my papers, that's the proof." Rocking on the bench, one hand reached across to clutch, to knead her shoulder, "You know," she's saying. "You know where it comes from. I had the papers. It's all in there. That's why they took it. Fight or flight, the needles, juice the blood.

Crush it into silver, sugar water. Sugar." Her rocking slows. She takes a deep and gentling breath. "You know," she says, and closes her eyes.

Jo opens hers, essays a sidelong look. The woman, still holding her shoulder with a slackening hand, crisp-haired head tipped back against white tiles, asleep. Shifting, working her head back and forth, Jo stretches out her legs, up her arms, lunging to catch the blanket as it slips. Looking about. She frowns.

The three women across the room, the one in the puffy ski vest, her head's tipped forward chin on chest, the one in the middle, knees jackknifed, hiking that vinyl skirt, she's sagged to one side, pillowed on the shoulder of the third, her head tipped back, cartoon orange bouffant crushed against the tiles, the snuffle of a snore resumed. She's asleep. They're all asleep.

Jo gets to her feet, paper slippers crinkling. Out into the space between benches, past the toilet and the sink there, dulled hunks of stainless steel obscenely sprouted from the wall, up to the thick round bars of the door of the cell. Taking hold she presses close, looks out into the hall, blank cinderblocks of a white that seems at once dingy and freshly painted, speckled linoleum scuffed and scarred, to the left, the right, she starts. Somebody's slumped on the floor there, a woman in a uniform of clashing greens, legs splayed out at an awkward angle like the truncheon from her duty belt, eyes shut, unconscious, asleep, maybe asleep.

The bars thrum under her hands with a weighty thunk, she lets go, steps back, a clack, somewhere a clank. Tentatively, she pushes the bars. They slide to one side easily with a well-greased hiss.

After a moment, she shuffles out into the hall.

Past the sleeping deputy, under a bank of fluorescents that snaps off, stutters back to life. Some alarm, buzzing ahead, cuts off with a tinny ding, she stops a moment, listening. Steps out of the rustling paper slippers, leaves them behind.

Around a corner, past an alcove, another green-clad deputy collapsed over a boxy camera-printer before a lit wall hashed with height marks, five foot, five foot six, six foot. Out in the empty utilitarian lobby, glass doors reflect harsh light against the dimness of what looks to be a parking garage beyond. In the middle of the floor a police officer's sprawled atop a big round-shouldered man in a sleeveless hoodie, arms cruelly bound by whitely stretched zip-ties, the sluff and wheeze of sleeping breath, bubbling catch of a snore, the scribble-scratch of nib on paper. Someone's writing something.

Across from the doors a counter takes up most of the wall, topped by panes of glass a handspan thick. Behind it, a woman in a charcoal suit, her hair all tiny corkscrew curls of brown and gold hung loose about her face, "A moment," she says, without looking up from her calligraphy.

Those two, asleep, the cop in his blacks and tactical vest lifted slowly, lowered, by the gently inexorable lungs of the man beneath. Her bare feet filthy on the scrubbed linoleum, nail of one big toe a dead grey curl. She starts as the buzzing alarm kicks off again, an elevator door trying to close itself beside her, track blocked by someone's heedless, green-sleeved arm, an ugly black watch about the wrist.

The woman behind the counter tucks away a thick-barreled pen of ruby tortoiseshell, lifts up her sheet of paper, eyeing the loops and whorls inked over it. "A moment more," she says, over the relentless buzz. Turning she reaches over the deputy asleep beside her to lift the lid of something, a copier, a scanner, she's laying the paper on the glass.

"You did this?" calls Jo.

The woman, bent over, eyes a monitor over the deputy's shoulder. "You'll have to be more specific," she says, loudly dull through the glass. Clack of keys, a sideways sliding flare of light.

"Okay," says Jo. "Who are you? What have you done? What the, *shit,*" as the buzzing shuts off again with a ding, the elevator door sighing back open in silence. "What the hell is going on?"

"Mrs. Upchurch," says the woman, looking up from the monitor with a pinched smile that doesn't reach her carefully painted eyes. "You're being extracted."

"Is that so."

"Had I not been called away last night," another key-clack, she does something with the mouse, "things would not have gotten so out of hand."

"So," says Jo, "you, sent that other guy, instead?"

"Mr. Loudermilk," she's lifting the lid of the scanner, "was there on other business entirely, and not at all prepared for what he found." Lifting the paper from the glass, she folds it once, and then again, impressing the creases with quick sure swipes. "The situation's more fluid than it seems."

"But you, ah," Jo swallows, "you're good. You got this."

Another fold. "They'll wake up, soon enough. They'll be vaguely embarrassed, and unable to keep in mind the matter of a woman, brought in for questioning in last night's shooting," swipe, "and," she says, "if they do think to look in their files for any such reports?" She lifts her hands, empty of any paper at all.

"Neat trick," says Jo. "Maybe next, you can pull a pair of shoes out of a hat? Or a," whirring, the elevator door's sliding shut again, fetching up against that prostrate wrist, and there's the frustrated alarm again, "shirt," says Jo, over the buzz, "hang on, let me just," heading for the elevator, but "Wait!" says Mrs. Upchurch, hastening down to the end of the counter, "you cannot disturb – "

Jo, stooped over the deputy's arm, looks over, back, her eyes meeting Mrs. Upchurch's for one charged instant.

"Don't," says Mrs. Upchurch.

Jo slips through the gap, into the elevator, dragging the arm in after. The buzz cuts off as the door slides shut on Mrs. Upchurch's lunging scowl. Jo's pressing every button she can on the panel, but only the one that says L lights up. She stabs it again and again with her finger. The elevator starts up.

Sudden squawk of an electric guitar, she jumps, sinister noodling that overdubs an echoing cascade, she rears back against the elevator wall as the drums kick in and the rest of the band revs up before it cuts off to start all over again, the snarling guitar by itself, a ringtone, the phone, there, in the deputy's other hand. She resettles the blanket about her shoulders. The elevator haltingly stops, with a ding, the door sliding open, and as it does Mrs. Upchurch reaches in to seize the blanket below her chin and haul her stumbling into an unlit lobby, and swung about by the force of it Jo wriggles free of the blanket bare feet slap the carpet crouching, arms a-ready, closed doors down the hall behind her, to the side, but daylight vaguely shining from the hall away down there, and Mrs. Upchurch stood before it. "Listen," says Jo, "lady, I – "

"Joliet Kendal Maguire, *you* will listen to *me,*" hisses Mrs. Upchurch. "I know," she says. "I know when you finally made up your mind. I know why you left. I know how it was you managed to come back. I even know where you learned to ride a horse, and who the father would have been. But most of all, girl, I know what's embedded in your heart. You cannot surprise me, and you will not thwart me. Are we clear?"

Jo, still crouched, takes a breath. "Okay," she says. "Sure. Except the whole what the fuck you want to do with me bit." One of her arms drawn back, her hand closed over her breast.

Straightening and softening at once, Mrs. Upchurch offers the blanket, "It's not you," she says. "It's that."

Jo lifts her hand away, "This?" she says. The pucker in her skin just visible over the hem of the bralette. "You can have it. Please, take it, I insist," but Mrs. Upchurch, still holding out the blanket, shakes her head. "It's not that simple," she says.

"Why would it be," says Jo, and takes the blanket.

"The qlifot's embedded, in you. Until it's done, there's nothing to be done."

"Qliphoth?" says Jo, trying the taste of it, "huh. We've been calling it quicksmoke." Looking down, as she drapes the blanket about her shoulders, "I mean, it's not either, at the moment, but trust me." And then, "You're a wizard, right?" and when Mrs. Upchurch, frowning, opens her mouth to demur, "I mean," says Jo, "you know shit. So. What happens, to the seed, when the flower sprouts?"

"You," says Mrs. Upchurch, "are *not* a seed, *that,*" and then, composing herself, "there are points," she says, "where similes fail. That's not a seed. There is no seed. And what comes, when it comes, will not be a flower."

"Whatever it is," says Jo, "it's something you want, isn't it. Something powerful."

"It's necessary," says Mrs. Upchurch.

"Yeah," says Jo, looking away. "I bet you say that to all the girls." Across the lobby from the elevator bank a display cabinet, and pinned within, curled and fading drawings in crayon and marker of police cars and police boats and helicopters, cops in black uniforms, and blue, guns in their hands, robbers with striped shirts and domino masks, and great big sacks of loot, Our Neighbors, say letters cut from construction paper, The Police. A notice in the corner says Mr. Chheda's Third Grade Class, Beverly Cleary Elementary. Light catches and drags across the dusty glass of it, shifting, brightening. Jo frowns. "We should go," Mrs. Upchurch is saying, "they'll be waking soon."

"Was there anything else?" says Jo.

"What?"

"Was there anything," starts Jo, sharply, and then, "did they grab any of my stuff? My phone, the, the gun? Or Jack, did they pick up Jack, too? Or May? Was there *anything* else?"

"There's nothing left," says Mrs. Upchurch, "that'll lead them back to you." The light behind her welling.

"That's not what I'm – "

"We don't have time for this. We have to *go*. We should've gone already. What is that."

That light, warming, swelling, reaches the lobby, flooding in to brighten everything, gleam trim and blaze the elevator doors, dazzle the glass, lap the walls and wash over them both as they turn to see the source of it, marching up the hall toward them.

"Did you know?" says Mrs. Upchurch, a hand lifted to shield her eyes, but her words can't be made out over the brilliance. She tries again, shouting, "Did you know!" but the terror in Jo's face, and the awe.

"The moon, under her feet," says Mrs. Upchurch, unheard in all that light. "About her head, a dozen stars, a crown."

The Queen enters the lobby, each of her steps a crack of dawn, and daylight flares from the sweep of her hands as she lifts them, shines from her blackly lustrous curls, burns from her terrible green gaze. "Jo," she says, and it's all so bright. Jo's closed up her eyes.

Mrs. Upchurch flinches as it all turns to regard her. "You have brought her forth already," says her majesty, her words at once quite close and much too far away. "That will go well for you. Release her to us now."

"Of course," says Mrs. Upchurch, quickly, flatly, small, and that's when Jo with a startling yelp begins to laugh, or sob, it's hard to say.

THIS TUB'S OF BEATEN COPPER, not of wood, set in the midst of the trim green lawn stretched flatly out to parapets of brick. Panels of palest gauzy blue shiver in an intermittent breeze, screening the tub from the backsides of the buildings at the high end of the block. Above, shreds and scuds of darkening clouds slink from the setting sun, and those last bright beams of daylight strike window-glass and metalled trim, shine slantwise over graveled roof and silhou-etted copse, softening as they fall to wash the edges and details away, dissolving all that distance to a deepening haze outshone already by storefront and streetlit intersection, artificial colors sharper, more precise, though small, and thin, to be so sharp. Jo's sat at the one end, shoulders lapped by faintly steaming water, head hung low. Knelt behind her on the grass Queen Ysabel in a rough white robe, leaned over the beaten rim of the tub to rub and knead Jo's wet-dark hair with sopping clouds of suds. Jo flinches, and she halts, her hands become cradles, "Did they hurt you?"

"They, ah," says Jo, turning away, "they weren't that careful, putting me in the car."

Her hands now combs, to sluice away the suds. "My poor Gallowglas."

"Are we done?" Slop of water restless against copper.

"Rinse," says Ysabel, lifting away her hands to blot them, front and back, on the nubbled lapels of her robe. Jo dunks her head, then pushes out into the middle of the bath, her wake a soapy iridescence. Ysabel looks back, over her shoulder, "It seems it's time," she says, to no one in particular, "for refreshment, and illumination." Parting those lapels to draw aside, let slip, down her arms and off. She lifts a bare leg over the rim, slowly to settle herself with a beatific wince, the water displaced rolled silkily across to lick the edges, lift Jo's hair, brush her ducked chin as she looks away. The sun gone down, away behind the hills, the city turned toward night below. "Quite the spread," she says. "Those from the old place?" She's pointing, down the lawn yet glimmering to the angled shadow-shapes of a couple of empty Adirondack chairs.

"You know, I think they are?" says Ysabel. "Gloria hasn't bought anything like that." Leaning back to soak her curls, sighing extravagantly. "We can have them taken back, if you'd prefer."

"What?" says Jo. "No, I don't," something, a flicker, she turns back to see the surface of the bath now littered with floating candles, a dozen or so, and Ysabel, smiling in their lambent glow. A small tray's been set beside her, on a stand, and on it a bottle in a silver pail, two slender fluted glasses. "What's that?" says Jo.

"Vodka," says Ysabel, plucking the stopper from the bottle, "infused with tarragon," pouring a gelidly viscous trickle, "and kept on ice," into one glass, then the other, "all day."

"So," says Jo, eyeing the liquor palely green that half-fills the glass she's offered. "That's a thing."

"Don't sip," says Ysabel. "Not yet. We must have a toast." A small brass box has been placed on the tray where the glasses had stood, and she flicks it open with a fingertip, prising out two slim brown cigarettes. Leaning forward, she tips one toward Jo, who shakes her head. "For the toast," says Ysabel. "A sip of liquor, through a mouthful of smoke. The spice," waggling the proffered cigarette, "complements the herb," lifting her own fluted glass.

"Clove?"

"Of course."

"I'm trying to quit."

"I know. But one, just one, won't hurt. I am the Queen; I do so decree it."

"Is that how it works." Jo takes the cigarette, and lights it, following Ysabel's lead, by bending over one of the floating candle-flames. A long and crackling drag. "My God," she says, sunk back in water, cigarette and glass held high.

"We toast," says Ysabel, enbowed in curling smoke and steam, "then inhale, then sip."

"Complicated," says Jo, sitting up, inclining her glass toward Ysabel's. "To what?"

"To your return." Clink of glass on glass, but Ysabel pauses, frowning, in the act of lifting her cigarette.

"I, ah," says Jo, her glass unmoved, her cigarette aside.

"You're back, and you've come back. What else could there be?"

The two of them, there, in that tub, flickeringly lit from below as night settles about them, Ysabel sat up, leaned forward, Jo almost submerged, and only her head and laden hands to break the surface.

"I haven't," says Ysabel, then, "asked. Anyone. Not since you told me you did not, again."

"So, what," says Jo, "you're coming up on your thirty-day sobriety chip?" and then, almost immediately, "I'm sorry," she says, looking away, the steam.

"It's only been three weeks," says Ysabel, quietly.

"Shit," says Jo.

"Since we restored the owr."

"Cinco de Mayo, yeah."

"I've asked no one but you, that once, since then."

"What," says Jo, "what is that, what does that even mean."

"They're free," says Ysabel. "All of them. Freed of the burden of the answer they'd given. And some of them, many, did leave. Go on to live their lives elsewhere, and they're happy, I suppose, but those who stayed? Anna, my mother's amanuensis, and Petra B from the coffee shop, with her camera? The Starling, and Chrissie, and her sister? Melissa, and Gloria our Chatelaine, who's somehow made this house into a splendid palace, for a queen," she takes a gliding slowly closer lowering step, glass and cigarette both high in one hand, her other reaching, her fingertips to brush Jo's cheek. "There is room here, in this house, for you."

Jo, eyes closed, takes in a breath. "I have to go back," she says. "What?"

Hiss of cigarette dropped in vodka, "I don't know," Jo's saying, turning away, "if they're okay, I don't know if they got picked up, too," gripping the rim of the tub, "if May or Hector," glass held high as over she throws a dripping leg, "fuck, Jack, he could've been in the next cell over, I never would've known," looking to set it down on the tray, but the pail's gone, and the brass box, and in their place a stack of neatly folded towels. "I gotta go back," she says, and lets her glass drop to the lawn.

"You've got to do no such thing," says Ysabel.

"You weren't there." Jo seizes a towel, shaking it out. "You didn't see what they did, the cops, when they showed up in force." Wrapping it about herself. "Yanking people around, smashing shit up, like they were *pissed,*" tucking it close, above her breast, "they had to be there at all, and they were gonna take it out, on whatever they could reach."

"There is nothing you can do tonight," says Ysabel, "that you cannot do as well, or better, tomorrow."

"Is that how it is," says Jo. "Your majesty."

Something, some tension, slips, or shifts, in Ysabel's expression, "Don't," she says. "Not between us, Jo," and a swallow. "Please," she says. "Do not."

"What else, am I supposed to say? You're the, the *Queen.* I'm just, a lowly Duchess, or whatever. You conjured up a hot tub, on a lawn, on the roof of your fucking *palace.* You," she says, catching her breath, "you were, lit up, like the goddamn *sun,* Ysabel. How do you even *do* that."

"I was furious," says Ysabel. "When your Shrieve told me what the Harper had done." Turning to her cigarette. "I should've assembled the knights," she says, and lets out a cloud of smoke.

"I doubt it would've gone any better," says Jo, "you'd rolled up with an army."

"Well." Ysabel sits up in the water, drinks off her vodka in a swallow. "It's not an army, or a sun, we've sent to chastise Chillicoathe."

"What?" says Jo, her hand closed over the knot tucked in her towel. "Why?"

"He betrayed your grace. Sold you, his liege, for a moment's advantage in a silly feud. He'll have to face our Huntsman."

A blink, looking away. Looking back. "Who?"

"Melissa Gallowglas. Don't be jealous, Jo. We are the Queen. We must have a Huntsman."

"Ysabel," says Jo. "My God. What have you done."

Over the door, red neon letters, VERN, they brightly say, the T and the A before them hung lightlessly from the crumpled frame. A boxy car pulls up beneath, the color uncertain in this light, dark green, perhaps, or purple. The back door on the sidewalk side pops open, letting out a bluesy riff, a chanting voice, got a good thing going, God damn, gotta give it to you, girl, you got game. Somebody's climbing out, but even as bootheels hit the curb she's rolling over, reaching back, jingle of buckles as she hauls out a bundle long and heavily awkward, "Careful!" calls the driver, over the music. "Heck is that, anyway, is that a sword?"

"Yeah," she says, rough with effort, "a goddamn," yank, "sword," stepping back, swung around to clang the tip of it planted on pavement, scabbard rising wooden frame and iron fittings, thickly felted wool, handle of it long and straight above the wide strong quillions, topped by a gleaming faceted pommel. "Gonna take it in there, put the fear of God in some asshole, because *that* is apparently what I do, these days."

"You?" says the driver, leaned back, peering up. "With that?"

Leaned there, hands on the quillions, motorcycle jacket over her sundress of pink and spangled marigolds, she lets out a bark of a laugh. "As if. This?" hefting, dropping, clang and chime, "it's a prop, for a music video. Band's inside."

"Hey!" he says, leaning even further back as she's about to close the door. "You can leave a tip in the app, whenever you want."

"Sure thing," she says, shutting the door. Watches the car pull away. Gripping the hilt with a grimace she yanks, lifts, the long and leather-wrapped ricasso tugged free of the quilted throat, and then, there, an inch, another, of the bare steel blade, sharply gleaming in the mean red light. She drives it home with a grunt. Hauls the scabbard up to brace the weight of it against her shoulder, tipped back the hilt and quillions, weight of it balanced by her hand laid lightly. The door there, under the light, a sign by the narrow window of it, NO MINORS, it says, Permitted Anywhere On This Premises. "Well," she says, "here we go," and makes her way up the poured concrete steps to take hold of the handle of it.

I taught myself
the only way to vaguely get along in love
is to like the other slightly less
than you get in return.

I keep feeling like I'm being undercut.

—Tom Campesinos! & Gareth Campesinos!

NO. 40
" – dirty white noise – "

AN OFFICER IN BLACK beckons from poured concrete steps, "Who's got the scene?" she calls to him, pointing to a van parked close by the curb, Portland Police it says on the side, Forensic Evidence Division.

"Logan," he says, "and what's her name. Hidaka."

"Fuck," under her breath. "They done with the fibers and shit? Because I am not putting on a bunny sut." Her white pullover gone pale magenta in this light, her close-cropped silver hair stained pink, tipped back, she's looking up, VERN, say those lit-up letters above them, lurid, red.

He holds out a pair of paper booties. "You're gonna want these."

Inside, the bar's a pool of jukebox colors diffusely dim, a woman behind the bar, man on the stool before her, coffee cup in hand, "Bartender," says the officer, "waitstaff, they didn't see it go down, but they got good looks at the perp."

"And have their statements been taken?"

"Of course."

"Cut 'em loose." She sets a couple of business cards on the bar, snap. "It's two o'clock in the morning." Sends them skating away with a flick of her fingers to fetch up next to the coffee cup. "Get yourselves home. Call if you think of anything. Detective Bauer."

"We gotta lock up when you're done," says the man on the stool.

269

"Then, as quick as we can. So! Officer…"

"Villaraldo," he says, tapping the nametag there on his tactical vest, but she's bent over, tugging a bootie on over a hiking boot. "Corey Villaraldo. We've met, like, before."

"What is this, Officer Villaraldo, number thirty-six for the year?" Yanking the elastic of the other bootie over and around her heel. "And it's not even June."

"I thought last night was thirty-six. Out by the airport?"

"What out by the airport."

"I thought," he's frowning, "you caught it."

"Officer Villaraldo," she says, straightening, "I caught a body, last night? Out by the airport? I'd be sleeping in, working that, and it'd be Christgau here, having to deal with Ted the FED." She points toward the back of the bar. "I presume the scene's through there?"

Past a service window that opens on a still white kitchen, through a low wide doorway into the side room, the dimness here shoved aside by bright white worklights set on tripods at the far end, relentlessly revealing the scuffs that draggle the carpet, the chips and dings in the formica, the rips in the leatherette, the dust that glazes the video poker screens, the nubbled nap of bright green felt, but the lake of blood's still somehow resolutely dark, harsh highlights struck from the glossily untroubled surface of it, but otherwise quite black. In the middle of it, slumped against one cyclopean leg of the pool table, black boots tipped over, bare knees crooked, marred by streaks and laps of the only red the blood can muster, a motorcycle jacket skewed open over the ruin of a sundress. Two figures in coveralls shapelessly white in all that brightness, one of them cradling the long lens of a camera, lifting it to snap a photo, the other stooped over the body, paper booties islands in that lake.

"What do we got," says Bauer.

"Samples," says the stooped figure, his hood up. "Data, to analyze." Intent on the tweezers in his hand, peeling back a ripped and sticky flap of cloth.

"Melissa De Voor," says Villaraldo, flipping back the cover of a notepad, "twenty-seven, Sixty-two Aught Six, Southeast Fifty-second is what it says on her license, but a, ah, former roommate there says she moved out over a month ago. Current address unknown. Cash and cards weren't touched."

"So what you're saying, Officer Villaraldo, is that robbery doesn't appear to be the motive." Turning back to the figure still stooped over the body. "Have we settled on a Cee Oh Dee?"

He spares a look back over a paper-white shoulder. "It'll be in my report." The hood's elastic frames a clean-cheeked face, glasses rimmed with golden wire.

"C'mon, Ted," she says.

He looks to the other figure in white. "Almost done?" She nods, snapping another photo.

"Criminalist Logan," says Bauer, then, tone sharpened, arms akimboed. "Upon the conclusion of your preliminary examination of the scene, what, in your considered opinion, is the most likely cause of death?"

He lifts away the tweezers, props a crinkling elbow on a knee. "Exsanguination," he says.

"And that was the instrument?" She points. Laid in the blood on the other side of the body an enormous sword, the great long blade of it tipped away at an angle, gleaming highlights sedimenting where the tip of it and the edges break the gelling surface.

He shakes a rustling head. "That, she was holding."

"That?" Stepping to one side for a better view, booties fastidious on the verge of the lake. "Christ, it's longer'n she is."

"Perp had two, witnesses said." The photographer, camera lifted up and away, peers at something beneath a table.

"Two, what," says Bauer. "Knives? Cleavers? Machetes? Claymores?"

"Actually," says Villaraldo behind her, pointing, "that's more like what's known as a Zweihänder?" blinking as she cocks a dubious brow at him, "a classic claymore," gesturing with his fingers, "has more of a forward-angled, ah – "

"Is a renaissance fair in town?" she says. "Maniac running loose, Officer, two bladed weapons, positively dripping blood, and you guys can't turn up anything on the canvass?"

"We got units rolling. We got a BOLO." And then, "There's a, lack of clarity? What happened, when he left? There was a car, but he maybe didn't get in the car. You want us to pull back? Go house-to-house?"

Bauer's closed her eyes. "How many wounds," she says. "On the body, how many wounds."

"Detective," says the criminalist, "I can't possibly answer that question yet."

"One," she says, stepping close to point, "just one. It's a damn big hole, but there's only the one, you can take that to the bank. And she was loaded for bear. This was a confrontation, this was," grimacing, at the sight of her bootie planted in blood, "personal," she says. "Our boy's scared out of his mind, laying as low as he can. Dumped the weapons for sure within a couple of blocks." Lifting her foot, wobbling a little to keep her balance, she tugs off the bootie and drops it, plop, to the blood, as she sets her bared boot on dry carpet. "Find them, maybe, we can't turn him up."

"Hey," says the photographer.

"What." The criminalist hikes up to look over the corner of the pool table. She's knelt down by one of the red-upholstered booths, peering at something pinched in her fingers, "I don't know," she says.

"Let me see," says Bauer, crinkle-stumping boot and bootie around the pool table, "hold it up, I'm not gonna touch." The photographer lifts her blue-gloved hand. "It's a bone," says Bauer.

"Metatarsal," says the photographer.

"It's a bone, covered in purple glitter."

"That's not what I don't know about it," says the photographer.

"Well, heck, bag it," says Bauer. "Might just break the case wide open."

A Hightop, Fire-engine Red – how to Help – deal Sealed
nor Yet the Butcher's son – what he Might do

A fire-engine red Chuck Taylor hightop, toe-cap snowily spotless, nudges aside a leaning sheaf of long green-yellow grass. The ragged shreds beneath it, short acrylic fur a white gone wetly grey, marred by streaks of grimy mud, a stuffed toy animal, belly of it twisted, torn, and matted clumps of fiber stuffing spilt from the wound. All in black Jo Gallowglas lowers her foot, pushing back more grass with one bared arm. The head of the toy's vaguely equine, with a short black mane of some material stiffer than the fur, and sewn there, just above the blackly glassy eyes, stripes of rainbow colors spiraled into a horn-shape stiffened, perhaps, by a length of wire within. Gingerly she lifts it, sagging, limp, out from its dew-damp hollow, tenderly she turns it about, to cradle it in the crook of her arm. More loose stuffing drifts from the rip to float away, snagged by the lightening grass. There's a tag, sewn to the seam of one stubby leg, and over the faded washing instructions blocky letters have been written in a child's per-snickety hand, ROY G BIV.

"Boss! Hey! Hey, boss!"

She looks up, eyes hidden away behind small round sun-glasses. Sweetloaf, pompadour a-bob, stumbles toward her over junk-strewn tummocks, holding up a flat black something, "I think I fucking found it! Over there, by the," looking back, missing a step, "shit!" waving an arm for balance, "that fucking tent, right?" The debris trailed off behind him, cinder blocks and bicycle wheels, boards from broken pallets, an upright shopping cart, that bent torchiere at a drunken angle, all spread from a raggedly irregular mound, edges of it knocked and tossed about in churns of mud and torn-up grass, surmounted by a small dome tent uprooted, tossed aside but still intact, a-wobble beige and orange in the morning breeze. "I mean," Sweetloaf's saying, "I don't fucking know, I can't turn it on. Not sure if it's the fucking battery or, you know," handing it to her, "that."

The screen of the phone is softly misshapen by a web of countless whitely splintering cracks where there isn't, here and there, a missing shard to offer a glimpse of the occulted inner works. She hands it back. "Get rid of it."

"You sure?" He frowns, to see it back in his hand. "There's a guy, out by Mall Two Oh Five, he's a fucking wizard with that Gorilla Glass shit. Which," but she's turning, walking away, "fun fact," he's hastening after, "is not fucking made by gorillas!"

Past the trailer tipped over, hitch driven into the grass, past the van its side door gaping, unshaded, on toward the dull green motorcoach, stranded at the edge of the field, spray-painted bedsheet still hung by a hook or two on the side, and littering the ground before it, beside it, around it, tumbled from it hundreds of, thousands of magazines tossed, torn, crumpled, ground into mud, all of them each and every with the same bright yellow frame edging their covers. Picking her steps with care, Jo wades into them, over them, through them, across toward the door of the coach hung askew, reaching there to lay the stuffed toy on a cleared bit of the coach's floor.

"Boss?" calls Sweetloaf, over the yellow-lapped field. "The fuck is all this? Somebody's chucked, like, fucking," he kicks something, *"kibble*, everywhere."

Jo's started clearing the steps, picking up magazines, stacking them neatly on the grass.

"Boss?" calls Sweetloaf. "Hey. Boss. Everything okay?" Offering a hapless shrug to Astolfo, coming up in his grey sweatsuit.

"Go on," says Jo, flatly quiet, stacking magazines. "Get out of here. You're done."

"Boss," says Sweetloaf. "Come the fuck on."

"Your grace," says Astolfo.

"You want to help?" snaps Jo. "Drag over some plastic. A tarp. Somewhere to stack the clean ones, go on. The ones they, they fucking," tamp, tamp, evening the magazines in her hands, "trashed," she says, stacking them with the others on the grass. "Set those aside. We'll, figure something out. You." She points to the third of them, young, slender, ashen hair in curls to his shoulders. "You're new."

He lifts a hand to his neatly knotted tie of gold, tucked safely within the placket of his fine white shirt. "Jeffeory, your grace. The Axe."

"You're the Axe."

"I am but freshly dubbed."

"Yeah," she says. "If you're the Axe, shouldn't you be over across the river? With the Count?"

He looks to either side, but Astolfo's already off that way, tugging at the van's downed awning, and Sweetloaf's stooped to gather magazines. "I serve the Queen," he says.

"Yeah?" says Jo. "Well, okay. Let's go. Hop to." Smoothing a torn cover with her hand, the yellow of it framing what's left of an image of an iridescent beetle, with great curving horns, that almost fills the palm of an unconcerned hand. She tips back her head, eyes hidden away behind those sunglasses, then sets the ruined magazine aside.

The weakly brightening air is breathless, still, untroubled by even a rumor of engine-rumble or tire-roll. By the back door, under the flight of stairs bolted to the brick, he leans out the doorway, one hand on the jamb, to peer at them, three worn plain cardboard boxes stacked one atop the others, hard by the foundation. The sky above a ceiling of flat pale shapeless clouds without definition.

Inside, through a cramped dark kitchen, down a narrow hall lined with cubbyholes, stuffed neatly each with mismatched pairs of shoes, and more of them lining the floor below, croc by stiletto, wedge by boot, sneaker by moccasin, he's awkwardly looking around the two boxes in his arms so as not to step on anything. Clatter through a beaded curtain, strings of it rattling loud as they drag the cardboard, up to a worktable mounded unstably with yet more shoes, and more besides, fallen and tumbled in piles on the floor. He squats to let drop the boxes, shoving shoes out from under till they both sit flat. Lifts a hand to the mighty round of tight black curls crowning his head, but pulls away at the touch of them, scowl twisting. Up on his feet in a practiced, stoop-shouldered stance somehow at odds with the lanky power in his frame. Out through the curtain left swaying in his wake.

The beads, slowly, still. Silence for a moment, or two, before a slithery, shifting slip, a Chelsea boot, destabilized, disturbed, tips toppling flop from the worktable to the floor, taking with it buckle-clack an undone sandal, a brogue a-slide the slope of shoes, a plimsoll tumbling end over end to fetch up at the edge of the table, buffered by a shower shoe, rustle and settling slump until all is once more still.

Back through the clattering beads with the third box, that he sets atop the other two, brushing down the front of his dull blue shirt. He pries up a stiff flap and reaches into a tangled nest of footwear to pull out a running shoe of teal and neon green. Eyes it, the pile on the table, the alluvium littering the floor, and lets it drop. Reaches in for another.

Unlocking the door he swings it open with a jingle of the bell, "Okay," he's growling, "okay, come on in," and "I'm sorry," says the woman stood there, shoulders draped in a wide pink scarf, "are you open?"

"Might as well be," he says, switching on the lights in the front window. George's, say the letters painted in red and yellow in an arc across the glass. Shoes Repaired.

"Is the," she's saying, "old man, here?" That pink scarf, her blue jeans palimpsested with felt-tip graffiti, her scuffed suede mules. The floppy knit toque on her head. "I heard," she says, "he ran a sort of, lost-and-found?" Turning over what's in her hands, a worn brown low-topped boot, panels of darker elastic on either side. "This is ridiculous," she says. "Who cares about a shoe on the sidewalk. Lost and found. I could've just, I should just throw it away."

"You could," he says, his stern expression not quite a frown. She looks up to meet it. "No," she says, looking away. "No." Down to the boot in her hands. "If there's a chance."

He tips back that black-crowned head, his expression reluctantly letting go. A flick of a gesture, another, at her hands, the boot, she holds it up for him. "I might've seen the like," he says, looking over his shoulder to the worktable, the whelming mound of shoes. "But it might take a bit."

There's a knock at the door, "A moment," he says, but quietly, to himself, dabbing the mottled back of the photograph before him with the rubber-stoppered top of a small brown bottle. Presses a yellowed strip of paper to the glistening daubs of mucilage, 6/17/1983 Law Firm Seals Deal For Top Floor, the browning typescript stretched across it, (l – r) S. Yoelin, J. Dunn, G. Welund, F. Pinabel, G. Rhythidd, A. Pinabel, J. Sap, ending there in a feathery torn edge. He unscrews the cap from a fountain pen and sets to inking a second p there, beside the first, deftly counterfeiting slabby umber serifs. Again, a knock. "A moment!" he calls, louder this time.

"Package!" Muffled, from the other side of the door. "For the Outlaw!"

"She's not within!" He starts on an e, finickily etching the curl.

"Well could you maybe take it for her? Come on!"

He lifts the pen, eyes the cap in his hand, looks up, lips pursed in a put-upon moue. Unfolds his legs to get to his feet.

He's young, the man at the door, cheekbones hunched like shoulders under a squint at the effort of hauling the box in his arms over the threshold, "Where do you want it," into the kitchen, and "Wait," he's left to say, hastening after, screwing the cap on his pen.

"Right here?" The young man hoists the weight of the box up onto the counter there, overlooking the room beyond.

"What, what," he's blustering, tucking the capped pen away in his vest, "what is that."

The young man, stepping back, shrugs, his oversized yellow plaid shirt new enough that sharp creases still clench the back of it, and the sleeves. "For the Outlaw. Came to the warehouse for some reason," he's headed around the counter, looking down into the room beyond. "I drew the short straw."

He nods at that, poking the box with his long and slender fingers, prodding it about. A bright red logo haltingly turns into view, Archie McPhee, it says. Home of the Original Horse Head Mask.

"So, like, what is this?" says the young man, headed down the three short steps, and he starts up, eyes owled with alarm, "No!" he cries, bustling around the counter, "Wait! Stop!"

"It's, okay, it's okay," says the young man, hands held up, away, stood among all those banker's boxes white and brown stacked in that room beyond, its windowed walls narrowing to a point. "What is all this? It's not the Outlaw's, is it."

Arrested there at the top of the three steps, his still-wide eyes dart back and forth, the unsettled boxes, the photographs stacked here and there, the low table laden with his work, his tools, the onionskin paper, bits of newsprint, the tweezers, the scissors, the small brown bottle. "This one," he says, slender fingers twining, one hand folding up the other over his narrow breast, "does maintain the morgue, at the direction of her grace, much as was done for the Devil."

"Morgue?"

"Moments," he says, those slender-fingered hands now firmly clasped, "fished from the river of time," taking one step down, and another, "laid out for solemn and dispassionate consideration."

"These are from, newspapers?" Looking over the boxes, a lid skewed here and there, the papers, folders, photographs within. "Like, their, paper files?"

"Clippings, and other ephemera, there, there," a hand released, to vaguely point, "the bulk of the collection does consist of photographs, along with their accompanying captions, indices, and tags," that hand withdrawn, refolded, "there are, several archives represented," a wince, that's almost a shrug, "and thus several such, systems, protocols, codes," he frowns, not unhappily.

"What," says the young man, unsquinted eyes gone serious, "what do you got on the Black Panthers?"

His frown pinches contemplatively. "Panthers?"

"Portland chapter of the Black Panther Party. Nineteen sixty-nine, seventy – Kent Ford? Johnson, Oscar Johnson? Sandra Ford? George," he says, "Honeycutt?"

"This one must humbly admit the effort to secure the Skanner's files was not met with much success."

Those cheekbones hunch again, higher than before. "Then what have you got on Vanport?"

"Ah!" Eyes brightening, frown swept away, "yes, of course," stepping among the boxes, "the Vanport flood, thirtieth of May, nineteen and forty-eight. The files should be," one long hand lifted, wavering, but "No, no," the young man's saying, "not the flood. Anything but the flood."

Those brows pinch again, lips pursing, "Construction, and the opening, would've been nineteen and forty-two, there may be files," turning to point, but *"Not* the beginning," says the young man. "Not the end. Just, what it was like, in the middle. Regular, everyday, whatever, you know? Anything like that."

Those slender hands spread in an apology. "If it did not make the news, it will not be in this collection." Arms folding, one long finger lifted to tap at thoughtful lips. "Perhaps," he says, "the Historical Society?"

"Forget it," says the young man, heading up three quick steps, "forget it," but then, his hand on the doorknob, "Cora Bunch, okay?" he says. "You want the news, you find out what happened to Cora Bunch. She lived in Vanport."

He doesn't slam the door when he leaves. The short man looks away, back to his low table, "But, that would be absurd," he mutters. "This one does not investigate." He plucks the pen from his vest, and sets to unscrewing the cap.

"Tell her, Gee!" a burst of spangles and glitter, "you *tell* that bitch she can't *have* my fucking song!"

"I've asked you not to call me that," he says, without looking up from his ledger.

"Tell *her,* Gav," says the woman following after, loosely wrapped in green terrycloth, "remix is not song. Song is not remix."

"And I've asked you not to call me *that*," he says, but the first woman's whipped about, "The *beat*, it's the fucking *beat* is the same, whenever everybody *hear* Charli kick in that Pink Diamond beat, that bip bip, doo boop-dee-boop, they know it's about to be the Merch on the pole, only no, no, they hear that beat, that *Pink* Diamond *beat*, only it's a fucking *remix*, and it's *your* skanky Slavic ass in*stead!*"

He looks up, then, rich red hair a-flop from a high widow's peak. "This is about a song?"

"It's about *respect*," snaps the first woman.

"This is about a song," he says, looking back to his ledger. "Play whatever you want."

The second woman smirks at the first, who throws up her spangled hands, "No, Gee, goddammit!"

"Don't shout, Merch."

"Is Galveston," says the second woman. "Like Glen Campbell. Galveston, oh Galveston – "

"My aim is true," croons a newcomer, crowding the doorway to that tiny, white-lit office.

"Rocky," he says, shaking his head, "you aren't helping."

"Not in the job description." She jerks a thumb over her shoulder. "Company."

"It's Saturday. It's hardly almost noon. Who could possibly," but his expression collapses, from indulgent bemusement to affronted disgust, "what," he says, suddenly vehement, "under all the stars above, could you *possibly* want here?"

Rocky squeezes back against the wall of the hallway, making room as the Merch, glittering, shrugs back against the paper-piled cabinet, and Gina, resettling her robe, smiles bitterly to see who stands revealed. "Hello, old boss," she says.

"Ladies," says Chilli, yellow beard a-blaze in the white office light. "Been a while. Maybe head out front, get a party started? Need a word with your new boss."

"Gina," calls Gaveston, over the rash of departure. "Find another blasted song. Merch, don't ever yell in this office again. And Rocky?"

"I know, I know," she says, "make some damn money."

He turns back to his ledger. "Get out," he says, after a moment, companionably enough, but without looking up.

"There's nowhere else I can go," says Chilli.

"Not a problem," turning a long lined page, "I need to address."

"Oh," says Chilli, "but Stirrup. You've been with us at every step of this path we have taken. Together."

Gaveston looks up, then, and makes a show of turning his head to the left, then the right. "I see no us. I see you. Who sought a boon from the Gammers. Who abandoned that quest, to pick a fight with the Outlaw. Who – "

"That was a *duel,*" snarls Chilli. "I *prevailed.*"

"Whose hand, last night, was on the hilt," says Gaveston, quiet, cold. "Yours, and no one else's."

"That?" spits Chilli. "Is *that* why, that's why you, that mewling sack of berry juice? She *drew* on me!"

"She was the Queen's Huntsman, you rotten fool. You will not speak so, of her."

"Whyever not?" The words too loud, and with a ragged edge. His gesture too sudden, his smile too ostentatious. "You think she'll mind?"

"She was sent," says Gaveston, flatly, "by the Queen, and you must – "

"The Queen!" That big yellow head thrown back. "You said it yourself, Stirrup: the Queen? Is done!"

"No!" roars Gaveston, up on his feet, "no." Leaned forward, planting balled fists on the cluttered desk. "I said, and I maintain, that an open Apportionment is dangerously foolish. I worry now, as I did then, that we will never see another bounty enough to keep it possible. But to say her majesty is done? Those words are *yours,* Harper. *Not* mine."

"When I spoke them," says Chilli, and his is now the quiet voice, and cold, "you were with me."

Gaveston straightens, fingertips on the desktop now, not fists. "Do you know, Harper, where I was, but a year ago?"

A blink, another, uncertain at the slackening of the tension he'd been leaning on. "Sellwood?" says Chilli.

"I was a banneret, in Sellwood," says Gaveston. "Four streets, and all their folk: Tenino, Umatilla, Harney, Sherrett. Their medhu mine to glean; mine the hand that received their portion, direct from her generous majesty."

"Yeah, yeah," says Chilli.

"Then you remember, how it was never enough. How they would give, and give, and all we ever brought back were miserable pinches. You remember, how it was, just one short year ago."

A wave of dismissive agreement from Chilli.

"September, then," says Gaveston. "Eight months gone. Not even three full seasons – the Bride's champion, in his foolish pride, lost a duel to a mortal slip of a girl, and the Bride and the Queen fallen out over it. And I thought to myself, it must be time, time to pass, from the one, to the other, and what harm could there be, in helping it along?"

Chilli, arms folded, beard hunched about his grim-set mouth.

"I went to the Duke, and urged him take the Bride, for with her hand would come the Throne. So was I there, the night a mortal slip of a girl sent Tommy Rawhead down to dust, and for my pains," says Gaveston, sat back in his chair, "for his grace's embarrassment," adjusting the drape and knot of his burgundy tie, "my arms were sworn in service to the Hawk, my streets pledged to his coffers, and now," a hand laid on the open pages of the ledger, "I manage a bawdyhouse on Foster Road, and it's been far too long, since last I was in Sellwood."

"And when the wind blows?" says Chilli, hoarsely gruff. "The one that doesn't stop? That whittles her majesty's bounty back down to generous pinches? Who will you whisper to then, Stirrup?"

"You miss my point," says Gaveston. "I may grumble, I may growl, I may well have a beer, but I'll take the pinch and be glad of it. My politicking days are done." Smoothing the long page of the ledger with his hand. "Go on," he says. "Get out. Bruno will soon enough know you're here."

"You," says Chilli, "you wouldn't call him, on me."

Gaveston opens a drawer of the desk and pulls out a little phone, flipping it open. Chilli's yellow beard gathers in a scowl, and he turns and steps without a word from white-lit office into the cramped shadows of the hall. The light shifts, as out there the door to the bar's swung open, music coming into focus, snapping drums, relentless riff, a woman coolly chanting would you like us to assign someone to worry your mother, muffling again as the door swings shut. Gaveston deliberately folds up the phone. "Soon enough," he says, and drops it back in the drawer.

FIRST, A BOX — WHAT THEY GOT WRONG
THE STONEY STRAND, THE SALTY SEA
WHAT'S KNOWN, WHAT'S NOT

FIRST A CARDBOARD BOX, printed with blue diamonds and pink, Mezcal, says the logo, 400 Conejos, and atop it in his arms a blue milk crate with a dozen or so albums inside, and an awkwardly tilted gooseneck lamp. Next a sleekly slender turntable under a couple of boxy speakers braced with his chin, cords neatly wrapped about one grasping hand, following the first through the parlor and out the front door. A third backs down the staircase in his shirtsleeves, craning up over the unwieldy bulk of a thick rolled futon toward a presumable fourth, presumably clutching the other end. "Your pardon, miss," says Pyrocles, there in the middle of the parlor in his dark blue suit, a smile polite beneath his mustaches. "We've not been introduced."

Becker beside him turns to see the woman stood in the archway from parlor to dining room, her baggy T-shirt, hacked-off sweats and fuzzy socks, "right," he says, as she says "Oz," and he says, "Oz, this is Oz, meet Pyrocles."

"Don't *I* get an introduction?" calls a heavyset man over the futon, as it's squeezed through the front door out onto the porch.

"You've already met," mutters Becker, peevishly.

"Context, Arnie," stepping within as the doorway clears, his enormous cardigan a-sway. "Never open your mouth till you know the shot; what flies in the street's not fit for a drawing room." Looking past Becker to Pyrocles. "Whoever told you that you could work with men."

"Actually, Jimmy," says Becker, "about the – "

"Nah ah ah," says Jimmy, lifting an implacable finger, "never quit a job, Arnie, if instead you can get yourself fired." He produces a plain white envelope, folded once in half. "State law mandates that, by the close of the day upon which one's employment is terminated, any monies outstanding are due, and so: eight hours' wages, at fourteen an hour. Less taxes, of course." Handing the envelope to Becker with a flourish. "You'll note it's dated yesterday."

"Oh," says Becker.

"And but also." Jimmy produces from another pocket a glossy black phone.

"Oh," says Becker, again. "Right," as he takes it. "Sorry."

"I believe this concludes our business."

"Jimmy, seriously, I'm sorry, it all just – "

"Enough, Arnie," and there's that finger again. "Live the dream," he says, not unkindly. "Follow thy bliss."

The shirt-sleeved man leans in from the porch, "Anything more, Anvil?"

Pyrocles shakes his head, but holds up a hand as Oz, who's looking to her fuzzy rainbow socks, mutters mostly to herself, "This is all well and good, but I don't suppose," looking up, "I can't imagine," she says, a little louder, "anybody knows somebody who needs a room? Six hundred a month, communal kitchen," trailing off.

"Good friend Oz," says Pyrocles, and he holds out something to her, a tightly neat roll of bills wrapped about with a rubber band. "Go on," he says. "Funds freely given, to be taken freely."

"That's, ah," she says, but she takes it.

"And with them, this advice," says Pyrocles, "a glass of cold, fresh milk, set nightly by your kitchen sink, will work wonders."

Out the front door then, and off the porch. A sandwich board's set up on the scraggled strip of frontage grass, Piano Lessons, it says, Weekday Appointments. Parked on the street a black late-model suv and an older, smaller pickup truck, pale blue, meticulously clean, futon laid in the back of it, the milk crate, boxes. The last of the men climbs into the suv, offering a wave of a salute to Pyrocles, and he nods in turn as that big engine clears its throat.

"Now what," says Becker, taking hold of the handle of the pickup's passenger door.

Pyrocles looks over the hood between them. "The haberdasher's, I think," he says. "You need a proper suit."

"Charles Harlib," says the delivery woman.

"I see that," he says, "I mean, it's just – "

"That's the address?" Her manner brusque.

"It's," he says, "yeah."

"Can you sign for it?" Her shorts of baggy brown.

"I," he says. "Yes."

Back through the house, eyeing the box, it's flat, not especially deep, a bit longer than his forearm. Past an empty mantel, into a narrow sitting room, a girl stood in the middle of it, face squeezed up in rapturous attention. Enormous headphones pinkly cup her ears, the music in them loud enough to leak a jouncing beat she's nodding along with, "Grace," he's saying, he says, "Grace," a flick of a gesture at his ear, push off, and seeing him she shoves back the headphones, chorus suddenly swelling, sinking down in this void like a crater, and she shakes her head, brow cocked, what?

"Momsicle about?"

"In here," says Carol, past the cluttered breakfast bar, there in the kitchen in her brown and yellow serape, book bag slung from her shoulder. He pinches a corner of the shipping label on the box and yanks, a ripping strip.

"Jason?" says Carol. "What is that?"

"I was going to ask you," heading toward her, into the kitchen, away from heedless, prancing Grace. "I can guess, but," shrugging, the box in his hands.

"They said it was coming tomorrow."

"Well, that's something else they got wrong."

"So, happy Memorial Day, I guess, or whatever." And then, "It's for you, jackass. The retro keyboard you've been jonesing for."

He looks up, stunned. "We can't possibly afford this."

"Don't worry about it."

"Which card did you even put it on? OnPoint's just about full, and Citi would've alerted – "

"It's not any card you have to worry about."

"You can't just *say* that, Charley, I have to – "

"Hey," she says, not loud, but sharp.

Jason closes his eyes, "I *have* to keep track of these things," he says, and opens them again, but she's looking, turning away, calling over the breakfast bar, "Not on the couch, Gloria, Gloria! Not on the couch." Out in the narrow sitting room, Gloria hops off the cushions of the low couch to resume her yearning pose feet planted on the rug. "I swear," says Carol, turning back, "I don't know what it is right now, with her, and show tunes."

"That's a," he says, "bit racist, don't you think? Policing, what she ought to listen to, or not, just because of," trailing off, "her," a gesture, toward the living room.

"The point *I* was trying to make," says Carol then, slowly, "is that show tunes, as a rule, are grotesquely overproduced, tragically underwritten, and, inevitably, mawkish. She can do better. A good murder ballad, maybe."

"Carol," he says, and winces at the force of it. "We're running the ragged edge, these last couple months. Especially with you being gone so much, doing, whatever it is you, do, with those people, I *have* to keep track, so we don't – "

"Keep track," she says, so witheringly quiet. She hauls up her book bag. Yanks it open. "How about," she says, rummaging, "that last run to Trader Joe's? Or the other night, when Grace and I snagged dinner from FoPo? Did *that* show up on your cards or alerts, or," she's plucked something out, "did you even notice that it didn't?"

It's a gold credit card. MasterCard, it says. Bank of Trebizond. Carol L. Harlib. Good thru 21/45.

"I only put a couple things on it, at first," she says, "because I didn't really believe that it would do what they said it would. But it does."

"They," he says. "Who, they."

"Gloria. Those people. This is for expenses. Within reason. Groceries. Take-out. The occasional gift."

"For, what?" he says. "Singing? Sometimes? Hanging out?" She's savagely hauling the book bag up on her shoulder. "Will they at least provide us a ten ninety-nine?"

"You're welcome, Jason," she snaps, pushing past him, out of the kitchen, away, leaving him with his box, and Gloria with her headphones, reaching up for a big finish.

She taps the last of a string of numbers written on the slip, "Thirty-seven," she mutters, and then, pushing her narrow glasses back in place, "he wants what?"

"To speak with the owner?" says Petra B. "Or manager, or whatever."

"Isn't this what Gloria's for?"

"I can't find her, Anna, I'm sorry," stepping out of the way as Anna shoves back her chair, "If it's one more thing," she mutters, on her way out the door, and Petra B left bobbing in her wake.

Out onto the balcony ringing, the warehouse spread below, overhead doors cranked open to either side to let in cooling, greying light, and all the hobs and clods, urisks and domestics, penates, broonies, mechanicals and here and there a peer, all about their various businesses, but it's not the chopping, the rustling, the rattling, the scraping and tearing, the brushing and mixing, it's not the indications and adumbrations, the attestations, the raucous laughter and that angered yelp, it's the singing that's most notable, as they make their way down the skeletal staircase bolted to the wall, it's that lone baritone booming from out on the loading dock, "Fetch me some a thy father's gold, and some a thy mother's fee," and the chorus, well-pitched, raggedly timed, an two a the steeds from the castle stalls, which hold em thirty an three!

Black battleship of a pickup, parked by the loading dock, facing the hitch of the flatbed trailer, and stood in the back of it Big Jim Turk, hoisting one end of a bundle of yellow two-by-fours, hefting his big deep voice, "I'll mount me on my milk-white steed, an thou the scarlet roan," and at the other end there's Lustucru, swinging the bundle in time, as Cherry-coke wrestles a roll of chicken wire up and over the tailgate, Cinædus and Brether Ned humping up twine-wrapped stacks of newsprint, we'll ride till we reach the stoney strand, an hour afore the dawn!

Anna makes her way past all the unloading, keeping a prudent distance, there's Powys stood on the corrugated flatbed, and paint-spattered Trucos beside, Getulos crouched behind them, but instead of a husband I've found me here a grave in the salty sea! as Petra hops out of Christian's way, he's leaping onto the flatbed with an awkward armload of rolled-up papers.

Down by the foot of the trailer, there on the pavement, a man's stood in drab coveralls, arms pointedly folded, seething under a scowl as he takes Anna in, her smart blouse crisply white, her trousers neatly tartaned, "You in charge?" he belts.

"What can," but "Pull off, pull off," Jim Turk's launched the next verse, "your rings and pearls, and deliver them up to me!" and she waits for the cæsura, "How might we help you?" she says, quickly, but solicitously clear, for I think it not fit such a glittering tip should rust in the salty sea!

"This has to stop!" shouts the man in the coveralls, a patch at his chest that says Gatto & Sons, much as the sign on the warehouse across the street, Gatto and Sons, Wholesale Produce. "The music! At all hours, the coming and going! Living here, and this ain't a residential block! And the, that goddamn street fair!" throwing his arms frustratedly wide, for I think it not fit such a silky slip should be roughened by the sea!

Anna hitches up her trousers at the knee to squat there, on the dock, head now at a level with his. "We let your trucks through," she says. "There was no impediment to your trucks."

"If I'm to doff my holland smock, then turn your back to me!" booms Big Jim Turk, swinging another bundle of lumber. "You shouldn't've had to!" shouts the man in the coveralls, and Anna manages not to flinch. "Tell me, sir," she says, but she looks away as she does so, "are you Mr. Gatto," somewhere up past the trailer, "or, ah, one of the sons?"

"Derek!" he shouts. "I'm the fucking day-shift manager!"

"And I would be Anna Nirdlinger. A moment." Hand on the edge of the dock, she hops down, "Hey!" he shouts, but click-tock of heels she's headed away around the foot of the trailer, for I think it not fit such a ruffian bent my beauty for to see!

Coming toward them all down the middle of the street a man on foot, his vest and trousers of rumpled plaid, expression slackly grave. "Shrieve?" calls Anna, hastening toward him, and another "Hey!" from the man from Gatto and Sons. "I did then turn my back to you, and laughed to hear you weep!" but there's a commotion up on the trailer, "ahead!" yells Trucos, marching with an imploring gesture down toward the foot, "to see where she's going!" but "She won't be *driving*," insists Getulos still crouched at the head of it, "she's to draw everyone *after!*" and Christian beside him, trying to keep the plans from rolling back up, but I caught you by your shoulders wide, and tumbled you into the sea! For six pretty maidens drowned thou here, but the seventh did drown thee!

"Oh!" cries Anna, there by the man in plaid, or "No!"

"Hey!" shouts Derek, one more time. "Can somebody! Anybody! Please! Who the *hell* is in charge, here?"

The dim air's doldrummed by arabesques of smoke that leak from the coal of the cigarette in her fingers poised, untapped, over a plastic coffee lid. She's sat herself on the yellow table among the six of them set close together, red shoes propped on the cushion of a rolling chair, black trousers loosely baggy, black top sleeveless, rising to a low turtleneck. "I'd heard your grace had quit," says Bruno, closing the double doors behind him.

She looks over her shoulder, eyes hidden away behind small round sunglasses despite the dimly haze. "It's a process," she says. Ash tumbles as she lifts it to her lips, stopping just short of a breath, "What do we know."

He leans a hand on the back of another of those scattered rolling chairs, "Nothing more, I fear. But – "

"Nothing," she says. "Is that what there is? Or just what you've been able to find out?"

"Your grace," he says, strained.

"Sorry," she says, a wave of that cigarette, the cigarette she lowers to crush out on the coffee lid. "There's no record," he's saying, "of anyone with the name May, or Hector, being processed into the Detention Center in the past two days. There was a Jack listed, as an alias, but too old to be whom you described."

"What about Johanna?"

"And no record of a Johanna Draper. Of course, there's no record of your incarceration, either."

"Right," she says.

"My lady," says Bruno, "the Queen's Huntsman is dead."

Squeak of the wheels as her feet drag that chair toward the table, "I told her," she says, folding her arms atop her canted knees. "Where's Luys?"

"I – couldn't say. He, is, where he is."

"I ask for help this morning, I get Astolfo, I get Sweetloaf, I get one of Agravante's boys, and that's it?"

"Jeffeory's no more with the Hound. Her majesty's named him her Axe."

"Yeah, I," she says, straightening, "I don't care," she says. Looking to him, down at the corner of the lavender table. "Where's the Mason?"

He takes in a breath, examining a moment the cracked leather of his worn brown brogues. "Your grace," he says, "does yet stand with her majesty?"

Her own inhalation's sharp, through her nose, "Jesus," she says. "The hell kind of question is that."

"Unfortunately apposite."

"Shit," says Jo, tipping back her head.

"I would not disagree," says Bruno.

"I can't," says Jo, and then, with a kick that spins the chair away, she hops off the table. "I can't. There's too much – if they didn't get picked up by the cops, they must've, at least, one or two of them, I need somebody, I need several somebodies, who know the current, ah, situation, where the camps are, who to talk to," but Bruno's shaking his head, "what," she says. "What."

"For that sort of work, we've always gone outside the company. There's the gentleman who fancies himself the Commanding Officer of the city's indigents, but," a grimace of a grin, as he notes the blank expression she's offering, "of course, your grace knows the co."

"We're not going that way," she says. "Shit."

"There's still the matter of the Huntsman's death," and then, as she turns away, "my lady – it appears to have come at the hands of the Harper."

"Christ!" she roars, and he flinches, "Bruno! I know!" Both hands up to her face, "You think," she says, "I got *any* sleep last night," removing her sunglasses to glare, directly, at him.

"Your grace," he says, and ducks his head.

She steps away, toward the darkening windows, folding up those glasses. "Okay," she says. "So. Smart guy. What's the play." Looking back, over her shoulder. "What's your plan."

He spreads his hands. "I, have no plan, your grace. I never do. My dearest wish is only to see that, those who do? Have everything, and everyone, they need, to see them done."

She closes up her eyes, and after a moment opens them again. "Bruno," she says. "Shrieve. You're getting sentimental on us."

His lips quirk with a touch of rue. "Assume, for the moment, that I don't believe her majesty, when she tells us Count Pinabel's no longer himself. Assume I don't account your grace a blasted fool for trying to bear – "

"Hey," she says, sharply.

He leans into an avuncular smile. "Our counterfactual is you *don't* shoulder a terrible burden you refuse to share."

"You have *no* idea – "

"Indeed, your grace," he says, quietly, even tenderly, and she bites back what she'd been about to say. "My point is this," he says. "Downstairs from us, right now, a Queen's ransom sits in a great wooden tub, open to all, knight, or churl, or peer of the court, that any might take what they would, and none," he says, "not one, ever takes more than they need. I don't know that your grace appreciates the magnitude of what her majesty has done. What you, Jo, helped her to do." He takes a breath, a shadow in the hazy unlit shadows. "It's returned to me a faith I hadn't realized I'd lost," says Bruno. "For that, alone, I'd follow her majesty over the very rim of the world."

"And the rest of us tumbling after," says Jo. "Shit."

"It is even as your grace has said," says Bruno.

RUBBER STRIKES GLASS – SPIT & IMAGE
POTTED CLIFFS – TRANSACTIONAL ANALYSIS

THE SOUR GONG OF RUBBER MALLET STRIKING GLASS, jagged top edge held secure by a hand gloved in nubby canvas, another strike, the snap of it breaking loose amidst a ringing showerfall of splinters and shards, the smash when it's tossed to the growing pile of broken glass on the blue tarp spread below, another gong, another, four of them in rough dungarees, T-shirts, coveralls, clambering about the scaffolding erected before the great curving wall of broken glass, criss-crossed by an erratically angled grid of wide blue strips of tape, a detuned, arrhythmic carillon, rung out over a constant drizzle of broken glass.

"It is done," says Agravante, under all that racket.

He's stood at the head of a folding table, the only furniture as such in that wide room, and set on it before him a napkin folded carelessly, dotted with crumbs, a shaker tipped over, salt spilled from its silver cap, a small brass lamp, snuff of smoke uncoiling from the tip, a little white ceramic dog, ears and tail of it painted black, a tightly curled netsuke rabbit, carved from yellowing wood. "Seems odd," says the man in the green denim jacket, taking up the last item, a ragged little cloth chimera, body of it striped, legs of iridescent fabric suggesting scales, head of it roughly wooled, with button eyes, and two limp horns. "Doing such a thing without the benefit of her majesty."

"Yours the hand that gives, Soames Thomas," says Agravante. "Yours it is, to take away. How," waiting out a vigorous smash, "how goes the work?"

"New panel's due from Wilsonville in a matter of hours," says the man in the green jacket, settling a white cap on his thickly greasy hair, "it will be in place in time for tonight. But, my lord," pitched low now, so as not to carry much further than themselves, "assurances were made, as to supportment, for our work?"

"You'll have your portion, my lord," says Agravante, just as low. "This very night." And then, raising his voice up over the clamor, "Next!" he bellows, turning away, only to "oh!" at the glumly narrow man stood there, "we are done," says Agravante, voice pitched once more low, "nothing should need be said." A gesture back toward the table, the items still littered on it.

"Excellency," says the glumly narrow man, chin tucked behind the fenceposts of a high white collar, "this household's complement has been," the next word lost in a crash of glass, and "What?" snaps Agravante, an irritated shake of his white locks.

"Decimated!" says the glum man, flinching at his volume. "Sir. There's aught to polish the plate."

Agravante claps a hand to a narrow, black-jacketed shoulder, and the glum man flinches again. "You are the Majordomo! Master of any domain. I leave it, all, in your hands so very capable. Next!"

A young man, pale hair elaborately braided, gestures toward the doorway, inclines himself to murmur something as Agravante passes, into the relative quiet of the long dim hall, and another man stood there, blinking at the milky light, the clanging glass, his safety orange coveralls, his red velvet frock coat pricked and dimpled by intricate embroidery. Agravante leans to one side, looking past him, "I'd thought there were to be two of you?" he says.

"Excellency?" says the man in the frock coat.

"You'd be the Hawk's Cinquedea. Not the Harper. Why are you here."

"Hawk's Widow's," says Pwyll. "Frankly, excellency, it's all a wreck. Gradasso's gone, you see. The Kern. It's a wreck, sir, all of it, and coming down around us, and I need a place to stand. I'd just as soon," leaning close, "other guys," he says, hoarsely forceful, "have come over, last few days. I heard."

"The Spadone," says Agravante. "The Axle. The Estoc; the Flammard. And the Mason, Luys. But you, I was told, came here, with the Harper."

Pwyll looks back, over his shoulder. The front door, at the end of the hall.

"You understand," says Agravante, leaning close in turn, "whatever my position on her majesty's choice of Huntsman, it would be, impolitic, for me to be," out in the wide room the tenor of the tumult's overwhelmed by shouts and cries and an enormous shattering crash, but Agravante's pressing home his point, "seen," he says, "rewarding anyone who'd had a hand in the demise of that particular gallowglas."

The gonging has, for the moment, stopped, replaced by heated conference. Out there in the wide room an enormous portion of the window's fallen loose, smashed to tempered bits, and the Soames has taken off his cap. "Pwyll," says Agravante, "tell me," as Pwyll drags his attention back, "who was it, that ended the Kern."

"I didn't," says Pwyll, and then, "I do not know, my lord."

Agravante smiles. "A judicious response. Welcome aboard."

A dozen cans on the tip-top shelf, Campbell's, they say, over and over, Tomato Soup, he seizes one, his other hand busily disengaging spindly spectacles from a shirt pocket, holding them up still folded to peer through at the label, contents, suggestions, directions, but he's blinking, shaking his head, moving the spectacles in and out until he closes up his eyes. A sigh, somewhat peeved. Lifting the spectacles away. "Stir in one can water," he mutters, hand to the back of his head, wincing as he touches there a mighty round of black curls.

The jingle of a bell, up front.

Setting the can on the counter he turns and starts to see the little man stood unexpected there, beads of the curtain behind undisturbed by any passage. "Out," says Gordon Porter.

The little man smiles around far too many teeth. "We are loathsome in their eyes," he says, cheerfully. "Strewn panting on an unknown shore, overcome by weariness. No god nor mortal will have truck with us. We were born – "

"Don't need this," Gordon growls.

"We were born," that word stretched through those teeth, "for all that is not right, by their lights, and that is why we're left to fend for ourselves in the barn, the crib, the cellar and the sty, we make of their crumbs our feasts, our wine their dregs. We've dogged their footsteps everywhere they've been, across the sere dead grass of continents since sunk, over storm-chilled waves, to cities that would one day scrape the sky, and gardens there, with oceans all about – "

"Somebody," says Gordon, but "we hum!" cries the little man, taking a step toward him, "mere snatches of their half-remembered songs, as we set about the work they will not do," and another, "what else, is there, for us?"

"There's what we do," says Gordon, "and there's how we go about the doing of it. No need for all the bowing and scraping, the yassuhs and the no-milords. Your nasty little self is proof enough of that."

"We all must do as we are bidden."

"Yeah? Who's bidden you, these days?"

"I'll eat your birds, youngster," a sudden, savage snarl. "Their quills will make my toothpicks, and such delicate baubles of their skulls."

"House is free," says Gordon, with a lurch of a step angled toward the gap between the little man puffing himself up and the beaded curtain. "Kitchen ain't. Get yourself gone."

Out in the front room there's an old man in a brown suit much too big, frowning to see Gordon stepping through the shoe-choked doorway. "Looking for Gordon," he says. "He about?"

Gordon blinks.

"He ain't been at the table," says the old man, looking away to the window. George's, it says. "He didn't say nothing about having up family."

Gordon blinks, again. "I know the kid," he blurts. "Christian. He's a, a friend."

"Christian," says the old man. "I swear, you are the spit and image."

"I got," says Gordon, a vague gesture at all the shoes, "work, so, I'll say you stopped by?"

"Tell him Duckie say he got nuts to lose."

"Yes, sir," says Gordon, after a moment, and Duckie nods. "I got a nap to see to, meantime," he says, and turns away, limping slowly toward the door. Gordon watches, until the bell over the door jingles again.

Thick-knuckled fingers snap by the padlock, and again, loud and sharp in the still grey afternoon. He seizes the lock, shakes it, nothing. "Leugh," he says, leaning against the smooth bright orange door, *"leug."* Letting go of the lock, he stoops close to it, "Stone and Salt," he whispers to it. "Lugubrio."

Open it pops.

Rattle and crash with a shove he throws up the door, looking about, the empty alley and all those other orange overhead doors side by side still closed, still locked, still silent. His bald head ruddy, as if picking up some color from them all, his cloth coat, much too short in the sleeves, shawled with fur the color of cheap lime candy, his wide-waled trousers belling over bare and filthy feet as he steps inside.

A couple-three gear carts, a trunk, all blackly anonymous in the shadows, a keyboard there, leather sack beneath it, a careless splay of wood and ivory pipes, a partially assembled drum kit, tom on a spindly stand, rakish hi-hat, big bass that says Stone & Salt on the head in fresh black vinyl letters. He squats by a canvas shopping bag to rummage up a pale drumstick that he spins about suddenly unclumsy fingers. Eyes it resting, there, in his hand. Tucks it back away.

Past the kit a fleet of instrument cases laid with casual reverence on the concrete floor, a couple of fiddles, or maybe one's a mandolin, the hulk of an acoustic bass, beached on its side in stiff nylon, something long and low and flatly rectangular, but he sits himself heavily beside a battered old guitar case of felt and cardboard, marked by a lone demure sticker, pasted at an angle, Play Anything, it says. Raps the lid of it, once, then scoots himself back.

The lid trembles and then, with a protesting creak, lifts. Up from within a slender hand, joined by another, reaching, stretching, a fusillade of knuckles cracked, joints popped, fingers wriggling now, limberly loose. The case scrapes the floor, shifted by the shift of weight within, a curled back breasting the lid, a long bare leg lifted out to slap a blue flip-flop on the concrete, a skinny red-headed man standing himself up out of the case, blinking thickly, cropped grey sweatshirt, Y-font underpants laundered to a dingy ivory. "Otto," he says, looking away. "Or, it's *Sir* Otto, now, isn't it."

"Not no more," says Otto Dogstongue.

"Not no more what."

"They say you can feel it? When it happens? Well, I'm here to tell you they're right. Bread, oil, salt, pop, pop, pop," savoring each plosive smack, "and once more," a sigh, a flick of those fingers, "court's light a Bullbeggar." A shrug. "Had no idea ol' Tommy Tom'd go for all that pomp and circumstance. Must be trying to impress the Barons."

"So what did you do," says the red-headed man, stepping away, snagging the stool from behind the drum kit.

"It's what I *didn't* do. I didn't swan off across the river, with him and the rest of the Local brass. Kamali and Stevedore,

Jackstaff and Gaffer, and Luthier, who can't win a duel for a nickel, but not no more meself." Sitting back, resettling that furry collar on his shoulders. "Meeting's next week," he says. "What am I, not supposed to go?"

"So why am I awake?" says the red-headed man, skinny gammons planted on the stool.

"Come back with me, John Wharfinger. Come back, to the Queen's new digs. She's done so much more, in a month, for far so many more, than the Local's ever dreamed. You have any idea why it's so quiet here, now, and empty?"

"I like it."

"It's because everybody's there," says Otto. "They're all there."

The red-headed man looks up, out toward the open door, the orange doors across the alley, scowling at the marginally brighter afternoon.

"And there'd be music. We'd all play together, again."

"Herself?" says John Wharfinger.

"The Axe may have foresworn us, but my lady Outlaw's piped for Carol, and I did rattle a drum betimes."

"And the kid?"

"Streak's yet Blue," says Otto, unfolding a giddy smile.

John Wharfinger nods, looking down at the case on the floor.

"I mean, come on," says Otto, smile crumpling. "We could, we could get a truck, load all this up, it wouldn't take, come on, John."

"I said yes," says John Wharfinger. "But I wouldn't say no to a truck."

"No, but, see?" he's saying, "they fucking get fogged," holding up the goggles, "I wear 'em," up against his forehead, "here, right?" shrugging the flop of his pompadour aside, "fucking cool, right? But when I want to actually fucking *wear* them," lowering a brass-ringed lens over one glaring eye, "they're all fucking *fogged!*" whipping it away, leather straps a-flap. "There has to be some fucking treatment, or something, a fucking spray, some fucking, I don't know, fuck is the word, unguent? Something?"

The Dinny-Mara shrugs without looking up, as he adjusts scrape and chime the placement of upright leaves and shards of dark grey slate set neatly close one flat before another in a small cast-iron pot.

"Seriously," says Sweetloaf, "they don't fuck up like this in the fucking movies." And then, as the Dinny-Mara sits back, eyeing his arrangement of slate, a stark little cartoon of sheer mountain cliffs, "Don't fucking *do* me like this," says Sweetloaf, aggrieved. "Moisture's, like, your fucking *thing.*" The Dinny-Mara's pouring a cup of water into the pot, and bends down to flick a switch. The gurgle of a hidden pump, and a sudden skin of water coats those leaves of slate, rinsing dull greys away to every possible shade of black, iridescent indigos through all the blues and wetly ruddy browns to hints of green, as a mist seeps up, flowing between and about those cliffs, lopping the lip of the pot. "Fuck it," says Sweetloaf, turning away with a scowl. The Dinny-Mara carefully lifts the pot, mountains, fog, and all, and sets it on a shelf with a dozen other potfuls of mist-sodden cliffscapes.

Sweetloaf stalks away up the aisle between those stalls, lit here and there against the cloudy gloom without, and the gently lambent glow of the great wooden tub. Past it, there before the empty, unlit stage, a dozen or so are crowded about great sheets of paper unrolled on the boards, murmuring, pointing, "Fuck," mutters Sweetloaf, "still fucking at it," turning about, goggle-straps flapping, he stops suddenly, "Oh," he says. "Hey."

The young man crouched on the floor of the otherwise empty stall doesn't look up.

"Hey," says Sweetloaf. "Butterlocks. How the fuck you doing."

"Stop calling me that." His oversized shirt of yellow plaid, he's crouched over a broad sheet of rough brown paper, scribbling over the shape he'd just begun to draw with a grease pencil. "Well," says Sweetloaf, "the fuck should we call you?

We already got a Goodhill, used to fucking do for a house up in Montavilla."

"Christian," he growls, starting again, two quick strokes to either side, a long wobbly line to connect them, and another, a low rectangle.

"Like *that's* gonna fucking last."

Those murmurs at the other end climb to a pelting absolutely, answered by a rousing chorus of negations and dubious groans. Christian sits up to look over his work. The thick blank painstaken strokes are now clearly the outline of a long façade, topped by a low-hipped roof. He addes a shape at one end of it, suggesting a shallow porch, and two doors, side by side.

"Fuck is that? A strip mall?"

"Apartments," growls Christian, duckwalking down to the other end of the sketch, "where people lived, and, and," strokes now quick, assured, "worked, and," another porch, the same two doors, "cooked," he says, and winces, "dreamed," he says, and scowls.

"The fuck ever," says Sweetloaf, looking away. The kerfluffle by the stage drops away, stilling, as all those domestics and mechanicals turn, look, duck heads, a couple of them bowing, "Hey," says Sweetloaf, "look alive. It's the Duchess."

Up there, Jo Gallowglas, all in black, a hand held up, nodding, as Trucos, or is it Getulos, says something earnestly emphatic, pointing to the plans, and Getulos, no, it's Trucos, vociferously disagrees, as Jo, still nodding, backs away, that hand still up, pushing back against their collective enthusiasm.

"Shit," spits Christian, stuffing the grease pencil in a pocket, scrabbling to roll up his drawing, clambering to his feet as Sweetloaf steps out of his way, "I gotta," he says, but "Christian!" calls Jo, rounding the tub, heading down that wide aisle toward them, past stalls filled with art and tools and debris. "I was looking for you. *Really* wish you had a phone."

"Well," says Christian, looking down toward the other end of that aisle, the arch, the shadows beyond. "I don't."

"You still up on the camps?" she says, and a "hey" for Sweetloaf. "Where folks these days jungle up? I need to find somebody, and Bruno's people are useless for this. Little old lady named May, had a big damn camper out by the airport and a metric fuckton of National Geographics," but "Nah," he's saying, raising his voice, "nah, co's gone and ain't neither of us want nothing to do with the new xo. Trust me."

"I want, you," she says. "I have to find her. And, Jack, and Hector – cops trashed the camp, Thursday night, and they didn't get picked up, but otherwise I got no idea where they went. You need to get out to whoever you can who knows about or's in charge of this shit, and tell me, I mean, is Springwater still a deal? What?"

He's shaking his head. "I help you, you gotta do something for me."

"Since when," she says, "did this become transactional?"

"Since when I never worked for you, is when."

"You," she snaps, but catches herself, "what," she says. "What is it."

His chin juts, points toward the crowd of them, up by the stage. "They're working out what to build, on the float out there. I mean, they know what, just not which way it'll go. It's a map, or a model, of the city, that'll sit in the lap of the Queen."

"Lap," says Jo.

"Of a statue, of the Queen. So, you, have to tell them. Vanport has to be in there. One way or another, they gotta put Vanport in there, too. That's what I need you to do, for me." The glare over his hunched cheekbones. The rolled-up drawing crumpled under one arm. The free hand curled in a heedless fist.

"The fuck is Vanport?" says Jo.

It's abrupt, how Christian turns away, sets off, slap of his grimy running shoes, "Hey!" shouts Jo. "Christian! God-dammit. Christian! You want anything with that, that fucking float? You gotta run it past Gloria! It's her show! *Christian!*"

He's gone, under the arch, into the shadows.

"Shit," says Jo.

"Hey," says Sweetloaf, then. "Boss. I know some a them fucking camps."

"So do I," says Jo. "I need all of the camps. Everything. I have to find them."

Sweetloaf shrugs, goggles glinting. "I can drive."

A HALF-DOZEN DREAM-CATCHERS – HOW HE'LL DO IT
THE ONLY MORTAL HERE – ALREADY UNLOCKED
A DISAGREEMENT

A HALF-DOZEN DREAM-CATCHERS dangle before a broad window, colors washed away by the glooming on the other side of the glass, relieved only by the pinpoint brilliance of a lamp across the street, there before a three- or four-storey pile of bricks, the huge high windows of it as dark as everything else. She lifts a hand, surprising the shadows, reaches along the sill to nudge a small round mirror in an octagonal frame, shifting it until the silvered surface catches a corner of streetlight flaring, she blinks, lashes artfully thickened by mascara, lids carefully lined. Scoots the mirror back as clack of latch, key-jangle, lights flick on out in the front room, "what we've been doing," someone's saying, "I think you'll see," and she sits up, smoothing wrinkles from her lap.

Lights flick on in here, and there she is, sat on the couch in her charcoal suit, corkscrew curls, dourly patient mien, but he doesn't seem to see her as he bustles in, grizzled and jowly, doughy in tie-dye, to lean over the big desk, shuffling through an assortment of red- and blue-jacketed files. The second man stays in the doorway, tall and achingly slender in a long pale cardigan, and he does seem to see her, a smile cocked in his lush brown beard, so neatly combed.

"Here we are," says the grizzled man, manila folder held up, a trophy, "participation," he says, and then he sees her, too, and his bluster's whisked away. "Who," he says, "how, how did you, what are you doing here?"

"Might we have the room, Mr. Stiles?"

"I," he says, looking to the man in the doorway, who, still smiling, shrugs a slender shoulder.

"A few minutes only," she says.

"I could just," he says, pointing, past the man in the doorway, out. "I'll wait in the car," he says, stepping back into the front room. At the sound of the outer door closing, she says, "You despise him."

"Nelson?" says the man in the doorway. "That's a strong word, despise. I merely prefer when I don't have to think of him."

"And why do you have to think of him now?"

"Can we skip, to where you tell me I'm in your way, I need to get out of it?" he's stepping out of the doorway, into that back room, "you'll have to forgive me, I'm not up on the etiquette in this sort of situation."

"What sort of situation is that, Mr. Lake?"

"Luke," he snaps, and then, "the situation," gathering up his splintered insouciance, "of being ambushed by an occult operator."

"Are you feeling ambushed, Mr. Luke?"

"Just, Luke."

"Plain, simple Luke."

"That was you, wasn't it. The sunburst, downtown, a couple days ago."

She looks to the mirror on the sill, the reds and greens of the frame now clear in the artificial light. "We're not the only players at this table, Luke."

"What I don't know," he says, folding his arms, "is if it means your little excursion across town was a success, or a failure."

"Why do you find yourself having to think of Mr. Stiles?"

That smile in his beard flashes teeth. "You must have some idea," he says. "You knew enough to meet me here."

Her arm, stretched out along the back of that couch. The rumples shadowy soft of her charcoal sleeve, of her exactingly baggy trousers, one leg crossed over the other, glossy grey pump tocking aloft there, a metronome portentously adagio. The expertly painted expression brightly expectant.

"He has something I want."

That expectancy dims a little, disappointed. The metronome ceases.

"Need," he says. "His, contacts. The good name of this, organization," with a gesture that takes in the back room, the front room, the desk, the files.

"The Urban Restoration squad," she says. "Founded by Nelson Stiles, and Michael Sinjin Lake."

Not a trace of that smile can be found in his beard.

"What I don't know," she says, "what I can't, quite, discern, is, well," a fillip of her fingers, "why."

He looks down, lush beard lapping his shoulder, thick hair brushing the cardigan lopped open over a stark white shirt, his khakis the color of sand, his monk-strap sandals. "Surely," he says, and then, looking back up to her, a hint of that smile returning, "you've heard my speeches."

"Oh, indeed," she says. "And read, the interview, in Street Roots. You've managed quite a lot in little over a week."

"Then you know."

"One bad day," she says, limned eyes widening as she relishes the quote. "Your message discipline is admirable. All the petit lumpen. But," leaning forward, elbows braced on her knees, "to what end, Luke. Toward what purpose."

"That," he says, and there's his smile complete again, and his teeth. "That's how I'm going to do it. No one, not a one of you, believes, that I say only what I mean. That I'll do everything I say."

"The dispossessed," she says, "reclaiming what was theirs. Well." Hands on her knees now, pushing, up on her feet. "You are not in our way today, Luke." Stepping close beside him, she takes in a long, savoring sniff. Favors him with a benedictive nod.

He doesn't watch her leave. But when there is no clack of latch or groan of hinge, he turns in the doorway, with a snort, to see that front room empty.

His suit, his shirt, his tie, all coolly subtle blues and greys and here and there a touch of pink, and what's left of his hair's been slicked straight back. Arms crossed before him, he worries at the watch about his wrist, shining silver, bulbous crystal and a heavy, segmented band.

A laugh bursts over the burble and hum of polite conversation and startled, blinking, he looks up, across the spare crowd in that wide room, there's Pyrocles in shimmery blue, there by the great curving wall of glass, and hard beside him a squat man, thickly thewed, shoulders still a-wobble with hilarity, glossy black hair wrapped in a blue scarf, his two-tone shirt of pink and ivory, embroidered across the back with calligraphy that says Gutter Perfection, crossed by the worn brown leather strap of a sling holster.

Becker looks away.

It's a varied crowd, these knights and peers and sundry others gathered in this room. The man at the makeshift bar beside him, a folding table, really, dull green jacket and white mesh-back cap, nodding as he lifts a plastic coupe of fizzing wine from the ranks of identical coupes. The short woman across the table, her black dress brief, taking up two coupes to hand one to another woman, willowy tall, her jacket of black leather. The man there in a linen suit, his sun-browned head quite bald, explaining something desultorily to the woman uncomfortably buttoned up in cyan and bared skin, her close-cropped hair a virulent chartreuse. The stone-faced man, impassive in his olive-green fleece vest. The young man holding court by a waist-high pane of glass, a balustrade about a stairwell leading down somewhere, his pale white tangled dreads just touched with gold, his slim blue suit, his shirt and tie the same flat shade of dusty pink, directing with a magnanimous gesture the attention of those about him to the man at his side, wide face warmly red, jacket of indigo twill.

Becker seizes a coupe, wincing at the slosh of pink wine that dribbles his fingers, takes up a second with more care, and sets off through tendrils of converse toward that great high wall of glass, the evening outside flatly black, blown out by the bright lights here within, and the two men stood before. He offers one of the coupes to Pyrocles, even as he sips from the other, "sorry," he says, a winsome shrug. "Only two hands."

The squat man doesn't seem put out. "Good to see you again, Arnold," he says, with grave bonhomie. Becker's eyes slip side-long to Pyrocles, who lifts his coupe, "Joaquin," he says, "is to be named this night the Shootist, of our court."

"Provisionally," says the squat man. "Needs must we await your next Samani to make it official." The matte black butt of a pistol grip peeps from that brown leather holster, strapped across his chest, snugged up under a pectoral. "Soon enough," Pyrocles says, turning aside, "soon enough. Excellency!" to the young man approaching, his blue suit and his pale, pale locks, "how provident, that we might supplement our ranks with the likes of friend Joaquin!"

"Indeed," says the Viscount. "It seems roses, in the end, do trump saltwater."

"Excellency, I unfolded a map," says Joaquin, "and with a finger traced the route from where I'd been, to here, to there, and when I saw just how much further north I'd have to go?" He shakes his scarf-wrapped head. "There's rain enough in Oregon for my taste."

The Viscount reaches back, beckoning, then hands a plastic coupe to Joaquin, "We merely await the arrival of Southeast," he's saying, "and then we'll be about our Apportionment." Looking off to one side, "Someone!" he calls, "play music!" Turning back, smiling tightly as with a clack there's heard the groaning eloquence of an unseen cello. "Of course, Shootist, you've no streets yet to till, but nonetheless you'll have tonight your measure and your due."

Joaquin's nod is one of phlegmatic approbation. "Southeast," he says. "This would be the gallowglas," but then, a puzzled frown at the Viscount's admonishing hand, "I'd thought the Duchess to be a gallowglas?"

"Her grace," says Pyrocles, "does not," as the Viscount says, "I fear the only mortal to grace us with his presence is the Anvil's, ah, companion," a knuckle to his chin, "it's on the tip of my tongue."

"Becker," says Pyrocles. "Arnold," says Joaquin. Becker empties his coupe with a gulp. "Even so," says the Viscount, looking to a bustle at the doorway of that wide room, "ah!" he says. "And here's Southeast. Clear the table! Make room, make room!"

Stepping from the hall, his rough brown jacket pattered with fresh rain, his hair a jet black cap, beside him an older man in a blue coat, shoving back a damp grey mane, up to the folding table that's been cleared, not a coupe left in sight, as the Viscount stands himself at the other end. "Luys!" he says. "Good Sir Mason, what bricks have you brought us tonight?"

Luys sets a modest canvas sack on the table, "There was no time to press and mold, I fear," he says, tugging open the mouth of it to reveal a plastic bag within, sealed up about a heap of loosely golden dust.

"Beauty's in the stuff itself, and not the shape it takes," says the Viscount. Looking up, from the sack to the crowd of them, thick about the table, "Friends," he says, "peers, neighbors, gentles all, before we divvy up our dower, a moment, to mark the loss of the Glaive Rhythidd, wise counselor, trusted advisor, dear friend, beloved brother," an inclination toward the bald man in the linen suit, who does not look up to meet it. "A Huntsman, murdered in the street; an awful parody sent to accost us – let us hope her majesty's – "

"Your sister," says someone in that crowd, quite low, but audible enough.

"I," says the Viscount, suddenly cold and terrible, "have. No. Sister. Therefore," a deep breath, "it cannot be said my sister has done," lifting his hands, fingers spread, "anything. Now. Let us take another moment, more pleasant, I assure – "

"What of the Count?"

"To admire," grits the Viscount, turning away, a gesture back, toward the great dark empty window behind, "the labor undertaken by our Soames, to restore this hall to its former grandeur – "

"At great expense!" says the man in the meshback cap, and the tension run through them all relaxes, then, with chuckles, nudges, though their attentions all return to fix upon the bright sack on the table. "All hail the Soames," says the Viscount, "and his mighty rabbits. Now – "

"Where is the Count?" It's the stone-faced man, off to one side, glaring fixedly not at the sack but the Viscount, whose hands are on the table now, by a small set of silver scales, the precise brass cylinders of graduated weights. "Grandfather," he says, "is indisposed."

"And the Princess?" says the woman in black leather. "Also indisposed?"

"Baronness," says the Viscount, "Barons, peers and delegates – let us cut and weigh and portion out our bounty. There's time enough for business, at another time." He's lifted a slender glass tube from the neat wooden rack of them, there, gleamingly upright, empty, and the breath of the room is held as he dips it into the modest sack of light.

Becker looks down, the pinkly sticky coupe in his hand, the sharp crease of his trousers, the grey of them shot through with threads of blue and lavender and silver, his softly polished shoes. Shuff of a sliding step aside. Under a threadbare scrim of freshly unswept sawdust, spangled still with crumbs of broken glass, a coprolite of caulk, the floor, it's faded, but an unmistakable stain, an irregularly ruddy brown, blotching once-polished boards. Becker steps back, and back again, away and off, "I'll, uh," he says, "bathroom," but Pyrocles has pressed close about the table with the rest of them.

Out, into the hall, long and dim, lit only by a spot at the far end striking shadows from the rails and stiles of a yellow front door. Becker feels his hesitant way along until there, to the left of that door, can be made out a stairwell climbing its shadowy way up in an enclosed spiral, and a man stood on the first step, arms folded in a suit forbiddingly dark, skeptically chewing his lower lip. Becker turning about steps right, blinkingly into a lemon-bright kitchen, a woman in a white apron, kerchief about her hair, halted in the clattering act of unloading an armful of empty plastic coupes into an ungainly garbage bag, "Not yet!" barks someone, someone else, a grumpily narrow man, shirtsleeves tightly rolled above his elbows, flat black vest buttoned up to the white collar upright like a fence about his gin-blossomed jowls. He's roughly stripping the plastic wrap from a plastic tray of chopped raw vegetables, cucumber slices, pepper strips of red and yellow and green, whole cherry tomatoes, baby carrots orange and magenta and yellowing white, florets of broccoli and cauliflower, "Not yet!" he snaps, again, more plastic trays of crudités stacked one on another beside him, "it will come, it will come," and he flings a gesture at the doorway, but Becker's already backing through it, "Sorry," he's saying, "sorry," back out into the hall.

"Moody!" he bellows, boots loud on the boards in this darkly narrow alley between boat-bows crowded close, the unlit façades of floating homes, "Moody!" over the lop and slap of the water below, the ringing chimes of fittings jostled, taut buzz of cables strummed by wayward gusts. "You will answer for what you've done!" Kicking a cleat wound about with thick grey line that stretches a-sag out over the water to the blocky snout of a house-boat, porched-over bow of it blankly anonymous behind those darkling screens. "Hey!" No gangplank braced between wharf and deck, no sign of one laid about anywhere. He plants himself on that very edge, slopping water below, cargo shorts and a bulky sweater, pale tangle of beard and unkempt hair. What little light there is to be found here snags the edges of the swords he carries, one in either hand, spread challengingly wide as he roars once more, "Moody!"

A flare dazzles over him and wharf and bow and all, he steps back, an arm thrown up to shade his eyes, blade bright in his hand, "Moody?" he says. A step toward the light, and another, "Face me, you wretch!"

"Ain't nobody here, Harper," the snarl in response. "But keep it down anyway." The light swoops away, settles brightly to reveal the rough grey boards between them, his boots, her enormous canvas deck shoes. "Peg-Meg?" he says, querulously.

"Always the games."

"You went over to *Moody?*"

A guttural plosive that might be a laugh, or a spit, or a cough. "Moody works for the Commanding Officer. Commanding

Officer rents. This dock?" That light swings back and forth between them, tarries, lapped a ways up his bare shins. "The Soames," she says.

"You've gone over to the *rabbits?*" he says, even more incredulously, and the light swoops away, back down the length of that alley, "Needed a watchman," she says.

"Meg Greentooth, gone to the rabbits," he says. "Five-fingered Pwyll to the hounds. Red Gaveston to his doxies, all in a day, I just don't – "

"Kern Gradasso gone to dust," she says. The light's switched off.

"Margie," he says, thickly.

"Go," she says.

The colorless key stops just short of the lock, bobs a moment, is folded back into fingers that seize the handle, lever it easily down, unlocked already. He opens the flimsy door, and a groan of springs as he steps his weight within, head and shoulders stooped against the close curl of the ceiling. A step to the right, and he sits himself with a creak in the booth there in the nose of the unlit trailer. A crackle across the little table, from a cigarette's glowing coal.

"Your grace," he says.

"My lord the Mason," says Jo Maguire.

"I had thought you'd meant to quit."

"I meant," she says, "to walk out of the city and never come back." Another crackling flare. "Lately I'm shit with the grand pronouncements."

"Where had you meant to go, on foot?" he asks, gently, genuinely interested.

"I don't know," she says. "East."

"That way lies the desert."

"Not like any thought went into it." The coal swoops to be swiftly snuffed, a ruddy glimpse of the rim of a plate, his closed hands on the table, bit of leather tied about one wide wrist. "But there," she says. "That was it. Last one."

"As pronouncements go, that's not so grand."

"It's a promise," she says. "Big difference. Whatcha got, there."

His one hand's tucking away that key. His other, the one that leaks a faintest glimmer through his fingers' interstices, he opens to reveal a slender glass tube, capped by dark-waxed cork, and within a filament of gold. "A portion," he says. "Same as any other."

"Didn't know we'd started giving 'em out in test tubes," she says. "Classier than sandwich bags, I guess."

"Do you believe her majesty?"

"Do I what now?"

"Is that not," his voice like gravel underfoot, "the crux of this conversation?"

"You weren't there," she says, flatly. "You didn't see him, you didn't *hear* him. You weren't there."

"I have, now. If he's truly what you say."

"If you had, if you truly had? There'd be no doubt."

"Yet there is," he says, simply.

A moment passes, before Jo says, "So. You don't. Believe her."

A shuff, of corduroy on naugahyde, the clink of crockery displaced. "On this particular point," he says, picking his careful way, "I do maintain, her majesty's mistaken," and then, in a rush, "for I do not doubt the most undeniably compelling of reasons." A heavy breath, taken in. "I do not doubt her majesty believes. But what she's done, my lady, because of that belief? Threatens to sunder court, and city, all."

Click, chime, something in her hands. "What is it she's done, Luys."

"Denied the Hound his portion. Banished a fifth entire. Charged them with impossible demands."

Click, rasp, a pop of flame from the lighter in her hand, that brings out the color in his rough brown jacket, her pale bare arms, "That it?" she says. Couple-three unwashed plates at her elbow, the cigarette butt, a desiccated tea bag crumped against a mug. "That's all that's got you upset?"

"My lady," he says, his expression grave, "it is more than enough."

Whick, and darkness once more. Squeak as she sits back on her bench.

"Your," he says, after a moment, considering, "absence," he says, testing the weight of each word, "did greatly, upset, her majesty."

"So it's my fault."

"I mean only that it was upon your grace's vanishment that she retreated, to that woman's warehouse." Table-creak as he leans toward her. "When you found your way back, it filled us all with hope. And when you helped her turn the owr, that hope was fulfilled, to overflowing," his voice a husk, he swallows. "But then you left. Again. Walked away. And she announced her plan to give it freely, to any and all, save Southwest."

Click, chime. Click. "You left out the bits," she says, "where Southwest attacked her."

"An exaggeration," he says.

"Where you there, for the first one?"

"A disagreement, over how best to safeguard her majesty."

"What, whether to fuck, marry, or kill?"

"No harm was intended – "

"Were you there?" Slip and pop as she leans toward him, clack of plates, "way I heard it, Marfisa had to throw the goddamn throne through the window to get them both out safe."

"The window," he says, "has been restored."

"Well thank God for that. And the throne? How about the King, Luys? How come nobody talks about that?" And then, "I swear, if you'd asked me, who'd be the true believer, and who's the triangulating, equivocating fuck-up – "

"My lady!" He starts back, blinking, as the lighter's flame licks up once more between them. "Am I?" she says.

"Of course."

"Then this?" says Jo. "Stops." Click, the flame is gone, and sudden once more darkness, and complete. "No more footsie with Agravante. Got it?"

Scrape, a grunt, groan of trailer-springs, a gasp, "Let *go,*" she says.

"We will be *torn apart.*"

"And you're the only one can hold it together?"

"Someone," he says, "has to," slip, scuff, the hiss of her breath, *"Jo,"* he says, a roughly secret whisper. "Her majesty is *mad.* This scheme of hers, her mulish stubbornness, her wasteful dalliances – she sent her *Huntsman,* it could have been *you,* to a needless, useless *death.* Jo. Listen to me. *Jo.* There is no *Bride.* A Queen, two Crones, and there is no Bride. Do you," clink, a clunk, "do you understand?"

Squeak, and a sigh of the cushion, released, she's getting to her feet. "Tomorrow," she says. "First thing. As many of everybody as you can, meet me at that, woman's warehouse." A step away. "Some friends are missing. We're gonna find them." Clack of latch, the flimsy door swings open, streetlight spilling silvery thin, and there she stands, harshly limned against her silhouette. "Now. You want me to send in Sweetloaf? Or you gonna dally yourself?"

"Lady," he says, choked, but the trailer judders, and she's gone.

THE LAST CHORD

THE LAST CHORD floats from his strings, a brightness falling shimmering dissolve, and his fingers lift from the fretboard, the soundbox, but his arms remain curled about that big-bellied guitar, his head hung low, face obscured by a lone long lock dyed blue. There's no applause, but the stillness all about him breaks as one by they lower hands, or lift them, look to their friend, their neighbor, to him there on the stool by the cold and empty hearth, the crowd of them in that big front room, lit only by dim lamps set in elaborately fronded sconces, and somewhere in the middle of them all she takes a deep and shivering breath, "Oh, my," she says.

"White boys shouldn't ought to play the blues," murmurs the woman beside her, "always ends up something different when they're done with it."

"Now, Mother," she says, but frowns as she looks to her, much too tall, head and shoulders draped in the hood of some loose, brief jacket of pale gold, or brassy silver, high black boots laced up past her knees, but her dark thighs bare between for anyone to see. "Forgive me," she says, "I had thought – "

"You keep doing that," says the woman, not unkindly, moving away through the crowd, leaving her to herself, her long full navy skirt, prim pink sweater, hair neatly tucked in an up-do, folding her arms as the crowd, released, moves about. Up there by the hearth the guitarist speaks quietly with a short man all in black, his beard a whisper of curls to line his jaw.

"I shouldn't be here," she mutters, and casts about, the front door there, she sets out toward it, but her first step stumbles, something clatter-thump underfoot, and she kneels, skirt pooling, to take it up, a lone shoe, a loafer with a strap across the softly wrinkled vamp of it, and tucked there the winking copper of a penny.

"Is someone," she says, looking up, but there is no one, every-one has gone, there's just the stool there, by the hearth, and otherwise that big front room is empty.

It was a quarter to nine
We were running on Las Vegas time
Show's about to start, so stand in line
Can't blame us, boys
We all sigh above the dirty white noise

—*Patty Larkin*

NO. 41
" – arms - legs - heaven) – "

THE TABLE IS LONG, to stretch the unlit length of that long porch, suspended beneath the enormity of the house above, propped out over the steepening slope below. That table's long, and scrubbed so meticulously clean it might catch even the faintest hint of what light's available down here and hold it, a reflection, suspended, so it seems, a fraction of an inch or so above that ruthlessly polished surface. A thick orange cord's been laid along the top of it in a mostly straight and unkinked line until about halfway down, where it ends in a plug, and the line's taken up by a thin brown cord, continuing on until it in turn ends in a plug joined by a smooth white cord, this one relaxed, looped in a couple-three lazy coils to fetch up at the base of a small white desk lamp, set here at the very head of the table to thinly shine on a lone white saucer laden with three unbitten slices of pressed meat, rectangularly pink. A figure's sat in a chair, turned away from table, lamp, and plate, a silhouette wrapped in a blanket, arms and legs presumably tucked away, head tipped forward, chin pressed to sunken chest, sharp shoulders rising slowly and settling, slowly, with sleepingly regular breaths, gently stirring a wild crown of loose thin hair.

Agravante's stood to one side, a hand on the balustrade, a tiny knife in that hand, the wickedly pointed blade maybe half the length of its handle. The collar of his shirt's undone, the knot of his tie loosened, the both of the same dull color, uncertain in the darkness. He lifts the knife up to balance on its point, held in place by a fingertip, lets it topple to catch it, quick. Lays it gently, clink, on the railing.

"Trumpets," croaks the other, and Agravante looks to see that head lifted, woozily a-wobble, but those tiny dark eyes are fixed on something far away, over and past the glower of downtown that rusts the bellies of the clouds hung low above, something away out past the unseen horizon. "Blow," says the other. "Horns. For that is the law, on this day, when the moon has risen," something of a struggle, then, wriggling weakly in that chair, to free, perhaps, an arm, to point, but those blankets, it seems, are tightly wrapped. "In half an hour, if even that, the sun will also rise, to give chase over the clouds, and down there," those tiny eyes shift, that attention shifts, to fix on the city below, "they will cast about for me, but they will not find me," that head turns, then, and those eyes find Agravante, "for you have done me this great wrong, and hidden me from sight." A sigh, and that head tips precipitously back, the weight too much for such a frail neck. "The new moon has now risen that will swallow them whole."

Agravante watches, waiting, tiny knife now tightly in his hand.

"The levain," says the other. The words, no longer clear, struggle through a hoarse and rough-edged whisper. "Must be fed." That head pulls itself upright, but tips slowly to one side, the weight as yet too much, and those black eyes jerk and dart. "A measure of Camas wheat, and good clean Bull Run water, but, but but, but," the head struggling upright, and there, a small but definite smile of accomplishment, perhaps, even pride. Agravante steps away from the balustrade, toward the blanket-wrapped other in that chair. "The water must be left out, open to the air, an hour or so, or more," the words clearing, strengthening, "there are reagents, that must dissipate, I brought it with us, the levain, when first we did come over, a crock tucked in my shirt, against the warmth of my breast, and every loaf that I've made since has started with a dollop of that levain, and is this," that smile, sharpening, Agravante halting, the look on his face slipping, from one valence, to another, "what you want? Is this why you coddle me? Feed me? Keep me," that tongue licking out, a slickery sheen in the darkness, "warm? Ah ah," as Agravante steps close, presses close with that knife in his hand, "let's not be rash, boy, boy, son, grandson, after all," swallowing thickly, chin drawn back, those black eyes craned down to the wicked point, "there may yet be," says the other, "a chance," letting the word linger, stretch into a question, a possibility, those eyes squeezing shut as Agravante lifts the knife, high up above his head, and drives it down to thunk into the table, stuck upright, just out of reach.

"Would've been such a waste," mutters the other, and then, calling after Agravante, who's making his way back up the length of the porch, "Regret is a luxury! Much too expensive. Best to make peace, with what is, and fire up the grill! I'll have six lambs, and a ram, without blemish, and a whole young bull, and none of your oxen, and no incense, do you hear me? None! It is a rancid stench, in my nostrils!"

Chuckling, at the creak of stairs behind, shaking that wild-crowned head. Out there the darkness has lightened, the horizon now a reddening jagged line to break apart earth and sky. The other looks down, to the meat on the plate in the puddle of lamp-light, and leans toward it, a struggle again within those blankets tightly wrapped, too tight. Slumping in the chair, leaning over, mouth opening, straining, yearning, but still it's just a bit too low, too far. Straightening, that head tipped back to blow out a defeated sigh.

"Shit," hisses the other.

THE UNDERWEAR FIRST – THE REST OF THEM
THE FILTHY KITCHEN – EIGHT & EIGHT & EIGHT AGAIN
AGILE SAFFRON COLOR GLASS

FIRST, THE UNDERWEAR, blue jockey shorts he finds among the tangled bedclothes and clumsily works over long and skinny feet, kicking up to yank them along his shanks and teuks, snugly snapping them about his loins, working his fit within. Something clunks free as he unwinds a pants-leg from the blankets, and he bends over the foot of the low bed to fish it up, a pair of goggles, leather straps a-dangle, lenses framed by round brass rings. Frowning through them in the dim light, he huffs over one of the lenses, misting the glass with his breath, and scrubs at it with a pinched-up wrinkle of bedsheet. Peers through them again, turning this way and that, the only light in here diffused through gauzy curtains hung in slender windows there and there. Careful of his slumping pompadour, he works the straps over around the back of his head, fitting the lenses over his eyes, blinking behind the glass, then lifts the lenses up to his forehead, just beneath his pile of matted curls. Then he casts about until he comes up with a grubby white T-shirt.

Clack and creak, the trailer's flimsy door pops open and below springs groan as the Mason climbs within, Luys in yellow corduroy and rough brown serge, his hair a neat black cap, two white paper cups in the cardboard caddy in his hand. "Hey," says Sweetloaf, turning the T-shirt around, inside-out and back again, "you have any fucking idea what the fuck time it is? Because I did *not* mean to sleep this fucking late."

Luys smiles. It's a gentle smile, to see Sweetloaf there, knelt on the alcoved bed, jockey shorts and goggles, terribly delicate shoulders, those knees too great for his thighs, the T-shirt slowing, stilling in his hands, "sun's fucking up," he's saying, "we gotta get the fuck on our way, is that chai?"

Luys sets the caddy on the table of the booth there in the nose of the trailer, then steps down the length of it, heavy steps one, two, three, "wait a fucking," says Sweetloaf, as a big brown hand reaches to cradle the side of his head, thumb of it quite gently stroking his cheek, a bit of leather tied about the wrist. "My lord," murmurs Sweetloaf, even as he presses a kiss to the rough-edged palm. "We have to go."

Both those hands now, cupping his shoulders, and Luys stoops as Sweetloaf lifts his mouth for a kiss, a lightly gentle kiss, and brief, but then another too quickly opening to something hungry, forceful, mouth seizing mouth, tongue parting lips, a grunt from Sweetloaf, his own hands pushing against Luys's shoulders, fingers crumpling yellow corduroy even as he sighs into a third and savoring kiss.

"Her grace," says Sweetloaf, when Luys lets go his lips, "expects us," opening his eyes, *"expected* us, at sunup this very whoop!" as Luys pushes him back on the rumpled umber comforter, serge knees dimpling the bedsheets, pinning Sweetloaf's hips between them, the one hand still gripping a shoulder, the other wrenching aside the tails of his yellow shirt, slither of belt and jangling clank of buckle undone, "wait," Sweetloaf's saying, "sir," as Luys releases his burgeoning cock from the lopping flap of his fly, "we have to," as Luys folds over him one hand driven into the sheets a strut the other gripping Sweetloaf's pompadour, "her grace," says Sweetloaf, but lever and sway and hips and hand, the glistening mauve that brushes his chin, his cheek, his mouth a grimace turned away, "my lord," he says, "my fucking *lord,"* as his head's turned, tipped, placed, thick fingers crimping his curls, he sputters, "the father, father of our lord, by my good father and by the ghost and the apostles twelve," Luys has pushed himself up and drooping back, and Sweetloaf beneath him's braced up on his elbows, "and the *seven* who *stand* with *me,"* he's saying, he's chanting, "and *list*en to the *things* that *drop* from his *mouth, back* the fuck *off!* Celta*tal*babal! Io Sabaoth!" and he spits. Luys has drawn the one leg back and off the bed, and now the other, taking a step uncertain, back. "Rous!" shouts Sweetloaf, sitting up, and Luys takes back another step, "Rous!" and another, "Rous!" until he fetches up against the booth, "Rous!" yelps Sweetloaf once more, tossing blankets and sheets aside, yanking his dungarees into his lap. Luys puts a hand back, trembling, and presses it to the table to still it, then leans a pivot to swing himself into the booth, the clink of his loosened belt against the tabletop.

Sweetloaf's got his dungarees on, he's buttoning them up, "the *taste,"* he's muttering, and then, "I got *no* fucking idea," wrestling into his T-shirt, goggles pompadour and all, "maybe Beaumont's rubbing off on me," kicking himself to the end of the bed, "fucking Christy-Ann," snatching his shoes from the floor. Luys watches, impassive, that hand of his quite still there by the cups still in the caddy.

"Well?" says Sweetloaf, his hand on the handle of the door. "You coming? Cause I'm sure as shit going."

Luys takes in a deep breath, but then looks away, down the cramped length of the trailer, past the spill of garbage from under the little sideboard sink, to the ruin of the bed tucked at the end.

"Yeah," says Sweetloaf, opening the flimsy door. "My lord, sir, you want some fucking advice?"

"Not especially," says the Mason.

"Get yourself the fuck together," says Sweetloaf, and out he steps.

"My lady Chatelaine!" cries one of them, and five or six steps above she stops with a clang, lowering her head before swinging back to glare down at them both brought up quite short behind, beneath, Trucos and Getulos in worn coveralls streaked and smeared with smatters of differing colors, side by side on those skeletal stairs, each with a paint-speckled boot on the same perforated tread.

"Don't," she says, "call me that. And if you are gonna call me that, don't fucking say my lady. Are we clear?"

"Of course" and "Yes, my – of course."

"Cause I wanted to think we were clear the *last* time," she says, "but here we are again," and she lifts the steaming paper cup in her hand, an admonition, "so, are we?" Her enormous grey T-shirt says Dirtbag Algorithm. "Absolutely, fucking, clear?"

A look, between the two of them. The one says, "Absolutely, my lady, but," and the other winces. "What must we do?"

"What should we do?"

"We need a decision!"

"He *can't* be right!" and a shove, against the railing, "He's wrong! He's wrong!" pushed back, into the wall. "Which way," and "Where," and "should she look" and "Guys," says Gloria, but "should she be facing," they continue, "forwards?" and "guys," she says, "guys," but "toward the rear!" and "Leading them on!" and "Drawing them in!" and *"Guys!"* she shouts, and the ringing clomp of her cork-soled wedge on the stair. "Enough! Geeze. Just, make the call. This is your show, your deal, it's your call. Okay? I can't, I can't make it for you. I'm not gonna do that," turning away, another step up, but then she looks back, a gesture with her cup, "but make it quick, okay? It's already Monday. We roll on Saturday," and up and up she goes, leaving them stood there, turning slowly to face each other's consternation.

Up on the balcony, Gloria's stopped before the door, now a pink so glossily soft it almost seems to give under the exploratory pressure of a fingertip, to tack as it's lifted away, and maybe a ghost of a print left behind. The pink's been laced with tendrils of feathery barely white, leaf-shapes stenciled in curls and coils that twine together but never repeat. She looks to the two of them clanking back down the staircase, into the hurl and the burl, the palettes of those spattered coveralls predominately pink, overlaid with drips and splotches of ivory and white. She takes hold of the knob of rose-tinted crystal, turns it, and opens the door.

The office within is still too small, too bright, the carpet still grimy, the escritoire remains half-buried under papers. "They painted the door again," says Gloria.

"Hadn't noticed," says Anna, sat before the desk, brief grey shorts and a frilly blouse, sorting the papers, this precarious pile, that teetering stack.

"Why would you," says Gloria, taking a wincing sip from her cup. "I mean, it's not like it's ever off its hinges, or we're tripping over dropcloths, or hey, are those the rest of them?"

Anna can only watch helplessly as Gloria seizes the papers from her hands, "I told you," she says, her patience distressed, "it was put through Saturday. To be delivered this morning. Despite the holiday."

The papers, of a size, are oddly weighted, plastic cards affixed to the bottom thirds, "Yeah, I know," Gloria's saying as she rummages ungainly through them, cards click-clacking, "but still," Trebizond, Trebizond, Trebizond, the letters stamped in flashing golden plastic.

"This brings the total number drawing from your account to thirty-seven," says Anna.

"Yeah?" says Gloria, tapping the papers against an edge of the desk, neatening up the edges, looking up to see Anna's sternly frown. "I thought you said this wouldn't be a problem."

"I said I could get them. I never said," a sigh, both sharp and pointed, "no one," she says, "has ever done anything on this," a gesture toward the sheaf in Gloria's hands, "scale," she says, "before. I couldn't," and a slow shake of her head, *"possibly,* tell you if, or if not, *this,"* sitting heavily back with a creak, "was or was not to be a problem, which," taking off her spectacles, "is," she says, wiping the one lens, and the other, with a tail of her blouse, "a problem," slipping them back into place, lips pursed in a pinch.

"Well," says Gloria, "okay then," dropping the pages indiscriminately atop another pile, "all the more reason." Zipping pop of unstripping stickum, she rips the card from the topmost page, tossing the paper aside. Another zip, toss, and another, zip, clack of cards together in her fingers, paper fluttering settling onto the carpet.

"Gloria," says Anna, a monishment.

"What, it's not like they need to read the letter," says Gloria, zip, toss. "Study the terms." Zip, clack. "Weigh pros and cons." Pop, flap. *"Sign* anything." Zip, click. Flutter. "All they have to do," she says, "all. They have. To do."

"Is what, Suzette?"

Gloria, holding out the next denuded letter, lets it fall, flop. "I thought you were all in on this," she says.

"All in," says Anna, with a questioning lilt.

"Dammit, Anna, this is *not* something you do just because," and "I didn't," Anna's saying, but, "because, because this *only* works," says Gloria, forcefully, "this only works if we're all, all of us, all in."

"All in what?"

"All in!" shouts Gloria. "Agreement! Together! On this!" Knocking the rest of the freighted pages clumsily into the air, toppling the stack they'd been resting on to slither and flittering slide as Anna scrambles to stem the flood, Gloria, opening her mouth, shutting it up again.

"There's no need for histrionics," says Anna stiffly, gathering papers up from the floor.

"I'm just," says Gloria, "I'm trying to *help* people."

"I know," says Anna, sitting back up. "I know." She's folding discarded letters together along their creases, setting the tidy bundles aside. "But you get so angry, doing it."

"Shouldn't I?" snarls Gloria, shuffling quickly click-clack through the cards in her hands, "Here," she says, "I'll go call Thorpe," holding one of them up between a couple of fingers, "least we could do for her. And here," winging another, "get that to Addison," she's heading for the door as Anna fumble-juggling manages to catch it. "I mean, thank God for what happened to Melissa, right?" says Gloria, scowl souring even as she does, "else we'd be up to thirty-eight."

The door's jerked open, slams shut. Anna flinches. Turns back to the stacks of paper, resettling her spectacles, "One might think," she mutters, tucking the folded letters into a pigeon-hole, "the books would be more easily kept, an it all flows just one way."

Rattle of gunfire, whoop of triumph, but he's knelt here in the bathroom, unconcerned, shoulders draped in a robe of worn brown terrycloth. Whump of an explosion forced through television speakers, loud enough yet to rattle the bottles and cans that litter the bismuth-pink tub. He nudges one with a fingertip, an empty chime, the clack and hollow rattle of vacated cans against damp fiberglass unevenly stained with something rustily brown, distributed in swipes and smears that rise up the sides to an abruptly level ring a couple inches below the rim, well above the garbage within. The xo, the co,

Chad, sits heavily back on his heels, "Shit," he grunts. "I just wanted a fucking *beer.*"

Staccato ostinatos of small-arms fire, hectoring shouts, get him, get him get him, tempo raggedly hastening as the timbre shrills until, shuffling down the hall he grimaces at the volume, waving a hand irritatedly as if to brush away a swarm of percussive pop-pop-pops, he scowls at the howls of disappointment, you utter chud, how did you miss, he was standing right there!

He turns away from that boisterous front room, out onto an awkward landing, a short flight of stairs dropping from it, treads hacked and gouged, into a kitchen, checkerboard floor obscured by smears and streaks of mud and grease and other stuff, the stickily rippled playa orange and brown and dull dark red left by whatever might've seeped from the grim black garbage bags and paper sacks piled about the almost unseen can, overburdened themselves with spilling slopping garbage, more empty bottles and cans and also wadded crumpled wrappers and paper towels, tailings of food half-eaten, pizza crusts and burrito rinds, glistening slimy plops of this or crumbling ridges of that, deposits of wetly dark coffee grounds and there what might once have been a handful of jojos. He steps off the stairs, off the track of something dragged at some point through the filth across the kitchen toward the back door, leaving a wake of rusted, ruddied stains through and under, displacing the mud and the grease and whatever else, but he's headed for the fridge, there by the big sheet of plywood leaned up against the cabinets. Yanks open the door on over-stuffed unlit chaos, "shit," he says, to himself, "right," expression souring about that stiffly slick white scar, "Jesus, it's starting to smell." Gently, gingerly closing the door of it, clink.

"Say the word," growls the man behind him, and "Jesus!" he yelps, a faltering step to one side, turning, as the growling heedlessly continues. "I'll have her up to core it out. Somebody's got to deal with this mess."

"Don't," says Chad, says the co, "don't fucking *do* that," a freighted breath, "don't," he says, again.

"Don't?" Heavy steps toward him, that broad-brimmed black hat pulled low, that jacket of army-surplus green. "We still gotta get something straight," a kick at a ringingly empty can, squelch into filth, *"you* don't *tell* me don't."

"Don't you fucking," says the co, staggered back, fumble-hand catching the railing behind him, as explosions redouble out front, he's struggling gulping trying to catch his breath, "Moody, I swear to God – "

"Swear to me," snarls Moody, shoving back a ragged cuff, flash of gold, light slung from a crystal dial, and the co turning his head away opens eyes squeezed shut and stood there before him, breathing like a bellows, the co, one knobble-knuckled hand clenched in a fist on the linoleum table-top scrubbed clean, the other lifting up a glossy blue brochure rolled in a crumpled tube, shaking it in the co's face as he draws back, trembling, "No," he manages to say.

"Annapolis," the co's sneering, "the Naval fucking Academy, is *that* what you think you want?"

"They, they," the co's stammering, "they said they, they want me," and "What?" the co barks, "What is it they want?" and "they said, because of the," and "tell me what, what is it," shaking that crumpled brochure with every imperative, "the test score, the test," the co's saying, "the, the PSAT," wincing at a slap of laughter from the co. "The test? They don't give a good God *damn* about any damn test or your brains, your moral character, any of that shit. They got your *name,* boy," uncrumpling the brochure, stabbing the mailing label with a finger, "because you are my witless, worthless son," rattle of glossy paper as the brochure's hurled away, "and *I* sank a *God* damned *Japanese* sub for them, right in the *God* damn mouth of the Columbia, nineteen and forty three, and *look* what good it got me!"

But the co's looking away, toward that oblong of ocean brightly blue on the spotless checkerboard floor, a slender destroyer, unfussily grey, steaming serenely across it. His T-shirt's striped with orange and yellow and brown, his jawline smoothly un-troubled by stubble, cheek unstiffened by any scar. Flinching at the sudden crack of an explosion, loud, but not so loud enough to be so close, to ring and shake the cans and bottles piled up with the garbage and, pinch of a frown, he looks up from the filth to see sharp-scowling Moody, the hat, that jacket, those eyes, the heavy gold watch about his wrist. "You *know* what has to be done," says Moody.

Blinking, mouth twisted about some sour taste, *"Fuck* you," spits the CO.

"Jasper's dead! Bambi shot him! Cops ain't doing a goddamn thing! It's a conspiracy, dammit, all the way up to the top of this stinking city! Chad!" but the CO's lurching away up the steps to the awkward landing, "You *know* what you have to do, you worthless, useless sack of – "

"Useful," says the CO, turning abruptly, one hand on the balustrade. "You want useful?" Gunfire rising once more somewhere behind him. "Go get me a bottle of something. Whiskey. Old Crow, I don't give a shit. I," he takes a step, as if to come back down, and Moody, clutching the crown of his hat, takes his foot off the bottom stair, "I am the commanding officer," says the CO. "You will not speak to me that way again."

Moody lowers his hand, "Oh yeah?" he says. "Or what? Or *what?*" But the CO's gone, through the doorway, past the hall, into the clamorous front room.

"That is *exactly,* what I said," she mutters to herself, unknotting the soft bow from about her throat. "Six, it was six of them." Lets it drop to join the jacket already crumpled on the tightly woven carpet. "But that's okay with me." Kicking off her kitten heels, shaking back her corkscrew curls, she sets to unbuttoning her blouse.

Naked but for sturdy briefs, she steps to the heavy curtains, checking the drape of them, smoothing their opaquely heavy fall with a sweep of her hand. "Tuesday," she says, turning back to the bed, draped with blankets a touch more brown than the carpet. "Time to pay for the hamburgers." She pushes the underpants over her hips and down.

There on the bed by a shut-up laptop a parcel, wrapped in burlap, and a small tin box. She takes up the parcel, unfolding the wrapping until what's left in her hand is the stub of a candle the width, perhaps, of a finger, but not even so long anymore as a knuckled joint. She sets it with exaggerated care on the carpet. "King and Queen of Caledon," she says, taking up the tin, "how many miles to Babylon?" Sliding back the lid of it. "Eight, and eight, and eight again," she says, pinching out a match, bulbously white-tipped. "Shall I get there by candlelight?" Striking the match on the bottom of the tin, the sudden rushing flare of light in her hands, she squats as it settles into itself, a steady, silent flame above the candle, its ragged tallow collar, the sooty crumble of wick. "Aye," she says, "and back again," but there's only a candle, burning on the carpet at the foot of the bed, the discarded suit, the closed-up laptop, and otherwise that dimly generic room is empty.

The carpet under her hands, her knees, a loose grey shag, and it's been some time since it was last vacuumed. She pushes herself to her feet, glossy corkscrew ringlets dulled, her back, her arms gone ashen in the green-white light of fluorescent tubes caged in lines above, the meticulous definition of her painted lips and eyelids washed away. She coughs, once. The man at the head of the table does not look up from the cards he's adeptly sorting despite the cigarette that smolders between two fingers, reaching to snap down card after index card, there, and there, pastel blue, pink, yellow, each with a word or phrase or passage handwritten in thin blue ink. His shirt is white, his jacket a rope-stripe of indigo and ivory, his round glasses rimmed with clear plastic, black hair oiled and combed in a severe part. "Jasmine," he says, "then absence, then jasmine."

"I only have a couple minutes," she says. "Four at most."

He looks up, light flaring from his glasses. "Jasmine. Absence. Jasmine. Countersign."

Her lips pinch. "Carnation," she says. "Offal. Jasmine. And it's cold."

"Dr. Uniform," he says, and returns to his cards.

"Mother," she says.

Snap. Snap. He lifts the cigarette to his lips for a ruminative drag, picks up a card to sweep it across to the other side of the array, where he taps it once, twice, then takes up another and pushes back from the table, getting to his feet. The wall behind him's panes of frosted glass, and more green light behind, covered over with index cards fixed in neatly ordered ranks and files. "You lost another operator Thursday night," he says, sticking one of the cards to the bottom of one of those lines.

"I wasn't informed there'd be one to lose," she says, arms folded, pebbled with gooseflesh.

He sticks the second card to the glass by itself, alone. "As you have made abundantly clear, you are Station Rose." Lifting the cigarette to his lips. "A good head of station is always already aware of whatever might happen within her purview." A sip of smoke. He turns to look to her again.

"It helps, if we get read in, whenever Ops decides to go walkabout within our, as you put it, purview."

A dismissive wave, as he sits back down, "A simple errand to fetch an item, one of many, that ought to have taken an hour or more at most. There was no need to distract you."

Shivering, "You," she snaps, and then, collecting herself, "had one of your contractors, try a smash and grab for a by-blow right in the middle of surveillance critical to our end of Agile Saffron. And you didn't think I needed to be distracted."

He shifts the position of another card, snap. "So you *were* aware of the details."

"After the fact."

"Tell me, Dr. Uniform: why is surveillance by the airport critical to Agile Saffron?"

He doesn't look up to see the twist of her lips as she considers how to say what she says next. "The night I invoked Setebos protocols. The night Saffron Rose was reactivated. Something, else, came back, with it." A deep, shuddering breath. "Color Glass," she says.

At that he looks up, glasses blanked over with light. "There's been nothing in your reports."

"I had to be certain," she says. "The situation's, delicate, as I'm sure you can appreciate."

Snap, he sets down a card, sherbet green. Moves another, cornflower blue. "You ascertained this on Friday, then, when you, Frances, put yourself in the same room as a queen, and a dormant scale of qlippoth?"

She looks down at that, away.

"You will document this thoroughly in a report that should have been on my desk that afternoon." Snap a pale pink card. "You will keep the two of them otherwise apart until an action's been approved," shuff, goldenrod slid from here to there, "for the permanent sequestration of Color Glass. Said action to be conducted under the auspices of this Directorate, and not Station Rose." Looking up. "Is that," he says, but she's not there anymore.

"Ah," he says. "Of course. Nevertheless." Snap, another card.

The candle's just a rim of wax on the beige carpet, a smoking nubbin of char where once had been a wick. She unfolds an arm to seize the blanket from the bed, tumbling the laptop to the floor as she wraps it draggled about herself, lowering her shoulders as her shivering, slowly, subsides. "Should've been a goddamn phone call," she mutters, stooping to snatch up her underpants.

HANDS ON A BARE HIP – NOT NOW
HOW TO GET NOTICED – THE NEWIS SPREAD

HANDS BY A BARE HIP, sun-browned, water-beaded, undo the knot of a bikini string, A hint of things to come, the caption, 2,421 likes. Don't tease us, Sooeurs! says the first comment, followed by a string of emojis, hearts red and purple, a peach, a spurt of pale blue droplets. "What's wrong?" says Ysabel, leaning close.

Chrissie swipes the photo away, shuts off the phone, "Ettie," she says. "Posted that, to our feed. Without telling me."

"From, ah, Los Angeles?" Ysabel presses a kiss to her shoulder. "Do you regret not going with her?"

Chrissie curls her fingers in artful tangles, inky black in the shadows, "No," she says, quite firmly, and it's her mouth that's kissed next. "Though," she murmurs, when it's over, "it has only been sixty-seven hours and forty-five minutes. Or so. But she shouldn't've done that." Her hair's been shorn to a fuzz of candlelit gold that clings to the curve of her skull.

"Very rude," says the Starling, sat up on the other side, her yellow bob mussed to disarray, collarbone ruddied by a smudge of lipstick.

"Then you must post something of your own." Ysabel sits up. "We should stage a tableau! Have Petra photograph it, I'm certain she'd be superior to," a dismissive fillip of her fingers toward the phone, "whoever did *that,*" but Chrissie's shaking her head, "I don't want to bug her," she says, nestled among the pillows. "And anyway, there's the show, tomorrow." Rugs and wraps now lopped up to her chin. "That's enough."

"Your television début!" Ysabel claps once, delighted, looking from one to the other, "as sexy devil-spirits, how could I forget."

"As tulpas, my lady," says the Starling.

"I'll be the tulpa," says Chrissie. "Both, I guess."

"What will you look like? What will you wear?"

The Starling shrugs. "We'll find out tomorrow."

"Fitting's at six," says Chrissie.

"But you must have some ideas – go on," nudging the Starling, nudging Chrissie, "whip something up. Dress in character. Your Queen commands!"

Leaning over Ysabel, the Starling offers a hand to Chrissie, who takes it with a sigh to pull herself up and, hand in hand, shedding silk and satin and brocade, bolsters and cushions bumped and slippingly tumbled, they step through the ring of candles flickering in their wake, padding toward the dressing screen set up there, between two of the blocky columns, and the frame of it is whitewashed wood, and the panels of pale linen. Ysabel smiling tugs cushions and pillows to arrange a comfortably makeshift throne against the side of the widely empty bed, and drapes her lap with a diaphanous scarf of purple roses and blue, edged with orange tassels. Laid out on the far side of that bed atop the blankets smoothly spread and tucked a black T-shirt, a kilt tartaned with black and red and white, an assortment of tights in blacks and greys, neatly rolled, a pair of fingerless cycling gloves.

"Majesty," says someone in the shadows off that way.

"Not now," says Ysabel. "Set the scene: music, something good for a dramatic entrance, at a nightclub. And a glass of the vodka, the vanilla vodka."

A clack, and the space is filled with a humming chord of voices stretched, a simple echoing phrase plucked from a guitar, breathy vocals, I'm in bed, texting girls, but I'm thinkin bout you baby, and Ysabel takes a colorless sip from the slender fluted glass in her hand.

Buckled platform pumps step from behind the screen, the one, the other, hand still in hand, yellow hair in ringlets tumbled to their shoulders, bodices of ivory folds plunging from their necks in scoops that shift and sway and somehow gather in tightly brief hip-hugging skirts, and clattering bracelets about their wrists, and filigreed armbands of gold, as the chorus swells to a thumping crescendo, you might be someone I could love, or you're just somebody I fucked once. "Oh, that's a start," says Ysabel, but the Starling straightens, hips unslung, arm lowering, as Chrissie steps close, behind, "We have an audience," she says.

Ysabel's wryly merry leer melts as the music abruptly ceases with a clack. Next to a column there a figure fitfully limned by candlelight, the crease and placket of a fine white shirt, the knot and drape of a tie, the curls of his long hair. "I created you my Axe," she says, quite cold and steely sharp. "Shall I have you uncreated? Transformed to a stag, and set upon by hounds?"

"Majesty, I've news – "

"Not! *Now!*" The candles flare, a slop of light past the columns round about to show the gold of his tie, the gleaming grey of his trousers, the ashen surplus of those curls. "You should be out, with her grace, in the field," says the Queen, her green eyes fiercely stern.

All in a rush, "Majesty your humble servant has," he says, "been," a breath, "tasked, with remaining here, to coordinate her grace's efforts. But it's from this vantage that I might report Luys, the Mason, is not either in the field, nor here, nor seen today by any of the court. Her grace is wrothly vexed by this development."

The Queen's head droops, with a sigh, black tresses slipping to curtain her breast. "This news," she says, her words pitched low, "might've waited, till we had finished our ablutions." Chrissie takes a step away from the Starling, but doesn't lift her hand from the Starling's arm. Ysabel's looking back up, her smile considering a return. "But you're here now," she says. "You might as well favor us with an opinion: are they not lovely?"

"Majesty?" says Jeffeory, the Axe. Chrissie's hand slips away as the Starling looks to her with eyes that are green, not blue.

"Play on!" cries Ysabel then, getting abruptly to her feet. "Vodka for all!" Arms out for balance as she negotiates the slippery tumble of pillows and rugs. "I'll outfit myself as well," she says, skipping past the candles as the music resumes mid-beat, you this but fuck it, here's my confession, as Ysabel catches Chrissie's hand, lifts it for a kiss, "We'll have dancing!" Leaning in to quickly kiss the Starling's lips even as she's letting go, twisting away, "Vodka!" she calls. "Shots for all!"

"My lady," says the Starling, "it's only just past ten."

"Not in the Dvůr Sto Věží!" says Ysabel, her smile now wickedly bright, and she ducks behind the screen.

"I couldn't possibly."

"No," says Gloria, "seriously, it's not," a hand up as if to push it away, but the gold card doesn't waver in Anne Thorpe's hand. She's sat at one end of the nubbled green couch, black trousers crossed at the knee, mustard-yellow sweater vest, her snap-brim at a jaunty angle on her head. "It's not anything you'd ever have to worry about," says Gloria. "That's the beauty of it."

"It's precisely why I *would* have to worry about it," says Thorpe, but Gloria's resolutely folding her arms, stood at the edge of the unlit stage, the cavernously busy warehouse opening out behind and below. Thorpe lowers the card, setting it precisely on the arm of the couch. "It's been a couple-three weeks. Why call me today?"

"You're still," says Gloria, "working on the story."

"I'm always working on a story."

"Well, this," a gesture toward the card, "is part of that. I mean, you don't think it all," a gesture tossed over her shoulder, at all the daily bustle, "came from my father's estate, did you? That's still tied up in, who knows what. Legal shit."

Drawing back her hand, Thorpe peers down her nose at the shining card, "Bank of," she says, "Trebizond? Okay, it's *definitely* not just the ethics I'm worried about."

"It's totally legit."

"Sure."

"Anything you need. Within reason."

"This," says Thorpe, looking pointedly past Gloria toward the activity below, the overflowing stalls to either side, the yammer and chatter, jangle and strum, the rattle-thump and clang and chime and the clack-lack blunder surrounding that great wooden tub in the middle of it all, the scaffolding at the other end framing a half-painted mural, great sharp fang of a mountain lit up in orange and magenta, unearthly pinks and greens and an appalling blue that looms over what might soon become a tree-stuffed town, "all this?" says Thorpe. "Is within reason?"

Gloria shrugs winsomely. "Reason is," she says, "as reason does. Don't you need something like this?"

"Christ," says Thorpe, studiously refusing to look at the card, "of *course* I do. That's the whole fucking point. Why. Did you. Call me. Today." And then, as Gloria looks toward the half-opened overhead door, "Are you really going to make me ask? About the truck, out there? The trailer? What you're going to do with it?"

"You saw that?" says Gloria, and she snorts at the stone-faced look of patience depleted that Thorpe offers up in response.

"It's, another part of the story. Might make a good ending. We're building a float. We're gonna crash the Starlight Parade."

The stone holds a moment before it cracks in an exasperated, a perplexed, an admiring chortle of a sigh. "Good lord, girl," says Thorpe. "You are bound and determined to get yourself noticed."

"It's a celebration!" cries Gloria, throwing up her hands, turning about, "all of this, of everything we've been able to do," looking about, turning back, "we *deserve* to get noticed. It's gonna be epic. It *has* to be."

"And the very next day, you're shut the fuck down."

"You forget a step or two?" Gloria throws wide her arms, taking all of it in, "This whole place is mine! Free and clear!"

Another complex guffaw. "You mean that circus, a couple-three weeks ago? Sweetie, absolutely *nothing* about *any* of that was a legally binding document."

"They can," says Gloria, but she's looking down, turning away, a change in the tenor of the bustle below, a sharpness, a stentoriousness, a shift in focus surging about that tub. "I mean," Thorpe's saying, "did you think you saved the Lovejoy Ramp, too? Gloria?" But Gloria's stooping, a hand on the edge there, stepping off from the stage to drop to the floor below, "Hey!" making her way toward the knot of hobs and cods coalesced to one side of the wooden tub, faces concerned about something in the middle of them all, arms outstretched, helping hands, all suddenly undone, shoved back, flung up, away, some stumbled to the concrete floor, some against the staves of that tub, a haze of golden dust a-shimmer in the air with a yelping coughing whoop, and hands on the lucent Himmelbarb's shoulders Gloria steps between Cherrycoke and Dewslip, past Loati and Angavelle, to come to the hunch of a girl on the floor, blowsy madras shorts, black hair in curls, shaking with sobs, "Olivia?" says Gloria, small, appalled.

The girl looks up, eyes far too wide, gold smeared about her lips, her cheeks, sheen of it split by the blackening tracks of welling rolling tears, "Gloria," she says, "oh my God, Gloria," lunging for her, grasping with hands that drip gold, "She's had," says someone, but "Only what you need!" pipes someone else, "Only what you need!" a refrain taken up by others, "Only, only what you need! What you need!"

Gloria kneels to catch her by the elbow, "Olivia," she's saying, the waist, "what are you," but "I'm sorry, I'm sorry," Olivia's saying, "I never, I didn't know, I had to know, Chloe, Chloe said it was just, but it's, it's so much," those eyes, and nothing but darkness between and beneath the lids of them, filling up so wide, "I can see," she's saying, "it's all so," twisting in Gloria's grip, "wait," says Gloria, "Olivia, wait," but those eyes look past her, up to all the rest of them pressed close about, "the hands," says Olivia, "the noses, the cheeks! I see it now! The clothes! It's, it's like," and Gloria flinches as that wondrous mask of cracked and grimy gold, as those eyes turn back to her, "Muppets!" cries Olivia, "Brian Froud! Brian Froud Muppets!" Brows flaking brilliance as they lift in amused bemusement over those depthless eyes, "You're wearing a wimple!"

On the other side of the tub Ellen Oh lurches with a shove against her tattooed shoulder, and turns to catch the end of a baseball bat before it can poke her again, sweat gleaming her cloak of sharp-drawn ink, blinked from frowning eyes. Marfisa draws back the bat to an angle en garde, "They have it well enough in hand," she says. "Let's resume." White-gold hair in a ruthlessly braided queue, grey shorts and T-shirt, sleekly seamless running shoes, both hands on the black-taped handle of the bat she twirls once, slowly, swings a slow deliberate blow that Ellen parries with a quick shift of the staff in her hands, clack, stepping to one side bare feet deftly crossing one before another beneath the belling cuffs of yoga pants. Another deliberate blow, caught by another jerk of that staff, slender and long, lemony palely troubled by a hint of grain, held warily, hands wide apart. Marfisa sets to with one-handed alacrity, slinging blows that Ellen grimly blocks, down from above, up from below, roundabout into a jab of a thrust clack-lack, whack, whack, pressing forth, falling back, leaning in, to and fro this emptied stretch of aisle between the stalls. "Hit me," says Marfisa. "Hit me. You're not trying to hit me."

"I don't," says Ellen, clack, "see the point," lack-crack, as Marfisa tosses the bat from hand to hand, turns a chop to an uppercut that Ellen whacks aside, "none of this," stepping back, swing ducked, "will do, any good," whick, "against that monster," clack-crack, but back she steps again, and back.

"Exercise!" cries Marfisa, whirling the bat above her head. "Is it not the case," a chop, and Ellen blocks, "every day you cannot manage to race your heart," chop, and block, "a measurable stretch, why, then," crack, "a day is stricken from the brief allotment given you to live!" another chop, but Ellen ducking skips back from it, "Make room! Make room!" someone's bellowing.

Marfisa lets the unchecked force of that last blow swing her bat down around and up, readily cocked in both hands above her shoulder. "Make room!" It's Templemass, waving his red-draped arms as he backs his way down the aisle ahead of Gloria and Big Jim Turk and, cradled in Jim's arms, Olivia. His shirtfront smeared with gold where she's clutched it groaning, sniveling, gleaming cheeks beneath those black and empty eyes, and the mass of others pressing after, far more than Templemass might hope to clear with his exhortations. Ellen steps back into a stall lined with racks of shawls and bandanas and cravats, as Marfisa, bat still at the ready, steps into a stall across the aisle, hung about with garishly dour portraits on fields of velvety black. "Make room!" cries Templemass once more.

As they're passing Olivia cranes up in Big Jim's arms to look to the one side, the other, that cracking golden mask hollowing about an opening mouth, those empty eyes, and she points a golden hand at Marfisa, "Horse!" she cries, she screams, pointing at Ellen, "Horse!" struggling against Jim's unyielding arms, throwing off Gloria's comforting hand, and with another "Make room!" they're off, away down the aisle, headed for the arch at the far end, followed by the tremulously murmurous crowd of those about, the rest stood watching, looking away, resuming what they'd been doing before, and but none of them left there by the wooden tub.

Marfisa her bat yet cocked steps back into the clearing aisle with an expectant look for Ellen, leaned there on her staff in the stall opposite, but Ellen's looking up past the tub, not to the unlit stage, not to the woman watching there in black and ugly yellow, but to the man headed toward them both, quite short, rough moleskin over discreetly checkered shirtsleeves, trousers of rumpled corduroy, "You," he says, to Marfisa, "you should not be here."

"This hall's as open to me," she says, "as to anyone, whose jacket isn't blue," tock, the tip of her bat on concrete.

"You should not be here," he says, again. "The news has spread, of what your brother's said you've gone and done."

Ellen's laid down her staff, she's taken up a roughly simple jacket, shrugging it over her tattoos. "I have no brother, Shrieve," Marfisa's saying.

"Let's not mince words, my lady Outlaw. The Viscount has told of a figure with the head of a horse, that broached the house at King's Heights, and did there murther the Glaive Rhythidd, and cut him to the bone."

"His excellency's mistaken," says Marfisa, flatly quiet.

"Of this, I have no doubt," says Bruno. "Nonetheless. The Glaive is gone, and her Majesty's Huntsman is gone. It were best if the Outlaw were not to be seen so openly at court, for the next few days."

"Few," says Marfisa, looking past him, over his shoulder, to Ellen, the staff once more in her hands. "I wonder if the Shrieve's not optimistic."

Bruno claps a hand to Marfisa's shoulder. "I've no doubt the perpetrator will be soon found," he says, smile faltering as she blinks, once, and he lifts his hand away. "A violation, of this magnitude." He steps back, starting at how close Ellen has come. "I trust you'll – both, agree."

"Well," says Ellen, when Bruno's out of earshot, "it's not as if we'll find the monster here."

"Nor my brother, neither," says Marfisa.

EARLY, DIM, & SODDEN – WHAT SHE WOULD HAVE SAID
THE PHOTOS ON THE MANTEL – UNDER THE LIGHTS
NO SMALL ACCOMPLISHMENT

IT'S EARLY, OF A DIM AND SODDEN MORNING. Thin light seeps through enormous flower-shapes painted across the window-glass to settle on the high thick mattress laid upon the floor, gently picking rumples and folds from among the tangled sheets, the pillows piled, lightening them, but not enough to draw out any differences between the pastels lurked within, only just enough to define the heights, the crumpled peaks and ridgelines, the window-facing slopes. He shifts, the shape of him turning from side to back, a massif obliterating, remaking the bedscape, crumpling ranges, raising up plains, geologic time made legible for one brief turbulent moment before all is settled in a new configuration. His face now visible, the summit of his nose, that light too weak to find many at all of the white hairs hatching the lush black copse of his mustache. A snort, air roaring through the caverns of his nostrils, and he blinking opens the lightless tarns of his eyes, "Gloria?" he says, when he can.

She's sat at the foot of the mattress, jet-black hair a finely threaded shawl to drape the bulk of her shoulders, spill down her pale bare back.

"Sweetling," he says. "Your friend will be fine. All is well."

That hair unsettles as her shoulders lift, a sigh, a slump to still again. "You don't know Olivia."

He sits up, sheets slipping, "It happens," he says, "the first time one," a breath, "overindulges," he reaches for her, but falters, falls short, his hand settling instead on his sheeted knee. "An embarrassment, yes, but hardly more than a wince and a blush, and it's not as if she's part and parcel of what goes on hereabouts, your friend from school. And when her father came to fetch her, he was none the wiser," but he surges up sheets falling away to take hold of those heaving shoulders as she chokes out a sob, "oh," he says, roughly gentle, "my deckled dove, my darling dear, what is it, what," his arms about her now, rough cheek against hers shining wetly, holding her until she catches hold of herself, her sobs resolving in a deeply determined breath. "Melissa," she says. "Not Olivia. *Melissa.* She didn't, didn't have to," as she curls herself against him, "you told me to, play the game, change it, stay at the table and change the game. But I couldn't, I couldn't, if I had, if I did," and he says, "Sweetling, don't," but she's saying "she wouldn't have, she wouldn't be, *dead.*"

A kiss for the top of her head, grizzled mustache pressed to sleek black hair. "That's not on you. None of that could be on you."

"Isn't it?" Pulling away, looking up. "This is my place, Jim. It's supposed to be my place. I mean, fuck, you wouldn't be here, you wouldn't have, if I wasn't, calling the shots around here? Admit it. You wouldn't look twice at me. If I wasn't."

His broad brow ripples with concern. "Well," he says, agreeably enough, "and it may well be you have the right of it, my deftly diddle. Iffen you weren't the ball-busting bitch of the walk who every living day is the one to whip this hall into whatever shape it can manage, well," a smile tenderly hints the corners of his mouth, "it's true enough, you'd not be resting sweetly in Jim Turk's arms of a night. You'd not be yourself, but someone else," and he soothes her scowl with a fleeting brush of his fingertips, "and it's not anyone else I'd want to be holding," words worn down to a softly burr, "not anyone, but the entirety, that's you."

"Oh, and you think you're sweet."

"Ah, no," he says, "that, for certain, I do not. Sweet ain't for the likes of you, no. Sweet is what your friend'd want." She snorts at that, a smile forming in spite of itself. "I declare," he says, "you spoil me, my morning glory, with your grit, your gumption, your, don't," as she pushes away, as laughter threatens her smile, "your accomplishments. Don't shy away from this. Your friend, what was her name?"

"Olivia."

"Olivia," he says, savoring the syllables. "When Olivia's father came, yesterday, to fetch her from this place, your place, the place that you have built, and did you see, the look, on his face, in his eyes, as he did so?" His guilelessly open smile, his gentling joy. "I never had a daughter, that I know, but rest assured, you, as you are, here and now, what you've done: there's never a cause in this world that would have a father look as peevishly on you," but at that she shudders, yanks away, scowly souring, "My father?" she spits. "How would he, look at me? At what I did, with his, bullshit dream?" Ostentatiously looking about, the walls of plaster crumbling, the layer of paint drooped away from the ceiling there, the elaborate bloom of a water stain, details coming into focus as morning stretches to fill the room. "He was gonna have all this torn down, because he couldn't be fucking bothered. You think," and the look turned to him then, and he blinks, "you think I give a good God *damn* how he'd look at me, or even if? You know, you have any idea, what I'd *say* to him? If he was here, right now? I'd say, go *fuck* yourself, is what."

"Sweetling," he says, hushed, "I never meant," but she holds up a forestalling hand, "Did you hear something?" she says, looking to the brightening windows. "Like a crack?"

Yearning rings in the piano notes, as a bitterly chipper voice sings for you, cause blondes here don't jump out of cakes. Two women crowded close on stools before a mirror far too bright, both with the same blue eyes, that same nose, the same yellow hair blown out and rounded in enameled bobs. The one to the left shapes her eyes with charcoal daubed about the lids, above, beneath, as the one to the right limns her lips, leaning toward herself in the mirror as rich thick red's stroked along, around, and the piano changes gears, chin up, put on a pair of these roseys.

"How's this," says Chrissie, to her left.

"Let me," says the Starling, taking Chrissie's chin in one hand, delicately, lipstick in the other, peering a moment before touching it to those painted lips. "There," she says, letting go. "Wait." Neatening a line with a fingertip, lifting away a crumb of color.

"Spoiled, I guess," says Chrissie, taking up a mascara brush. "You'd think it'd be like riding a bicycle." The Starling, moueing herself in the mirror, sets to with the lipstick.

"Y'all should already be *dressed,*" says the harried man in the doorway, an aloha shirt predominately blue over an ivory Henley, "y'all needed on set, like, now."

"Having to do our own makeup," says Chrissie, blinking, "takes time."

"And we're supposed to," says the Starling, checking her lips, "whatshername," says Chrissie, "the intimacy, uh," a quick stroke, "Terry," says the Starling.

"I don't," says the man in the doorway, scrolling through his phone, "have anything, I just, they're rigging lights and need you there to check, like, now, so, please, just, get dressed, and, like, go?"

"Dressed?" says the Starling, looking up to him. "In what?"

He looks about the cramped room, the littered counter, the mirror, the two of them perched there, "Shit," he says. "Costumes. Shit. Let me, just, let me go," pointing away, ducking out.

"You do that," says Chrissie, with a sigh.

Closing the door on the din, the ringing chains, the swaying paper-laden baskets, the shun and ponk of pneumatic tubes, all subsumed by the howling whine of that brutishly enormous shredder grinding away beneath the balcony. The latch clicks, and a silence falls to strenuously complement the coziness of the decor stuffed within.

He jerkily undoes the buttons of his linen jacket, shrugs it free of one shoulder, the other, folds it to drape it over the back of a floral armchair stood before that polished desk. His sun-browned head quite bald, slack cheeks grizzled with a dusting of white stubble, eyes bereft of any appreciable emotion, or intent. Turning toward the brick fireplace set in the opposite wall, mantel crowded with a gaggle of matryoshka dolls, a white porcelain vase top-heavy with roses so deeply red they're black, a throng of sepia-tinted photos in elaborate frames that his emptied eyes seem to fix on, even as his fingers undo the white cuffs of his smoothly cerulean shirt.

He lifts a photo from among the rest, a pudgy woman in a stodgy dress, pillbox hat to swallow her sculpted curls, a smidge shorter than the men to either side of her, the one in rumpled linen and a wide knit tie, the other in three sharp pieces and hand-painted silk, both quite bald, though their cheeks are each neatly grizzled. He strokes the frame of it once, elegant curlicues of brass suggesting tendrils, or vines, then lets it fall, crack, to the coldly empty grate. Another, the short and pudgy woman in a differently stodgy pantsuit, stood at the very desk behind him, proudly displaying the squat black box of a machine, a lever upright to one side of it. The frame's an asymmetric thing of slender, overlapping arches that falls from his fingers to the grate with a broken chime of glass. Another, he doesn't even bother to look at it, and another, this one thrown, smash, and again. Somewhere outside a dim alarm's begun to sound, just loud enough to trouble the silence here.

The clamor redoubles as the doors swing open, a harshly monotonous blare so loud the shattering of another photograph is lost. The man in the doorway, ink-dappled apron and a blue-backed sheet of paper in his hand, tosses a brusquely dismissive wave at someone, and the klaxon abruptly cuts off. "My lord," he says. "My lord Welund."

The last photograph, lifted from the mantel. "It's been three weeks or more," says Welund, and drops it to the grate with the clattering others. "Why was none of this cleared away."

"My lord the Glaive never asked that her, my lord!" as Welund turns away from the hearth. "Your, your brother's, tie!"

Welund's hand to the lopsided knot of it, silk striped rigorously blue and rosy pink. "Do you see my brother here?" he says.

"My lord?"

"Do you see my brother in this room?" suddenly sharp, and loud. "Then do not speak of him. Why has the work stopped?" Looking past him, out to the chains hung still, freighted baskets restlessly a-sway with the momentum of their halting, tubes and valves all holding their great breaths, even the monstrous shredder's stopped, teeth of it quivering visible, and all the clerks in their striped shirts and aprons stood by their roll-top desks. "My lord," says the clerk beside him, handing over the blue-backed sheet of paper. Welund takes it, then looks down at it, then frowns. "I don't know this account," he says.

"It is quite large, my lord."

"I see that. It mentions subordinancies?"

"Thirty-seven, sir."

"So many!" Blinking, peering more closely at the fine print. "How is it I'm not familiar with this account?"

"We'll pull the file, milord. But note," the clerk leans over the paper, seeking a clause, pointing it out, "one is held by the Queen's Outlaw."

Expressions did animate Welund's face, of concern, annoyance, puzzlement, but all of them now fall away to leave a slackly chill. "I see," he says, looking up, from the document, to the clerk. "The closure's noted as of shortly before six," he turns his wrist to check the watch about it, a silver nest of gears and dials, numbers and hashes picked out in something that gleams like mother-of-pearl. "Three hours lost, already. This account," handing back the document, "is now a top priority. Any and all collections, re-possessions, foreclosures, are to be taken immediately, and thoroughly." The clerk nods, crisply. "What are you called?"

"Illicuddy, milord."

Welund collects his jacket from the back of the armchair. "Empty this office. Arrange it as might best suit you. It's been long enough without a director here on the floor. I trust," looking the clerk up and down, the white gloves, the gartered sleeves, the ink-splotched apron, gabardine trousers with the cuffs rolled, "you'll dress accordingly."

"My lord," says Illicuddy.

"Get back to *work!*" bellows Welund, shoving his arms into the sleeves of his jacket, rattling down the stairs even as switches are thrown, pumps chug to life, tubes trembling hum and ring, chains set to back and forth motion and their baskets swinging with them, and with one final decisive flick, the great churning shredder is set in tumultuous motion.

"I'm sorry – wait – "

"It's all right – "

"No, but – "

"Cut," the patiently exasperated annoyance, "cut." Crisply, from over in the corner, "Reset?"

"No," that patient weariness. Someone else says, "Position two?"

"I'm so sorry."

"No," that patience, nearly exhausted, audibly reins in its edge. "No, let's just, break a moment, in the moment, and then we'll pick it, we'll pick it right back up, we've got, we've still got – "

"Really. Sorry."

"Don't," that sharpness, loosed, the reins sawn, hauled back, "we've got, just a few more moments, to capture, from this vantage, let's use this, as an opportunity, play it out, play with it, let's let it take a shape we can, we can use, in the master, these are, these would be, intercuts, I mean, easy money at the brick factory, right? Still rolling?"

"Hadn't stopped," crisp as ever, from the corner.

"We got bytes," slowly lugubrious, "what we don't got, is time."

"Okay. Ladies. Gus. You're looking, fantastic. The, ah, tableau, it's, it's working. Now. Assuming we're, we're all ready to, get back to it, let's roll with it again, let it play out, don't worry so much about – "

"He can't touch her," says the Starling, brightly lit there, on her knees at the foot of the shining white expanse of bed, smokey stockings and a wisp of underwear about her hips and her yellow hair blown out in a rounded bob. "It's all right," says Chrissie, sitting up beside her, stockings of smoke, underwear a wisp, "it's all right," yellow hair a-bob, "I can," taking the Starling's hand, "he can," her other hand, her arm held awkwardly over her breasts.

"We, ah, talked about that, restriction, when there were, there were three of you."

"Triplettes," two syllables ludicrously mournful.

"We talked about it," says the Starling. "We agreed. Where's Terry Prudhomme?"

"It's okay, Star," says Chrissie, but the Starling's shaking her head, "No, it's not."

"Actually?" says the tanly smoothly man, supinated between them under all that bright bright light, naked the stretch of him from close-cropped hair and clean-shaven cheeks past the broadly sculpted utterly hairless planes and angles of his pecs, the shining tight-packed ridges of his abdomen, the sleekly length of his thighs, his calves to his gleamingly pedicured toes, "this merkin-thingie's pinching something fierce, the glue or something, I don't know," an oddly delicate gesture with one wide hand coming not at all close to the stark green bit of cloth that cups his genitals. "I could use a minute to adjust, if that would help y'all get more, ah, comfortable? Too?"

"I'm sorry," says Chrissie, and both arms wrapped about herself now, "it was, it won't, it won't happen again."

"Doing fine, darlin," says the naked man, sitting up to swing his big feet over away off one side of the bed.

"Where," says the Starling, peering into the darkness beyond all that bright light, "is Terry Prudhomme?"

"It was, her flight got, screwed, the holiday, logistics, are, she'll be here, when she gets here, but we've got this room, this room we've got today, we need this, today, it's all we've got, but we're all professionals, this is good, this is fine, it's a break, mandated break, definitely a cut now, let's, let Gus get himself settled, we'll reconvene in fifteen and pick up right back here, and can somebody get Gus a robe?"

"I'm sorry," Chrissie's saying, as the Starling yanks loose a sheet, "I'm sorry, it was just a, like a, flinch. It won't happen again."

"This is not," mutters the Starling, draping that sheet about Chrissie's shoulders, "what we agreed."

The first card turned over a single, unmarked color, a brightly yellow laid on the blue-painted floorboards, fnap. The next a metalled bronze, sheened in floating daylight, set down off to the right of the first. The third a glimmering russet placed, after a moment's hesitation, between and above, and the fourth, turned quickly over, placed below, a dull nut brown, quartering the circle.

She contemplates them a moment, sat on the smooth blue floor at the foot of the mattress on the pallet in the middle of the room, the floor, the sloping ceiling, the attenuated walls all the same flawless eggshell blue, clear and plain and cloudless, her white briefs, her cloak of tattooed ink.

The fifth card is much smaller, eggshell white, cut not from glossy stock but something more like linen. She sets it in the center of that square, taps the back of it, once, then quickly turns it over, snap. Frances Upchurch, say slender, sans-serif letters, and beneath them, in the same font, a simple, ten-digit number. "Two," she reads, "two, zero. One. One. Sev – "

"Must you?" says the woman now in the room with her, not too tall, hair bound tightly in a sheaf of tiny corkscrew curls, broad shoulders bared by a sturdy grey tanktop, Miner Normal, it says on the front of it, over a stylized Corinthian capital.

"You're driving," says Ellen Oh, setting the rest of the cards to one side. To the other, laid on the smooth blue floor, the flop-empty goggle-eyed head of a horse. Mrs. Upchurch purses her lips. "That so."

"Why were you in the house, that night."

"I should've thought that was obvious," but then, with a sigh, Mrs. Upchurch plucks at the knees of her baggy blue sweatpants and, wincing, sits herself across the spread from Ellen. "Forgive my tone, and appearance. Yesterday was an utter bear. Today was to have been a me day."

"You, ah," Ellen frowns, "took my call."

"You *summoned* me, Ellen Oh."

"But," Ellen looks down, at that card, "you gave me your number."

"I wasn't expecting you'd," says Mrs. Upchurch, as Ellen says, "I never thought you'd," and they both bite off frustrated stops.

"I forget," says Mrs. Upchurch. "Who you've known. What you might've picked up, along the way."

"I wasn't thinking you'd actually, appear," says Ellen. "Physically. I'd, uh, would've had something, to drink. Snacks."

A snort too brief to be considered a laugh. "All right," says Mrs. Upchurch, "so. Tell me why I'm here."

"The monster," says Ellen. "How do I kill it."

Mrs. Upchurch shrugs. "How should I know."

"You," Ellen frowns. "That's what you *do*. You *know* things."

A hand to her breast, "You flatter me, truly," and the performance of a smile, an eloquently simple mask of those naked eyes, unpainted lips, "but I do have my limits."

Looking down, at the cards between them. "But you want it dead."

That smile folds into something at once admonishing and disappointed. "You're the one who wants to kill, Ellen. Do try to keep up." And then, head tipping judiciously to one side, "Awfully first-person singular, this morning. Where's your partner in vengeance?" Ellen, still looking down, her hands on her knees. "Too distracted? Her celebrity crush, perhaps?" Mrs. Upchurch looks up, away, around, the bed, the blue, the gently sifting daylight. The cards. "Her troublesome brother?" The only other anything besides themselves a photograph, hung out in the air of the room, invisible threads secured to unseen anchors set in plaster, between the floorboards, a hand, the back of it roped with veins in rich greys, crisp blacks, reaching for something, or warding it off.

"The monster," says Mrs. Upchurch. "Let's call him, Charley, for the sake of convenience. Charley was, once, something of a colleague."

"Not," says Ellen, "their grandfather."

"What? No. No, the Pinabel is, gone. Destroyed. Overwritten. Charley has, gone through some changes."

"You," says Ellen, "you were there to see what would happen. When it was threatened. What it could do."

"You took your shot. You failed – but you did make it out alive, which is no small accomplishment."

"And," says Ellen, looking up, small smile slipping into place, "now I know how to hit it."

"What you hit," says Mrs. Upchurch, "was only there to hold the teeth he was using to rip you open. That gonna be your strategy for round two?"

Ellen lifts a hand to the crook of her neck, where leaves and vines have been tangled by a jagged discontinuity, a frozen slash of lightning violent through them.

"The meatmongers," says Mrs. Upchurch. "Renny, and Brankowicz, his daughter, Jill. Have you told them you've quit? Or were you just going to leave them to figure it out, eventually?"

Ellen, both hands back on her knees.

"Your housemates, Daniel, Montaigne. You're just going to leave them in the lurch, with the rent?"

The corners of Ellen's lips, pinched.

"You must know," says Mrs. Upchurch. "This is the last time you will ever get to leave a place. It would be well to do so properly."

"I was, already," says Ellen, tipping back her head, looking up, and up, into all that seamless smoothly blue. "This room," she says. "I'd finally made it what I'd seen it could be, would be, when Monty and me first found this place. I walked in here, and I saw it, and I made it, and I was done. I was thinking, maybe Accra. There's a guy there, usually sets up by the Makola, he does, just, amazing shit, with goat. So I was already thinking, maybe, Accra. When Phil climbed into my car."

"It is a lovely room," says Mrs. Upchurch.

Ellen looks down, takes up the horse's head, there by her knee. "I used to live in a world," she says, "wherever I was, whatever I was doing, I'd know, any minute, he could just, be there. Both of us in the popcorn line at the Qaraghandy Zoo, or, or he'd be sitting at the only other table in a gasthaus, in Bissen, or just, I can't even remember where, Antananarivo, not looking where I was going, and boom, and just, knowing that? It was, like, an echo, that never stopped ringing."

Both her hands on that mask now in her lap.

"I don't live there anymore," she says. "I've already left. Just one last thing to tidy up."

Mrs. Upchurch leans forward, looking over the cards spread between them. "Purpose," she says, musing, "through a sense of propriety, and – oh, but I'm reading it upside down. The body," she says, with a gesture to her right, "through grounding, and firm boundaries, achieves a purity of purpose." Looking up. "What else could we require."

Ellen picks up the fifth card, small and pale. "Do I need to," she says, but "No, no," says Mrs. Upchurch, getting to her feet. "I'll show myself out. I know the way."

Disappearing into a sweatshirt, wrestling her way up and through, glossy bob now mussed, a suggestion of yellow curls unsprung, as sharp notes toggle a simple phrase over an airy space of strings, can't plan for anything, except the rain. "I guess we won't be getting a check today, either." She bends to scoop up a squiggle of tie-dye.

Wiping the last of the cold cream from her face in the far too brightly mirror, the flags will all fly green at the embassies, you're here next to me, except you're not. She frowns. Turns away from herself in the too brightly mirror to look to her there, pulling up swirling tights, "Hey," she says, "you're," a gesture, up by her face, her hair.

"What?" Leaning close, there beside her in the mirror, their hair of a length, thereabouts, but hers undoing itself in artfully definite curls, and noticeably darker, and her blinking eyes bright green. "Oh," she says.

"You should probably," says Chrissie.

"Why bother," says the Starling.

Chrissie smiles. "Would've been funny, if it happened out there."

"Funny," says the Starling, skeptically. "Go on, get dressed. I want ever so much to be gone from here."

"I miss Cos, and Aya," says Chrissie, dabbing the corner of her jaw with the greasy cloth. "Why don't they ever come out to play anymore?"

"Should've just brought the blasted screen with us," mutters the Starling, plucking up jars and vials and tubes from before the mirror, dropping them clink and clatter in the bag at her feet.

THE LETTERS ON THE WALL – HER QUESTION
TROUBLE WITH THE TRUCK

HUNG ON THE WALL THE LETTERS, deep and wide, precisely serifed forms cut from some dully leaden metal dark against the pale wood paneling, and the man in the brown coveralls up on the stepladder grunts as he lifts the capital R from its hooks, grimaces as he twists to lower it, carefully, to the floor. "Welund Barlowe and Lackland," murmurs the receptionist, beard meticulously trimmed, a small but ornate brass telephone headset clipped to one ear. "How might I direct your call."

Out in that lobby all chrome and cream and beige she's vivid, her pink track suit, bright blue piping down the sleeves, her hair, close-cropped, a virulent chartreuse. Behind her a confusion of reflections and refractions interleaved, glass walls lightstruck by lamps discreetly tucked away delineating this hall, that conference room, until at last the high grey gloomy clouds without.

Reflections shift and swing, a suggestion of movement, and she stands herself alacritously up. He's coming out alone, his navy suit, his shirt and tie of the same chalky blue, his white white hair in dreaded locks gathered loosely together, expression grimly set. She hastens to the elevator bank, pressing the button to summon one, checking within as the doors open, allowing him brusquely to step in first, taking up a position beside him as the doors slide shut.

"Send word," he murmurs. "The Barons, the Soames, the Mason, all to the house in King's Heights this very afternoon, ready to move in strength. And our knights to assemble, and Joaquin as well, under the Anvil's hand."

"My lord," she says, outwardly unperturbed.

"And I need a meeting with Reginald Davies, as soon as it might be arranged. You can reach him through his firm, Maieutics, or possibly his development concern, Anaphenics."

"Is this to be a drink, my lord? Dinner? A phone call?"

"Whatever it might take," he says, "logistically, to get us speaking, together, as soon as possible," and a sigh, "so be it."

Elevator doors slide open on a dim garage filled with ranks of close-packed automobiles. Iona in pink leads the way toward a black suv, looming there on a rumple of concrete hard by a thickset pillar. Agravante, white head lowered in thought, crisply follows after. She stops, abruptly, there by the tail of it, lifting a hand, fob in her fingers, thumb poised, "My lord," she says, but the fob drops with a clank as light blooms about her hand to banish shadows lighting up the figure leaping spring-squonk and panel-crump from the trunk of a sedan to swinging bring a long staff down from overhead a savage whipping chop that's caught, just, by Iona's shivering blade.

Press, a twirl, whack, click-clack, the staff spinning, swinging, jabbing to test Iona's parries and ripostes, black tights and a baggy black jacket, flop-muzzled goggle-eyed horse's head, the mane of it stiffly upright. Agravante shakes out his white-locked head, stretches out his navy arms, a long-bladed dagger in either hand, hilts of them wrapped in blued wire, "Stop," he says, politely enough. "Outlaw," he says, "you should not have," but then revelation dawns, as his shoulder's shoved from behind, by the tip of a bat, "come," he says, "alone," lowering his daggers, annoyed.

"Never alone, in a herd," says the figure stepping out from behind him, white T-shirt and grey running tights, baseball bat delivering another insouciant push, and rising wobbly from the shoulders a limp-snouted bristle-maned horse head, glaring at him somehow through pop eyes skewed in differing directions.

"Put up, Chariot," says Agravante, stepping with the push of the bat, "stand down," his arms still open wide, but now his hands are empty. "This is bark, not bite."

"Bite enough, for a lie direct," says the horse with the bat.

"A lie?" says Agravante, suddenly concerned. "How so?"

"You," a poke of the bat, "have a day, and a night, to put it about that you misspoke. To say, where any and all might hear, that the Queen's Outlaw," a shove, rocking his shoulder back, "has been most grievous wronged by your own words. A day, and a night, and if you do not? It will then be proved upon your body," and another thrust, but this one he catches, one hand whipped in to grip the end of the bat, hold it firm against a briefly push-pull struggle.

"I spoke nothing but the truth," says Agravante. "Someone wearing a horse mask broke into the house at King's Heights. The Glaive was murthered, then and there. Cut down to bone, as if struck, perhaps, by a gallowglas," looking from the horse with the bat, to the horse with the staff. "There is no lie in that."

"A day, and a night," says the horse with the bat, backing away. "Make it right, or it will be made right."

"And then we come for your monster," says the horse with the staff, lifting it up, away. Those floppy snouts turn toward each other, a look shared between them. Then they're off, into the shadows among the cars.

"Well," says Agravante. Iona stoops to find the fob.

Six tables of a length, pushed together in two close lines of three tables each, the tops of them differing colors, dully scrubbed white and sunny yellow, pale green and sinister gleaming red, stolid brown and lavender, but she's not sat at any of them, she's standing there, at the one end with the mullioned windows darkening in the wall above, pale feet bare, laddered tights printed with clockwork gears, vast blue T-shirt, her long black hair undone, and one hand balled in a fist.

"Chatelaine?" says the Queen.

She's stepped through the open double doors, black curls artfully tangled, loosely belted robe of lace. "What," says Gloria, turning away from the windows, "you don't even bother to dress, now?"

"I was told it was urgent."

"Close the," Gloria's free hand gestures, "doors. Come here."

The double doors swing shut together as the Queen, golden slippers on her feet, lace frothing about her knees, her shins, steps to the end of the table, "Well?" she says.

"Just," says Gloria, still stood there by the windows, "first, actually, first. Ask me your question."

The Queen looks down to her hand, fingers spread on the brown tabletop. "What?" she says, looking back up to Gloria.

"Ask your *question*. Whenever you want, something, a cup of coffee, a ride to the store, to feel, better, about, your fucking *self*, you ask it, so go on, ask. Ask the goddamn question."

The Queen lifts her hand from the table, folds up her arms.

"I was *dead,*" says Gloria, and the ragged edge of that word. "I said *yes,* I told you *yes,* I would've done *anything* for you, I did all of those horrible *things* to you, and he, he *killed* me, I was *dead,* and you, you," blinking rapidly, "your brought me back," says Gloria, simply, quietly. "Why did you bring me back."

"Gloria," says the Queen, gently, even tenderly. "What is this about."

Gloria lurches toward the table, "I haven't," she says, unclenching her fist, "painted a goddamn thing in *weeks.*" She lays out what she's been holding in it all this time, click, click, click.

A moment's hesitation, and then, with uncertain steps, the Queen makes her way up the line of tables, past lavender spun with threads of violet, past deeply banked red a-glitter with silver and black, there to look down on sunny yellow formica and set atop it three black jagged shards of plastic, embossed with a broken string of numerals. Printed there, at what had been a corner, interlocking circles of red and orange. Bank of Trebi, on another, continuing across the third, zond. Gloria Monday. Good perhaps, 8 maybe, or 7, the date's been sundered by a crack.

"It's the end," says Gloria. "Is what it's about. Happened this morning. I'm pretty sure. But the Safeway delivery just got canceled, so there's, we're out the, toilet paper, cleaning supplies, and Doe refused our order, so that's, ah, no donuts, or coffee, in the morning, we were gonna, we have to put in the Rubinette's order, next day or two, I'm not sure how we're gonna, Anna, Anna has some, she's gonna make some calls, about, ah, about my father's, uh, but," shaking her head, pink bangs a-swish.

"Who did you tell," says the Queen.

"Christ," Gloria's saying, "the internet, the phones, wait – what?"

"These," says the Queen, pressing one daintily manicured fingertip there by the broken card, "are always secured by an awful secret. If that secret is shared, with anyone, that security is," lifting her hand away, "broken. The value," to her breast, clutching closed the lace. "I hope," she says, so very tenderly, "it was worth it."

Turning away, walking away, back down the length of the tables. "Ysabel?" calls Gloria, after her. "Ysabel!"

One of the two double doors bursts open, well before the Queen has reached them, forcefully enough to bounce off the stuttering twang of a doorstop. Stood there, wide-eyed with chagrin as that door swings slowly back, "Lady," he calls, catching the handle, pushing within, "my lady," but he's looking to Gloria, not the Queen, "there's trouble, with the truck. You must come."

"The truck," says Gloria, coming down by the Queen.

"Rabbits have come, lady," he says, "on behalf, they say, of the Guisarme," his neatly knotted tie of gold, his ashen curls, brushing his shoulders, "they mean to take the truck, but Jim Turk does refuse – lady!" pressed back against the door as she bulls past him, out of the room, into the hall, away. "Majesty?" he says, turning to the Queen, stood there, stricken.

Bare feet slapping, down the stairs, around and past the scaffolding skewed through gloomy foyer, under the wide low arch, bulbs strung along the ceiling of it dark, out into the cavernous warehouse, echoing with the commotion of the crowd about the open overhead door at the other end, there before the empty unlit stage. She breaks from her hasty harried trot into a plunging arm-pumping run past stalls filled with garbage and equipment and art, up to and around the lustrous wooden tub as shouts break over the clamor, "Hey!" and "Whoa!" and "Stop!" and "Gallowglas, gallowglas approaching! Gallowglas to the field!"

Hands grab, torsos interpose, she's stumbled, buffeted, shoves in turn, "Dammit," she snaps, and yelps *"Out* of my *way!"* shouldering on, but "Lady!" cries someone, and someone else, "Chatelaine!" There, suddenly, before her, wee Goggie, eyes wide, cheeks flushed, hands up, halt, stop, "you mustn't, you can't," she's saying, "he's horribly wounded, if you set foot out there, he'll be done to dust, and for sure!"

A clatter, shouts from without, they're all surged forward, jamming the doorway to see, "Why," growls Gloria, "why aren't," struggling, yanking, wrenching against the hands that grasp that clench that hold, that bar, *"help him!"* she roars.

A mighty crash out there, the splash of glass, a howl of rage, hoots and taunts, Gloria hurls herself about, against those implacable hands, but someone out there, someone, a high clear voice is singing, "Was on a jolly summer's morn," and another voice leaps to join, "the twenty-ninth of May!" as a wornly ragged chorus assembles itself, "that we took up, our turmut hoes, and *here,* we means, to *stay!"* and oh, the cheers at that. One last shrug of a yank from Gloria against slackening grips, hands falling away, bodies that step back, as out there a single voice, deep, but threadily hesitant, "For some delights, in hay-makin," and a heavy, hacking cough, Gloria shoving abruptly forward and again the grabbing clutching gripping, "and some they fancies mowin!" strengthening with every word, "but of all the jobs, what we like best, give us, the turmut-hoein!"

The light, changing, changes.

Gloria turns away, from the door, the song, the crowd, to see her majesty then, approaching, up the aisle between the stalls, and that cavernous late afternoon swells with the daylight that shines from her face, her hands, and they all, all of them, falling silent, fall away, press close to either side an aisle of their own past the outshone tub, toward the open overhead door.

The Queen in sunlight and in lace steps out onto the loading dock, illuminating the scene below, the battleship of a pickup truck, intimidating grille dented to one side, fender crumpled, headlight shattered, and Big Jim Turk stood up on the hood of it, hunched over clutching himself, wobble of a hilt there winking in her daylight, a rapier shoved through his shoulder, tip of it a-gleam above his back, and a smile grimly twists beneath his mustache. On the pavement before and about there's bald Otto Dogstongue, and Mulciber behind him, doubled over a wound of his own, and Trucos and Getulos, side-by-side, paint-spattered fists up and ready, and Lustucru in his apron and looming, limber Fell Swinton. Arrayed against them a tidy knot of rabbits, the empty-handed Stevedore and the Gaffer, the Kamali with his jeweled gloves, lowering a scimitar, the Luthier with his chain, and there among them the Guerdon, glowering in pinstripes. Off around that way, by the side of the flatbed trailer, there's the snarling Buggane squared off against Swift and the Jackstaff, spinning away his stick, deferentially alarmed to see her, shining, there.

"What is the meaning of this," says the Queen.

Crumple-pop of the hood as Big Jim with a grunt sits himself, "They would," he says, taking hold of that workmanlike hilt, "repossess our truck," and, grimacing, prepares to pull.

"Majesty," says the Guerdon, smoothing away his glower, "if we might repair in camera?"

"You might address us here, before the court."

The Guerdon's expression, smoothed, betrays a squint of disdain. "It should be a matter simple enough, majesty. Funds for its purchase were drawn from an account found to be in arrears. Until we've ironed out the irregularities, which I'm sure we will, the truck must be," wincing, he pauses, as Big Jim Turk with a guttural groan hauls the rapier free from his body. "Must needs be secured," he says, then.

"The truck's secure with us," says the Queen. "There's no need to remove it, if all's so simple, and so certain, as you say."

"But, majesty, there are bonds beyond those of the court," again, he pauses, as Jim Turk tosses the freed blade to the Stevedore's feet, clang. "The damage, of course," a gesture, toward the dented grille, "must be seen to."

"*That,*" grits Mulciber, the word scraped thin by pain, "is on *you.*"

"You will leave the truck," says the Queen.

"What, then, majesty, are we to tell the Glaive?"

"That you failed," she says, and at that, he looks down, to his polished bluchers on the tarmacadam. He nods, once. "It shall be even as your majesty has said."

"It is always to be as we say."

The evening above, deepening to an eerily sullen blue, still held at bay, for the moment, by her warming golden light. The Guerdon lifts a hand, beckoning, and the Jackstaff heads back around the truck, followed by cautious Swift, and the Stevedore collects his sword. Big Jim scoots himself to the front of the hood, a hand clapped to his leaking shoulder, and there he plants a boot on the bumper to glare as the rabbits and the Guerdon retreat, up toward the two SUVs angled at the top of the darkening street, and then, as cheers break out, as applause smatters up from the crowd in the doorway, on the dock, as Otto offers an arm to Mulciber, and the Fell Swinton throws up her great big hands, and Trucos, shaking his head, looks over the broken headlight. Jim Turk steps off the bumper and hauls himself onto the dock with the help of many hands, hands that return to and redouble the applause, as he bows before the Queen. She waves a benison over them all, but turns away to step back into the warehouse without a word.

The applause patters to silence as evening falls all about. The Buggane hops onto the flatbed and from there to the dock as Getulos, pointing, insists something to Trucos. Big Jim, hand once more clutched to his shoulder, nods absently to Iemanya and to John Wharfinger, to beaming Charlichhold, as he joins with most of the rest of the crowd to filter back in under the overhead door, into that cavernous room as racks of fluorescents above flickering buzz to actinic life, dispelling shadows, and with them the warming ambience of the tub. And there's Gloria Monday stood before it, her T-shirt rumpled, askew, expressionlessly watching his approach.

"Sweetling," he says, lifting his hand from the hole torn through his shoulder, holding it wetly shining between them as she steps close, "but a moment with the owr, and I'll be right as rain."

She slaps him.

P. INTERROGATIONIS

P. INTERROGATIONIS, she writes in blue-black ink, hesitating only the briefest moment between that first r, and the second. Closing her little black notebook, capping the pen, she leaves her hands to these tasks as she leans forward, intent on the glass tank before her, the two white plastic pots within packed full of rich wet dirt and barky mulch upholding small copses of slender green stalks, topped by feathery fronds eaten away in countless brown-edged holes like lace, or ash. A dozen or so cocoons depend from this branch, that groin, rippled packets blackly umber but for that one, there, it's burst, shell of it no longer tight-packed darkness but whitely translucent and delicately struggling free of the last clinging shreds, wobbling its way atop the frond, ungainly with the brand-new bulk of furled and sodden wings, a butterfly.

"You're early," she murmurs.

Hesitantly precise, the butterfly picks its way to the very end of a frond that doesn't seem at all to notice the negligible weight, and there, achingly slowly, it unfurls its great frail span, russet-spotted ruby sheets filigreed and edged with ghostly white, shivering as they dry in the light of the lamp close-set above.

"New addition to the harem?"

She closes her eyes, dips her head. Takes up unseen from the foot of the bed beside her a round of fabric beigely grey, lifts it up over her head to tug it down, a stretchy yoke about her neck. Gathering the softly mass of her long black hair into a practiced bun she holds with one hand as the other pulls that yoke back, a clinging scarf to hold back her hair, to smoothly, closely, frame her face. Only then does she turn on her stool, the flutter of a couple-few other butterflies about the room at her sudden movement, and she looks up to the blurry silhouette there, a mass of white locks draped about dark shoulders on the other side of the cloudy gauze, there in the open doorway of the room. "You are always to knock, first," she says. "You did agree to that."

"Perhaps you didn't hear," says Agravante.

"I hear a great many voices below," she says. "Comings, and goings. Am I to be paraded at another gathering?"

"Circumstances," he says, the form of him shifting as he steps closer to the gauze, coming into focus, concern and resolve squaring off in his expression, "have forced our hand. We've made the first move."

She leans forward, hands on her knees somewhere beneath her long empurpled skirts. "You've made a move," she says. "I wonder: have you made a decision?"

"Action demands decision," he says.

"But not, so much, reaction," she says. "You've a certain renown for keeping options open, Viscount, but there's a fine line between such admirable reserve, and dithering till the iron's cold, and circumstances force." She takes, then, a deep and fortifying breath. "Which, then, is it to be? Am I to rule a city? Or a suburb?"

"A city," he says, after only a moment. "By this time tomorrow, I should imagine."

"So very sudden," she says. And then, "Are you, here, to quicken me? Is that the plan?"

"I will not be King. I've made that clear," a step back, his features blurring with the distance, and the gauze. "I've another in mind, for that."

"And will I get to meet Señor Another, before the event? Have a word or two, perhaps, with my Bridegroom, before he has my husbanding?"

"You will, you should," says Agravante, "stay here, and safe; the next two dozen hours or so will prove fraught. Knights will be posted, at your door. And food – are you, hungry? We have," he says, stepping back, into the hall, "pizza."

"I'm not," she says, a shake of her scarf-wrapped head, "hungry. Some tea, perhaps."

The door swings shut, more firmly, perhaps, than necessary. She sits, without moving, until she hears the scrape of the hasp, and the clack of the lock, snapping home.

Now, this here, this is a floating cathedral prairie
song. It used to be sung by the old prospectors
when they were waiting for the cathedral to arrive.
Back in the '20s, when the Bechtel corporation used
to take cheap labour out into the desert to complete
its massive projects—the big dams, and so forth—
the men weren't paid very much, and they couldn't
get any liquor, so they used to sit outside in groups,
in circles, and they'd wait for the cathedral to come
by: a big, floating, transparent glass cathedral, lit
by columns of light from underneath. When it
came by, they'd all stiffen, and howl.

—*Robyn Hitchcock*

NO. 42

" – sun, dust, Shadow – "

"We're closed" – four Golden cards
Cinnamon, Auburn, Chestnut & Wenge – not a Game
Tableau – Thundering bootheels – who They're looking for
Sweetwater; Springwater – why She came – a Rondel of Teeth
a history of Vanport – a word with Gordon – a Reason
Silently, & with Great care – enough – what her Majesty requires
so Uncertainly keen; such Delicate anguish
"Only what you need!"

"We're closed," says the man behind the counter, without looking up from his receipts.

"But sir," says the man at the door. "It was unlocked."

"That would be because Mel went for coffee," says the man behind the counter, "and Mel is a," his fingers punch punch punch the keys of an adding machine, "thoughtless," he says, at the rattling clack of calculation, "individual. Close it on up on your way out," punch punch punch, "come back tomorrow," clattering rap.

"But tomorrow is too late, and what I have in mind," stepping in from the door, his bulky oaten sweater, his dull green cargo shorts, his boots anonymous beneath dried mud and dust, "it will only take a moment of your time, or mine," his great big beard, his unbrushed head of hair quite yellow, even in this sparse light, "or anyone else's. Look, let me show you," and he lifts a hand, closing it in a fist before him about nothing at all, and it's as if every bulb in the shop has suddenly been over-whelmed, the flare from between his fingers striking brilliance from glass cases to either side, the phones and cameras lining the mirrored shelves within, and electronic devices more occult, the knives there, some sharply silver, some resolutely matte, and other bladed shapes and tactical accoutrements, the glittering glass tumblers there and silver flasks and lurid copper cups, the sparks and sheens from watchbands silver and gold, and all their crystal dials. That brightness, embering, falls, and his fist's now filled with the hilt of a short but serviceable sword, the pommel of it heavily golden.

"Neat trick, son," says the man behind the counter, "but, place like this? I got nine-one-one on speed dial." His vein-rumpled hands do not stir on the counter, the one rested on the adding machine, the other moved to cover those receipts. The Harper Chillicoathe hastens toward him, "No, no," he's saying, turning the sword about to present that pommel first, setting it on the glass countertop between them, "I mean to trade it."

The man behind the counter looks over the blade, then up to Chilli, his small square spectacles secured by a slender silver chain about his neck. "For what, exactly," he says.

Chilli looks over, past the man behind the counter, to what's racked back there, the shadowy file of shotguns, rifles, bullpups, long guns, there above the pistols and revolvers and handguns neatly lined on a middling canted shelf.

"Ah," says the man behind the counter, the one hand lifting from those receipts, thumb circling his fingertips, "well, cash, credit, or trade, it's a purchase, and as a purchase I have to run you through Ficus, which, this time of night, they won't come back till the morning. And we'll be needing some form of state-approved identification, fingerprints to be kept on file, all that pesky nonsense."

"I was," says Chilli, "hoping," and a smiling shrug, his hands still there on the countertop, not reaching for any of the pockets of his shorts, the pads of his fingertips curled away, tucked pro-tectively against his palms. "Hope," says the man behind the counter, and a deeply reluctant breath taken in, let out, as those small square lenses turn back to the sword on the glass between Chilli's hands, shortly sturdy, well-made, but well-used, the several nicks and dings and scrapes along the blade of it a-gleam in this depleted light. "I," he says, "couldn't do better than one, one twenty for this. You got a ways to go yet, for that."

Chilli lifts a hand, fingers rounding into another fist. "I have another sword," he says.

Four golden cards scattered over the nubbled green cushion, Bank of Trebizond, they say, Bank of Trebizond, Good thru, Good thru. Carol Harlib, says one, and John Wharfinger another, Otto Dogstongue, and the last one there, it can just be made out, The Blue Streak.

"Fun while it lasted," says Otto, knelt behind that couch, arms folded along the back of it, chin on his crossed wrists.

"Lasted?" says John Wharfinger, perched on an arm of it, slim black guitar case at his feet. "I just *got* here."

"They, they got my name right," says Blue, sat on the couch by the little pile. "I mean, y'know, I could only ever use it when nobody was paying any attention. Or, or self-checkout. That worked." Flicking a card with a fingertip. "But they got it right."

"Have to pack it all up again," mutters John Wharfinger.

"Cheat Death," says Carol, stood at the edge of the stage, looking out over the cavernous warehouse, and only a few of the overhead doors rolled up even halfway for the dour morning light. Here and there this subdued knot or that contemplative clump of lares and hobs, urisks, losells and phenodderee, cleaning, some of them, tinkering, others, fidgeting, quietly talking, one to another, looking up and off to nothing much at all. "Come on," she says, turning back to them all, quietly quizzical, "Dirty on Purpose? I played it for you. We were never as lucky as we'd like," she sing-songs, "the miracles are through," letting that last note linger as she theatrically lifts up her face, her hands, wryly smiling, her calico sundress, her tight white T-shirt, her skinny jeans.

"Lady Waters," says John Wharfinger. "And the Hooded One." His red hair tangled, a darkly iridescent vest crimping his voluminously white blouse. "Bit on the nose," says Carol, and then up pipes the Blue Streak, "Goodbye, Mr. Ed," he says, looking to John Wharfinger, "some tasty Gabrels noise you could munch on." His long-sleeved T-shirt says The Telegenic Dead in white letters on black.

And then ruddily bald Otto is crooning, "Anything, to feel weightless, again," his eyes closed, his fingers lifted to help carry the words. "I liked that one. Who was that by?"

"The Handsome Family," says Carol, mildly exasperated.

"There's a bed for me where'er I lie," says John Wharfinger, "and I don't pay no rent."

"If it's good enough for Nelson," warbles Otto, beaming widely, "it's quite good enough for me!"

"This was a Pizza Hut," sings the Blue Streak, the fingers of one hand dancing, "now it's all covered in daisies," pointing out the notes of the tune in the air.

"What was that, that beautiful day song?" says Otto.

"What, U2?" says John Wharfinger.

"No," says Otto, "no, it was, elbow? Yeah. The, ah – "

"One Day Like This," says Blue.

"Sure about that one? says Carol.

"One day like this a year'd see me right," sings Otto then, loud enough that out there on the floor this face turns up toward them, and that.

"Okay," says Carol, "but if we're doing that, we're doing A New England. Kirsty MacColl's, because it is objectively better."

"Oh, hey," says Blue, pointing to Carol, "we could do, you could do Let My People Go."

"What," says Otto, frowning, "from that mole thing?"

"No, no," says Blue, as Carol's saying "That's let my children live," and "no," says Blue, "the, the, like, Diamanda Galás. You know. You," pointing to John Wharfinger, "do something simple, stark, you know, electric piano, and you," back to Carol, "really stretch those cords, you know?"

But Carol's frowning, and John Wharfinger shakes his head. "Too much like what we already did," he says. "Nicodemus." He looks away.

"Where is her blasted nabs, anyway," says Otto, pushing up to his feet there behind the couch, and then, as they all turn to look at him, sternly, sadly, taken aback, "what," he says, did

I miss something? Are we not supposed to talk about her? What?"

A bit of a stir out in the warehouse, someone's come in under the main overhead door, a woman with a pink scarf about her neck and a floppy knit toque on her head, her jeans palimpsested with felt-tip graffiti, looking about, uncertain. "You never should have put that blasted Star Wars song on everybody's phones," John Wharfinger's saying to Blue.

"Star *Trek*. And it got us that write-up, didn't it?"

"After we split!" snaps Carol. "Fat lot of good *that* did."

Someone beckons to that woman, Powys, and there's Luchryman pointing, and others, gesturing, there, toward the great wooden tub out in the middle of it all, a dappling pool of sunlight faintly from a summer yet to come.

"No," says Carol, "what I'm thinking," as that woman makes her way toward the tub, "is maybe," says Carol, "Peter Pumpkinhead. Let's begin," lifting a hand, but she doesn't snap her fingers poised. The woman in the pink scarf has dipped a hand into the tub to pull it, shining, out.

"In sixteen forty-nine!" sings out John Wharfinger, and he's up on his feet, "to Saint George's Hill!" his voice quite loud and carrying clear, and startled, smiling, Carol's slinks in over his, smoothing the edges, "a ragged band they called the Diggers came to show the people's will!" The Blue Streak leaning forward on the couch helps them punch the next line, "They defied the landlords!" and the thump of Otto's big black boot on the boards of the stage. "They defied the laws!" thump! and everyone out there has turned to look up to them. "They were the dispossessed, reclaiming what was theirs!"

A breath ratchets up and up until it breaks a shuddering gasp and eyes pop open in blinking alarm, "No, no, don't stop, keep going, go!"

"Are you all right?"

"God, yes – "

"I could – "

"No, don't – "

"I should – "

"Yes, yes, like that – wait – your hair!"

A hand lifted from a buttock as hips still, and bellies, the shuff of skin on silk, breasts rise and fall, and shoulders, the labor of breathing. Fingers brush a dangled lock, the roots of it a yellow dulling quickly to a sandy buff, deepening to cinnamon, to auburn, through chestnut and wenge to glossy midnight tips.

"I'm," blue eyes blink, to green, "distracted."

"Look like her," the imperative no less forceful for being whispered. Those eyes clench. Braced arms shudder. Sweat patters satin as that hair's shook out so darkly black, so artfully tangled, "no," the whisper, "no. Look like her. Look like her."

Lifted up, all that hair is shoveled back, and again, back and away the shadowy bulk of it melting in the candlelight to reveal the corners and curves of the skull beneath, licked by the merest fuzz of gold, and that nose, and those eyes, now icy blue.

"Like this?"

"Like her."

"Like you," hiking up, falling forward, "like now," weight caught on hands planted to either side of all that yellow hair, belly over belly, breasts against breasts, thighs spread about hips that hitch and settle, rise and fall with every stroke the sigh the breath the look that's edging toward the everything to fall.

Sometime later she sits up alone among the wraps and rugs, the pillows and bolsters, the candles guttering about. Her hair a pile of tidy black curls, looking about, "Tina?" she says. And then, "Chris?"

"Up here."

Sat tailor-fashion there, at the foot of that wide bed so neatly made, her yellow hair severely straight to her shoulders and past, eerily lit from below by something, her phone, in her hands, in her lap.

"Did she post again?" Drawing a shawl to herself, blue-black and glimmering silver about her shoulders. "Chrissie, did Ettie post again?"

"What?" Looking absently up from the phone. "No, it's Gav. We can pick up a shift whenever we want. As the Sœurs. If you can hold it together."

"You want to dance again?" she says, her hair now severely straight, slithering yellow down her back.

"Want," she says, "is a strong word," looking up, her face underlit. "But we need money, and I don't think," a click, the phone goes dark, "we'll have much of a career in television," and it's a bitter twist, but there's something of a smile there, in the shadows.

"You should come down from there, Chris. You shouldn't be up there."

"What, on the bed?" Looking over, to the black shapes of clothing neatly laid out on the smooth white duvet. *"She's* never coming down here." To the white pillows neatly stacked, undimpled. "And her majesty won't be back anytime soon. I mean, the game's just about over, don't you think?" Down to her, knelt there on the rugs, wrapped in that shawl. "If you need somewhere to stay," she says.

"I have a place. I, should, have a place." A breath, taken in, let out a sigh. "Ettie, won't she, if she thinks I'm, replacing her? Won't she be angry?"

"Ettie bought a one-way ticket." Twisting about, her legs unfolding, a foot lowered to the bolsters below. "She knows how to get back. Come on," holding out a hand, gesturing with her chin, toward the screen there, the pale frame of it, and the panels of plain linen. "Let's go have one last spa day."

On his wrist the golden watch, face of it crammed with three ticking dials set in an encompassing fourth, each quartered and marked by exquisitely tiny numerals, sigils, runes, each with its set of slenderly filigreed hands pointing this way, that, and set atop them all a single ornately majestic sweep hand. Fingertips roughly oblate, the nails of them cruelly cut short, pinching the innermost bezel of it, squeezing, twist, click. Every hand on the face of it falls slack, even the sweep, swung loosely with gravity as he tilts it back and forth. He taps the crystal, brow furrowing over his frowning eyes, his sharp nose, his sharper chin. He twists the bezel back, tick-click.

Those hands immediately leap to resume their twitching, ticking, majestic sweeping, and she surges awake at his feet, sucks in a slobbering, overdue breath, "oh, Moody!" clutching his shins, "I saw her, she was real as anything, real as ever, as you," and he yanks a foot free, "Christ, Ada, get up, you're fucking disgusting." Planting a boot against her shoulder, shoving her back against the louvered closet door, rattling the mirror hung from it, pasted over with stickers mostly black, some red, a few grey, printed with letters white and silver and black in shapes like electric shocks or shards of glass, or words found in the oldest Bibles, Free Men, they say, and Wewelsburg Summer, Sovereign, a blocky red capital L. "Hnánpa," she's muttering, "xhnánpa ála, in'ála, oh, Moody, you got no idea," her black hair dulled with grey, shining with grease.

"Pretty sure I do," he mutters. Squatting beside her slumped there, folded in on herself all heavyset elbows and knees, beige bra-strap slipped from one wide shoulder, careworn hand curled a darker brown against the pale swell of her belly, grey-ridged slabs of her feet pinched by filthy green flip-flops, but her eyes, so wide, so liquidly wonderstruck, "Thank you," she murmurs.

"Shut up," he says, not unfondly. Looking to the ceiling close above. Off up that way, muffled voices, raised with an edge of stridency, "The hell?" he says.

"That damn game," she says.

"That's not," he's listening, stock still, "the game."

A thump shakes the ceiling. He starts up, heads out, through the door, into the hall. "Moody?" she says, getting to her feet. "Moody?" One step, two, towards the door, a-stumble at the sound of the first gunshot.

Loud, and flatly definite, an immensely crack however many rooms away, and then a second as irruptive, and she squeaks, then jumps at the third shot, higher, sharper, "Fuck!" she shouts, and then stuffs a fist in her mouth, cowering.

Silence, falling, spreads, seeping through the house until the scuff of her flip-flop against the carpet is unimaginably loud. She lifts her foot with elaborate care for her next step, and her next, through the doorway, into the unlit hall, the short flight of steps ahead, and daylight, however indirect. Two more gunshots in quick succession, back to those flat cracks, a third, a fourth, she crouches at the top of those stairs, the garbage piled beyond, the filth-streaked checkerboard floor, the daylit kitchen, empty.

"Moody?" she whispers.

"*xo!*" someone bellows, up at the front of the house. "Danny *Moody!* Come out and get what's *coming!*"

Hunched over she scuttles into the kitchen, around toward the back door, but tumbles to a sudden flopping stop. Someone's stood there, blocking the way to the garage, a little man with an outsized head, and seeing her, he unfurls a smile, his thin lips parting about far too many teeth. Ada Minthorn screams.

She screams, and there's an immediate scuffle from the front of the house, heavy footsteps dopplering toward the back the kitchen her, and the little man looks up to the awkward landing in the far corner, the man burst onto it, baggy shorts, bulky sweater, his head a great bush of yellow, and in his hand, his hand is filled with, planted atop his hand a polished black cylinder set in a dulled silver frame that sprouts a long and slender barrel pointed this way, that, toward the hall behind, back to her, she's looking right up into an empty black hole rimmed by a perfect round of grey that holds her, fixed, for an inscrutable moment before it jerks away. "Cearb," he says, the name tearing itself from his heaving breath. "This isn't," he says, "what I asked for. This isn't what I wanted!"

"Boon," says the little man, lips pursed over those teeth, savoring the word's taste. "Bane," he says. "Bone." A shake of that head. "It's all in the shape of the mouth."

"Please," says Ada then, a squeak of a word. "Please." Looking to the little man in the doorway to the garage, the armed man on the landing, the empty doorway back down to the basement. "Please."

"Danny Moody hurt her grace," says the Harper Chillicoathe. Lowering the gun to point at her again. "You all did." His free hand, trembling, reaches across to press the heel of it against the revolver's hammer. The click-tack as it's cocked. "So. You all have to go."

He pulls the trigger. The hammer springs forward as the cylinder lurches a widdershins notch. The empty click is barely audible.

Chilli blinks. Ada opens her eyes.

He cocks the gun again. Click. And again, click. "No," he says, and "no," he says, click, "no, he told me, he said, it wouldn't do this, no!" Click. A sleeve of army-surplus green reaches around him, a hand clamps about the revolver to wrench it aside, twisting the fist, and Chilli hisses.

"Never dry-fire a piece of shit like this," says Moody, the revolver now upside-down in his hand. "You'll lock up the mechanism."

"He said revolvers *never jam!*"

"It didn't." Moody shoves Chilli to stumble a step or two down. "You just can't count." He turns away, off toward the front of the house. "Moody!" shouts Chilli, starting back up after him. "Blast it, Moody!"

Ada, slowly, turns herself about in the suddenly empty kitchen, the door to the garage unblocked, the little man gone, and his teeth, the unlit stairs down to the basement, the pop and shuck of her flip-flops as she makes her way toward the steps up to the awkward landing, and the front of that little house.

The hiss of a signalless channel carried by patient speakers. An agent decked in tactical gear, frozen on an enormous television screen, an effortful rictus just discernible through a rectilinear blizzard of rainbow snow, and the cracks that radiate up the screen from a jagged hole blown through it, close by a corner. At one end of the couch a guy's sitting, a kid, really, head tipped back at an alarming angle, both hands on the controller in the blood that puddles his lap, spilled from the hole punched through his chest. Another guy's crumpled by the other end of the couch, "Christ," says Moody, his knee on that guy's chest, the heel of his hand clamped over that guy's mouth, fingers pinching shut his nose, holding it there despite a weakly bucking struggle, knocking aside the flop of a bloodstained hand. "You can't even make a mess properly."

"What are you doing," says Chilli, folding up his arms, leaning his back against the wall.

"What you couldn't." Moody tilts his head to one side, considering. That bloodstained hand's fallen to the carpet, motionless there by the emptied revolver, laid to one side by a second gun, stubby black barrel set on a compact khaki grip. "This one got the teevee, huh? Trying to shoot back?" Getting to his feet, he scoops up the second gun. "Bet that scared the bejesus out of you."

"Why are they still *here,*" says Chilli.

Wiping the grip and the barrel with a corner of his jacket, Moody steps over to the leather recliner, and Chad, the co, laid back in it, brown robe sprawled about the bloody ruin of his naked chest, hands flopped over to either side hung low, one bare foot kicked out, quite still. "You know what?" says Moody. "I take it back. Six shots, four hits, center-mass, two kills, and he," jerking a thumb back, "would've bled out before anybody got here. Not bad, for your first massacre." He drops the pistol into the co's lap.

"What are you doing," says Chilli, shaking that yellow head.

"Used to stage scenes like this all the time for the Gulf Clan, and the Norte boys." Kneeling by the recliner, peering about, that body, this. "Give cops a simple story, easy to read," getting back to his feet, "they won't go looking for anything else." Shoving back a ragged cuff to eye the golden watch about his wrist. "Ada!" he calls, stepping away from the recliner. "Ada, baby, time to go!"

The kid, at the far end of the sofa, his head recently shaved, the naked scalp unbearably pale, and whatever his T-shirt once said can no longer be made out. The guy crumpled at this end, the revolver there on the floor by his bloodstained hand. The co's head, right there, sightlessly staring up at the pop-corned ceiling. Chilli, trembling, braces a hand gingerly on the back of the recliner to shuddering leaning reach, over the body, the flopped-open robe, the blood-sodden boxers, to take up that pistol, so small in his hand, two fingers curling naturally enough about the blocky brown grip, and his thumb, his index finger longer than the barrel of it, grimly flatly black.

Lurching out of the front room across the hall out onto the awkward landing, gripping the railing. Footsteps thumping up from the basement, there's Moody, stepping into the kitchen, his broad-brimmed hat on his head, muttering to himself, "where did she," but stopping as he looks up to see Chilli there, and what's in his hand. "Well," he says. "Would you look at that."

So high, too sharp, a barrage of popping strikes at an immense snare drum too loud in that close space. When the pistol stops jerking, when the silence returns, almost as immense as what it displaces, Chilli opens his eyes to see

and sees

Jo Gallowglas, Jo Maguire, Hawk's Widow and Queen's Favorite, Duchess of Southeast, her trousers black and baggy, her black turtleneck sleeveless, both hands clutching her breast, "what," she says, "the," and drops to her knees as a feather sprouts from between her fingers, long, slender, vanes of a grey so iridescent it seems to contain every possible color paling to a clean white down about the quill, and another, another, "shit," she says, as each of them glittering sheenly shining silvery erupts from her breast to tip, slip, drift away, shed even as they emerge to float to the checkerboard floor, and Chilli, shrieking, drops

the pistol, dropped into the co's lap.

"What are you," says Chilli, but then his hands leap to cover his dumbstruck mouth.

"Setting the scene," says Moody. "Remember?" Shoving back a ragged cuff to eye the golden watch about his wrist, grinning sharply, "Hot *damn,* I wasn't sure that was going to work. I'm telling you, this thing," looking up to Chilli, down to the pistol, the mirth leaking out of him, shoulders settling, grin dissolving. "Want to try again?" he says.

Chilli pitches forward, heaves up an eruction of white-gold fluid that splashes between his clutching fingers, spatters the carpet, his boots, the leather of the recliner, the body. An arm about himself, he groans.

"I'll get my hat," says Moody, stepping away. "Maybe go find Ada. This ain't the kind of place you want to stick around."

Stepping stumbling Chilli crashes back against the wall, blotting his beard with the back of his hand. The co, his head just visible, staring gormlessly up at the ceiling. The kid at the end of the couch, somehow staring still at the color-drenched television. He'd recently shaved off all his hair, that kid. The naked scalp so unbearably pale.

BOOTHEELS THUNDER down stairs from weakly sunstruck balustrades of glass above past yellow and grey of underlayment atop those joists and beams the color of old coffee into the softly shadows of that long and slender open porch beneath, and the screams, the relentless raw, full-throated screams from that far end, frantic pulsing bleats shoved out between desperate yelping breaths hauled in enough to draw another ragged howl of anguish, rage, of pain and terror, harrowing despair, wordless, shapeless, formless, ceaseless, echoing over the vertiginous drop beyond, the screen of trees quite dark against a whitely haze of sky. Luys leaps the last few steps at the bottom to crouching lope the length of the porch, the table gleaming endlessly to one side, the wall to the other opening on a widely solid bannister, the needled trees beyond, rattled thunder become a scuffled scrape as he skids to a halt at the far end, reaches for the squalling squealing screaming tangle of blankets in the slant of sunlight there, "My lord!" from the stairs behind, the Viscount Agravante descending with only a whit more deliberation, a dash less alacrity, "my lord Mason, do not!"

A fold of blanket loosening as he seizes it, drooping from a pinkly enormous white-crowned burden, and the screams it seems had until now been muffled, as that burden tips up, that nose, those crinkled eyes, those cracked lips yawling spreading wide to make room for a piercing yowl so much louder than any that had come before, and wincing, grimacing Luys yanks at the blankets, tugging them free, digging for something, a shoulder, an arm to grip, but there's nothing, nothing but blankets and that enormous rolling shrieking head that he catches in his hands, pressing palm to cheek as that scream is swallowed by a sobbing breath, air desperately sucked into nowhere at all, and another, another, quick yelps as percussive as hiccups as Luys struggles to hold the twisting yanking slowing twitching gentling breaths that come more easily now, and the screaming's stopped. "My lord Pinabel?" says Luys, perplexed.

Tiny eyes blink open to focus, darkly, on him. "Candy floss," mutters the other, swiveling savagely to clamp that mouth about the heel of Luys's hand.

Gurgling, blanching, Luys rears up, slapping the floor with his free hand, but even as those pink cheeks hollow, those tiny eyes bulge, the butt end of a polished wooden haft is pressed to the temple of that head, crumples whitely hair against pink skin, pressing, "Stop," says Agravante, shifting the butt to pinch a crimple of earlobe, press. "Let go."

Spitting, growling, the other does, that somehow guttural snarl grinding itself into a word, words, "How, long, how *long*," as Luys sits heavily back, "must I wait patiently, as you catch me out, again and again, and *again!* How long must I wait, to avenge my iquor you have spilled upon the stones!"

Luys, fallen back, weight propped on the one hand, the other held up before a bewildered scowl, the heel of it marred, a purpled black arc stippling the skin, seeping into the flesh. The bit of leather tied about the wrist. He opens his mouth, but can't seem to find a word. "Hold, there, Joaquin," calls Agravante, somewhere above, "let no one other any further down the stairs but the Anvil, call for the Anvil, let him through," he's stooped to busy himself with gathering up the blankets, "I was *shot,*" the other's sputtering, "somebody *shot* me, how did a goddamn *gun,*" and Luys hunches over his lap, cradling that darkening, puffening hand, his bewilderment eaten away by a growing consternation, "oh," he manages to vocalize, "I," and "my," as the other's strained and fraying monologue, "goddamn *bullet,* goddamn *hole,*" dissolves in hacking coughs that culminate in an extended heaving syncopato, "oh," the other, groaning, "oh, oh that's not right. That's not right at all."

"My lords," a new voice somewhere above, taken aback, and "Good sir Anvil," Agravante, smoothly stood back up, "take charge of the Mason, and with Joaquin take him away through the main room and up the stairs, as discreetly as you might. I'll see to the Count and join you, presently."

"My lord," says Pyrocles, concerned. Agravante murmurs reassurances, even as the swaddled other spits and snivels and moans, but Luys, Luys is focused on the feather that's drifted across the floor to settle softly by his knee. Long, and long, a foot or more, thick quill no less substantial for being translucently pale, the sudden puff of bright white down, the neatly layered vanes an innocuous, a deceptively plain and simple grey that within its color somehow iridescently contains so very many fleeting others. A hand is on his shoulder, a suggestion he might stand, why not, he does, with some little effort. A step's proposed, he takes it, and another, along the table, out of the sunlight, away from the babbling, and the feather, that gleaming feather, but his hand, his hand's still there before him, in his hand.

"Careful," says someone, Agravante, holding an axehandle, or is it a blanket, but no, he's back there, in the sunlight with the other, it's Pyrocles so very large and puzzled, blue jacket stretched by those broad shoulders, glint of pewter beads at the ends of his mustaches, "take his arm," but someone's already holding his arm, and yet a rough brown hand takes hold of his elbow, gently, but still he winces, swollen fingers curling even at that distant touch. He looks up from his hand to the man stood beside him on the stairs, squat and powerfully built, slick hair tied back with a red scarf, strap of a holster snugly crossing the front of his two-tone shirt, slight smile so gently solicitous under such dark eyes, and Luys, blinking, crumples in a faint.

A hand clamps his shoulder, crumpling the leather, "Hey!" he shouts, turning with it as he's getting to his feet, "the fuck," and "you fucking," arms flapping, catching his balance, shuffle-slap of rubber on cardboard, crackle of gravel, "fuck!" and the man who's grabbed him lets go, a step back, "You," he's saying, "you, what are you, who are you looking for? What did you say?" and the woman crouched on the flattened box looks away from them both, huddled in her once-white sweatshirt, mumbling something under her breath. "Who are you looking for?" says the taller man again, black jeans and a tight T-shirt that says I Fix Things in antique letters, It's What I Do.

"Man," snarls Sweetloaf, resettling his brown bomber jacket, "you do *not* just *grab* a guy like that, I mean, fuck!" His pompadour a-flop, the brass-rimmed goggles perched on his forehead. "I mean, shit, *manners,* you know? I mean, *Jesus,*" but at that he catches himself, blinks away, "fuck," he's muttering, "fuck, *fuck.*"

"I'm sorry," says the taller man, "but this is important. You were saying something, you were describing someone, someone you're looking for?"

"Ā gōng zǎi bo zhǔ xián," chants the crouching woman then, her mumbling bubbling to the surface with an edge of hilarity, "ā gōng! Ā gōng!"

"There's this kid," says Sweetloaf, cautiously, still scowling. "Not too tall, not too short," a hand, lifted to wobble right about there, "dark hair, lots of buttons on the jacket, jean jacket, young, I guess, I don't know," a shrug, "name's Jack."

The taller man seizes his shoulders, "No," he's not quite shouting, "no, it was somebody else, who else, who else are you looking for?" but he stops, suddenly, panting, wild eyes staring not at his hands or Sweetloaf's face but letting go nonetheless, stepping once more back. "Ā gōng zǎi bo zhǔ xián, ā mā zǐ bo zhǔ jǐng," sings the woman, rocking back and forth. Sweetloaf steps into the space the taller man's ceded, "You are *not* doing that *again.* Are we absofucking*lutely* clear, on that?"

"I'm sorry," the taller man's saying, "I'm sorry, please," wiping his hands on the front of his shirt, "please."

"A woman," says Sweetloaf, warily. "Short. Lived out by the airport with all these fucking cats. Wore, like," lifting his hands to his face, his eyes, below those propped-up goggles, "super-dark fucking glasses all the time."

"May," says the taller man.

"Her name's," Sweetloaf's saying, "yeah, how'd you fucking know?"

"How do you know my mother?"

"Whoa," says Sweetloaf, "whoa whoa whoa," but the taller man isn't reaching for him, and he lowers his hands, "I don't, man. I never even fucking met her."

"Èr gè xiāng!" chirp the woman, popping suddenly to her feet. "I know about the cats. I heard about the cats."

The taller man, suddenly solicitous, "What did you hear, about my mother?"

"I need a dollar," says the woman, "I need five dollars, twenty. Twenty dollars."

"What do you know," says the taller man, leaning over her, her sagging sweatshirt, her drooping hospital pants, dingy white spotted with blue, her black hair all a-kilter. "What have you heard, about my mother?"

"I heard," she says, "about the cats. I heard she lives, with cats. Up by the airport, but you gotta fly to San Francisco first, Ess Eff Oh. Ess Eff Oh."

"But," says the taller man, May's son, "*how* do you know her?" as he stuffs a hand in a pocket, "have you seen her? is she here?" even as Sweetloaf's shaking his head, "Nah, man, she doesn't know a fucking thing, I already *asked* her," reaching to slap that proffering hand, "she's fucking *scamming* you," but May's son persists, with a sidelong look at Sweetloaf, handing the woman a folded bill she reverently takes. "A gōng," she mutters, "a mā," sinking back to her crouch on the cardboard.

"You shouldn't oughtoa done that," Sweetloaf's saying, but May's son stalks off, away out from under the bridges above into the sunlight. Sweetloaf hastens after, away from the woman, the cardboard, the draped and suspended blue tarps, the bedraggled, mud-rumpled tents, the catawampish stacks of rough-hewn wooden pallets, the drifts and ramparts of garbage and junk, plastic jugs and discarded clothing, shreds of cardboard and trampled paper, an abandoned cooler, a massive truck hub turned on its side, sheet of raffled plywood set atop it, a makeshift table waiting for lunch, or a game of cards. May's son has stepped off the narrow paved track that stretches off through grass and scrub to either side, copses of trees there and along there, and up ahead another little knot of tents and trash and taut blue tarps in the shade. "Rovers and ramblers," says Sweetloaf, "tinkers and vagabonds, you can't do a one a them any fucking favors," but May's son lifts a hand, shaking his head, "Where do you get off, asking about my mother like you are?"

"Hey, it's okay," says Sweetloaf, "it's all fucking okay, all right? My, ah, my boss, your mother did her a solid, let her stay a couple a fucking weeks, you know? Fed her cats, and shit, until the fucking cops showed up and fucked everything up, and we've been out here just about every day since, hitting up every fucking hobo jungle and vagrant camp we can find, checking with the jefes, looking for her, and Jack, and, and," snapping his fingers, "whatsisname, okay? Because she's fucking worried, my boss, okay? About your mother. Okay?"

May's son looks away, back toward those highway bridges, busy with traffic oddly silent. "They're telling me," he says, "the RV is abandoned. The cops. They're telling me because it's abandoned they have to test it for hazardous chemicals, because abandoned RVs get used as meth labs. I'm telling them this is ridiculous because this is my mother and she has never had anything to do with meth but it doesn't matter because it's abandoned and this is what they have to do. They're telling me it's probably going to cost thirty thousand dollars at a minimum. They're telling me I have to pay for it because even though it's abandoned my mother was living there which makes it her responsibility, which makes it mine. They're telling me the owner of the property can sue me for the cost to have it tested and removed if I don't." He aims a kick at a tummock of grass. "I never should've gone to them for help."

"Well," says Sweetloaf, after a moment, "sympathies, for whatever fucking troubles, man, but I'll tell you what I *could* maybe – "

"Mike," says May's son. "Mike Holmdahl." He offers a hand. Sweetloaf cocks a brow, draws back, "Yeah?" he says, "What I *maybe* could do, see, me and my boss? We parked up by the fucking electrical thingy-whatsit, up at a Hundred and Second, and she went east, and I went fucking west, so I can tell you that from there," pointing up, along the length of paved trail, "to here," pointing back, toward the overpass, "it's no fucking dice. But. But!" spreading his hands, "the two of us, we make our way back up the Springwater, catch up with her before she fucking makes it all the way to fucking Beggars Tick, and the three of us, we compare notes, where the fuck we've all been, what the fuck we've learned, coordinate our future fucking plans," lowering his hands, shake of his head, "to find," he says, "your fucking mother."

"Hey," says Mike, May's son, but without heat.

"Okay?" says Sweetloaf.

"Okay," says Mike, after a moment.

"Okay." With a jerk, Sweetloaf starts away up the paved track, looking back with a gesture, come on, let's go.

"You know," says Mike, as he starts up after, "Driving out here, that guy Lake was on the radio? You heard about him? Anyway, he was saying that right now, today, this whole, the Sweetwater Corridor, it's currently – "

"*Spring*water," says Sweetloaf.

"Springwater, the Springwater, it's the largest homeless camp in the entire country, right now. Isn't that, amazing? All these, people?"

"And did you bring enough folding fiat for every single fucking one of them? You gotta stop *doing* that, man. Ain't a fucking *one* a those bums worth a fucking shinplaster. You know, you want to know what the worst part of this fucking hopeless search is? It's the fucking *smell*. These fucking losers can't even be bothered to *take* a fucking *bath*."

"Hey," says Mike, "buddy," with some little concern. "They can't take baths because they don't have *houses*. That's why they're here."

Sweetloaf rounds on him, "I *sleep*," he snarls, "on a fucking *threshold*, more nights than not. I never had a goddamn *bed*, excuse me, your fucking pardon, but I wake up every fucking morning and I take the time to look like *this*," drawing his hands, an exaggerated gesture, up and down himself, dungarees, bomber jacket, pompadour, goggles, "so *fuck* them if they fucking can't be bothered," stalking away on up along the path.

She crouches over a white wooden box of a frame easily as long as she is tall, if she were to stand to her full height, but only half that in width, and the walls of it less than a foot high. Her white hair's tied back in a ruthlessly glossy queue, her shoulders bunch and shift within a loose white tank as she wrestles with a great but flimsy sheet of pressboard, unfolding it along the scores pressed there and there down the length of it. That frame has been assembled half in the blue and white kitchen, half in the hall beyond, under the little yellow lights strung along the ceiling, and she awkwardly stretches past the jamb, leaned out over the pressboard to adjust its fit to the corners just out of reach, muttering an imprecation as she does.

"You know, you could have that done for you," says Ysabel, stood behind her, one hand on the knob of the door to the apartment.

Marfisa lets go of the pressboard, pushing herself a-twist back out of the hallway to sit on her heels by the frame. "To have it done, majesty," she says, "I'd need someone to do it, and he," a desultory gesture, off that way, "is all I have."

Ysabel follows the gesture, looking back over her shoulder down the three short steps into the room beyond, filled with bankers boxes brown and white stacked stacked three or four high in rows before the couches, around the coffee table where Inchwick's hunched over his work, the tweezers, the mucilage, the scraps of paper and photographs, studiously paying them no mind at all.

"So," says Ysabel, turning back to Marfisa, "what is that you're building for yourself."

Marfisa, a hammer in her hand, cups her other hand to catch the tiny nails she lets fall from her lips. "Bookshelves," she says, pointing that cupped fist toward the flat packs stacked within the kitchen, five of them all of a length, BILLY, each says, in bold sans-serif on their narrow sides.

"You do love your books," says Ysabel. "I'd no idea you had so many."

"Abby Tinker does. And when she comes to live here, I must have these shelves ready for them."

"These were purchased on the Chatelaine's account?"

"With Anna's assistance." Opening her fist to let the tiny nails rattle down to the pressboard sheet. "She showed me how to have them delivered directly here," pinching one up, leaning back through the doorway, "they arrived yesterday, while I was," tap tap tap, she drives it home, securing the sheet to the frame. "Out," she says. Tap tap tap. "The mechanism, for assembling the frame," rapping a white wooden wall with a knuckle, "turned out to be quite clever. Almost a shame it's now down to hammer and tacks." Tap tap tap.

Ysabel folds her arms about herself. Her white coat soft and loose, open over a briefly golden halter, and her trousers loosely soft and white. "This must be the last thing purchased with her cards," she says, quietly.

Marfisa stiffens at that, sits up, the hammer set aside. "You've come here," she says, "your royal self, to deny me once more what you've freely given."

"We," says Ysabel, "deny, nothing. Gloria has broken with the bank, and I," a deep breath, looking up, those artful tangles slipping from her shoulders, "came, myself, to tell you so."

"The bank is yours," says Marfisa, curtly. "Break with them, and unbreak the account."

"The bank has never been ours."

"Your majesty is Queen."

"It's *done,*" snaps Ysabel. "Out of ignorance, or," a brief shiver, she tightens her grip about herself, "love," she says, "it matters little enough. It's done, and not to be undone, not even by my majesty."

"So," says Marfisa, folding her legs tailor-fashion, propping her hands on her knees. "There's to be no more," and a sidelong look at those flat packs, "things. That's disappointing. I'm starting to think that these won't be enough."

"I imagine the Shrieve has plenty of shelves in his jackdaw-nest. If you were to – "

"Why is it your majesty is here?"

Ysabel's mien of gentle concern is troubled, then, by a hint of frown. "To make, certain, that you'd know."

"A dozen dozen others might've served that certainty – why, then, should it have fallen to your majesty, to bring this news to me?" Sat there, by the half-built shelf laid prone, under those little yellow lights, her expression inscrutably patient, as Ysabel looks up, away, hands folding one about the other.

"It's been six weeks," she says, finally, "since I last spoke with my brother."

"He's gone," says Marfisa, bluntly.

"He's been gone before. And when he was," still looking off, away, "I'd speak to him, when I was otherwise alone." The soggy light out the window over the sink, weakly grey but bright enough to fill the room, to softly silhouette her, all in white and glimmering gold. "Sometimes, he would speak back. Sometimes, I'd almost see him, a shadow, in the corner of my eye, a reflection, in a windowpane, I," she says, "the shortest night? When you and I first, kissed? I told him, after, and he laughed, and asked what had taken us so long."

Marfisa, intent on the hammer turning about in her hands, the head of it set on the floorboards, tink.

"But since that early morning when I looked into his eyes and saw he was no longer there," says Ysabel, "nothing. Not a word. Not a glimpse. And I cannot even bring myself to," a weighty sigh. "He's gone."

"You will not find him here."

Ysabel with a shake of her head says, "That's not why I came." And then, a step closer to Marfisa, away from the door, "Last week, you came to me, to tell me something, but turned and left me there, before you did. I'd not have another five weeks pass between us, without a word."

Marfisa, still sat there upon the floor, shrugs. "Whatever I meant to say was said."

"Marfisa," Ysabel kneels then, reaching out, but not to take her hand, "whatever else has happened, we were *friends*. Before that kiss, and after, after everything – "

"There *is* no after," snarls Marfisa, suddenly forceful, suddenly bitter, and Ysabel recoils, and Marfisa, blanching to see it, lets go the clattering hammer to reach out, to seize, but not her hand, "Lady," she says, hoarsely, "I *still love you.*"

Her hands, gripping Ysabel's arms, her upper arms, crumpling that soft white coat. "I never," says Marfisa, *"stopped.* Loving. You."

Ysabel, starkly upright, lips parted, blinking, once, twice.

"When you, when we, kissed, in that room, in Goodfellow's house, you took, my heart," and Marfisa lets go the one arm, withdrawing her hand a fist to her breast. "Try as I might, I cannot take it back."

Ysabel, stiffly drawn back, blinking, once again.

"When I refused your oil," says Marfisa, "your salt, your bread, I still," a shuddering shake, "loved you. When I, set out. To leave the city. I," but she shakes her head, lets go her other hand, sits back, folding her arms, tucking her chin, looking down, away. "When the owr turned to ash?" she says, "and all your spells, were broken?" Ysabel leans back at that, weight braced on one propped arm. "I woke up that next morning, *still,* in *love,* with *you.* I," says Marfisa, "will always," arms still folded, head tipped low, eyes closed away, "love you, my lady. Until the last of the stars falls away from out our sight, until the end of all the days to come, I will love you." Lifting up her head then, those fathomlessly dark eyes meeting Ysabel's dulled green. "But I do not think," she says, "that I will ever be able to like you."

Tink of the hammer, taken in hand. Rattle of tacks scooped up from the pressboard. Leaning back into the hall, over the overturned frame, she sets to hammering them home, one after another, tap tap tap. Ysabel pulls herself to her feet. Takes a step back, and another. Looks about, the sink, the window, the light, the room beyond, the boxes stacked, and Inchwick, assiduous about his work. The door to the apartment, still ajar. She opens it enough to step through, and closes it, quietly, after.

A Rondel of Teeth – a history of Vanport
a word with Gordon – a Reason

The rondel of purpled toothmarks pressed into the glossily tautened heel of his hand, and jagged red lines like rays from an angry sun stitch the palm across to the meat of the thumb, the base of the fingers, the bit of leather about his wrist. His puffy hand laid gingerly on his lap of brown corduroy, by the untucked tail of his yellow chamois shirt, dimly pale in this dark room. Curtains have been drawn across a window there, daylight leaking along the edges, but otherwise unlit. Wide bed neatly made, color uncertain in the shadows. The armchair that he's sat in, generically dark. Low mass of the dresser there, obscure against the wall. Under his boots a rug of some white stuff, too loosely soft to be any actual fur, and set on it before him a wide round porcelain basin, and a plain white saucer, and on that a slim little knife, all of a silvery piece. His other hand he runs through his neat black cap of hair, strands of it falling back into place as his fingers pass. He jumps a little as the door to the room opens just enough to admit her, whisking shut behind. Her sweeping gown, so richly dark, still manages a glimmer in the shadows, and the sudden contrast with the pale scarf wrapped about her head, framing her face, cooly composed, a hint of concern.

"Highness," he says, struggling to his feet.

"My lord the Mason," and she hastens toward him, "do not stand on my account," and nodding, he sits himself again, wincing as his hand is once more laid upon his lap. Chime of the knife as she kneels before him to peer at that bite, slop of something, water, from the jostled basin, "Highness," he says, "you've wet your hem."

"Hush, my lord," she murmurs, lightly brushing the tight-stretched skin with her fingertips. "It's quite hot."

"My lady." He swallows. "Why have you come."

"It would seem," she says, touching the tip of his thumb, the yellow rumple of his rolled-up sleeve, the knot in the bit of leather about his wrist, "the Viscount has finally dropped the dice into his cup." Sitting back, her hand now hesitant over the saucer, the knife.

"Highness?" he says, and then hisses as she shifts his hand, making room to set the saucer on his lap. "Hold still," she says, and presses the point of that slim knife to the angry heel of his hand.

His teeth clench. He strangles a yelp. What oozes up and out of the heel of his hand to bulge a weighty droplet dangling to slowly, slowly fall, thick as tar, or treacle, a dollop settling melting slowly into a purple slick on the saucer.

"Oh," she says, lowering the knife, the tip of it daintily stained. "I do not think that this will do."

"Lady," he groans, shifting in the chair, "I've, what's left of, my portion," digging in a pocket with his other hand, a shivering shake of his head, he's come up with a slender glass tube, and within, a fragment, of a filament, of gold, but "Oh," she says, "I do not think that will nearly be enough."

He closes his hand a fist about the tube, lowering his black-capped head. "There's more, about the house. There must be more."

"That's not why I am here." She untucks the impromptu cuff of his sleeve. "Are you especially fond of this shirt?"

"Not, especially – Princess – why?"

"They've given us a knife," tugging the sleeve down to blot the fresh wound, gently, but determinedly. "A dish of water," one last press, then carefully peeling the chamois away, eyeing the smeary mess that's left. "But nothing to serve as diapering." A shake of her swaddled head. "Can you unbutton yourself?"

386

"Your pardon, highness?"

"The shirt," she says, bending down to start picking at the knot in the laces of his boot. "It will need to come off. It will all need to come off."

"Highness?" he says, perplexed, even as his unwounded hand begins to work the buttons free, one by fumbled one.

"Ana," she says, widening the mouth of the boot, "Annisa," tugging it from his foot, "hight," she says, setting it aside. "And here, my lord the Mason, it's your pardon I must seek." She sets to untying the other boot. "I know your office, but not, I fear, your name."

"Luys," he says, his shirt unbuttoned, lopped open over his bare chest.

"Luys," she says, removing his other boot.

"Annisa," he says. "What happens next."

"Well." She sits back with a rustle of gown. "There's medhu enough in your other hand." Looking away, reaching up, she undoes a fold of her scarf, and another. "We'll clean the knife," she says. "Make the cut. Let it fall direct into the water." Deftly gathering up the scarf as she unwinds it until she can set it aside on the rug, neatly bundled. "But after that?" Looking up at him, now, dark eyes meeting his, her face in the shadows so much larger, somehow, framed only by the smooth close underscarf, beigely grey.

"After?" he says.

"My mother," she says, "is the Dearborn Queen, and her majesty, my sister, High Queen of all the Court of Engines, but even so," both her hands take hold of that scarf just there, beneath her delicate chin, "what happens next's a mystery." Peeling it up and back and away, to let fall unbound the softly mass of her long black hair. "Shall we find out together, my good sir knight?"

"Cora," he says, those long dark hands of his lifting from the top of her desk, "Bunch. Bee You Enn Cee Aitch." Frowning. "I think."

She sits forward, an elbow on the edge of her desk, "And who was she to you? Great-grandmother? Elder auntie?" Her hair a darkly afro loosely wafted with the breeze of her movement. "Go on," she says. "Sit."

"No," he says, "nothing like that," and he does, in one of the two narrow wooden chairs in that tight space, his oversized shirt of orange plaid still sharply creased from its factory folds. "I'm just curious."

"And you are?"

"Chris," he says. "Beaumont." Pointing back, over his shoulder, the half-open door, illuminated by a pane of frosted glass. "You got, office hours. I just," and he sighs.

"You're not in any of my classes."

The scrape of the chair abruptly loud as he pushes back, "I can go," he says, but she lays a hand on her desk, and he doesn't get to his feet. "Curious is fine," she says. "I don't mind satisfying a little curiosity. But I'm curious, myself. This doesn't happen too often, somebody coming in off the street."

"Duckie," he says. "Told me you were the person to talk to."

"Duckie," she says. "You mean, Howard Chiles?"

Christian's scowling, "I don't know about that," he says. "Duckie. Plays poker most afternoons with, with Mr. Mills, and Mr. Ford, back of, uh, George Honeycutt's old shop."

"Mr. Ford," she says. "Kent Ford."

He shrugs, somewhere in that shirt. "All I know is, Duckie says, you got a question about Black history in Oregon? Then you talk to Professor Yadira Dini, Portland State."

A cushion sighs as she sits back, both hands on black plastic arms, a judicious nod, a small smile, briefly pleased. "The thing about Vanport," she says, "it was the second-largest city by far in the state, but only for six years: built up from nothing in about three and a half months, in 1942; washed away in the Memorial Day flood of 1948. Maybe fifty thousand people lived there, at one point or another, over those six years, all for the war effort – Henry J. Kaiser needed labor to build cargo ships for the British, and then warships for the Americans, and all the white men were being drafted, so," her own shrug's more

388

of a definite thing, the wildly patterned reds and blues of her blouse rising as her hands lift, spread rhetorically, "Vanport trebled, quadrupled the state's Black population in the course of a year or so. What's arguably the first racially integrated housing development in these United States, and all of it only due to an accident of capital and war, but: enough of the canned lecture." She shifts a couple-three books on the cluttered desk to reveal a trimly silver laptop. "What all that means, is," lifting the screen of it, "there's seven or eight thousand people, coming and going over the course of those six years," typing something, soft clack of keys, the hard drive chuckling to itself, "any one of whom could be your Cora Bunch. And you ought to notice, how specifically imprecise I'm being, with these numbers," swipe at the laptop's trackpad, click, a quick burst of typing, another. "Vanport," she says, "might've had a post office, and a library, a movie theater, a shopping center, a hospital and a high school – PSU?" She taps her crowded desk. "Founded as the Vanport Extension Center. Postwar higher education for returning vets. The U by the Slough."

Christian draw back in his narrow chair, that scowl of his turning, cheekbones hunching quizzically.

"What I'm getting at," she lifts a hand at once inviting, forestalling, placatory, "Vanport might've been the second-largest city in Oregon, but it was never incorporated. It never had the chance to develop the means of seeing, and counting, and remembering, that cities need in order to build up archives." Her attention returned to the laptop, type, swipe, twiddle, click.

"So that's it?" says Christian. "Nothing we can do? Nothing to look up?"

"Not," she says, "nothing," clack, tap, "necessarily." Pointing to something, there on her screen. "March of 1947, the telephone exchanges were rearranged to give Vanport a switchboard of their own. Used to be they had a hotchpotch of exchanges, ah, Trinity, Tuxedo, University, Webster, but they all became Tyler. So: they printed a directory." She moves some of the clutter out of the way, a couple-few file folders, a stack of books, making room to turn the laptop about to face him, "and there you go," peering around to tap, there, a blotchily printed column of tight-packed names from some old sheet of typescript, he leans forward, cheekbones hunched in concentration, Bunch, A., TYler 4-5642, Bunch, Jos., TYler 4-0181, Burdell, Geo., TYler 2-1712. "That's it?" he says, looking up.

"That's," she says, turning the laptop back around, "two possibilities. Which is two more than you had," tap, tap, click, "when you came in. That ain't nothing."

"Yeah, but," his scowl shifting from concentration to annoyance, "what do I *do* with that, I don't," shaking his head.

"I can only get you so far," she says. "Talk to your elders. Talk to Duckie. See what they can make of those names."

"Duckie wasn't ever in Vanport."

"True," she says. "But I'm sure he knows folks who were."

"How many died in," he says, in a rush, and then, a breath, "the flood?"

"The official count," she says, "is fifteen. And I can tell you the name Cora Bunch isn't on that list. But that's the official count. There's no way to know for sure how many, or who, but there's more. That flood came on awful fast."

"Yeah," says Christian. "I know."

Up past the jumble of bicycles, parked along the edge of the overgrown yard, a cyclopean ziggurat of poured concrete steps leads up to a comically cramped front porch framed in peeling pink siding. An enormous figure takes up most of one corner of it, a crude suit of wicker armor, the warp and weft darkened in streaks and patches by old rain. He looks up at it, one foot on the concrete steps, stooped in a barn jacket made for a much wider man, and he shakes his head, crowned as it is by a mighty round of black curls.

"Will you knock?" she says, stood behind him, draped in a rough grey himation over an ivory chiton, her left arm sleeved in sleekly shimmering mail.

"You should get back," he says. "I didn't mean to interrupt your rehearsal."

"It's fine," she says. Her face painted, the shapes of her lips and eyes theatrically elaborate on a whitely powdered ground. "Matty will appreciate some time to fix her Jupiter lights." A nod, toward the front door the color of liver. "Well?"

It's opened by a round little man in a cocktail dress, "Yeah?" he snarls, but as he peers up at them his ruddied scowl softens in vague disappointment. "Oh," he says.

A brownish sofa at an angle before an unlit hearth in that dim, high-ceilinged room. Two women dressed in black are sat upon it, leaned back against either arm, outstretched legs entwined beneath a garish god's eye afghan, the one of them her white hair tightly knotted in glossily ruthless braids, the other her white hair unbound, a-float in wisps about her head and shoulders. "Do we mistake our eyes?"

"Has Aphrodite stepped down from Olympus?"

"Look more closely, it's but the landlady."

"Fickle fashion does but wax nostalgic."

"To what do we owe."

"I would not," says Linesse, lifting her bared hand, "lay claim to aught of yours today, no more than but an ounce of your attentions. It's Gordon," stepping aside, that hand swooping, a gesture, "who'd have a word with you," but he looks away from the both of them, and her as well, away down the length of a table littered with folded newspapers and stacks of magazines, "I should," he says, "go," taking a step away, and another, another, until, "George Honeycutt," calls the one of them, there on the sofa.

"Porter Foresworn," the other.

He halts, a hand on the dusty tabletop. "Gordon," he says, looking back over his shoulder. "The kids call me Gordon."

"Called, they did."

"And kids."

"So long ago."

"And we, you see, are not."

"What would you have of us, Porter?"

"I," he says, turning slowly, reluctantly, but about, "am not myself."

"Why, and who else would you be?"

He straightens, *"This,"* he booms, and Linesse at the other end of the table starts at the force of his voice, "is not *me,"* his hands up about his exuberantly dark hair, his glaring, unlined face, his shoulders broad, up and back, his chest swelling with a great breath taken in, but deflating, sagging, slumping as he lets it out, shoulders stooped once more, chin drooping, hands lowered. "I was born," he says, "in nineteen and *forty-four*. I can't be *looking* like this. *They don't know me."*

"But they never did."

"They knew George Honeycutt."

"Son and namesake of George Honeycutt."

"Nephew to Eddie Unthank."

"Good friend of Kent Ford, and Oscar Johnson."

"The children called him Gordon."

"When he served them breakfast."

Gordon, scoffing, looks away, but one of them lifts up a spindly finger, "George Honeycutt, who, in nineteen, was it, seventy-one?"

"It was."

"At the corner of Vancouver and," snap, snap.

"Was it Beech?"

"North Vancouver, anyway."

"Three witnesses saw him – "

"A third was never confirmed."

" – get manhandled into the back of a prowler."

"By two uniformed Portland police officers."

"But, to this day."

"The Portland Police Bureau insists."

"To this day!"

"No car was patrolling that neighborhood."

"Not at that time."

"He was never seen again, George Honeycutt."

"But the protests?"

"Were *spectacular."*

Not a clock ticks, not a board creaks, not a drop drips, not the faintest breath of a breeze, not until Linesse says, "Gordon?"

"Who you mourn never was," says the one of them.

"I *was*," he insists.

"You were," says the other, "a young man."

"Twenty-seven."

"Twenty-six, he's a Sagittarius."

"And we will always have been who we are."

"But I was," he says, his words crumbling, hoarsely, "old, with them, for a time," and then, barely vocalized at all, "why."

"A mystery?"

"A gift."

"A precious gift."

"Too precious?"

"What is it you tell your hopeful charges?"

"As you usher them through the door?"

"I," says Gordon, frowning, but the one of them calls out, "Heed thy own advice!"

"Heal thyself, Porter."

"Howsomever foresworn."

"I give no drop," he says, fiercely quiet. "I take no pinch. *That,* would be how."

"That would be how you serve your Queen?"

"That would be how you serve this Court?"

"Sacramento!" he shouts, and slaps the flat of his hand on the table, and Linesse jumps. The one of them there on the couch lifts her nose, and the other lowers her chin. "The Court of Camellias *fell*. Two months ago. Their Queen deposed, without a Bride. King, fled. Knights, torn to pieces in the street. This *city,*" he snarls, stomping toward them, one, two, three, "is on the verge of following after, am I *wrong,*" and he slaps the table again, and Linesse flinches. "Tell me I am wrong."

The one of them lifts up her head judiciously. The other looks down, lips pointedly moued.

"Tell me how you would have me best serve my hopeful charges," says Gordon, quietly, his hand a fist, knuckles down on the tabletop.

"There's the work, to be done," says the one of them, then.

"There's always the work," the other.
"The shoes."
"The shoes."
"They never."
"Never."
"Stop."

Silently, & with Great care – enough
what her Majesty requires

Silently and with infinite care he slips between jamb and door opened just enough to admit him, shutting it after with such delicate precision, and the faintest click of the latch.

The room's unlit but for daylight weakly seeping from the edges of heavy curtains drawn, not enough to clearly determine the color of the duvet and pillows neatly spread, just enough to make out the mass of a dresser against the wall, to render the figure, sprawled insensate, palely naked, in what must be some sort of armchair, black-capped head tipped back, one arm flung aside, the other folded tucked against his flank, and the darkly swollen mass at the end of it cradled on his breast. One soundless step after another to the foot of the bed reveals a second figure crumpled on an oblong rug of singed fake fur, delineated by thickly regular strokes of long dark hair laid in drooping hanks about and over the slim round of a shoulder, the slope of a waist, the swell of a hip. Between the two of them, by a bare foot, a hand closed about a little silver knife, there's a wide round soot-smudged basin, half-filled with greasy smoking water, and hung within a cloud of darkening yellowish grey unskeined in sluggish threads and tatters, and he sucks his teeth to see it.

Hiking up his sharp-creased trousers he kneels by that tableau, pale hair in dreadlocks swaying in the shadows. He plucks forth a pocket square, ivory edged with a pink insistent even in this darkness, and shakes it out to twist and wad it up again, and dips it in the basin, dredging up that slimy cloud as best he can, dunk and swipe to lift it, dripping, from the water. He stuffs the whole mess under the bed, distastefully flicking his fingers, wiping them back to front on an unscorched stretch of rug.

The man in the chair, unmoving. The woman, still, fœtally curled, not even the hint of breath.

An energetic plinking as he digs in the pocket of his jacket to produce a couple of slender glass tubes, each capped with dark blue wax, and within them threads of golden warmth, shining enough to ruddy up his hand. He sets one on the fur, and snaps off the top of the other with a quick clean clink of sundered glass. Tipping it over the basin he taps out golden dust, some falling to spark and pop and blacken on the greyly greasy surface of what water's left, but mostly drifting in clumps and streaks of gleaming gold on the sooty porcelain rim. The tube, emptied, he whips beneath the bed as well.

The second tube.

Tink as he breaks off the top of it. Sits up there by the armchair, leaning over, careful of those canted ash-splashed knees, the bare thighs slackly muscled, hatched with thick black hair. Focused intently on that shape that had once been a hand, fingers lost in the purpled bloat, a glint of quick-bitten nail capsized in the swell of it, the ghost of a knuckle knurling the darkly taut skin. The bit of leather tied about the wrist. The arm then, drained pale, held close against that chiseled flank. He tips the second tube up over his palm and taps out the golden dust into a tidy little pile. The woman, still curled, unmoving, behind him now. The basin gently steaming by his knee, the little silver knife, the saucer, daubed with a wine-dark paste. He frowns.

He slaps his laden hand down on that shape.

Shuddering jolt the man in the chair surges struggling wrestles to yowling shrieking hissing smoke, but Agravante will not be dislodged, holding tight as yanked and wrenched he's chucked from side to side, knee-thump and kick-chime and slop a hissing gasp, but keening up from Luys's throat such a lost and hopeless howl that gathers strength, volume, a vector, weight, well on its way to becoming a vowel, perhaps a syllable that might've opened into a word, but roughly ragging as he thrashes in the chair, hoarsening, raveling, shredding, crumbling into a lowering hacking cough of a sigh as his body relaxes, slumping beneath Agravante yet between his knees, hunched over until a gasp, that broad bare chest beneath him rising, falling, a breath taken in, let out, another, and another, and.

Hanks of long hair shifting slip from her shoulder as hips, rolling, lift above pivoting knees, her hands still pressed to the scorched and sodden fur, and her face, "My lord," she says, the words half-swallowed, pushing up her head, "my lord," she says, again, and something somewhere's dripping. "You mustn't, my lord. I have failed you all." Wavering, unsteady, she looks up to his arched back jacketed in midnight, bent over Luys's lap. "I must," she says, wincing as she sits herself back on her settling heels. "Gather myself," she says, head hung low, hands lifting to the hair spilled long and loosely damp about her. "I must wash."

"Your majesty did not fail," says Agravante.

"I could not," she says, combing those dark wet tresses with her fingers, "turn," she says, "the owr, it all, it all," tugging, snarled in a knot, a hiss, "it all," she says, "went *off*," her hands suddenly ceasing. Caught on the back of her hand a glimmering crumb of gold, and more, a-sparkle along the verges of the rug, flashing from this half-molten strand of fur, or that, somehow, incredibly, gilding the rim of the tumbled basin.

"It was never all," says Agravante, "or nothing at all." Dark shoulders gather themselves, bracing, "Our fortunes only ever turn on just so much: enough." Pushing himself up, and back, silhouetted by a sudden flare of gold, gold that brightly lights Luys's chest and shoulders, limning even as it fades the edges of his cheeks, his chin, glimmering the dark cap of his hair, falling into the black pools of his wide eyes staring aghast at the arm he's lifted in Agravante's wake, the bit of leather tied about his wrist and the hand, there, five fingers unfolding, turned this way about and that, ruddily mottled, a bit darker, perhaps, than the rest of him, but otherwise hale and whole.

"Enough," says Agravante, again, and a burbling cough. His arms fold about himself, that midnight jacket pouching open, his white shirt, his pinkly lustrous tie still smoldering, spotted with a last few golden embers dying even now, and his drooping white locks singed. "Enough, to heal a hand. Enough to quicken a queen. Enough," a deep breath, "to save our court." Shrugs to resettle his jacket, hands still tucked away. "I'll leave your majesties to compose yourselves." Turning, stepping away. He winces as he reaches in the shadows for the doorknob, but stops before stepping through. Looks back. "Unless you'd have me send someone to assist?"

Luys, sat up with no little effort, stares in horror not at his hand, but Agravante, "My lord," he manages to say. "You can't possibly, my lord. You can't!"

"But, your majesty," says Agravante, stepping out, into the hall. "I didn't."

Over, through, down, and switch, then up around and through again, and switch, around and through once more, fingertips patting the knot to shift, adjust, but "No," says Agravante, "no, no, stop," slapping those fingers away, "it's lopsided. Stop."

"My lord," says the Majordomo, glumly, "allow me to, if you would," lifting his hands away even as he reaches again for the tie, glossy blue and red and buttery yellow to pick out paramecial paisleys, crumpled by the half-done knot, "I said stop!" snaps Agravante, slapping again, wincing as he strikes the Majordomo's hand. "Go on," he mutters. "See to the court." Tugging to loosen the knot, fingers clumsy in gloves the color of fawn, sawing the tie back and forth until he can hurl it away. "My lord!" cries the Majordomo, reaching for him even as he rears away, but "Enough!" snarls Agravante. "Go on, about your business."

"Your tie, my lord – "

"I'll do without!" Tugging the gloves, one hand, the other, resettling the fit of them, eyes closing definitively as he presses the one thumb against the other palm. "I'll do without," he says, again, and opens up his eyes, and with those newly stiff, tight-wrapped fingers, undoes the top button of his shirt.

Clunk of a key, turned in a lock, the body of it dropping enough to free the shank, twist and she lifts it from the hasp, her other hand turning the knob to open the door, "Your majesty," she says, stepping to one side.

"I," says Annisa, but then, words fail. She doesn't take the proffered step through the doorway, into the room, the gauzy wall beyond, the scraps of shadow fluttering against it, in the lamplight. "We," she says, still stood there in the hall, loosely wrapped in a rough green robe, and only an underscarf of beigely grey to bundle up her hair.

Set on a stool before the wall of gauze an overweening bouquet of roses, the buds and blossoms so very round and full and richly winey red and purple against the paler green of their foliage, so droopingly heavy they threaten to topple in any available direction, a-tremble with possible catastrophe.

"Majesty," says Florimell, the Laguiole, in her jacket of salmon pink, "will you require assistance, with your ablutions, and preparations?"

"We," says Annisa, and a deep breath, squaring her shoulders. "We would have that," a gesture, toward the exuberant bouquet, "removed. The odor, in such a profusion, cloys."

"Of course, majesty." Florimell's looking down to her suede magenta booties, pressed together side-by-side, pink-painted nails just visible through the cut-outs at the toes.

"We would have my clothing, our clothing, our personal effects, brought to the bedroom where I was," another breath, and a shake of that tight-wrapped head. "Where we were, this morning. My subjects, and equipment," looking past the roses to those palpitating shadows, "will remain; this is to become my laboratory." Looking to Florimell then, waiting, patiently, until Florimell looks up, those softly light brown eyes. "We would speak with the Majordomo at his earliest convenience."

"Of course, your majesty," says the Laguiole.

Shrugging into the yellow kitchen, those high white cabinets, his chamois shirt more of a goldenrod, really, in all this brightness, the crash of running water, there, at the sink beneath sunlit curtains, a tall broad man in buff coveralls looks over his shoulder and smiles. Shuts off the faucet, turns about, drying his hands on a dishcloth, "Sir Mason," he says. "How good to see you."

"Don't," says Luys, quiet and quick, unsteadily lurching the lemony length of floor to fetch up there at the end, and the tall man stood between him and the sink, "don't," he says, "presume, to such familiarity," and a brusque gesture, "Scuppernong," he says, "your pardon, but I've need, of the sink." And then, "It's, good, to see you, too," he mutters, as Scuppernong steps aside.

He catches water in cupped hands, splash to his face, and again, and he takes the dishtowel Scuppernong offers, blotting his brow, his cheeks, wiping his hands. "I had heard," he says, "there were few enough to see to the house, these days." Still wiping his hands, the front of his shirt wetly dappled.

"Oh," says Scuppernong, "I work the grounds, mostly. He never sees me. I do hear him, of a morning," reaching to take the cloth from Luys, "chattering to himself on the porch," and Luys is left with the one of his hands cradling the other, darker, mottled, the palm angrily ruddied, and there the ghostly rondel of faintly darker toothmarks, the memory marked of a bite almost taken. "What is he," says Luys, a merest whisper Scuppernong leans close to catch.

"My lord," he says, drawn back. "He is the Grandfather Count."

But Luys is shaking his head, no, he says, a soundless puff of a word. Scuppernong's genial puzzlement crumples to a frown, "My lord," he says, but Luys is turning the one red hand over and back again, squeezing the mottle of it with his thumb, his fingertips, and the bit of leather swings about his wrist, "my lord," says Scuppernong again, reaching hesitantly, to take both hands in his, to stop them, soothe them, press them close between his own.

"You will show the deference his majesty is due," says Agravante, calmly stern there in the doorway, his midnight suit, his white shirt open at the throat, hands clasped behind his back.

Scuppernong looks from him there back to Luys, something dawning in his expression, a whelming horror to slack his lips, smooth his brow, dull his blinking eyes, his hands leap apart, releasing Luys, and with an awkward rustle, a thump of cabinet doors, he sinks to one knee before the King, bowing that tow head, and Luys all the while yet shaking his head, no, he's mouthing, no, no.

Striding the length of the kitchen footsteps heavy a hand swept out to clasp a buff-shrouded shoulder, "Up," says Agravante imperiously, "and be about your work," that hand gloved in pale fawn, lifted away as Scuppernong gets to his feet, but Luys catches him, his own hands on those shoulders, and Scuppernong stiffens, uncertain where to look. Luys hikes up off his heels, leans close, to press a kiss to Scuppernong's forehead, nosing aside those towy curls.

"Go," says his majesty.

Scuppernong steps away, back down the lemony length of the kitchen. Luys looks to his hands, there on the counter. Takes up the dishcloth to wipe them again, and over again. Agravante looks him up and down, brushes the chamois shirtfront with the backs of his gloved fingers. "We should change this."

"No," says Luys.

"Your majesty," says Agravante, but then, at the look he is given, stops.

"Do you know," says Luys, sternly, quietly cold, "what you have done," but also shakily, and hoarse.

"What has happened," says Agravante, "happened, because it had to. We cannot be without a Queen. A Queen must have a King, to quicken her. It's as simple as that, your majesty." He moves to step away, but Luys catches him by the elbow, "When the time comes, for her to turn more than a pinch of owr," dragging him close, "what will happen then?"

"What has to happen," says Agravante, looking down at the clutching hand, mottled so angrily, "will happen, but it will not be for quite some time. In a moment, after I make a call," shrugging himself free from Luys's grasp, "we will step out to address the court, and your majesty will rally the knights. We

400

have a city's ransom to secure, and a foolish wrong to right." Again, those fawn-gloved fingers brush yellow chamois. "You really ought to change this shirt."

so Uncertainly keen; such Delicate anguish
"Only what you need!"

A look of such keen uncertainty, such anguished delicacy, as her breath catches, a happy sob, a nod, her face tipped up, to spill black curls along her heaving back.

He closes up the phone in his hand, scowl losing itself in the shadows as the light of the screen is folded away.

She's overwhelmed, again, eyes widening in greenly consternation as her head's jerked upright, oohing mouth as her white jacket slips from her shoulders as she lowers a hand, her hands, golden halter draped over her rising breast and falling with a breath, fingers stroking severely yellow hair, the head of the woman knelt before her, the head of the woman knelt behind, the same pale naked swoops of torsos that bookend her, pale hands clutching olive thighs, bare hips, white trousers loosely pooled about her ankles, there on the lapping rugs.

Light blooms unnoticed beside him, flaring from his hand, lasting barely long enough to glimpse once more that scowl, yes, framed by ashen curls, his necktie neatly knotted, the smoothly gleaming wooden haft his descending fingers curl about, the tooling that filigrees the butt and cheek of the axe-head at the top before slipping entirely back to darkness.

Pale shoulders rolling those yellow heads swiveling twisting pressing mouths to work, to lick, kissing sucking nipping and licking again together until the one behind lifts up, sits back, removing her lips to make way for fingers, and between the two of them she throws out her free hand for balance.

He steps from behind the column, toward the three of them, the spread of rugs and pillows, the brightly burning candles, the haft of that axe in both his hands the head of it dropped down swung back and then up, behind and above his shoulders. The one knelt behind sees him coming and starting back her hand slipped free a swallowed yelp of shock at the swinging glint of that axe through the air and between them ungainly she looks up in time to lurch forward falling managing just to duck the uselessly murderous blow and tumble a-sprawling to fall to one side on the pillows.

The one yellow-headed woman getting her bare feet under herself as the other pushes herself upright to blinking wipe her mouth with the back of her forearm but starting to see that axe held high, his one hand choked up hard by the head of it, reaching with his other hand to shove her aside, stumble to crash into her twin. "False Queen," he snarls, stepping a polished black brogue onto the rugs.

"Jeffeory," says Ysabel, rolled over on her back, still trying to kick her feet free of her trousers, "put that – "

"You," he says, falling on her, his suited knee driving into her belly, "are deposed," the words too calm, too cold, too steady, as he hauls the axe around, the edge of it over her throat, his grip tightening. "Your gallowglas whores will," but that last word snags on something, a puzzlement pinching his brow. He falls away to reveal the Starling crouched behind him, the wide flat blade of an ornate punch dagger protruding from her fist, yellow hair severely straight still swaying from the force of her blow, blinking, sternly worried, but blinking, those eyes of hers changing from blue to brightly green, to icy blue again, to the more earthly color of mud.

"What," says Ysabel, staring at the bit of bone, a patella, landed on her belly, spangled with a chilly silvery glitter, but that's when Chrissie, sitting up, finds her breath, and starts to scream.

"Hello?" he's calling, peevishly loud. "Anybody? I'm looking for a, is there, anybody?" Turning about, tall but stooped, plain grey sweats, his dwindling hair clipped close. "Hello?" Up on the unlit stage behind him, to one side of the nubbled green couch, a battered acoustic guitar upright on a stand, the frayed ends of the strings of it, unsprung from the tuning pegs, glinting in the shadows, and the whitely striated shellac yet glossy enough to catch and hold a trace of glow, the afternoon daylight sloped through the windows above, perhaps, and the opened stalls, or maybe the gentle golden light that shimmers just over the rim of that wooden tub, out in the middle of it all. A half-dozen or so, scattered desultorily about, a lar and a lutin, a kobold, a clod, a couple of broonies, a slouching hob, murmur or sip or tinker or pack this or that away, but each of them all of them studiously avoiding any notice at all of his agitation, his frustration, "Anybody?" he calls, headed back toward the one great overhead door, but veering from the threshold toward the foot of that skeletal staircase, bolted to the wall there, under the painted letter-shapes of some long-faded sign.

He's only halfway clanging up those steps when the door at the top of them bursts open and she steps out, willowy tall and determined, loose white blouse and brief knit shorts of an incongruous check, russet hair framing a pair of narrow black-rimmed glasses. He draws himself up as she ringingly hurries down, "Excuse me," he says, and louder, "excuse me," but she's focused on the bottom of the stairs, angling to slip past, and he reaches to impede her, *"excuse* me," he says, "I need to find Marfisa."

Stopped there she looks up, from his arm to his face bent over her, abashedly stern, "And who are you?" she says.

"Eddie," he says. "Auchincloss. I'm, is she," looking away from the darkly irked eyes behind those narrow lenses, out over the warehouse below, "this is," wonder creeping, distractedly, into his words, "all this, it's her place, right? Y'all've been busy."

"Marfisa isn't here," she says, stepping down and past, but, his attention yanked back, he reaches to catch her arm, "It's *important,"* he snaps. "She doesn't even have a *phone,* as far as I can tell, I'm sorry," letting go, "but I really need to find her."

"Twentieth and Hawthorne, sometimes," she says. "The older building, dark brown. Number three one two." Down below, someone's ducking in under the overhead door, thinning blond curls and a turquoise summer suit, and she's turning away again, but Eddie hustles a couple steps down after her, "If you," he's saying, "if you see her, before I can find her, can you, could you give her a message?"

She doesn't nod, looking back up at him, but she doesn't shake her head, either. Down below the man in the summer suit's looking back outside, lifting a beckoning hand.

"Tell her," says Eddie, "tell Marfisa, that Abby Tinker is," but then he stops, and takes a breath. "Tell her it's about Abby. And that I need to see her as soon as possible."

"I will," she says, but another half-dozen or so men in suits of navy and periwinkle, Prussian, steel and azure and sky, all march in to join the man in turquoise, and after but a moment's conference fan out to ring the tub. "God *damn* it," she mutters, and leans out over the railing to spit. They're unfolding burlap sacks from their jackets, shaking them open, lofting them over the walls of the tub, some with more reluctance, perhaps, or less alacrity, than others, to settle, limply empty, atop the golden dust within, and the light about them dims, the warmth of it falters.

"Only what you need," calls a domestic, hesitantly, out from one of the stalls, but "Not a Hound!" cries another, and "Not a Hound!" the chant's taken up, "Not a Hound!" and she's clanging away down the skeletal staircase, "Stop!" she calls, but "Begin!" booms the man in the Prussian blue suit, and they all, some with more enthusiasm, perhaps, and less trepidation, than others, set to scooping handfuls of spilling golden dust into those burlap sacks.

"Stop!" she cries again, hurling herself toward them as the chants collapse in peals of alarm, seizing a dark blue shoulder even as someone shoves her aside, silence falling as she hits concrete beneath a trident braced against a turquoise hip, the middled prong of it dimpling her blouse. "Keep on," says the knight in Prussian blue, though the slither and shuff of shoveled dust never stopped, and he steps to the side of the knight in turquoise, holding that trident, and squats beside her, "Now," he says. "Who is it you think you are, to interfere so with knights of the court, about royal business?"

"Some of you!" she calls, then, "go! Find Big Jim! Call for the Shrieve! Gloria! Send word to the Helm! Some," faltering, as the knight in turquoise leans on the trident, but the knight in Prussian lifts a hand, "No, no," he smiling says, "let them go. We'll need strong backs to load these on the truck."

The trident's lifted away, turned about thump to set the butt of it on concrete, and sitting up on her elbows, she reaches to resettle her spectacles, and suddenly alarm, "Petra!" she cries, surging to her feet. "Stay there! Do *not* set foot on the floor!"

Halfway up those skeletal stairs, Eddie turns to see a few steps above a woman caught in the act of coming down, black hair in angled swoops to her chin, a bit of black lace ringing her throat.

"Oh, *do* come down, little gallowglas!" taunts the knight in turquoise, hoisting his trident. About the tub, another knight his shoulders straining a navy blue jacket, stops his scooping, bag gaped darkly in one hand, gold light warming the side of his face, sparking the rough weights that tremble at the ends of his mustaches a moment before redoubling his shoveling with frustrated anger. The bottom of the tub can be seen in growing patches, all about the rim, and they're having to lean well out over the pile now, to scoop up dust enough. "You'd be the Glaive's secretary, wouldn't you," says the knight in Prussian blue, leaned patronizingly over her. "I am," she snaps, stepping back, "Anna Nirdlinger, I keep the books, for her majesty, and *you*, Guerdon," she sneers, "would be trying to take what isn't yours!"

"Not *ours?*" turning to sweep an arm toward the tub, the knights busy about it, "this is the very heart and treasure of the court," he's saying, "to be held close, and tight, and safe, portioned out to peers and knights, not piled up in the marketplace!" even as the first of the filled sacks' hefted heavily out. "And we!" he shouts, eyes wildly wide, "are! the court! We are about the Queen's business! We are bidden by the King!"

"You," says Anna, as horror crawls into her voice, her eyes, "he's," she says, "you," and her head begins to shake, from side, to side. "It's ours!" someone pipes up, and "Ours!" the call taken up, "It comes, it comes from us!" from someone else, and "It comes to us! It comes to us!" and "From us! To us!" the building chant, and "Ours! Ours!"

"In good time!" booms the Guerdon, the Trident beside him, weapon ready, as another sack's hauled out of the tub. "And in such manner as is prudent, and in such amounts as are provident. The owr," raising his voice over the mutterings and murmurings, the yelps, the shouts, "the owr is once more safe and secure! The owr is in her majesty's hands!"

Something happened: it happened inside her head; it
happened to her mind, and its effect spread through her
body like a chill, or a warmth, and was realer than either.
She gasped and blinked, looked at the sun, dust, shadow,
tried to apprehend what had just changed, and felt a
stray thread on her sleeve tickle her arm in the breeze, a
leather crease across her instep from her soft leather
shoe, the air passing in through the rims of her nostrils
breathing, the moisture at the corners of her eyes.

—Samuel R. Delany

NO. 43

" – the Five Pointſ – "

CLATTERING BUTTONS – AN APRON OF DIRT
INTO THE GROTTO – DON'T ASK – THE SPLINTERED WRACK BELOW
ADMINISTRATIVE MATTERS – HIPPOCREPIS COMOSA – RABBIT STEW
NOTICE: ILLEGAL CAMPSITE – BREAKING FAST – COFFEE, HOT
A MOMENT PASSES – AGAIN, SUNSET – PREPARING HIS DOSES
NUMBER TEN – WHAT KIND OF GHOST – THE SOUND OF WATER FALLING
WHERE SHE IS, AND WHAT SHE IS TO DO

BUTTONS CLATTER and clack as spindled fingers clamp his shoulders, push the one, pull the other, twisting him about, "whoa," he's saying, "whoa," as he plants his feet to hold him fast, but the elderly man's relentless, tugging and shoving as all over his grimy denim jacket those badges and buttons and pins so strikingly colored, distinctly sloganed, PROTECT Each OTHER, says one, and Star Grease another, ACT-UP, HE / HIM, Think Younger '74, Queer But Tired jangle and clank until he's turned about just so, his back to the ruddy, low-slung sedan parked athwart an otherwise empty street, "Boy," the elderly man is saying, "I put up with *far* too much the last few days to have *any* patience left in these my bones," the face of him weathered away to extraordinary furrows and prominences, eyes sunk deep in calderas beneath the whitely shagged escarpment of his brow, pinched mouth set in a wrinkled moraine, "so kindly do us a *solid,* and hold *still.*"

"What he said," from the kid, sat back against the fender, scowling under a matted pompadour.

The elderly man opens the long driver-side door, squats in his shapeless linen suit to lever up the front seat, "Go on," he's saying as he does so, "she just wants to talk."

"Who?" says the young man in the denim jacket, *"Who?"* even as the elderly man is tugging and pushing, folding him into the back seat of the car, closing up the door of it with a gentle chunk that's nonetheless terribly loud in the silence about them, and not even a susurrant rumble or whir of traffic on the overpasses laced above.

"Jack," she says.

Her hair a bit too ruddy to be brown, per se, pushed back to sweep her shoulders, black top turtlenecked, sleeveless, bare arms folded, those eyes the color of mud to either side of that nose, looking at him with such, such concern.

"Fuck you," he says, looking away with a clack of buttons.

"I've been looking for you," she says. "All week, ever since, Jack. Do you know what happened to May. Her son, her son's worried sick."

"I bet," he snaps.

"Do you know where she ended up? Just, tell me, Jack, yes or no, and I – "

"You mean, after the cops arrested you? Busted everything up, kicked us all out? No, Jo. No fucking clue. Been too busy, trying to put my *life* back together."

"Jack," she says, reaching out a hand, "I'm so, so sorry, about," but before she can lay it on his knee he jerks away, "Don't," he spits, "don't you dare."

She draws back her hand. "You know I didn't shoot anybody. You know that was bullshit."

"What do I know!" he shouts, and she flinches. "You," he says. "Look at you, some, what is it. Duchess. And your goons? Driving you around in this," and *"Jack,"* she says, sharply, but he plows on, "this fucking *car,"* he snarls, and "Jack!" she barks, flatly loud in these confines, and then, as he's catching his breath, "I had to find you," she says. "I used what I had. Those guys?" and she looks away, with a sigh. "Who you saw, out by the airport, that's me, Jack. That's, who I am. Not," a hand, laid on the back of the seat before her, "not this."

"Yeah?" he says. "Well, which one of you's looking for May? You with the goons? They can round up all her cats, maybe. Put all her magazines back together. Wouldn't *that* be swell."

"We've already," she says, "done, what we can, with that, already. You," leaned back, away from him, against the passenger-side door, "you're here, but you can leave, whenever you want. But. You might want, a hot bath? Change of clothes? Something to eat, a bed, perhaps, under a roof?"

A moment, then, as he doesn't look at her, but doesn't reach for the handle of the door, either. And then, leaning over him, she reaches across to rap on the window-glass, and nods to Sweetloaf when he leans down to scowl through it at them both.

AN APRON OF DIRT – INTO THE GROTTO
DON'T ASK

AN APRON OF BARE DIRT slopes from a retaining wall down to a row of slender columns upholding the bridge above, a file of proscenia framing the quietly empty cross street, dimly lit, the one-lane ramps arising close by either side. A couple of old dome tents pitched right up against the wall, beneath criss-crossed stripes of whitewash palimpsesting old graffiti, before flattened cardboard laid out, an impromptu parquet floor, but everyone hooting and hollering's gathered about the wide circle scratched in the dirt, down by the arches, where all is vaguely lit by an orange haze of sodium vapor. She's on her hands and knees in that circle, coughing, groaning, wrapped in a puffy ski jacket of some filthy color, impossible to name, and he's strutting shirt-less about her, preening for the crowd, skinny arms spread wide, fingers beckoning for more, nodding that head under a slop of dark hair, stringily greasy, sharp nose, sharp chin, those sharply eager eyes, "Another?" he roars, and they all bellow their approval. He rears back a heavy brown boot and hurls it forward, an unsteadying kick to her belly that lifts her bodily off the dirt, and a plosive burst of breath. He drops to a squat, sharp-bent elbows braced on sharply bended knees, teeth bared, waggling his tongue. Moaning she's pushed herself back up on hands and knees, her mismatched shoes scuffing the dirt, "Oh, no!" he cries, sharp angles unfolding to lever him upright. "You ain't got permission to *leave*, Bambi!" Stalking around to plant those boots once more between her and the sketchy edge of the circle as, grimacing with a labored sob, she pulls herself down, in, curling about herself as the crowd about them jeers. "Oh, no, indeed," he says, quiet and close, as he tugs something free from the small of his back. "Bambi Jo, you ain't never gonna leave." An elaborate swing of his goosefleshed arm to bring to bear a long and tapered poignard, the hilt of it wrapped in wire.

"Dread Paladin."

Silence falls about those two words, spoken, not loudly, but with cuttingly definite purpose. She's stood with the others, outside the circle, older than all of them, taller than most, rough hair unkemptly dark, craggy cheeks and a jut of a nose, frame of her softened by a puffy coat of her own, greasily bright, pink or orange or yellowy gold, perhaps. "That's enough tax."

"Oh, no," he says, "no, jefe, we ain't talking tax, not for what she's done," reaching, seizing, yanking up by that hair-colored hair a face crumpled with effort, or terror, or grief, perhaps. "Not for what she thought she was gonna do," he says, hunching close with that knife.

"Moody."

She steps out of the crowd, into the circle, hands still tucked in the pockets of her puffy coat. He looks up, heaving his breath, ribs broadening, yielding, sharply defined by shadows, and the awful look upon his face.

"We got no sanction," she says, stepping closer to them both.

"*Fuck* that," he spits, with a savage shake of the head in his hand, "she thinks she's gonna *leave* us. Thinks a job and a room in a *box* is enough to get her out of here. No *way*," and another shake, "we let that go. No *way*," leaning close, tip of his tapered blade sinking into the puffy nylon of her jacket, "and here," he says, the rage drained out of his voice gone cold, "right here, is where I should've done it. Split you open," shifting the tip from yielding nylon to slick taut flesh, "throat to cunt, dumped you out, there and then, *fuck* the chief and the fucking commandant, and *fuck* Bambi, I'd've been *done* with her. *That* time would've been *worth* the doing." Standing abruptly, letting her drop to the dirt. "Instead of letting whichever one of *you*,"

411

swinging the blade in a wide circle, taking in that crowd of still and silent silhouettes, "gets beat to hell, down by the tracks," that flash of anger once more muttering away as he looks to her, crumpled in the dirt, the face of her turned away, the back of her head a darker shadow among shadows. "At least you know what it's like, now," arms at his sides, his blade hung low, "doing time for for someone else's crime. Jacked for what you didn't fucking do. But," and, suddenly sputtering, "damn, the, the *look*," a gasping cough of a laugh, "on poor, poor Jasper, on his fucking *face*," shaking his head, *"bang!"* doubling over with paroxysmal giggles.

"She ain't there, Moody," says the tall woman, and his giggles pull up short, he turns to look up to her stood there, hands still in those pockets, looking not so much at him as where he'd used to be. "She ain't in jail, Moody," she's saying, but the voice that seeps from those barely moving lips is thicker, lower, softer, slurred. "You said you put her in jail, but she ain't there."

"Ada?" he says, incredulous, pushing himself to his feet, "but I don't meet you yet, not yet, not till way after," looking down, to his hands, but instead of a glinting silvery knife there's a heavy golden watch. He shoves back the cuff of the jacket he's wearing to stare at the dials of it, the majestic sweep hand atop them all swung slowly, inexorably widdershins until it reaches the bottom of its arc where it shivers to a halt, pointed straight at him for one long stretch of a moment, before soundlessly resuming its clockwise course.

Rattle and scratching crackling pop he scrambles crabwise up off flattened cardboard, out from under sunstruck blue tarpaulin, shouldering past Ada flapped over and back in her bone-dry purple rain shell to hunch up and clanging claw at a kiltered panel of cyclone fence. Out there in the street a low-slung ruddy car, black stripe down the side of it, an elderly man in a shapeless suit lowering himself into the front passenger seat. "Hey!" shouts Moody, but the engine's rumbled to life, swallowing the rattle of the fence in his hands and whatever it is he hollers next. Tires squeal and the car leaps away, tail of it shuddering slewing until the velocity catches up with it straightening, accelerating, gone.

"Hold up," says Jo, one hand lifted, a warning gesture tossed back over her shoulder, her other held to her chest, loosely curled.

"Problem?" says Jack on the top step, behind her, above her.

"No," she says, "probably," taking another step down, "probably not. Still," as she makes her way down step by quick but careful step, passing from thinly daylight, muralled walls, yellowing tile, down into rough-poured concrete grotto, a darkness shaped and ranked by blocky columns thrust up to groin a ceiling lost in shadows, hiding and revealing by turns an archipelago of candlelight at the far end, about a cluttered nest of pillows bolsters rugs and wraps and Persian carpets laid upon the floor and a figure stood there, two, silhouettes uncertain in the glimmering flicker.

"Hello?" calls Jo, as she makes her way along the unlit aisle between the columns. "Excuse me, hello?"

One of them, thickset in a long white coat, looks away from the candles, peering into the darkness to see who called, but turns back to the light with a shrug. The other, shorter and more slender, doesn't look away from whatever it is it seems they're both awaiting.

"I don't mean to interrupt," she calls, "I thought this was, I mean, I'm looking," but they've drawn themselves upright at some signal or sign, as what they've been watching for appears, stepped out from behind the screen stood there, linen panels set in frames of white-washed wood, a figure tall and slim, draped in frothy white and spangled with gold, and black curls artfully tangled about her shoulders.

"Ysabel?" says Jo, brought up short.

The woman in the white coat turns again to look to her, candle-light slipping to pool in the roundly concave mirror she wears on a band about her temples. The shorter man, his shirtsleeves gartered, doesn't deign to register Jo as he steps to Ysabel's side, lifting from about his neck a loop of tape-measure that he fussily deploys. Ysabel stands impassively, tugged this way, nudged that, as he takes the measure of a length of sleeve, the stretch of a seam, noting the results on a minuscule notepad, and all the while Ysabel's gazing down at Jo with a vaguely imperious disappointment, and Jo closes her eyes, then opens them, a gesture far too considered to be thought of as a blink.

"Starling," says Jo.

"Duchess," says the Starling. "Have you come to stay?" A half-step forward as the shorter man kneels behind, twisting to reach with his tape-measure.

"I, ah," says Jo, "what?"

"Your grace's things are laid out on the bed, there. No one has, interfered, with any of that," a gesture made awkward by an attempt to measure a hem.

"I, ah, I'm not," says Jo, looking over to the high wide bed on the other side of that puddle of candlelight, "here for, ah, this," she says, and the dark clothing laid out to one side of the pillowy white duvet. "That," she says. "Um."

"All's intact and as you'd left it. We'll just be a moment longer," looking down to the shorter man as he tucks his pad away in the bib of his apron.

"That's fine," says Jo, brows pinching, "we're just, I'm," a gesture, toward the dressing screen, "just here to use the, ah," looking back, over her shoulder, "I thought I told you to wait," she says.

"Yeah," says Jack, stood at the very verge of the light that glints and winks the buttons pinned up and down his denim jacket, he's staring, wide-eyed, slack-jawed, one hand lifted, reaching, but not exactly, toward, but not precisely, the Starling. "You, ah," he says, blinking, "said. There wouldn't be, ah. Problem."

"There isn't?" says Jo, as the Starling's saying "And you are?" and Jack leans back, suddenly, away, into the shadows. "It's not," says Jo, "nothing's, can we just, Jack? If you could, okay?"

"A moment more," the Starling says, turning away from them all, back toward the screen, "and we'll be out of your grace's hair."

"No!" says Jo, a sharply interrupted gesture, "wait," she says, "nobody, I'm not here to, kick anybody out, or anything, Starling, just, hang on a minute," but the Starling's stepped herself back behind the screen, "I, ah," says Jo. The woman in the white coat looks down, brushes something from a sleeve. The man in the leather apron pushes himself up off his knees.

"What," says Jack, "is going on?"

"You," says Jo, that interrupted gesture resuming askew, yanked back at him, "are in dire need of a shower, a bath, whatever, a change of clothes," and he closes his arms protectively about his clattering jacket, "Then what the hell are we doing here?" he says.

The Starling steps out from behind the screen, taller, wrapped in an oversized hoodie of pale pink gently overwhelmed by the cornflower seeping from those puffily broad shoulders, the hood of it lowered to lap her shoulders like a ruff of richly royal blue. Squeak of spotless white sneakers as she kneels by a black gym bag, unzipping it enough to slip a handful of filmy lace within. "I'm not, moving in, or anything," says Jo, quickly, "so you don't have to go anywhere, I'm not, kicking you out, Starling, you're, you're okay."

"Wait," says Jack, unnoticed, "what?"

"Rest assured that your grace in no way is putting me out," says the Starling, hauling up the gym bag as she gets to her feet. Looking about the guttering island of light, the pillows, and the rugs. "I'd meant to leave regardless."

"Starling," says Jo, as she turns to leave, "wait, is there a light switch somewhere, or, like, any lights, at all, besides," looking down, at all those burning candles.

"All else is packed away," says the Starling, setting off.

"Yeah, but," says Jo, "is she," and at that, the Starling stops, there in the shadows.

"Is she okay?" says Jo.

The Starling looks back, over her shoulder. "No," she says, and she's gone.

"Jo," says Jack, an unvoiced cough to catch no one's attention but hers. And then, again, *"Jo,"* more urgently insistent, "Jo!" She turns to him, slowly, with a shake of her head. "Come on," she says, stepping off the rugs.

"Where'd they go?" the same hoarsely insistent not-quite whisper. "The other two."

"They left," she says, looking up at the screen. And then, "Jack," she says, and he jerks away from the shadows, peering back at her through the candlelight, "some of this shit," she's saying, "you don't know the answer, just don't ask. Trust me." Beckoning. "Get over here."

"What is that," he says, without stepping onto the rugs between them.

"It's just," a gesture at the three tall folds of it, shallowly zigzagged, linen panels obscure in that light, "you go behind it, they'll clean you up, change your clothes, fix your hair, cut it, rearrange, whatever. Whatever."

"Whatever," he says, "I want?" Looking back, over his shoulder, into the shadows.

"Yeah," says Jo, but then, "I mean, it's not like you'll have time to, to tell them what you want, or anything, they're pretty damn fast. But just, have an idea, in your head, they'll do whatever's best for you, and, you know, what's going on. You, uh, Jack?" He's slowly turning back, staring not at her, but the screen, expressionless. "You want me to go first?" she says. "I mean," looking to the screen herself, a sour twist of her lips, "they like to fuck with me, sometimes, but that's because they think they can get away with it. I'll make sure they know they can't get away with fucking with you. Okay?"

Jack's still staring, flatly, at the screen.

"Jack," she says, and then, a bit more forcefully, somewhat more loudly, "Jack," she says. *"Jack."*

The hand on her knee laid so gently it doesn't trouble the rumpled corduroy. "Sarandib," she says, voice cracking about the name. "There were," she says, "three princes," her own hand, so knobby and so spare, liver spots laid loosely over knuckles, veins, lifted shakily to press two fingertips quite deliberately to her wrinkled, lowered forehead. "I can," she says, and the man knelt before her leans close to catch her whispered words, sandals shifting scratchily on gravel, hem of his pale cardigan heedlessly brushing the dust, but not an ounce of the weight of him leaned on the hand he's lightly laid on her knee. "I can see them," she says, "such, brightly beautiful robes, and gowns, the turbans, and the jewelry, they were," lowering her hand, then, to set it, quivering, atop his, "on the right-hand page," she says, her other hand a-tremble, laid palm-up on her other knee, "and they pointed to the lovely map, on the left," lifting up her head, but her eyes are closed, looking away into somewhere else. "A teardrop, in the ocean," she says, "amber, and gold, and the names, written in black ink, Sandocanda," she says. "Bumathani. Nagadisu. Anuro," and she takes a deep breath, "Grammi," and a sigh. "All those houses, the corners they would turn, their flowers grown up to meet their balconies, where they would eat their breakfasts, fruit and tea, rice puddings, sweet and sticky," her next breath taken in stepwise sips, like little sobs. "All gone," she says. "All lost, forgotten, but all, somehow, still there, in that map, those lines, that ink," and one more thready inhalation, "the princes," she says. "They ripped it," no longer a whisper, "the map," lifting up both her hands, "the three of them, torn apart," and her hands drop, nerveless to the mattress she's sat upon, quilted, filthy, formerly white. "They tore it all apart," she says, and he tips his head to better catch her words, sere ghosts of consonant-shapes now, barely bound by unvoiced vowels. "The princes, tossed away, the map, crumpled, under their boots, so, so many of them, photographs, interviews, drawings, stories, maps, the maps," her last few words so many suppositions, drawn from twitches of those lowered lips.

He lifts up his head, straightens his shoulders, pats her knee with that hand once, twice, but leaves it there, fingertips brushing the corduroy. "A terrible thing, Mother," he says. "We are so very sorry it happened to you."

She looks up, blinking quickly, "Mike?" she says, those eyes of hers darting back and forth before she squeezes them shut against the light, cloudily weak though it is, "Mike?" she says, again, "that you?"

"No," he says, and now he lifts his hand away, looks over his shoulder, a mildly impatient snap of his fingers. "But you are someone's mother." The woman behind him turns away from an older man, who snatches the plastic-wrapped packet of clean white underwear from her unresisting hand as she sets down an overstuffed shopping bag, Ross, it says on the side of it, rounded purple letters, Dress For Less. She digs into it, past more packets of underwear and bundled-up socks, white and athletic grey, maroon and navy blue, each wrapped in clear un-labeled plastic crinkling to come up with something smaller, wrapped in plastic that's anonymously grey. She slaps it into his waiting hand and he draws it to himself, slitting it open with an unzipping flick of his thumb, tipping it over to shake out the contents, a pair of black plastic sunglasses, oversized, flimsy, wraparound, that he presses into her hands, knobbled and spotted. "Oh," she says, shakily unfolding them, lifting them into place, over those milkily tremulous eyes, "oh thank you, thank you, sir. They broke mine, when they pushed me down. Thank you, sir. Thank you."

"Lake," he says. "Call me Lake. And, Mother," taking those hands of hers in his, squeezing them, gently, as his lush brown beard lifts and spreads in a smile of grim determination, "what was done to you is inexcusable. Unforgivable." His brown eyes darkening, hardening. "And we will make them very sorry that they ever did it."

THE SPLINTERED WRACK BELOW – ADMINISTRATIVE MATTERS
HIPPOCREPIS COMOSA – RABBIT STEW

BELOW, THE SPLINTERED WRACK can still be seen, ensconced within the shadow of the house, weathered upholstery torn and some few shreds of draggled filthy stuffing, all the lush green grass grown high all up around and through it, and about it, even now, glass shards glint in the failing light. His one hand on the wide wood balustrade, the other folded, tucked against his breast, his loose shirt of a sunny golden yellow, silk, perhaps. He takes a breath.

"My lord the Mason," says someone there behind him, and he turns.

The Marquess Linesse, Northeast's Helm, all in monochrome, her gunmetal hair cut short, her black leather jacket hung open over a halter of heather grey, a plain steel helmet in one hand.

"You asked us for a conference," she says.

"And we are pleased that you have come," he says, stepping away from the balustrade toward the long table jutted out from under the house above, but still within its shadow. He gestures toward a chair to his left, even as he sits him at the head. She hauls up to set that helmet on the table, mirroring metal on polished wood, even as she pulls out the chair to take her seat. "So," she says. "Yourself would be the King of Roses."

"Say, rather, that her majesty Annisa's now our Queen."

"You quickened her."

He unfolds his hand, holds it up, and there, about, across the heel of it, that purpled rondel of toothmarks. "She turned owr enough to heal this hand, that would otherwise have done for me." Closing it up again. "Not so much as yet, perhaps, but more will come, with time."

"And while we wait?"

He looks down to the polished wood between them, that gathers up and banks away the falling light. "We have," he says, "secured, what remains, of the court's existing stores."

The corner of her mouth downturning just, even as her brow so slightly angles up. "How much," she says.

"More than enough," he says, "to fill a puncheon, but not so much as might fill a pipe."

"So," she says. "Plenty."

"The stores of the court are once more under controlment, that," laying his unclosed hand definitively on the table, "is the import, of what's been done."

She looks away with a shake of her head.

"Linesse," he says, leaning forward. "In the wake of her mother's infirmity, her brother's loss, to have left those stores, our treasure, out in the open, where anyone might," but "I know," she says, *"what* I know, Luys, is I've four knights sworn, not even a handful, who must glean the medhu from the Northeast Marches," and both her hands are laid as flat as his upon the tabletop, "and yet, from the moment her majesty offered up the owr to any and all, not a moment has passed that one of those four has not been keeping watch, from the great hall of her palace, or the streets about it, ready to step in at the slightest provocation, and not once, Luys, in all this turbulent month of May, not a once has any of them had to. But I must admit," drawing back her hands with a faint squeak, "not a one of us thought to keep that bounty safe from theft by stealing it."

His expression flattens, and his voice, "We cannot steal," he says, "what's ours."

"Chop logic," she says. "There was but one exception, to her majesty's largesse. No sworn Hound might partake. Yet Udom, yesterday, saw those bullies as they crept into the palace with their sacks, and every man Jack of them dressed in blue."

"They came not as bullies, nor as Hounds, but knights, in service to their Queen."

"At the order of the Viscount."

"As directed by their King," he snaps, and then, a breath, a gesture, "Linesse," he says. "You and I, Mason and Helm, did serve his grace the Duke for many years, together. We're practiced, in forestalling the, exuberance, of others, long before it curdles to unfortunate excess. The Spadone's shenanigans, or the Cater, and the Harper. Sidney Dagger."

"Lymond," she says, with a warning lilt, but he holds up a hand, his left hand, his mottled, bitten hand, "What she did," he says, "with what is all of ours," and then, finger by finger, counting off, "is just. Like. That: exuberant. But," laying his hand back down, "doomed. In need of," sitting back, in his chair, the light fading about him, "curbing," he says. "You must see that. Beset on all sides by outlaws and warlords, and she would prosecute this vendetta, against a dozen of her knights, a fifth of her court, turn your coats, or be turned away, and for what?" A shake of his head. "But a dozen burlap sacks proved her a fool."

"You proved nothing of her majesty," she says, "but that she is correct to scorn the Hound."

"There's the crux!" he says. "We can no more be merely Hounds, or Hawks, we can't only serve the Helm, or the Hive. We must, all of us, every one, be for the Rose."

"And that would be yourself."

"That would be her majesty, Annisa Baydoun, our Queen of Roses."

"But you," she says, "would be King."

"I am," he says.

She draws her helmet to her with a scrape. "John Perry ruled five years," she says. "Lymond for five months. We'll see you last five days."

"Marquess," he says, in such a tone that she holds that helmet still at the table's edge. "In a moment, upstairs, the firstly portioning of what's been taken back will be laid out, securely. Prudently. Orderly. One for Northwest, of course, and Southwest. Southeast. North. And, one for Northeast, also." Pushing back his chair, he gets to his feet, the shadows now so long the light can't brush his sleek black cap of hair. "Take a moment," he steps around, across the table from her, "think, for a moment, and then come back upstairs. Take what's parceled out for you, for your fifth, give back, to your people, what they have freely given."

Away down the long length of that table, fingertips trailing from chair-back to chair-back, down and down to the end of it and the high and narrow flight of steps beyond, and up and up he goes, without once looking back.

At the top he comes around the balustrade of glass into that wide room, where a folding table's been set up, and there atop it five neat parcels bundled up in wraps of iridescent pink, of burnt orange, dull gold, of a leafy green, and a cooly silvery grey. Stood beside it a woman uncomfortably strapped in raddled cyan and bared skin, her close-cropped hair a virulent chartreuse, expression forbiddingly grim, and some few more already about that otherwise empty space beneath the great and curving wall of glass, the Soames in his jacket of kelly tweed, turning and folding up a yellow meshback cap in his hands, the Anvil Pyrocles in slatey seersucker, his widely knotted tie of royal blue, and there beside him Becker, in a vested suit of darkest navy and a crisp white shirt, what's left of his hair slicked back, still, he reaches to discreetly tuck an errant sprig behind his ear, "Why," he murmurs, "why not, the lawyer? From the bank?"

Pyrocles leans close, speaks quietly, but clear, "He will also sit the council, but as an advisor in matters fiscal, as befits his expertise. I am to represent the fifth, and see to our portion. Administrative matters, little more. Much as, ah, yes," as through the doorway steps a thin man, entirely bald, his suit of bone over a brown silk shirt, "Calidore, the Flammard, will sit across the river from us, and Bodenay," a taller man in a slimly outmoded suit of popping daffodil, "the Gladius, will do for the," but Pyrocles, still looking toward the doorway, frowns, "Hive," he says. A third man's come into the room, squatly powerful in a satiny black kimono jacket over a two-tone shirt of orange and magenta, his long black hair held at bay by a pink bandana, his faintly puzzled amusement brightening as he catches sight of Pyrocles. He makes his way toward them with a quick salute of a wave, "Sir Anvil!" he calls, "how good it is to see you."

"Good Sir Shootist!" says Pyrocles, with much the same bonhomie, "if I might be so bold."

"Ah, in but an hour's time, if that," says Joaquin, "you might say so in earnest, and not so bold a jest."

"You're to be knighted?" says Pyrocles, beaming.

"It seems his majesty's determined a coronation does for a Samani, and he'd have new knights, for every fifth," and an inward deprecation twists his grin. "From provisional, to formal, at a touch. And might I say," shifting his attention from the one, to the other, "how splendid it is to see you here as well, Arnold," and that deprecation turns itself about within his lips. "Think you his majesty would name himself a Huntsman?"

"Wait, but," says Becker, alarm lighting on his brow, "you mean, I mean, like Jo?" but Pyrocles with a heavy step closer sets a firm hand on Becker's shoulder, "No," he says. "He's said nothing to that point."

"To you, perhaps," says Joaquin.

"He'd've asked," says Pyrocles, and Becker, blinking, looks from the one to the other, and neither looking to him.

"As you say," says Joaquin, turning with the rest of them toward the doorway to that wide room and the the woman stood there, gowned in purpled midnight, and a neatly figured scarf of blue and white to bundle up her hair, looking over the crowd of them all bowing their heads to her. Behind her in the shadowed hall the Viscount Agravante's white locks head and shoulders above her, and his blankly satisfied expression, looked out over them all as they lift in unison their solemn heads to see their Queen, all of them but the King himself, stood by that table, looking not to her and not to the court scattered about that wide room, not down, to the bricks on the table before him, each in its colored wrap, but back, over his shoulder, to the glass balustrade about the stairwell down, and there, on the top step, Linesse all in monochrome, plain steel helmet under one arm, one black boot lifted to the clean-swept floor of that wide room, looking not to her majesty, nor his, not to the rest of them all, but to those bricks neatly wrapped, cool green, dull gold, dim orange, and pink, and the grey, rendered by some trick of the light as a mirror, shining.

Evening light still strong enough to harshly slant through crooked blinds beneath the warm glow unobscured of a great half-circle of glass above, radially mullioned, orangely bright. The office so lit is small and lined with towering bookshelves about an overlarge overstuffed desk, and each and every shelf and otherwise available surface is covered, filled, crammed, piled high with books set upright, side by side, or shoved side-long above them, here and there laid open face-down atop this precarious stack or that more promiscuous mound, a couple-few more across the top of the desk, and one on the pile on the leather cushion of the only chair, all left splayed open, pages curling, pressed flat with other books, words exposed to the slanting light and all those other spines, gleaming leather or leatherette beside wrinkled bowed and crackling paperbacks, jackets shining wrapped in plastic or dustily matte, crumpled, creased, a few smoothly unblemished, and all those downcast names, printed in gold or silver or white or black or some contrasting color, Stewart Holbrook, Mark Fisher, John Michell, Ioan Culianu, Nik Cohn, Alan Moore, David Graeber and David Wengrow, Ron Sakolsky and James Koehnline, A. Bartlett Giamatti, E. Kimbark MacColl, Henry Farrell and Abraham Newman, Reza Negarestani, Christopher Chitty, Julian Jaynes, Avram Davidson, Alfred Hutton, FSA, Sudhir Alladi Venkatesh, a Wordsworth Dictionary of Proverbs, an Encyclopedia of Witchcraft and Demonology, an enormous two-volume Oxford English Dictionary, a Dictionary of Imaginary Places, one whole shelf consumed by the 1997 edition of the Oregon Revised Statutes, bound in pebbled black, along with a handful of brick-red volumes from 2007, the slick grey width of Title 11 of the Code of Federal Regulations there by an imposing bulk of leather worn to blackening crumbling flakes and faded golden lettering that says Deady & Lane's, over and about the buckled ridges of it, General Laws of Oregon. A rattle, a click, someone's trying the door of the office, an afterthought tucked between a couple of bookcases.

Another rattle, a clink, the door swings, hesitantly, open. She steps through, the sheen of her pearly jacket brightening in that light, rendering the color of it difficult to ascertain. Hands held up and out, away from the stacks and piles as she steps once, twice toward the desk, around to the side of it. One hand holds a little sprig of greenery capped with a couple of clusters of bright yellow flowers, tiny petals of them loosening, drooping in her fingers curled. Looking about, left, right, up, around, the shelves, the books, the desk, the window, the light, the dust. Shifting a couple of books on the desk, she unearths a burnished laptop wide and flat and heavy enough it's with some little effort that she levers up the screen of it. Considers it a moment, pursing her precisely painted lips. Brushes the keys of it with that sprig. The screen flickers to life, filled with a photo of a lighthouse stubbily upthrust from a rocky promontory, icons winking into place along the bottom, including one outlined as a battery-shape colored with a sliver of red, 7%, say the characters beside it.

She brushes the keys once more with the sprig, and again, as applications spring to life, windows stuttering open one after another, password challenges answered even as they appear. Mindful of her nails, she swipes and clicks the trackpad, presses keys, browses a queue of unread messages, subjects modulating from angry apprehension where are you answer your phone's dead where through less heated concerns about that proposal what are you how about a drink into a flurry of dated congratulations on a fight hard fought and a campaign won and a handful of genial what's nexts as she scrolls down and back in time. Swipe, click, now the screen displays the ordering information for a pack of tarot cards, inscribed by Giani Siri, buyer pays shipping. A shake of her head, swipe, click. Inscrutable numbers tightly columned in a spreadsheet. Clack-click, swipe. She frowns.

Setting aside the sprig she reaches past the laptop into a gap between stacks of books to fish out a micro-cassette recorder, slim and silvery, the dotted grille of the speaker, the plastic window scored and cracked, obscuring the tape within. She strokes the buttons along the side, markings worn away to illegibility, then punches one. The tape whirls, rewinding itself, jerks to a stop, button popping back up. Finger shifting, she punches another.

"Yeah, so," says the voice of David Kerr, "item one, get Avery off my back regarding the whole onsite meeting bullshit situation, Item two," click, whirr of the tape fast-forwarding, clack, "thing with the situation is, I'm fairly certain he knows exactly what he's walking into, and," click, whirr, clack, "sparkle like burnished bronze, the likeness of lightning, and draped," click. She sets the recorder down on top of the book before her, there on the corner of the desk, The Thirty-Six Dramatic Situations, it says.

Whirr. Clack.

"What he's walking into," says David Kerr, "and that more than anything else, I mean, thinking about it, he couldn't possibly, not and be so," sucking his teeth, "certain. It would really be helpful to have some idea what his handlers have been telling him. So," unseen, he shifts himself, rustle of clothing, clack of the recorder's housing against the mike, "Frances Upchurch, though that is not your name. What did you hop our boy up on."

Her hand hovers over the recorder, a finger over the buttons, but she's looked up, away from it, at all the books on all the shelves about. "I've done my homework, Dr. Uniform," he says, a bit louder. "So if you're hearing this," and she turns sharply back to the recorder, "it's because I haven't made it back, and if I haven't made it back, well, I probably won't. So. Here's hoping you're just, really alacritously fast, at doing what it is you do, poking about, snooping, whatnot." Squeak of the take-up spindle, hiss of tape, her finger poised over the buttons. "Maybe our boy Phil doesn't really know what's slouching toward him up in that house on the hill, but you know I know you do. They all have four faces, and I bet you've seen each of them. Every one has four wings, their feet are straight, and the soles of them like calves' feet, and they sparkle like burnished bronze, the likeness of lightning, and draped in garments white as snow, two four six many of them, crowding the room, and their names, all their names, the names of them all begin with," click.

"There's only the one," says Frances Upchurch. Punching another button, and the drawer of the recorder pops open. She plucks out the cassette, small, clear plastic smoked with grey, unlabeled, unmarked. Tosses it, once, high in the orange light to catch it and tuck it away in a pocket of her jacket.

Night's fallen. Nestled between three emptily narrow streets a little lot, filled with stilled and silent cars, the colors of them uncertain in the streetlight brightly thin from lanterns set on poles among the bordering trees. New Seasons Market, says the discreetly spotlit sign above a grass-grown awning. High broad windows filled with light offer glimpses of well-stocked shelves and no one at all to make their way between or about them or to go in or out through unmoving glass doors.

"Can y'all *hear me?*" she yells.

Jaggedly abrupt in all this cloistered stillness, her lurching searching steps, her wildly lashing arms, each ended in skillful grips about the hilts of whip-thin rapiers, "Can you," and

426

she leans into the roar, drawing it out, jaw rictused, tendons distended, *"hear! me!"* Swung about, her bare feet slapping pavement with every swiveling, loping step, clacking the vivid layers of beads that lap her shoulders and her breast. "Bad moon rising, how I'm signified! Blades too quick, how I'm dignified! Draw down on me, that's suicide!" Throws up her hands, those rapiers shining, "Rabbits!" and a loudly flat clack as she whacks them together, "Can you!" Clack. "Hear!" Whick. "Me!" Stalking back down the short lines of cars to either side, toward the trees thinly screening the far end of the lot, "Y'all *rabbits,* y'all *rabbits,"* she chants to the beat of her feet, "union strong, always wrong, hiding back behind that label all day long," spun about, those swords spread wide to take in the whole space, "mechanicals please, looking to seize and you come upon these?" crossing the blades high above her, "you drop to your *knees!* Take a page from Brer Possum, learn how to play dead, bow your head, droop them ears when you hide up under your bed, you heard what I said, here come the Child of the Moon that you dread, you'll be mystified as you're nullified when you testify so to certify how my expertise with my snickersnees leads over and all to my victories!" Leaning into it again, *"Hasenpfeffer!"* she bellows. "Incorporate!"

But already the pop of mockingly languid applause, there, and there, she straightens, shaking her beaded twists away from her wolfish grin, pointing with the one rapier to the man stepped out from behind an anonymously pale panel truck, lifting the other toward the man leaned against the trunk of that sports car, jerking away to cover the man stepping onto the lot through the thin scrim of trees, and each of the three of them with empty, clapping hands.

"She hasn't heard," says one of them.

"Nobody told her?" says another.

"She ain't been told, Boggs," says the third.

"Who's first," she says, blades still up and out, pointing together now, to the third of them, the first, the second, but "We're all on the same side now," he says, pushing up off the trunk, wrapped in a dark pea coat, fisherman's cap pulled low.

"Your Marquess took her portion," says the third man, his long coat of dark leather.

"It all begins a strenuous return to normalcy," says the first, his robes of white, and jewels glinting, green, blue, brilliant, all on the backs of his hands.

"So there's no need to fight, tonight."

"Or evermore."

"Then let's play!" she roars, whacking her rapiers against each other again. "Come *on!* Right now, all at once, y'all snuffling dizzy-eared lop-wits!" but they're turning away, slipping away, one by one back between those cars, into the trees, gone. "Rabbits!" she yells, there in the middle of the lot. "Y'all rabbits!" But a bleep behind her, the whoosh of sliding glass, a burst of music, slippery, jangled, timeless, and she whirls about to the shock of the woman stepping out, freighted canvas bag slung from one hand, sleeveless dress and a puff-ball of curls, taken aback to see the Mooncalfe, barefoot and shirtless, blades in her hands, blocking the way, and all falls still once more, quite suddenly.

"Rah!" shouts Zeina, throwing up her empty hands, leaping away to the bumper of one car, roof of another, crumpling pop the hood of a third and off through the trees, over the sidewalk, before a honking squealing truck and away, leaving that woman stood there with her groceries, blinking, as the doors slide shut behind her, whist.

Notice: Illegal Campsite — Breaking fast
coffee, Hot — a Moment passes

Notice, says the bright orange flyer, Illegal Campsite, attached to the smaller door with careless strips of tape, It is the policy of the City of Portland to provide notice, and here a corner of the flyer's curled, obscuring the text, shelters erected at illegal campsites, it continues, This campsite will be cleared, and then, twenty-four (24) hours after and seven (7) days of: and, hand-written there, the date, 6/1. Notificación, it continues, beneath,

Campamento Illegal. He brushes it with considering fingers before ducking away beneath the much larger overhead door half-lifted beside it.

The vastly cavernous hall is empty, dim, stalls marching away to either side and no one in them, about them, around, though here and there the signs of activity interrupted, boxes left open, frames stacked and canvases half-draped with quilts and wraps of felt and bubbled plastic, a cookstove dismantled, the scaffolding at the far end abandoned, dusty polyethelene sheeting hung from this pole, or that, obscuring an unfinished mural, a great sharp fang of a mountain lit up unearthly, pink and green, orange and magenta limning an appalling massive blue loomed over a suggestion of a thickly darkly deeply haunted forest, but overwhelming all that empty, quiet hall are neatly stacks of yellow two-by-fours, chest-high, depending, there in the aisle between those stalls, and spiky rolls of chicken wire leaned up against them, tipped before them, there among the twine-wrapped packages of newsprint one atop another, some tumbled from this height, or that, rolled or pushed or kicked almost to the verge of those pallets there, laid out beneath an enormous wooden tub, knee-high, unlit, empty.

His steps clack slowly, measured, as he makes his way from that half-opened overhead door toward the tub, until a footstep doesn't clack, but rustles. Looking down, to his cracked brown wingtip set upon a crumpled corner torn from some much larger page. He lifts his shoe away to see the ghost of an intricate framework, a figure sat, resplendent, and in the lap of it a tumble of households and of towers, all sketched in charcoal long since smudged, smeared, worn away to ashen smoke.

The clack resumes, measuredly stepping toward that tub, around it, to find her there, sat on the pallet, clocked black socks up over her knees and big black boots, brief red skirt and a soft black sweater, puffily oversized. Her hair's been tucked away beneath a stocking cap of black, and her scowl lightens somewhat to see him. "Bruno," she says.

"My lady. Did we lose a bet?"

Her scowl tightens, she tugs at the hem of her skirt, pressing it into her lap, but says nothing as he hitches up his trousers to lower himself beside her, braced against the wooden staves of the tub. "I take it you have found them?"

"One of them," she says, tilting her knees away. "He's off getting us coffee. Thinks he's being galant," she says, archly stressed. He stares at her lips, the same brightly artificial red as her skirt, and she shakes her head away, annoyed. A lock of hair escapes the confines of her cap, a fakely glossy platinum slither there behind her ear, and his brow quirks, "What," he says, "did you do – "

"He thinks it's cute," she says, tersely tucking it away. "How bad has it got, that there isn't any coffee?"

He sighs, and shifts himself to sit his back against the tub. "It was bad, when the Chatelaine's credit was revoked. They finally took her new truck yesterday, and the trailer, and now," he sighs, "it appears there may be trouble with our tenancy. But. What was done, here, on Wednesday?" Looking up, to the faintly buzzing fluorescents racked so far above. "A whole new word is needed, for what did happen then."

She hikes up to look over the rim of the tub, the floor of it swept almost utterly clean, a half-dozen, maybe, no more than a dozen crumbs of gold left to sparkle in the rough whorls of the grain. "They really polished it off," she says.

"No one was here," he says.

"Well, but, who's left?" she says, sitting back down. "Sweetloaf, whatsisname, Cullock? Astolfo, maybe? You?"

"Anyone," he says, with a wave toward the detritus of all those half-finished tasks before them, "but specifically," turning with a stern look for her, and "Oh, sure, Bruno," she says, with a bitterly mocking lilt. "All of us all lined up against the lot of them, just a big old knock-down drag-out donny-fuckin-brook right here in the middle of the," her hand, reaching in the air before them, "the, this, palace," she says, "and a gallowglas smack in the middle of it all, that's, that's," shaking her head, looking away.

"The right word, at the right time, from the right person, and enough stood up behind you?" leaning forward, to catch her eye. "Rebellion's a fickle, fragile thing, your grace, a kettle easily knocked from the flame, before it comes to boil. They would have folded."

"Rebellion?" she says, incredulous. "They're the ones with everything sewn up, the whole fucking court, lock, stock, and the goddamn barrel. They're the fucking *empire,* Bruno."

"They may well have the barrel, but they will never fill it. Has your grace spoken with her majesty."

"What, today? I just woke up, Bruno. I have not had my coffee, yet."

"My liege," he says, with some concern, "do you happen, even, to know, where her majesty is, of the moment?"

She looks to him, brow quirked, considering. "Anna," she says, then, "said, last night, said that she'd said she meant to, to *be* with," a breath, "the, ah, the strippers, exotic dancers, those, the, I, I didn't want to get in the middle of that. Interrupt," she says, "anything."

"Her majesty," says Bruno, "did quit this palace yestereve, for the apartment of her sometime dalliance, Christina Halliwell, who has worked as an exotic dancer, and also as an actor, singer, and model, under the names Christienne Limoges and Tina Triplette. Number Seventeen, Twelve Forty-five, Southeast Forty-ninth; rooms shared with her sister and partner, Stephanie Halliwell, currently in Los Angeles. Her majesty did spend the night, but slept alone, on a couch. I'm told there's plans for brunch at Surabaya in a bit."

"The couch," says Jo. "You're well-informed."

"Your grace must be, when it comes to her majesty."

"You're saying they, they'd actually, are you saying she's, in danger?"

"Her majesty is always in danger. Put away your delicacy: your grace must always be in the middle of it, now, or at the very uttermost least, know where that middle, and her majesty, might be found."

"Dammit, Bruno – "

"Blast it, Duchess," and she flinches, though he has not raised his voice, "you," he says, that syllable quieting punching the air between them, "are Southeast. You are the Widow, of my lord the Duke. Favorite of the Queen. You are the Hawk, my lady. Your grace has authority, which is power, but also a terrible duty. You are the last of her majesty's court, and your grace must – my lady!"

She's lurched herself to her feet, stalking away around the tub to fetch up suddenly before Jack, stood there just out of sight, his denim jacket of a softer, brighter blue, verbosely spangled with badges, and beneath his nose, above his lip, a neatly penciled mustache. He holds a couple of tall white paper cups striped yellow and red and blue down the sides and a plain white paper bag, and as the Shrieve Bruno cries "Duchess!" Jo seizes Jack by an elbow and yanks him stumbling after, back away from the unlit stage the overhead door the tub and Bruno, reaching after her, "Jo Gallowglas!" as she drags burdened Jack with her past lumber and paper, chicken wire and stalls, dismantled stove and scaffolding, into the archway under the mural and through the tunnel and all the while "Wait" he's saying, Jack, and "Jo, stop" and "I'm gonna drop, Jo! Wait!" as they spill out onto the yellowing tiles of the vaguely daylit foyer, "The hell?"

"I just," letting go, turning about, resettling the cap on her head, "wanted some, peace, and quiet, for," looking to his cups, the bag, "what did you get?"

"Uh," he says, "ah, lemon, lemon poppyseed, and, and chocolate chip. Muffin-tops, I mean. And, uh, they had," lifting one of the cups, "protein lattes? Which, I figured – "

"Come on," she says, grabbing his elbow again, yanking him after, toward the dark stairs down as, down the flight from above, one two many sets of footsteps clack-tocking, thumping, "have to," someone's saying, Gloria Monday, "no, *we* have to, get it all in, every last scrap off the dock," coming down into the foyer, followed closely by Jim Turk, and then Getulos, Trucos, and more besides, "the *paper* especially," says Gloria, across those little hexagonal tiles and into the tunnel, her jet-black hair and her great brown T-shirt that says Sheriff of Hong Kong in lurid red across the front, "some of it's already got rained on," she says, "and more's on the way, so we need to figure out," turning about before the archway, shuffle-scuff of her dingy shower slippers, "who," she says, thrusting a finger at Big Jim brought up short, "is gonna," she says, but beneath that bushy mustache of his, the black of it hatched with white, his satisfied smile spreads wide, and without a word but a simple wave of his hand he steps past her, out from under, into the great high hall, his loose white shirt wide open at the throat, his corduroy kilt a-sway, "we have to," she says, turning after him, "what the," stepping after him, "happened," she says, taking in the lumber, the wire, the bundles of newsprint, "you," she says, hastening after him, "you already," catching him by a sleeve, "you already *did* it," hauling him about even as she launches a shove at his shoulder, "you let me just, natter on, like that, and the whole time, we, you, you!" Another shove of a punch. "You let me pontificate, like a goddamn *asshole,*" crashing her whole self into him, wrapping him in an enormous hug, "you big fucking *jerk,*" she says, muffled against his chest.

"Sure, and of late, sweetling," he says, and a kiss for the top of her head, "you've a lot on your mind."

"Jesus," she says, pushing away from him, his big hand gentle on her shoulder, "the fuck is that?" pointing, past the lumber, the empty tub, to the space before the opened overhead door, where a man in a pale work shirt is stooping to set down a couple of heavy cardboard boxes he's been carrying by the handles up-folded from the tops of them, his bent head topped by a mighty round of tight black curls. Straightening, shoulders hunched despite his powerful frame, he looks about to spy a folding table, leaned up against the wall there, and crosses over, pulls it away, unlimbers the one set of legs with a resonant clank, kicks the other set down, clank, and easily lifts the table to spin it about and set it lightly down. Heads back to, with some little effort, take up the burden of those boxes and shuffle them over to, one after the other, haul them up and set them on the table. "You!" he calls, pointing to Teacup Tall, stood there by Jim Turk, and tosses something a-jangle that juggling dandling Teacup happens to catch, a ring of keys. "Two more in the sedan outside, in the trunk. And the cups, bring 'em. Help!" he barks at Charlichhold, with a sweep of his now-empty hand. "Go on! Do *not* scratch the finish, you hear me?" A woman's ducking in beneath that half-opened door, her stodgily utilitarian dress of taupe and umber, and an apron not quite so white as once perhaps it had been, and two wide milkily translucent plastic bins stacked one atop another in her arms, and she's careful not to tip or shift them as she straightens and makes a beeline for the table, where he's crouched to poke a perforated notch at the base of one of those boxes, digging into it with a darkly thickly finger, hissing, to wrestle out a plastic spigot, shaking his hand away.

"Everything is okey-doke?" she says, setting the bins down one by the other, popping the lids off them to reveal ranks and rows of donuts glistening, gleaming, dusted with sugar, white and yellow-gold and densely chocolate and burgundy blue.

"Turns out, hot coffee's hot," he says, moving on to punch in the notch at the base of the second box. There's Teacup and Charlichhold with two more, and long ungainly plastic sleeves of paper cups, and up comes Dick-a-Tuesday to take a sleeve in his hands and gnaw a hole in the plastic wrap, tipping out and stacking up the cups as the stoop-shouldered man in the pale shirt pushes himself to his feet, a hand to the back of his black-curled head, "You saw the napkins? Cup jackets? Creamer, sugar? Go on, go on, go get 'em," shooing them with both his hands, turning about, taking in the smattering of others slowly approaching, from this stall or that, the arch at the end of the hall, the balcony above, "and tell everybody it's coffee!" he booms. Brushing down the front of his shirt. "Better than the alternative," he mutters, to himself.

"That's Gordon?" says Gloria, still stood there by the lumber.

"You know Gordon," says Big Jim behind her, hands on her shoulders, watching as Gordon starts filling cups from one of the boxes, handing them around, and Teacup Tall is scowling at Getulos's paint-flecked fingers hovered contemplatively over the donuts, as Danarey and Herwydh, Hob and the lucent Himmelbord, Nicky Nack and Cragflower, Cherrycoke, the Flynn and flat Peg Powler, Joli with her rainbow braids and Tumble Tom, gigantic head thrown back, laughing fit to fill the hall, and Val demurely ducking, her greasy unwashed hair hung well down past her shoulders, Sproat, the Buggane, and Petra B in black, tugging a stray bit of tape from the heel of her hand. "Shall we, sweet?" says Big Jim, leaning around her.

"What?" she says, shaking her head. "Sure, yeah," stepping away from him, out from under his hands, looking from table, coffee, crowd, back to the lumber and the supplies, laid out there in the aisle. "We, we don't need a truck," she's saying. "We don't need a truck! Trucos!" she calls, beckoning. "C'mere! I wanna run something by you guys."

And then, afterwards, her smile spreads in fits and starts almost in spite of itself, and, blinking, the breath she's catching turns to puffs of laughter. She rolls onto her side on the white expanse of softly deflating comforter, pressing her thighs together as his hand slips from between them.

"God," he says, knelt beside her, still in his fresh white T-shirt, those newly stiffly selvedge jeans, his curls a-glimmer in the candlelight, and that neatly penciled mustache, "you are so fucking beautiful," he says.

"Shut up," she says, half-muffled, but she doesn't flinch at the hand he lays on her bare hip. Still in that copious black sweater rucked and tangled, those black socks stretched well up over her knees, but the cap is gone, and tousled on the pillows her short hair glossily bleached to a fakely translucent platinum, stripped of all lingering colors as if to leave room for any possible color to somehow come rushing in.

"You are," he says, that hand of his slid up, along her hip, her flank.

"You're just saying that," she says, "because I'm here. Available."

"I'm saying it because you're beautiful," he says, that hand of his tugging the hem of her sweater, lifting it. "Go on," he says. "Take this off. Go on."

"Stop," she says. "Jack. Stop it. Stop," jerking away, she claws back a corner of the comforter to slip under it, "I'm chilly. Anyway, it's your turn. Shimmy out of them jeans, already," but he's looking away, shifted to sit on his haunch. "I know you like being galant and shit, but it's supposed to be, like, a reciprocal act, you know? Sex? Couple-few more goes, I'm gonna start feeling guilty. You keep picking at that, it'll never heal."

He yanks his hand from his upper lip, the mustache thinly dark and sparse, "It was supposed to be bigger," he grumbles.

"They can only work with what you've got," she says, elbows leaning on her knees tented under that comforter.

"That's not," he says, "not what we saw. Yesterday."

"What, who, the Starling? Trust me, Jack, that was, mostly? Her."

"Yeah?" he says, sitting up, seizing handfuls comforter, tugging, "and what about," he says, yanking it free of her grasp, "you," he says, pulling away dim white to reveal the featureless black, that sweater pulled down over her bare lap, the clocking of those long socks lost in the shadows.

"*You* thought this was cute," she says.

"You don't?" He looks back, over his shoulder, past the nimbus of candlelight from the floor there to the pale linen screen just visible, "so go put on something else," he's saying, but she sighs, leans forward, hooking her thumbs in the top of one of those socks, pushing it, down her thigh, around her knee, down and down, "I don't care," she mutters, working it over her ankle and off, wiggling her freed toes.

"All right," he says, as she's wadding up the sock to toss it away, into the shadows on the unlit side of the bed. "What's next."

"With what," she says, hooking her thumbs in the top of the other sock.

"For us! What are we gonna do next."

"I don't know, Mr. Draper," she says. "You tell me."

He blinks, his expression falling away. "That's, not my name," he says.

Her hands stop, that sock down over her knee, bunched about her shin. "Okay," she says, without looking up.

"That's, that's not me. That's not my name."

"Okay," she says. "Jack. Just Jack. I didn't, mean anything by it."

"Yes you did," he says.

She looks up, then, to meet his eyes as fiercely stern as hers, that mustache arched over an incipient snarl, the corner of her own mouth so absolutely motionless before, with a breath, relaxing. "Okay," she says. "Jack. What is it you think we ought to be doing."

"You," he says, "yesterday *you* was the one all fired up to go find May, and hell, I don't know, maybe Hector, but instead we've done," he shrugs, "fuck-all. Just, holed up down here, a day, a day and a half, I mean, do you even have any idea what time it is?" but "I'm," she says, "tired, Jack. I'm just," working the sock the rest of the way off, "so. Fucking. Tired." Tossing it away.

"So, what," he says, "is that it? You're just, gonna give up?"

"I," says Jo, lifting the corner of the comforter to crawl back under it, "am going to lie down and maybe sleep for a bit, I don't know. I might get hungry enough I'll, actually, maybe, go look for some way to scrounge something to eat, and that," lying back against the pillows, "is pretty much all I got."

"You wanted my pants off a minute ago," he says.

"Moment's passed."

"You've got," he says, "people, who would," a breath, an irruption of animation, "you have *money,*" he says, sat up, "cars, people, you've got," an arm flung up, pointing above, "all *this,*" but she's rolling over, up on an elbow, "Jack," she says, and then *"Jack,"* and, shaking his head, that hand drops back to his lap. "Precisely none of any of that is mine," she says.

"But – "

"You have *no* fucking idea what I, I've," she closes up her eyes, a fortifying breath, "I wanted to find you, and fix things. Put them right. But," lying back on the pillows, "I can't. Roy's dead, Jack." One arm curling protectively over herself, shapelessly black atop white. "Roy's gone. I'm sorry."

"You're," he says, looking down at his hands, one beside the other in his lap. "Sorry," he says, and then, "what about May, what about, getting her back to her, to what's hers. Her cats. Those damn National Geographics."

"She has people."

"She, she has, what?"

"She has people, her son, whatsisname. Mike."

"He lives in *Wilsonville!* He drives a goddamn stormtrooper *pickup truck!* The *fuck* does he know about jungles."

"She knows his phone number, Jack. Yours?" Opening, blinking, her eyes. "I bet she doesn't. And me," closing them up again, "I don't even have one, anymore."

"You, you're," sputters Jack, "so, that's, that's it. You're giving up."

"Looks like."

"Well, I'm not," he snaps. "I'm gonna go out there, I'm gonna find her, and I'm gonna make sure everything, I mean everything, is back the way it was. With or without you."

"Okay," says Jo, her eyes still closed. "I mean, you know how to catch a bus."

AGAIN, SUNSET – PREPARING HIS DOSES
NUMBER TEN – WHAT KIND OF GHOST

AND NOW THE SUN IS SETTING ONCE AGAIN, to hurl against a towering wall of clouds such brilliant washes of a wildly nameless color that deepens as it rounds, and fades, to merest orange, and red, and ruddy gold, and greening, there, along that edge, and blueing into greys, receding across and beyond the river, sailing away into oncoming night. The city below lit up as well in painful gleamings struck by those last few lances from glass and steel and even here and there the clean white stone of this climbing tower, the interlaced yellow timbering of that construction site, it's all too bright to look upon for long. The trees that crowd the slope to seat and frame the view provide a darkly cool relief about the city far below so crisp it almost seems too close against those cyclopean clouds, so close and small enough to reach out, from here, among those trees, against a stone wall risen up abruptly on this side of the street, but even as those towers so bright so close so small she might reach out with her hand to cup them, lift them in the palm of her hand, all that brightness swelling up from darkening streets to climb those delicate planes and edges of stone and glass and steel, it all takes on a fiery rose, a blush that falters, fades, sinking away before it might escape the falling fulness of night.

She steps off the sidewalk into the street, two lanes of dimming tarmacadam, the high stone wall behind her, the gap in the trees ahead. Not even a crumble of sidewalk on that other side, not yet, just a verge of grass where she twists a quarter turn and sets to striding, one definite foot before the other along the edge there, of yellowing grass against pavement, matte black soft-soled shoes, bare shins and knees up to loose black shorts, grey jacket zipped up to her sternum, where ink climbs in spikily knotty thickets up from under along the lines and cords of her throat, up and under to the point of her jaw. Slowly, languidly lifting her arms to either side, as if walking a tightrope, as if reaching for the stone wall to her left, out over the dropping grass and treetops to her right. One of those hands holds an awkward rubbery bundle, oxblood edged with black, the other a slender boning knife, the single edge of it curling to a needly point.

Ahead, the grass slope gentles, the verge widens, enough for a sidewalk to start itself and even more for the side yard of a low house built out on stilts over the drop. She stops short of that first step onto concrete, lowering her laden hands. Eyes the next house along, and the next. Each of them from the street seems nondescript, and all much like the others, but she fixes on that one, there, fourth along, a meander of paving stones set in the scrap of yard leading to a yellow front door, the shallow curl of a driveway leading to a white garage shut tight.

Ellen Oh shakes out the bundle in the one hand and, careful of the knife, tugs it on over her head, a goggle-eyed horse's head with a stiff black mane. "Take two," she says. But it's another long moment before steps onto that sidewalk.

A dozen or so clear and empty capsules piled on the island countertop, translucently soft, yielding under his fingertips as he plucks one up, pinches it apart, tucks the one end upright, there, in a small hole drilled in the slender plank before him, and the other end laid beside it. Another plucked, pinched, tucked and laid, and another, again, six holes neatly and evenly drilled in that end of the plank, six capsules so prepared. He takes up in one hand a little silver funnel, carefully fitting the slender stem of it into the first cap-end held upright in the plank, and in his other hand a tiny scoop at the end of a longly delicate handle. He dips the scoop into a spill of golden dust tipped out on a square of paper, there by an empty glass tube, lifting up a pinch of a portion of it, glimmering in the harsh light shining down from above. Leaning close to eye the amount, pewter weights a-dangle at the ends of his long grey mustaches, he taps the delicate handle with a precisely trembling fingertip, and again, knocking just enough of a puff back carefully onto the paper and then, with a sure swift shift and twist, deposits the pay-load into the mouth of the funnel, then strikes the rim of it once, a silvery clink, dislodging any lingering trickles of brightness. "We must be parsimonious," he says, setting aside funnel and scoop to squeeze the two ends of the cap back together, "at least until our new Queen finds her footing. But our lot's enough," taking up funnel and scoop to set to filling the next, "more than enough, for a dozen pills, twelve days, and some," tap, twist, clink, "left over." Looking up from his work. Lifting up to perch on his forehead a pair of glasses, the half-moon lenses set in wire rims. "More than enough," he says.

Out past the otherwise pristinely empty island, beyond that belvedere of focused light, the darkly glossy kitchen floor ends in a featureless surf of pale shag stretched untroubled by table or sofa or armchair to a sweeping upright wall of glass that looks out over the bright night beyond, and just before that glass untroubled by any reflection he's sat tailor-fashion, bare feet tucked beneath bare knees, bare shoulders rounded, slumped, hands laid limply in his bare lap, and Pyrocles smiles to see him. "Becker," he says, gently, lowering his glasses, taking up funnel and scoop once more. "When you're ready, I've a dose prepared."

A moment more, and then, with a sigh, Becker sets himself in motion, leaning forward as he hikes his haunches, arms spreading as they lift, legs unfolding as his head works back and forth, the wince of a crick. "Did you," he says, turning, frowning, nakedly unconcerned, "what did you," he says, looking across that wide and empty space to Pyrocles, iron-bright beneath the kitchen lamp, busy about his work, "what *do* you," he says, setting out across the shag, "think, of Joaquin?"

Six filled capsules glimmer on the island, discretely separate from the larger pile of empties, and Pyrocles doesn't look up from his hands as they set to preparing another six, pluck, pinch, tuck, "What do I think of him?" he says, mildly puzzled.

"He's a, he's new," says Becker, the color of him warming as he approaches the light. "I mean, Sacramento. You've, none of you has ever, worked with him. Before." Blinking against the brightness. "So. What do you think?"

"He is," says Pyrocles, intent on scoop and funnel, "a doughty knight."

"Doughty," says Becker. "That's, that's a word. Yeah." Shadows deepen, sharpen to underline wrinkles and sags, defining the shift of tendon and muscle as he lifts a hand to brush back what's left of his hair. "Did you, ah," he says, "I mean, when we, um," gesturing fruitlessly, "you know, did you," as "Yes," says Pyrocles, looking up. Lifting his glasses back up onto his forehead. "As did you."

"Yeah, yeah, that's, I know, that's not what I, that's, I just, I mean," and Pyrocles, smiling, says, "Pleasures of the flesh, and treasures of the heart, lie in very different realms, love. So long as we keep that borderline in mind," laying his hand, palm up, on the island countertop, "we'll be fine," as Becker clasps it, "That's you," he says.

"I rather think," says Pyrocles, "our Shootist's attentions, pleasure and treasure, are currently occupied elsewhere."

"No, I mean, you're ringing."

"Am I?" says Pyrocles, frowning.

"Your phone, it's the buzzing, on silent, it's, mine," Becker points, "mine's in the bedroom, charging, and anyway," looking down, "no pockets, so," as Pyrocles, leaning back on his stool, pats about himself, "I will never," he mutters, lifting out a glossy white plaque, the screen of it lit up, Incoming Call, it says, Viscount, the buzz of it strident in the open air, "understand," he says, poking a green icon, "hello?" he says, lifting it to his ear. "Yes. The Anvil, yes."

He frowns. "I see," he says, and then, "of course," and sets the phone down on the countertop.

Becker tilts his head to take in the expression Pyrocles turns away from him. "Is," he says, "is everything," but Pyrocles takes off his glasses, setting them clink by the phone, pinching the corners of his eyes. "Something's happened," he says.

Abruptly up in the darkness, a gasp, a retching groan of a cough. Throws back a drift of comforter, lunging for the edge of the sliding to heavily thump that high wide bed and slippery flap a pillow tumbles those oversized bolsters littering Persian rugs spread each over another on the concrete floor, "shit," she gets herself on hands and knees but tangled still in kicking loose, "shit," again as a flame blooms, a candle, lit, another, and another, off on the verges of this upholstered confusion, "cut it out," she snarls, "*stop* it," as yet another flares to life, "go *away,* leave me *alone,* I *told* you, just, *go,*" she snaps, "I don't," the slither, of long black strands of hair dragged with the motion of her head across marbled brown marmoleum, "need, anything," she says, the patterfall of more long strands falling from about her shoulders, from where they had been pooled in the small of her back, as she sits up, back, on her heels. The sway of all that black hair, squirming about her arms, coiling up to lap her knees, lofting suddenly as if in some unfelt gust to shimmying float, all that long black mane a crown a cloud a tree above her, and slowly, so slowly, she lifts her hands to her face, to the mask over her face, shaped like a skull, her eyes behind the empty staring eyeholes of it, the crude teeth hung from the upper only jaw limned with thick black ink. "No," she says, with some little force behind the word. *"No."*

"Huntsman," says whoever it is who's stood behind her. She turns about, getting up on one bare foot, still crouched, her movement troubling the upward cascade of that mane, a sinisterly languid ripple to shadow the ceiling above.

"I wish," says the man stood there across the crepuscular lobby, "I could say," his brownly baggy boilersuit unzipped enough to reveal a lushly knotted necktie of paisleys in orange and gold and pink, "I were surprised," the tone of that word left hanging, as if another clause might be forthcoming, but he stands there, the marbled stretch of earthen brown between them, hints within of numerous incongruous shades suggested by the light of a dimmed chandelier above, he's stood there, waiting, and his strenuously flattened affect of disdain barely papers over an expression that trembles with an urge to slink away.

"This isn't," says Jo, lowering one hand from her mask to clutch, a fist, at her breast. The other lifting, tipping back that mask, the mane of it still a billowing tower above. "This isn't how it went down."

Puzzlement troubles his mien. "I don't understand," he says.

"This already happened," says Jo, pushing herself up, onto her feet, her bare legs, her shapeless black sweater, that mask sitting atop her fakely colorless hair. "You're Cotlap, the Lovejoy Earl. Tight with the Soames. Started running your mouth about how the King was a pretender and the Queen a bona roba, which, I had to look that up. You," and a deep breath taken in, held, as the mane shivers above her, and then, let out. "You were number ten," she says.

"I don't," he says, "understand – "

"You don't *have* to," she snaps, a stomp of a step and another over that floor, yanking the mane in her wake as more and more of it loops in tendrils up and out, and up, "this *already happened,*" she snaps, as the chandelier above jangles, loose crystals shoved about by seeking darkness, and the light begins to fade. "You were the tenth. Early March, the eighth," she says, "a Thursday," and lifts the mask away entirely. That thunderhead of darkness collapses, the terrible weight of the mane slapping the marmoleum, whipping her sweatered shoulders, her arms, slipping away down her back.

"Today," he says, hesitantly, as darkness restlessly settles.

"Three months ago!" she bellows. "Not even!" Letting the mask drop from her hand. "I," she says, "I'm not, dreaming," she winces, her other hand tightening at her breast. "So this, you, you aren't you. This, I've, been here before. This has happened before. You, you're Daniel fucking Moody, and I am fucking *sick* of this."

"I," he says, "who? *I,*" thumping his sternum once with his knuckles, "am the Cotlap Grady, Earl of Lovejoy, I take my portion from the Guisarme's hand direct, and see to the needs of a dozen and one in this building," those knuckles lifting, fingers spreading, a gesture to take in the lobby, the night-blanked glass doors there, the two gold-flecked elevator doors behind them, "that his majesty would would see demolished, and that, dear Huntsman, not the truths I've spoken through my running mouth, but this nagging impediment, that would be why you are here."

"Christ," she says, that fist still clenched, "it was boring the *first* time. We are not going through this again, Moody. You're not him, I'm not here, and, and, oh, oh *God,*" doubling over as her knee buckles, refusing her weight, slumping sidelong wretching for breath, and, for one fleeting instant, as he stands there, watching her struggle, a spark flares in his eyes, and his chapped lips quirk in the briefest, but clearest, most savage little smile. She's wrestling her arms up under the hem of that sweater, heedless of her exposure, grappling, grasping at something, quivering with the effort, and some growling climbing groan claws out of her mouth with a sudden ripping yank her hands beneath the sweater churn their way out, her fingers unfolding as she stares, appalled, aghast, astonished, at a feather so very long and slender as it is, the vanes of it a grey so iridescent it might contain all other possible colors paling to a clean and simple white about the quill, "shit," she says, as glittering sheenly shining silvery dropping from the palm of her hand to the darkness draping the marmoleum below, "what," she spits, "I, what?"

"Do me this honor," he says, that trembling slinking urge returned but ducked again behind his flat attempt at chilly disdain looked up, and out, to where she had been standing but a moment before, and not to herself there crouched on the lobby floor, over the black locks of that fallen mane, the feather in her hands. "Draw your blade and show it me before you strike," he says, to where she'd been, not where she is. "Do this, for me. I will not take it amiss. I do still hold it true," bracing himself, "as anyone must, that our King Lymond Perry's a bastard illegitimate, spawned of the Gammer's gallowglas lover, Handless Vincent Erne," a shuddering breath at the effort of having said that, let halfway out, for the effort of what's to come, "and I will tell you," he says, as she laboriously pulls herself unseen to her feet, "you, and anyone who'd listen, that his sister Ysabel's a lust-drunk strumpet no more now fit to be Queen than a cat! But I would never," and he swallows, "I would never raise a hand to any Huntsman of the court. And I will never shift my people nor my feet from off these floors. So." Still not looking to her stood wavering there at all, he tightens the knot of his necktie, adjusts its drape. "Show me your blade, then cleave me to the bone. For I," and he sighs, heavily, "am so, so very tired," but "Grady," she's saying, with some effort, "Grady. Earl." Snapping her fingers before his gaze, and he blinking looks from where she'd been, to where she is, half-slumped before him, sweater hiked, askew over her other hand, clutched at her heaving breast within. "I'm, sorry," she says. He steps back.

"I'm sorry," she says, again, and takes in a breath that lifts up, steadies, "I thought, you were someone else." Dragging her hand out from under, tugging the hem of the sweater discreetly down about her hips. "I'm sorry," she says, "that I did, what I did. You said some shit, you said *that* shit, and it, but, that's not a reason. If I had to do it over again I wouldn't, but that doesn't, excuse, any of it. All I can do is tell you I'm sorry but that doesn't, I don't, I've got no *idea,* how much of you this," the heel of her hand, thumping her chest, "this fucking *thing,*" and again, eyes squeezing shut in a wince, "I don't," she says, "know, what kind of, ghost, but you," she says, looking up to him again, "are here. And I," she says, but, trailing off, "am, sorry..?"

He's smiling.

He's grinning, lips spread, teeth bared, corners of that mouth dragged back and back to crumple his cheeks in a horrific rictus of surprised delight, an upwelling of malevolent joy that erupts in a snapped-off bark of laughter, "You," he says, his head shook slowly, one side to the other, "still," he says, "don't *get it.*"

She screams, a ragged burst of wordless rage as she lurches backwards, making room to find her footing on slipping hanks of mane, that one fist white-knuckled over her breast but her other even as she lets out another scream, as rough, as loudly raging, but longer, thinning, drawn out as that other hand curls in the air between them, fingers closing about a brightly aching white-hot flare that dimming subsides to reveal the hilt in her hand, three fingers gripping the glossy black tape wound about it, index finger against the stubby wodge of a barrel angled down, to one side, top of it slickly blued above the pebbled black of the frame, and the letters Kel-Tec stamped there, where her thumb is curled.

"Lucinda!" he crows, and throws up his hands. "You done growed up!"

Those hands flop forward, his chest punched back, the crack of the gunshot too much for the lobby followed quickly by another that powders the side of his rocked-back head, the whole of him collapsing withered to mane-strewn marmoleum and one step, two, she's stood over arm stretched down at what's leaving of him, pistol banging once more and again, too enormous to echo. The silence, stunned, returns to find an oiled spring-wound click of a mechanism, and another, another, the pistol in her hand not leaping but still reflexively kicking, braced for something that doesn't happen, over and over again. She groans, click, a choked-off sob, click, rising click by click to a shriek, click, until her arm jerks upright, cocked and poised to throw the pistol.

She doesn't throw the pistol.

The rug before her, beneath her feet a threadbare Persian, tangled knots of pomegranate and gold laid over damp concrete, and fitful candlelight picks out a single smoking scorch-edged hole, no bigger than a fingertip.

The pistol still in her upraised hand.

She lowers it, slowly, her other hand taking hold of the hem of the sweater. Yanking it suddenly up, under her chin, baring belly, breast, the slender white scar that climbs to end there as a nodule set in a pucker of blotchily ruddied flesh. She holds the pistol out away from herself, turns it about, brings it close to press the mouth of it right up against the darkly glassy surface of the thing, clink. She closes her eyes.

Click.

A splash, at her feet. The gun's been dropped. Her emptied hands at her sides. Somewhere, in the distance, the sound of falling water.

THE SOUND OF WATER FALLING
WHERE SHE IS, AND WHAT SHE IS TO DO

THE SOUND OF WATER, FALLING, in the distance, not the constancy of rainfall, not the singular trickle of a faucet or the focused plash of a fountain, but many differing streams and sources, here and there and there, the varying rhythms falling in and out of phase with each other, and their echoes, and now and then a sudden sputtering gout or exuberant overflow. Jo opens her eyes.

The light's brighter, whitely sifted from fluorescents bolted to green concrete beams along with oh so many pipes, black lengths of acrylonitrile butadiene styrene criss-crossing clean white polyvinyl chloride interspersed with much more slender tubes of gleam-nicked steel, and all of them every one leaking from joints and elbows, caps and seams, water falling from all that plumbing to spang and thump and plack and tock the roofs and hoods, the windshield glass of cars that have been parked in spottily ordered rows on a concrete floor awash with troubled dimpled spattered water, with water stretched in placid sheets, with rippled runnels gurgling down choked and sucking drains, water lapping over her bare feet, over the gleaming pistol dropped to the concrete before her, submerged.

"Ahuh," she says, she sobs, slosh-stepping back, "ah, aheh," arms wrapped about her oversized sweater, "Ys," she's saying, "Ysabel!" slap and spatter, "Ysabel!" turning about and around again, stilling, stalling, water-slash stop. He's stood there, at the far end in the moonlight slanting through the open garage door, not as bright as the fluorescents but limning him with a pearly sheen, for all that everything about him's grey, his trousers a roughly woven shade of ash, his loosely rumpled shirt the speckled hue of gravel, his lugubrious expression the color of cold oatmeal.

"John," she says, pitched to carry over the drip and tinkle.

"Joliet," he says, reverberantly. "You've changed your hair."

"What is this," she says, headed toward him. "Is it all melting?"

He looks, up, about, "No," he says, a considering shake of his head, "no. This, this is just, shoddy construction."

"Where are we?"

He shrugs expressively. "I, am here. You? Are, where you were."

She pulls up short, a couple-three car trunks between them, water slopping her ankles, her shivering grip about herself tightening. "This, isn't the warehouse," she says. "I didn't, unless this is, more, Moody bullshit," and at that, he moves to close the distance between them, slurp and plop about his grey shoes wetly blackening, "Do not," he says, "be so quick with that name, here and now. This is, perhaps," a sweep of an arm, taking in the garage about them, "what might have become of that warehouse, had it burned to the ground some years ago. If your Chatelaine's father had not completed his purchase, or made a better go, of the deal he'd had in mind."

"If he hadn't been cut down by Orlando," she says.

"You're shivering cold. Let's get you in, out of this," looking up, about, "rain," he says. Looking back, over his shoulder, the open door, the moonlight. "There must be a shop close by with something suitable. Once more, it seems," turning back to her, with something like a smile, "I'm called upon to see you outfitted."

"Well," she says, "if you'd maybe call first." Shivering enough now to chatter her teeth. Her one hand still closed, over the top of her breast. "Give a girl some notice."

A small bird, perched on the roof-rack of a low-slung, slope-hooded car, looking here there there, sharp black eye, wicked beak, head of it a pale grey cape shading to white at the throat, the body a canary yellow almost green in this uncertain light, there, then gone, a furor of wings darted over the sidewalk between steel and glass and a row of young trees freshly planted, all of a scrawny size, and those wings settle, and hold, a swoop of a glide over a yawning garage entrance, PARKING, say the steel-rimmed letters above it, past that turning climbing over clambering steps and concrete bleachers that lead up to a narrow alley and a couple-few more of those young trees lost in the steepening shadows of a falling night, or a breaking day. Wings flutter to dip sharply, rear up, alight, of a sudden, atop a demure blue sandwich board, Goat Blocks, it says, Leasing Office, and an arrow pointing. Looking there, there, up, over, a storefront tucked away here in this narrow crook of an alley, Alouyiscious, maybe, says the swirl-ingly calligraphed sign over the open door. Clearance Sale, says the hastily lettered cardboard sign in the window. Everything Must Go.

A look, away, again, and instantly the bird's not there, a rattle of wings, whip of air through that opened doorway into the unlit shop to find the edge of a rough grey hand and stop as if it had always been folded, tiny, there, up, out, there. "No, no, an actual, like, flower," Jo's saying, "grown up out of the, this, this thing, like it was a seed," from somewhere unseen, that curtained alcove, maybe, "looped, like, around my neck? This big fucking thing, always in the way, it was, like, a poppy? But, like. Pink."

Grey John lifts his hand, mindful of the bird's wariness, up and up until it's there by his listening ear.

"Anyway. She said, the, the wizard, Upchurch, said, it's not a seed. That there wouldn't be a flower. I mean, there was, but, that was, like, a dream? And I mean, just now, in what Moody, him, he, tried to, fuck me up with, I, it was, a feather, John, that came out of it. I mean, is it an egg? Is that what it is?"

The bird leaps away as that curtain's yanked open with a scrape of rings, and Jo steps out in a dull red running jacket, zipping it up to her chin. "What happens when it hatches?" she says.

He turns his grey head back from the palely open doorway to her in those uncertain shadows, red and black and white by other clothing racked in mistily pastel gradients. "Quicksmoke," he says, "does not hatch. It makes a shell, of scales, for itself, of what it takes from the world, that it might securely slumber, till it might safely wake."

"Yeah, well," she says, "I think it's getting restless," sitting herself on the low rim of steps about the little open foyer. In her hand a pair of long thick woolen booties, heavy socks with papery leather soles, that she sets to pulling on. "No shoes?" he says, frowning.

"I'm not wearing any of those," she says, pointing back to a low table decorously littered with slenderly spike-heeled pumps and insubstantial sandals. "I swear, everything in here's either lululemon knock-offs or, I don't know. Trophy wife goes to the bank. I think I know why they're going out of business. Okay," sitting back, hands braced on the floor behind her, "where am I going."

"I don't know," he says.

"Well, what am I supposed to do?"

"I don't know," he says.

"John," she says, sitting up. The face of him looking back, stonily impassive. "Then," she says, "how do I get back."

"You never left," he says, and steps toward the open door.

"I never," she says, and then, "I need to, John! I need to, you said. All this," a sweep of her arm, taking it all in, shop and clothing, shoes, the doorway, the alley beyond, but somehow also steel and glass, and brick, and pipes, and falling water, "it's what it could've, should have been. I need to get back to what it was, is, to what it is. How. How do I get back, to, to," and as she trails away, he half-turns, on the threshold, looking back to her. "How have you ever made it back?" he says.

She blinks. "Jesus, John," she whispers.

"It is given to you to see me but once more," he says. "It is my fondest hope," turning away, but not before that grey face is lighted by a smile, "that when that time does come, I shall see you, both, together."

And out he steps, into the alley. Up she springs and out, after him, into the burgeoning sunlight, "John!" she calls, but stumbles headlong reaching managing barely not to fall over a tummock twisting turned about upright again her footing not on brick or concrete but on grass, lushly rumpled grass, a great long vacant block of it tilted from the far high end yonder down and down, past a somnolent backhoe drooped there, struck by the rising sun, past the parking lot over across that street, Zipcars Live Here, say green signs hung from the cyclone fence, past the low olive warehouse across the street to the other side, Gatto and Sons, it says, over the bay doors, Wholesale Produce, down and gentling down past where she's stood to the low end of the block below, the hulking workshop across the short street there, Creative Woodworking NW, says the sign over the door. Down there, a corner of the lot's been cordoned off, a low and temporary fence of wooden stakes upholding sheets of startling orange plastic netting about a closecropped patch of grass. A couple haphazard structures within, makeshift sheds, waist-high at most, bridged by a wide bowed plank, and an erratic causeway of tree-trunk segments set on end about them.

Jo makes her way toward it all, carefully through the grass in those heavy woolen booties. Movement within one of those sheds, crunch of straw, a sleepy bleat. She could easily step over that low orange fence, but sits herself before it in the grass, and, as the light grows and warms, watches the goats, a couple of billies, a half-dozen nannies, three little kids all stepping from their hutches, chewing their breakfasts, greeting the day, one after another leaping onto those tree-trunks, and the clattering clack of their hooves.

Her eyes close.

The arc of the rising sun clears the treetops off to the left there.

She doesn't look up or around at the soft footstep behind her, the wisp of gauze over grass. She doesn't open her eyes to look to the hand, laid gently on her shoulder. Her mouth sets, holding something back. She lifts her own hand, to reach for those fingers there, unseen, and take them with her own, and squeeze.

Now Peter denied, and Judas betrayed;
I'll pay with the roll of the drum.
And the wind will tell the turn from the wheel
and the watchman is making his rounds.
Well you leave me hanging
by the skin of my teeth;
I've only got one leg to stand—

You can send me to hell
but I'll never let go of your hand.

—Tom Waits

NO. 44

"That was the river – "

SIDE BY SIDE – AFTER THE HUNT – EVERYTHING
AN EMPTY PAPER CUP – EXECUTRIX – A TERRIBLE MESS
DANCING IN THE STREET – ALL THAT'S LEFT – THE TALENT PORTION
PAPIER-MÂCHÉ – TYLER 4-0180 – ROUGHLY SHAGGY WOOLEN GREY
YOU WILL DISPERSE – WHAT HAS BECOME, WHAT WILL BECOME
COOLING HEELS – EYES JERKED OPEN – "SHE'S FINE"
AISLES OF PILLARS – DOWN THE LINE
NEXT EXIT

SIDE BY SIDE on the grass, the one draped in lace and black curls artfully tangled, the head of her pillowed on the shoulder beside, red jacket tightly zipped, glossily platinum hair against those curls, hands of them tightly clasped, fingers interlinked, as together they watch a wee kid, black and tan, white ears stood out like little wings in the sunlight, gathering itself at the edge of the one tree-trunk segment to spring, suddenly, to the next, a cele-bratory peep, an answering yammer from one of the nannies below. A murmured question, cold? maybe, a negatory shake of those curls. Another murmur, jacket, perhaps, but those curls shake again. Pulling apart, each turns to look to the other, green eyes blinking, calm eyes the color of mud, "I'm sorry," they say, at the same time.

A cough of a laugh, a smile, tipped together, forehead to temple, nose to cheek, a kiss, gently pressed. "I should not have cast you out," says Ysabel.

"I never should've left," says Jo, looking away, down to the goats in their corner of the lot, enclosed by that temporary fence of orange webbing. "This is all, too late to be from, before it was built, so it must be from after it, ah, got torn down? or whatever?"

"If," says Ysabel, that shoulder once more her pillow. "*If* it had."

"How did you find me?" says Jo, cheek brushing curls. "Or is this just what, I mean, you lost the goods, right? So they took your palace?"

"And who," says Ysabel, "do you imagine, might do that?"

"I, I don't know," says Jo. "The, you know. Powers that be."

"I assure you," says Ysabel, "my palace is where it always has been." Sitting up. "Would you like to go within?"

The light's changed, the warming sunlight brighter, the slanting sunlight shining upon, reflected out from, so much yellow stone, and white.

"Oh," says Jo.

Lift then the helm, tufts of the red and black panache a-bob, set it aside. Unfasten the gorget, tinted a watery rose, edged with gold, lift it from her shoulders. Undo the lacings of her nylon coif, peel it from her forehead, brush her glossily colorless locks from the blast shield. Reach in to pick apart a waxed knot from the riveted point on the gambeson. Grunt with the effort of un-coupling the power cables from the butt of the lance. Pop the spring-catch at the palm of the gauntleted right hand, allowing steel-mittened fingers to unfold from about the clear glass haft, swivel that blast shield away and hoist off the mighty powldron, unknotted ties a-dangle. Tug off the bridle gauntlet with a clack of laves to find wound about the elastane underglove a length of lacey ribbon, finework crushed and matted with sweat. Unbuckle the gilded plackart, and a clatter of tassets, then the mail skirt, links tinted a rosy gold, a weighty segment sag-ging where the mail's been torn from the burgundy velveteen lining, "Sorry," she says, "I don't know how," she winces, falls silent, as the skirt's unwound from about her hips. Pick at the waxed knots revealed, lashed to the points hung from the gambeson's lycra waistband, clatter and clack of cuisse and poleyn as loosened they settle about her thighs and knees. Brace her against the force of relaxation as the clamps are undone of the breast-plate brightly polished, etched with golden filigree about a single wine-dark beryl, big as a fist, set just above her heart. Lay the front plate aside as the back plate's lifted away, cable lopping from the battery-pack, and laid by the great glass lance on its silken wrap. Undo the greaves as the gambeson's unzipped, peeled open, tugged down her arms, then help her step from the clanking sabatons. Unbutton the hose at the back and tug them down her legs and, finally, off.

Take up amphoras of uncolored bisque and pour bright oil along her shoulders, her breast, her back, sluggish runnels down her belly, her thighs, set to rubbing the oil in, slap of palm against flesh, industriously stroking, smack and squelch of oil, "Wait," she says, "don't, don't touch," as slickened fingers lift from her breast, from the nodule there, just below her sternum, above her heart, opaquely clouded but flaked with delicate colors, the whitened pucker about it the end of a long pale scar stretched the length of her torso. Take up instead the golden strigils to scrape away, sluicing oil, grime, filth, dead skin, dried sweat, the dust of the road, water-stains and mud-stains and streaks left by leather, copper, mithril, of ruddy umber shaded to deeply red where it's still tackily wet enough to marble the oil, mingled but not mixed, splatters of ashen black, powdery flakes of white that slough off resolutely dry, refusing to soak in the oil, carrying with them glittering sparks of violet and of indigo, cyan and viridian, canary and vermillion, magenta winking, flashing, gone, all of it slopped and spattered with the oil to the tiles at her feet.

Break the ice stretched over a narrow pool, knock the plates and floating shards aside, help her wincing shivering into the pool and down. Look away discreetly as she spits a forceful "Jesus *Christ*" through chattering teeth, sunk to her shoulders, the oily residue lifted away in listless swirls atop the gelid water. Take up towels of thick white terry cotton from the heated ceramic stand, hold them ready as she climbs dripping up and out to rub, pat, wrap her about even as she brusquely pushes past beneath the arch into an antechamber about another pool, surface of it gently steaming, warmly lit within. Secure an urn of unguent, a cake of soap from a floating platter laden with phials and bowls and folded cloths, but scramble to steady it all from toppling in the sudden wake kicked up as she dunks herself, clumsily stroking away, toward the opening at the end of the pool, between the pillars, out into a vast wide basin beneath a cloud-stacked sky. The churn of her passage disturbs the mirror-still surface, ripples the reflected lines and angles of yellow stone and white risen up behind her, wing walls to either side of that water gate sloped to a curtain wall stretched between mural towers, white-capped turrets at the corners, about the yellow bulk of a donjon piled storey upon storey behind a criss-crossing welter of arcades and alures to a high-peaked steep-sloped roof, and more and slender towers under white conical caps that reach for the clouds.

Out and out with each gulping stroke toward the far side, the rim of dressed yellow stone a flat straight line cut across the infinity of blue sky set with sculpted clouds. There atop it, the confluence of the wake she bobbingly draws across that breathless water, a café table and two spindly chairs of wrought iron, and sat in one the Queen, her kaftan stiff with gold embroidery, her long black curls held back by a simple band of white, smoking a cigarette. Help her out of the water when she reaches the stepped edge of that rim, pat her down with more soft terry cotton, then unfurl a chlamys of grey wool and drape it about her, pin it at her shoulder with a brooch of bronze, a quartered circle set with a single glowering cabochon of garnet. Dressed, she steps past the empty chair to kneel at the Queen's feet, and lay her head in her majesty's lap.

"My Huntsman," says the Queen, running her fingers through glossily colorless hair.

The Huntsman lifts up her head, then plucks the cigarette thin and brown from the Queen's fingers for a deeply appreciative drag.

"I thought you'd meant to quit," says the Queen.

"These don't count," says the Huntsman.

Set the egg coddler on the glass tabletop, and the plate laden with soldiers of crispy toast, a smear of ruddy marmalade. Pour foaming coffee from the long-handled cezve into a demitasse cup. Bring the folded napkin, knife and fork, but she's already dunking a soldier in the egg, munching it hungrily down, working with her right hand freed from the opening in the chlamys, her left tucked away. "Your grace's hunt went well?" says the Queen.

The Huntsman waggles her emptied cup.

"They tell me," says the Queen, "your lance was utterly spent on your return. It'll take a day, at least, to fully recharge."

The Huntsman's cup is full again. She looks back, over her shoulder, the empty rim, and no one there.

"You don't want to talk about it," says the Queen.

"Tell me," says the Huntsman, "how is it you happened to meet me there, that day, that place, that particular," dunking another soldier, "angle," she says, "of the world."

The Queen tips ash from her cigarette.

"I mean, I know why *I* dropped out of everything, but you haven't said a word about what happened to land *you* there."

"Jo," says the Queen, but then she looks away.

"So, I guess," says the Huntsman, "you don't want to talk about it."

The Queen looks away, out over the rim of the moat, where the talus of the outer wall slopes down, the regular courses of ashlar blocks roughening to meet the living rock all overgrown with sprawling mats of rockrose bloomed in purple and yellow and pink above the swell of the great silver envelope serenely floated over the earth so very far below. "Perhaps," she says, "we were concerned for our favorite, out of all our – "

"Ysabel," says the Huntsman.

"My very best of friends," says the Queen, stubbing out her cigarette, "returned, at last, to me, but so, so angry," she says, with a questioning lilt, "driven," she says, and then, "hidden, where I couldn't reach," a breath, "to let you know how very much you're loved. How very, sorry, I am. That, alone, might've been enough. But," lifting her own cup for a sip, "it's much more sordid." Dabbing a drip of coffee from her lip. "Marfisa does love me, but that is not enough, for her. The Starling's ever cautious, and chary with her heart. I understand. Etienne? Was never mine, but that's all right. Christienne, though," and here she sets her cup down, clink. "Such a silly girl."

"How was brunch," says the Huntsman.

"She's leaving," says the Queen. "Tonight, tomorrow, perhaps she's already gone. To the City of Angels, to be with her sister. It will not go well for them, I fear." Sitting back in her chair with a creak. "That would be the impetus for catching a bus at half-past five in the morning, and riding it to the stop at Twelfth, where I disembarked to walk up and over to find," a smile struggles for her lips, "my palace a field, tended by goats, and my Huntsman, waiting for me. And that would be the why and how of it."

"You rode the bus, by yourself. I'd've liked to've seen that."

"Then I wouldn't have been by myself."

The Huntsman looks down at the crumbs on her plate, the residue of egg in the coddler. "I am," says the Queen, "sorry, for what happened to Melis – "

"Don't," says the Huntsman.

"But – "

"I haven't forgiven you for that."

"It was a mistake," says the Queen. "We should never have sent her alone. We shouldn't have named her to the office. We're, I, am sorry." Her hands laid flat on the empty glass. The plates, the cups, the utensils and napkins gone from between them. "So," says the Queen. "Here we are."

"For how long," says the Huntsman.

"What do you mean?"

"Is this it?"

"This?" The Queen looks out, the water, the castle, the clouds, the sky. "This is everything."

"Then everything's in trouble." The Huntsman tugs a lop of that chlamys aside to expose the nodule lodged there, in her breast, all of a single color now, a terrible dark red.

"That?" says the Queen. "That's nothing."

"I know." Chair-scrape on stone, "I'm maybe the only one who could possibly know." The Huntsman gets to her feet, looking away, from her majesty, from the castle, out over the edge of the wall. "Jo," says the Queen.

"This is just a dream," says the Huntsman, taking a step.

"No," says the Queen. "It's not."

"All the more reason," says the Huntsman, taking another.

"We have all we might ever want, here. We have *time.*"

"That's all it needs, Ysabel."

"We will not let it," says the Queen, standing now, white and gold and crowned in black, but, "I can't," says the Huntsman, palely colorless, wrapped in grey. "We can't," she says, looking back over her shoulder, "take that chance," and steps over the edge.

Steps over tipped forward to topple, but doesn't. Hung in midair, chlamys unwinding as she wrenches herself about, wall-rim just out of reach of her reaching foot. Twists to sit up, struggling for purchase in thin air, scowling with dismayed frustration as she wraps the chlamys back about herself. The Queen stood there at the edge of the rim of the wall, one arm lifted, the heavily embroidered sleeve slipped down to her elbow crooked, hand loosely curled in what's not quite a fist.

"Let me go," says the Huntsman.

"If you would fall," the Queen opens her hand, "we fall together," and off she steps from stone, into air, arms spread to gather the Huntsman to her as they drop, twining white and black, gold and grey, down and faster down past rocks and roses, the silvery ridged swell where they bounce, softly, once, clung together, slipping, sliding, tumble and dropping, gone.

AN EMPTY PAPER CUP – EXECUTRIX
A TERRIBLE MESS

AN EMPTY PAPER CUP rattles between two funneling flanges behind a clear plastic door, as machinery hidden within the cabinet grinds to humming life. There's a prolonged hiss. Enjoy a delicious cup of coffee! says the sign above the door, a steaming ceramic cup nestled amidst mounds of rich dark beans. She jumps when something spurts into the cup, the whole cabinet gurgles, and a thin but steady stream fills it until hiss, spit, the gurgle stops, the grinding hum, she blinks.

"It's done," he says. "You can, ah," he crouches, grey tracksuit flapping open, jerks up the plastic door to carefully, gripped by the rim, pull out the steaming cup. Offers it up to her, his dwindling hair clipped close, an abstract frown, "Go on," he says. "Take it."

She does, wincing. Switches to her other hand gripped carefully by the rim, sucking air through her teeth as she shakes the heat from her fingertips. White-gold hair unsprung from an otherwise ruthless queue a snarly halo in the light. A tentative sip, another wince, "This is *terrible,*" she says.

"It's coffee," he says, getting to his feet. "And hot."

The room is dim, cramped, overwhelmed by the enormous bed set at an angle, away from any wall, safety rails engaged to either side, the head of it ramped up in a semi-sitting position, foot of it lowered, a rumpled throne surrounded by monitors on carts, pumps, stands laden with drip bags, watchful courtiers clustered about. He's sat in the one chair, before a curtained window, poking at the phone in his hand, "Mackenzie missed her connection," he says, hushed.

"What?" she says, hunched on the only other chair in the room, paper cup in her hands, almost empty, now.

"Her flight from Denver." He looks up. "She won't be here till after midnight."

She looks down to the cup, back up to him. "Okay," she says.

Neither of them look to her also there in the room, laid back on that bed, so very tiny under white sheets and a pale pink blanket, closed eyes lost among those wrinkles without Coke-bottle lenses to magnify them, and the rest of her face swallowed by a clouded plastic mask held in place by elastic straps of vivid green, and the constant susurral seep of flowing air.

He's fallen asleep in that chair, an inhalation step by snoring, snorting step until a peak is reached, the breath released, a sigh, slumping till it ratchets up again. She hisses, suddenly, paper cup full and steaming, she manages bent over to set it on the floor, "Don't *do* that," she whispers, harshly. He's lurched upright, blinking. "Nothing," she says. The faintly regular beeps, a chime, the quietly constant push of air. She looks down to the cup, now capped with a fluff of whipped cream.

Up on her feet, cup in hand, she steps into a hallway fluorescently bright. An alcove, there, across the way, a garbage can sheltered somewhat from the relentless glare. She pushes open the flapping lid and lifts the cup over it, "But it's good," says someone close behind her.

"How dare you," she mutters.

"It's from the cafeteria, not that machine," quiet and low. "Fresh."

"I am the Outlaw," all the more forceful for being whispered. "You do not do for me."

"You are," even more quietly, "the Queen's Outlaw. And we do love our Queen."

She lets the cup drop, clang and slosh. Turns about, in the utterly empty hall.

Tinker, Abigail scrawled in fuzzy blue on the whiteboard, COPD, Emph, 6/2 05.30 FEV1 28%, the percentage circled, Group E, the letter underlined, twice. 6/2 again, in red, RN Fanshaw, Attending Sokolit. His tracksuit's black, now, his T-shirt white, and she's sat in the chair in the corner, still in her loose tank top, a few more strands of hair unkinked from that raveling queue. Neither of them look to the fourth figure crowded into the room, the tall woman by the bed, thickset in a long dark dress, greying hair swept up and back, a hand at the edge of that pink blanket, and the trembling of her fingers there, far from that hissing mask, those hidden eyes.

He says, "We should talk," looking toward the half-open door. "Mack."

She looks up, looks over, looks to Marfisa sat in the chair, back up. He's pointing toward the door. Rustle and thump of an effortful limp, she follows him out.

Marfisa looks, then, from her hands, between her knees, to Abby Tinker, unmoved within that crowd of monitors and devices. "She *what?*" the voice from outside, not his, flatly hoarse, and Marfisa looks back to her hands.

Thump and brush of skirts returning to the room, "This will not stand," says Mackenzie, harsh and flat and hoarse. "You are not equipped."

"She trusts me," says Marfisa, without looking up.

"You're not equipped!" shouts Mackenzie. "Hey," says Eddie, come in behind her, but a touch too mollificatory, "Those books," Mackenzie's grating, "her library, it's a national treasure!"

"And I am building shelves for it," says Marfisa, and now she lifts up her head. "She trusts me."

"We will get," snarls Mackenzie, "an injection, you hear me? Prostate! Rebate! Estoppel! I'm not," curling a shaking fist between them, "a lawyer, but I know *so* many lawyers, let me tell you," and "Mackenzie," Eddie's been saying, all along, "Mack," but it's not until the tip of the bat panks against the linoleum that Mackenzie, "you *scruffy,*" jerks to a halt. Steps back. Marfisa, leaning her weight against the braced bat, pushes herself to her feet. "You," says Mackenzie, "don't you threaten me," but Marfisa's reaching out and over to lay a knuckled finger against a sliver of dark cheek, just above that mask.

"Mack," says Eddie.

"We will stop you," says Mackenzie.

Marfisa, bat in hand, steps away from the bed, deftly slips between them, out of the room, into the hall, away.

The sparks, the smoke, the flaring licks of flame, the soughing collapse of gypsum, something topples, crack of glass, a picture from the crumbled wall, thumping rumbles, something, someone tumbled down and away to shouts and cries below, the banging clang of an impact that roils the smoke, even up here, that shivers more dust into the air, but stood in the midst of it all he only lifts a hand to touch his cheek, then looks to his fingertips, gloved in leather the color of fawn, smudged now with greasy soot and bright red blood. Rubs them absently against his shirtfront, but the poplin's already marred with tarry ooze and more wet blood, and he only dirties them further. Tugs that glove with the other, resettling the fit. Closes his eyes, pressing the clean thumb to that other palm, and twist.

Shakily he makes his way down the enclosed spiral staircase, flames flickering flaring orange and yellow behind him, down and out into a hall of bedlam, "she didn't!" bellows the Oubliette, hammer in hand, "their majesties?" says the Laguiole, in her pink suit, "the kitchen!" shouts the Chariot, pointing with her sword, and behind her the Majordomo, eyes widening in alarm to see him, stepped from the stairs, "Excellency!" he cries.

Agravante points with his filthy hand, unsteadily, behind him. "The upper storey, is on fire," he says. "See to it. Their majesties," pointing to the Chariot, "get them outside, now, until we are certain it's safe. The garage," pointing to the Oubliette. "Go around the front. Make certain it's secured."

"My lord," says the Laguiole, "your hair!"

He touches his right temple, the back of his head with his clean hand, brushing away the ash of the burnt remains of his locks. "The Pinabel is final," he says, "finally, gone, and I," a breath, "am now, the Pinabel." Lowering his hand. "Go. Time is of the essence."

"Excellency," says the Oubliette, his hand on the knob of the front door, "what of the assassin?"

With his filthy hand, Agravante points to the floor, the blood streaked and splattered from the staircase beneath his feet across the hall and into the lemon yellow kitchen. "That's why," he says, "I'd have you out front, to see she does not escape through the garage. Go!"

He lurches into the bright-lit kitchen, dragging blood with every step, following the trail as it thickens, widens, pooled before the closed door at the other end, and the smear of blood a shock about the knob, and the clean white frame. He takes hold of that knob with his filthy hand and twists, and shoulders open the door.

Shadows fall as he pushes it shut behind him. What dim light's left shines down on two white suvs, both with the same gold trim, interiors anonymously dark, and the handprint of blood smeared on the fender of the nearest.

She's huddled, a fœtal crouch in the shadowed space between rear bumpers and the closed overhead door, the head of her a snouted oblong, and one goggled, sightless eye. "Take that thing off," he growls, stood over her, the weight of him on his shoulder against the back glass of the suv. "My sister," he says. "The Outlaw. Marfisa. Where is she?" Nudging her with a foot. "Is she here?"

No response. No movement.

Groaning, he sinks to his knees beside her on the sticky concrete. "This was," he says, "personal. Wasn't it." Taking hold of the snout of that mask with his filthy hand, tugging it with some little effort from her spike-haired head, hung limply from the ruin of her ink-stitched throat.

"You think you have your revenge," he says, and lets the mask drop with a soggy slap. "All you've done is make a terrible mess."

The light changes, the door behind him swung open to brighten the hulks of those suvs. "Agravante?" says the King in a patterned silk gown, longsword in his hand. "The assault would seem to have been quelled. The fire's put out, though it has done some damage." That lemon light, bouncing off the white panels of the overhead door, sifting down enough to bring out the pale blue of Agravante's shirt, beneath the blood and ash. "I fear we've lost the Count, your grandfather." And then, "Have you the assailant?"

Those shoulders shift, and Agravante turns to look up in that light, his white locks clearly burned away, and the face of him singed black, and redly smeared with blood. "She's fled," he says, gently.

Dancing in the street — all That's left
the Talent portion — Papier-mâché — TYler 4-0180

Dancing in the street, purple pool-ring like an octopus about his waist, stubby inflated tentacles bobbing to the music from the speakers clipped to his rainbow suspenders, lyrics striding over a slinking beat, fuck the lease, I'm on my knees, he's an atheist, I give him reason to believe, God bless, tiny white lights strung about his shoulders against the falling night, and glow sticks of every prismal color lopped about his purple capotain, stole his heart cause my cheeks thick as thieves. Half a dozen men and a woman in lederhosen and Tyrolean hats, and cradled in their arms the brassy curls of tubas, a euphonium, a sousaphone, Trebel Frei, says the sternly Gothic blackletter on the white cap over the big bell end of it, someone cheers. A squad of transparent umbrellas, the poles of them neon tubes of actinic pinks and yellows and greens twirled about to more applause. "Friends!" an amplified voice from speakers somewhere oddly distant, pointed away, "Neighbors! Honored guests!" and "Here we go," says the man with the contrabass bugle, "Visitors from far and wide!" that booming voice, "Gracing our not-too-chilly and only somewhat rainy waterfront! Welcome, as we light up the Rose Festival with the one, the only, the best to ever do it, the greatest west of the Mississippi, welcome here and now, tonight, to the CareOregon! Starlight! Parade!"

"Okay," she says, and sets a clipboard on the table between them, "okay. So I'm gonna read you your rights, and when I'm done, you're gonna sign that, to show you understand."

"I don't need any rights," he says.

"First, you have the right to remain silent."

"I don't *want* to be silent!"

She holds up a hand. "Bear with me. We'll get through this. Anything you say can, and will, be used against you, in a court of law."

"There's no *need!*" he almost wails, "I came here to confess!"

"You have the right to an attorney," and he slaps the table with both his hands. She starts back, blinking, slowly getting to her feet. "I need you to let go of that," she says. "Leave it there, good. Lift up your hands, up and obviously empty, now: leave

466

them there, okay? Or shit gets ugly, fast." She leans back, without taking her eyes off him, "Officer Villaraldo? Could you, maybe, join us a minute? Keep 'em up, you're doing fine," as an officer in black fills the doorway, "Corey," she says to him, "mind telling me if y'all patted him down already?"

"Yeah," he says, "of course we, Jesus!" hand leaping to hip, "ut, ut," she says, raising that hand of hers.

There on the middle of the round grey table a revolver, laid on its side, black cylinder in a silver frame that sprouts a barrel long and slender pointed nowhere in particular, darkened hammer uncocked, handle of it paneled with black, inset with silver smudged and nicked.

"I'm giving that to you," says Chillicoathe, the Harper.

"You're doing fine," she says. "Officer Villaraldo, you mind bagging and tagging that piece in accordance with our clearly stated protocols and procedures?" He slips sideways past her, nitrile glove clutched loosely in his fingers to keep the skin of them from touching the revolver. "Now. Where'd you have that?"

"Wherever it was," says Chilli.

"And where is that?"

"It's mine, now. I put my hand to it when I've need of it."

"Wheel's empty, Detective," says Villaraldo. "Frisk him again?"

"You've done enough on that front, Officer. Get it squared away. Chilli? Chilli. Eyes on me."

"I traded my sword for it," he's saying, "and the Outlaw's sword, that I took as mine. And now I'm giving it to you! All I've left are my spurs."

"Let's, table that. You're saying, you killed the girl, Melissa De Voor, with one of those swords."

"Yes."

"And then you traded the swords for that gun?"

"Yes!"

"Chilli," she says. "Tell me. What did you do with the gun?"

"Abso*lutely* not," he says.

"Chicken."

"Oz, you are positively *frisky* in a crowd."

"Well, you're a chicken, and now everyone knows." She's wrapped in a red down coat, white socks on her feet, and striated clogs of purple and red, a black broad-brimmed bolero hat that turns to follow the group all dressed in red T-shirts over flannels and sweats, Portland Firefighters, they say in white, carrying a great round life net between them, beckoning as they do to the crowds along either side, come on, it's okay, try it!

"I will be pleased to tell them one and all," says Jimmy, with a distractedly disapproving mien, "I've proved myself a coward." His cardigan patterned with yellow feathers and red berries. Someone's stepping out from the crowd, black jacket, purple hair, and the firefighters lower the life net to help them, laughing, step aboard. A bass drum thumps a regular cadence, a rattling line of snares, a shimmering carillon of xylophones and glocken-spiels, a marimba, PSU Pedestrian Percussion, says the banner across the front of it, "Wait a minute," says Oz, "that, sounds awfully familiar."

"I believe," says Jimmy, "they mean to essay Radiohead's seminal composition, Paranoid Android. There – those are supposed to be the guitars," as meanwhile, ahead, the firefighters haul up the life net in sudden unison, hurling the laughing black-jacketed someone laughing into the air, "and there, see?" says Jimmy, pointing with his chin. "Thus am I vindicated."

Oz squawks, grabs his arm jerking back, and unrest ripples through the crowd about. He looks down to see a gurgling freshet slickening the bricks, slopping his black running shoes, a grunt and he joins them all, pressed back from the wee flood slipping away down the slope of the street, while out on the pavement, seemingly unconcerned, the parade marches on.

"How did you get this number?"

"I, don't have the countersign for that," says the phone.

"Dr. Uniform," he says, black hair oiled and combed in a part, round glasses rimmed with clear plastic. "Let's not play games."

"Let's not play games," says the phone, "is that, I'm sorry, Mother, is that boots without shoes? Solve mu for mi?"

"We shall," he says, "forego the challenge. Why are you not here."

"Even burning at one end, you eventually run out of candle."

"Expense another."

"Can you source for me a felon, on the West Coast, who's been hanged by the neck until dead?"

He looks up, glasses glossed over with green-white fluorescence. The man to his right, dull black suit, crisp white shirt, shrugs haplessly. "There are other paths," he says, looking back down to the phone. "You're needed here."

"Did you get my report."

"Your," he says.

"Should be in the drawer to your right."

"Drawer," he says, and yanks it open with a grating squeal. Draws out a manila folder that he opens to reveal a stapled sheaf of laserprint, TO MOTHER/HQ, it says, across the front in a boldly serifed font, FROM UNIFORM/ROSE, AGILE SAFFRON COLOR GLASS SITUATIONAL ASSESSMENT. "How," he says.

"November owed me a favor."

He looks up, sharply. The man to his left, white linen jacket, shirt of silky grey, shakes his head, an elaborate pantomime of disavowal.

"I must warn you," says the phone, "events on the ground have already outstripped the projections on page four. I was," a briefly considering pause, "too conservative."

"Uniform," he says, and takes a swig of smoke from his cigarette. "Station Rose hereby stands relieved." Exhaling a tenuated stream of smoke. "You are ordered back to Home Office by whatever available means."

"Mother? You're breaking up. Can you repeat that?"

"Uniform!" he snaps, "this is no time for," but the phone's muttering away, "If you can hear me, Mother," and "Uniform!" he roars, the man in the white suit flinches, "as events warrant," the phone's saying, and the man in the black suit's blinking rapidly. Smoke seeps up from the cigarette held high. "Uniform," he says, quietly, and more calm. "Answer me."

The phone says nothing.

A sip of smoke, a more considered inhalation. He folds the phone shut, snap. "Color Glass?" says the man in the black suit.

"Gluon saturate," says the man in the white suit. "Decelerating from a significant percentage of c."

"Antethesis?" says the man in the black suit.

"Gentlemen!" He gets to his feet, cigarette upright. "Saddlebag protocols are to be maintained at all times, without exception."

"Sir," says the one, and "Mother," the other, heads contritely ducked.

"The infraction has been noted," he says, closing up the folder. Looking over the index cards arrayed on the tabletop beyond it, goldenrod, salmon, cornflower, peashoot, each with a neat word precisely centered in blue ink, Apple, Engine, Nickel, Rocket, Camellia, Rose, Fountain, Angel, Electric, Sand. "Leave me the room," he says. "There's recalibration to be done."

"Try reading the *sign*, Lizzi," says the girl with the bangles about her wrists.

"Marysville Strawberry Festival," says Lizzi, peering through rain-speckled glass. "The sign isn't helping. And she's *singing.*"

"Talent is an important consideration of any beauty pageant," says the blond girl in the camisole.

"She's singing Pink *Pony* Club."

"The Marysville Strawberry Festival Queen," says the girl in the hijab, reading from her phone, "and all her princesses, *and* princes, have come to Portland's Rose Festival as ambassadors of all things strawberry, from Marysville, obviously enough, some thirty-five miles north of Seattle, on the Snohomish River delta, though still very much a part of the greater Seattle metropolitan area."

"Viva viva viva SeaTac!" shouts the girl in tights and big black boots.

"Ladies, there's a pickleball tournament," says the girl in the hijab, "how can we resist," but the girl in the paint-spattered smock's leaning over to shove the girl in boots, "Shut *up,* Penelope," she hisses, "they're gonna kick us *out."*

"Edith," says the blond girl, "nobody's kicking anyone out."

"Chloe," says the girl in the smock, with an acidic twist, "we're not supposed to *be here."*

"Leave, if you're nervous," says the blond girl. "Now, let's all wave bye-bye to the Strawberries," she steps up onto the bottom rail of the balustrade by Lizzi, "Sanaa," she says, "careful," steadying the girl in the hijab, and Penelope to one side of them all, Edith to the other, all of them leaned forward, foreheads pressed to the glass, looking down as the lit-up float swans beneath, sparks of white light sprinkled over lumpish plastic grass, Pink Pony Club, the queen and her court in rich dark red, blouses and gowns, black trousers, I'm gonna keep on dancin down in West Hollywood, waving laconically to the crowds before display windows left and right, Godiva Chocolatier, say the awnings, and True Religion Brand Jeans, Ann Taylor, say placards in the window there, they're on a bridge, the five of them, enclosed in glass a couple-three storeys up, stretched over the street between two beigely concrete midrise blocks of a downtown shopping mall, either end of it opening onto genteel walkways, glass-fronted shops about open atriums, but each end blocked by velvet ropes slung between stanchions, Closed, says a sign hung askew, CareOregon® Starlight Parade.

"What do you think Gloria would say, with a real queen here like this," says Penelope, as the float trundles away below.

"Who gives a shit about Suzie Gloria Monday freaking Wilson," mutters Chloe, even as Lizzi says, "Gloria! Whatever. Where the fuck is *Olivia?"*

"Ready?" she says, all in black but for the pink and silver ribbons in her hair, jet black but for the bangs dyed pink, crouched beneath the stiff cloth tented above them, hefting the two-by-four stretched horizontally to the bracketed cross-bar ahead, a frame obscured by drooping golden cloth.

"Always, sweetling," he says, with a quick kiss for her mouth, the black of his mustache hatched with white, and stooped he takes up his two-by-four, parallel to hers, hoisted, braced, he looks about, to all the others darkly dressed, hunched beneath that tenting gold, hands on poles and struts, and out there the laughter and the cheers, a whoop, the cheerful buzzing of what sounds like a flotilla of kazoos, "Ready?" he bellows, and then, *"Go!"*

The flimsy door of the motorcoach bangs open, fluttering the yellow strip of tape, CRIME SCENE, say the black letters printed over and over the length of it. Down he stumps, a hissing camp lantern held out in one hand, balancing his short but portly frame to the grass. An awning's hung, blue plastic tarp held up by a couple of canted poles, protecting what's laid out on more blue tarp beneath, stacks and piles of magazines, and pages ripped from magazines and fragments of pages filling a plastic tub there, and more spilled from black plastic bags, and the crumples and twists of them all, the softly ragged edges torn, split spines all painfully evident even in the thin lantern light, gleams shifting, limns slipping as he sets it on the ground. His fingers long and slender take up a candidate from the pile there by the door, careful of the pages loosely tucked within, lingering over the imprint of a bootheel cruelly pressed into the cover, marring the title, Planet or Plastic? it asks, over a floating shopping bag, all framed in rumpled jonquil yellow.

A rustle, out there, he looks up. Sets down the pages, steps away from pile, and coach, and light, slowly, into shadow. There, out in the grass, a small pale shape, sat looking back at him, the glint of one fierce eye. He steps back toward light's verge, slips a little notebook from his pocket, peeking quickly within. "You are," he says, looking up to the small pale shape, "Malocchio, the Great and," a quick look back down, "Great and Terrible. This one," a hand pressed to his sternum, where the lapels of his windowpane vest give way to his green linen shirt, "serves the Duchess," he says. "There's kibble, and fresh water. Go," a gesture, that hand reaching out, but the pale shape spooks, "tell your brothers and sisters," he says, lowering his hand. "This one is charged with setting things to rights."

The first of them leaps from the onlooking crowd, "Hup!" a darkling figure on prancing, stamping boots, spinning to flare the skirts of a long dark coat, "Ho!" the head, the head too large and round, the great long corvid beak of it gleaming with rainwater whipped with the spinning jerk and point, jerk and point, dancing between the trundling tail of the float ahead, a complex interplay of swirling ribbons of light that tangle high in the air above the men and women in spotless white coveralls pulling it along, between them and the vanguard of the band that marches after, all in black with strings of colored lights about their foreheads and their necks and shoulders, Black Cross Marching Kazoo Band and Temperance Society, says the banner folding up as the bearers at either end are jostled pushed and shoved aside by comrades pushed themselves, the buzzing tootle of their chorus snarled into aimlessly arhythmic atonality by a second figure leaping whirling splashing among them, flap and slapping whip of a great wide ankle-length dress, the head an oversized crudely shaped snub-nosed prick-eared cat's. A drum pops to thumping life, a fiddle skirls through a squall of feedback, a third figure, a fourth, a crocodile's head, a bull's, crudely shaped, hastily painted, too clumsily large as they dip and bob in frenetic time, splashing slashes of rainwater, "Ha!" and here comes the whistle, whirling and twirling around and about the fiddle line, punctuating the melody with piercing rills and runs, and then, the first of the puppets.

Wriggled from the exit there of the parking garage a ripple of gold held out and up on a pole pushed high and followed by another to become the arms of an enormous figure unfolding, the people beneath it, four, five, hoisting upright the poles they hold to open those long arms wide, the gown of gold gleamed rain-wet in the streetlights, head of it lifted slowly, a mass of paper pulp dried to a hard shell over shaped chickenwire, suggesting a mass of artful black curls hung loose to drape the canvas tarp sprayed with glitter over sturdy shoulders of two-by-four, the whole of it crowned by, click, a wheel of countless white lights as this towering queen a-sway lumbers vertiginously into the route of the parade, scattering kazooers before the prow of her already soaking hem, to the manifest wonder and evident surprise of the crowd, and also delight, but, as well, the growing alarm, as a second puppet appears.

Long skinny arms jank their way out and up, draped in tattered swathes and fluttering ribbons of glossy black, the length of it levering up to become another towering height all in black, and a hood made from a black garbage bag, and within two bright white spots light up as eyes to peer this way, that, those long and skinny arms outstretched, hands reaching, click, shining, powerful spots now blaze from each palm, lighting upturned faces to either side, gasping and squealing and shrieking in playful terror in that drifting not-quite rain, the water running more quickly now down the street, wavelets, rivulets ripple the pavement, plop and splash with every dancing leap and twirl and kick, with every step of the puppeteers up that onrushing stream, slopping the curbs to slick the sidewalks and lick at the shrinking, retreating, con-sternated crowds, as a wallop of white lops from the exit, a third puppet emerging.

Sharply angular shoulder, whipping slap of enormous lacey veil splashed in all that water, but it flutters, the lace. The air's changing, rising to a sound, the rush and wash of water become a rumble to drown out shouts and cries and screams, the float ahead swamped by a rising swell, ribbons of light lashing as it twists and tilts, abandoned by white-suited attendants scrambling away with band and dancers and clowns and acrobats and firefighters, the crowd all full-tilt fleeing the water that rises shoving spilling slosh, the lit-up float lifted, skewing, sparking, picking up speed with the churn, rushed back toward the golden puppet already a-sway, one arm dangled, abandoned, so slowly toppling back and back into the collapsing arms of the second all in black, sparks and pops from the great crown of light, and the third puppet slumps not even half out the gate.

Around the corner, riding the last of the failing swell, here comes a canoe, a ponderous dugout of a thing a-wallow on the settling slosh through and past the detritus, piloted by a couple of men, one in a black suit coat and a beaverskin chimney-pot hat, the other in shearling and a coonskin cap, the both of them paddles held up and out, ready, waiting as they look around, astonished, aghast, at the walls, the windows, the lights all reaching up and up to a starless sky.

"Nah," says Sweetloaf, ducking around behind the concierge desk, "it's, ah, it's fucking under here," rattle and thump, and up he comes to set on top of it a Bakelite telephone, dusty face angled with a worn dial, sleekly angular handset in the cradle. "There," says Sweetloaf. "Oldest fucking working phone in the city." Light sweeps the lobby, passing headlights overwhelming for a moment the chandelier, brightening the gold that threads the wallpaper. "Go on, pick it up. It's all wired in, you get the fucking tone and everything. You, ah," twirling a finger in the air, "you know how to fucking dial it, right?"

"I, yeah," says Christian, taking up the handset, turning it about, the unkinked cloth cord trailed awkwardly, pressing it to his ear, his other hand over the dial, but he frowns, "Hello?" he says, and then, "Op, operator? Do you, um, can you hook me to, a, Vanport number? The, the Vanport exchange, yeah, that's it." Tilting the handset away from his mouth, "She just, started talking," he says to Sweetloaf, his other hand digging through the pockets of his oversized jeans. "Yeah," he says, unfolding a much-folded sheet, "can you, um, put me through to," peering in the dim light at the printed image of an old sheet of typescript,

"Tyler four, five six, four two?" Tilting the handset away again, "It's ringing," he says.

Sweetloaf, looking away, distracted, nods.

"Still ringing. Uh. Operator? Can we try another number? Can we try Tyler, ah, Tyler four, oh one eight oh? Thanks."

Sweetloaf, stepping away, ostentatiously rolls his eyes.

"It's, ah," says Christian, and then, leaning over the concierge desk, "Hello? Ah, is this, is this Mrs. Bunch?" Angles sifting from cheekbones to brow, skepticism perplexing toward something like wonder. "This is," he says, "I'm Christian Beaumont, ma'am." Sweetloaf nudges his elbow, he shifts, "I was looking for Cora? Is she there?" Sweetloaf grabs his sleeve, irritated, he pulls it away, "went to the, I'm sorry," something's dripping, Sweetloaf tugs, *"Christian,"* he hisses, "did you say," says Christian, turning to glare, "cakestand?" His glare faltering, fading, he turns more fully around, his back to the concierge desk, "Tell her," he says, "I called," lowering the handset, reaching back, hanging up by fumbling touch. "Holy fuck," he breathes.

The short man before him blinks behind thick spectacles, his brow a mighty shelf of disapproval, "Language, son," he rumbles.

"Reverend Lee!" The woman behind him seizes his arm for comfort, for balance, but her grip squelches. He's soaked, the Reverend, his pastoral lavender rendered more of a violet by the water dripping from his suit. "I will not tolerate," he growls, turning to her, but "Reverend?" says someone else, and "Where," and "Oh, my," and someone's calling "Pearl! Pearl!" and a shriek of "What *happened?*" and wailing, wailing. Water's dripping from all of them, everyone, trousers and dungarees heavily pasted, skirts of various dresses runneled, clinging, water flung from outthrust, pointing, reaching hands, water squeezed from grips and embraces, water swamping the marbled marmoleum floor.

Roughly shaggy Woolen grey – YOU WILL DISPERSE
what Has become, what Will become – cooling Heels

Roughly shaggy woolen greyly fold and crumple dropping fall a limply scribble down the sunlit sky to finally so dribbled down collapse a puddle lopped upon a stretch of close-shorn grass, and then the sharp plop of a pin, a single glowering cabochon of garnet. Chanting below, harshly barking anger, simmering resolve, a rumble as something draws itself tighter and more tightly about the air, the sun, the light, the trim green lawn stretched flatly toward the parapets of brick that line the roof, a sudden rush of air, a dopplered squeak, a disorganized stumbling thump. She rolls heavily over to lie on her back atop that crumple of grey. Blinking at the shadow darkening the air above, the grass about, clenching up her eyes to brace herself as with a wallop a great white drapery stiff with gold lands beside her, a softly settling collapse, a drawn-out groan.

Jo's up on her hands and knees, "Ysabel," she's pushing aside confusing folds of kaftan, "Ysabel!" but "I'm here," says Ysabel, muffled, "it's all right, I'm okay," and a half-hearted laugh as Jo throws a placket aside to reveal her black-haired head, "I wasn't expecting that."

"You fall, you're gonna land, sooner or later." Jo sets to yanking free that length of rough grey wool, hunched over, away. Ysabel sits suddenly up, heel of a hand pressed to her frown, "You're," she says, and then, "we're still."

"What," says Jo, draping the wool about her shoulders.

"I would've thought," says Ysabel.

"What," says Jo, snatching up the brooch.

"What *is* that," says Ysabel, getting to her feet, heading toward the parapet yonder, where the menace is loudest. The sky above a mighty bowl of cobalt blue piled high with stark white sharp-edged clouds that do nothing to dim the sun, and the hills away across the river and the towers downtown before them stand in merciless focus beneath it all. Somewhat more slowly Jo follows after, looking out over the parapet and down.

A crowd fills the street below, a couple-three dozen or more folks thronging the loading deck, but so many more in knots and clusters a ragged arc between the warehouse and Gatto & Sons across the street, and in the space between these two imminent camps a handful of police cars, three, no, four of those trim black-and-white SUVs, a white sedan striped green and gold, officers in black uniforms and tactical vests stood about, seemingly unfazed by the shouts and jeers from either side, and a couple more, there by the sedan, conferring with two deputies in uniforms of clashing mismatched kelly greens.

"What on earth," says Ysabel, but Jo grabs her arm, "It's the eviction, Jesus, get back!"

One of the officers by the sedan is pointing, up, another turns, a deputy lifts something, a bullhorn, YOU THERE, his voice amplified to an order of magnitude above the ambient animosity, YOU ARE TRESPASSING, and Jo yanks Ysabel stumble-flap back from the parapet, out of sight, OFF THE ROOF, and the swoop and whirl of it all, GET DOWN OFF THE ROOF, the attention of those below, turned away from each other, the cops, turned up, that flap of white at the edge of the long flat roof. YOU WILL DISPERSE, that brassy voice, THIS IS AN ILLEGAL GATHERING, and the awful attention atomizes, the yammer resuming, YOU WILL DISPERSE, that voice overwhelming it all, as unperturbed as ever.

Ysabel tries to yank herself free from Jo's grip, "They *need* us," she's saying, hushed, but firm, "they need our *help*."

"The cops will *fuck you up*," says Jo. "We have to get *down* from here, somewhere safe, figure out what's going on, find some fucking *clothes,* where's that goddamn *hatch,*" looking about, the close-cropped grass, the Adirondack chairs. "There was a winch, or a lift," says Ysabel, "when they laid the turf, but," a shrug, "that will have been taken down," as another COME DOWN OFF THE ROOF YOU WILL DISPERSE erupts below. "They could not hurt me," she says, looking back toward the parapet. "They would scatter and flee if I showed my face."

"Gotta be something," mutters Jo.

"Oh," says Ysabel then. "Of course." She tugs at Jo's chlamys, Jo yanking it back into place, turning as she does, "The hell?" she says.

The brick backsides of the buildings at the head of the block, rising two and three storeys above the lawn, and one of the few windows looking out has been opened. Leaned out through the gauzy curtains there's Marfisa, her cloud of white-gold hair lit up by the sun, imperatively beckoning to them both.

And, once more, below, YOU WILL DISPERSE

The King looks up from the book in his lap. Closes it, about his finger, keeping his place, Retornamos como sombras, say the lurid orange letters on the cover. "Your pardon, majesty," says Joaquin, a hand against the jamb. "I was passing. The door was ajar." His two-tone shirt of cream and orange, crimped by the strap of his holster.

"We are rather on top of each other, aren't we," says the King, looking about the bedroom, the unmade bed, the baggage stacked against the walls papered in royal blue, sketched with white to suggest columns, a mighty portico.

"The repairs take longer than they should," says Joaquin.

"They'll take as long as they take. Hasn't the Vicar's council begun?"

"He sent me up here, to see to your majesties – "

"Khara!" harshly shouted from somewhere back that way, a thump, a crash, the other door bursts open, the Laguiole Florimell stumbles out, clutching the various pieces of her suit to herself in a wad of salmon pink, dangled white sleeve of a blouse as head down around and past the foot of the bed, heedless past the King to the door swung wide as Joaquin steps quickly back, but not quick enough, there's a collision, she gasps, he grunts, helps her along as she yanks herself free from his supporting hands, a flutter of pink, he's left to pick up her abandoned jacket. "My lord?" he says, looking to the King, who sets his book aside, "Go," he says. "I'll see to her majesty."

The bathroom off the bedroom's tiled in blue and pink, chrome fixtures and a mirror over matching sinks, one small window to look out on branches laden with leaves. She's sat in the pale blue tub hunched forward, hair uncovered and undone in inky tendrils to drape her shoulders, cloak her back, pool in coils to float along with indistinct clouds of white that thread the shallow water. He steps over the ewer tipped on the white bath rug, drizzle of something slimily white from the lip of it, and sits himself on the edge of the tub. Offers his hand, after a moment, held low to trouble the surface of the water, there beneath her face tipped down, and after a moment ripple and slosh she lifts her hand to take it, and squeeze it as he squeezes.

"We'll try again," he says.

"We scatter the police," says Ysabel, in the middle of the empty storefront, hands spread at the self-evidence, unfolding the kaftan. "It's easily done."

"*Hell* no," says Jo, sat on the sill of the wide front window, and the empty sunlit street behind her, the murmur of an unseen crowd. Dressed in a sweatshirt now, black, No Gods, it says, No Billionaires, her tights spangled with stardrift. "You ain't going anywhere *near* any goddamn cops."

"The people, out there," says Marfisa, leaned back against sheets of graffiti'd plywood stood up along the wall, "they aren't your," shaking her head, white hair an undone cloud, "they're not us."

"You mean to say they're sworn to Agravante's creature?" says Ysabel.

"They're with that mountebank," says the Shrieve Bruno, sat off to one side on a folding chair, "Lake," and "Who?" say Jo and Ysabel, pretty much at once. "He preaches, on the radio," Bruno brushes something from the knee of his summerweight suit, grey with delicate white stripes, "to the homeless, the luckless, the abandoned and forsaked."

"But that's absurd," says Ysabel.

"Your Chatelaine invited him," says Marfisa.

"When?" says Ysabel, turning back to her. "How? When?"

"Ah, folks?" says Jo. "What, what day is it?"

"Friday," says Marfisa.

"It can't be," says Ysabel. "It's Saturday afternoon, at least."

"Ysabel," says Jo, tone sharpened. "The date. What's the date."

Marfisa frowns. "Eighth June," says Bruno. Ysabel lowers her hand. "A week," says Jo. "A whole freaking week." The restless mutter of the unseen crowd, a distantly amplified yawp. Ysabel turns away from Marfisa, back toward Bruno, "What," she says, hushed, "what's become of them all."

"Those knights," says Bruno, "domestics, hobs and clods still with a house to keep, have mostly, largely, returned. Were you here for the parade? Gloria had them build great puppets, when her float fell through. But there was," blowing out a sigh, "a flood. Something to do with the digging, for the Big Pipe project. Storm sewers backed up downtown. So the city's said."

"But," says Jo.

Bruno shrugs. "Without a queen, or rather, with another queen to look to, the omens seemed clear. They've even held an Apportionment."

"From my stores!" snaps Ysabel.

"Obviously, majesty," says Bruno. "But from her hand. Which would seem to be consequential."

"And anybody who didn't have a house to go back to?" says Jo. Bruno shrugs, again.

"You stayed," says Ysabel, to Marfisa.

"Not for the palace." She gestures over her shoulder. "That was Abby Tinker's flat."

"Who the hell is Abby Tinker?" says Jo, but Ysabel snaps her fingers, *"She* wrote those space stories! That you like so much."

"She wrote the Caravan stories," says Marfisa, "and she wrote Cynara's World, which I like best." A deep breath. "She left her papers to me, and her books. That's why I'm still here." Head tipped forward, looking down. "Not for the palace."

"What's to become of it all," says Ysabel, to no one in particular.

"Demolition," says Bruno. "Condominiums. Ground-level retail, perhaps a parking garage, should development resume," a gesture, toward the plastic signs lapped one over another against the mural on the back wall, Wilson Properties, they say, and Anaphenics, beneath a sketch of a leaning, red-roofed tower, suggestions of olive trees. "Lake would have it become public housing, for his flock, though there's far too many ever to fit within. But the palace isn't the point, majesty," leaning forward, elbows on his knees, "if I were to gather what medhu I might, a drop at least from every fifth, if you were to turn it, even a fraction of what was turned before, and before the other queen might turn her own – that, too, would prove, consequential."

"Is that all," mutters Ysabel. Jo's frown tightens. "Until then," Bruno's saying, sitting back, "we must find somewhere safe, where your majesty might stay. Your things are still in the grotto, but we can hardly take you there. The pied-à-terre on Hawthorne's been emptied, I think?" looking to Marfisa, who doesn't seem to notice.

"Why are we even," says Ysabel, spreading wide her arms again, turning about in that storefront room, the golden embroidery pricking the dazzling white of her kaftan. "Have it done," she says. "Take our things to the Hawthorne apartment. Turn down the bed and make ready for us, and when all's in place, we shall merely walk there, it's not far," but "Majesty," Bruno's saying, and "That's not," says Marfisa, "your majesty, you must," but "you haven't," and "understand, there are," and *"heard,"* says Marfisa, voice rising as she pushes off the upright plywood, "issues," says Bruno, trailing away as Marfisa steps up to Ysabel, "a *blasted, rotten,"* she's snarling, and then, a shout, "There is! No one! Else!" her icy blue eyes locked with Ysabel's green.

Bruno says, gently, "For now, majesty, all that is left of your court is met here, in this room."

"Well," says Ysabel, lowering her arms, and again, "well."

"Stay here," says Marfisa, her voice cracked. She swallows. "Stay in Abby Tinker's flat," more certain, and direct. "A night, or two. It's close, but out of sight. I will see you're safe."

"That, that might well do," says Bruno, considering. "Between the unrest on the marches, the refugees in North, King Luys has a very full plate. The last thing he'd want is anything further stirred between the Outlaw, and the Vicar." Pushing himself to his feet. "Let's get you upstairs, then, majesty, and I'll set about the swelling of your ranks, and our stores."

"I'm sorry," says Jo, still sat there, on the sill. "King who the what, now?"

Walls paneled in rich wood, ceiling of pressed tin between dark box beams. The heavy drapes are drawn, and the only light from blue-shaded lamps that line the middle of the table. Sat at the head of it, white locks cut short, white shirt buttoned to the throat, hands laid before him, in gloves the color of fawn, Agravante clears his throat and says, "Your agreement – "

"Treaty," grates Wu Song, sat at the foot.

The briefest smile crooks the corner of Agravante's mouth. "Your agreement was with another king, another court, another line entirely. It no longer obtains."

"I see, no king," says Wu Song, his jacket of burgundy and black, the blocky hexagrams at his temples blurred by silvery stubble. "I see no queen. No duke. I see," looking about the table, "a baroness, a marquess," to Sigrid and Clothilde, in white and black, the helm Linesse, her left arm sheathed in a gleaming rerebrace and cowter, "I see the, spokesman, of a labor union," the Soames Twice Thomas there, by Bodenay, the tallest of them all, across the table from Calidore. "I see," says Wu Song, looking back to Agravante, and Pyrocles sat at his left, "no court."

"I am his majesty's Vicar," says Agravante, "in every matter under his encompassing hand. These men about you hold each of them a fifth of this city, and its portion. The Baroness is here to speak for our neighbors to the west, much as you, General, are here to speak for our neighbors to the east."

"You'd have us truckle with Hopper John."

"I'd have you avail yourself of the same privileges and opportunities afforded anyone in the hinterlands. No one is being slighted here."

"Piecework," snarls Wu Song, looking from Sigrid, to Clothilde. "*They* do piecework," he says. "We never did piecework."

"Even so," says Agravante, but that heavy chair at the foot of the table scrapes back, and everyone about it tenses, Pyrocles' hands leap to grip the edge of it, as Wu Song gets to his feet, "Should've waited a couple of weeks," he's saying. "Could've sent a boy with an empty hat. Would've saved us all the bother."

A beagle, white coat spotted with black, and tan, stood proudly in a field, and brushstrokes somehow suggest a foreboding copse of low trees in the distance, and a blue sky streaked with feathery clouds. The frame about it of ornately carved and gilded wood, tipped back up on the mantel over the hearth beneath of yellow brick, and embers a-simmer on the grate. He turns from it, folding up his arms in that two-tone shirt of orange and cream, creased by the worn brown leather strap of his sling holster. The black butt of his gun, poked out just above the crook of his elbow. Looking to the only other person in the room, sat in one of the two wingback chairs before the hearth, Becker, his sport coat of blue and grey over a trim fleece vest.

"Left to cool our heels," says Joaquin.

Becker looks away from whatever middle distance, blinking, befuddled, as if noticing him for the first time, "I'm, I'm sorry?" he says.

"The King doesn't want me," says Joaquin, taking a step away from the hearth. "His Vicar doesn't need me," and another step, closer to Becker, and another, inclining his head. "Your Anvil's left you here, as he sees to his duty." The denim of his faded jeans shellacked with old oil, grease, dirt ground deeply in, and long ago. The buckle of his belt a massive thing, enameled in blue, the chromed paisleys of it suggesting a bandana. "So, here we are," he says. "Cooling our heels."

Becker swallows. "I," he says, looking to Joaquin's hand there, braced on the arm of the chair, but that hand leaps to the butt of the gun, a slam out there, and heavy footsteps. Joaquin's suddenly by the doors, sliding one open just enough to peer into the hall, gun out, held high against his chest. The door across the hall's swung open, there's Agravante, looking about, "Vicar?" says Joaquin.

"Wu Song was," says Agravante, "called away. Our council resumes. You should see to their majesties."

"But," says Joaquin, "my lord – "

"We'll be fine," says Agravante, letting the door swing shut.

"Ah, well." Joaquin looks back to Becker. "Up and down and up again I go." He tilts the gun back toward the holster, but dips his head to kiss the rear sight of it, first. "Until next time."

Becker gets up out of the chair as the pocket door's slid shut, looking from the doorway, to the embers on the grate, then up, to the portrait on the mantel, the hound there, so serenely alert.

All the books on all the mismatched shelves about seem somehow to be leaning in and over, closing themselves about the one lone lamp, a fantasia of blue glass and beads, shining to one side of an overstuffed loveseat. Colorless hair's splayed over the arm of it where she's laid her head, turning a page of the book in her upturned lap, running her fingers along the text, dissolving into the maternal character like a drop of blood into another drop of blood. Closing the book, she sets it on the floor among the stacks and piles of so many others, sitting up to carefully place her feet among the stacks and piles. Reaches down for a drinking glass, tipping it in the light to confirm its emptiness, then sets off gingerly through through that darkly crowded room.

The kitchen lit by streetlight bright enough to make out the sink, and all the books that line the countertop, leaned one against another, sloppily piled on the glass plate of the stovetop, by an empty pizza box. She fills her glass at the sink and drinks maybe half of it down, stood there, looking out the window at nothing in particular.

To her left, the book-lined room, the burning lamp, ahead, the unlit hall, closed doors to either side among more books, the curtained window at the end, defined by street-glow. A sound-less, barefoot step, another, head cocked, listening, her attention focused not so much on the closed door to the right, as the left, where a thread of light shines dim along the carpet. Somewhere on the other side of it a quiet flutter of laughter, something's said, a sigh.

Into the book-lined room, she drinks down the rest of the water. Sits herself on the loveseat, lifting up her feet to turn herself sidelong, reaching for a knitted throw. Drags it back over herself, but there's a slithering avalanche of paper and she halts, mid-tug, as some portion of a manuscript settles to the floor with a flump.

"Shit," she breathes.

Falls back against the arm of the loveseat, legs at least tucked under the throw. Reaches up to shut off the lamp, clack. Closes up her eyes.

EYES JERKED OPEN – "SHE'S FINE"

JERKS THEM OPEN, awake, the lamp's burning, someone, Ysabel's leaning over her, "Wake up," she's shaking her shoulder. "I *am* awake," says Jo.

"Come on," says Ysabel, hushed, into the hall, opening the door to the right on a narrow bathroom, tile and fixtures barely a-gleam in the darkness. Ushering Jo inside, closing the door, Ysabel hunts about reaching, patting, finding the light switch, chipped gold trim, white tile, white sink, white toilet, lid of it covered by a plush brown cushion, a bathtub, dingily white.

"Go on," says Ysabel, skinning her ivory nightgown up and off, awkwardly, with just the one hand. Dropping it to the floor, she reaches to tug at Jo's sweatshirt, "Run a bath," she says.

"Get ready." Her other hand closed about something. Jo kneels, skroink, skoink, adjusting the taps for water hot and cold. Fits the plug in place. Ysabel's holding whatever she has in both hands, now, and watches. The sound of the water falling deepens as it fills, thickens, loses its trebled edge.

"Jo," says Ysabel.

She looks up from the filling tub to Ysabel, up the bare brown length of her, black curls about her shoulders, the green of her cooly expectant gaze. Wrestles her way out of the sweatshirt, drops it to the floor, shoves off her briefs. Her one hand to her chest, she holds out the other, but Ysabel doesn't take it, instead, she drops into it what she's been holding, a weightily sodden handkerchief.

"That better not be," says Jo, hoarsely wry.

"Don't be a child," murmurs Ysabel, stepping into the water, lowering herself with a hiss to sloshing sit, water gurgling, steaming, lips pursed, she looks to Jo, crouched beside the tub. "Show me," she says.

"What?"

"Let me see it."

The handkerchief still in her one hand, she lifts the other from over the nodule there, at the end of the long pale scar stitched from hip across belly up and up between her breasts to end in a whitened pucker about that thumb-sized gem, all of a single color now, a red so rich, so full, so very opaque.

"Oh," says Ysabel. "It's as dark as it was."

"Believe me, I know." That free hand reaching out, skroink, squonk, shutting off the water. Looking down, to Ysabel's knees, "So," she says, "what do I, just, squeeze, or," and, annoyed, Ysabel says, "Yes, Jo. As you have done before. Pour the medhu, into the water, over me," and "Yeah," Jo says, "I know, I just" but "I *need* to know," says Ysabel. "I don't. And I need to be sure."

"I get it," says Jo. "I do. I was asking, I mean, logistically. Squeeze it, or, I could dunk it? Let it, seep out? We might get more," but Ysabel's shaking her head, "Squeeze," she says. "Let it fall."

Jo nods, both her hands together. A deep sigh. "Ready?"

Ysabel shakes her head, but closes her eyes, lowers herself, black curls spreading, a-float, till the water laps her chin. Jo squeezes, bundling the handkerchief more tightly in her grip, and squeezes. Oozing out from her clenched fingers a droplet, white of it dimmed by gold, swelling, trembling, dangling till it's heavy enough to break free, to float, for a moment, in the air, beneath her hands, over the water, turning as it shivering starts to fall, followed quickly enough by a couple-few more in an uncertain trickle, pop-plop, splip. Milkiness unrolls from the impacts, spreading in thready tendrils through the water, over, around, about Ysabel's lap.

"Maybe," says Jo, shaking out the handkerchief, twisting it about, wringing another thin stream of milky droplets into the water, "I, ah," says Jo, and then the world hiccups, and the tub is full of gold.

Ysabel sits up, squeak of dust about her hips, under her pressing hands, her shoulders rising, falling with each deep breath. Plop of the handkerchief dropping from Jo's hands to the brightness. "Holy shit," she says.

"Yes," says Ysabel, muffled.

"No," says Jo, "I mean, it's not as much as, but, I mean, from just what, holy fucking shit."

"Yes," says Ysabel, holding up a hand. "Help me out." Glittering shimmerfall of dust as she levers herself up, pulling on Jo's offered hand, hiking a leg over the edge of the tub, dust falling with the unsteady shift of her foot on the water-slick floor, catching, floating, blackening to peppery flecks. Ysabel stands there, hands at her sides, looking back down at all that gold. Jo's tugging her sweatshirt back on, "Hey," she says, as her head appears, gesturing toward the discarded nightgown, but Ysabel reaches to scoop up a handful of dust, turns to pour it out in a tidy little pile on the counter by the sink. Leans down to scoop up more. "Turn on the water," she says.

"What?"

"I've portioned out what my court requires," she says, and three piles now, set forlornly by the sink, "the rest, as we've been told, is but superfluous. It would be, imprudent? to leave it here, out in the open, where anyone might take it," and then, when Jo doesn't move, or open her mouth to say anything, "turn *on,*" snarls Ysabel, lunging for the faucets, "the blasted *water,*" twisting one with an horrific squeal, a sudden gush of water crashing into the golden dust with a hissing spitting whistling plosion of steam, *"Jesus,"* from Jo, knocked back, backing up, as Ysabel wrenches a lever around and, up, above, the showerhead gurgles, chugs, spurts out a strengthening widening fall of water splashing over rippled golden piles of popping blackening smoking shriveling dust.

Jerks them open, awake, sunlight shining low and indirect from the window there, but no one, not anyone else about, at all.

Sits up in that oversized sweatshirt, No Gods, No Billionaires, places her feet among the stacks and piles of books and papers, "Ysabel?" she says, barely disturbing the air.

In the hall she opens the door to the right on a sunlit bathroom, white tile, chipped gold trim, the tub she squints scummed over with a brackish slurry faintly steaming still she backs abruptly out, stifling a cough, "Ysabel," she manages, blinking.

The door to the left.

The door to the left opens on a room filled with so many more books, a frozen turbulence piled and stacked to the walls, knee-high, hip-high under the windows there that look out over the flat green lawn, all about a wide bed, brass headboard and footboard, blankets and sheets all tangled about the one lone figure splayed across it, Marfisa, face down, her white-gold cloud of hair about her shoulders bare and back, rising and falling with a lustily rattling snore.

She pulls on tights, stardrift spangled over midnight purple, shoves bare feet into running shoes, tightens the velcro straps, they're a little unsteadily loose with every step out the front door and down the stairs, "Ysabel!" she calls, out onto the sidewalk, looking about, dark storefronts to either side, the brick garage across the street, high narrow windows blankly dark in the early light above a singular overhead door. Someone's getting out of a car there, hard by the curb, a sleekly anonymous grey sedan. Blocks away down the hill a bus gathers itself for the climb. The street is otherwise empty. Down the sidewalk, past the sedan, windows of the storefront there say Monte Carlo in red letters freshly painted, Pizza, Steaks, around the corner, the façade of the warehouse stretching away down the gentling slope, the litter of the long-gone crowd, a lone police car at a somnolent angle before the loading dock, but otherwise the street, the block, the morning's empty. Her hands press the heels of them to either side of her forehead. Shoulders rise and fall with shallowly accelerating breaths.

"She's fine," says someone behind her.

A woman, leaned back against the rear fender of that sedan, loosely tailored suit of pearly grey, amber aviators peering out from under the bleached brim of a jipijapa fedora set atop her corkscrew curls.

"Ysabel?" says Jo.

"She's fine."

"Where *is* she?" Soles slapping as she heads back up the sidewalk from the corner, "you know where she is, you fucking *tell* me," but the woman lifts a hand, hold up, "She's about her business. You should be about yours. It's gotten heavier, hasn't it."

That hauls Jo up short. "What," she says.

"Warmer, too, sometimes. Is the color changing, yet?"

"You're," says Jo, "Upchurch. That's your name. Right?"

"Joliet Kendal Maguire," says Mrs. Upchurch. "You need to deal with the qlifot."

"Quicksmoke," says Jo.

"Antethesis," says Mrs. Upchurch. "So long as we're listing names. Get in the car; I want to show you something."

"Show me what," says Jo.

"If I could just, tell you, I would. You need to see." Opening the passenger door of the sedan. "Go on. Get in."

"I've developed this complex, see? As to wizards, and second locations."

"Luckily for us both," says Mrs. Upchurch, heading around the front of the sedan to the other side. "I'm not a wizard."

"She scares the shit out of you, doesn't she," says Jo.

Mrs. Upchurch opens the driver's door, those carefully painted lips judiciously pursed. "That's how you know she'll be fine," she says.

"That's not," says Jo, stepping toward the passenger door, "she's not all I'm worried about."

"I'll take you right to her, when we're done, if you want," says Mrs. Upchurch.

Jo sits herself on the passenger seat. "Can you at least tell me," she says, a hand on the seatbelt, "where it is we're going?"

"Salem," says Mrs. Upchurch.

"Oh," says Jo. Fastening the buckle. She pulls the door shut.

AISLES OF PILLARS – DOWN THE LINE
NEXT EXIT

AISLES OF PILLARS stretch ahead, reached up to bear the weight of the viaduct above. It's not all that much darker here beneath it, the slanted morning light strikes crumbled grass-choked pavement all about, and the embedded rail lines cross gleaming straight and true. The blocky hulks of warehouses closing in to either side ahead still steep in cooling shadows, and while out in the open the white siding of a double-wide trailer's dazzled, the pallets offloaded beside it are still dimly uncertain, bundled panels of cyclone fencing, perhaps, Jersey barricades waiting to be deployed, and all the unhung signs leaned up against them in anticipation, Umpqua Bank, they say, and Crutchfield Evans, Sogge Enterprises, Hoyt Street Properties, Hoyt Yards, Coming Soon, Hoyt Yards.

The pillars, though. This one, here, one of the central file, flat grey face of it figured with a hermit in chalky white, a lantern held high in one hand, and calligraphed above, well out of reach, faded letters that say Diogenes the Greek Cynic Philosopher walking the

Streets of Athens with a lantern looking for an honest man. He was born about the year 412 B.C. She reaches up to lightly brush the chalked rays of light stroked out from the lantern-shape, just above her head. Black curls hang loose in artless tangles about her shoulders. Her slender, knee-length gown of ivory satin, edged with lace the color of bone. One last tap at the pillar as she steps away, slowly, even regally, despite the hint of a limp. Her feet are bare, and filthy, stickily damp, glistening amidst the grime.

The deck of the viaduct slopes gently down and closer until some dozen yards ahead it declines much more sharply to end, of a sudden, in a blank flat concrete wall. She looks down, at the random assemblage of litter strewn about between the pillars here, the screwed-up twist of paper, an uncrimped can, Washington's Viking Beer, it says, the crisp plastic wrap spilling soy sauce packets, a grimy yellow dish-glove, ripped half inside-out. She looks back along the length of the viaduct, the pillars. Shading her eyes against the rising light.

Her limp is more pronounced, crossing the sunstruck pavement. She leaves the most faintly glistening footprints.

Hitching up the skirt of her gown, she kneels by one of the smaller signs, a white placard that says Hoyt Yards in dark blue letters, and marks a number of organizations along the bottom as smaller sigils and logotypes in the same dark shade. She touches one, toward the right of the sign, Welund Barlowe & Lackland, it says. When she lifts her fingers away, smoke unspools from the spot where those names had been.

Scrape and clanking grind she drags that sign back with her, both hands held behind her, rattle and clack, head down curls swaying with the effort of it back toward the deepening shadow beneath the viaduct, back between the ranks and files of pillars, back to let it drop, clang, its own small island, cleared, clean, smooth, laid flat on the pavement there.

Pushing back all that tangled black hair, blowing out a resolute sigh. Bending down she sits herself tailor-fashion on the sign, tucking the one foot on top of the other knee, wincing as she wipes the grit from the edge and the sole of it. Settling her hands in her lap.

492

"All right," says Ysabel Perry. "Here we go."

He spritzes her hand with something, "Wait," she says, "what?"

"Photo ID," he says.

"No, with the hand," she says.

"Photo ID," he says, with a come-hither gesture, tucking the little spray bottle away on top of the hulking X-ray scanner.

"Thing about that," she's looking over her shoulder to Mrs. Upchurch, making her way past the row of metal lockers toward them, "hey," she calls out to her, just loud enough to catch attention, "we, ah, there's a problem," as Mrs. Upchurch reaches into her jacket, "I have no idea what happened to my license since the, ah," faltering, as Mrs. Upchurch pulls a card from a slender wallet and hands it to the guard, then holds up the opened wallet itself. He peers at what's within, holds the card up to check Jo's face against it, then returns it to Mrs. Upchurch. "Hand," he says, and spritzes the back of Mrs. Upchurch's hand. "Nothing blue, good," he says. "Belt, jacket, keys. Shoes should be fine. Underwire?"

"What?" says Jo, as Mrs. Upchurch lays her folded jacket on the conveyor belt of the scanner. "Underwire," says the guard. "In your bra."

"We're," says Jo, "we're good."

"Down the hall," he says, as she steps through the gate of the metal detector, "left at the end," as Mrs. Upchurch collects her jacket. "Stay to the right of the line."

Dim, long, the hall's pitched down at a moderately steep angle, a dark line painted straight and true along the polished linoleum, leading the way. "Here," says Mrs. Upchurch, handing the card to Jo, "you'll want this." Oregon, it says. Driver License. Her photo, expressionlessly surly, hair of her blond, cropped close, here and there a couple locks left long, dyed black. "Neat trick," she says. "Cops had it, is that it? And you just, held onto it, till you could whip it out, all dramatic-like?"

"A wise man once said," says Mrs. Upchurch, "magic is usually someone spending more time and effort on something than anyone might expect."

At the bottom of the hall, that line right-angles left into a dimly empty lobby, a heavy sliding door lit by thick glass reinforced with chicken wire, and more chicken wire strung over the apertures of an unlit booth to one side, "IDs," says a gruff voice within.

"But," says Jo, as Mrs. Upchurch steps over the line, holding her wallet up to the wire for inspection. Jo, with a shrug, steps over the line, holding up her license. "Hands," says the voice.

"But," says Jo, as Mrs. Upchurch offers up her hand, "you were just, up there," as a little buzzing wand's waved over the back of Mrs. Upchurch's hand, a patch there glowing a sickly indistinct blue-white. "You let us in."

"Hand," he says.

"You were the one who," she says, offering up her own hand. He lights it up. "Wait for the door," he says. "You'll be shown to a room. They're looking for him."

"Protocol," murmurs Mrs. Upchurch, leaned close as keys jangle. "They're short-staffed."

"I don't want to be here," says Jo.

"I know," says Mrs. Upchurch.

The heavy door slowly, smoothly slides to one side, revealing another guard, taller, beefier, but the uniform's the same, shirt a grey touched with lavender, trousers a black touched with grey, the same heavy gear hung below his paunch, same patch on his shoulder, Penitentiary, it says, Oregon Department of Corrections. He ushers them into a room immediately beyond the door, just big enough within for a small round table and three plastic chairs. "It'll be a minute," he says. "They're looking for him." Behind him, the space opens out, a common room filled with rows of picnic tables, men sat at them, paired over a checkerboard, alone, conversing, joking, discussing in small, muted groups, all of them dressed in another, different uniform, of rough, ill-fitting denim.

Mrs. Upchurch directs Jo toward the chair across the table, then sits herself in the chair to the side. "He's not gonna want his back to the door," says Jo.

"Do you?" says Mrs. Upchurch. She pats the tabletop. "Go on, sit. I don't imagine we'll be here very long."

Scrape of the chair against linoleum. Creak of plastic, taking her weight.

"Where were you?" says Mrs. Upchurch, after a moment.

"What?"

"You were, gone." The nails of her, carefully shaped and polished to gleam in the harsh fluorescence. "Completely. Utterly. Until about eleven o'clock, yesterday morning, just over a hundred and fifty hours. Gone." Her lips, the color of plum, widen in a welcoming smile. "Where?"

"You're, tracking me," says Jo. "Down to the hour."

"There's a lot riding on you, Miss Maguire," but the door to the room's pushed open, the guard leaning in to make room for a man in one of those denim uniforms, his black hair a greasy, spiky shock, and under his beak of a nose a pointed smile that sharpens in evident delight, "Bambi Jo!" he cries, with gusto. "I swear, you are just about the *last* person I ever would've expected to pay a visit to little old *me.*"

Mrs. Upchurch looks from him as he sits himself easily with his back to the door, to Jo, sat bolt upright, frozen until she manages, just, a whisper, "Dread," she says, "Paladin."

That grin folds itself into a look of some concern, somehow still sharp, "Aw, shit, girl, you shouldn't ought to call me that, not no more. I hope," he lays a hand on the denim over his breast, "you ain't still mixed up in those wicked, evil games. They only lead to darkness. As you can plainly see." His hand, set back on the table, the knuckles of the pinkie and the ring-finger not so much swollen as knobbled and twisted out of shape by some old incident, or accident. "But seeing as how the business of this place I've found myself is penitence, and I always take my business seriously," and here he leans forward, across the table, Jo flinching violently, Mrs. Upchurch quickly shifting a hand toward her, but just as quickly holding it back,

"I got to ask you, Bambi Jo," he says, seemingly unawares, "have you sought forgiveness for what it is you did," that crooked hand laid open, waiting to clasp the hand she isn't lifting from her lap, "have you, girl, accepted the love and grace of Our Lord Jesus Christ into your heart?"

They sit together, unmoving, for some time, in the silent sedan, still in its stall in the parking lot, before Mrs. Upchurch says, "He's been there the entire," and Jo says, "I know."

"So the Daniel Moody in town," and "Yeah," says Jo, "I know."

"There was a home invasion last week. Wednesday. In St. Johns."

"Bruno said. The, co. Couple of his boys. Moody did that?"

"He was involved."

"More names for my list."

"*You* didn't do it," says Mrs. Upchurch, suddenly insistent, sitting forward to look across to Jo beside her. "The qlifot has begun to put things into the world, now, instead of taking them out. All you did was to suggest a form."

"All I did," says Jo. "A hundred and fifty hours, you said, we were gone. So. Tell me. In the hundred and fifty hours, those six days, or whatever, did anybody happen to see Mr. Danny Moody walking about the greater TriMet area?"

Mrs. Upchurch sits back, curls against the headrest. "I can't say for certain," she says.

"But as far as you know?"

A deep breath drawn in through her nostrils, blown out through her lips. "No," says Mrs. Upchurch.

Green signs sail by overhead, indicating exits, distances, Kuebler Blvd., Delaney Rd., Albany 19, Springfield 62, Grants Pass 198, and blue signs off to the side, State Police Exit 252, and Food, a sequence of logos, Chick-fil-A, Carl's Jr., McDonald's, Applebee's, presumably hidden away behind the trees grown lushly green to either side, behind the immediate berms of turf, and the evidence of the mowing of it, brightly green, and the signs, the endless stretch of dull grey pavement, the rush and flow of traffic up this way, down that, the only signs of habitation here about, those, and the occasional glimpse of a parking lot, of a concrete wall, of a red tin roof, snatched from among the whipping greenery.

Another, different sign juts from the trees off to the left, atop a pole, over a glimpse of parked cars, a white suggestion of crenelated wall and towers to either side, with conical caps red and yellow, and an egg sat atop in a red top hat, waving to the freeway below. Enchanted Forest, it says. Next Exit. Jo swivels in the passenger seat, looking past Mrs. Upchurch at the wheel to watch it go by, ducking to peer back through the inconveniently small rear window, the other side of the sign much the same, castle wall, towers, that smiling egg who's somehow turned about to wave its other hand to everyone else as it recedes. Another of those green signs floats by, alerting those headed the other way, Salem 8, it says. Portland 53.

Trees dwindle as the rolling flattens into seemingly empty farmland, and now and then a stretch of frontage road, a pocket of low commercial buildings, a motel, a strip mall, an entire subdivision of blankly grey townhouses crowded cheek by jowl behind a high thick wall, and only here and there a tiny darkling window to look out over it, and gone, behind them. A green field dotted with unconcerned sheep, and in the tall grass alongside another green sign, 34, it says, Lebanon, Corvallis, 1 Mile, and the sedan gathers itself, surging past the semi to the right to close on the pickup ahead, signaling quickly, neatly slipping from behind the one truck ahead of the other, and then, as an overpass approaches, angling for the off-ramp.

This highway's scaled down, four lanes but without a median strip, the pavement of it older, so many cracks blackly repaired with ragged strips of tar. The traffic about's not so thick or all-enveloping, and the sedan seems to relish the chance to let loose and glide, past more farmland, garages and anonymous warehouses, more blank walls around townhouses clustered so closely together despite all the emptiness about. A tensely tuned harp and a lonely saxophone trade breathless passages over sauntering bass, shaking bells, a haphazard tanpura, and Jo closes her eyes. Mrs. Upchurch signals a lane change.

The trees close in again, and climbing rise as hazes up ahead, under a high hazed sky. The road narrows from four lanes to two. A sign that says Philomath. A sign that says Noon. A sign that says Cardwell Hill Cellars. Those hazily rising trees become hills around about and above, the road curling as it climbs to find its best way among the slopes and rounded peaks and down. Toledo, says the sign approaching, pointing off to the left. Newport, it says, and points away ahead. The distant blur of slopes ahead has fallen away behind the onrushing trees, and now an emptiness seems to grow there, patiently.

Guardrails emerge, those trees thin, off to the left that emptiness appears within, behind, beyond, a deeper, weightier blue out under the unfocused sky. The tenor of the traffic's changing, slowing, intermittently dispersing, as turn-offs proliferate, as intersections assemble themselves about thickening blocks of houses, of storefronts, a gas station, a lot lined with tractors and cherry-pickers, a lumberyard, and that vast emptiness somehow behind it all, around them, now. The largest intersection yet ahead, arrays of stoplights to regulate various flows of traffic. The sedan slips into the rightmost lane, signaling a turn, taking it against the light. Thriftway, Momiji Sushi Bar. Rodeway Inn, Free Wifi. Off to the left, between low roofs and scrubby tangles of trees, there, you can just catch sight of the ocean, so enormously far, so very coldly blue.

The sedan turns right into a small and nearly empty lot, Sea Breeze Budget Motel, says the short sign planted in the dead grass on the corner, the office and the low one-storey wing of rooms painted a sea-foam green, the trim about the windows more of a forest, and across a side street a two-storey block of rooms in those selfsame colors. The sedan stops, brake lights shining. The passenger door, after a moment, pops open, and Jo climbs out. Watches as the sedan neatly wheels itself about, slows briefly to gauge the traffic, pulls smoothly out of the lot, turning left, away.

Dim within, the office shaded, cramped, a low voice muttering somewhere, a radio, an unseen television, this is what I'm talking about, this is what we have to watch out for, we must be vigilant, there's no excuse, no one else to be seen, behind the counter, sat in the one lone vinyl chair, looking over the rack of brochures and cards under a curved sign that says Sightseeing. "Hello?" says Jo.

An older woman looks around the doorway to one side of the counter, her expression of expectant concern becoming something, something else, as she takes in the figure stood there, the colorless hair, those thin lips, that nose, the muddy, wary eyes.

"Hey, Mom," says Jo Maguire. "I'm back."

Once, you were tethered,
And now you are free.
Once you were tethered?
Well, now you are free.

That was the river.
This is the sea.

—Mike Scott

"That was the river – "

The text has been set in Tribute, a typeface designed by Frank Heine from types cut in the 16th century by Françoise Guyot; specifically, a specimen printed around 1565 in the Netherlands.

Kɪᴘ Mᴀɴʟᴇʏ lives in Portland, Oregon, with a cartoonist, a blooming ᴅᴍ, and (at last count) two cats.

He may be contacted via email at kipmanley@yahoo.com. His general-interest website is available for viewing at www.longstoryshortpier.com.

THE REASON WHY

"YOU COULD ASK YOURSELF A QUESTION," he says, doing up the last button. "Why is it, d'you think, her majesty comes to find herself here, to be doing such things? Of all places." Rolling up the sleeves of his union suit. She folds her arms, leaned back against the credenza, "I don't know," she says. "Some fight or something, with," shrugging, "somebody's grandfather, hers, maybe, I don't know. I can't keep track. It's family and it goes back years, so I don't think anybody could really explain it, but there's probably a lot of money, which means lawyers," she sniffs. "Our lawyers."

"That's why she's not there," he says. "Why is it *here* her majesty finds herself?" He fishes out a cracked brown boot. She snorts. "I haven't kicked her out yet."

"Sweetling," he says, "attend the line of inquiry with a modicum of the gravity I'd like to think it's due?"

"Here is where the action is," she says. "Simple. But now, she's got everything she needs, to fuck it all up. Again. And *that,* is the gravity of *my,* whatever the fuck it is. My query."

"The point, my nonpareil," he says, working a boot onto his foot, "that must be taken into account, is this: even," tightening the laces with a grunt, "even the most capable skipper in all the world, with the sun itself that shines from his very arse," tugging on the other boot, "why, even such as he'd be utterly lost, at sea, you might say, useless, in point of fact," snugging the heel of it home with a sigh. "When stood by himself," he says, looking up, "at the wheel of a mighty clipper, without he has a couple a dozen of these," and he holds up his hands, the backs of them up to the first knuckles furred with wiry black, the heels of them and the palms edged with rough thick callus, and about the thumb of the left a simple ring of pale gold.

"She's here, her majesty's here, for you guys," she says.

"Who else, to wash her dishes, and fold her unmentionables?" He gets to his feet. "Light her candles when it's time, and snuff 'em when it's done? Beat the rugs and polish the glazing? Lay pipe, fit bolt to camlock, joist against beam, set brick atop brick? How else might her palace assemble itself?"